Dreaming the Maya Fifth Sun

A Novel of Maya Wisdom
and
the 2012 Shift in
Consciousness

Leonide Martin

Artwork Property of David Leonard

ISBN 0-7414-3454-7

Published by:

INFINITY
PUBLISHING.COM

1094 New DeHaven Street, Suite 100
West Conshohocken, PA 19428-2713
Info@buybooksontheweb.com
www.buybooksontheweb.com
Toll-free (877) BUY BOOK
Local Phone (610) 941-9999
Fax (610) 941-9959

Printed in the United States of America

Printed on Recycled Paper

Published July 2006

Rabbit Scribe writing in folding-screen codex
with jaguar skin covers. From Late Classic vase,
northern Peten or southern Campeche,
8th Century CE.

Here we shall inscribe, we shall implant the Ancient Word.
A place to see it, a Council Book.
By the Maker, Modeler, mother-father of life, of humankind.
Of those born in the light, begotten in the light.
Knower of everything, whatever there is.

Popul Vuh

Mayan Book of the Dawn of Life

Acknowledgements

Many people, events and books have contributed to the realization of this story. Grateful acknowledgement is made to the Guides and Masters who inspired and propelled the process of bringing ideas into manifest form. Special appreciation goes to my teachers on this plane, the Surface World, including Hunbatz Men, Drunvalo Melchizedek, Caroline Myss, and Aum Rak Sapper. John Major Jenkins guided my approach to Maya cosmovision concerning 2012. Editing assistance was provided by several friends, with particular thanks to Stephanie Costanza for her precise eye for details, Cynthia Gutierrez for updating Spanish phrases, and Larry Kiser for expanding my vision.

To David "Lionfire" Leonard for his photos and illustrations, and the love we share for the Maya.

To my husband David Gortner, my unending appreciation for his consistent support and insightful suggestions.

To the archeologists and the Maya wisdom-keepers, whose visions often diverge, but whose passions for this ancient culture provide continuing inspiration.

For those who seek the ancient wisdom
That guides the cycles of our planet
And keeps harmony with the Cosmos.

Leonide Martin
lenniem07@yahoo.com
www.mayafifthsun.com

Dreaming the Maya Fifth Sun

Chapters	Dates	Page
1 The Dream	*Fall 2002 CE*	1
2 Mundo Maya	*Fall 2002 CE*	39
3 Tikal (Mutul)	*376 CE*	73
4 Belize Vacation	*Winter 2003 CE*	126
5 Izapan Cosmology	*Winter 2003 CE*	180
6 Call to Pilgrimage	*Early Spring 2003 CE*	225
7 Xunantunich	*377 CE*	268
8 Sunrise at Dzibilchaltún	*Spring Equinox 2003 CE*	307
9 Tikal and Uaxactun: Venus-Tlaloc Star Wars	*378-396 CE*	345
10 Priestess Return	*Spring Equinox 2003 CE*	397
11 Uxmal	*889-910 CE*	428
12 Sacred Ceremony at Chichén Itzá	*Spring Equinox 2003 CE*	471
13 Perfect Balance	*Spring-Summer 2003 CE*	500

Contemporary Characters

Jana Sinclair	Emergency room nurse in Oakland, CA, metaphysical and menopausal
Robert Sinclair	Her husband, music professor at Mills College, creative and talented with Midwest values
Marissa Sinclair	Their college age daughter
Carmen Wilson	Jana's friend at Unity Church, half Mexican
Carla Hernandez	Psychologist and metaphysical teacher
Harry Delgardo	Robert's anthropology colleague at Mills College
Francine Rappele	Maya expert at University of Texas, Austin
Angelina Menchu	Diabetic patient in hospital, old Maya curandera
Tuwa Waki	Hopi medicine woman
Aurora Nakin Hill	Contemporary Maya Priestess, Clearlake School of Maya Mysteries, classes and tours
Hanab Xiu (Hah-<u>nahb</u> Shoo)	Maya elder, Daykeeper, leads pilgrimage to Chichén Itzá
Fire Eagle	White American shaman, co-leads pilgrimage to Chichén Itzá
Evita	Possessed Columbian woman on pilgrimage

iv

Women's Group	Carmen Wilson, real estate agent, half Mexican
	Mary, RN colleague works in emergency room
	Grace, mixed African and Native American, indigenous artist
	Claire, blonde UC Berkeley psychology professor
	Sarah, lawyer and group humorist
	Lydia, naturalist, biologist, Marin Marine Institute
Michael, Julia, Steve	Friends at Clearlake School of Maya Mysteries, go on pilgrimage with Hanab Xiu

Maya Characters
(Phonetic pronunciation given in parentheses)

Yalucha (Yah-loo-cha)	Maya priestess of Ix Chel, from the Izapa tradition, with lifehoods in Tikal and Uxmal
Chan Hun (Chahn Hoon)	Noble from Uaxactun, Yalucha's lover
Xoc Ikal (Shock Ee-kal)	Mother of Yalucha, also a Priestess of Ix Chel
K'an Nab Ku (K'ahn Naab Koo)	Father of Yalucha
Hunbatz (Hoon-bahtz)	Older brother of Yalucha
K'in Pakal (K'een Pah-kahl)	Uncle of Yalucha, brother of K'an Nab Ku
Chuen (Choo-en)	Aunt of Yalucha, sister of K'an Nab Ku
Yo'nal Ac (Yo'nahl Ahck)	Chief Daykeeper Priest of Tikal
Chitam (Chee-tahm)	Son of Yo'nal Ac, suitor of Yalucha
Chak Toh Ich'ak (Chahk Toe Eech'ahk)	Ruler of Tikal, ahau/lord (317-378 CE, 9th ruler), Called Jaguar Claw I, Great Jaguar Claw
K'ak Sih (K'ahk Seeh)	Ruler of Tikal, kalomte/overlord (378-379 CE), Ruler of Uaxactun

Yax Ain I (Yash Aeen)	(378-402 CE). Called Smoking Frog, Fire-Born, from Teotihuacan Ruler of Tikal, ahau/lord (379-420 CE, 10th ruler) Called Curl Snout, First Crocodile, from Teotihuacan
Olal (Oh-lahl)	Priestess acolyte, friend of Yalucha's at Xunantunich
Zac Kuk (Sock Kook)	High Priestess at Xunantunich
Chan Chak K'ak'nal (Chan Chahk K-ak-nahl)	Ruler of Uxmal, ahau/lord (910 CE)
Mac Ceel (Mak Seel)	High Priest of Uxmal
Huntan Pasah (Hoon-tahn Pah-sah)	Chief Warrior of Uxmal

Other Historical Maya Rulers Mentioned in Story

Yax Ch'aktel Xoc (Yash Ch-ahk-tel Shock)	Ruler of Tikal, ahau (219 CE, 1st dynastic ruler), founder of Tikal's Jaguar dynasty
Hasaw Chan K'awil (Hah-saw Chahn K-ah-weel)	Ruler of Tikal, ahau (682-743 CE, 26th ruler), restored Tikal to glory after the Hiatus

Maya and Mexican Cities

Tikal (Tee-kahl)	Guatemala, Peten
Xunantunich (Shoo-nan-toon-ich)	Belize, Cayo
Cahal Pech (Ka-hahl Pech)	Belize, Cayo
Uaxactun (Wah-shak-toon)	Guatemala, Peten
Kalakmul (Kah-lahk-muhl)	Guatemala, Peten
Dzibilchaltún (Zh-beel-chal-toon)	México, Yucatan
Uxmal (Oosh-mahl)	México, Yucatan
Chichén Itzá (Chee-chen Eet-zah)	México, Yucatán
Piste (Pees-tay)	México, Yucatan
Mérida (Mare-ee-dah)	México, Yucatán

Jana woke with a start. It was that same dream again. She felt the familiar chill creeping up her back, raising hairs at the nape of her neck. A deep sense of unease accompanied the gripping sensation in her solar plexus. The image was still clear as she opened her eyes and stared into the darkness of her bedroom.

All she saw were the hands, always the same hands. The child's small brown hand gently stroked the old woman's bony fingers. Small fingers that were supple and round followed the ropy veins snaking across the back of the shriveled hand. Thin and nearly transparent, the brown skin was speckled with dark spots. After tracing the protruding veins, the child's hand slipped into the larger palm, gripped it for an instant, and withdrew. The old hand stretched, fingers fanning slightly, feebly trying to reach for something. But it was too dark to see.

The old woman's hand, thought Jana. *How do I know it's a woman, when all I can see is the hand?* It didn't make sense, but she knew it was an old woman.

What was the hand reaching for? What did it want, and why did the exact same image repeat itself over and over in her dreams? At least a dozen times in the last six months.

She took a deep breath and exhaled a quiet sigh. The disturbing physical sensations were dissipating, but she felt disquieted inside. Eyes now adjusted to the dark, she glanced over at her husband whose regular breathing informed her that he was deep asleep.

One thing you can say for Robert, he really does sleep well.

Feeling envious, she turned on her side, adjusted her pillow and tried to let the dream fade from her mind.

It's just so persistent, she mused. She could recall a few repeating themes in previous dreams, but not with such unerring precision and relentless frequency. This dream was uncanny. It was certainly no ordinary dream. There must be some meaning in this dream, something she needed to know.

OK, Jana conceded, *tomorrow I am going to seriously explore this dream.*

Standing by the bay window in the breakfast nook, Jana savored the early morning sunlight warming her face. She was still drowsy, although sleep had finally come after what seemed an inordinately long time. The aroma of dripping coffee caused her to sniff eagerly. The first morning cup was always the best, exciting her taste buds and sparking a welcome shower of adrenalin to awaken her brain. The coffee maker popped and gurgled a few final drips and sounded its little bell. The black nectar was ready.

Pouring herself a cup, Jana sipped carefully and savored the rich earthy aroma of Guatemala coffee. She and Robert were coffee connoisseurs. They favored organic, fair traded coffees in keeping with their ecological principles.

"Superbly aromatic, well-balanced with medium body, lively acidity and overtones of chocolate and spice" exuded the rainforest green bag. Swirling a sip expertly, Jana could detect "aromatic and lively" but "chocolate and spice" were subtle. Drinking more deeply, she cradled the warm cup between her palms, elbows on the round breakfast table. Morning sunlight emblazoned orange zinnias and yellow marigolds cheerfully bordering the small back yard. Taller shrubs by the fence were shrouded in shade.

Jana turned her head as Robert entered the breakfast nook.

"Hi, dear" he said, pouring his coffee and joining her at the table. "Sleep well?"

Robert Sinclair was tall, well built and attractive with a youthful physical vitality that belied his nearly 53 years. When the sun reflected off his ash blonde hair, it turned the gray streaks at his temples into silver highlights. Jana smiled and admired her husband yet again. His lop-sided smile, that certain turn of his shoulders, still evoked a thrill in her heart. Their 23 year marriage, the second for both, had been happy and satisfying though not without its challenges.

"I had the dream again," Jana said. "Had a hard time getting back to sleep."

"The one with the old woman's hand?"

"Yes. The stomach sensations and chills were really strong this time. It makes me feel so uneasy."

"Are you sure it wasn't a hot flash?" Robert queried mischievously.

"I don't think it was," Jana replied thoughtfully. She was 51 years old and going through menopause. These surges of heat wakened her often, starting as deep uneasiness in the mid-chest, then flooding upward causing her neck and face to burst into rosy sweat. Then a chill followed the uncomfortable heat. As a nurse, Jana understood the physiology of rampant hormones playing havoc with the brain's temperature regulating center. But, the flashes were tolerable, and would subside in a year or two. She wanted to do menopause naturally and avoid hormone replacement.

"I didn't sweat or feel hot," she continued. "The chill is different, up the spine rather than in front. No, it's just that the dream makes me apprehensive. It must mean something, to recur so often."

Robert poured more coffee, then brought cereal and set out bowls and spoons deftly. They combined all bran cereal with high protein-low fat granola. Jana liked soymilk for its isoflavones that helped menopause; Robert used 2% milk. Jana and Robert Sinclair were health conscious Californians, ate organic frequently and emphasized vegetables, fruit and whole grains. Both were trim and physically fit thanks to regular exercise regimens.

Jana tousled her light brown hair, causing glints of sunlight to dance on the golden highlights. Loose shoulder-length curls were natural, but the lovely color was compliments of a skilled hairdresser; she wasn't ready to become gray. Her clear skin revealed some fine lines around lips and eyes, less odious than the sagging neck that she kept at bay by a rigorous facial routine.

Her hazel eyes looked up into Robert's blue eyes, fixing his gaze with her earnestness.

"I'm going to do dream analysis," she announced. "I've got to get to the bottom of this."

"You know, dreams aren't always significant," Robert remarked. "I was reading in *Science Discoveries* about dreams. Said the big increases in electrical activity when you dream just gives the brain a workout, revving up neurons that don't get exercised during the day. When we're asleep the usual brain gatekeepers go into deep relaxation. Like the prefrontal cortex; it goes off line and can't censor brain functions the way it does when we're awake. There's more activity in parts of the brain that handle sensations, emotions and memories. But the parts of the brain that make sense of these are shut down."

He took another sip of coffee, waving his hand professorially.

"So, our dreams are filled with impossible things, uninhibited actions and emotions. You can breathe underwater, fly in the air, communicate telepathically, speak strange languages, do outrageous things. It's just random firings of neurons in the absence of brain processes that organize and integrate things."

Jana watched Robert with a bemused expression.

For a right-brain musician, he certainly does a lot of left-brain linear thinking, she observed to herself. He was like other technical creatives, that curious combination of science and art that causes so many doctors to play classical music as a hobby. But he did it the other way, a music teacher whose hobby was computers. He knew more about computers than most geeks and was a whiz at computer games.

She fixed Robert with a haughty gaze.

"I've heard the theory that dreams are just meaningless biology," she retorted. "Bursts of activity from the primitive brain, random stimuli that neurons transpose into weird images. Or that dreams are psychological garbage, debris left over from cellular metabolism that the brain needs to get rid of. But I don't believe that dreams have no real function. I think they *are* meaningful, maybe not always but many times. I tend to agree with what Carl Jung said about dreams: they are doors into the deepest and most intimate sanctums of the soul. My dream about the old woman's hand is too precise to be random. It repeats in exactly the same sequence every time, every detail is the same. And the feelings that go with it are always the same, too."

"Well, I sure don't have the answer," admitted Robert. He shot his engaging smile at Jana, halfway apologetic. "You probably should explore it more, it does seem unusual."

They munched cereal in silence for a while, watching assorted birds exchanging places at the feeder hanging by the fence. Their house in the low Piedmont hills on the east side of San Francisco Bay was a modest, older two-story structure. The back yard was small, with just enough space for a tiny patio, thin strip of grass and narrow flower garden bordering the fence. A few mature maple and bay trees created welcome shade in summer and graced the fall with lively colors. The area was favored by faculty at Mills College in Oakland, where Robert taught in the Music Department. The neighborhood was kept quiet by narrow, winding streets that discouraged through traffic. Some homes higher in the hills had spectacular views of the bay.

"Marissa called yesterday," Robert broke their silence. "She's coming over next weekend. Some friend is having a wedding shower, I think."

Marissa was Jana and Robert's 21-year old daughter, now a junior at the University of California, Santa Cruz. Robert's son from his former marriage lived in Los Angeles; they were on friendly terms but not close. Marissa was their "love child," born during the second

4

year of marriage, planned and anticipated. She had always been delightful, a bright, good-natured girl. Given considerable free rein by her doting parents, Marissa developed a strong sense of self with resultant willfulness. The adolescent years had been trying, especially for Jana. Marissa challenged her mother's authority and manipulated her father in typical Princess fashion. This led to family therapy for a couple of years, which defused tension enough to avoid serious blowups. After Marissa graduated from high school, family dynamics changed and she became more harmonious with her mother. Maybe it was growing up, or the new distractions of college, or better self-understanding that recognized shared values. Whatever the cause, Jana welcomed easing of tensions with her daughter.

"Oh, that's good," Jana said. "I can give her the new book I found on grail mythology."

Mother and daughter shared an interest in spirituality and mythology, alerting each other to books and seminars. They were intrigued with new ideas rapidly spreading about early Christianity, the relationship of Jesus and Mary Magdalen, and secret societies preserving hidden knowledge about the Holy Grail and Christ's bloodline.

"Is it another book on Magdalen as the bride of Christ?" asked Robert. He had reservations about this whole theory, in part because of his traditional Episcopalian upbringing, though he'd moved away from much of it. Now he and Jana were members of a local Unity Church with a philosophy of commonality among religious teachings. The Jesus-Mary Magdalen thing stretched his credulity too much, however, and he felt the evidence was not strong.

"No," replied Jana, "it goes into the modern symbology of the Fisher King legend. It has a good psychological analysis of how the wounded king has to heal before his kingdom—a man's life—can be prosperous and abundant again. Percival and the Holy Grail represent the king's own search to find and integrate his lost feminine side. The wounded male psyche can become whole and healed only by re-discovering the value of his feminine part. Men have to accept and integrate it. Integrating our masculine and feminine sides is something Marissa is really interested in right now."

"Uh-huh," said Robert. He often felt vaguely uneasy when this topic came up.

"And its something the world needs to do, also," said Jana emphatically. "That's why there's so much interest in the Jesus-Magdalen story, aside from how it makes people think of Jesus differently, more like us, more human and accessible. The big upsurge of goddess energy is also part of this. The planet has gotten unbalanced toward the masculine side. Five thousand years of the patriarchy has brought the world to the brink of destruction. We've got to balance that with feminine qualities of caring and nurturing life."

Jana glanced at Robert, reading his body language. He got uncomfortable if she pursued this topic too vigorously. She sensed his tension more than observed the slight narrowing of his eyes and tightening of small muscles around his lips. Reaching over and stroking his shoulder, she smiled warmly.

"Don't worry, sweetheart, you're one of the good guys. You've already integrated your feminine and masculine a lot. Artists and musicians are more balanced than most men."

"Creativity isn't just feminine." Robert tried not to sound defensive.

"Of course not," Jana demurred. "And sometimes amazing creativity flows out of our wounds, becomes part of the healing process. It's a question of balance, of inner harmony, of honoring and acknowledging all the parts of ourselves. And," she added thoughtfully, "we've got so many hidden parts of ourselves. So much can lie in that unexplored terrain of our being. I think my dream about the old woman's hand is coming from some deep, hidden area of my subconscious. I need to find out more about it."

"So, that's behind your plans to do some dream work."

"Yes."

"More coffee?" Robert asked, allotting the remainder equally in their cups. They sipped in silence, each lost in their own thoughts. They thoroughly enjoyed these morning conversations over breakfast. Sometimes their exchange was so animated and intense that they lost track of time, causing Robert to rush off to work. But today he rose from the table purposefully.

"I've got to get going. I need to stop by the library and review a couple of new articles before my music theory class this morning."

Jana acknowledged this with a nod, contemplating how Robert often did eleventh-hour preparation for classes. He was so self-assured as a teacher, drawing on over 30 years of experience, that browsing through a few last minute articles was enough to prime his mind for a provocative discussion with his students. She admired his confidence, wishing she were more at ease with teaching. She spent

6

hours over-preparing for her occasional classes, getting quite a case of performance anxiety.

"I'm going for a walk with Mary in Tilden Park around noon, but I should still beat you home," she called after him as he left the room.

"OK," echoed from the hall as Robert disappeared toward the bathroom.

Jana and Mary, both emergency room nurses, did a few warm-up stretches before starting their five-mile hike. Lightly dressed for the sunny, warm fall day, they wore t-shirts and loose shorts that allowed easy movement. Saying little after their initial greetings, the two women strode along briskly, soon breaking a sweat. Two loops through Tilden Park brought them around Jewel Lake, nestled like a glassy sapphire in the gentle hills, and past groves of mixed trees at higher elevations. Each carried a water bottle attached to their belts.

Patches of shade dappled the path, cast by the park's many eucalyptus, bay, sycamore and oak trees. A few pines and coast redwoods soared at higher elevations. Shrubby scotch broom, salvias and manzanita beneath the trees offered haven for wildlife. Periodic calls of scrub jays, Brewer's blackbirds, quail, crows and chickadees punctuated the still air. In mid-week the park was lightly used, and the women encountered few other hikers. After walking briskly for 45 minutes, they stopped for a break, sitting in the shade of a large sycamore tree and drinking from their water bottles.

Jana broke the silence.

"Mary, I've told you about my recurring dream of the old woman's hand, haven't I?" she asked.

"Yes, you did. It happened again?"

"Last night. The feelings I always have during the dream were especially strong. I'm really disturbed by this, Mary. I've got to find out what it's all about. I want to do some serious dream analysis. Any ideas?"

"Well, it's something of a coincidence, but last week I got a brochure for a dream workshop by Carla Hernandez. I've taken classes with her before; she's a Jungian psychologist who's branched out into transpersonal work. Does a lot with imagery and dreams, bridging different levels of reality. I enjoyed her classes. Maybe this one would help you. It's coming up soon, next week."

"Do you remember what day?" Jana had to plan around her work schedule, which was set up two months in advance.

7

"Saturday, I think," said Mary. "Not this coming, but the next."

"Hmmm," said Jana, "I'm off that day. Another coincidence?"

"Maybe a signal from the universe," laughed Mary. "I think the word now is synchronicity, the invisible forces of fate bringing into our field what we're slated to experience. Seems like you're meant to take this dream class."

"Yeah, seems so."

"Shall we get on with our walk?" Mary liked to keep moving.

"OK," Jana replied, getting up. "Thanks for the suggestion."

"I'll bring the brochure to work tomorrow," Mary replied, taking a couple of quick stretches then setting off at an energetic pace.

Jana dawdled, enjoying the pungent odor of eucalyptus on the warm air. The birdcalls were rhythmic, hypnotic. As the path skirted a large grove of trees, she strayed toward a clearing in their center. Her mind was semi-somnolent, intoxicated with aromatic resins of pine, eucalyptus and bay. An unseen force pulled her farther into the grove, as her somnolence increased and darkness began creeping around her vision. Numbed and blurry, she stumbled over tree roots and teetered precariously.

Watch out!

A tiny bubble of awareness percolated from the dim recesses of her mind. She reached toward the tree to steady herself, just as cold talons clamped the back of her neck. Sharp claws dug in, dangerously close to the jugular veins. Reaching with both hands to free her neck, she staggered. Then a force propelled her forward and she crashed full-face into an immense trunk, crumpling to its leaf-strewn base.

Shaking with fear and inexplicable cold, Jana rolled away from the tree, trying to get her eyes to focus. Dry leaves and twigs crackled beneath her, releasing more heady oils. She fought to stay conscious, lifting her head a few inches from the ground. Raucous crow caws buffeted her ears, too loud, too close. Through wavy vision, she looked around seeking the black offenders. For a second, ephemeral forms flickered in the clearing, transparent wraiths dancing in a circle, something native about them, a drum throbbing—no, it was her heartbeat. Fading again into darkness, she dropped her head onto the bed of leaves in a blanket of silence.

"Jana! Jana!"

Mary's voice seemed far in the distance. Then she was being held, cradled, given water to drink. Her neck hurt.

"Jana, what happened? Are you OK?"

Mary's concerned voice gradually pulled Jana's wayward mind into the present. As her vision cleared, Jana put one hand to her neck, seeking blood from the claws. There was nothing. Not even a bump.

"I, uh . . . I tripped and . . . uh, fainted," Jana said weakly.

"Drink some more water. You look awfully pale," Mary observed. "Have you been feeling all right? Had flu lately? How's your blood pressure?"

Jana drank as warmth returned to her body. Her neck still ached.

"It's been normal, I haven't been sick," she replied. Turning her head back and forth, she looked quizzically at Mary.

"Is my neck OK? Can you see anything there?"

"No," said Mary as she checked. "Does it hurt?"

"Yeah."

"Maybe you twisted it when you fell. Did you just black out?"

"Sort of . . . I went into a daze, lost balance, and something . . . " Jana paused. She couldn't get a grasp on the strange force. Maybe it was all her imagination. "It's hot . . guess I didn't drink enough water."

She shifted position, feeling the back of her neck, perplexed at its unbroken skin.

"Probably just orthostatic hypotension," she offered tentatively.

The nurses often used technical shorthand, a few words conveying an entire diagnostic profile. The dense words meant a sudden drop in blood pressure from postural changes. Dehydration could cause it.

"Yeah, or vasovagal reflex," added Mary as she helped Jana to her feet. This meant fainting from over-stimulation of the vagus nerve, altering heart rate and breathing.

"Um-hmm," Jana murmured, feeling steadier with each step.

They walked sedately back at the parking area, Mary watchful for any signs of faintness. Jana insisted she was feeling normal, but Mary advised that she get the ER doctor to check her over at next shift.

*   *   *   *   *

Carla Hernandez looked more like a fortuneteller than a psychologist. Short and plump, everything about her was round from ample bosom to swelling hips, divided sharply by a surprisingly small waist that turned her into a voluptuous hourglass. Tawny golden skin, the shade coveted by sunbathers, was hers by genetic inheritance. A wispy halo of unruly hair with a copper sheen framed her round face.

9

Golden-green eyes accentuated by dark mascara struck a bright contrast as sensuous lips curved under a strong but not unduly large nose.

Dangling gold earrings jangled and thin gold bracelets clinked softly as she gestured. To complete the gypsy motif, she wore a silk purple blouse with slit sleeves and a many-hued skirt with a metallic belt clasping her small waist tightly.

Her presence was commanding, despite being incongruous. She exuded a certain magnetism that hinted at mastery of hidden knowledge. Archetypal impressions given by her exotic appearance—Mystic, Alchemist, Magus—spoke of ancient traditions delving into life's mysteries.

In the brightly lit multipurpose room of the community center, 15 students sat facing a small desk and white board. Carla's animated speech had just a hint of accent, a slight roll on the "r" and long "i" making "pill" sound like "peel." Frequent gestures emphasized her points. Jana, always the diligent student, took notes in a spiral bound notebook.

"Dreams are gateways to our inner resources," Carla enunciated carefully. "They're on many levels, sometimes very personal and sometimes symbolic. Dreams serve different purposes, everything from re-living painful situations so they can be healed, to giving guidance about making decisions, solving problems, or answering questions. They let you explore hidden meanings that your logical mind can't figure out. Or, they bring messages from other levels of consciousness, from the spirit world or your own higher self.

"Sometimes dreams seem meaningless, you can't see any connections. Maybe some dreams are just random firing of neurons in the brain; one scientific school of thought believes that. But my experience with hundreds of clients leads me to believe there is meaning in nearly all dreams. You need to grasp the symbols, read the obtuse signs put together in unexpected ways by a brain freed from rules of rationality."

She paused, glancing around the group. Flashing white teeth in a knowing smile, she observed emphatically:

"You're all here because there is something in your dreams you want to understand. Something to get from dreaming. I will try to help. We dream a lot, about 20% of sleep time is spent dreaming, that's around an hour and a half. In a lifetime we dream more than 50,000 hours; that's six years, enough to get a university degree!"

Everyone chuckled as Carla tossed her head and laughed. Neon light glinted off her crystal and gold adornments.

"In spite of this, science still knows relatively little about dreams. What we do know is that dreams occur during REM sleep, when rapid eye movements happen. We have several REM cycles per night, during which vivid images occur along with increased metabolism and irregular heartbeat and breathing. Small muscles in the fingers twitch, while larger muscles go limp. Blood flow to the brain increases forty percent. Research using PET scans showed big increases in the limbic system that controls emotions. Blood flow also increased in subcortical areas for memory, sensory processing and muscle movement. And the brain stem regions regulating breathing and heart rate also had more blood during REM sleep.

"More blood flow shows there's a jump in activity in brain regions that work with visual patterns. That's why you have such vivid images during dreams. But, the part of the visual cortex that analyzes images, and the brain stem areas controlling large muscles, both virtually shut down.

"What does all this mean? You're basically paralyzed and unable to put sensations, images and memories into a logical context—at the same time that intense imagery and emotions flood brain regions without the usual inhibitory and self-disciplining mechanisms. You get to experience just about anything without any mental censorship. That's why dreams are so outrageous, impossible, and overwhelming."

Carla nodded, satisfied that she conveyed the power of dreams to her students. Her earrings bobbled in agreement.

Jana reflected on Robert's insinuation that dreams were biological garbage or senseless brain workouts. No doubt Carla wouldn't agree.

Glancing again around the group, Carla's eyes connected with Jana's and lingered for a moment. Jana felt a funny little "blip" around her heart, gone almost before she registered it.

"Dreams are a universal symbolic language," Carla continued, her eyes becoming dreamy. "There are lots of common dream images around the world, like water for emotions or intuition and fire for power or transformation. Carl Jung—" she pronounced the famous psychologist's first name car-o-lyn—"believed that dreams tap into the collective unconscious through archetypal symbols that represent the wisdom of all humanity. He thought these ancestral memories were inherited by people, just as we inherit physical characteristics.

So, dreams are revelations of our own hidden wisdom, part of our personal unconscious passed down through ancestral memories. Through this, we tap into a huge realm of ancient knowledge, of collective wisdom from eons of experiences, in our dreams."

Wow! That must be what's happening in my dream of the old woman's hand, thought Jana.

"Metaphysically speaking, dreams put you in touch with inner realms and open your psychic abilities. Don Juan, the Yaqui shaman, taught Carlos Castenada that through lucid dreaming—remaining aware while having a dream—he could expand his psychic powers into other realities. Edgar Cayce, aptly called 'The Sleeping Prophet' did his amazing clairvoyant work while in a dream state. Cayce emphasized that dream symbols were meant to alert the dreamer to something. Certain symbols signified it was time to change your beliefs, to take more responsibility for life, to be more accepting, or to let something go. Some dreams were meant to develop new qualities in the dreamer, such as non-judgment, humility, self-acceptance, love and courage."

Carla paused to emphasize her next point. Her earrings danced as she tossed her head.

"Cayce also thought that some dreams are prophetic, providing symbols that indicate a new energy, an important change, is coming into your life. He regarded dreams as a way to problem-solve, and often advised dream incubation, a deliberate invoking of dreams for specific purposes, to seek solutions for daytime problems."

It's a prophetic dream! Something is coming into my life. Jana was sure of it.

Carla wrote a few main points on the white board. Turning quickly to the class, her colorful skirt swirling, she continued:

"One last aspect of dream theories, then we'll take some examples. Dreams can be used to work out karma. As we reincarnate, our spirit brings along patterns that we set up for ourselves through past life actions. Each incarnation is an opportunity to clear and resolve these karmic patterns, so we can grow and progress spiritually. Most of our karma gets expressed during waking hours, but it can be experienced in our dreams. Recurring dreams are most often connected with karma. And, sometimes guides come to us in dreams, providing valuable information and insight. These guides are usually non-physical beings with whom you've been connected in previous lifetimes, or a teacher or family member who has passed on. These beings give support in your present challenges. When the rational mind turns off during sleep, guides have easier access to your inner self."

Jana's ears perked up. In the San Francisco Bay area in the early 21st century, no explanation of karma, reincarnation or spirit guides was necessary. These were part of the common culture. But the connection between recurrent dreams and karma was new for her.

"Any questions?" asked Carla, leaning back against the small desk.

"Can you say more about recurring dreams?" Jana quickly queried.

"Sure. They often re-enact some situation that is long-standing, either in this life or previously. When the same dream keeps recurring, it could mean you haven't worked out the issue and the deep psyche is pushing you to do it. Or, there can be a message the dream is trying to convey, but you're just not getting it. The dream content usually gives clues."

Carla tilted her head and eyed Jana quizzically.

"You've been having a recurring dream?"

Without waiting for an answer, she addressed the entire class.

"This would be a good time to do some individual dream work. Write down a dream you've had in as much detail as you can. Then we'll take some examples."

Jana wrote rapidly in her notebook, capturing every detail she could remember about her dream, including physical and emotional sensations that accompanied it. After a few minutes, Carla nodded at Jana, glancing at the enrollment list.

"Would you tell us about your dream? It's Jana, right?"

Jana nodded, then read the dream although she could easily tell it be heart. She didn't want to leave any detail out, however small. Carla listened carefully, then queried Jana.

"Can you recall any other details? Like what the old woman or the girl were wearing, the place they were in, whether it was night or day, anything else?"

Closing her eyes, Jana strained to remember but drew a blank. All she could see were the woman's and the girl's hands. She did have a sense that the setting was dark.

"Well, it's hard to know the dream's meaning without some more details," Carla said. "I can say in general, though, that hands represent doing something, handling or grasping. Hands might indicate that you can handle it, or that you're having trouble handling or grasping it. The young girl tracing the old woman's fingers and

13

veins gives the impression of exploring, examining, maybe learning. When she slips her hand into the woman's palm that implies supporting or comforting. It's also a sign of linking people together. They obviously have an important connection. To really understand the meaning of the dream, Jana, you need to expand it, to develop it more. This afternoon I'll cover the technique of dream incubation, which you should use to obtain more details about the scenario. Thanks, Jana."

Carla turned her attention to other students, who discussed their dreams. Jana was perplexed, listening to the rich detail and colorful experiences many other students had in their dreams.

Why is this powerful, recurrent dream so limited? You'd think as often as it happens, more details would have emerged.

In the afternoon session, Jana paid special attention to the technique for dream incubation and took extensive notes. In her mind she set the stage as she wrote:

Set your intention clearly. Phrase the question positively— tonight I will see more details of the dream about the old woman's hand. Do a purification ritual, such as burning sage or incense, and refrain from alcohol, drugs and heavy food. Review the issue before going to sleep. Place your dream journal and flashlight beside the bed. Instruct your subconscious to awaken you just after the dream so you can record it. As you fall asleep, repeat your request several times, then release all thoughts, attitudes and feelings about the issue. Take time in the morning to reflect and process dream information.

Carla explained that incubated dreams usually occur the same night you request them, but could take a couple of nights. She concluded:

"Although you might not be able to find associations between the dream and the issue at first, be patient, wait for understanding. Trust that within the dream is the answer to your issue or problem, and that your higher self already knows the solution."

Jana's attempts at dream incubation were remarkably unsuccessful. Though she followed each step meticulously and earnestly, no new imagery occurred. Neither did a ritual bath by candlelight nor cedar incense purify her energy field enough. She prayed for insight and guidance. She fasted from lunch until bedtime, which was hard because her finely tuned metabolism insisted on regular food. That night all she could focus on was hunger pains and what she would have the next morning for breakfast. She decided not to try that tactic again.

With frustration creeping in, Jana decided to take the dream to her women's group. These seven women had been meeting regularly for three years, drawn together by Carmen Wilson, Jana's long-time friend from East Bay Unity Church. Carmen was a dynamic, talkative person who always brought out people's talents. An inveterate networker, she loved the process of linking others, an attribute that served her well selling real estate at which she was notably successful, aided by her animated presence: short wavy brown hair, lively dark eyes, and a flashing smile packaged in her stocky frame.

Carmen's house was a charming Victorian in the better area of Oakland's historic district. It was the kind of house real estate agents loved, a real find that tripled in value after restoration work. Cheerful yellow and blue gingerbread trim, gracious porches and shiny gold turrets invited visitors into the warmth of shared friendships over tea and cookies—and Carmen always provided aromatic Ceylon teas and the richest and gooiest treats in Oakland. When they met at health-conscious Jana's house, the fare was green tea and wheat-free oatmeal-raisin cookies. Jana admitted sheepishly that she really loved indulging in Carmen's decadent treats.

The women gathered in the bright living room, sitting in a loose circle on brocade sofa and chairs tastefully complemented by lavish oriental rugs. They chatted while enjoying tea and goodies, catching up on each other's lives.

After a short meditation was "check in" time during which the women reported on what was up in their lives. If someone had a really big issue, it became the focus. Their understanding, not perfectly followed, was that no advice was given unless requested. The group leader, at whose home the group met, was responsible to keep order as much as feasible, often using a "talking stick." Only the person holding the stick could speak.

During "check in" time, Jana brought up her recent dream experiences, Carla Hernandez' class and her own fruitless attempts at dream incubation.

"I just haven't had any luck," Jana said. "The dream stays exactly the same, no matter how clearly I set intentions or how carefully I prepare for it. I'm really getting frustrated."

"Dreams are a threshold in liminal time," stated Claire, the youngest member. Claire was a slender blonde whose classic beauty belied her incisive intelligence. She amused herself by unsettling

15

men, who all too often were deceived by her looks and pigeonholed her as a blonde sexpot. The startled and dismayed expression on their faces when she shot forth a laser-sharp intellectual missile that blasted their opinions was its own reward.

"What's liminal time?" asked Carmen.

"It's a state of timelessness that reaches into other dimensions." Claire looked nonchalant. "The word comes from the Latin root *limen*, which means threshold. These thresholds are portals that open doorways into other states of being. They move us from *Chronos* or linear third-dimension time, into *Kairos* time, or timelessness. Some people think this timelessness is the archetypal realm, or the astral world, or a way of tapping into the collective unconscious of the planet. Liminal experiences open up sacred portals, mysterious places that are thresholds between the worlds."

"So dreams are portals to other worlds," observed Jana thoughtfully.

"Yes, I believe they are" replied Claire. "And so are those coincidences that we later recognize as synchronicities—significant events that converge to change our lives. Synchronicities are like a hole in the fabric of space-time, a place where the psychic field intersects with the field of matter. We all have those kinds of experiences, such as thinking about someone and right then they call us, or knowing in advance exactly what someone is going to say. But the higher-level synchronicities are numinous, meaning they have a sacred, special meaning that stirs our souls. These numinous experiences are overwhelmingly intense. That's why people call them spiritual. They have the power to transform you. We never forget a numinous experience."

"Bravo, professor!" chimed in Sarah. Witty and incisive, she liked to poke fun at high-flown rhetoric. Dark curls framed her olive-hued face with deep tawny eyes and thick curved lashes to die for. With aquiline nose and full lips—and also full hips as she was quick to admit—her lawyer training equipped her well for expounding the counter-argument whenever there was too much group agreement.

"Einstein himself would heartily agree. No doubt you've also found liminal connections to the unified field?" she said, tilting her head provocatively.

Claire was eminently unruffled, another part of her M.O. She actually was a professor, an Assistant Professor Step II to be precise, in the Psychology Department at the University of California,

Berkeley. That she had attained this level in Cal's competitive tenure track system was a testimony to her drive and intelligence.

"Why certainly, its elemental," she quipped in return. "As you know, Einstein spent the last years of his life searching for a unification theory that would encompass both quantum physics and relativity. Physics is getting close now with string and membrane theories. But where physics has flagged, psychology bravely moves ahead with its own theory of Unitarian Reality, as Jung put it."

"Well, Unity Church will go for that!" Carmen beamed.

Claire cast a denigrating glance, wearied at her friend's religious fervor.

"There is this universal field of consciousness," she continued with the expert's measured emphasis when lecturing novices, "called the quantum field or psi-field in physics. It's a web or membrane—something like string theory—that connects everything in the universe through all dimensions of reality. People, creatures, everything is linked through the collective unconscious. It's an immense psychic field that exists around the earth. Energy and consciousness are two different fields within the universal field. They interact with each other and with the field of physical matter. Energy and consciousness connect through vibration; vibration manifests on various levels, the most dense being physical matter."

"Strings and membranes?" puzzled Carmen, brow furrowed.

A new voice entered the discussion.

"They're the two most promising TOE's in physics: 'Theories of Everything' that can unite what physicists know about very large things—stars, planets, galaxies and the forces affecting them—and very small things like quantum particles and waves," said Lydia, a wiry tousle-haired naturalist. Her work at the Marin Institute of Marine Biology and Oceanography connected her with scientists of many disciplines. Understanding behavioral systems from their tiniest molecular elements to their relationship with the cosmos was her passion. Gazing around the group through her thick glasses, she continued:

"Unification theories explain how the universe works. What we see is only a small part of a much larger reality, most existing in non-visible dimensions. Different realities are very close, less than a proton apart, but they can't see each other because they exist at different frequencies. Physicists say all matter is made of tiny vibrating strings—actually the *harmonies* created by these strings. If you magnified any subatomic particle, you'd see a tiny vibrating string. Each type of particle is a string that vibrates only at a certain frequency, though the possibilities are infinite. Superstring theory ties all this together.

"What's really interesting are pictures of the membranes that form the universe. They have lots of lines all over their surfaces, looks exactly like strings. Hanging in space right next to each other, the membranes bump together and cause a Big Bang. This fiery explosion expands to create galaxies that keep expanding like ours is doing now. When everything gets so far apart there's virtually nothing left in the universe, some mysterious force draws the membranes back together. This starts up a new cycle for another Big Bang, and keeps happening for infinity."

"That's fascinating," Jana remarked. "It reminds me of the Hindu view of the universe as expanding and contracting in endless immense cycles, probably millions of years long. They call it the 'Breath of Brahman' the creator—the inbreath contracts matter and consciousness and the outbreath expands them."

Jana was steeped in Eastern philosophy since childhood. She was a second generation Californian, raised by parents on the fringe of the 1960's hippie movement. Despite two preteen children and steady jobs, they still took part in the free-spirited lifestyle that saw its epitome in the San Francisco Bay area: an Indian guru, yoga and meditation, and smoking a little pot. Jana's mom loved all things metaphysical, traipsing from one self-styled mystic to another, a true dilettante. Wispy scarves and flowing skirts reminiscent of the flower children still adorned her thin aging frame. Jana's dad fancied himself a semi-enlightened sage, full of spiritual advice to anyone who would listen. His mellow humor mitigated this irksome trait; often Jana felt he was laughing mostly at himself.

"Oh, this is getting too thick," protested Sarah, tossing her curly hair theatrically. "I thought we were discussing Jana's dream! What's it got to do with membranes, strings and the synchronicity hole in space-time?"

An unwelcome wave of irritation swept over Jana. As un-yogic as it was, she often felt annoyed by Sarah's sharpness.

"We're exploring the physics of liminal phenomena," retorted Claire, who shared Jana's ungracious view. Her voice tone was just short of disdain. "Grounding mysticism in science, if you will."

"I'll tell you a story to show how these things work," said Lydia on a gentler note. "How this network of vibrations, of strings, connects things to create synchronicity. My brother had a synchronicity happen that changed his life, big time. He was going through a lot of stuff during college. His grades were falling, he hated his major in business, didn't feel he was cut out for it. Life was pretty meaningless, and he'd broken up with his teenage sweetheart a few months before. Thought they'd be together forever. Basketball was all that kept him from falling apart, and then he broke his finger in a game. He wasn't a spiritual guy, but things were desperate. He remembers saying: 'If there is a God, he-she-it better show up soon and do something about my life.'

"One night his friends tried to cheer him up by taking him to a party. It was the last thing he wanted to do, they were a hard-drinking bunch, real party animals. He tried to say no, but they literally dragged him out. At the party, he just couldn't get into it. He left and went to a late-night café. He almost didn't go there because it was a stormy night, raining hard. He ran all the way, but got soaking wet. While he was shivering over a cup of hot cocoa, a pretty girl came over and draped a wool poncho over his shoulders. When their eyes met, he knew she was the one. They talked until the café closed, started dating and were married within the year.

"My brother calls her his café angel, sent by Spirit, because things really turned around for him. He switched majors from business to history, which he loves, and found purpose teaching kids to appreciate their heritage. He's a great guy now. Every time he tells the story, he marvels at the *string* of events. It all looked accidental, but if any one piece hadn't happened, if he'd done one thing differently, they would've never met. Then he'd have gone down the path of despair and maybe even suicide."

"Wow! That's a great bunch of synchronicities," said Carmen.

"Or happy coincidences," muttered Sarah.

"Do you really believe in a random universe?" shot Jana angrily.

Sarah shrugged. The faintest smirk betrayed her pleasure at goading Jana.

"There may be chaos, but it's not random," pronounced Claire with professorial certainty. "Now try this imagery, to get a sense of how the universal web works. Everyone close your eyes. Imagine the Planet Earth floating in space, like you're on a space shuttle orbiting around it. Now see a bunch of lacy filaments like a spider web surrounding the whole planet. Every living thing—people, animals, plants, bugs—has a filament. The filaments of the web interconnect, criss-crossing back and forth, working down through layer after layer until they reach the earth's surface, and even continue below into earth's central core. It looks like a three-dimensional holograph. At points where the web filaments intersect, there's a synchronistic window, a portal. These convergence points provide 'holes' into liminal time. They link different layers of reality, different dimensions. When our filaments converge with filaments of other beings—in whatever dimensions—then we have a threshold experience. We have connections with other realms. Does that help?"

Jana was lost in the lacy filaments of earth's web, caught up in the luminous beauty of silvery threads weaving around the blue-green planet with its white cloud patches. She could float in space indefinitely, peaceful and joyous, just observing this exquisite planet of untold possibilities. Hearing voices of the women indistinctly, she breathed a deep sigh, pulled her awareness back into her body and opened her eyes.

"So the universal web is made up of these strings?" asked Mary, Jana's nurse colleague.

"Maybe, but its hard to completely merge theoretical physics and consciousness," Claire observed. "Here's what I think is the best way to understand threshold experiences like dreams and synchronicities: the idea of interacting fields. We know biological organisms create morphic fields, some kind of emanation that leaves an imprint on their surroundings. Right, Lydia?"

The biologist nodded as Claire continued:

"When certain things occur over and over in a place, a field of morphic resonance is created. How do you pick up the sense of danger when you're in a cave that turns out to be a lion's den? Something happens in your awareness, more than what you see or smell. A subtle field operates there, the psi-field. It encodes, stores and transmits information. I think that field is what we pick up."

"Like the strong sense people get of being in sacred space when they enter a cathedral or monastery?" asked Jana.

"Exactly!" Claire was always pleased when her point got across. "If you're tuned into a field, you can receive its information, but if you're not then it's as if the field didn't exist. Everyone's mind seems to have a 'band-width' of psi-field receptivity, which gets wider in altered states of consciousness. This explains prophetic dreams, telepathy, past life recall, and simultaneous inventions."

"So we might be able to tune our minds to certain fields, like tuning a radio to different stations," Mary suggested.

"Something like that," agreed Claire.

"Along all the multiple dimensions?" Sarah seemed sincerely interested. "Would that put us into past and future, or parallel universes?"

"Maybe so," Jana ventured. "There's a group of physicists who think there are millions of parallel universes, we just don't know how to access them."

"You know, I think I had a psi experience," Sarah said thoughtfully. "The first time my parents took me to Israel, I was about eight. I was wandering around some ruins way out in the desert, just a bunch of low stone walls that had once been a village near the Dead Sea. All of a sudden my vision went fuzzy. As I looked down at my feet, they seemed dark brown, wearing rope sandals. I could sense the village humming all around me, almost hear voices and goats bleating. It was like I was there, in Judea a long time ago."

"That really does sound like tuning into another dimension, a psi phenomenon," Claire agreed, giving Sarah a forgiving look.

"Or almost slipping through a hole in space-time," remarked Lydia.

"Yeah, and traveling into the past," Mary said with a perplexed expression.

"Are we talking about traveling *physically* to other dimensions or universes, or doing it mentally?" Carmen asked.

"Physicists want to do it physically—same root for both words," quipped Sarah.

"Yes, but mystics and shamans do it with their consciousness," said Grace. In her typical quiet style, she waited until the group's discussion moved to areas that touched her life. Part Native and part African American, she knew something of shamans.

"Shamans enter an altered state of consciousness, a kind of trance, often by using substances like mushrooms but sometimes without any. In this state they can project their consciousness into other realms. Native people believe shamans travel among spirits and gods, gaining special knowledge while in the supernatural realms. They may use animals or plants as naguals or familiars, and go to places of power to enter other dimensions, places where shamans have made journeys over many years, because these have special energy. Scientific studies of these power places show higher than normal electromagnetic frequencies."

"Huh! Sounds like morphic fields," Mary observed.

"I've always wondered about shamanic journeying," said Jana. "Do they actually go to other realms? Does their body move to another dimension?"

"Exactly the question Carlos Castenada posed to the Yaqui shaman Don Juan," Sarah declared triumphantly. She liked getting a jump on the intellectuals. "Carlos had the experience while in an altered state of being a crow and flying over the village landscape. He saw trees and huts from the air just as a flying crow would. So he asked if he actually was the crow or if his consciousness was identified with it. And do you know what Don Juan said?" She paused for dramatic emphasis.

"He said 'What difference does it make'?" answered Grace.

"Exactly," Sarah conceded, deflated and a little annoyed.

Jana's attention came into sharp focus.

The crow. The shaman became the crow.

Chills ran up her spine as cold talons pressed against her neck. A wave of darkness clouded her vision and the sound of flapping wings filled her ears. Reaching quickly to grasp her neck, the sensations abated as mocking caws faded into the distance.

"Some say shamans project their subtle body, the energy double of our physical form that hovers an inch or so around us," said Claire.

Jana couldn't follow the rest of Claire's discourse. The chilliness would not leave her body. Her neck hurt, although she couldn't feel anything unusual.

"When they use a power place to launch their subtle body, they're taking advantage of field resonances built up over years or centuries. These fields tap into the archetypal realm, where a lot of the symbolism used by shamans comes from. Their power animals, gods and ancestral beings are all archetypal forms."

"That's right," said Grace. "Where did you learn about shamans?"

"Psychology is a big field," Claire remarked with a shrug. "Shamans also go to different levels of the spirit realm, don't they?"

"Uh-huh. They see the universe in three levels—the underworld, the middle world that we inhabit as humans, and the upper world of celestial beings. They learn specific routes to travel to each level, and power animals or familiars often assist them."

"Like crows?" Jana asked weakly.

"Crows are common naguals of Native American shamans," Grace replied, noticing Jana's uneasy energy. Then she looked around at Sarah and said:

"You're right too about what Don Juan told Carlos. Shamans don't distinguish the real from the unreal. They believe all experience is valid. To them, what happens is real in the dimension it occurs in. What they learn is brought back into our ordinary world, the middle level, to benefit individual people or their tribe. Some journeys can be dangerous, and sometimes shamans don't return. When this happens their body might die, or they may become mentally deranged."

"Wow, that sounds a lot like the movie 'Matrix'," said Carmen. "The good guys, you know, Neo, Morpheus and Trinity, did almost exactly the same thing. They got hooked up to these plugs—kind of like a web—that catapulted them into the apparent real world we live in. But actually this world was like a holograph, a creation of images. In reality the people in it were hooked to plugs that fed their electrical energy to the fiendish machines, but they were drugged into believing they lived in that 'real world.' The good guys had just become aware of the hookup and gone through a process to disconnect."

Most of the women were nodding that they had seen the movie.

"But here's the interesting thing," continued Carmen. "When the good guys deliberately got hooked up, and went to the holographic world to rescue others, they had to fight humanoids working for the machines. In the fighting, they could get killed and that would mean their actual body, in a trance state while plugged in, would also die. Like shamanic journeys, huh?"

"Yeah, into different levels of reality," observed Mary thoughtfully.

"You're changed by what you experience when you return from these journeys," Claire declared. "You've connected with an archetypal field in the collective consciousness. This sets up a magnetic tendency to attract experiences that fit the patterns. When we're hooked up with an archetype, certain events happen in our life.

"Here's the key point: archetypes and their fields orchestrate synchronicity. Magnetic forces are set into motion, move along strings through inter-dimensional portals and put us into liminal time. Then we have 'real world' experiences that magically correspond to what's in our consciousness, at times even before we're aware of it! I think this is the field that mystics and visionaries tap into, the realm of gods and goddesses, guides and masters, mythic and spiritual figures. The field that brings matter and consciousness together."

Everyone was quiet for a few moments after Claire finished.

"So what can we conclude from all this?" asked Carmen, bringing the group's evening toward closure.

23

"I believe that most of what exists in the universe is invisible, at least to ordinary sight," Grace ventured. "Some kind of matrix holds all possibilities, hovering out there in suspended animation, waiting to pop into being. Maybe all parallel universes and all time are in this matrix—so that past, present and future are occurring simultaneously. But, we're mostly tuned into the present, 3-D world. When we're in liminal states, portals open for us into these other realities."

"So, our ability to tune our consciousness to other dimensions is what allows us to have experiences that are called mystical," mused Jana.

"Or, these experiences can come knocking on our door through dreams and synchronicities, which brings our discussion full circle," concluded Sarah with a touch of self-satisfaction.

Everyone laughed.

"More tea?" asked Carmen.

Most of the women pursued tea in the kitchen or sought the bathroom. Grace looked thoughtfully at Jana and said:

"I've had some puzzling dreams too. One turned out to be really important. Would you like to hear it?"

"Oh, yes," said Jana.

They moved to the far corner of the room, standing close together. In a soft voice, Grace told her story:

"When I was 14 and growing up in Oakland, I had a serious depression. I didn't feel like I belonged anywhere, I just didn't fit in. I couldn't identify with the black kids at school; I wasn't part of their culture. But I wasn't really white either. My mom is mostly white with a little Native American, but was distant from that side of her family. My dad is maybe 25% black, but moved so many times he didn't have any local ties. We moved a lot during my childhood. I felt like a racial and cultural mish-mash. I hardly had any friends and wasn't interested in school or much of anything else. I read lots of fantasy and sci-fi books to escape my pain and loneliness. I was especially intrigued by stories about dragons. Images of these huge scaly fire-breathing creatures with wings and slitted eyes filled my daydreams.

"Then I started noticing lizards. They were everywhere—on the sidewalk, on my doorstep, skittering over rocks in the park, climbing the fence behind my house. They looked more and more like miniature dragons and I loved to see them, they brought light into my dreary days. I started having dreams about lizards, but not the little ones around home. These were about a foot long and had heavy heads, thick bumpy skin, short legs and fat tails. After weeks of these dreams, I went to the library and looked at a lizard book. There they were! Gila monsters, native to the desert southwest. I was amazed. I knew I had to go where these big lizards lived, it was like they were calling me.

"After grilling my mom, I found out she had an uncle in Tucson. I convinced her to let me visit Uncle Willy. She was actually relieved that I was interested in doing anything. He was a kind, wise old man and took me to wildlife parks and museums to see Gila monsters. As I learned about his life, a window opened to my Native American lineage. We visited distant relatives at a reservation. I totally resonated with so many aspects of that culture, the desert, native jewelry and crafts, and indigenous worldviews that I felt a whole unknown part of myself come alive. From native elders I learned that lizards are guardians of the inner world, and connect you with the primordial earth and your own steadiness of purpose. This led to my career in indigenous art. And, I discovered inner guides through native rituals. In one vision quest I met my main guide, White Buffalo Woman. She has taught me so much, and assisted me in lots of situations over the years.

"There were real synchronicities in all this, from animal messengers to dreams to finding a mentor and a spirit guide."

Jana listened intently, enraptured by Grace's descriptions.

"That's a great story," Jana said, "thanks so much for telling me. How do you communicate with White Buffalo Woman?"

"She seems to put thoughts or ideas into my head," said Grace. "Sometimes I see faint images of her in my inner vision during meditation. Once on a vision quest in the desert, she appeared like a semi-transparent figure floating in the sky. But I'm really aware of her presence most of the time. Have you had contact with guides?"

Jana shook her head.

"No. I've read a lot about guides but I'm not aware of any."

"Don't lose hope. Your guides are there anyway. If you ask, they show up in ways you can recognize them. You may need a helper, an archetype or power animal. They help you create the energy field that draws the guides to you. A guide can help you understand the meaning of your dream."

Jana hugged Grace with new appreciation. As she said good-byes to the group, a wisp of thought floated through her awareness: this evening's focus was fuel for her quest.

Looking appraisingly in the mirror at her wrinkles, Jana applied make-up strategically. Her looks were the last thing most ER patients cared about. The 3 to 11 shift at Bayside Community Hospital near downtown Oakland could be a zoo, handling traumas and serious illness. Or, it could be quiet, one never knew. Anyhow, she liked to look presentable. The staff had to look at her, after all. Maybe it was just a habit, a social custom.

How much of what we do is just a string of chemical reactions coursing through our brains. Strings again! She laughed softly to herself.

"Did you say something, sweetie?" came Robert's voice from the adjacent office. "No, I was just laughing to myself about my thoughts."

"That good, huh?" Robert walked over and stood in the bathroom door. "Was it something from your group last night?"

"You must be psychic." Jana smiled at him as she put her make-up away. "That's what we talked about. Psychic phenomena, quantum physics and altered states of consciousness. It was really interesting. I learned some things about Grace that I never knew before."

She brushed her hair and settled the soft curls to her satisfaction.

"You'll have to tell me more tomorrow," Robert said.

"OK. Well, I'm off," said Jana, giving him a quick kiss as she grabbed her purse and threw on her sweater.

"You're fine," Mario pronounced, draping stethoscope around neck as he finished Jana's exam. "Excellent prognosis for no further fainting episodes."

"Thanks, Mario."

Jana was minimally reassured by the young ER doctor's confident manner. The powerful sensations of her "episodes," impossible to describe clearly, troubled her deeply.

It's more than physiology. There's no way I can tell him what it is.

She joined Mary for change of shift report at the nurses' station. So far it appeared pretty quiet.

"Who's on tonight?" asked Mary.

"Mario and that new doc, Frank," said the nurse going off shift. "Narcotic count correct, all rooms re-stocked. Mike's finishing up a laceration in Room 1. There's a call from 3 West, they're waiting for more information about an admit this morning. Husband was supposed to bring it in, patient's name is Silverman. That's about it. Well, except for Tony's new car."

The nurse nodded toward the admissions clerk sitting across the room at his desk.

Tony looked up at the nurses and smiled. His dark soulful eyes danced with delight, and sensuously curved lips displayed the absolutely charming smile that women found irresistible. However, Tony was gay and up-front about it. Wavy black hair styled back from the forehead was sculpted to just below the ears, giving him a 1928 look with an exotic twist. With the frame of a bodybuilder going to flab, his well-muscled torso slopped into expanding waist and hips, a fullness that resolved into muscular and shapely thighs. Tight jeans and polo shirt revealed his form suggestively with unfortunate emphasis on "love handles" bulging just above the belt.

"So, Tony, tell us about the new car," said Mary.

Tony stood and used graceful limpid hand motions to emphasize his points.

"You won't believe this, I hardly can myself," he said. "My partner Joe has a friend who's an auto mechanic. This guy has an arrangement with a couple of used car dealers, that when they get a real bargain car in they call him for first option to buy. Joe told him I was looking, and he told Joe about this one. I went to the lot and couldn't believe my eyes."

He paused to dramatize the story.

"It's a 1999 Jaguar, mint condition, 56,000 miles, silver-green with tan leather interior, and all the dealer wanted was $15,000!"

"Hey, that's great Tony," said Mary. "I've always admired Jaguars, they're so sleek and classy. Aren't they expensive to maintain?"

"You know, it's not so bad now that Ford owns Jaguar. I hear parts are expensive," Tony replied. "But what the heck, I saved a lot and hopefully it won't need much. For sure I'm driving this one carefully. Can't get in a wreck like I did with the last car. It's got that cool silver jaguar ornament on the hood. If you get a chance tonight, take a look. It's in the staff lot."

"How wonderful," Jana added. "I'll try to see it."

Tony threw his charming smile at the two women again, then sat down at his desk to continue work. A moment later he spun his chair around and held out an open magazine.

"Take a look, this is similar but a later model," he said.

Jana took the magazine and gazed at the smooth contours of a metallic gold Jaguar speeding down a jungle road. The hood ornament depicted a silver jaguar in mid-leap, front legs extended together. Looking admiringly from the side of the road were a couple of actual jaguars, their tawny coats blanketed with round black spots, their long tails trailing close to the ground. The ad was captioned simply "No contest."

Well, I'm not sure I agree with that, Jana thought. But she had to admit it was a beautiful car. She passed the magazine to Mary, who looked at the ad and handed it back to Tony.

"Well, Tony," Mary said, "it's a great car and you deserve it. Congratulations."

"Thanks, its kind of symbolic for me," Tony said with a touch of shyness.

The phone rang and Mary picked it up, getting involved in answering questions about when a child's fever would become cause for concern.

Jana mused about the Jaguar car being symbolic for Tony. Did it represent strength, courage, cunning, power? She had never thought much about jaguars before. They lived in forests in South America and were the biggest predators there, like pumas in the western United States. Were jaguars power animals for the native people in South America? She recalled last night's discussion with Grace. Might the jaguar hold some meaning for her?

Before she could pursue these thoughts, two men entered the emergency room lobby. One held a washcloth over his right eye, mumbling about getting stuck by a branch. While Tony got the patient registered, Jana stuck her head into the doctor's room to notify Frank and then set up Room 2 with an eye tray. Within five minutes, Frank was examining the patient's eye, with Jana assisting. The minor injury was quickly treated.

The rest of the evening saw little action. Jana had enough time to sneak out and look at Tony's new-used Jaguar car in the staff parking lot.

She had to admit it was a thing of beauty. Moonlight gleamed off pale contours, the leaping jaguar on the hood casting an elongated shadow. In the dim light, Jana almost thought the jaguar ornament moved. As her fingers stroked its cool metal smoothness, an eerie feeling crept over her neck and shoulders. Wings flapped in a nearby tree. Startled, Jana grabbed her neck protectively and turned quickly. Nothing was there. Soft wind sighed in treetops. Traffic noise roared in the distance. Muffled voices drifted from somewhere near the hospital entrance.

The near-full moon hovered low against the night sky. Few stars were visible, most lacking brilliance to shine through the city's ambient light. Just below the moon, one large star twinkled defiantly.

The evening star that appears just after dusk. What's that star? Geez, I should know.

Jana rolled over star rhymes in her mind.

Venus! The evening star is Venus. . . Wish I may, wish I might, have the wish I wish tonight. . . Venus, the jaguar, the crow . . . I wish to know.

The star held her secrets. Jana returned to the ER.

An hour before end of shift, the ER door flew open and a crowd burst noisily into the lobby. Four children ran to the check-in window, gesturing wildly and breathlessly chattering in a mixture of Spanish and English. Squeezing through the entry doors came a man and woman, half dragging and half carrying a rotund older woman whose arms hung limply, head bobbing erratically as she was transported awkwardly across the lobby.

"Nurses!" Tony called loudly.

Jana and Mary leaped into action, quickly taking in the situation.

"Get a wheelchair," Mary told the nursing assistant Peg who scurried down the hall.

Jana dealt with the family while Mary alerted the doctors and set up Room 3.

"Mee moo-ther, she seeek." The middle age woman holding up her lethargic cargo spoke in halting English with a thick Spanish accent.

"Está diabética," offered the man in Spanish.

"OK, we'll help her out, endiendo problema," reassured Jana as Peg came with the wheelchair. Easing the old woman into the wheelchair, Jana felt her pulse, which was slow but full. Quickly wheeling into Room 3, the nurses lifted and heaved the plump little Mexican woman onto the exam table. Mary took vital signs while Jana assessed her state of consciousness.

"Señora?" Jana spoke close to the woman's ear, smelling the fruity odor of ketosis on her breath. The old woman moaned and muttered something unintelligible in Spanish.

Turning to Peg, Jana said:

"Go get Mario, he's Spanish."

"I thought he was Italian," said Peg.

"Last name Fuentes, he's Spanish," Jana said.

"OK," Peg conceded as she rushed off.

"She's diabetic," Jana said to Mary. "We'll need some stat blood."

Mario whisked into the exam room, a fair-skinned young man with close-cut brown beard and blue eyes. He exuded an air of self-confidence blended with humane concern and calmness; the epitome of the new breed of ER physicians who liked the fast paced action and lack of entanglement that emergency medicine offered.

"What do we know about her?" he asked, feeling her pulse while reading vital signs.

"Diabetic, speaks Spanish, probably in ketoacidosis," said Jana.

"Low blood pressure—100/60, rapid pulse and respiration," said Mary.

"Hola Señora," Mario spoke loudly to the old woman. "¿Como está? ¿Tiene dolor?"

She moaned again and shook her head, but she was too obfuscated to really respond.

"Mary, go get as much history as you can from her folks," Mario directed. "Jana, we'll need an IV with ½ NS and a CBC and SMA-7 stat. Get a finger stick glucose now. We'll get ABG's once we've got an IV going." He listened to her heart and lungs with his stethoscope, concentrating.

Jana knew the ABG's—arterial blood gasses—would be diagnostic of the old woman's degree of acidosis, caused by burning body fat for energy when glucose (blood sugar) was not readily available due to lack of insulin, the underlying problem in diabetes. The by-products of burning fat include ketones, which build up in the blood, making it too acidic. This causes the symptoms of ketoacidosis, including thirst, frequent urination, vomiting, abdominal pain, fruity breath odor, and mental stupor that can progress to coma.

Jana moved quickly, getting an autolance and glucometer from the counter top. Holding the old woman's right hand palm up, she pressed the autolance against the tip of the woman's middle finger, noting that no reflex withdrawal movement occurred. In a couple of seconds, a small droplet of dark red blood formed on the fingertip. When it was nicely rounded, suspended and almost ready to drip she pressed the test strip against the blood droplet, soaked it well and inserted it into the glucometer. In another couple of seconds the small digital screen blinked red numbers reporting the old woman's blood glucose: 620.

"620," Jana told Mario. This was severely elevated; normal blood glucose was around 120 mg/dL. Values above 300 mg/dL were considered very high.

"Just as I thought," he said. "Out of control diabetes. As soon as you draw blood for labs, give her a bolus of regular insulin 20 units and start a liter of ½ NS with regular insulin, 7 units per hour."

Mario checked the old woman's pupils.

"Responsive," he said with satisfaction. "Vitals are stable, she's not too deep."

Jana gathered equipment for the blood draw and IV. She extended the old woman's right arm, placed a tourniquet around the biceps and searched for good veins. Not surprisingly, fat layers buried the forearm veins deep inside, even the inner elbow veins were buried. Jana sighed softly and decided to examine the back of the hand for good veins.

She turned the old woman's hand. A shock of recognition caused her to inhale sharply and freeze.

The old woman's fingers were amazingly long and slender for her obese body. There was very little fat on her hand, making several large veins stand out starkly. They traced snaking patterns across the surface. Light brown skin, thin and nearly transparent, contrasted with darker splotches from aging spots. Huge knuckles stood out against slender fingers.

It's the hand from my dream!

Jana felt the familiar chill with tingling sensations moving up her spine, causing hairs to rise at the nape of the neck. Heart pounding, she broke into a cold sweat, feeling shaky inside. For what seemed like a timeless moment she sat transfixed—not long enough for Mario to notice, however, as he continued writing in the chart.

With Herculean effort, she pulled herself back into the present. Her mind was numb as she functioned on automatic pilot, deftly threaded the IV needle into one of the old woman's large veins, collected blood specimens, hooked up the IV and administered the bolus of insulin. After securing the IV in place, she added insulin to the bag of ½ NS solution hanging from the IV pole, labeled it and adjusted the drip rate.

Mary entered the exam room with paperwork obtained from the old woman's family and handed it to Mario. As the two talked, Jana moved around the exam table, took the old woman's other hand and gently uncurled the long fingers. Turning the hand over, she gazed again on the uncanny resemblance to the dream hand. No clear

31

thoughts formed in her mind; she swam in a sea of sensations ranging from awe to visceral uneasiness deep in her solar plexus. She was dimly aware that her heart was pounding rapidly.

". . . a 74 year old Mexican visiting her family, name Angelina Menchu, long time diabetic but not good about checking blood sugars and taking meds," Mary was saying as Jana's mind became more present. "She's been feeling unwell the past 2-3 days, appetite down. They thought she might have a cold coming on. No known fever. No one paid attention to voiding or diarrhea, but no complaints of abdominal pain. No vomiting. She was taking more naps than usual. Tonight after dinner the daughter went to check on her and couldn't arouse her, that's when they decided to bring her in."

"Do they know her meds?" asked Mario.

"No, but they did bring in the bottles," said Mary, handing him three small plastic medicine bottles. "Its all in Spanish."

Mario perused the labels, easily translating the medications: Metformin, a common oral medicine for diabetes; ibuprofen for joint and arthritis pain, and lisinopril for high blood pressure.

"Diabetes type II, hypertension, arthritis," he said, writing in the chart. "Seems pretty straight-forward, but lets rule out infection and see how bad the ketoacidosis is. Can you run the blood over to the lab?"

"Sure, I'll have Peg do it," Mary replied, gathering the blood specimens.

"Jana, let me know if there's any change in vitals. Do another glucometer reading in 30 minutes. Should have most of the lab back by then."

Mario and Mary left the exam room.

Jana sat beside the semi-conscious old woman, holding her left hand. She slipped her fingers into the woman's palm, as she had seen the young girl do innumerable times in the dream. The long big-knuckled fingers closed and pressed softly. Jana's entire arm felt electrified, currents of tingling energy coursing from hand to shoulder. She sat very still, attuned intensely to her inner sensations. Her heart rate had slowed down and her breathing was shallow. Taking a few deep breaths, she became aware of something vibrating in her mid-chest, the heart chakra region. The electrical energy was activating something, a pulsing vibration that was not unpleasant but rather strange, unusual, energizing.

After a few minutes the old woman's grip loosened and Jana's fingers slipped out of her palm. By reflex of many years' nursing practice, Jana snapped to attention and began checking the woman's vital signs.

Blood pressure 116/68, pulse 110 and regular, respiration 24. Doing OK. IV dripping evenly and secure. She inserted a catheter to check on urinary output and did a dipstick; values were as expected for diabetic ketoacidosis. There were no signs of urinary tract infection, which might have pushed diabetes out of control. Jana wondered what caused the old woman's problem.

For the first time, Jana really looked at the old woman's face.

Angelina Menchu—different last name for a Mexican, Jana thought.

Angelina's face was broad and square, with prominent cheekbones. Her temples seemed too narrow, but cascading silver hair with several dark strands compensated nicely. The dominant feature of Angelina's face was the nose—large and curved, like a mountain arising suddenly from a broad plain. However, the nose was narrower than expected for its impressive size. Thankfully, her mouth was also large and wide. Although wrinkled, her brown skin was remarkably supple for one so old. Closed eyes were sunken into cavernous sockets.

Who is she?

Jana queried no one in particular. Her mind was still not able to wrap around this event. Floating in the recesses of awareness were snippets of her women's group discussion the night before. Synchronicities, apparent coincidences with deeper meanings, networking strings, openings in the fabric of space-time, liminal portals . . . something unusual was happening.

Angelina's hand matches the old woman's hand in my dream perfectly. This must be a synchronicity, a portal in space-time.

Jana was in the mind-warp of three distinct realities. She kept drifting into the dream and its sensations, and remembering flashes of the women's group conversation. A moment later she was mentally processing as a nurse, watching the IV and catheter, taking vital signs, observing the old woman's condition. She had a rather disembodied sense, like an aspect of her consciousness was standing apart, observing the interplay of mental processes and physical actions. It was a state of hyper-awareness, and things seemed in slow motion.

Glancing at the clock, Jana realized 30 minutes had elapsed and she needed to get another glucometer reading. This time Angelina twitched her hand as Jana used the autolance to prick a finger; a good sign that she was getting more responsive. The digital readout appeared: 545. The blood glucose was coming down in response to IV insulin.

A few minutes later a lab technician came to draw arterial blood gasses and left a preliminary lab report. Before Jana could call, Mario appeared and she gave him an update. He perused the report, nodded and went to examine Angelina. The lab values were as expected for diabetic ketoacidosis. A slightly elevated white blood count was not enough to point to an infection. Maybe Angelina had simply been over-eating, enjoying her children and grandchildren, not paying attention to her sugars.

Peg brought Angelina's daughter into the exam room. In fluent Spanish, Mario explained the old woman's condition and plans for admission to the hospital for several days. Jana caught a word here and there, for her Spanish was limited. The daughter looked relieved and grateful, saying "Gracias, Doctor," over and over. Señora Menchu would be taken to the medical unit called 3 West. The family could visit her in the morning. Her condition was stabilizing now and she was out of danger.

Jana ushered Angelina's daughter back to the ER waiting room, and watched the family's animated interchange. Some of the children had fallen asleep on the floor. The parents gathered them up and waved good-by.

It was 11:00 pm, time for the nursing shift change. Jana went to the nurses' station to report out: Angelina Menchu, 74 year old Mexican woman visiting her family locally, in diabetic ketoacidosis, now stabilizing, to be admitted to 3 West. All labs done, IV insulin drip and foley catheter in place, still minimally responsive.

And with the hands of the old woman in my dream.

The next day Jana went to Bayside Hospital an hour early. She felt compelled to visit Angelina Menchu. At the 3 West nurses station, she got an update on Angelina's condition. Ms. Menchu was alert, responsive and had ambulated briefly that morning. She was still on IV's but was tolerating oral liquids and would be advanced to a diabetic diet. Her glucose was almost normal and the acidosis had been largely corrected. The doctors were still uncertain what precipitated the ketoacidosis, as they had not found any source of infection. She was in Room 314 and had visitors.

Jana hesitated outside Room 314, feeling uncertain of what to do or say. It wasn't every day you got to talk with someone in your dreams. Angelina probably didn't speak English anyway.

34

Oh well, I'll give it a try, Jana thought and entered the room.

Angelina sat propped up in bed, the IV from last night still in place. Sitting beside her bed were two girls, one a well developed teenager and the other about 7 or 8 years old. They were all watching the TV attached high on the wall. Jana could not help glancing at the TV, as a silken female voice with a faint British accent said:

" . . the ultimate driving machine—Jaguar—for the discriminating few." There on the screen was a metallic red Jaguar accelerating gracefully across a manicured countryside, it could have been Middlesex in England or horse country in Kentucky, with rich green fields bordered by white fences, gently sloping into the distance as a few majestic oaks fanned wide branches over contentedly grazing thoroughbreds.

Jaguar! Synapses sizzled in Jana's brain. Power animals, guides bringing a communication from the spirit world. In Angelina Menchu's room. There was no doubt that a link was being given between Jana's dream and what this old woman represented.

Shaken, Jana hardly knew how to begin as three pairs of eyes focused on her.

"Buenos dias, Señora Menchu," Jana said. "¿Como está? Yo no hablo espanol bien, y entiendo poquito." She explained that she did not speak Spanish well, and understood little. "Estoy su enfermera de anoche en la sala de emergencia." She attempted to say that she was her nurse in the emergency room last night.

Angelina's broad face broke into a beaming smile. Her deep black eyes twinkled giving amazing life to her face, taking some of the focus from her huge nose. She began speaking rapidly in Spanish, the gist of which Jana took to be thanking her for her help. Jana smiled and shrugged, indicating she did not understand.

The older girl spoke: "Grandma says thank you for taking care of her. She does not remember much but there was a woman with soft hands who cared. That must be you."

Jana was surprised momentarily at the girl's perfect English without noticeable accent. Then she realized the girls were probably born in the States.

"Well, yes," Jana said, "that was probably me. I was her nurse in the ER. I just wanted to see how she is doing."

The girl translated, listened to another barrage of enthusiastic Spanish from Angelina, and told Jana that her grandmother was feeling like herself again, thanks to your wonderful hospital and doctors and you. She was sorry she had not taken her medicine, and would surely do this without fail in the future, as the doctors emphasized. The girl added on her own that the family celebrated two birthdays and grandma ate too much cake.

Jana nodded, unable to take her eyes off Angelina's face. She asked where Angelina lived, where she was from.

The girl half-translated and half-injected her own views, saying her grandmother was from a small town in the Yucatan called Piste. It was near the famous Mayan ruin, Chichén Itzá; many people came there for equinox celebrations. Not far away was the colonial town of Mérida, a wonderful city of white buildings and numerous plazas; she had visited there last year. Every night there were dances in the plazas, and lots of shops with crafts, clothing and jewelry as well as many stalls for food and drink. Obviously the girl had thoroughly enjoyed her visit to Mérida. She suggested that Jana would really enjoy the city.

The younger girl, with large dark eyes and a slender face, added that grandma had been visiting them for almost a month. Her English was also excellent. Jana remarked that they must be enjoying grandma's visit, which the girls affirmed with gestures and patting Angelina's hands. Their open affection was sweet to Jana.

Then a discussion ensued among the girls and their grandmother, in Spanish. The older girl looked puzzled, shaking her head. Angelina kept repeating herself, seemed to be insisting on something. She looked at Jana, gesturing with her left hand that was free of the IV tubing. Jana heard her say "Es muy importante,"—very important— several times. Finally the younger girl acquiesced to her grandmother's request to communicate something to Jana. But the older girl rolled her eyes, stepped back and appeared quite embarrassed.

"My grandmother wants me to tell you something very important," the young girl said. "My grandmother is a curendera, a medicine women among the people of her village. She knows things, I don't understand how. She says the spirits want to tell you something."

The girl paused, shyly glancing at Jana, aware of the cultural gap that her generation was trying to span, hoping not to be thought of badly.

Jana felt her heart rate accelerating, and the tingling sensation coursed up her spine.

This is it, she thought, *this is the message from the dream.*

"Please tell me," Jana said in a reassuring tone. "I know there's something I'm meant to hear from your grandmother."

"It doesn't make any sense," said the girl apologetically. "Grandma says that Chak wants to see you. He wants you to come to his place after you go to Tikal."

Jana looked perplexed. Angelina spoke again to her younger granddaughter, seeing that the girl was at least minimally willing to communicate her message to Jana. They exchanged several sentences, and then Angelina said emphatically "¡Háblale!"

The younger girl sighed at this command to speak and continued:

"Grandma says that she is not the one you are seeking. She is just a messenger. You must go to the place of the jaguar, which I think is around Tikal, to find what you are seeking. Then you will go see Chak."

"Who is Chak?" Jana asked. She was dimly aware that Tikal was another famous Maya ruin.

"Chak is the rain god," said the young girl. "I don't know much about all that. It's part of the old religion that Grandma still follows, though we're Catholic. She, uh . . . talks to the old Maya gods."

"Is your grandmother Maya?" asked Jana.

"Yes, our family is half-Maya mixed with Spanish," the girl answered. "And Tikal, it's a Maya ruin in the jungle."

"En Guatemala," Angelina added, understanding a little of what was transpiring.

The teenage girl had turned her attention to the TV, obviously not wanting any part of this conversation. The younger girl fell silent, looking embarrassed. Jana decided not to pursue it farther, as Angelina was beaming and seemed satisfied. Jana took the old woman's free hand, looking once again at the prominent veins snaking across the back, and the long slender big-knuckled fingers she had seen so often in the dream. Angelina pressed Jana's hand warmly.

"Muchas gracias, Señora," Jana said.

"De nada," Angelina replied. Sensing that Jana was leaving, she added, "Adiós, hija."

Jana knew hija meant daughter—strange that the old woman called her that. Saying good-by to the girls, she glanced once more at Angelina, and left.

Images flooded Jana's mind. The jaguar in Tikal, a Maya ruin in the jungle of Guatemala. A mysterious rain god called Chak summoning her to his place, wherever that might be. Was an archetypal field reaching out to her across dimensions? Were these synchronicities popping through openings in space-time to give her an important message? Jana had an eerie feeling that a huge force field was enveloping her, changing things in her life indelibly.

Chak Mask, Labnah

Clouds drifted across San Francisco Bay, caressing the hilltops and forming wispy fingers in canyons punctuating the low mountains. Streaks of pale sunlight penetrated the clouds at irregular intervals, brightening the breakfast nook where Jana and Robert sat. Off work that day, they were enjoying a leisurely breakfast.

"I think the clouds will burn off by noon," Robert predicted. It was a common fall pattern in the bay area microclimate.

"Probably," Jana agreed. She cradled a warm cup of Indonesian blend, fair-traded organic coffee. Inhaling the tantalizing aroma then sipping the strong dark brew, she savored the "complex earthy, nutty flavor with a broad smooth finish," as the label described.

All of the above and more, Jana concluded, exhaling with satisfaction.

Jana was mulling over how to tell Robert about Angelina Menchu. She felt unsettled, pushed out of her comfort zone by the strange but synchronistic events of the past month. As Robert read the morning paper, she glanced at his profile. His clean-shaven jaw line was strong and well defined; though loosening neck skin hinted that he was older than he looked. The straight line of his nose with a high bridge reminded Jana of classic Greek statues. Wide-set blue eyes brought balance and grace to his face. Altogether, a handsome man, Jana reflected. But, a man who found reason and logic more comfortable terrain than the swirling domains of consciousness and metaphysics. She had to begin somewhere, so she jumped in.

"What do you know about the Maya?"

Robert shot her a quizzical look, raising his left eyebrow.

"The Maya?" he repeated, setting down the newspaper. The very unexpectedness of her question set his mental computer into high gear.

"Well . . . they were an ancient civilization in Central America, highly developed, who built large cities in the jungles. They had a hieroglyphic type of writing and kept amazingly precise calendars based on advanced knowledge of astronomy. Their civilization peaked then rather suddenly disappeared before the Spaniards invaded México, I'm not sure about the exact time frame. I really don't know much more."

Turning full face to Jana, he asked intently:

"Why on earth do you want to know about the Maya?"

Jana took a deep breath, letting it out slowly. She looked straight into his eyes.

"There might be some connection with my dream about the old woman's hand," she said slowly. "Several coincidences—though it's hard to believe they were accidental—happened in my women's group and at work. I'll tell you the details, but here is the bottom line: I took care of an old Maya woman from México visiting her family here, she was in diabetic crisis, and when I started an IV in her hand, I recognized that it was *exactly* the same hand as in my dream."

"No kidding!" Robert exclaimed. His face registered genuine surprise.

"*Exactly* the same," Jana repeated for emphasis. "It was uncanny, and it sent me for a loop. So I went to see her in the hospital the next day. She told me, through her English-speaking granddaughters, that she was a messenger for some spirit who wanted me to go visit the place of Chak, but only after I'd gone to the place of the jaguar, Tikal. The granddaughter told me Chak was a Maya rain god, and that Tikal is a Maya ruin in Guatemala. I know it sounds weird, but with so many unusual links, I can't help feeling this is something really important."

"Whew! That's a bizarre story," Robert said, shaking his head. "Can you fill me in on more details?"

Nodding, Jana got up and poured them each another cup of coffee. Then she retold the events starting with the women's group discussion about synchronicities, liminal time, thresholds between dimensions, morphic and archetype fields, and the radical views of reality brought by quantum physics. She left out shamanic journeying; that would push the envelope too much for Robert. Nor did she mention the sinister experiences with crows; these were still too baffling.

She summarized Grace's story about lizards that guided her to connect with native roots and find her life work. Jana pointed out the role of power animals and linked this to the emergency room scenario with Tony's new Jaguar auto, the Jaguar commercial on TV just as she entered Angelina's hospital room, and the connection between jaguars and the jungle ruins of Tikal.

Nearly two hours passed before Jana finished giving Robert the details. He interjected questions at certain points, genuinely interested in understanding his wife's strange experiences as best he could. His logical mind kept checking these events against his view of reality, coming up with "does not compute." However, Jana was completely sincere and unerringly precise in her descriptions, so he could not doubt they were real. Robert was rapidly approaching a state of cognitive dissonance and Jana was clearly distressed.

True to his predictions, the low clouds had dissipated and now the sun shone fully through the bay window into their breakfast nook. Both had lost track of time, but the bright sunlight caught their attention.

Robert looked at his watch.

"Nearly noon," he remarked. It comforted him to relate to linear time, he reflected somewhat sheepishly. Looking empathetically as his lovely wife, now distraught and confused, he admitted with candor: "I don't know what to think."

Silence lasted for a long moment. Jana sensed both the subtle tension between them and his desire to be supportive.

"I don't blame you," she proffered. "I hardly know what to think myself."

"What will you do next?" he asked.

"I need to learn about the Maya."

"I think I know someone who can help," Robert enjoined with that masculine sense of relief when a concrete suggestion eases a difficult situation.

"Why don't you get together with Harry Delgardo?" Harry was their mutual friend, and a colleague at Mills College who taught in the Anthropology Department. "New World civilizations aren't his specialty, but I'm sure he knows enough to steer you in the right direction."

"That's a great idea," Jana said, her face brightening. "Harry knows a lot about cultural symbolism. He'll be able to help me piece things together. Thanks for the idea, sweetheart." She smiled and Robert reciprocated, the tension between them melting away.

Rising from the table simultaneously, Jana and Robert hugged each other, their lips touching in a soft kiss.

"Come to campus with me on Monday," Robert said, his arms still around her. "I'll call Harry this weekend and set up a time. You're off work, right?"

Jana nodded in confirmation. She leaned gently into his body, feeling inexplicably comforted by their physical contact. She always loved the feeling of Robert's arms around her. From the first embrace it felt like coming home, being united with her beloved whom she had known forever. And it stayed this way for all these years.

41

Hazy morning sunshine sparkled on dewdrops covering the lush verdant lawns of the Mills College campus. Cement walkways wended their way through groves of sycamore and spruce, eucalyptus and bay trees accenting white stucco walls and red tile roofs. An occasional tall palm showered a graceful cascade of serrated branches. Arched doorways and long wings added to the mission flavor of the architecture.

As Jana and Robert walked toward the Mills Center for Contemporary Music, the bells of El Campanil, the famous clock tower designed by architect Julia Morgan, sounded the quarter until the hour. Erected in 1904, El Campanil was billed as the first concrete structure on the west coast. Towering sycamores lined the road approaching the music building, whose venerable brick walls bespoke dignity and scholarship. At the entrance, Robert bent over and kissed Jana, lightly brushing her lips.

"Got to hurry," he said. "Meet you at the Rothwell Center for lunch."

"OK," Jana replied, appreciating his long muscular strides toward the entryway. Proceeding along the shaded sidewalk, she drew her sweater tight against the chill of late fall air.

Mills College, nestled in the Oakland foothills, is a small liberal arts school founded by a Christian missionary couple in 1852 as a "Young Ladies' Seminary". Offering the first BA degree to women west of the Mississippi River, Mills College added a Master's degree in 1921 giving graduate education to both women and men. Always forward thinking, the college hosted controversial speakers such as Mark Twain, Gertrude Stein, Margaret Mead, and notably Martin Luther and Coretta King during the desegregation movement in the late 1950's.

The music department at Mills College was world famous. Started in the 1870s, it hosted such luminaries as Emma Nevada, an internationally known opera singer and graduate of the college, and the famous Spanish cellist Pablo Casals. The French modern music composer Darius Milhaud was a professor at Mills for 30 years. According to Robert, who admittedly had a more highly developed appreciation for contemporary music than most, Milhaud's compositions were "intriguing and innovative," though his atonal structures did not appeal to "the masses." Dave Brubeck, the respected jazz improviser, studied with Milhaud at Mills College.

Jana finished the short walk from the music building to Lucie Stern Hall, home of the Anthropology department. Stern Hall was a large square structure of white stucco with an interesting six-sided roof design, showcasing red tile and long low arcade. Entering the main door, she quickly walked the familiar hall.

Harry Delgado's office door was characteristically open, unlike many of his colleagues who valued their privacy. Harry was outgoing and talkative, perennially hoping someone would drop by so he could engage in conversation, his favorite pastime. As Jana knocked, he swiveled his wooden chair eliciting a couple of creaks, waved toward the equally uncomfortable wooden armchair near the desk, and smiled gleefully.

"So good to see you," Harry gesticulated in an effusive style. He was small and wiry, with frizzled gray hair cropped unevenly. Bushy gray eyebrows projected haphazardly over the metal rims of his thick glasses. Clear gray eyes peered out quizzically, distorted by the trifocal lines but unmistakably twinkling.

Jana attempted to sit in the chair, but the seat was covered with magazines and haphazardly placed papers. Smiling apologetically, Harry leaned forward and grabbed the unruly pile, tossing it onto a small mountain of journals, papers and books that occupied the corner behind his desk. The new additions slid around then settled into the mess. Glancing around Harry's office, Jana noted the general disarray with books tilted precariously along shelves, papers hanging out erratically, and crumpled wads littering the floor among precarious stacks of books. A long spider web draped gracefully across the top of the curtain-less window. Harry's desk was even more daunting. There was not a clear spot, the phone was half-buried under manuscripts, and a small pile of books threatened to fall off one edge. Even the computer keyboard was partially covered with papers. Of course, the trashcan was overflowing. It was exactly as Jana remembered from her prior visits.

She wondered how Harry ever found anything, but somehow his keen spatial sense allowed him to hone in, making paradoxical order out of disorder. As always, he was oblivious to her bemusement at the disarray.

"So you want to learn about the Maya," Harry threw out, not one to waste precious conversation on social amenities. "Robert told me a little about your new fascination. Are you interested in modern Maya, ancient ones or both?"

Jana reflected briefly, then said thoughtfully:

"Both, I guess."

"That covers a lot of territory," Harry almost chortled, hitching his uncooperative swivel chair closer to Jana. After a few tugs, as the wheels stuck on a pile of journals, he gave up and continued:

"I can tell you a little about the contemporary Maya, as a cultural anthropologist. But for the ancients, you'll need other more knowledgeable sources. The field of Maya studies has become rather large and complex. Several disciplines are now collaborating, including archeology, epigraphy, biology, ethnology, ceramics, linguistics and art history. I've checked on a few sources and have suggestions for books you can get at the library."

Map of Maya Region

"Did the Maya people mostly die out?" Jana asked. "Robert said their civilization collapsed before the arrival of the Spanish conquistadors."

"Not at all!" exclaimed Harry, with animated hand gestures. "Today there are over seven million people of Maya descent living in southern México and Central America. Mostly in Guatemala, Belize, Honduras, the Yucatan and Chiapas, I believe. They've resisted the infusion of Spanish culture with remarkable tenacity, and preserved a great deal of their ancient customs and traditions. Altogether about 28-odd Mayan dialects are still spoken. These Maya people are largely rural farmers, living a life whose rhythms follow seasonal planting and harvesting of corn, beans and squash even as their ancestors did. They also sell fabric and weavings, pottery, foods and plant medicines at local markets to supplement their incomes."

"I had no idea there were so many Maya now," Jana remarked.

"Yes, but their living conditions are poor. In Central American countries there's a sharp division between the indigenous Maya and the elites descended from the Spaniards. The basic equation has been the same since the conquest: A small group of wealthy families owns most of the fertile land, and the indigenous people serve as laborers. Large plantations produce export crops like coffee, cotton, sugar and fruit; while the rural farmers have the poorest land on steep hillsides or tropical forests where soil becomes exhausted in a few years. Since farmers can't support their families, they work on the plantations—called *latifundios*—for terrible wages."

Harry clacked his tongue disapprovingly, shaking his shaggy mane.

"Maya families tend to be large, like all rural cultures. You know, cultural traditions, lack of birth control, the need for more working hands in the fields and homes. Entire families often live in one palapa, without water and electricity. The political system supports the elite; there's little motive for social reform that would reduce the cheap labor source. In recent years, wealthy countries including the U.S. have bought land and products from Central America for a pittance, often intervening politically to maintain a favorable regime. Over the years, there were uprisings and pockets of Maya resistance, suppressed with brutality and fear tactics. It's not a pretty picture, and our country's role is less than admirable."

"Wow," said Jana, "I've heard a little about guerilla warfare and exploitation of resources in Central America. Is the situation improving now?"

"Yes, there are numerous efforts underway, both local and international," Harry replied in a satisfied tone. "Amnesty International, the Oslo Peace Accords, the Rainforest Action Network, Heifer International and the Earth Island Institute are some groups working on human rights, ecological balance and economic reform for tribal peoples. Local initiatives such as farming co-ops and rural clinics get support from abroad."

He paused for a moment, as if recalling another important point.

"The situation in México is different," he added. "Its population is much more blended, about 90% are mestizo, a mixture of indigenous peoples and Spanish. After their war of independence in 1821, mestizos rose to leadership positions everywhere. There are still big gaps in wealth, with more traditional Mayas at the bottom rung. But in-between, you see mestizos in politics, education, arts, business, at all social levels."

"Tell me more about the current Maya preserving their customs and traditions," Jana requested.

"I'm no expert in this area," Harry reminded her, bushy eyebrows crawling over glasses rims as he furrowed his brow. "Here's what I do know. Traditional Maya in the wet areas live in square houses built of stone and plaster with palm thatch roofs. In the drier Yucatan regions, palapas have round walls of slender poles tied together; sometimes mud and plaster are used for finish. The high-pitched roof is covered by palm thatch. There's a single room with a central hearth; three stones are placed in a triangle where cooking pots are set. This is exactly the home and hearth arrangement used by ancient Maya. Today as in the past, the hearth is considered the center of home and family, a symbol of beliefs about the core of the universe. They often bury the afterbirth of children under the hearth. Modern Maya may ask where you're from by saying 'Where is your umbilicus buried?'

"The hearth has important spiritual symbolism. Maya creation mythology centers the cosmos in a three-stone hearth that lies in the constellation Orion with its three dominant stars. Each Maya home reflects this cosmos. Dedication rituals imbue homes with the soul-force that permeates the universe. Ancestral shrines and family altars have always been part of Maya residences from earliest times."

"So family life for the common people may not be a whole lot different now than in earlier times," Jana surmised.

"There is a lot of similarity," Harry agreed. "Their religious rituals and healing practices are still based on ancient customs, although with a Christianized overlay. In fact, Spanish and Maya religious institutions and beliefs were very similar in many respects: both burned incense during rituals, had images which they worshiped, had priests, built impressive temples or churches, conducted elaborate pilgrimages, and followed a sacred calendar. Both had a hero god who died and was resurrected—Jesus Christ for the Spaniards, and the Maize God for the Maya. Over the centuries, the Maya have blended together these gods, saints and rituals.

"One dramatic example is the Quiche Maya ceremony called Eight Monkey. This takes place every 260 days, following the old Maya Calendar Round, or sacred calendar. On that day, tens of thousands of Maya gather at dawn in the Guatemala highlands community of Momostenango. They form groups around many altars made from mounds of broken pottery, while over 200 shamans act as intermediaries between individual petitioners and the supreme deity *Dios Mundo (God World)*. The shamans pray that sins be forgiven and requests be granted, while each person adds a potsherd to the pile.

"Wherever we see the 260 day Calendar Round in use, there are shaman-priests or *daykeepers* whose job is to keep track of the days, so rituals take place at the right time. Another important function of shamans is divination, done using the calendar day signs or by casting red seeds or maize kernels. This is a deeply rooted, very old practice far out-dating the Spanish influence."

Jana felt that subtle whirring sensation in her mid-chest as Harry talked about shamans. She was coming to identify this sensation as the physical sign of a synchronistic connection, a moment when the window of space-time opens and two different realities interact. Her women's group discussion about shamans, and Angelina Menchu's status as a medicine woman in her village, flashed through her mind.

"So the shaman tradition of the ancient Maya is still strong today?"

"Right. The first shamans showed up in the Maya creation story, told in the *Popul Vuh*. Let's see if I can remember." He scratched his head. "Oh, yeah. The first two attempts by the creator gods to make human beings failed. So, they sought the counsel of an elderly husband and wife who were called the grandparents, because they were older than all the other gods. They both were daykeepers and diviners—shamans who knew secrets of the sacred calendar. They cast corn kernels and coral seeds, just like modern Maya diviners, for how to create proper humans. The husband was a matchmaker and the wife a midwife, roles that exist now in contemporary Maya society.

47

When the gods finally got it right they were successful in creating people from maize made of water and ground corn."

"What about healing practices?" Jana asked. "I'll bet ancient customs carry over in that area."

"Right," said Harry gleefully. He was thoroughly enjoying this discussion with such an avid listener. "Contemporary local healers are called *h'men,* which means 'performer' or 'doer.' They devise medicinal cures for sick people, and lead agricultural ceremonies for successful crops. A shaman has greater knowledge of spiritual and religious ceremonies, though there is overlap. H'men combine physical cures with spiritual practices. For instance, taking a plant medicine for nine days has more to do with the sacredness of the number nine than it does with properties of the medicine. During rituals, shamans speak to spirits of the otherworld or ancestors; burn incense and candles, and offer tobacco or a chicken as a sacrifice. These rituals usually take place at an old ruin site, the mouth of a cave, by a mound of rubble such as pottery shards, or by a cross erected on a hill."

"Are shamans dangerous? Can't they do harm to people?"

Harry nodded seriously.

"There are both good and bad shamans and h'men. People who wish ill on someone employ a bad shaman, called *brujo or bruja,* which is a Spanish word. The brujo conjures a spell that can lead to illness, possession by an evil spirit, or bad luck in general. To break these spells, the afflicted person visits a good shaman who uses techniques to drive the evil spirits out or dissolve the spell."

A growing sense of uneasiness crept into Jana. She was both repelled and fascinated by the discussion of shamans. Flitting at the edges of awareness were crow caws, cold talons and flapping wings.

"They use animal familiars sometimes, right?"

"Yes, often. These animal companions are called naguals by Native Americans. The shamanic arts—witchcraft to the Europeans—have long associations with animal magic and shapeshifting."

Shapeshifting! Chills ran up Jana's spine.

Harry seemed distracted, looking for something on his disorderly desk. Shaking his head, he muttered:

"It was here a minute ago . . ."

Jana didn't want to, but she was compelled to ask:

"Can . . . uh, can shamans become animals, like . . . like crows?"

"Well, yes, at least that's what they say," he replied, still rummaging through hopeless messes of papers. Turning back to Jana as his chair protested with a loud squeak, he either failed to notice or chose not to acknowledge her uneasiness.

"It's definitely part of the shamanic tradition. In some way they harness energies of animal familiars to bring about real-world effects. Still a mystery to me, but well-documented in anthropological studies."

"Are curenderas also shamans?" Jana was thinking of Angelina.

"I think they're Mexicanized female h'men," Harry offered. "More focused on plant medicine and spirit forces for healing, but they can do shamanic work. Curenderas are widely used in Hispanic populations."

Harry scrunched his forehead in an effort to remember. Suddenly his bushy eyebrows leapt as his eyes glowed with memory access.

"There's one ceremony that really shows the shamanic tradition continuing among modern Maya," he spoke with keen emphasis. "The Tzotzil Maya living in the highland community of Zinacantan have an end-of-year ceremony, rituals that are a heady mixture of Christian and Maya-pagan elements. Plenty of pure theatricals, with actors impersonating monkeys, jaguars, and Spaniards. The whole village goes to a sacred mountain shrine that represents a pyramid. People take place in these activities according to social ranks—a parallel to the highly stratified society of the ancient Maya.

"They call on their animal alter-ego; each villager has an animal counterpart just like the ancient Maya. These animals can be anything from a jaguar to a mouse, though some are fantastic composite creatures. Oh! I just remembered. The Maya word for the animal familiar is *uay,* pronounced 'why.' Using these supernatural forces, the rituals are aimed at curing illness as well as bolstering well-being of the community."

Jana tilted her head quizzically.

"Does this relate to Native American concepts of power animals?" she asked.

"Probably serve the same purposes," Harry answered. "*Uay* is a word also associated with buildings called 'sleeping places' that we think the Maya used for vision quests. Like our Native Americans, the Maya used substances and rituals to attain altered states of consciousness so they could commune with the spirit world. These animals were often helpers in this process."

That's it! Jana thought, flashing on jaguars. *Another thread in the web of synchronicities.*

"Tell me more about the ancient Maya," Jana entreated. She knew answers were there, hidden in veils of time. "You really know lots for someone out of their major field. I'm impressed."

Harry smiled and shrugged.

"One does accumulate a surprising assortment of information after thirty years in the field," he said with some humility. "Well, let me give you a birds eye view of ancient Maya civilization. The Maya were an amazing people. They were master builders."

With a dreamy expression, Harry conjured images as he entered story-telling mode.

"Imagine a huge city rising out of the dense green jungle canopy. Gleaming red and white pyramids tower hundreds of feet, their intricately carved roof combs soaring above the tallest trees. Stone mountains, reaching up into the sky, bringing shaman-kings and priests closer to the gods of the cosmos. Broad plazas paved with white plaster create huge open areas between pyramids, palaces and administrative structures. Multiple levels of stairs connect these immense structures. Long white roads, also of stone covered with plaster, fan in many directions, some stretching 10-30 miles. Called *sakbeob,* they lead to ceremonial outposts or subject cities. Around the large cities are thousands of huts, covered with thatch roofs, from which spirals of smoke ascend. Cultivated fields surround the cities for many miles.

"The lowland jungles, western mountains and dry plains of the Yucatan were covered with hundreds of cities, spreading all the way from southern México to Honduras. The population density of the Maya civilization at its apex rivaled that of China—600 people per square mile over a 36,000 square mile area. They used intense farming methods, built raised fields and diverted water. In the drier areas cities were built near *cenotes,* deep pools of water in limestone craters often 30-40 feet below ground level. Or, cisterns were created in the limestone ground to hold rainwater.

"The Maya had complex social and political structures, with a stratified society. The ruler or king, his relatives and other nobles were the elite class. There were merchants and artisans. Peasants provided most of the labor. Several royal lineages became dominant, forging alliances through marriages and trade. The royalty and nobles were much involved in warfare, some cities having long-standing rivalries. Conquest and dominance of rival cities brought resources and wealth to the victor. The triumphs and accomplishments of kings were inscribed on stone slabs or stelae, a cross between history and propaganda to impress their people and enemies with their prowess."

"Just like kings, emperors, dictators and presidents have done throughout history," Jana observed sardonically. "What about their religion?"

"They had a sophisticated religion that was linked with movements of planets, constellations and the Milky Way. We now realize that the Maya had perhaps the most advanced knowledge of astronomy in the ancient world. They were obsessed with tracking time. They believed cycles kept repeating endlessly, and each cycle had a distinct quality. What occurred the last time in a particular cycle was sure to happen when it recurred. All aspects of life were affected by time cycles.

"Numbers were sacred in themselves, and each held particular meanings. The most sacred calendar was the *tzolk'in,* a 260-day cycle created by intermeshing 13 numbers with 20 day names. Every day had omens and qualities that guided people's activities. It was used for divination. Remember I told you that wherever you find modern Maya people using the 260-day calendar, the old traditions are very strong?

"There was another solar calendar of 360 plus 5 unlucky days. Now, being the astrologers they were, the Maya knew that the solar year actually has 365 ¼ days. They called this the "Vague Year" and made adjustments. In addition, they had the Long Count calendar that goes backward and forward in time over millions of years. It's very precise, an absolute calendar that has run like some great clock from a beginning point in the mythical past. It allowed them to date any event within the span of historical time without ambiguity."

"So, calendars shaped their lives," Jana reflected.

"Exactly. The hieroglyphic code was first deciphered by identifying number symbols and the Maya system of counting. The story of cracking the Maya code is an exciting one, with tremendous discoveries quite recently. Now about 90% of the glyphs are understood. By firmly connecting Maya dates with the Gregorian calendar, we can determine exactly when events occurred. The origin of the Maya calendars is mysterious, because they suddenly appeared in highly developed form."

"When was the Maya civilization happening?" asked Jana.

"It flourished for over 3000 years, from around 2000 BCE to 1000 CE, though I believe the collapse of the classic Maya culture

51

happened in the 900's," Harry replied. "But an advanced civilization continued, with Mexican and Toltec influences, until the arrival of the Spaniards in the late 15th century."

"Where did the Maya come from? How did they acquire their advanced knowledge and complex society?" Jana was intrigued and puzzled. She thought the most advanced ancient civilizations were in Egypt, the Middle East and Asia.

"Now you're asking questions that not only myself, but others more specialized in the field have trouble answering," Harry chortled, half-amused at his own limitations. "There's controversy about the origins of the Maya. The old theory was migration from Asia across the frozen Bering Straits to Alaska at the end of the last Ice Age. But new archeological evidence throws that idea into question. Quite developed cultures have been excavated in Peru and Chile dating back as far as 12,000 BCE. Since this crossing would have occurred 10,000 years ago—that was when glacial conditions were favorable—people couldn't have migrated all the way down from Alaska to Chile in that time span. It takes thousands of years for migrations over such distances. The new theories say that these early settlers came from Asia, navigating across the ocean to warm, unglaciated islands of South America. Then they migrated north as continental glaciers receded. Or, they might have come from Europe using boats along the eastern coasts.

"We really don't know, there's mystery about Maya origins. Archeologists date the earliest occupation of the Maya area at 13,000 BCE; these were hunter-gatherer peoples. There's evidence for cultivation of squash as early as 10,000 years ago, and corn by 5,000 BCE, much earlier than previously thought. A Gulf Coast civilization called the Olmec appears to be the immediate cultural predecessor of the Maya. As their influence spread across Mesoamerica, we find prototypes of classic Maya civilization: cities with large structures, burial of rulers in jade-lavished tombs, use of serpents and jaguars, carved stone slabs, hieroglyphic writing, and a dot-and-bar counting system.

"Archeologists have divided Maya civilization into 3 phases: Preclassic, Classic and Postclassic, with an associated timeline based on Long Count Calendar dates. You'll need to read some books to get the exact dates."

"Why did the Maya civilization fall?" Jana queried.

"Most Mayanists now agree it was due to a combination of factors. Overuse of natural resources, failure of agricultural techniques, and centuries of incessant internal warfare are probably the keys. Studies of climate changes in the lowlands show that the wet climate of the Preclassic shifted to drier conditions during the Classic. A severe drought started around 800 CE and lasted over 200 years. This coincided with abandonment of major late Classic cities. Conquests broke up city-states and reduced centralized power. There may have been revolt against kings and elite classes, when living conditions deteriorated for the commoners. While there's no strong evidence of disease as a factor, skeletal remains do show decreased nutrition in the late Classic. Some sites had sudden changes in pottery, architecture and sculpture, suggesting takeover by an outside group, most likely from central México. The seafaring Putun Maya from Tabasco took over the Yucatan by the Postclassic period. Trade routes also shifted toward the coast, affecting the economy of inland sites.

"Whatever the reasons, this great Maya civilization in the jungles and mountains of southern and western Central America collapsed. Vast cities fell into ruin, swallowed gradually over centuries by the relentlessly encroaching jungle. Impressive sites continued in the drier Yucatan, overtaken and expanded by the Mexicanized Maya, until a series of battles with the Spanish conquistadors drove the Maya farther and farther into the jungle. Those who stayed abandoned their cities and re-formed in the village structure that persists until the present.

"The legacy of the ancient Maya culture was not rediscovered until the late 1800's when some British adventurers braved their way into the thick jungles in search of legendary lost cities. The excavation and study of Maya sites really took off in the late 1950s as museums and universities sent teams out. There's been a kind of renaissance in Maya studies the past decade or two, I believe."

Harry realized that he had been talking for a long time. He glanced at his wristwatch, noting that it was nearly noon. He needed to go to a meeting soon.

"Well, Jana, I've filled your ears with a lot of information, more than I thought!" He seemed pleased with himself. "I do have to go. Are there any particular questions you have? I've got time for one or two."

"Thanks, Harry," she said. "I really appreciate everything you've told me. Looks like I've got a lot of reading to do. I do have a couple of questions, but maybe the answers are too involved."

Jana paused, watching for Harry's reaction. He didn't seem too ready to leap up. Nodding at her, he said:

"Shoot."

"What to you know about the Maya god, Chak? And, what about the city of Tikal?"

"Chak is easy," Harry replied, "because I don't know much, just that he is a very ancient god associated with rain, thunder and lightning. He's one of the few deities whose cult has survived among the living Maya. Tikal is a long story, however. It was the dominant city in the Guatemala lowlands during most of the Classic period. Its fortunes had several ups and downs, since it engaged in endless alliances and warfare with neighboring cities. It grew into a huge city, with a population that might have topped 100,000 at its apex. We know more about Tikal's kings, dynastic politics, battles and ceremonies than most other sites, because it's been excavated extensively. The Tikal kings, mostly of the jaguar lineage, carved their history on multiple stelae, a virtual 'forest of tree stones' as the Mayanists say. So, they left a good record, more complete than any others."

Kings of the jaguar lineage. Jana felt a little "ping" in her chest.

Harry checked his watch again.

"Sorry, Jana, I've got to get going. There are lots of books that cover Tikal. I've made a short list for you, its somewhere here."

Harry began digging through the stacks on his desk. With uncanny precision this time, he shoved aside a few report folders, journals and small notes to pull out a handwritten list on a ragged-edged page torn from a spiral notebook. Handing it to Jana, he said:

"This is a list of some major Mayanists, you can find books by them in the library. They're among the big names in contemporary Maya studies: Michael Coe, David Freidel, Linda Schele, Peter Mathews, Nikolai Grube, Tatiana Proskouriakoff, David Drew, Simon Martin, Mary Miller, Karl Taube, Peter Harrison, David Webster. It's a big field; there are lots of experts from various disciplines. But this is a start."

Harry stood up. Jana also arose, getting relief from the hard wooden seat that had made her buttocks a bit numb.

"Oh, there's one more contact for you," Harry muttered, again searching his disordered desktop. "Where the heck did I put it? Never mind, I'll write her information on your page."

He reached toward Jana who obligingly returned the notebook page. Scribbling furiously on the back, he advised:

"This is the email of a leading Maya archeologist at the University of Texas, Austin. Name is Francine Rappele. I met her at a conference several years ago, and we've kept in touch since then. Hummm, that's probably why I know as much as I do about the Maya. She's a friendly woman, she'll be happy to help you."

Harry gave Jana a brief hug and ushered her out of his office, waved good-by and hurried down the corridor to his meeting. Jana watched fondly as his wiry form broke into a power walk and disappeared quickly around the corner. She felt appreciative and a bit overwhelmed. How was she going to find clues to her dream in all of this? Heaving a deep sigh, Jana turned and headed toward the entrance, carefully folding the ragged page and putting it into her purse.

Curved sidewalks took Jana past Olin Library where she would search for Maya books, to the Rothwell Center, a large teashop-bookstore complex. Its open plaza was a favorite place for lunch, lattes and conversations. Wisteria twined along a trellis, shading one side of the plaza. The noon sun was warm; she shrugged off her sweater without noticing, so preoccupied was her mind.

Rounding the corner to the plaza, she caught sight of Robert sitting at a table with a student. The young woman's straight blonde hair fanned across her shoulders and down her back. She seemed enraptured with what Robert was saying, her focus so intent that she failed to notice Jana approaching. Robert was animated and in his element, gesturing as he spoke, very professorial.

Robert Sinclair was, by his own admission, an escapee from the Midwest. He grew up in a midsize town with conservative family values. By all measures, he should have stayed close to home like the rest of his relatives. But he was smitten by the West Coast, and moved his disgruntled wife and small son to California. After a few years scraping by doing music gigs, he landed a teaching job that eventually led to Mills College. Before that, however, his thoroughly disillusioned wife divorced him and returned to a more contained life in the heartland.

Music was his passion. His talented and doting mother encouraged him in the music career she had given up for marriage. His engineer father never thought it was a good idea; who could earn a living doing music? Robert's success as a music teacher, and his swing to liberal values, caused his dad much consternation.

Jana caught snippets of the conversation as she drew near; the topic was French impressionist composers. Robert was covering these musical experimenters of the late 19th and early 20th centuries in his contemporary music class.

". . and Debussy brought back the renaissance modal scale, which created a whole new way of writing music. It was actually the foundation of impressionistic composition. Just dropping out the two half tones in the standard scale made a huge difference. Ravel, Satie and many others took this technique and gave it their own voices, writing music that creates images, mental pictures in the listener's mind."

He stopped as Jana walked up to the table.

"Hi, there you are" Robert said.

The blonde turned to face Jana.

"Jana, this is Veronica, a student in my class. Veronica, my wife Jana."

Jana was sure she saw a flicker of disappointment in the young woman's limpid violet eyes. Smiling appropriately, the women shook hands with the obligatory "nice to meet you."

Reflexively, Jana took a rapid mental inventory of the lithe young woman's attributes. Tastefully understated eye makeup accented long lashes and deepened her unusual eyes. Precisely applied lip liner emphasized her classic lips. The straight nose, high cheeks and forehead gave her face symmetry that would be envied by fashion models. Her clear, warm-toned skin had a radiant glow.

She ought to try fashion design or modeling instead of studying contemporary music. Why is it that the gorgeous women are always the ones who follow the professor after class to ask questions?

Jana was petulant. It must be the alpha-male effect, she reflected. Beautiful women were drawn to powerful, in charge men. And what man is more powerful than a college professor, in the context of his work? Talk about the captain of the ship! Professors have total command in the classroom. They mold their student's lives and grade their success. They're experts, guides, gurus if you will, in the topics students aspire to master. They bear the mantle of ancient wisdom and mastery of life's mysteries.

Well aware of the inevitable attraction between professors and students, Jana recognized this as an occupational hazard. Of course, the fact that Robert was a handsome man, a senior professor in his department, and a delightful conversationalist added some high voltage energy to this equation. Take Harry, for instance. He certainly didn't have the same magnetism for women students. Though she sometimes wondered about it, as far as she knew these attractions remained strictly Platonic. Robert talked of the code of ethics forbidding professors to step over the line into intimacy with students, as this violated the sacred trust of the teacher archetype: to offer knowledge impartially and to develop students' minds, without personal agendas.

Huh! That one bites the dust pretty frequently, Jana thought with a touch of cynicism.

Veronica and Robert exchanged a few more words as Jana processed these thoughts. The young woman rose to leave, but Robert stayed seated, typical of the un-knightly behavior of modern "emancipated" men. As Veronica leaned to sling her backpack over one shoulder, the knit shirt pulled away from her hip-huggers, exposing a golden-tan amazingly flat belly. Her navel was pierced with a small gold ring sporting a tiny diamond, tasteful and expensive. Waving and giving Jana a contained smile, she sauntered off with a rolling gait that accentuated the sway of her well-formed hips.

With a spark of envy, Jana pictured the belly pad that inevitably seemed to develop around menopause. Even with effort, midlife women never had that taut, flat belly. Nor the navel rings. Tribal piercing, Jana concluded. A statement of their generation. Could piercing relate to native practices, reflect a dawning awareness of indigenous values that the planet needs now? This was a more promising perspective.

"How was your meeting with Harry?" Robert asked as Jana sat down.

"Really good," she replied. "He was lots more knowledgeable than he lets on. I learned quite a bit about both the modern and ancient Maya. He gave me a list of authors in the field; I'll look them up at the library this afternoon. A colleague of his is a leading Mayanist at the University of Texas, Austin. That was an interesting coincidence. He gave me her email and said she'd be happy to correspond with me. Do you know her? Name is Francine Rappele."

Robert thought for a moment, then shook his head.

"I'll get in touch with her after I've learned more," Jana continued. "I need to formulate questions to ask. I'm still in a haze about what I'm looking for. Maybe as I read things will get more clear."

"I'm sure they will," Robert agreed cheerfully. "Ready for lunch?"

"OK."

After obtaining a couple of Thai wraps and apple juice, they returned to their table. A few umbrellas were open to shield diners from the bright sun. The low buzz of conversation wafted through the open area; the plaza was nearly full. An occasional loud laugh, or voices raised in friendly argument punctuated the air.

"That student of yours, Veronica, is very lovely," she said pensively.

"Veronica? Yes, she's pretty," Robert agreed casually. "Really sharp, too. She's got a good mind and an inquisitive nature. Music's not her major, this is an elective for her."

"She seems to enjoy talking to you," Jana proposed.

"Her term paper is focusing on French impressionists. She wanted more insight into their techniques. She does get intense about her topic and relentlessly pursues it."

"As long as she doesn't relentlessly pursue you." The words were out of Jana's mouth before she could edit them. She felt a bit embarrassed.

Robert raised his eyebrows and looked startled. Then he laughed out loud, throwing his head back and exposing his straight white teeth.

"Really, Jana, there's nothing to worry about" he said reassuringly. "She is attractive, but so are the majority of Mills College women students. If I let that get to me, I'd be in deep trouble. My gosh, they're all young enough to be my daughters!"

"That hasn't stopped a lot of professors," Jana reminded him.

"Well, its bad form," Robert observed, "and worse, it's damaging to both parties. Not to mention putting a black mark on your career. I know professor-student affairs happen, but it creates a terrible mess. No thanks! I'm steering clear of that."

He smiled and reached out to touch her arm.

"And anyway, I'm in love with you," he said with sincerity. "I've got no interest in those young things, except to develop their minds. You're the woman of my heart."

A slight misting of tears touched Jana's eyelashes. She was a little surprised at her emotional response to his words. She nodded, leaning toward him to receive his kiss.

"Thanks, sweetheart," she said. "I don't know why that came up. I'm feeling so unsettled about my dream being connected with the

Maya. I've no idea where it's going to lead. Maybe all this is making me feel vulnerable."

"That makes perfect sense," he replied. "I must admit, it all seems strange to me. You're doing the right thing, though, exploring the field to see where it takes you. I'm glad Harry was able to give you some resources so you can delve more deeply into it."

Jana nodded, thinking:

And clues about jaguars and shamans.

*   *   *   *   *

A stack of books surrounded Jana in the bedroom-turned-office that she shared with Robert. Her expedition to Olin Library had been notably successful. The better part of last week was devoted to organizing the enormous amount of information in archeological and ethnographic books. She kept an electronic journal to record facts and impressions.

Her notes started with a concise summary of what gave Maya culture its unique characteristics, from Michael Coe's book *The Maya*. These traits, shared by all the Mesoamerican peoples, were more or less peculiar to them, being absent or rare in other American Indian cultures:

- Hieroglyphic writing
- Books of fig-bark or deerskin paper folded like screens
- Complex permutation calendars
- Knowledge of astronomy, movements of planets and stars
- Ball courts and ballgame with a hard rubber ball
- Highly specialized markets
- Highly complex pantheistic religion with nature divinities and deities emblematic of royal descent
- Blood-letting ceremonial practices with self-induced bleeding from ears, tongue or penis by royalty and elites
- Human sacrifice including removal of the head or heart
- The idea of a cosmic cycle of creation and destruction, and a universe oriented to the four directions with specific colors and gods assigned to cardinal points and center (not exclusive to the Maya)

Because of these shared traits, archeologists concluded there must be a common origin. The most likely source was the Olmec of southern México, who demonstrated many of these traits over 3,000 years ago. All Jana's books mentioned the Olmec, and she found David Drew's description in *The Lost Chronicles of the Maya Kings* most interesting. She wrote in her notes:

The Olmec were an enigma who appeared suddenly on the Mesoamerican scene. Through sophisticated art and huge monuments, they left behind a powerful record of rulers and gods, and a completely new kind of society. Between 1100 and 900 BCE they transformed an egalitarian small village society into a hierarchical social structure with elites and kings, inhabiting large cities with massive monuments and ceremonial centers. Excavations near Vera Cruz, México found an extraordinary subterranean system for drainage, stone basins and even fountains.

A revolutionary architectural form, a mound pyramid on a raised square platform, was first found there. A badly eroded mound, 98 feet high, appeared to be a ceremonial center. It was embellished with basalt columns and mosaic pavements of serpentine carved in the form of abstract masks. Each serpentine block weighs about 900 tons.

The Olmec were best known for carving colossal human heads of basalt, weighing up to 20 tons and standing 6 ½ feet high. These huge basalt boulders must have been dragged or floated on rafts from ancient quarries in the Tuxtla mountains 37 miles away. The square faces have a Negroid appearance with a flat nose, flared nostrils and thick full lips. Some looked like baby-faced jaguars.

Elaborate burial tombs containing serpentine and jade indicate a ruling class. Olmec rulers played an important religious role, and may have been the first shaman-kings. Their deities included gods of rain, earth and sky. They used animal symbolism. This formalized religious structure required priests or shamans, distinct from the healers or diviners of local villages, the h-men.

Olmec influence is widespread after about 1000 BCE, visible from western México down to El Salvador. They were traders who established distant outposts.

The Olmec, Jana concluded, were the "mother culture" of Mesoamerica. Out of this cultural matrix, the Maya civilization emerged. But, no one knew where the Olmec came from.

The Maya civilization arose in 2000 BCE. Archeologists divided the time-line for cultural development into three phases: Preclassic, Classic, and Postclassic periods. Jana wrote down the characteristics of each period, searching for clues. She kept a map handy to locate Maya sites.

The **Preclassic** period went from 2000 BCE to 250 CE. The early village tribes were well on the road to a complex hierarchical society by 800 BCE. What may well be the largest city the Maya ever built, El Mirador, once had immense pyramids and platforms larger than those in Tikal. One temple has monstrous jaguar masks and paws, teeth and claws painted red. These vast structures, built early in Maya civilization, invite comparison with the great pyramids of Egypt. With population in tens of thousands, this city dominated the north Peten area for 500 years.

Jaguar symbols have been with the Maya a long, long time, Jana mused.

Tikal had been settled since 800 BCE but remained little more than a farming village for centuries. Around 200-100 BCE it burst into growth, its leaders building temples, platforms and plazas in rapid succession, including the North Acropolis, which became the

religious heart of Tikal. Many kings are buried in pyramids there. A peculiar structure, the corbel vault or arch, was used in the stone burial chambers. This technique is typical of all Maya stone buildings.

Corbel Arch, Labnah

To make corbel arches, the masons built vertical walls to the desired height, then closed the top portion by stacking each successive stone a little farther inward than the one below. The gap on top was closed with a capstone. Corbel arches can achieve great height, but the rooms they create must be narrow. If the angle of the stacked stones is not steep, the arch will fall; thus a wide angle put the ceiling in danger of collapsing. Maya buildings have long, narrow maze-like rooms.

Tikal is the place of the jaguar. .

The **Classic** period went from 250 CE to 900 CE. This was the florescence of Maya civilization. Large city-states dotted the southern lowlands in what is now Guatemala, Honduras, Belize and southern México. Cities were laid out around central plazas, bordered by pyramid temples, palaces and "administrative structures" where kings and nobles conducted business.

At the height of the Classic, Maya population reached 10 million, though recently that estimate was doubled. Sixty or more city-states had 60,000 to 100,000 people. Ruling dynasties formed and warred, cities made then broke alliances, the elite lived in wealth, and intensive farming along with widespread trading sustained the population. The renowned Jaguar Claw family of Tikal became the longest lineage of kings in any Maya city.

The Jaguar Claw kings! What do they have to do with my dream?

Tikal had an alliance with the central México city of Teotihuacan, the most powerful empire of its time. It influenced Tikal's art, stucco imagery, and warfare. Using a spear-throwing device acquired from Teotihuacan, called *atlatl*, Tikal rose to dominate the Peten region, conquering several nearby cities. At least two rulers of Tikal were from Teotihuacan, probably marrying into the ruling family.

A powerful alliance formed against Tikal. Long-time rival Calakmul joined forces with Caracol, Naranjo and Dos Pilas to virtually surround the colossus, bringing it to defeat and killing the king in 562 CE. For the next 125 years, no stelae or monuments were carved at Tikal—the "Hiatus." Tikal's greatest king in the jaguar lineage revived the city and brought it back to power 130 years later. His creative genius built the famous Pyramids I & II, Tikal's trademark. Soaring in austere magnificence over the verdant jungle, they continue to inspire awe in modern visitors.

Why does looking at these pyramids make my heart leap? Jana felt their powerful magnetism drawing her into the picture.

The Classic ended with disappearance of the Maya from the southern lowlands. By the late 800's virtually all the great cities were abandoned. Archeologists thought the Maya culture fell apart from the inside, collapsing under combined pressures of exhausted farm lands, incessant warfare, drought, and loss of belief in the king's ability to appease the gods.

Maybe drought brought by the ubiquitous Chak was the final straw. But he's found everywhere among Maya sites, which could be 'The place of Chak'?

Temple 1, Tikal

The **Postclassic** period went from 900 CE to 1520 CE. The northern lowlands saw an upsurgence of Maya civilization, led by the Mexicanized Putun Maya. They built new cities in the Yucatan and forged different trade routes. An era of new cultural practices began. Instead of kings, a supreme council ruled the cities. These councils consisted of a group of brothers and cousins, who formed alliances and conducted wars against other cities. Priests had lesser roles.

The Toltec culture from México penetrated the Yucatan, bringing its god Quetzalcoatl, the "feathered serpent" who became identified with the Maya sun god, Kukulkán. Chichén Itzá rose to dominance in northern Yucatan as a major ceremonial center. It was settled and abandoned twice over a period of 870 years. The famous Pyramid of the Sun continued as a sacred site for equinox ceremonies until the Spanish conquest. The Itza people later joined forces with the city of Itzamal to overcome the great city of Mayapan in 1263 CE.

In the mountain regions near the Pacific coast, the Quiche and Cakchiquel kingdoms formed after 1200 CE. These groups united into an empire in 1470, but broke apart around 1500.

The Spaniard Hernando Cortes landed on Cozumel Island in 1519. Seafaring Maya in 50-foot canoes had a brief encounter with the pale bearded strangers. Both Maya and Toltec prophesy foretold their coming. This was a sign that the Maya people would undergo a long period of subjugation and anonymity. Keepers of Maya knowledge, their science and cosmology, had to bring this wisdom underground.

Pockets of Maya resistance to the conquistadors lasted another 178 years. Retreating into the dense jungles and distant mountains, the Itza, Quiche and Cakchiquel people fought Alvarado and his successors until the last Maya kingdom fell in 1697.

And so it ended. Or did it?

Jana had to stop. Her wrists ached from typing, and a bone-tired weariness crept over her body. Glancing at the clock, she was surprised at the time: 12:20 am. With a sigh, she sat up straight, stretched and arched her shoulders back, relieving tense muscles. Quickly saving her work and closing down the computer, she got ready for bed. Slipping quietly beside the soundly sleeping Robert, she snuggled into her pillow and drifted into the soft darkness of sleep.

Some time later the dream recurred. This time, however, she was vaguely aware that she was dreaming. Part of her consciousness seemed to be watching, knowing it was an observer and yet fully involved with the dream images. Again she saw the old woman's hand, with long thin fingers, large knuckles, and ropy veins snaking across the back. The young girl's small brown fingers traced along the veins, gently, affectionately. Soon the small hand slipped into the old palm, which curled thin fingers to enclose it. There was darkness, and the stillness of well-advanced night. The girl withdrew her hand after a while, and the old fingers fanned outward as if reaching for something.

The dream had always ended there. But Jana's awareness as the Observer insisted on more. The darkness became less dense, and a vague outline of the old woman's body lying on an elevated surface became faintly visible. The room was made of stone, and the surface on which the old woman lay was a stone bench attached to a wall. The girl had moved toward a doorway, drawing a heavy curtain back. Faint dawn light crept through the doorway, highlighting its corbel arch. The girl was about 9 or 10 years old, slender and barefoot. As the dawn light played across her face, its most pronounced feature was highlighted—a very large nose that dominated its contours. She wore a white shift hanging loosely from shoulders to mid-calf. A single braid of dark hair hung down her back. After lingering a moment in the doorway, and glancing inside at the old woman, the girl departed.

Morning light began to dispel the dark shadows inside the room. The stone walls were bare but covered with white stucco, the floor was of stone and had a small hearth in the center harboring a few dying embers. Three rounded stones flanked the hearth. The old woman was lying on a woven reed mat, covered by a colorful blanket with zigzag geometric patterns. Her breathing was raspy and erratic. Jana knew she was dying.

Jana woke with a pounding heart and tingly sensations up her spine. Through her bedroom window, early dawn light was just beginning to change night's darkness into gray tones, harbingers of sunrise. She lay very still, replaying the dream in her mind to imprint its details indelibly. There was no doubt that this dream was a Mayan image.

Did my imagination invent this?

Maybe all her reading about the Maya, learning details of their life, created these new dream images. But what comes first? Does what we learn create our images, or does the act of learning release pent up memories that allow the images to come forth in our minds?

At this point it didn't matter to Jana. The important thing was that the dream progressed, and the corbel arch linked it solidly to the Maya. Knowing that the old woman was dying lent a sense of urgency. The old woman wanted to communicate with her, of that Jana was certain. It might be related to the message given through Angelina Menchu. She needed to unravel this mystery.

The next morning at breakfast, when they were on their last cup of coffee, Jana told Robert about the new images in the dream. He listened attentively, his blue eyes watching her face closely as if searching for clues to understand more deeply. When she finished, he questioned her.

"Do you think your studying about the Maya might have created the rest of the dream?" he asked.

"It must have some influence on the dream," Jana thoughtfully replied, "but I don't believe it created what I saw. Its more like my studying opened a window so what was already there could be seen."

"Uh-huh," Robert responded.

Jana knew he really didn't buy into that view. She was not ready to be logical about the dream, to explain it away rationally. She wanted to hold onto its magic, to allow the possibility of synchronicity. In the dream she felt what it was like to be on the threshold between worlds, to stand in the liminal moment, with the shimmering unmanifest just about to take form. In the long silence that followed her last statement, she drifted into another reality, mesmerized by images of wide plazas surrounded by tall pyramids, jungle canopies, stucco masks and carved monuments.

"Was the population of the ancient Maya very large?"

Robert's question startled Jana, pulling her back to the present. She blinked a few times, refocused and responded almost by rote.

"Yes, up to 10 or 20 million at the height of their civilization," she said. "That would be in the 7th and 8th centuries CE."

"How did they feed such a large population?" Robert asked. "With cities located in jungles, conditions for farming must have been less than ideal."

"They used several techniques for farming," Jana replied. "Slash-and-burn methods are well-suited to low fertility jungle soil. The Maya farmers would clear off a plot of jungle land, cultivate it and grow crops for 3-4 years. Burning maize stalks after harvesting put nutrients into the soil for the next crop. Then they had to leave that plot fallow for around 8 years, so the soil could rebuild. They developed an adjoining plot, and followed this procedure again. But when cities got really large—some had populations of 100,000 people—more intense farming methods were needed. Rectangular raised beds bordering rivers or swamps have been found. The Maya would dig out channels and pile the ground up to create raised beds. They had means to direct water flow through the channels. Often they could get two crops per year from these."

"What did they eat?" Robert was genuinely curious.

"Maize, beans, squash, peppers mostly," Jana told him. "Various fruits, avocados, spices and cacao, which they made into a drink. They kept little dogs and turkeys for meat, and hunted deer, peccaries, some birds. If close to the sea, they obtained mollusks and fish. They traded across great distances for things like salt and cacao."

"Interesting," said Robert. "So they didn't have any large animals?"

"No, the largest was the tapir, standing around 3 feet and weighing 200 lbs. It has a long snout, slick brown hair and a short tail, sort of a cross between an anteater and a pig." She thought for a moment, then added: "Jaguars are the biggest predators. But the Maya didn't have any pack animals. People had to carry the burdens. They never used the wheel."

"Maybe wheels would sink in the jungle mud," offered Robert. "A litter or pole sling dragged behind might have been easier."

"That could be," said Jana. "They did use rivers and swamps for transportation, especially in the lowlands. It's amazing that they quarried and transported huge limestone blocks over considerable distances in the jungle. They needed enormous amounts of stone to build their cities."

The conversation continued along more practical lines as Robert asked questions about Maya cities, buildings and lifestyles. Jana enjoyed sharing her newly acquired information and was pleased at how much she could recall. But in the back of her mind hovered the new images in the dream that confirmed Maya links. A sense of urgency kept percolating inside.

At work later that evening, Jana and Mary sat in the nurses' station enjoying a cup of coffee during a lull in the action. It was an opportunity for Jana to explore new details of her dream with Mary, who had been doing dream work for some time.

"Last night I had my recurrent dream again," Jana said, "but finally it went farther and I could see the old woman and the girl more clearly." She described the new details precisely; they were emblazoned in her memory. "Most striking, though, I was aware during the dream that I was dreaming. Some part of my consciousness was hovering there, observing the whole thing."

"Jana, you had a lucid dream!" Mary exclaimed with uncharacteristic excitement. Her unflappable style served well in emergency room work, where she was eminently calm in the midst of chaos and crisis. Her intense response now showed how deeply she was affected by Jana's experience.

"What's the significance of that?" asked Jana.

"Lucid dreams are powerful tools," Mary said with enthusiasm. "You have experiences way beyond ordinary life, where almost anything is possible. You can actually learn to direct lucid dreams, and create new outcomes for things that happened. Or, you can go deeply into spiritual teachings, past lives, psychological issues, problems. Lucid dreams express your deepest identity, who you really are. The old woman and girl must be deeply connected to your inner self."

"Wow," Jana said. "That's fascinating. But I don't feel identified with either person, like I was one of them."

"Dream science says we actually *are* every character in our dreams," Mary replied. "They represent different aspects of our psyche, like a symbol for some part of ourselves that we need to acknowledge or integrate."

"I've got to go deeper," Jana said, feeling the urgency again. "But it's so hard for me. Look how long it took for the dream to progress even a little."

"Jana, I've got an idea," said Mary. "Do some individual work with Carla Hernandez. She uses regression techniques and imaginal journeying to help people delve into things like this. You've got to get beyond the mental gatekeeper who tries to prevent access to deeper stuff, probably out of fear that it's too overwhelming."

"Well, you've got that right," Jana said ruefully. "I must have one really great gatekeeper!"

The sound of an ambulance siren interrupted their talk. Both nurses jumped to their feet, instantly focused and ready for action.

*   *   *   *   *

A few days later, Jana sat across from Carla Hernandez in her subdued office. Carla's dress was less flamboyant; slacks and shirt-jacket of ochre and lavender, with only the purple-fringed scarf draped casually around her neck hinting at the gypsy. Ever unruly hair haloed her face, wisps jutting erratically, and heavy make-up brought her green eyes into prominence.

Jana retold her recurring dream, the new details, and Mary's observation that it was a lucid dream.

"Mary said you'd help me go deeper, so I can understand its significance and get the message. I'm certain there's some kind of message, but it's eluding me."

"OK, there's a way to access deeper layers of your dream state. It's a technique called imaginal journeying."

Carla explained this involved a relaxation sequence, then entering subconscious realms through a "descent" process. They would dialogue during this experience, though Jana would remain lying down with her eyes closed. The dialogue would be taped for later reference. After finishing the exploration, Carla would bring Jana back to present with an "ascent" process.

With some trepidation, Jana stretched out on the massage table. Carla made her comfortable with a pillow and light blanket. Dimming the lights and playing soft music, Carla sat beside Jana and guided her in deep breathing, followed by tensing and relaxing muscle groups from toes to scalp. Then she began the descent process.

"Picture yourself at the top of stairs that are going down into the earth. The entrance looks life a cave cut into a small hill. Begin walking down the steps, one at a time. I'll count as you descend. Take note of everything you see, smell, or hear. One-two-three, feel the cool stone on your feet. Four-five-six, it's getting darker and you can feel dampness, hear the sound of water dripping. Seven-eight, now it's really dark, you place your hands against the walls, which are cool and damp, stepping carefully down. Nine-ten, you're at the bottom of the stairs, its totally dark, quiet, still.

'Now bring the image of your dream to mind. Replay it from start to finish. At the end, ask to be taken to the place of the dream, or to a related place."

Carla waited a few moments, then asked:

"Where are you?"

"In a long room," Jana said dreamily. "It's dim inside, only a few small windows in the stone walls letting in some light, rectangular windows, no coverings. There's a tall doorway in one wall, but no door. It lets in more light."

"What do you see inside the room?" Carla queried.

"A woman is standing in the center . . . a teacher, she's teaching the younger girls. I'm one of the girls, I'm listening avidly to her."

"Can you see yourself, or the woman, what you are wearing?"

"White dresses, like shifts, loose and comfortable. Her dress is embroidered along the hem and sleeves, colorful patterns of red, yellow, blue. My dress is plain. I'm sitting on the floor, its hard and cool beneath the mat. I have black hair in a long single braid down my back. I can't see her face, but I'm very fond of her."

"What is she saying?"

Jana was silent for some time. Inwardly she strained to hear, but no distinct words were audible. She watched as the stately woman, who had a commanding but gentle presence, gestured while picking up objects, discussing their use. But nothing specific came to Jana.

"I'm just not getting it," Jana whispered.

"Do you have a sense of anything else?"

"It all feels . . . precious, sacred, this gathering I'm in with the teacher. We girls are very committed, this involves our life calling." Jana's voice trembled with emotion as tears formed in the corners of her eyes.

Carla noticed Jana's emotion. She asked softly:

"What are you feeling, Jana?"

"I—I'm not sure," Jana said unsteadily. "Something like heart yearning, sweetness mixed with sadness . . . love, apprehension . . . really mixed feelings . . ." Her voice trailed off into silence.

Carla waited. The music wafted gentle, serene melodies of flute and strings. Jana's breathing slowed, became more rhythmic.

"Is there anything else in this scene?" Carla asked.

"We all have brown skin and dark hair," Jana reported. "Bird calls come through the window, they sound like parrots squawking mixed with chirping and warbling."

"Ask to see where this place is," Carla prompted.

Jana requested inwardly to know its location. Images appeared of thick forests, vines twining through tree branches, stubby palms, steamy humid ground.

"Its in a forest, no, more like a jungle," she said. "The temperature is quite hot, lots of moisture, tropical feeling."

"Ask for a sign to help you identify the place," urged Carla.

Jana presented this request in her mind, and waited. A strange image flashed through her inner sight then disappeared. Carla noticed the frown that furrowed Jana's eyebrows ever so slightly.

"What did you see?"

"Its odd. It looked like thick hair tied in a knot behind someone's head. That's all, and it passed very quickly."

"OK, remember that image and wait for it to show up in your life. It's a clue about this place." Carla refocused the imagery journey, asking:

"Can you get a sense of how what you've seen relates to your dream?"

"It must be a Maya city," Jana said. "The building style, hair, skin color and clothes of the people fit. This place is definitely in a jungle, like in the dream, but I'm not clear about the surrounding terrain."

"Are any of the people the same?"

"I don't know, I don't think so . . . at least I'm not sure if they are," Jana murmured. "They're not the same ages, the woman is younger and the girl older than in my dream. The girl's face doesn't look the same."

"OK," said Carla. "This may be another phase in their lives, or a different incarnation, if they are actually the same beings. It's almost

70

time to return. Ask for any other images that can be shown to you at this time."

Jana did ask, but no further imagery was forthcoming. Her mental screen returned to the rectangular room with the teacher and the girls. She savored the feeling of belonging, being at home, having an important calling that this teaching involved. Again she felt deep heart connections with the teacher, bringing a few more teardrops to her eyes.

"Anything else?" asked Carla.

Jana simply shook her head.

"Now prepare to return to present," Carla instructed. "Envision yourself at the bottom of the stairs, in deep darkness. As you ascend, there will gradually be more light and warmth. I will count each step: Ten-nine-eight, feel your hands against the damp moist walls guiding you up. Seven-six-five, you step carefully feeling the cool stones and noting its getting lighter. Four-three-two, you're nearly at the top, your eyes are adjusting to the light, its warmer. One, you step out through the cave entrance into the warmth of the sun shining on a beautiful meadow. Stand there for a moment, take a few deep breaths of the fresh clean air, then open your eyes when you are ready. Move your arms and legs a little, bringing your body into the present"

Jana blinked several times, her eyes adjusting to the light in the room.

"You may want to lie there for a few minutes," Carla said. "Get up when you are ready, I'll be back at my desk."

After a few minutes Jana rose from the table and joined Carla. They went through a de-briefing of the experience.

"How was that for you?" Carla asked.

"Really vivid," said Jana, "I was there, the place was almost as real as this room. But I'm frustrated that I couldn't get more details."

"That's not uncommon for people just starting to do imaginal journeying," Carla reassured. "Your ability to get specific information increases with practice."

"Can I do this on my own?"

"Of course, here's a hand-out with instructions for a couple of techniques, including the one we used today. The observer part of your mind guides you in and asks the questions. I call it an imaginal dialogue. It's really effective."

"Yeah. For sure the images I had today are connected with my dream, even though I don't understand exactly how," Jana observed.

"Stay alert to subtle clues," Carla advised. "Often they are so small that it's easy to miss them. Clues may come in the most unexpected ways. Listen carefully to what people say to you; often the spirit world uses other people to transmit communications into this reality. Memories might come, what looks like unrelated things in the past. Pay attention, write them down because later you may find connections."

"Thanks so much, Carla. This has really been helpful. I've still got so much to discover . . . I wish I didn't have such a strong gatekeeper to the deeper recesses of my mind."

"Gatekeepers do serve us," Carla reminded her. "You might think of them as divine timekeepers, giving us access to hidden material in the time that's best in our lives. Make friends with yours, show appreciation for its role in keeping you from getting into more than you can handle at the moment."

A quiver of uneasiness coursed through Jana. Specters of crows hovered momentarily in her awareness. Crows, the *uay* of shamans.

After the session, Jana stashed Carla's tape carefully in her purse; it would be her teacher for doing imaginal journeying on her own. If only she could break through the wall that separated her from finishing the dream—then she could understand the Maya synchronicities, and the message these held for her.

Darn that gatekeeper! Jana thought. Or should she be thankful?

3 Tikal (Mutul)

The dawn sky was growing brighter as Yalucha set out on the errand given by her mother. At the edge of the eastern bajo, where the immense swamp met with higher ground, a special herb grew that was sacred to Ix Chel. Yalucha was to gather this herb for the katun end ceremony her mother was conducting in their small home temple tomorrow. Xoc Ikal placed high importance on serving the Great Mother Ix Chel, and had instilled deep respect for this feminine creative force in her daughter Yalucha.

The brown-skinned girl strode purposefully forward, her slender legs reaching forth in large steps while her arms swung gracefully, one hand grasping her herb basket. Her small rounded breasts bounced slightly with each stride, and she noticed them again with a touch of surprise. She had not yet gotten used to these protrusions that were growing quickly in the past several months. Her loose white huipil with geometric blue trim around the skirt flapped gently against her thighs. Bare feet skimmed across the cool stones laid out in straight paths between clusters of buildings set on white plaster platforms.

She glanced upward as a group of brown jays made an unusually loud commotion. Their harsh caws were a frequent sound at Mutul (Tikal). They hopped in an animated argument among branches high in the tall ceiba trees. Wispy arms of white mist swirled around the upper canopy, turning pale pink when catching the sun's early rays. Parrots began their sharp screeches and the twitters of hundreds of awakening birds were music to Yalucha's ears. She loved the sounds and sights of her home, the great Maya city of Mutul. Thin columns of smoke curled upward from thousands of thatched roofs, homes grouped in clusters around the city's periphery. Wails of babies mixed with rhythmic episodes of barking as the city's small dogs notified each other of their presence. Ocellated turkeys gobbled to greet the sun, and far in the distance she heard the eerie roars of howler monkeys. Deep-throated and resonant, these roars evoked images of huge mystical creatures yelling at each other from the distant stars.

Xoc Ikal's instructions had been very specific.

"Find only the newly sprouted Kaba yax nik (Vervain), which have pale green leaves. If the tips are darkened, they have past their greatest power. Ix Chel requires only the best herbs for the katun ritual. We are coming to a difficult yet potent time, and we must keep the spirit forces in balance to help our people. The feminine is much needed to balance the power of K'inich Ahau, the Sun God. With the most potent Kaba yax nik, I can infuse Ix Chel's energies into the coming katun and maintain the balance."

Yalucha admired her mother, a priestess of Ix Chel trained in the old religion from Izapa, an ancient city on the western coast. This tradition stretched back some 75 katuns (1500 years) and mingled in the girl's mind with the origin stories of her people. The long count calendar and the sacred katun cycles of 20 tuns (years) were developed by the astronomers of Izapa, who learned to read the stars in distant millennia.

Xoc Ikal was not born in Mutul; she came from the small city of Kanhol (Sky-portal) located in the mountainous region three kins walk to the west. Her family had passed on the tradition of serving Ix Chel through their ancient lineages from Izapa. Yalucha too was part of this lineage, and had been selected for priestess training while still a small child.

And I'm almost finished with the first stages, she thought proudly. Her mother often complimented her on how quickly she learned the rituals and herbal lore. There was a deep rapport between mother and daughter; they often knew what the other was thinking before any words were spoken.

The sounds of stone chiseling broke Yalucha's reverie. As she approached the West Plaza of the city, the stone path merged into a wide stairway of five steep steps. She sprang lightly up the steps onto the wide West Plaza, made of huge flat stones covered with limestone plaster. Across the plaza she spotted the stone carvers, close to the stairs rising the height of two people, leading to the Great Plaza. Engrossed in their work, they chipped deftly on the pale gray stone slab towering two heads above them, propped by support scaffolding that held it almost upright. The carvers were carefully pounding both sides of the stela with sharp black chisels, made of very hard and highly prized obsidian. Intricate glyphs and complex details of the ruler's figure were etched in medium relief onto the slab.

Yalucha's father was a stone carver, but had not been chosen to carve the ruler's katun end stela. Although from a noble family living many generations in Mutul, he was not related to the ruler. The three men assiduously working on the slab were relatives of Chak Toh Ich'ak, the 9th ruler of Mutul. A powerful ahau, he was a direct descendant of Yax Ch'aktel Xok, the founder of Mutul's royal dynasty. The ambitious Yax expanded the city and had important events recorded on stelae.

Although Mutul had been inhabited by Maya people for over 60 katuns (1200 years), they lived in scattered clusters of villages until shortly before Yax Ch'aktel Xok's time. Under his influence, the city developed different zones for residences, public ceremony, court business, markets, and royal palaces. Over the past seven katuns, the low hilly forests between two large swamps or bajos had been cleared in many areas, creating space for the impressive city with its huge plazas and pyramid temples. The next three rulers added many new temples, plazas, ball courts, palaces, administrative centers, and homes for nobles and commoners. Yalucha knew that her city was one of the largest in the land of the Maya, but she had not traveled to other cities yet.

I wonder if I will think our temples and palaces are still so grand once I've seen others, she thought. *But I'll get a chance soon!* The conversation she overheard between her parents last night replayed in her mind:

"I'm sending Yalucha early tomorrow morning to gather herbs for our temple ceremony," her mother remarked.

"Um," her father, K'an Nab Ku mumbled, sipping his warm cup of spicy cacao mixed with pepper that he often enjoyed after dinner. A few minutes of silence ensued, then he said: "She's growing up. Has it now been a full year since she started her moon cycles? It's time for her to marry."

"Not until she completes her priestess apprenticeship at an Ix Chel training temple," said her mother. "I'm thinking of sending her to Xunantunich or Altun Ha. Maybe before her birth month of Uo starts with the heavy rains."

"Is this really necessary? There are fewer and fewer Ix Chel temples. People worship K'inich Ahau now. The ruler brings the sun god's power to our city." K'an Nab Ku knew this was a delicate subject with his wife. Though her expression did not change, the quick hitch of her left shoulder always alerted him of her annoyance.

"Yes," she replied softly, "and all the more reason to maintain the goddess' tradition. The masculine gods like the display of power on earth, and are amused by warfare. Look at how the rulers have taken over sacred ritual from the shaman-priests. They concentrate their power too much, and seek glory and riches by warring against our neighbors. This is not like the old ways when our people lived in harmony with each other and the earth. It *is* necessary for Yalucha to complete her training."

75

Another period of silence. Yalucha could imagine the wheels of her father's mind turning over, considering his reply. Xoc Ikal was a very strong woman, with a mind of her own and a fierce allegiance to her values. K'an Nab Ku loved her deeply, and had found their marriage rich and fulfilling ever since he wooed her during his visit to Kanhol more than a katun ago. He was scouting for special quartz stone in the mountains around her city, staying with distant relatives who knew her parents. The attraction was instantaneous, and he determined to marry the lithe mysterious young woman who seemed a little foreign. Her parents were delighted, for he was from a venerable family of Mutul, a fine noble and excellent match for their daughter.

But he was no push-over, and had his opinions too. He enjoyed the prosperity and reputation of his city, now becoming a dominant force in the southern lowland region. Mutul had recently won the overland trade route competition with Caracol, a large city located three and a half kins (days) southeast of Mutul, nearer to the eastern sea. The rulers and their worship of the sun god K'inich Ahau had been key factors in this economic advancement.

Just look at the fine buildings and monuments of Mutul, he thought. *Much more impressive than a small mountain city where the tallest structure was barely the height of two men.*

"The rulers and K'inich Ahau have brought Mutul great benefit," he finally replied. "We live very well. But do send Yalucha to complete her priestess training. I am happy to provide the gifts required by the Ix Chel temple for her apprenticeship."

This last remark was his gentle prod reminding Xoc Ikal that their family's prosperity would allow the training to be completed. And, by implication, this supported the new religious-political structure. She chose to skip the opportunity for further dispute over the gods and goddesses. She said simply:

"Yes, we have much to be grateful for. After the katun ceremony, I will seek omens to select which temple and send an emissary to set up her apprenticeship."

Yalucha loved her father, who was playful and gentle with his second child. It was good the first was a boy, so he could relax about the family lineage. Her father was handsome by Maya standards, with a prominent nose, full lips and the sloping forehead favored by the nobility. Her brother endured the boards strapped to his head as an infant, forcing the skull to elongate from front to back as the line from nose bridge to crown was made as straight as possible. She and her mother were required to wear the boards for a much shorter time, thus their foreheads did not slope nearly as much as the men's did. For that, she was happy.

Going away to an Ix Chel training temple! She felt eager anticipation rise with a fluttering sensation in her solar plexus. As long as she could remember, she had been fascinated with goddess lore and sacred rituals that would bring blessings to people and affect the workings of nature. Not many in Mutul knew these secrets, nor set the feminine deities in high position. Most paid homage to the male figures such as Hun Hunahpu, First Father and the mythic Hero Twins who outwitted the Xibalba lords of the underworld to bring the Maya people into existence. And now the cult of K'inich Ahau, with the city's ruler as his earthly expression, had gained ascendance.

Yalucha relished the opportunity to delve more deeply into the feminine divinities while completing her priestess training.

Then the next part of her parent's conversation struck her with a force. Her father said it was time for her to marry. She did not feel ready. Unlike most girls she knew, who spoke longingly about their future husbands and babies, she was not very drawn to the domestic life. The desire to learn, to explore life's mysteries, to engage the forces of nature held much more appeal.

I suppose it is inevitable that I must marry, she mused. But there must be a way to keep up priestess work, as her mother did. Surely there would be a suitable husband who could support her calling. At least she did not have to think about that while doing apprenticeship.

With the confidence of youth, she dropped these thoughts and just assumed things would work out. Now she was mounting the steep steps leading to the Great Plaza, the center of public ceremony and royal social life in Mutul. As she stepped onto the immense white expanse, the morning sun broke through an opening in the trees and blazed brilliant golden light into her eyes. To her left, the tall pyramid-temples of the Sacred World-Tree Complex[1] loomed overhead, glistening white stone structures with multiple tiers and a central staircase leading to the ceremonial platform on top.

Atop the ceremonial platform was the temple, a stone structure consisting of small rooms one behind the other with connecting entryways. The front room had two to four doors, but the central door always lined up with those into the rooms behind. Long poles laced

---

[1] Called the North Acropolis by archeologists many centuries later.

together by vines supported a palm-thatch roof. The ruler, ahauob (nobles) and priests would appear from within the back rooms, where they had been in preparation, and stand on the upper platform to perform public ceremonies.

Several platforms built over 25 katuns elevated the temples well above the Great Plaza level. The four pyramid-temples all had steep stairways on the side facing the Great Plaza. These had been built over earlier structures in typical Maya fashion. The tallest was on the north edge, completed before Yalucha's birth by the Mutul ruler, Chak Toh Ich'ak. The outer walls were elaborately decorated with large plastered and painted masks. This north temple was the revered ruler's burial place, on sacred land long used for ceremony and royal burial. Several stelae stood erect in front of the wide stairs leading to the temple platforms. These intricately carved stones recorded important dates, persons and events of Mutul's history.

Yalucha stool still for a few moments, transfixed by the majestic heights and harmonious proportions of the Sacred World-Tree Complex, gleaming white walls and stairs contrasting with vibrant blue, red and yellow designs painted on masks and around the lower tiers. The temple complex always took her breath away. She felt human aspiration reaching skyward to connect with the deities who inhabited the Upperworld domains, the sky and the stars. For her people, the human and spiritual realms were inseparably interwoven. The physical world that the Maya inhabited was understood as the material manifestation of spiritual realities, and the spiritual realm was the essence of the material world. The Maya's experiences encompassed multiple dimensions; one was the world of their lives on the earth, the Middleworld, and others were the realms of gods, goddesses, ancestors, and other supernatural beings, the Upperworld and Underworld.

The actions and interactions of these Otherworld beings had great influences on events of the physical world, and could bring health or disease, victory or disaster, life or death, prosperity or misfortune to the lives of human beings. But the influences were not just in one direction. The Otherworld beings needed the actions of humans to bring them what they required for their existence. Psychic and material sustenance were necessary, and only living humans could provide this nourishment to them. Humans also were the source of souls who would be reborn in the Otherworld as the ancestors, to serve as wise guides and counselors to beings of all worlds. Maya shamans were able to operate in all dimensions, using the power of ritual to keep the worlds in balance. Kings, rulers, priests and priestesses were all capable of being shamans. They had abilities to attune their inner awareness and infuse ritual objects with power to penetrate into supernatural domains.

Voices far across the Great Plaza drew Yalucha's attention from the temple complex. Several women on an early morning errand were passing the Palace of the Ahauob[2] on the south side of the plaza. They glanced briefly at the girl standing silently near the temple complex, waved and proceeded on their way. Yalucha continued eastward past the Palace of the Ahauob, a grouping of residential and administrative buildings that formed a dense complex of several levels, each supported by a platform. Several stairs gave access at various points into the complex. The buildings were square or rectangular, with thatched roofs. One long building immediately facing the plaza contained eight doors, each opening into a separate small windowless room. These rooms were used for meetings, adjudication of disputes, consultations, and planning. Behind them, on a higher platform, were residences of elite nobles. These multi-room structures had interconnecting doors, with small courts beside them. Narrow passageways between residences formed a maze giving access to those farther behind.

At the eastern edge of the Great Plaza, Yalucha descended five wide stairs onto the East Plaza. Long, empty and dazzling white in the morning sun, the plaza was flanked on the south by the ruler's palace, a graceful structure of perfect symmetry built by Chak Toh Ich'ak, "Great Jaguar Claw," early in his reign. Known as Jaguar Claw House, it was the residence for members of the Jaguar Claw lineage. The building was considered sacred and important to the city's very identity. Over the baktuns to follow, no one dared touch this structure except to make small additions and embellishments.

Standing alone on a high platform, Jaguar Claw House originally had seven rooms on the first floor. Oriented equally to east and west, it had 3 doorways on each side. From the west a grand staircase of 14 steps rose to the palace platform. The middle door opened to the central room, the largest in the complex. This central room served as a household shrine, and had no interior access to other rooms. The two flanking doors led into residential areas with linking entryways into a maze of adjacent rooms. Interior stairs gave access to second story rooms, a recent addition to accommodate an expanding royal

---

[2] Called the Central Acropolis by archeologists.

family. A thatched roof with support poles covered the top. The exterior walls were coated with white plaster, and the lower levels painted with the Maya colors of red, blue, green and yellow.

Smoke curled upward from the kitchen room on the southeast corner of Jaguar Claw House. Yalucha heard the typical sounds of a household awakening to the morning routine: muffled women's voices, clinking of cooking vessels, babies wailing, dogs barking, and someone pounding on stones, probably making repairs. The smell of maize porridge stimulated her own hunger, as she had not eaten before leaving home. She quickened her steps, for it would take at least an hour to reach the bajo, gather the herbs, and walk back home. Hurrying past Jaguar Claw House, Yalucha reached the edge of the East Plaza, descended the stairs and entered the forest.

Trees, shrubs and vines lined the stone path and the smell of damp peat filled Yalucha's nose. Last night's rain moistened the foliage and soils, encouraging tiny mosses to grow between the stones, but these would soon brown and shrivel as the hot season progressed. The forest was no longer dense, as it was frequently harvested for building timber and vines. At regular intervals the stone path branched into additional walkways leading to housing clusters, partially visible through a network of branches. Residential clusters perched on the gentle hills that dotted the landscape around Mutul.

The tallest trees—ceiba, mahogany, cedar, guanacaste—soared high into the sky to form the upper canopy of the wet forest. These tall trees provided a perch for hawks to scan the expanse of forest for prey. The next layer consisted of medium height, waxy-leaved trees with brilliant green colors such as cacao, fiddlewood, xate hembra, copal, ramon and vanilla. Home to monkeys, toucans and macaws, the canopy created by leaves and branches shaded the rest of the forest and the ground. Lianas emerged from the forest floor, weaving around trunks and branches toward the upper canopy, seeking light. Strangler figs followed suit, mingling their viney branches with lianas to form a dense mat that spread horizontally seeking sunlight. Below the canopy was another layer of palms, saplings, ferns and shrubs, keeping temperature and humidity even and protecting the fragile forest floor from the pounding of tropical rainstorms. In areas where the canopy was opened due to harvesting or fallen trees, the saplings raced upward to fill in the gap.

As she rounded a curve in the path, Yalucha came upon a flock of ocellated turkeys feeding along the edge. The large male turkey eyed her coldly, lifting his head high. Periwinkle-blue skin covered his neck and head, dotted with bright orange warts. Glossy ink-blue feathers covered his body with rainbow ripples where the sun played across them. His colorful, peacock-like tail feathers each had a ring, circling a small blue orb. Four females, smaller and plain brown, and three young males were in his flock. They skittered quickly into the underbrush as the alpha male straightened his neck and spit out a screechy gobble, then followed them into the forest. Ocellated turkeys abounded in Mutul. Often raised in pens as well as trapped in the wild for their meat, turkeys were considered most succulent. Their tail and wing feathers were used for headdresses and fans.

Yalucha delighted in the creatures of the forest. Her father called her his Nature Child because she brought assorted critters home to study or nurse back to health. She "cooled the heart," *sikub avolonton,* and the animals became tame. They often approached her when she sat very still, showing little fear unless she moved. Mimicking animal calls was a favorite childhood game.

Glancing down, she saw a dark beetle struggling in a puddle beside the path. Its tiny legs churned as it unsuccessfully sought footing to climb the steep gully. Murmuring "poor little one" she scooped it into her palm, smiling as the horny legs scratched against her skin. Gently she set the beetle on its legs at the forest edge and watched it creep with measured strides into the underbrush.

Soon the forest gave way to vast cultivated fields on either side of the path. Raised rows with deep trenches between were laden with maize beginning to ripen. Beans and squash grew on the edges and sides of the ridges. A series of wooden gates controlled water flow from networks of canals, drawing from the bajo or from reservoirs dug into the limestone bedrock. A vast field of maguey (Agave) plants grew in characteristic disarray, since new plants sprouted from roots of parents. Agave was an important crop; its leaves were de-pulped to produce strong fibers for twine and cord. A few farmers were already at work weeding, pruning and shifting water flows. Farther along the path were raised rows of manioc, pinuela, and macoyas that yielded fine fibers for thread. At the edge of the fields were groves of avocado trees, fruit palms, nuts, and annatto trees that produce achiote, a spice giving rich taste and deep yellow color.

A line of green marsh grasses, punctuated by occasional palms and avocado trees, signaled the edge of the bajo. Yalucha turned onto a dirt path following the bajo edge. She recalled her mother finding a cluster of Kaba yax nik herbs beside a large rock outcropping not far from the stone path's end. A few more minutes of brisk walking brought her to the smooth wind-worn limestone rocks piled upon each other with wispy weeds growing out of cracks here and there. She climbed to the top for a better view. Before her, to the east stretched the vast swampy bajo, now a collection of small ponds with muddy reed-filled flats in between. Once the bajo was a huge lake that never went dry, even at the height of the dry season. Now water was becoming a bigger concern at Mutul. Ten reservoirs had been dug to hold precious rainwater and store it for future use. Canals were cut into the bajo and arroyos dammed to direct water from the nearby river to the city's agricultural fields. The intensive farming done by Mutul to support it's population of nearly 50,000 often allowed the city to obtain three or four crops annually. This demanded a steady supply of water.

A few herons waded in shallow ponds, their long pointed beaks poised to spear incautious fish. Ducks called while flapping in low flight across the marshy stretches. The sun was now well above the horizon, rapidly warming the air and dissipating the mists.

I must hurry, Yalucha thought. She glanced left and right along the bajo bank, seeking the herbs. To her left was a stand of broad-leafed pathos, keeping the soil moist beneath.

That's it! She clambered down the rocks and pushed aside the pathos leaves, revealing a vigorous cluster of Kaba yax nik. The herbaceous plant was knee height, now half the size it would attain later in the season, with 3 to 4 inch serrated leaves opposite each other along the stems. A few early flower spikes protruded from some stems, beginning to form the purple-red buds that would open into tiny flowers. This sacred plant was used for many rituals and ceremonies. It contained a fine ethereal energy that drew the spirit beings closer to earth.

Eagerly she knelt, pulling out her sharp obsidian knife.

Wait, she thought, *give thanks to the spirit of the plants and ask permission to take their leaves.* She knelt perfectly still, lifted her palms up, and with a gracious nodding head motion chanted softly the prayer of appreciation for the plant spirits.

"I thank you for your gifts, oh Spirit of Plants. With these gifts we, your earth children, sustain our bodies and souls. Now I ask permission to take these herbs as a sacred offering to Ix Chel. I am Yalucha, the one who follows your sacred ways and serves the goddess."

She waited a moment, listening. Insects hummed, birds sang in the distance, and the Spirit of Plants whispered softly to her inner hearing "Take the herbs with blessings, daughter."

All nature was alive. Often she talked with spirits of plants, communed with animals, heard soft sighs in the wind and caught faint memories of the rocks. She cried tears of gratitude with the rain, danced with moonbeams, sang to the stars, bowed to the sun.

Respectfully and deftly Yalucha cut a small bundle of Kaba yax nik, placing them carefully in her herb basket, covering them with a cloth dampened in bajo water. She rose and retraced her steps back to the city.

Avoiding the Great Plaza, already filled with people and bustling with activity, Yalucha skirted the north border of the city using a well-worn path through the forest. The path passed behind the Sacred World-Tree Complex, pyramid-temples rising above the trees, and wended around a large t'zonot holding water for the city. Several women were drawing water into elongated ceramic containers, which they balanced on their backs and stabilized with forehead cords. The path disappeared into thick forests where only a dappling of sunlight hit the moist dirt underfoot. Soon it forked, and the left section shortly joined a stone-paved walkway that led to a series of residential clusters. The homes of many nobles were spread around the city borders, a way to decentralize elite authority and maintain daily influence upon the people. The highest nobles and relatives of the ruler lived in elegant palaces near the Great Plaza.

Yalucha's home was in one of the outlying residential clusters, on the extreme northwestern edge of the city. She crossed several paved walkways, nodding a greeting to people as she passed. Her family's compound consisted of four homes with contiguous walls built in a U-shape, added over the course of three generations. Her great-grandfather had built the original house, now the home of her grandparents on her father's side. Theirs was the central home facing an open plaza, with three wide steps leading to the main door. Yalucha's father, K'an Nab Ku as eldest son lived in the home to the right; his brother and sister's families lived in two homes to the left, forming the wings of the U-shape.

In the center was a private courtyard, paved with limestone plaster and shared by the families. One large kitchen served the complex, adjoining Yalucha's home with a substantial garden on the outside. Each home had a main room in which a fire was kept during cold weather, often used for separate family cooking. One or two smaller rooms branched from the main room and were used for sleeping. A stone bench lined the walls of the main rooms, used for sitting.

In typical Mayan style, the homes sat on rock platforms and were constructed of large stones with mortar in between, covered by smooth limestone plaster. Carved columns bordered the main doorways, and carved hardwood lintels, made from mahogany, cedar or sapodilla trunks, added grace and strength over entryways. Symbols of Maya deities and stylized sacred letters decorated columns and lintels. Roofs were made of hardwood logs strapped together with strong liana vines, then covered in multiple layers of palm leaves. Palm leaves for roofs were cut only during the final waxing phase of the moon, for then the sap retreated into the trunk and left the leaves drier so they cured properly, avoiding mildew and rotting.[3]

Approaching the back of her family complex, Yalucha walked through the garden to the common kitchen. She knew her mother would be there. The garden was special to them; a place of nature spirits with many herbs for healing and ceremonies. Already the corn was waist high, the squash bearing golden and green gourds, and the beans full of pods swelling with their black and speckled red seeds. Various peppers sported dark green or red, oval to wedge-shaped fruits. A few rows of manioc and maguey grew in front of several avocado and guayaba trees already forming fruit. The herbs, planted closest to the kitchen doorway, presented a splash of variegated green, white and red leaves in small clusters bordering the walkway.

As Yalucha entered the kitchen, the delicious smell of maize porridge filled her nostrils and her stomach growled hungrily. She was happy to be home and ready for breakfast. Inside the kitchen a small fire burned in the pit located in the room's center, smoke rising through a vent hole in the palm thatched roof. The porridge bubbled in a large ceramic pot perched on hearthstones at the fire's edge. Xoc Ikal turned as her daughter entered.

"My heart is glad to see you," she said. "Were you successful in your quest?"

---

[3] This practice is still followed by modern Maya, who live in stone-plaster houses with palm thatch roofs very similar to ancient dwellings.

"Yes, Mother," Yalucha replied, lifting the cloth from her herb basket and showing her mother the Kaba yax nik that she had collected.

"Oh, those are perfect!" exclaimed Xoc Ikal, touching some serrated leaves gently. "Ix Chel will be most pleased. I've prepared a bowl with water to keep them fresh, over here." She gestured toward a beautifully painted polychrome pottery bowl with a basal flange. It was decorated with intricate, symmetrical and interlocking patterns in three rows around its sides. Yalucha carefully removed the herbs from her basket and placed them in the bowl.

Gratefully she accepted a bowl of steaming maize porridge from Xoc Ikal, settling down on the stone bench that wrapped around the kitchen walls at sitting height. Using a small hollowed gourd, she scooped up porridge and savored its creamy sweetness and welcome warmth. Through the inside door opening onto the courtyard, she heard children's voices. Her two younger brothers were playing with their cousins in the noisy garrulous way of boys. She felt a rush of love for her mother. Glancing at Xoc Ikal, she admired her mother's skillful hands preparing food offerings for the goddess' ceremony tonight.

Xoc Ikal was taller than the average Maya woman, standing tall as a man, not counting her topknot of dark hair. From the topknot, bound with a black cord, her hair hung in a heavy braid down her back to below the waist, swinging gently as she moved. Her nose was less prominent than usual, and her full lips were complimented by large almond eyes. Though well developed and strong, she was not stocky and appeared long-limbed. She wore a white huipil with a narrow border of blue around the hem.

Yalucha reflected on the ease with which her mother transitioned from her domestic role to her priestess activities. Everything seemed so natural with Xoc Ikal. She was fully herself in every situation and flowed gracefully with the pace of events. Tonight's Ix Chel ceremony was special because it celebrated the katun end. Her mother would perform a vision quest seeking guidance for the coming katun.

"Yalucha," Xoc Ikal spoke as if reading her daughter's thoughts, "tonight you will assist me as the gift bearer of the sacred herbs. Later you must prepare the Kaba yax nik in the traditional way, and perform the activation ritual for the herbs just before our ceremony."

Yalucha knew that meant she would need to fast from noon on, but she did not care. It was a great honor to present the sacred herbs during the ceremony, and she was thrilled to be selected for this.

"Thank you, Mother," she said. "I am honored and will follow the tradition carefully." She finished the maize porridge, scraping the walls of the bowl with her gourd to get the last morsels.

"You've learned the traditions very well," said Xoc Ikal. "It is decided and your father agrees that you will go for priestess training before your birth month of Uo this tun (year). As soon as the katun end ceremonies are over, I will make the arrangements and decide which Ix Chel temple. I'm considering Xunantunich or Altun Ha. Both have fine temples and very active traditions for healing and serving their people spiritually. You will be there for two tuns. Is this appealing to your heart?"

Yalucha felt the heady rush of anticipated adventure, mixed almost instantly with trepidation. She had never been away from home before for such a long time. Her biggest forays outside Mutul lasted a few kins (days) while she accompanied her mother on visits to outlying villages for healing or ceremonial work. Quickly she gathered up her courage.

"My heart dances with joy. I am eager to do apprenticeship at an Ix Chel temple, so I may become a full priestess. Can you tell me something about these temple cities?" she asked. Xoc Ikal replied:

"Both are small cities compared to Mutul. Their purpose is religious works, so the temples and the training of priests and priestesses are the main focus of city life. There is no ruler as we have here, and only a few nobles not in religious functions. People from the surrounding areas come daily for healings, or to request special ceremonies for guidance or boons. A regular ritual calendar is followed, with frequent ceremonies for each important date and event. Although Ix Chel is the primary deity, there also are ceremonies important to Itzamna, Hunab K'u and Chak. This will give you a well-rounded background for relating to the many faces of Spirit. As you know, the essence of all deities and all life is the One Great Spirit. From its many forms and guises, individual people, the plants, earth and animals find what expression is most precious to them and draw inspiration from it. Always remember this, Yalucha. No one form of Spirit is superior to another. Honoring of form is a choice, but all are to be respected."

Yalucha nodded silently, acknowledging this great truth she had been taught as long as she could remember. Like a chant, this teaching played through her memory as she had first heard it: *The letter, the stone monument and the god are all the same.* She shook her head and frowned, her movements so subtle that her mother did not notice. It was still hard for her to grasp this concept. These three levels of being—a letter, a stone monument, a deity—seemed different. Maybe this would clear up during her priestess apprenticeship.

Approaching footsteps brought Yalucha back to the practical life of the kitchen. She glanced up at the young women who flung aside the door drape and entered with a forceful stride. It was her aunt, her father's younger sister Chuen, who lived alone in the smallest house along the left wing.

"Greetings of the morning," said Chuen, "is there porridge left?"

She grabbed a cup and was ladling the remaining maize porridge out of the pot almost before Xoc Ikal had time to return her greeting. Chuen was anything but timid. Her strong-headed manner offended some people, but Yalucha found her stimulating. She certainly knew her mind and did not wait for approval before taking action. This troubled Yalucha's grandmother, who was less assertive than her daughter. Quite a few feelings were stirred when Chuen decided to divorce her husband a couple of tuns ago. Maya women had considerable freedom of personal choice and nearly equal civil rights as men. Couples could divorce by simply agreeing to do so, or by one party leaving and going to live elsewhere. Chuen's husband resisted their parting for a while, creating tension in the extended household for many months. But finally Chuen's insistence, and her failure to conceive after five tuns of marriage, convinced him that the better path was finding a more compliant wife. Yalucha was sure that her mother had helped Chuen avoid conception with herbs that prevented pregnancy. This secret knowledge was never revealed to those outside priestess training, but the city and village women knew such herbs existed and sought them from the adepts when needed.

Chuen was a musician, playing flute and ocarinas with exceptional skill. In addition, she was a fine dancer with a short compact body and muscled arms and legs. She was often hired to perform with her entourage at weddings and other family celebrations. Art was her life, and she had no time for husband or children. She taught dance and music to augment her income, conveying her passion to students and creating quite a following of young admirers.

"I'm late for a lesson," Chuen mumbled between quick gulps of maize porridge. "May your hearts enjoy the day," she said in departing, tossing her bowl aside and leaving it to the other women to clean. Yalucha and Xoc Ikal exchanged bemused glances, smiled and began cleaning the bowls and cooking pot, using a large wide-mouthed jug filled with water and a sudsy root powder applied to small cloths. They talked softly about details for the ceremony that would begin at sunset.

*   *   *   *   *

Shortly after Yalucha had left to gather herbs that morning, her father K'an Nab Ku and her older brother Hunbatz waited in the plaza fronting their home complex. The sun warmed the white plaster while the maize porridge served by Xoc Ikal for the morning meal warmed their stomachs. Soon a heavily muscled, powerfully built man emerged from the smaller home complex across the plaza. K'in Pakal crossed the distance in several springing strides, his smooth coordinated movements almost surprising. Brother to K'an Nab Ku, K'in Pakal was a respected warrior. Although only in his mid-20s, he was a veteran of many battles and had received praise from the ruler for his bravery.

K'in Pakal smiled greetings to his brother and nephew. The sun glinted on the inlaid gold and sparkled off precious stones embedded in his front teeth, which were filed into points in the fashion of warriors. He enjoyed flashing his showy teeth, smiling often and broadly. A light multicolored cape was thrown over his wide shoulders, but his chest was bare. Around his thick waist was a leather band decorated with shells and beads, from which hung a green obsidian dagger. Breeches of white cotton fit his bulging thighs closely, tied beneath the knees with woven cords. Warriors seldom wore the common skirt garb of Maya men, as they wanted greater freedom of leg movement.

"Greetings of the rising sun, brother," said K'in Pakal, "and to you, nephew." He added this with a touch of diffidence.

Hunbatz prickled at the subtle slight. His uncle was full of himself, proud of being a great warrior.

Because we're stone-carvers, Hunbatz thought to himself, *this war hawk thinks less of us. But what we create will long outlive all memory of his deeds.*

This thought comforted Hunbatz. He grunted a greeting, but his father seemed unperturbed and joined arms with K'in Pakal to begin their walk to the city center.

The two stone-carvers wore white cotton skirts to mid-thigh, with a waistband of woven fabric. Geometric patterns in bright colors decorated the waistbands, loin and cheek cloths that hung knee-length in front and back. Their chests were also bare, decorated by pendants of silver or copper inlaid with colored stones. To ward off the morning coolness, they threw short white capes over their shoulders. Maya men generally wore their hair long, tied in a topknot behind the crown with a ponytail hanging to the upper back. Sandals of tightly woven maguey cords formed the soles and leather thongs laced around the ankles. Tied to their belts were pouches holding the currency they would use for trading at the market: cacao bean pods, small seashells, and semi-precious stones. K'an Nab Ku also had several small bags filled with herbs prepared by Xoc Ikal. Medicinal herbs for treating diarrhea, upset stomach, fevers and infections were greatly valued and often needed. These he would keep in reserve for particularly hard bargaining.

The three men were going to Mutul's large cosmopolitan market. It drew merchants and traders from distant cities, as well as a host of local artisans and craftspeople. Now the market was especially teeming with goods, because of the katun end celebrations. Many people from outlying villages had swelled the city's population. Everyone of means would want a fine offering for the gods as part of the ruler's katun end ceremony tomorrow. It was also a good opportunity to obtain special products not usually available, and stock up on staples. The marketplace would be closed tomorrow, so the men left home early to beat the crowds and ensure the widest selection of goods.

Walking briskly down the stone pathway, they soon came to the West Plaza where stone-carvers were finishing the ruler's katun end stela. K'an Nab Ku and Hunbatz cast appraising glances as they passed by, and were struck with admiration for the fine quality of carving. They did not begrudge the ruler's choice of his relatives to carve this memorial stela. It was simply the way those in power acted, an accepted fact of life. There was plenty of work, as stone carving was always in demand in Mutul.

After crossing the West Plaza, the men veered off to the right instead of mounting the wide stairs to the Great Plaza as Yalucha had done earlier. They took the three-person wide sakbe that led to the marketplace. Raised nearly a man's height above ground level, the sakbe was a straight masonry causeway that gave easy access to the marketplace even during the rainy season. Sakbeob, "white roads," were used by the Maya to connect important areas of their cities, and link with outlying sites. These causeways stretched like long, white arteries through the green canopy of the forest.

89

It was a short walk from the West Plaza to the marketplace, a straight line due south. The rising sun warmed the air as the three men walked along the sakbe. Green shrubs and trees bordered the raised causeway, as the sounds of calling birds and chattering monkeys kept up a constant symphony. Although the men had started early, the sakbe was already host to a stream of people, most going toward the marketplace. Nodding occasionally to acquaintances, the two older men pursued an on-going conversation about politics at Mutul.

"Chak Toh Ich'ak will be giving the foreigners a place of honor at the katun end ceremony," said K'in Pakal, his voice revealing a touch of annoyance. "He has hinted that we have much to learn from their methods of war."

"The ruler does seem to favor our visitors from Teotihuacan," K'an Nab Ku observed. "Perhaps it is prudent that he does so. Look at their dominance in the highland cities. Kaminaljuyu is in essence an outpost of their empire. Their influence spreads throughout the western trade routes, and makes an impact here also."

"Yes," replied K'in Pakal, "that is just my concern. Although their intentions seem peaceful, I am worried about their ultimate goals. Mutul sits in a key location for overland trade from the east coast, and we are a rich and prestigious city. To bring us under the Teotihuacan wing would advance K'ak Sih's ambitions and gain him great favor from his ruler."

"K'ak Sih appears an ambitious man to me," said K'an Nab Ku. He reflected on the Teotihuacano warrior's demeanor. As strongly built but taller than K'in Pakal, K'ak Sih had intense black eyes and a fierce aura. A man of middle age, he was reputed to outfight younger warriors and demonstrate fury in battle that terrified his opponents. He was a master at their innovative method of warfare, the atlatl or spear-thrower.

"Have you seen him demonstrate use of the atlatl?" asked K'an Nab Ku.

"Yes, many warriors were called to observe K'ak Sih and his retinue use their atlatls," said K'in Pakal. "It is a curious device, about the length of a man's arm. At the far end from where they grip it, a curved hook serves as a seat for a short spear. They balance the spear against the thrower, using a side arm motion to pitch the spear forward. This method allows spears to fly much farther than hand thrown ones. And it gives the masters of the art, such as K'ak Sih, an uncanny accuracy in hitting targets."

"How would that affect warfare?"

"It gives the spear-throwers a much greater range," K'in Pakal commented. "That would allow a first assault, before the enemy could reach hand spear range. It could impose great damage, if enough warriors used the atlatl. I have heard that the Teotihuacan methods of war differ from ours. They seem bent upon destroying the entire army of their opponents, rather than taking noble captives as we do. Then they invade the enemy city and kill its ruling family and nobles. After that, they take over the city and make it another outpost for their empire."

"This requires an immense army, both for battles and populating conquered cities," observed K'an Nab Ku. "It does not appeal to me."

"Nor to me," agreed K'in Pakal. "Mutul has done well by intimidating our enemies and keeping their leaders wary of attacking us. We gain much tribute that adds to our wealth, more than taking over other cities. And we obtain royal blood for sacrifice, in the manner required by K'inich Ahau. It makes no sense to adopt such foreign methods."

Even as he said this, however, K'in Pakal sensed that Chak Toh Ich'ak had plans to train his army in the atlatl method. He added:

"I worry about the ruler's ambitions."

"His main ambition is to keep the kingship of Mutul in his direct line," said K'an Nab Ku. "Now that his second son has been killed, only his daughter remains. But others of Jaguar Claw lineage, his nephews and cousins, have greater claim to kingship. Chak Toh Ich'ak is old, nearly three katuns (60 years) and cannot live much longer. I wonder if his cultivation of the Teotihuacanos is connected with some scheme to seat his daughter as ahau of Mutul."

"Humpf," retorted K'in Pakal. "The ahau of Mutul comes from among sons of ruling families, not daughters. How can he change that? Perhaps he's become demented in his old age. I expect we'll have a new ruler soon, but not of his choosing."

K'an Nab Ku kept his counsel, choosing not to respond to K'in Pakal's last remarks. He felt certain that Chak Toh Ich'ak was committed to maintaining the ruling line of Mutul in his direct family, and that meant finding some way to pass it through his daughter. Marriage to a first cousin was out of the question, but a second cousin would be acceptable. He passed images of the eligible young men through his mind, but none had the leadership qualities needed to rule a large city like Mutul. The ruler indeed had a dilemma on his hands.

K'in Pakal interrupted his thoughts, saying:

"You have to admit that the green obsidian blades from Teotihuacan are the finest anywhere. I plan to find myself a longer dagger and to select an especially slender one to offer K'inich Ahau at tomorrow's ceremony." He patted the green obsidian dagger in his belt.

K'an Nab Ku nodded.

"Yes, and the Teotihuacano traders are here in abundance. I want to get an unusual carved jade for my offering. Mexica jade has lovely pale shades swirled with creamy streaks. There is none finer, and their craftsmanship is impeccable. A worthy offering to K'inich Ahau."

Hunbatz, who had remained silent as the older men discussed politics and war, perked up as the conversation turned to crafts. He aspired to become a skilled carver of smaller objects such as jade, obsidian and bone.

"Father, I would like to obtain a carved jade also," he said. "Show me the merchant who brings the fine work from Mexica jade quarries."

"I will," replied K'an Nab Ku. "You must study their work carefully, for you can learn much from their techniques. Perhaps the carver himself will be there, and you can ask him for pointers." He supported his son's interest in fine carving, which was much in demand and would always provide a good living.

The sakbe joined a large plaza that held the market, called k'iwik. The men quickened their steps and entered the market area.

The marketplace at Mutul was immense. Line upon line of small stone and mortar structures stretched wall to wall in straight rows, facing each other across a wide alley. Thatched roofs covered the structures. There were 10 rows, filling the plaza from end to end. These structures served as both homes and shops for the merchants, artisans, and craftspeople. Most were single room structures, but some had two or even three attached rooms with interconnecting doors. These belonged to the wealthier merchants. Many artisans and craftspeople produced their wares here.

There were always some vacancies, used by traders from other cities while sojourning in Mutul. In front of their shops, the merchants spread colorful blankets upon which to display their wares. Both men and women worked in the marketplace, sitting outside on the blankets serving customers. Many structures had a roof overhang covered with palm thatching and supported by poles that protected the merchant, wares and customers from rain and sun.

The hum of human voices joined the sounds of musical instruments, clanking pottery, and occasional drumbeats as customers tried out the merchandise. Blending into the gathering crowd, the three men browsed past merchant's stalls. The huge selection of wares was nearly overwhelming. Local merchants offered pottery mostly of the Tzak'ol style: polychrome ceramics with stylized designs of cranes, parrots, anthropomorphic figures or geometric patterns painted on bowls with a basal flange. There were polychrome figurines of gods and goddesses, animals and people. Plant pigments of white, red, yellow, blue and green were used. Large flat plates for maize flatbreads, deep bowls for stews, small cups for cacao and taller cups for balche abounded. Often glyph texts accompanied figures, describing events or reciting prayers or poems.

Another type of pottery popular in Mutul was made of black ceramic with incised contrasting white or gray glyphs and geometric designs in shallow relief. These ceramics were polished and fired, bringing sheen to their smooth glazed texture. The black ceramics took many forms, but particularly striking were the deep cylinders with lids, often standing a forearm's length high.

The men had little interest in ceramics, although Hunbatz lingered to examine the carved black pots. All did pause, however, at two stalls near the end displaying a distinctly different type of pottery. Vases and bowls had tripod legs at the base, a feature never used by the Maya. A figurine on top served as a handle; most were animals or faces of people or gods. Small spouted jugs with handles and a flared base mingled with the three-legged pottery. The designs on these vessels had abstract swirls and leaf-like patterns without the glyphs typical of Maya pottery. Incense burners sported visages of Teotihuacan gods such as Xipe Totec, god of springtime, or the fierce appearing Tlaloc, god of storms, with his large circular ear plugs, down turned mouth and eyes ringed with white circles, like goggles. Already some Maya potters were copying the Teotihuacan style.

The merchants seated on striped blankets looked up quizzically but made no move to stand. They waited for a sign that the buyers were serious. Square-jawed faces, straight foreheads and small noses showed their Mexica origins.

Both K'an Nab Ku and K'in Pakal thought of their conversation on the way to the market. Catching each other's eyes, they shared the same thought:

These foreigners are having too much impact on Mutul.

The men continued to the next row where obsidian and jade were featured. Stall after stall of tools, jewelry and vessels made of black, green, cream and white colored stones stretched before them. Now they concentrated and carefully examined the wares laid out on blankets. Sunlight caught the edges of blades and reflected off shiny surfaces of pendants and vessels. Metals such as gold, copper and silver adorned the finer jewelry and knives.

K'in Pakal found the craftsman who made green obsidian blades of extraordinary quality. He turned the cool stone blades in his hands, feeling for weight and balance, carefully running his finger across the edges to test sharpness. He examined the hilts for hand fit and attachment to the blades. Expertly crafted blades were available in many shades of green, from light translucent jade-green to deep forest green with dusky hues. For himself, he chose a long forest green dagger with copper and silver patterns in the hilt. For his katun end ceremony offering, he selected a slender translucent green dagger whose handle was worked with gold and inlaid with red stones. It was very fine and very expensive, but a worthy gift for K'inich Ahau.

The bargaining began with an animated but friendly exchange. The merchant settled for a large amount of K'in Pakal's cacao beans and semi-precious stones. The warrior had only one-third left after buying both daggers, but he felt content for he knew the value of these blades.

K'an Nab Ku watched his brother, who bargained well. He nodded approval and admired the purchase. They walked on until K'an Nab Ku found a jade stall that caught his eye. This was the Mexica jade he had mentioned, brought by traders from areas not far from Teotihuacan. Local jade did not match this quality. For tuns these traders had journeyed from the upper peninsula, following the coast that bordered the great eastern sea in their large sea-worthy canoes, then taking smaller canoes up rivers that flowed eastward from the mountains west of Mutul. It was a hazardous and lengthy trip, with some overland trekking. The traders had been doing it for many tuns, since before K'an Nab Ku's birth, and were very adept in handling difficulties that might arise. These traders were not Teotihuacanos, but another smaller tribe living south of that great city. They worked the jade mines in nearby cliffs, and occasionally found veins of gold and marble. Marble sometimes found its way to Maya markets; it was more highly prized than gold.

Both father and son fingered, stroked, and closely examined the lovely carved jade pieces. Pendants, necklaces, rings, wrist and arm bracelets, earplugs, vases, large container vessels, flat plates, figurines, cups, and other objects abounded. K'an Nab Ku wanted a purely decorative carved jade, something not intended for everyday use or body adornment. It was his offering to satisfy the sun god's appreciation of pure beauty. After looking at many objects, he selected a hand-sized flat jade piece that could serve as a wall hanging. It was carved in deep relief with images of Maya creation mythology figures: the Hero Twins, Hun Ahau and Yax Balam[4], the false sun-bird Wuqub' Kaqix (Seven Macaw) whom they unseated from his perch in the sky, the Lords of Xibalba (Underworld) whom they outsmarted in order to resurrect their father the Maize God, seen emerging from a serpent's mouth.

The jade was pale green with swirls of subtle creamy streaks, polished until it gleamed. The stone carving was exquisite, done with deftness and skill that he envied. It was costly, but just the gift he wanted. With little bargaining, he paid the merchant's price, throwing in a couple of bags of herbs. The merchant's wife was especially interested in the herbs, looking very pleased when she learned that Xoc Ikal had prepared them. His wife's widespread reputation, even among foreigners, still continued to amaze him.

Hunbatz found his jade carving at the same stall. It was a smooth round pectoral pendant with a hole in the center, made of darker jade full of richness and mystery. Concentric circles in low relief traced delicate patterns around the opening. His father and uncle nodded their approval as he used half his cache of cacao beans to buy his offering.

Having fulfilled their mission, the men spent some time browsing and chatting with merchants and other shoppers. It was sunny, warm and pleasant. They admired colorful woven textiles, sandals, and belts. They fingered shells of many sizes, shapes and colors from the eastern and western coasts, especially noting the bright red thorny oyster called spondylus, whose shells were a favorite trade item and much favored for ceremonies and burials. The Maya scraped the white lining from the shell to reveal the orange-red under layer. This color was sacred, it was the color of the east, of rebirth. K'an Nab Ku bought some spondylus shells for Xoc Ikal to use in ceremonies.

---

[4] The Hero Twins are called Hunahpu and Xbalanque in the Quiche Maya version of the *Popul Vuh*, copied and translated by the Spanish friar Francisco Ximenez between 1701-1703.

At nearby stalls, bundles of stingray spines were tied together with thongs, leaving long ends for carrying. These sharp spines were used for sewing, ceramic working and bloodletting by priests, rulers and nobles seeking visionary experiences. The cups and bark paper used for catching blood and ceremonially burning it were also available.

Musical instruments were featured in several stalls. Merchants offered different sized drums, reed and ceramic flutes, figurine ocarinas, shell trumpets, plain gourd rattles and decorated maracas, large turtle carapaces with deer-antler beaters, and many types of wood percussion sticks. Other merchants offered pearls and semiprecious stones of rainbow colors, mirrors made of pyrite plates, feathers of many birds including the ocellated turkey and quetzal, flint and chert from deposits in the drier central regions, copal incense, and pigments for dyes including indigo, annatto and the precious red cinnabar used for burials.

Many foods were available, ranging from fresh fruits and vegetables to several varieties of dried beans, whole kernel and ground maize. Stones for grinding maize were featured, a flat dense stone with a shallow hollow combined with an oval stone pestle. Salt was a highly valued trade commodity, brought from salt flats on the coast of the eastern sea. Cacao beans and ground powder were present in abundance, along with dried peppercorns, honey, and beeswax. There was rat poison made from roots of the cardboard palm, perfume from the flowers of sweet acacia trees, and ink made from its pods. Birdcages were fashioned from bent branches of the Acalypha tree, some populated by brightly colored songbirds. Ceiba fiber and Agave twine were gathered in large heaps, and choice boards of cedar and mahogany offered for carving or building. Gum from the zapote or chicle tree was sold as a chew. Pelts of animals such as deer, gray fox and jaguar could be found in a few stalls.

The sun was approaching its noon apex when the three men completed their tour of the marketplace. Before returning to the sakbe for the walk home, they stopped at a food stall and bought maize cakes for their noon meal. A staple food and useful when traveling, these were made of ground maize cooked with chopped nuts and dried fruit, held together with rendered dog fat. The Maya had a long relationship with dogs, called *pek*, whose origins were lost in antiquity. There were two main types: a shorthaired dog and a hairless dog. The former was used primarily to chase prey during hunts; the latter was fattened for food and offered as sacrifices during ceremonies and burials. Black and white spotted shorthaired dogs were used for sacrifice, often depicted in Maya ritual art.

The three men munched their maize cakes while standing, exchanging greetings with passers-by and watching the burgeoning crowd filling the rows. Licking their fingers to enjoy the last morsels, they left the marketplace and began their walk back on the sakbe.

Halfway to the West Plaza they encountered the Chief Daykeeper Priest and his teenage son. K'an Nab Ku had a warm friendship with Yo'nal Ac, the Chief Daykeeper Priest of Mutul. The two men bowed and touched each other's palms in the formal greeting of respect for priests. All stopped and joined in conversation. K'an Nab Ku was pleased to see Yo'nal Ac's son, Chitam, who was in training with his father as a Daykeeper Priest. The young man was two tuns older than Yalucha and was attracted to her. He was from a respected noble family and a long line of priests with close ties to the ruler. Not only an excellent marital candidate, he was also the son of a good friend—a perfect match, in K'an Nab Ku's mind. Yalucha should be pleased to have a husband who was devoted to serving the gods, and steeped in the mysteries of the sacred calendars. They would have much in common. Her father had not yet mentioned these ideas to Yalucha or her mother; he was biding his time for the right moment.

"Greetings of this auspicious time," said K'an Nab Ku. "I trust K'in, the Sun, traces his course on schedule."

Yo'nal Ac acknowledged the inquiry with a positive hand signal. The Chief Daykeeper Priest was a thin, small man with a wizened right leg from nerve damage during birth. He used an intricately carved walking stick, covered with celestial icons and vision serpents. His face was angular, made even sharper by a huge hooked nose, larger than usual even for a Maya man. This prominent facial feature caused his thin lips to appear even terser. Intense black eyes burned out from deep sockets beneath thick, overhanging eyebrows. Mutul's residents and many from neighboring cities held Yo'nal Ac in awe because of his great intuitive powers. His skill in divination was sought by many, and used by Mutul's ruler for guidance in important decisions and actions.

"All is as the Tzolk'in predicted," he replied.

The Tzolk'in was the Maya's sacred calendar of 260 kins (days), used to guide everyday life. It had 13 uinals (months) of 20 kins that meshed together until all possible combinations were used. It took 260 kins for the entire sequence of combinations to occur. The Maya

97

used a cycle of 260 kins because it embodied the power of creation: a woman's pregnancy lasted 260 kins, and Venus' passage through the night skies averaged 260 kins. Venus traversed the Underworld for a time, not visible in the sky, and then rose in the east as Morningstar. First Father, Hun Hunahpu, was reborn as the Morningstar after Venus' death and passage through the Underworld.

Yo'nal Ac carried a great responsibility as Chief Daykeeper Priest of Mutul. He kept daily track of the sun's movements from solstice to equinox to solstice, to ensure that ceremonies occurred on exactly the correct date, and that Long Count dates inscribed on stelae meshed properly with the Tzolk'in and Haab dates. Haab was the solar calendar, also divided into 20 kins. The last kin in each cycle carried premonitory energies of the coming cycle. Every 52 tuns (years) the Haab and Tzolk'in completed their sequence of combinations, the Calendar Round period. Thus, there were 18,980 unique kins with a name from each calendar—and a unique set of spirit forces acting upon the lives of people and the environment.[5]

The Chief Daykeeper Priest had the grave responsibility to ensure that katun end ceremonies took place on exactly the right kin. The ruler's ability to invoke predictive visions and journey in the realm of spirits depended on following sacred calendars precisely.

The Long Count calendar tracked time in a never-ending, immensely long cycle going back to the origins of the world. It flowed into the dim past and distant future for eons. This highly accurate count completed its greatest cycle, a Sun (Age), in 25,650 tuns (years) then rolled over into the next age. A new Sun or Age began when the precession of the equinoxes completed its full circle.

Maya Calendar Terms

Kin	1 day
Uinal	20 kins (similar to a month)
Tun	360 kins (similar to a year)
Katun	20 tuns (7,200 kins or 19.72 years)
Baktun	20 katuns (400 tuns or 394 years)
Great Cycle	13 baktuns (5,130 years)
Sun (Age)	5 Great Cycles (25,650 years)

---

[5] Contemporary Maya still use the Tzolk'in calendar.

This very morning he and his son Chitam had risen before dawn and walked through the silent city to the Observatory Complex.[6] Located on a wide plaza southwest of the Great Plaza and connected by a raised sakbe, the Observatory Complex consisted of a square pyramid in the center and three small temples on the east edge. The square pyramid had two main stairways on its eastern and western sides, and two smaller stairways the other two sides. From the flat platform on top, the Daykeeper Priest could sight the positions of the rising sun in relation to the three small temples on the east. At the summer solstice, the sun rose behind the northern corner of the far north temple, at the equinoxes it rose behind the middle of the center temple, and at the winter solstice it rose behind the southern corner of the far south temple.

However, precision was required for the sightings of the rising sun. Yo'nal Ac climbed the eastern stairs slowly using his walking stick. His son Chitam lighted his steps with a hand torch, as the darkness was still deep in the hour just before dawn. He glanced up at the twinkling stars, and inwardly expressed gratitude to K'inich Ahau

Tzolk'in and Haab Calendars

Left smaller wheel has 260 teeth with 20 unique Tzolk'in day names plus numbers 1-13.
Right larger wheel (Haab) has 365 teeth with 18 unique months of 20 days, and one month of 5 days called uayab.

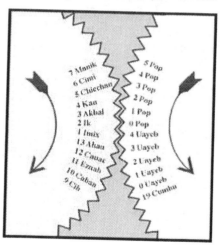

that the dawn would be clear. Sighting was challenging enough without having to contend with fog or clouds. He settled into a cross-legged position on a cushion brought by Chitam, facing the east. Here he would meditate and wait for the exact moment to begin the sightings. Chitam sat on his cushion just behind his father, placing the

---

[6] Called the Lost World Complex, Mundo Perdido, by archeologists.

torch in a holder. For what seemed a long time, the pre-dawn silence was broken only by an occasional night insect or owl call.

The eastern horizon began to lighten. Yo'nal Ac positioned himself sitting behind the central observation niche. This morning should herald the kin before true spring equinox, which was the seating kin of the new katun. The Daykeeper fixed his vision on a row of small grooves at eye level, carved on the surface of the observation niche. At equinox, the sun rose exactly through the center groove, which aligned with the small middle temple. By counting the grooves left of center, the Daykeeper knew how many kins remained until spring equinox.

It was a complex art and required exacting focus. The Daykeeper needed to precisely identify the exact center of the middle temple, despite his angle of viewing. Such precision often took years of practice. Yo'nal Ac was a master at this art. He hoped to impart his skills to his son, who was now sitting exactly behind him to learn the alignments. Since this was the seating kin of the new katun, it was one kin before true spring equinox. Yo'nal Ac focused his vision through the first groove to the left of center. He fixed his sight dead center upon the roofcomb of the middle temple. He waited, hardly blinking. As the sun rose he would have only a few seconds to ascertain if the alignment was correct. If clouds or mist obscured the horizon, the reading would be less accurate.

The sky became lighter in the east. Chitam felt tension rising in his body. He craned his head to see beyond his father's head in front, but knew only one person would have the exact view. On earlier kins leading to the equinox his father had let him sit in front, but today was too important. The Chief Daykeeper had to make the determination that indeed it was the kin before true spring equinox, so the ruler's katun end ceremony would fulfill the sacred calendar.

As the eastern sky became lighter, Yo'nal Ac could discern that only a few low clouds hung above the horizon, and there was not yet a sign of mist. The horizon would be clear, good for sighting. A bright golden-orange glow signaled the immanent rise of the sun. Yo'nal Ac squinted against glare as the fiery orb sent its first dawn rays across the roofcomb of the middle temple. With clockwork precision, the tip of the sun appeared in groove one to the left of center, filling the tiny space with dazzling light. A moment later, the sun's upper curve broke over the roofcomb and flooded the observation pyramid.

Yo'nal Ac breathed a sigh of relief. His tense shoulders relaxed and he turned to Chitam, smiling.

"The true spring equinox is tomorrow," he stated in a lilting tone. "The katun end ceremonies are correctly timed, and the gods will be pleased that we have abided by the sacred calendar."

Chitam smiled back in return. His face was a younger and softer version of his father's, having the same large hooked nose, thin lips and angular shape. These two would not be considered handsome by Maya standards. But they were Daykeeper Priests, a highly respected profession, and in good relationship with the ruler.

Now they were finishing their conversation with K'an Nab Ku, his son and his brother the warrior. Pleasantries were exchanged about the gifts the three men had just acquired for the katun end ceremony, and the richness of selections at the marketplace. Chitam edged his way toward Hunbatz, and asked to see his jade pendant as the older men talked about the political climate and foreign influences.

Hunbatz took the jade pendant out of his pouch and offered it to Chitam.

"What remarkable workmanship," said Chitam as he rubbed his fingers over the delicately carved surface. "The color is deep and mysterious, a fine offering to K'inich Ahau. I am sure he will be pleased."

"My heart is warmed by your appreciation of my gift," replied Hunbatz. "It was very costly, but I am glad to part with my abundance to honor the gods. Perhaps this will help bring favor upon us all, and upon Mutul."

"So might it well do," agreed Chitam. "I am searching the market myself for a sun effigy made of gold and copper, the colors of K'inich Ahau. Like to like, sun to Sun. It seems a proper gift."

Hunbatz nodded agreement. Chitam handed back the jade pendant thoughtfully. After a slight pause, he inquired:

"And how is it with your mother and your sister?"

"They are well," answered Hunbatz, with a quizzical expression. "They are both much involved in preparing for mother's Ix Chel ceremony tonight. She will invoke the vision serpents and seek messages about the coming katun. Yalucha is to be an assistant in the ceremony. Are you coming?"

"Sadly, no. I am required to attend my father as he prepares for the ruler's katun end ceremony tomorrow," said Chitam. "Will you convey to them that my heart sends blessings for their ceremony?"

101

"Certainly," Hunbatz agreed.

Having overheard the young men's last few words, K'an Nab Ku said warmly to Chitam:

"You must come to visit Yalucha soon, Chitam. I am sure she will be happy to see you and tell you about the Ix Chel ceremony."

Chitam nodded, and the two fathers exchanged knowing glances. A process was already at work, and they understood it well. The alliance suited them both.

Bidding each other farewell, the two groups of men parted company and began to walk in opposite directions along the busy sakbe.

The rest of the kin passed quickly for Yalucha. She spent the afternoon alone and in silence, fasting and preparing to be the gift bearer of the sacred herbs. She stayed in her bedroom, a small rectangle with one window. The door that opened into her parents' bedroom was covered with a heavy woven cotton drape. Artfully she selected through and arranged the Kaba yax nik on a flat ceramic platter inset with jade. Each leaf received a purification gesture and power invocation, as she removed it from the stalks and placed it in a fanned circle on the platter. When the platter was completely lined with serrated leaves, she placed it on her small stone altar in the wall with a carving of Ix Chel above. Then she sat and entered a state of inner stillness, holding her focus on the goddess and repeating chants mentally when her mind wandered.

The ceremony began at dusk. Shortly before sunset, Yalucha quietly left her room, carrying the platter covered with a multi-colored cloth. Avoiding others, she slipped along the edge of the courtyard and approached the temple complex on the west. The temple was a modest but harmoniously proportioned building, on a raised platform with five wide steps for ascent. Rectangular in shape, its single story had a vaulted stone roof. The narrow corbel arch above the central door led into the ceremonial room. Two smaller doors on either side opened into rooms where ritual clothing and objects were kept. On the portico in front where the priestess stood for ceremony was a round altar stone, knee high with intricate carvings all around its base.

Yalucha climbed the stairs and entered the room on the right, changing into ritual clothing. Her mother and an older woman, the temple assistant, were already there. The women kept silence; each knew her role well. They assisted each other in donning the white and green robes with bright yellow borders that represented the great mother goddess, Ix Chel. Unlike everyday huipils that hung loosely from the shoulders, these robes were belted with yellow twisted cords and fit the body closely. The deep v-neck exposed the upper chest for adornment with necklaces made of gold, jade and semi-precious stones. The sleeveless robes had skirts with side slits to the upper thigh, allowing freedom of arm and leg movements.

Xoc Ikal's headdress was the most elaborate. The temple assistant had wound her long hair into double-sided buns to help stabilize the headdress. Stiff woven cloth with embossed patterns held dangling carved beads falling onto her forehead. A wood frame anchored at her waist supported a tall fan of ocellated turkey feathers, shimmering translucent purples, greens and blues against a dark brown background. Three tall plumes soared up behind, bright red-orange tail feathers from the treasured quetzal bird. Additional beads swayed behind the headdress on thin yellow braided cords to the mid-back. Yalucha and the temple assistant wore smaller headdresses with similar embossing, beads and shorter feathers.

In full regalia, Xoc Ikal stood regally with a distant look in her eyes. Yalucha savored her mother's powerful presence as the temple assistant made minor adjustments to her headdress and straightened the hem of her robe. Tonight was a special ceremony for the katun ending. The girl knew her mother would enter a trance state and commune with the ancestors, goddess and gods. In the ancient tradition of Izapa, she would use a brew made from the spotted hallucinogenic mushroom to open her receptivity to the spirit world. Tonight Xoc Ikal would become one with Ix Chel, or other spirits who wanted to communicate with the people. She would speak as an oracle and convey their messages.

At tomorrow's katun end ceremony conducted by the ruler, the method of self-bloodletting would initiate Spirit contact. In more recent times, the offering of royal blood was favored by K'inich Ahau. Tomorrow the ruler, Chak Toh Ich'ak would let blood and bring forth the message of Spirit for the people of Mutul.

The sounds of a crowd gathering in the courtyard filtered through the temple doors. All of Yalucha's family members, neighbors and people from other areas of the city were gathering for the ceremony. These were people who maintained religious ties to the great mother goddess, who respected Xoc Ikal for her healing and wisdom. The courtyard was filled to near capacity with about 80 people. Women sat on thick blankets with babies and small children in front of the temple stairs. Elders also sat nearby, but most of the crowd would stand through the short ceremony.

As the sun's red globe descended behind the western horizon, torches were lit in wall sconces around the courtyard. Musicians began playing, hand drums beating a slow regular rhythm as flutes sounded reedy wails. Periodically the sharp percussions of maracas—decorated rattles—accented musical phrases. Off to the far left, behind the group of musicians, was a three-foot tall mother drum. She would sound her deep resonant voice later in the ceremony. The cadence gradually quickened, building an air of anticipation among the crowd. They began a spontaneous chant to the drumbeat, the nighttime prayer to Hunab K'u:

"Dzu bulul H'yum K'in, dzu tip'il X'yum Ak'ab ,(Already the Master Sun has set, and the Mistress Night has risen.)

C'tucule tian ti teche C'Hunab K'u." (Our thoughts are in you, dear God)

As the last rays of the sun faded from the horizon, the music suddenly stopped. A silence full of portent hung above the crowd. From the left doorway the temple assistant and Yalucha emerged with slow, measured gait. Each carried a small oil-filled bowl in which a flame flickered. Using a thin kindling stick, each woman lighted one torch on either side of the central doorway, then placed the bowls on the round altar. Yalucha put the platter with consecrated herbs on the right side of the altar, while the temple assistant placed another ceramic platter holding food offerings and the copal incensor on the left side. In the center of the ceramic platter was a tiny vial made of deep blue glassy stone; it contained the mushroom brew that opened the pathway to the spirit world. The two women took their places beside the torches.

The hand drums began a measured cadence. After a moment, Xoc Ikal emerged from the left doorway and a murmur of appreciation rose from the crowd. She was splendid as the torchlight reflected off gold and glass beads in her headdress and evoked a warm golden glow on her white robe. The long quetzal headdress feathers bobbled as she walked and the turkey feathers shimmered as they caught light. When she arrived behind the round altar, facing the crowd, the drums suddenly ceased their beat. Xoc Ikal raised her arms and began the ceremony:

"Great Spirit, First Father Hun Hunahpu—Hunab K'u, Cosmic Mother Ix Chel, I ask for your presence here with your people, your

Maya children. We now open our hearts for you, the sustainer of our life, to enter."

Xoc Ikal faced east. She lowered her arms making a ritualized motion with her right hand, and the crowd turned to face east for the honoring of the directions, an ancient procedure to initiate sacred space. She called to the east in a clear, pure voice:

"*Lik'in* (east), where the k'in (sun) rises, place of red maize, your fire is our blood, our heart, our emotions, the flowing of liquids. You bring forth the birth of life and rebirth each kin. Initiate in us the power to create a heart-felt life, so that we may keep good relations with the entire web of existence. *Yum Ha,* Master of the East, receive our homage."

The crowd intoned a long "*Yum Ha*" and shook rattles. All then turned to face the north with Xoc Ikal. She made another hand motion and spoke:

"*Xaman* (north), the cold sun, place of white maize, you are the air we breathe, the breath that brings harmony and peace to our bodies. Your winds cool our emotions, take us inward to refine our wisdom. Guide us into prayer where we may lose ourselves in the sacred and know Spirit. *Yum Ik,* Master of the North, receive our homage."

"*Yum Ik*" intoned the crowd, shaking rattles. All turned to face the west, and Xoc Ikal motioned with her hand and spoke:

"*Chik'in* (west), the dying sun, place of blue maize, you are the earth which provides our bodies. Your sacred waters give purification and healing. When our soul departs, you reclaim the body for another cycle of life. Activate in us deep transformation and peaceful repose as the light enters darkness. *Yum Caba*, Master of the West, receive our homage."

"*Yum Caba*" intoned the crowd, again shaking rattles then turning south as Xoc Ikal spoke the last direction.

"*Nohol* (south), the hot sun, place of yellow maize, you are the growing things of Mother Earth which sustain our lives. Your fiery heat brings abundance of vegetation, fruitfulness, and mature power. Guide us to ripen what we have started, to carry our intentions into manifestation. Show us how to act to keep the earth healthy. *Yum Kak*, Master of the South, receive our homage."

"*Yum Kak*" was intoned on a long, low note with louder rattling. Those who had stood for the directions settled down on their blankets. A few babies gurgled softly.

Xoc Ikal faced the altar and used kindling sticks to light copal in the ceramic incensor which she held by attached braided strings. Murmuring secret incantations, she swung the incensor in a large circle over the top of the altar. Soon the woody, pungent scent of burning resin drifted through the crowd, who sniffed eagerly to absorb its meditative effects. Copal was the most sacred incense used by the Maya, harvested from the resin of copal trees using diagonal slashes in the trunk. The bark was sliced when the moon was full, to ensure flow of the resin at the time when sap was highest in the tree. An old custom among copal harvesters was to drink a very hot cup of thick corn atole when they got home, to promote free flow of the sap.

Replacing the incensor on the altar, Xoc Ikal lifted the platter with its fan of Kaba yax nik leaves. Balancing the platter on one hand, she lifted it high above her head, then lowered it and breathed softly across the leaves. She called in a singsong chant to the sacred herbs, her body swaying slightly, asking the herbs to send forth their purifying vibrations and prepare a portal for contacting the spirit realm. She asked Ix Chel to receive these consecrated herbs, and be receptive to her quest tonight for insight into the coming katun. Slowly she walked inside the middle door of the temple, placing the platter on a ledge beneath a low-relief carved image of the great mother goddess, Ix Chel, that covered the far wall from ceiling to floor. As the torches cast shifting light into the room, shadows played across Ix Chel's image, and it seemed as if she moved.

Xoc Ikal returned to the altar, taking the gifts for Ix Chel one by one, blessing and offering them to the goddess inside the room: the finest white maize ground into a coarse grain, precious red cinnabar, dried fruits and nuts, crushed allspice, blue maize cakes filled with dried berries. As she incanted in her rhythmic singsong, the hand drums picked up the cadence. Returning to the altar after giving the last gift, she began a slow, sinuous dance.

The drum cadence increased and the flutes joined in with eerie minor melodies that created a sense of mystery. The sharp rattling of maracas punctuated the underlying rhythm. Xoc Ikal performed fluid, deliberate movements with her legs and arms, entering balanced poses that required great muscular coordination. The crowd held their breath as she maintained a pose. When she initiated the next movement, the crowd released their breaths in an explosive exhale making a "poh" sound. Dancer and audience became a single organism, swaying and breathing in synchrony. Even their heartbeats pulsated in unison to the drum rhythms. As the dance progressed, a sense of growing excitement became tangible.

Xoc Ikal paused, facing the crowd across the round altar. The music slowed and only the drums kept a soft, slow beat. Already her eyes held a distant vision, as she lifted the small blue glass vial holding the mushroom brew. At this moment the mother drum sounded her deep throaty voice, barely discernible as a low vibration. As the mother drum sounded more loudly, all present felt her resonance inside every cell of their bodies. Xoc Ikal brought the vial to her lips and took one small sip. She was experienced enough to know that too much of the hallucinogen would push her into a chaotic state of uncoordinated imagery that she would have difficulty understanding. Her goal was to obtain a clear message from Spirit about what to expect of the coming katun, so the people could prepare both practically and spiritually.

As she replaced the vial on the altar, the mother drum beat more insistently. It was the heartbeat of Mother Earth, the Cosmic Goddess, the pulse of life itself. Xoc Ikal released herself into the beat, swaying and twirling slowly. Her arms lifted and began a weaving sinuous movement, with all four fingers of each hand held together touching the thumbs. She opened and closed this thumb-four fingers gesture as her arms made weaving motions, an invocation of the vision serpent, the cosmic pathway to and from the spirit world. Her body became serpentine, making undulating movements. The flickering torchlight caught the reflection of fine sweat glistening on her bare arms and legs exposed through the slits of her robe.

The powerful impact of her dance drew appreciative sounds from the crowd, a sucking inbreath followed by a soft moaning outbreath. Continuing the snake-like movements, she entered the door into the temple's main room, danced a few minutes longer before the image of Ix Chel, then sat on a small stone bench against the wall. The drumming stopped and all was silence.

Yalucha and the temple assistant followed into the temple. They seated themselves on an opposite bench, facing Xoc Ikal who sat with closed eyes, already in deep trance. The two women had responsibility to anchor the priestess's physical body while her soul traveled in the spirit realm. They connected mentally with her persona, keeping their eyes open watching her body. If they did not maintain focus and constant contact, her soul might get lost in the spirit realm and be unable to find the thread of human consciousness that allowed her to retrace her path to the physical world. Years of training in maintaining this focus allowed Yalucha and the temple assistant to remain completely motionless except for their slow, shallow breathing.

Outside in the plaza, the people were stirring about. Women with young children, and the elderly rose from sitting, gathered their blankets and headed home. Children and elders needed to sleep, crocks of dinner stew needed attending, and animals needed to be fed. Many men departed to indulge in cups of balche, a fermented liquor made of ba'al che' tree bark mixed with honey and water. Whenever the Maya had ceremonies, balche was consumed in great quantities, mostly by men. People remaining in the courtyard engaged in muted conversation, catching up on gossip or speculating about what might lie ahead in the coming katun.

The Maya were both very serious and very relaxed about their ceremonies. Ritual was an integral part of their lives, as natural as breathing. They were accustomed to lengthy ceremonies; the katun end ceremonies would last for three kins. When the vision serpent was being invoked, the process could take many hours. Some people preferred to wait and stay more meditative, others socialized or resumed their daily tasks. Everyone was critically interested in the communication from the spirit realm brought by the vision quest, for they used this to make decisions in their lives. They knew a specific rapid drumbeat signaled that the vision quest was completed and the oracle would speak. All who could reassembled to hear the message.

Xoc Ikal's journey in the spirit realm was short. Her breathing shifted and the two anchors realized her soul was returning. They mentally called to her:

Welcome back, we acknowledge your return to this body of Xoc Ikal.

Soon she opened her eyes, still holding a dreamy gaze. Yalucha brought her a cup of water and encouraged her to drink it all. This would help remove the residue of the hallucinogenic mushroom brew from her body. The temple assistant walked outside and raised her hand to signal the drummers. They began the rapid drumbeat to summon people for the message from Spirit.

The courtyard quickly filled almost to capacity. The crowd murmured softly at first, then fell into silence ripe with anticipation. The temple assistant sounded a high-pitched, clear-voiced flute note seven times. To the Maya, the number seven was an invisible doorway between the realm of spirit and creation. It was like a two-sided mirror, showing both cosmic and physical reality, neither fully spirit nor body but both. It was the center of creative pulse, the converging point between the past and the future. Seven merged the realms.

Xoc Ikal walked from inside the temple and stood behind the round altar stone, facing the crowd. Still in semi-trance state, her voice was rich and resonant with an otherworldly quality, not her usual voice tones, as she spoke the message from the Spirit world:

"Ix Chel smiles and waves her hand over crops of fat maize. Cacao trees are laden with long full pods. Flowers burst in bloom and the fields are covered with abundant crops. The rains come in good measure. The people are well fed.

"The markets of Mutul abound with goods from near and far. Green and black obsidian, shells, gold, shining stones of many colors, rich fabrics and ceramics fill the stalls. Traders bring their best goods to the great city.

"The hair knot symbol of Mutul strikes fear and respect in the hearts of all our neighbors. There is great power, the 'bird of prognostication' flies high in the sky and is unopposed. K'inich Ahau smiles and shines his life-giving rays upon our city.

"The jaguar comes forth, and on his back sits an owl. The jaguar's eyes become large and very bright, become like owl eyes. His claws become longer and sharper. His power grows greater and his spots change as he takes on the owl spirit. The people of Mutul bow in honor of the owl-jaguar. He leads the warriors to many victories and builds many large structures in the city.

"Hear, oh people of Mutul. The spirits and ancestors have spoken for the coming katun."

The mother drum beat a low steady rhythm and the hand drums wove more rapid cadences for a few minutes. Xoc Ikal raised her arms, moving her hands in a benediction over the crowd, then turned and disappeared through the far right door of the temple. Yalucha moved forward to close the four directions, as the temple assistant followed to attend Xoc Ikal. Briefly but sincerely, Yalucha thanked the spirits of the four directions for being present in the ceremony, and the crowd bowed in honor to each. As the crowd dispersed, the girl removed the altar objects and brought them inside the temple.

The people were elated, and talked excitedly with each other. The predictions for the katun were outstanding! Every part of the message was positive, and Mutul could look forward to 20 tuns of prosperity, abundance, power, prestige, and dominance. Most thought the owl would bring far vision and wisdom to the jaguar, symbol of Mutul's ruling family.

But K'an Nab Ku read a more practical message in this imagery. He saw the influence of Teotihuacan becoming embedded in Mutul's leadership—just as he and his son had speculated this morning. Spearthrower Owl was the name of Teotihuacan's ruler, and stylized owl eyes represented their goggle-eyed god of war, Tlaloc. He wondered if the ruler's visions tomorrow would contain a similar message.

After helping her mother disrobe and put on a huipil, Yalucha guided her back to their home. Xoc Ikal would remain secluded the rest of the night, drinking copious amounts of water and tea of zutz pakal (sour orange leaves and flowers) which cleansed the liver, removed toxins and protected from negative effects of supernatural forces. No words were needed as the daughter's deft hands helped the mother wash off dried sweat using water from a ceramic vessel kept in the bedroom, don bedclothes, and lie down on her woven mat under a fresh cotton blanket scented with zutz pakal flowers. Bowing her head in respect, Yalucha slipped out of the room and carefully closed the heavy drape across the door.

*　　*　　*　　*　　*　　*

The sound of conches blown loudly from each of the four directions at the edges of Mutul awakened the city's residents to the first kin of the new katun. Dawn was just breaking and the underbellies of low clouds glowed pink on the eastern horizon. It was the beginning of three kins of celebration, eagerly awaited by the city's population, which had swollen to nearly 90,000 people due to the influx of merchants as well as nobles and commoners from neighbor cities and villages. All who could wanted to be present for the great lowland city's celebration of an important phase in the sacred Tzolk'in calendar. Rumors of a foreign presence from the powerful northern empire Teotihuacan added extra excitement to events at Mutul.

People began gathering in the Great Plaza shortly after dawn. Only with a good location would they be able to view the ruler of Mutul, Chak Toh Ich'ak, and his noble retinue perform their offerings and rituals. The main rituals would take place on the steep stairs and high platform of the central pyramid temple of the Sacred World-Tree Complex. Warriors were already present in the plaza, keeping a corridor clear for the royal procession. Across the plaza in the Palace

110

of the Ahauob, noble families found spots on the stairs, roofs and terraces around their homes that provided a good view. As people kept joining the crowd, the adjoining West and North Plazas also filled up. The view was not as good from these lower plazas, but it still allowed people to feel part of the ceremonies and participate in the emotional energies of the occasion.

The women and young boys in Yalucha's family found a reasonably good spot on the north corner of the West Plaza, just beyond the wide stairs. They could see the central pyramid temple from the side, providing a view of the steep temple stairs where processions would occur. The high platform where ruler would stand was visible from a side angle. The men had taken their katun end gifts and assembled with others of the city's nobility—the batab, sahal, priests and warriors—near the ruler's Jaguar Claw palace. For the women, their West Plaza location was the perfect distance from the bloodletting rites they knew would be occurring.

Xoc Ikal reflected upon this ritual, which had gained favor since the kings had risen to power. She knew blood was precious, and held magic powers for influencing the gods and ancestors. Women had long practiced sacred blood rituals that honored the important times in women's menstrual cycles: the first menses, afterbirth bleeding, and the retaining of blood after menstruation ended in older women. But all of these involved the body's natural discharge or retention of blood, not self-inflicted bleeding as ceremonies now in vogue required. She knew of occult rites that used the power of self-inflicted bleeding to invoke visions or carry psychic communications. These were infrequently used in her spiritual tradition, and only at times of great duress or extreme danger.

But, she pondered, men do not bleed unless wounded by self or others. There was no doubt great power in the ruler and noble's bloodletting for invoking vision serpents. The priests' ways of using hallucinogenic drinks or enemas had largely fallen into disuse among the royal leaders. For those with military ambitions, blood clearly held the greater power. The practice of capturing and sacrificing rulers and nobles from other cities was part of this blood ritual, believed to bring great favor from the gods, in particular, K'inich Ahau.

The mood of the crowd intensified as drums began sounding, echoing throughout the plazas. Soon the piercing wail of flutes and clay whistles accentuated the drumbeats. The initial core of musicians entered the Great Plaza, ascending the stairs from the East Plaza where they had congregated near the Jaguar Claw palace. Beating hand-held drums, thirty men marched four abreast, dressed in bright loincloths and headdresses with shells and feathers. Dozens of flute, ocarina and whistle players followed, both men and women, and several teenage children who were studying musical arts. Chuen, Yalucha's aunt, was among the flute players along with a few of her best students.

Next came a stream of dancers from many walks of life: masons, farmers, weavers, potters, merchants, any who had a bent for dancing. They wore ankle cuffs, made of numerous nutshell rattles. Bumping together as the dancers pranced and twirled, these rattles created constant hollow clacking sounds. Multi-colored costumes with trailing skirts or loin-beech cloths, flashing metals and stones on chest and arm jewelry, and waving headdress feathers added to the exotic appearance of the dancing group.

After the dancers came a cadre of priests, wearing long skirts of fine white cotton bound by waistbands dyed deep indigo, woven with thin silver strands to which small coin-like pendants were attached. These made a high-pitched clinking sound as the priests moved with studied dignity. On their chests were wide pectoral collars of stiff indigo-dyed cloth, sewn with rainbow hued stones and shells. Unlike other Maya men who wore their hair hanging down from a topknot, the priests kept their hair up, wound in tight loops around the crown with a headband of owl and turkey feathers. The higher ranked priests had short jaguar skin capes tied with braided thongs across one shoulder. Among the last of the higher ranked priests was Yo'nal Ac, hobbling slowly using his walking staff, flanked by his son Chitam and another young acolyte. They watched him solicitously, ready to lend support should he falter.

The final cluster of priests was composed of the royal drummers. They carried chest high, elongated drums of polished and finely painted wood, with single drumsticks of carved hardwood, one end covered with soft hide for percussion. Solemnly and silently the royal drummers processed, their arms wrapped around the tall drums until they reached the stairs leading to the Sacred World-Tree Complex. There they spaced themselves in two facing lines along the wide stairs, across the platform to the base of the central pyramid temple. The senior priests formed two groups on either side of the temple's steep stairway. The musicians and dancers preceding the priests had dispersed among the crowd.

The royal drummers began to beat a deep-throated, slow and compelling cadence in perfect unison. All other sounds ceased, and a hushed anticipation fell over the crowd. As the rhythm synchronized their heartbeats, the people and visitors of Mutul fixed their gazes upon the eastern edge of the Great Plaza.

Keeping in perfect step with the drumbeat, eight strong young nobles supporting the ruler's palanquin on their shoulders ascended the East Plaza stairs onto the Great Plaza. Four on each side, they bore shoulder poles that transected the palanquin base, and moved carefully to maintain an even keel up the stairs. The palanquin itself was sacred, considered a god-spirit of the Mutul ahau, Chak Toh Ich'ak. Made of wood, it was carved with masks, jaguar god images and the glyphic symbol of Mutul, a head with topknot viewed from

the rear, like a tied bundle. A canopy over the palanquin was held up with four slender, carved and painted poles. Feathers and magnificently woven red and yellow cloths covered the roof, signifying the ruler's wealth and power, and jaguar pelts on the floor proclaimed his descent from the founder of the jaguar family lineage, Yax Ch'aktel Xok. The ruler sat upon a raised dais in the center of the palanquin, in full royal regalia. As the palanquin bearers completed the ascent and reached the level plaster floor of the Great Plaza, the crowd burst into a roar of acknowledgement for their king.

Chak Toh Ich'ak was quite old for a Mayan, having ruled for over 60 tuns (3 katuns). His age was admirable for a ruler, because the city's ahau was the single greatest prize that could be attained in war, and the ultimate goal of every battle. Chak Toh Ich'ak had endured numerous battles, though his two sons had been killed many years ago in different skirmishes. Thin and wiry, his small form appeared much larger due to his prolific regalia.

Chak Toh Ich'ak

Virtually every inch of his body was covered with adornments. The sandal thongs between his bare toes merged into knee-high leggings of jaguar pelt bordered with fringed golden fabric, held in place by two bands with jade clasps. Above his knees were thigh bands of multiple jade pieces on leather, with sun god faces looking forward above the knees, ringed with white round beads.

More jade bracelets and wrist cuffs surrounded his lower and upper arms. An intricately decorated cloth skirt hung to mid-thigh with pieces of jaguar pelt sown on each hip. A yellow woven band with orange-red fringed trim formed the skirt's lower border; dark blue stones inset in white shells punctuated the fringe at regular intervals. His thick waistband had white and red geometric patterns.

Directly in front over his navel was carved obsidian in the shape of a human head, representing the enemies he had killed. From beneath the carved head, his loincloth hung in three diminishing tiers to mid-calf. White with pale blue borders, the loincloth bore a pendant of small royal symbols such as stingray spines, jaguar god images, red spondylus beads representing blood, and dark glass smoke curls of the vision serpent. Completely covering his chest was a huge jade and obsidian pectoral collar, each grouping of stones lined with polished white ceramic borders in circular and branching patterns. He held the stylized World Tree (Wakah Kan, "Raised-up Sky") that represented the central axis of the world, constantly recreated by sacrifices performed by the king. It symbolized the Milky Way, which harbors a passageway for rebirth of souls and ancestors. In Maya creation myth, First Father raised the Wakah Kan shortly after the last creation. The king personified the World Tree in his flesh.

As magnificent as was the ruler's attire, it was eclipsed by his immense headpiece. Set upon a turban of round jade beads, a large white god mask peered fiercely with great jaws open and teeth flashing. Another two rows of colored stones, jade and ceramics sat above the mask, rising an arm's length above the ruler's crown. From this headpiece a wide fan of feathers spread out forming a rectangle bordered by white ceramic beads with tiny jade insets. Slightly longer feathers fanned out behind his midback, held in place by a thin wooden frame along his spine, anchored in his waistband. At the very top of the headpiece four long quetzal tail plumes arched gracefully forward and backward. Large jade earplugs covered both ears with dangling white ceramic ceiba flowers reaching to his shoulders.

The ruler's face held an impervious expression, and his eyes were distant, looking ahead at the pyramid temple. The crowd quieted as the palanquin progressed slowly across the plaza, the bearers in step with the drum cadence. Immediately behind walked 13 nobles, scantily clad in loincloths and pectoral collars with jewelry and feather headdresses. Along with the ruler, these nobles had fasted and secluded for 3 kins in preparation for the vision serpent invocation. They would also shed blood to enrich the sustenance offered to the gods and ancestors.

For even as the gods had wanted creatures to "name their names, to praise them" as told in the Maya creation myth, the gods also needed humans to give them sustenance through life-supporting offerings: maize, cacao, other foods, but especially the essence of earthly life, blood. Among this group were three noble women, wives of the king's highest counselors. These women wore semi-transparent huipils of mesh in thatched square patterns and sported jeweled feather headdresses, the prescribed costume for women during bloodletting ceremonies.

When the ruler's palanquin reached the stairs of the Sacred World-Tree Complex, the bearers lowered it to the ground, and the ruler stepped off to ascend the stairs. He walked slowly across the platform, through the rows of drummers and priests, and mounted the steep stairway of the central pyramid, stopping about one-fourth of the distance to the top. There he turned to face the crowd gathered in the Great Plaza, as the midmorning sun shimmered off his feather headdress and set shining glints dancing in his jewelry. Again the crowd roared in appreciation of his magnificent appearance, now in full view. Never had a king looked so regal, so impressive, so powerful! For most of the Mutul population, Chak Toh Ich'ak was the only ruler they had known, for he had outlived nearly all his age contemporaries. He was a living legend, the greatest ahau, Jaguar Claw the Great. From this elevated position, he quietly watched the rest of the processional.

The nobles who had prepared for blood letting walked around the central pyramid and disappeared behind it. They would ascend to the ceremonial platform from the rear stairs after the ruler's ascent from the front stairs.

Another troupe of dancers now crossed the Great Plaza. A mixture of men and women, these dancers were from the nobility and had prepared with fasting and seclusion. They would perform the dances of jaguars and *uayob,* or spirit companions. Some would embody various gods or goddesses. Their costuming reflected these beings, with pants of jaguar pelts and masks of jaguar faces, *uayob* and important gods. They carried props such as snakes, flint-headed staves, eccentric carved flints and stones, battle-axes, seed bags, and skull rattles.

Following the dancers came nobles and warriors who had been granted special placement for observing the ceremonies. They would sit closest to the stairs of the pyramid platform. First among this group walked the warrior lord from Teotihuacan, K'ak Sih, with five of his main lieutenants. They were resplendently dressed in their characteristic Tlaloc warrior costumes and prominently displayed their spear-throwers, the atlatls. Their headdresses were more squared, broad and less tall than those of the Maya, decorated with circular bands around the base and fringed feather patterns they favored. Their ear flanges displayed white round ceramic Tlaloc goggles. The feathers on their headdresses were less abundant than the Mayan style and the posterior ones arched straight back in a row, rather than fanning all around the head and upper body. Bare brown chests rippled with dense musculature under metallic and woven fabric neck collars. Tight loin wraps that left their legs bare were topped with heavy stone and metal embedded belts that held long obsidian daggers. From behind their waists flowed a tier of long white feathers cut flat on the ends, the tips dyed brilliant red. Their footgear consisted of leather boots with two or three layers of colored fringes. Marching with measured determination, the foreign warrior lords exuded fierceness with a touch of arrogance; after all, theirs was the greatest empire the lands of Tamaunchan, Turtle Island, had ever seen.

The ten royal trumpeters came after this select group of nobles and warriors. Walking two abreast, the trumpeters carried three foot long carved wooden trumpets, made from a single mahogany branch. The sun glinted off the dark sheen of polished wood, shaped in slender shafts with flaring ends. There were no openings in the trumpet shafts; the sound was controlled completely by lip and tongue placements. The heavy trumpets were carried across their right shoulders, and would be used to announce the ruler's message for his people, after he performed his vision rites.

The constant pageantry and relentless drumbeats had mesmerized the huge crowd gathered in the plazas. They stood or sat as one transfixed being, some swaying slightly to the drum cadence. But heads snapped to alertness when the next group in the procession appeared up the stairs onto the Great Plaza platform. A group of Maya warriors in full combat gear surrounded a captive with bound hands. The young man was of the royal lineage of Uaxactun, Mutul's

116

primary rival city located less than a kin's walk to the north. These two large cities had battled intermittently for over two katuns. This captive was obtained during the most recent skirmish nearly one tun ago. He had been kept under guard for just this purpose—to serve as the crowning sacrifice of the katun end ritual.

Captives were often displayed during important calendar times, scantly clad and stripped of their symbols of power and status. Today the Uaxactun lord was dressed in full, fine noble regalia with his city's name glyph carved on his pectoral collar. This was to emphasize his importance and proclaim the value of this offering in honor of Mutul's protecting gods, thus cultivating their favor in future battles. Although he clearly knew his fate, the young warrior lord carried his head high and walked with self-assurance. Dying bravely was the true mark of a warrior, regardless of the circumstances. Murmurs of appreciation rose from the crowd, as they acknowledge the young lord's courage. He was a fine offering to the gods.

The procession ended with a long stream of Mutul nobles bearing gifts on large offering plates called *zac lac*. Their waists were thickly encircled by waist bands over hip cloths and skirts, made of fine cotton resplendent with woven and painted patterns in bright hues. Sandals and leggings had fringes, tassels and coins that bounced and clinked as they walked. Headdresses of colored cloth bound by leather headbands sported jade, pearls, shells, and semiprecious stones topped with elegant tail feathers that bobbed in time with the graceful, measured movement of the procession. Gleaming against their bare brown chests were pendants of deep-green jade and blood red spondylus shell ornaments, with matching earplugs of surprising size. Among this group were Yalucha's father, older brother and uncle. As the procession ended, the drumming stopped.

Numerous priests prepared cloths to receive the nobles' gifts. Each noble held his offering plate high to display his offerings before the ruler and the priests. The gifts reflected the entire richness of Mutul's marketplace: shells and coral, jade, obsidian and flint blades, jewelry of multicolored stones, ceramics, bone and wood carvings, beautifully colored woven fabrics, cured hides, foods and herbs. Seaweed, sponges, and other living sea creatures were conveyed inland in saltwater-filled crocks to keep them alive. Stingray spines and the backbones of fish were additional tokens of the primordial sea of creation, and symbols of bloodletting.

With expert grace, the priests lifted offerings from the plates and placed them on cloth squares, making decorative arrangements. As each cloth was filled, the priests tied it into a bundle while singing chants that told the story of the creation of this world, the Fourth Sun. They proclaimed the significance of katun end cycles in keeping the worlds in balance through proper timing of ceremonies. The sun was near noon apex when all the nobles' gifts had been received and bundled. A steady stream of priests carried the bundles to a trench recently dug in the center of the small plaza in between the four temple pyramids. Carefully they lowered the precious offerings into the trench, scattering red cinnabar powder over them. Later the trench would be sealed and re-covered with new plaster. The consecrated gifts would forever belong to K'inich Ahau and the other Maya gods, buried in the center of the four "sacred mountains" that represented the four directions, in the Sacred World-Tree Complex that symbolized the center of the Maya world.

Two chief priests ascended the central pyramid stairs, taking positions on either side of the ruler. Carefully they flanked him as all ascended the remaining steep, narrow steps to the top platform of the pyramid. The ruler's regalia were heavy, he had been fasting, and he was old. The kin had turned hot with a few puffy white clouds breaking the sun's relentless blaze. Ascending sideways to maintain balance, the three men slowly worked their way up without the ruler needing assistance. He disappeared from view as he entered the center room of the roof temple where the priests helped him remove most of his clothing. From behind the roof temple, the 13 fasting nobles appeared and sat on either side of the platform. Priests attended them with bloodletting paraphernalia that included stingray spines, rope to pull through wounds, bark paper to catch blood, and painted ceramic bowls for burning the bloodied papers. Sacred chants and incantations, barely audible to the crowd below, were sung by the priests.

One senior Daykeeper Priest used a hand-held sundial to track on the sun's progression. When it indicated high noon, he signaled for the ritual to begin. The deep-throated tall drums began a steady lively rhythm while the hand held drums beat a syncopated counterpoint. The ruler, clad scantily and wearing a small feather headdress, re-appeared from the roof temple room and sat on the platform facing the crowd. His priest attendant brought the bloodletting tools and squatted beside him. Using a sharp stingray spine, he cut lacerations into his penis, already scarred from multiple prior wounds. Through the lacerations he pulled lengths of rope to encourage bleeding, as the priest caught his blood on the bark papers. In a trance, the ruler's face showed no expression, no signs of pain.

At the same time, the 13 nobles began their bloodletting, piercing their penises, tongues, cheeks and earlobes with stingray spines, pulling rope through wounds. The priests collected blood-soaked papers and burned them in multiple ceramic bowls. Soon columns of dark smoke were curling around the rooftop temple. The bloodletting and burning continued for some time. A few of the younger nobles descended the steep pyramid steps, and danced below on the pyramid platform. Twirling and stepping high, the nobles caused the large triangular cloth panels tied under their loincloths to flare outward like two wings. Already spotted with blood, these panels became nearly saturated as the centrifugal force of twirling pulled blood from their genitals onto the panels. The gleaming white plaster of the platform became splattered with bright red blood. Dizzy with spinning and blood loss, the young nobles one-by-one collapsed into the arms of attending priests, who carried them behind the temple. The priests removed the blood-soaked panels and added them to a large fire behind the pyramid, burning stained clothing made sacred by the noble's sacrificial offering of their crimson life essence.

The insistent drumming and low toned chanting of priests mesmerized the crowd, while the sunlight and heat made them light-headed. With intense focus, they identified strongly with the ruler and nobles undergoing blood offerings to the gods. In the dark gray swirls of smoke, many could see shapes of the vision serpents undulating lazily in the noon light. They never doubted their ruler's ability to call forth visions that would open access to the spirit world and allow him to communicate with gods and ancestors.

When the sun reached one-quarter below apex, the ruler ceased his bloodletting practices, and the nobles followed suit. Attendant priests lifted him gently and carried him into the middle room of the rooftop temple. There they sat with him, serving as anchors while he traveled to the spirit realms. Other priests sat beside the nobles lining the top platform, serving the same purpose as their charges underwent their own otherworldly journeys.

The drums took up a violent, frenzied rhythm and the crowd let out a long moaning sound. The deep voices of priests intoned a low, sustained ominous note. It reverberated across the plaza, causing skin to prickle and stomachs to go queasy. This signaled the ultimate sacrifice. To ensure a successful vision journey, a human life would be given to the gods and ancestors.

119

Two Mutul warriors brought the young captive from Uaxactun to the platform fronting the Great Plaza. His regalia had been removed, and he wore only a loincloth. Three priests came forward to perform the sacrifice. The young noble appeared dazed but stood erect, awaiting his fate. As the warriors arched him back on the steep temple steps, one priest quickly inserted a long dagger under his left rib cage, directly into the heart. Death was instantaneous. The crowd roared as the other two priests collected blood pouring from his heart wound in two wide mouthed cups. This would be added to the blood offerings in the large fire. A trickle of blood dripped from the noble's limp body as the warriors removed him. The white plaster of the pyramid platform was saturated with the scarlet nectar of life, *itz* or cosmic life force, maker of magic, filling the stone mountain with *ch'ulul,* the soul's sacred essence that permeated the cosmos.

A period of waiting ensued. It was always uncertain how long the vision journey would take. Those involved in the procession and rituals were trained in the discipline of focused waiting. Most were in altered states of consciousness; sun, heat, thirst and hunger had no power to distract their concentration.

Not so with most of the crowd. Mutul's merchants, servers, laborers and commoners did not have this tradition of spiritual focus. They had not trained for it, and were not expected to remain still and focused through the waiting. Mothers had to tend babies and feed children, women needed to return to household tasks, the elderly and ill needed attending. Quietly the crowd began to thin, starting at the edges where most women and children had gathered. Voices were kept low and talking at a minimum among those who stayed. Many sat down or sought what shade was available. The sun was now nearly halfway through its afternoon descent.

Xoc Ikal, Yalucha and other women of their group moved to the green shrubs and small trees bordering the West Plaza. They drank from ceramic water jugs, and ate a few maize cakes. Children played quietly with insects in the greenery. Yalucha knew her mother would not return home until she heard the ruler's message from his vision journey. Yalucha too was keenly interested; would his communication from the spirit world confirm her mother's or contradict it? Although appearing calm outwardly, she felt tense anticipation inside.

She was also deeply disturbed by the bloodletting and sacrifice, the most extensive such ritual she had ever witnessed. As an apprentice in the healing arts, she had great respect for the human body and was dedicated to preserving its health and functions. Self-inflicted wounds, even for spiritual purposes, troubled her. Assisting her mother to attend people with illnesses, she had seen some of the complications that happened after bloodletting: serious infections that took months to heal, despite Xoc Ikal's considerable skills with herbs and incantations. These sufferers remained weak and fatigued for long times, and some never fully recovered their vitality. Some men and women remained scarred for life, their faces disfigured. At times speech was affected by thickening or tethering of tongues from excessive scar tissue. Repeated lacerations of the penis or perforations for purposes of inserting bones or sticks might have permanent effects on sexual functions. Xoc Ikal had tried to help men so afflicted, even calling upon shaman surgeons at times, but the excruciating pain with erection led some men to avoid sex altogether. And some were rather young, thought Yalucha, shaking her head at such choices.

Watching the young noble from Uaxactun die had sent shudders through her entire body. She felt some intangible connection with the unfortunate young man, very little older than she. Something deep within her reacted with revulsion against this practice, although periodic human sacrifices had long been part of her people's ceremonies. Taking human life in order to give life to the gods seemed excessive. After all, the Hero Twins' victory over the Lords of Xibalba won the right to substitute offerings. Her training and natural inclinations pulled her strongly to support and nurture life, not to destroy it.

Catching Xoc Ikal's glance, Yalucha was sure her mother shared these thoughts.

The old tradition is best, she reflected. *Is blood really necessary to give sustenance to the gods?* In previous times, they were satisfied with gifts from the bounty of the forests and fields. What had caused this change? She started to ask Xoc Ikal, when the trumpets sounded.

Standing on the top platforms of the other three temple pyramids of the Sacred World-Tree Complex, the royal trumpeters hefted long wooden trumpets to their lips and blew deep honking tones that carried throughout the city, resonating off stone walls in echoing cascades. Seven times the trumpeters blew in unison, announcing that the ruler's vision message was to be given. The ruler himself would not speak; exhausted and weak from fasting and blood loss, he had relayed the communications he received in whispered gasps to his chief scribe to record, and to the High Priest who would speak to the people.

121

The Great Plaza rapidly re-filled with Mutul's citizens and visitors. The women by the West Plaza returned to their vantage point, and watched as the High Priest strode majestically onto the top platform. The afternoon breeze caught his long white skirt and billowed it around his legs, while silver beads reflected sunlight from his waistband, pectoral collar and fathered headdress. Solemnly he pronounced each word slowly and clearly, his deep bass voice carrying easily across the plazas.

"People of Mutul," intoned the High Priest, "our ahau has communed with the spirit world. From the vision serpent's mouth first emerged Yax Ch'aktel Xoc, ancestor of our ahau and founder of the Jaguar Claw lineage. The revered ancestor spoke of even more greatness to come for Mutul. This will be accomplished through the true jaguar lineage, his direct line of descendents. Mutul's rulers of the true royal blood will be joined by allies of great power, and will bring our city to ascendancy even as the sun, K'inich Ahau, rises to his apex. Oh, yum K'inich Ahau!"

"Yum K'inich Ahau," murmured the gathered people, "Master Lord Sun."

The High Priest continued:

"The Maize God appeared from the vision serpent's mouth, and spoke of Mutul's abundance and wealth in the coming katun. Our people will be well fed, will enjoy many luxuries, and will grow in size and strength.

"The patron god of Mutul, the Baby Jaguar appeared to our ahau, and turned into *K'in Tan Bolay*, the Sun-Centered Jaguar. He showed our ahau the grandeur to come for Mutul; many new structures, tree stones (stelae) and sacred mountains (pyramid temples) will be built in the coming katuns.

"Our ahau saw his father and mother in the Upperworld, preparing a home for him to join the ancestors. But first, they said, a great victory must occur that will bring fame and glory to Mutul—a victory that will forever be celebrated by our people.

"Be of leaping heart, people of Mutul!" the High Priest raised his voice until it vibrated the very ear bones of the crowd below. "Celebrate this auspicious katun with joy, for abundance and greatness is foretold by the ancestors and gods."

The crowd roared with delight. No better prediction for the katun was possible. They were favored and blessed by K'inich Ahau, the other gods and ancestors. Mutul the great! Mutul the glorious! Led by the royal Jaguar Claw line, the greatest dynasty in all of Tamaunchan, land of the Maya, Turtle Island. Some people began dancing and leaping, but the High Priest raised his arms and the tall drums began a calming cadence. Warriors were alert to contain premature celebrating, for the recessional still had to take place.

The semi-comatose ruler had been carried by his attendants down the rear stairs of the pyramid temple, followed by the nobles who participated in the bloodletting ceremony. Chak Toh Ich'ak was laid on the jaguar pelts of his palanquin; the eight young nobles lifted and carried it back across the Great Plaza, followed by the entourage of nobles, warriors, and priests. All walked solemnly to the drum cadence, as the ruler was returned to his palace and the ministrations of his shaman-healer and family. The sun hung low on the western horizon, but one additional feat was necessary before the celebration would begin.

The stela carved with figures of the ruler, his parents and glyphs marking the Long Count date and telling of his accomplishments was to be seated at sunset. The warriors opened a new wide lane through the crowd from the stairs of the West Plaza to the platform stairs of the Sacred World-Tree Complex. Supervised by the stone carvers who had just completed the stela yesterday, a select group of strong young nobles strained their shoulders against the weight of the massive "tree stone."

The stela was cradled in a net of thick ropes suspended from strong poles that the nobles carried on their shoulders. With a unified cry, six men on each side straightened their backs and hoisted the stela up from the ground. With careful, small steps they maneuvered up the wide stairs onto the Great Plaza. Once level, they walked with larger steps, but slowly so the stela did not swing back and forth, for it could easily knock them over with this motion. The tall drums broke into a measured beat, punctuated by more rapid rhythms of hand drums and clacking rattles.

Long orange-gold shadows streaked across the Great Plaza as the sun began to set. Breathing heavily, the young nobles moved more quickly to bring the stela into position by its trench, recently dug into the plaza in front of the platform's wide stairs. Quickly removing most of the ropes after positioning the stela base on the edge of the trench, the nobles used four remaining ropes, two in front and two behind, to raise the stela. Adding muscle strength by pushing, they inched the stela forward until it dropped neatly into the perfectly sized trench. The massive stone monument settled with a loud thud, then stood erect as the sun's last rays played blood-red shadows across the exquisitely carved images. The number glyphs bearing the Long Count katun end date stood out in deep shadow relief:

8.17.0.0.0   (AD 376)

The warriors and crowd cheered and clapped at the smoothly coordinated effort. Removing the last ropes, the nobles stood in silent admiration for a few moments. Later a mason would fill in the trench with plaster, sealing the stela in its honored place in front of the central pyramid temple. In the minds of Mutul's people, this "tree stone" would remain standing forever, joining stelae previously erected by Mutul rulers, and being joined by later stelae created for rulers yet to come.

The drummers and warriors, tired nobles and remaining priests now were free to leave or join the evening festivities. As torches were lit all around the Great Plaza, servers came forth bringing food and drink from the ruler's kitchens for the people. There were huge vats of deer stew, enormous platters of maize cakes, fruits, nuts and berries, and large jugs from which balche and cacao drinks were served. New musicians appeared, playing lively melodies on flutes and whistles accompanied by hand drums in riotous cadences. Dancers dressed as jaguars, uayob and gods or goddesses burst into spontaneous performances at various spots around the plaza. The mood was boisterous as the crowd swarmed about, eating and drinking with abandon, and often joining the dancing in-between mouthfuls.

The people of Mutul were celebrating. The new katun brought wondrous good fortune. They were blessed by the gods and fated for greatness.

Yalucha, her mother and younger brothers left the West Plaza to return home after the ruler's palanquin proceeded back across the Great Plaza. They had listened intently to the High Priest as he spoke the ruler's vision journey message. Both women were struck by the close similarity in spirit communications Xoc Ikal and Chak Toh Ich'ak had received, although different spirit beings had appeared to each during their vision trances.

Tired and hungry, the women joined others of their household to prepare the evening meal. They knew the men would be feasting and celebrating in the Great Plaza, drinking too much balche and eating too much rich food. Tomorrow the women would give their men the herbs that assisted indigestion and counteracted effects of the fermented alcoholic beverage.

The women's mood was pensive. Yalucha felt overwhelmed by what she had witnessed and the issues it raised inside her. Xoc Ikal reflected on parts of the ruler's message that seemed to hold hidden meanings.

The High Priest had said "allies of great power" would join the Jaguar Claw rulers in bringing Mutul to ascendancy. This could only mean Teotihuacan. Xoc Ikal was well aware of the place of honor given to the emissaries of the great northern empire. But what did this exactly mean? The specific ways allies gave assistance could be problematic. Also, there must be a great victory before the ruler departed to the Upperworld, which surely could not be far in the future, given his advanced age. Mutul's warriors had won many victories in recent years, but somehow this one would be different. She sensed with a chill of dread that Teotihuacan would be involved in this "great victory."

The image from her own vision journey—the jaguar with the owl on its back—was emblazoned in her memory. The owl was a symbol of Teotihuacan. The jaguar of Mutul had changed its appearance because of the owl. The symbolism was clear; but she could not conjure up the earthly events that would take place to fulfill this vision.

Xoc Ikal tucked her children into bed with special tenderness that night. She lingered with her only daughter, Yalucha, stroking the girl's long dark hair until her breath settled into the deep steady patterns of sleep.

So beautiful and so intelligent, thought the mother. *And so devoted to the goddess.* What would the future hold for her daughter? Sadness pulled at Xoc Ikal's heart, despite the auspicious predictions for Mutul in the new katun.

"Let's go to Belize during semester break," Jana said with studied casualness.

Robert looked up from the music magazine he was reading.

"Belize? Why Belize?"

Jana waved the México and Central American tour book she was perusing.

"Belize has everything for the perfect vacation: beaches, barrier reefs for snorkeling, lots of interesting parks, hiking and river sports, and Maya ruins," she said.

"Aha! I see why you want to go there—Maya ruins."

"Well, yes, that's a big factor," Jana admitted. "Actually, I've had a yearning to go there since Grace went a couple of years ago. She told our women's group about it."

"Grace went to Belize? Whatever for?"

"She was searching for her roots, I think. She had this idea that some of her African American ancestors were Garifuna from the Caribbean, and Belize has a big population of them."

"What are Garifuna?"

"They're a mixture of Africans and Carib Indians. Grace saw pictures, and thought she looked more like them than our Afro-Americans. I don't think her trip shed much light on her ancestry, but she had a great time and really liked Belize. I remember being fascinated by her descriptions of Maya pyramids. Belize still has a large population of Maya descent, though mostly mixed with Spanish."

Jana gave the travel book to Robert. He flipped through several pages, stopping to read a few sentences here and there.

"This sounds really appealing," he said, reading a paragraph out loud: "There are thousands of places in Belize's Caribbean where you can don a mask and jump into an enchanted undersea world. Most are near the long barrier reef that lines an island chain off the coast. Belize has the second largest barrier reef in the world, after Australia. Hol Chan Marine Reserve near Ambergris Caye, the largest island, and Laughing Bird Caye, off Placencia on the southern coast offer colorful coral and a huge variety of fish, sharks, turtles and manta rays."

"Yes, I've heard that Belize has world-class diving and snorkeling," Jana agreed. "It's also a great place for ecotravel, with lots of wildlife you can't find anywhere else. It has rivers for canoeing, huge cave systems, mangrove forests, jungles, waterfalls, flowering trees, and several wildlife sanctuaries."

"Sounds impressive. Maybe you've got a good idea."

"And another plus," Jana added, "their official language is English. Belize used to be British Honduras, and remained a member of the British Commonwealth after it was granted independence in 1981. Most people are bi- or trilingual and speak English well."

"I'm open to going to Belize," Robert conceded. "But I'd really like to spend a good deal of time on the beach. Can we combine that with going to Maya ruins?"

Jana had actually done quite a bit of thinking about that very question. She knew Robert loved beach and ocean activities, and had a proposal to offer him.

"I thought we could divide the trip into two parts. One week going inland, visiting wildlife parks and scenic areas, and seeing Maya ruins. One week on Ambergris Caye, which has some of the best beaches and water activities. What do you think?"

Robert reflected for a few moments. He was curious about Maya ruins, those amazing ancient cities lost in the tropical jungles for centuries.

"That would work out fine," he said. "Lets do the inland part first, then spend the second week relaxing on the beach."

"Great!" Jana exclaimed. "Why don't you research Ambergris Caye, and I'll do the inland itinerary and check into flights."

Robert nodded and went back to his magazine.

Jana was elated that Robert agreed readily, but tried to keep a calm surface. She had to make choices; Belize had hundreds of Maya ruins, many unexcavated or requiring long rides over bumpy dirt roads that could be impassable during rains. And, she knew without a shadow of a doubt that she must go to Tikal, just across the border in Guatemala.

The message given to her through Angelina Menchu remained etched in her mind:

Chak wants to see you. He wants you to come to his place after you go to Tikal, the place of the jaguar.

Following Harry's advice, Jana initiated an email dialogue with Francine Rappele, the Maya expert from the University of Texas, Austin.

JS: What can you tell me about Tikal's connections with jaguars, and the place of the god Chak?

127

FR: The jaguar was an important symbol, an animal spirit or *uay*, for many lowland Maya cities. The Baby Jaguar was a patron god for Early Classic Tikal and Caracol. The Bearded Jaguar was a patron god of Tikal, Palenque and Naranjo in the Classic and Late Classic periods. The rulers of Tikal claimed the jaguar as their personal uay, often wearing jaguar images on belts, shields or armbands. This dynastic line came to be known as the Jaguar Claw lineage. We have limited information about the first six or seven kings, though we know one was called Hunal Balam or Foliated Jaguar. The king who brought Tikal to prominence in the 4th century CE was Chak Toh Ich'ak, Great Jaguar Claw I. He built the sacred clan house of the Jaguar Claw family, a magnificent structure still standing in Tikal, partially restored. He also created some of the early pyramid temples for which Tikal is famous. Kings and priests often wore jaguar costumes when performing rituals and sat on jaguar shaped thrones. The jaguar was the central power image for Tikal.

Chak is an ancient deity most often associated with rain and weather. Early versions of Chak with his typical protruding snout and reptile features appeared on monuments at Kaminaljuyu and Izapa around 300-100 BCE. In his benevolent form he is the bringer of rain, a critical role since the success of crops depended on proper timing of rainy and dry seasons. He had a destructive side, causing drought or storms and hurricanes. In Maya creation mythology, Chak cracked the Cosmic Turtle open with his lightning stone, allowing the Maize God to resurrect through the crack. They called their land Turtle Island, and believed their people were created from maize.

Chak is also associated with the constellation around Venus when it appears as Eveningstar in Virgo. The rising of Venus became a signal for initiating warfare during Classic times in Tikal. Chak was especially important to Maya peoples of the Yucatan peninsula, where drought was a constant threat and rainfall much less than in the Guatemala lowlands. In the Puuc style of architecture that flourished there in the Postclassic times, Chak masks were a dominant symbol. In Uxmal there are rows of masks adorning many structures. In Kabah, very near Uxmal, the entire front wall of one building is covered by hundreds of Chak masks. We find Chak masks at many other Yucatan sites including Sayil, Labna, and Chichén Itzá.

JS: Is there one particular place that is most strongly associated with Chak?

FR: I would say the Yucatan, because of the dry climate and topography devoid of rivers and lakes. If Chak could not be persuaded into benevolence, dire circumstances would result. Of interest, the contemporary Maya of the north Yucatan still make offerings to the rain god Chak. I hope this information has been helpful. Let me know if you need more.

Jana gazed out the airplane window at the slate gray waters of the Gulf of México, stretching endlessly toward the horizon. Their flight from Houston would arrive in Belize City in two hours. Mulling over Francine's email, Jana realized this visit to Tikal was a first step. It was the place of the jaguar. Going to the place of Chak, however, required a trip to the Yucatan. At the moment, she had no idea how that might happen.

Soon the flat landmass of the Yucatan Peninsula appeared. The flight skirted its eastern edge before crossing over the Caribbean. Jana watched the shores of the México peninsula come and go, feeling inextricably drawn to it. Maya ruins were everywhere in the Yucatan. Though she strained her eyes to detect hints of gleaming white stones, only a dappled sage coated the landscape.

Belize City was crowded and busy. The resort van lost no time heading west to the Cayo District. Leaving the savannah with its short pine trees and palmetto scrub mingled with swamps, they followed the Belize River valley past rolling hills molded by eons of rain draining into networks of rivers and creeks. Skirting the Maya Mountains to the south, they climbed the foothills to San Ignacio on the Macal River, the main town in the Cayo region. The van driver, a nearly black-skinned young man with a Creole accent, deposited Jana and Robert at the Cayo Hills Resort office.

Stepping out of the van, Jana drew her jacket tighter against the chilly late afternoon wind.

"Isn't it cold for this time of year?"

"Mon, it never be cold in Belize," the young man replied cheerfully. "But now a norther blow in, last few days. Pretty cold, ha?"

"Sure is," Robert agreed, sorry he hadn't brought more warm clothes.

He'd checked the weather shortly before their departure. It was cooler than usual for mid-January, around 60 degrees F instead of the usual high of 85. Intermittent rains were predicted although the rainy season usually ended by December. But, cold fronts called "northers" could blow through.

"The weather, it change often, now," said the driver. "It be pretty tomorrow. Maybe little rain, not much. Mostly sun this time of year."

Jana glanced at the charcoal clouds gathering on the northern horizon and doubted it would be sunny tomorrow. After checking in, they followed winding pathways between wet emerald lawns dotted with bushes sporting pink, orange and yellow flowers. Their thatched-roof cottage, made of dark weathered wood, had an inviting porch with a hammock slung across one end. Birds of paradise with bright beaky flowers and twining pink bougainvillea surrounded the cabins. It was cool inside, all dark wood with only shutters over the windows, a testimony to the usually warm climate. Robert immediately turned on the small electric heater.

"I'm going to need another pair of jeans if it stays this cool," remarked Jana.

"Good idea," replied Robert. "I'll bet you can find some at a shop in San Ignacio. What are we doing tomorrow?"

"Visiting two ruins nearby," Jana reminded him. "We've got a tour booked through the resort, takes most of the day."

"Let's go into San Ignacio the day after."

"No, we've got another tour to Mountain Pine Ridge then."

"The day after?" Robert queried hopefully.

"Yes, dear, we finally get to town," Jana said with an indulgent smile. "You can get your browsing fix and sample some local culture. Then we head to Tikal, but I need to get some jeans in case it's still this cold. Though it should be warmer there, the Peten in Guatemala is lower elevation, more a true tropical wet forest."

"I hope so. I had no idea it'd be this cold in Belize."

Rain fell softly during the night, waking Jana with steady drips as it collected along the roof edge. She snuggled closer to Robert, grateful for the warmth of his body. The weather was disappointing; she hoped it would not detract from her first experience of Maya ruins.

Xunantunich. Just thinking the word caused a thrill in her heart. Francine Rappele told her this meant "Stone Woman" in Maya. Dreamy images of the old woman's hand, the slender barefoot girl, the room made of stone with a corbel arch doorway floated in tantalizing fragments across the fringes of her awareness. Were they hidden in the ruins at Xunantunich? Would the meaning of her dream become clear tomorrow?

Thin rays of sunshine streamed through slits in the wooden shutters, falling on Jana's face as she woke the next morning.

Sun! She felt jubilant. Jumping out of bed, she threw the shutters open, allowing bright sunshine to hit Robert full face.

"Eeyoou!" he yelped, closing his eyes tight and burying his face in the pillow.

Jana laughed and bounced on the bed, shaking him gently.

"Time to get up," she chided him. "We've got the sun! I bet it'll be much warmer today. I'm starving, lets get some breakfast."

"Ok, Ok," Robert grumbled. "Try to remember we're on vacation, will you? What time is it, six am?"

"No, its almost seven-thirty. The tour leaves at nine, so we better get moving."

They wore long pants, tee shirts and light jackets to breakfast. Although the sun was bright when it broke through puffy white clouds, the air was still quite cool. Wet pathways glistened, melodic birdcalls mingled with squawks of macaws and parrots. The hearty breakfast of scrambled eggs, toast and ham—which Jana didn't eat— was delicious, topped off with fresh tropical fruit. But the coffee left a lot to be desired; it was weak and almost tasteless.

Commiserating about the anemic brew, they agreed to buy good coffee on their town excursion, plus some way to drip it. Jana regretted not bringing along a small cone dripper and filters, which she always did when traveling to areas with dubious coffee. But Belize was next to Guatemala, which produced great coffee, so she had expected the best.

Shortly after nine the resort van chugged up the highway for the three-mile drive to Xunantunich. A well-dressed middle-aged Mexican couple in good physical shape joined Jana and Robert for the tour. Tall grass covered the rolling hills like a thick carpet of velvet, glistening with moisture. A few shacks dotted the road, but one large, opulent house set far back in a meadow attested the presence of a wealthy class.

The van turned at the small village of San Jose Succotz, situated beside the Mopan River, the stopping off point for the ruins. Jose, the resort tour guide, informed his passengers that Succotz was a traditional Maya village whose residents identified strongly with their culture. Many worked as caretakers or guides in various ruins. The town featured an art gallery and gift shop selling superb wood and slate carvings. The tour would return here for lunch and shopping.

Jose navigated the van down a wet dirt road a few hundred feet to the Mopan River. Waiting at the bank was the venerable hand-winched ferry that was the sole means for crossing the river. Two cars

131

could fit single file, with room on the side for people and bicycles. Jose and the two couples piled out of the van to enjoy the short ride, joined by a young man sporting a long ponytail. Holding his bike, he responded to their "good morning" in a heavy German accent. Jose pointed out a large brown iguana perched in the branches of a tall tree on the river edge.

The smooth surface of the Mopan River stretched 100 feet bank-to-bank, belying the swift current that ran deeply beneath. Joining the Belize River that emptied into the Caribbean at Belize City, the rivers were an important means of transportation before roads. After the crossing they returned to the van for the winding uphill drive on a rutted dirt road that took them the final mile to Xunantunich. Parked near the Visitor Center, they stood in the cool morning air while Jose provided background about the ruins.

"Xunantunich, pronounced *Shoon-an-toon-itch*, means Stone Maiden," Jose began. His English was excellent. "It was built on a limestone ridge standing 183 meters above sea level. The top was leveled, creating a small area for the central structures. The site is 76 meters above the river valley, and its tallest pyramid, El Castillo, rises another 40 meters above the main plaza. Because it's placed on a hilltop, the central area is small and covers less than a square kilometer. It has six major plazas surrounded by more than 25 temples and palaces. Residential structures of the elite and working class spread a few kilometers into surrounding hillsides."

"Could you translate meters into feet?" Jana asked, feeling sheepish. She handily converted centimeters into inches because of her nursing work, but lost the ability when numbers got large.

"OK, let's see," Jose ran some quick calculations through his mind. "One meter is about three and a quarter feet. So the Castillo stands 130 feet above the plaza, which is about 250 feet above the river valley."

"Thanks," said Jana.

Jose continued his commentary. At times he broke into Spanish to clarify a point for the Mexican couple.

"There are four major architectural groups in the central area. Structure A-6, called El Castillo, dominates the main plaza. Though many call it a temple, this massive structure is actually a large palace complex. It probably served as the dwelling and administrative hub for the rulers. The structure has several layers, with the later ones built on top the earlier ones. This was a common practice among the Maya. At one time El Castillo had a decorative carved stucco frieze

132

that may have gone all the way around. What is remaining, on the eastern and western sides, was discovered in 1949 and restored. It's now covered with a protective layer of plaster. The frieze has astrological symbols, Maya day glyphs, human faces, serpents and jaguar heads, and a king performing rituals. Other structures in the A group served as temples and ancestral shrines, in which stelae were kept.

"You know what stelae are? They're carved stone slabs set upright, with images of kings and dates of events. Eight stelae and four altars were found in Plaza A, but most could not be read due to weathering. All the inscribed dates that can be read are in the Late Classic period. A ball court was also discovered in Group A.

"Group B contains mostly residential structures, seven buildings have been uncovered here. Group C located south of El Castillo has several structures that probably were residences of people with high status, and a small ball court. Group D is connected by a causeway, called *sakbe,* leading southeast from Group A. It has 16 unexcavated mounds, the largest is a pyramid bordering a courtyard group. Many structures in Xunantunich are only partly excavated. Recent work has given us a better map and idea of the city's cultural history."

Jose paused and invited questions.

"What were the time periods of Xunantunich's occupation?" asked Jana.

"A small village was established here in the Middle Preclassic, around 600-300 BCE. The site was consistently occupied, rising to prominence then declining between 700-1000 CE. Its late development is unusual, because most other cities in the region were waning during this time. Archeologists wondered why Xunantunich was on the rise. Recently a stela was found carved with what may be the emblem glyph of the large Peten city of Naranjo. This suggests that Xunantunich may have been a subordinate site allied with the power group that included Naranjo, Caracol and Calakmul. They formed a Late Classic alliance against Tikal.

"After the authority of this group faltered, the elite at Xunantunich must have taken control of their city and expended great effort to develop it. The city saw rapid growth and major construction on El Castillo during 700-800 CE. This flowering didn't last long, however. The last date recorded on a stela is 830 CE. After that, we know Maya activity continued in the site, but development really slowed down. During the Early Postclassic small groups briefly reoccupied the site after abandonment."

"What is an emblem glyph?" queried Jana, her attention caught by the words.

"Those are hieroglyphic signs that signify the name of cities," Jose answered. "Each city had its own emblem glyph."

He glanced around the group, noticing the other three people appeared restless. Although Jana was completely absorbed, the others clearly needed to move on.

"Let's go up to the main plaza," he suggested, leading the way past the Visitor's Center, where they would go later. The climb up a well-worn footpath was moderately steep.

Jana felt her heart racing, but not from the easy climb. She was thoroughly excited about seeing her first Maya ruin. Tall trees mingled bright green leaves with darker palm fronds, arcing over the path and obscuring the view until they were just at the entry to Plaza A-1, the main plaza.

Stepping onto level ground, Jana caught her breath at the sight. The rectangular plaza was covered with short grass, flanked on north and south ends by two huge structures. Just their immensity was overwhelming. The taller one, El Castillo, soared skyward as if reaching to embrace the white clouds overhead. Three distinct levels formed tiers, the topmost supporting a small building with several doors and roofcomb. Broad white stairs led to the first level, where an eroded fresco was visible. To ascend higher, there were footpaths on either side. The second level was covered with grass, its outline indistinct. Facing El Castillo at the other end of the plaza was a smaller structure about half as high, with extremely wide stairs descending to the plaza, and narrow stairs on the left side. A mysterious, small grassy mound sat on the otherwise flat top.

Jana stood transfixed, as the others followed Jose to the center of the plaza. For a moment, she felt outside of time and ordinary awareness. A palpable essence seemed to emanate from El Castillo that throbbed with each beat of her heart. Her eyes hungrily took in every detail, scanning and re-scanning the structure. Turning slightly toward the smaller structure, she felt a crosscurrent as though caught between two electromagnetic fields, each pulsating against and through her body. Tingling sensations crept up her spine and she felt the hairs rise at the nape of her neck. There was something very familiar yet oddly different about this place.

Robert called her name, summoning her to re-join the group. As she approached she caught Jose's discourse about El Castillo:

134

" . . and what remains is just a portion of the original structure. The lower level was a broad rectangular building with perhaps 18 rooms aligned in interconnected sets of three. The top level was built over this and had fewer rooms, an estimated 12 in the same pattern. Corbel arches created the roof, with long narrow rooms typical of elite Maya residential buildings. The inside rooms wouldn't have had any light or ventilation, and were most likely only used for sleeping. Most Maya activities took place outdoors. Beyond that square structure in the center of the plaza is another grouping of palaces. So far, archeologists are not sure what the square structure is."

Ceremonial temple for moon rituals. The thought popped into Jana's mind with uncanny certainty.

"These structures," Jose continued, pointing to three low mounds on the east side, "are thought to be temples. One is a stela house, where several carved stelae depicting rulers were found. The grouping on the other side has the ballcourt, and possibly administrative buildings. Please walk around, and climb El Castillo if you would like. Meet me back here in 30 minutes, and I can take you to other groupings."

"Pretty impressive," Robert said to Jana, as the other couple headed toward El Castillo. "The sheer scale of the buildings is quite something. I wonder how they got all the stones up this hill and into place?"

Jana pointed toward the lower square structure.

"Want to climb up?" she asked. Robert had acrophobia; heights made him dizzy and off balance. This structure seemed sedate enough for him to climb without difficulty.

Robert had already arrived at the same conclusion.

"Sure," he said, "but I'll forgo climbing El Castillo. You can go up that one, I'll get pictures."

The wide front stairs of the square structure looked unstable, so Jana and Robert used the narrow side stairs to ascend. It was an easy climb. They stood on the grassy knoll, a cool breeze flapping their jackets. Other structures came into view, covered with grass and shrubs. People in the plaza below looked like large insects crawling along criss-crossed paths. El Castillo loomed dominant above the tallest trees.

Putting his arm around Jana's shoulders, Robert asked:

"So how is your first Maya ruin?"

"Incredible," she replied. "I feel so connected with this place. When I first entered the plaza, I was bombarded with a powerful energy; I could feel its vibrations in my body. I love it here. It's a special place."

"It is special," Robert agreed.

They stood in silence for a while, the quiet almost palpable, heavy with the lost history of the people who lived in this city for over 1600 years. While Robert took pictures, Jana walked the entire rim of the platform, slowly and ceremonially. When she returned to where Robert was standing, he gestured toward the stairs, and she followed him down.

"OK if I go up El Castillo?" she asked.

"Sure. I'll wander around the plaza, and take a shot of you on top."

Jana set off to climb the wide stairs to the first level. She was surprised at how steep the steps were, yet they were not deep, causing her to place her feet sideways. She wondered if the Maya had tiny feet; they were a short people averaging around 5 feet in height. Walking along the ledge of the first level, she picked up the footpath on the right, following as it curved behind the next level. A series of steep, narrow switchback stairs led inside, giving access to the top structure after a giddying climb. Jana had to place her hands against the walls for balance.

The stairs ended in a long narrow room. She stood under a high corbel arch, observing how the stones came closer in increments to form the roof support.

Just as depicted in the Maya books. But not quite the same shape as in my dream.

Coming out of the narrow room created by the corbel arches, she faced the plaza and looked for Robert. He appeared as a tiny ant far below. Standing on the small ledge, arms outstretched to touch the walls, Jana felt the exhilaration of height and wind whipping through her hair. She stepped a little farther, just outside the room. It was dizzying to look straight down, so she quickly moved her gaze across the plaza, taking in the spectacular view. Beyond the square structure she and Robert had just been standing on was a palace group. North of these, the hill dropped off and the Mopan River valley spread in undulating hills toward the horizon. The distant hills were dark blue-green with sculpted clouds of gray and white hovering above. It was breath-takingly beautiful.

Jana waved at Robert, hoping he could see her and get a picture. Yelling was no use; the wind carried the sound away. She turned back to explore the rest of the structure. It was intriguing how the small, narrow rooms were joined by even more constricted passages. Did the Maya royalty really sleep in these rooms? They seemed unlikely choices for a comfortable rest.

Climbing down the perilous steps behind the top structure, she reached the middle ledge. Edging cautiously along, she looked west where the dense forests of Guatemala stretched endlessly. Looking southeast, she could see the faint outline of the Maya Mountains. So much green, so much jungle!

Descending to the first level ledge, she found the famous frieze still visible on the west and east sides. She had to stand close, as the ledge was only three feet wide. At first the frieze appeared to have only geometric patterns. Her eye was not accustomed to the ebullient imagery, and the size of the carvings made their patterns hard to discern. But soon she could make out human and animal figures in stylized positions wearing many adornments. At one end of the frieze she recognized a mask, a square face with inward curving eyes, an identifiable nose over square cheeks and jaws, a tooth hanging from the upper jaw. Gingerly she touched the lower part of the mask, feeling the plaster cool beneath her fingers. Each curve, each symbol, each figure had rich meaning to its creators, she reflected.

Watching Jana's descent, Robert approached the base of the pyramid. Jana waved and posed beside the frieze while he took a picture. She found another footpath down and joined him.

"Wow, that was an awesome experience," Jana reported. "I could see in all directions for miles. Its no wonder the Maya chose this site. They could watch activities all around, see anyone approaching. The rooms inside the top structure are really small. I doubt they were very comfortable as bedrooms, and probably pretty cold, too."

"Maybe they had some other uses," Robert said.

"Just my thought," agreed Jana.

Jose signaled them to rejoin the other couple in the main plaza. He suggested proceeding to Group C. As their group took the path bordering the west end of El Castillo, Jana was inextricably drawn to another path branching off to the right.

"What's down this path?" Jana asked Jose.

"That takes you to A-21. It's not well excavated, and we don't know for sure what kind of a structure it was. Not much to see."

"Could I go there by myself?"

Jose hesitated. He did not like his group to split up. But he sensed Jana's eagerness, and concluded she was no ordinary tourist.

He glanced at Robert, who shrugged making the universal "whatever" gesture.

"All right, but please be back at the main plaza in 30 minutes," Jose acceded. "We will meet you there."

Jana nodded, smiled at Robert and headed down the path to structure A-21. She had no idea why she made this request; it came out spontaneously. She knew inside that she must go to the structure. After a few minutes the forest closed in on either side of the path. She heard buzzing insects and birds, but no other sounds except her feet on the soft damp dirt. This path was much less traveled; weeds encroached along the edges. It followed a slight descent. After about 10 minutes walk, Jana entered a clearing with a grassy mound in the center. A few stones peeked out here and there along the corners of the rectangular structure that had a smaller, proportional mound on top. One flowering shrub with deep fuchsia flowers perched jauntily atop the small mound.

Walking up to the structure, Jana placed her hands on a partially exposed stone at shoulder height. It was moist, dark gray with several lichens clinging to its surface. She closed her eyes, receptive, inviting. A humming sound filled her ears. She quickly opened her eyes and looked around, suspecting a large bee was about to land on her head. But, no bees were anywhere near. She closed her eyes again, and the humming resumed. She relaxed into the sound, waiting, anticipating. Her fingers felt the coarse circular ridges of the lichen. Images of plants began to flood her inner vision. She could not see them distinctly, but they appeared to be herbs. Waves of pleasure coursed through her. Inexplicably, the humming sound and herbs made her feel very happy.

No further images were forthcoming, so Jana opened her eyes and walked around the structure. It was about 30 feet high with a base of 50 feet at its longer side. Not a very big structure, and there were no doors or designs to give clues to its purpose. Stepping through ankle high wet grass, she circumnavigated the entire mound. The forest was close behind, only five feet away. Jana peered into the dense web of trees and vines, but deepening shadows obscured her view. Nature reclaimed any unattended land with a vengeance.

Glancing at her watch, Jana realized she must return soon. Proceeding to the front of the mound, she stood in direct center, facing it. Looking up, then side-to-side, she felt compelled to memorize the mound's details, such as they were. Touching another exposed stone that jutted out from the grassy cover, she again closed her eyes and asked inwardly for information. She saw herself at work in the emergency room, attending a patient.

What on earth is that about?

She wondered why an ER scene appeared. Maybe it was random firing of brain synapses, as Robert would say.

No. Something happened here. Related to the dream . . . to me.

An aching sensation surrounded her heart. Something hovered just beyond the reach of her mind. Then practical thoughts took over.

I've got to return. Robert will be upset if I'm late.

Embarking up the path, she took one last look at the mound before dense foliage closed the view. This was important, she sensed, but its mystery was not revealing itself to her.

The uphill grade of the path made Jana a little breathless, as she walked briskly to rejoin her group. They were waiting in the main plaza, but could not have been there long. Robert appeared relaxed and happy to see her. He got easily annoyed when she was late, an occurrence that happened too often as far as he was concerned.

Jose led the group back to the Visitor's Center. There they viewed a fine scale model of the site, and a fiberglass replica of the famous hieroglyphic frieze, making it easier to identify the forms it contained. In the nearby museum, there were several well-preserved stelae. Jana looked with interest at the male figures carved on the stelae, surrounded by hieroglyphs recording their deeds.

Jose leaned against the rails surrounding the stelae. Jana was still studying them as Robert and the Mexican couple went to the gift shop.

"There's an interesting story told by the Maya of Succotz," Jose said softly to Jana.

She turned with keen attention, her eyes widening.

"Some years ago, when the present-day Maya discovered the ruins, one of them was hunting here in the morning," Jose related. "He was crossing the plaza in front of the temple we call El Castillo. Suddenly he stopped short, as there appeared before him a beautiful statuesque Maya maiden, of heroic size. She was of a dazzling, supernatural whiteness. As she stood in the rays of the rising sun, she looked with fixed and stony gaze toward the valley, in the direction of what is now Succotz. He sensed she meant for his people to build their village there, and they did."

"Was she ever seen again?" asked Jana.

"There are stories about the Stone Maidens that enchant men and lure them into the forest," Jose replied. "They say the name of the ruins was taken from this story."

"Stone Maiden, Xunantunich," Jana repeated.

"Maybe the man was hypnotized by his first view of an ancient stela lit by the sun. Maybe it awakened a mystery carried in his Maya blood from the past. But the Maya people of this area did separate themselves from the mestizos and created their own town of Succotz after this."

"Thanks for telling me. Me gusta mucho, I like the story very much."

Jose smiled and glanced at his watch. He nodded toward the Visitors Center, then led the way out of the small museum.

"Are you ready for lunch?" Jose queried the group. His eager smile made it clear that he certainly was. Getting affirmatives from everyone, he soon had them in the van, across the ferry and ensconced in the Plaza Café in Succotz. On the patio overlooking the river, they enjoyed the warm sun and lunch of pizza and fruit juices. After lunch, Jose took them to a gift shop featuring local art.

The shop had a large variety of items; ceramics, wood and slate carvings, clothing and woven goods, figurines and dolls, jewelry and paintings by local artisans. Jana was immediately taken by a female figure she saw featured in several mediums, usually dressed in a complex outfit—a wide belt with dangling attachments and a long sash down the front. She wore large earplugs and a heavy necklace, her hair tied in knots hanging down her back. An impressively sized serpent was coiled on her head, and in her hands she held what appeared to be a collection of leaves and plants.

One shopkeeper, a stocky woman, noticed Jana's interest and pointed to a slate carving of the figure, saying:

"Ix Chel," which she pronounced *Eesh Chel*. "She is goddess of healing, medicine woman. Very big goddess for Xunantunich. Muy importante aqui."

Jana smiled at the woman, trying out her Spanish.

"Soy enfermera en un hospital en Los Estados Unidos, en California."

"Ah, bueno," the shopkeeper beamed, then took off in a rapid outpouring of melodic Spanish, leaving Jana completely in the dust.

"Pero yo entiendo un poquito de Español," Jana said apologetically, explaining that she understood little Spanish.

140

"Si," the woman acknowledged, then said, "Ix Chel, she for you. You like this one?"

She lifted a round slate carving with the goddess of healing in shallow relief, kneeling in a gesture of offering with a meditative expression on her face. Its tones were warm and light, and the 6-inch size perfect. Jana did like it.

"Yes, I will take this one," Jana said. "Thank you, muchas gracias."

Dinner that evening at the Cayo Hills Resort was especially good by Jana's standards. The resort promised that vegetarian meals were "no problem" but their notion was to simply remove meat from the plate. Tonight the menu featured Belizean Rice & Beans, the country's signature dish; spicy red beans cooked in a Dutch oven with coconut milk and the assertive flavors of cumin, garlic, allspice and cilantro. On the side were fried ripe plantains, like bananas but more firm and starchy.

"Do you like the plantain?" Jana asked, after Robert had taken a few bites.

"Actually, I do. Its unusual but has a nice flavor. Not at all like bananas."

"At least I'm getting a reasonable amount of protein," Jana commented. The evening before she'd asked for cheese, and had been given two individually wrapped slices of cheese product.

Their conversation drifted into the day's experiences. In the afternoon they went to Cahal Pech. On a hill overlooking San Ignacio, the compact two-acre site had 34 structures: several plazas and temples, palaces, ballcourts and what is thought to be a sweathouse. The tallest structure was 77 feet. Archeologists believed the site was a ceremonial center and acropolis-palace of a royal family. The site was continually occupied from 900 BCE to at least 800 CE. The largest monuments were constructed in the Middle Preclassic, 400 BCE, when it probably dominated the central Belize River valley.

Cahal Pech was known for its excellent museum with a site model, painted murals of life in ancient times, and videos of excavations. Jana was fascinated by the murals' full-color renditions of Maya life and structures. Seeing the buildings with intact white plaster walls, painted with ruddy, ochre and deep turquoise tones gave an entirely different feeling. She got a better sense of how people related to the buildings. Steps to platforms of different heights were used to direct traffic flow, according to location and steepness.

In one mural, 3 men sat cross-legged on a bare hill overlooking the river valley. Scattered huts of villagers could be seen in a distant meadow with mountains behind. The men wore only white loincloths and had their long black hair tied on top of the head, secured with a white band. Facing each other, the men were gesturing and holding sticks, with four round stones forming a small circle between them and decorated ceramic vessels beside them. The plaque said they were shamans seeking omens for their people.

Another mural depicted a self-induced bloodletting scene. A richly dressed man wearing jade headdress and ornaments, probably a king, sat cross-legged on a small platform inside a bare room; the adjoining plaza visible through a corbel arch doorway. He held a pointed implement in one hand, aimed at the fingers of the other hand. An attendant stood nearby holding a ceramic pot toward the king. There was splattered blood on the white plaster floor beneath the king's platform. His face with closed eyes held an inscrutable expression.

"Weren't the murals at Cahal Pech great?" Jana offered, following her thoughts.

"They were," agreed Robert. "They gave a good idea of what Maya life was like, and how the Maya looked. They really had big noses, didn't they?"

Jana nodded, adding:

"Walking through the structures gave me the sense of a complex society. The rooms were like a maze; they had so many inter-connections. I was puzzled by the small rooms on that raised walkway around the largest plaza. With so much exposure at a public gathering place, they must have been used for ceremonies."

"Probably. It was a pleasant site, with lots of trees. Had some well-preserved corbel arches, too. An interesting building technique, since they didn't master the mechanics of true arches."

"So you *are* enjoying the ruins," Jana said playfully.

"Yes, I'm finding myself more interested in them that I expected," Robert admitted. He shook his head and smiled warmly at her. "You get me into the darndest experiences. I would never have come here on my own. But I have to admit I'm having a great time. Thanks, sweetheart."

She was always touched by his expressions of honest appreciation. One always knew where they stood with Robert, he did not conceal his emotions. And, after a little initial resistance, he was usually open to new experiences.

Jana reached across the table and took his hand, feeling a tingle of excitement as her fingers intertwined with his. Her heart felt open; she was aware of the familiar surge of attraction toward him that had remained constant over their years together. She sensed he was responding in the same way.

That night they made love with an eagerness and intensity that had not been present in their lovemaking for some time. Jana knew that sex was better on vacation, but this had a special quality, a sweetness that was deep and soulful.

As Robert embraced her, Jana arched her body into his, standing on her toes to reach upward for a long, lingering kiss. Lifting her off the floor, Robert gently laid her across the bed, lowering his body over her. He smothered her face with kisses, and she nuzzled under his neck, inhaling his masculine smell and savoring it. They undressed and caressed each other slowly, taking time to increase their level of desire. Slipping under the covers, for the night was quite cool, they felt the familiar contours of each other's bodies. Jana loved to run her fingers through Robert's chest hair, still golden and only touched with gray. He cupped his hands around her breasts and stimulated her nipples to become erect, then kissed them. She felt the hardness of his erection against her thigh, further driving her desire.

The urgency of their passion mounted, but Robert still held off until Jana pulled him insistently onto her. She felt the jolt of pleasure as he penetrated deeply, a warm fullness that spread throughout her pelvis. Robert's lips found hers in an insistent, open-mouthed kiss, his tongue probing. Jana surrendered to this double entry, melting away body boundaries to merge with him completely.

It was in these moments that she most fully understood the receptive feminine principle. Receptive of his maleness and encompassing it. Twining the kundalini energy running up each one's spine into a single unit, pulsating, palpating. She matched his strong thrusting in a building rhythm, increasing to the point of maximum intensity. Mind and thought ceased, there was only union and rhythm and wet warmth.

Jana built quickly toward orgasm, the waves of intense pleasure radiating from her pelvis throughout her entire body. Even her toes felt pleasure sensations. She moaned softly, lost in this ecstasy of body being. Having brought her to climax, Robert now plunged with joyous abandon as she followed his rhythm. After a few moments his excitement peaked, and the waves of pleasure wracked his body again and again and again. He made the series of groans she knew signified

143

an especially powerful orgasm. Then he rested on top of her. She welcomed the heaviness of his body, a moment she had always savored. The stillness after sex brought deep peace and unity to them.

After a minute or two, Robert rolled off Jana.

"Boy, that was great!" he exuded happily.

"Uh-huh," she murmured, not wanting to break the sweetness of their union. She felt special tenderness toward him, and immense appreciation that he was her partner in life. Soon the sound of his regular breathing informed her that he had fallen asleep. Careful not to disturb him, she slipped out of bed, cleaned up, and returned to snuggle beside him. Her lips brushed his forehead, as she whispered "Good night, sweet love."

The morning was sunny and warm as Jana and Robert set off for San Ignacio. It was a 20-minute walk from Cayo Hills Resort to downtown, giving interesting perspectives on how people lived. The small houses were built of wood with corrugated metal roofing; a few had palm-thatched roofs. Chickens and dogs were everywhere, coexisting peaceably for the most part. Barefoot children played in grassy yards, running along the streets pursuing some passing interest. They were simply dressed but not bedraggled. The nicer houses had tended lawns, porches framed with flowers, and large shade trees.

The business district, modest in size with curving streets, offered shops, banks, cafes, bars, tour agencies and the "best produce market in Belize" according to the guidebook. There were even a couple of internet cafes, testifying to San Ignacio's link with modern times. The friendly, brightly colored town had a long history. Located on a wedge formed by the junctions of the Mopan and Macal Rivers, it was a stopping off point for travelers when river traffic was the main mode of transportation. It started as a logging camp, then became a center for chicle, the sap of the sapodilla tree, used to make chewing gum. When the demand for Maya artifacts on the black market soared in the early 1900's, the self-reliant chicleros shifted from harvesting chicle to obtaining relics.

The local Maya strongly resisted Christianization, despite several waves of Spanish friars and soldiers. Tipu, a Maya city six miles downstream, became a symbol of independence, providing refuge for other Maya fleeing Spanish rule. In 1707 the entire population of Tipu was forcibly removed by the Spanish to Lake Peten Itza in Guatemala.

Taking in the sights and sounds, they appreciated the warmest day since their arrival in Belize. The streets were narrow, but allowed two small autos to pass easily. Motor vehicles shared the space with horse-drawn wagons driven by bearded men in black clothing. There was a large Mennonite community nearby, living their traditional lifestyle without use of modern equipment. The local population was mostly mestizos of mixed Spanish and Maya descent, with Creoles, Mopan and Yucatec Maya, Lebanese and a few Chinese and Sri Lankans. The American couple enjoyed the mixture of people whose skin tones shaded from black to café latte. The sounds of several languages mixed in with auto horns and lively rhythmic music.

After finding coffee filters and a good brand of Guatemala Antigua coffee recommended by the storekeeper, they searched for a cone dripper. This was more difficult; they finally had to settle for a plastic oil funnel that Robert found in a general merchandize store. Jana figured by using two filters and crimping the bottom, she could slow the drip down enough to brew decent coffee. It was worth a try.

They found the produce market, a large gathering of open stalls with tarps for protection against sun and rain. The brightly colored produce, artistically arranged in rows or clusters, had some familiar but many unknown varieties. They sampled fruits generously offered by merchants, including pineapple, oranges, papayas and bananas, buying some to take along.

Jana found jeans in a clothing booth at the edge of the market. Between the merchant's poor English and Jana's limited Spanish, communicating was not easy. But she managed to get directions to a bathroom, where she tried on the jeans. The fit was good except the hip-hugger waist that flared a couple of inches too wide. It was close enough. Jana bought the jeans, laughing to Robert about the teenage style with flared legs and a gold streak.

After snacking on some excellent yogurt and trail mix from a small market, they were delighted to find a bookstore and went in to browse, one of their favorite pastimes. Catering to tourists, the neatly arranged bookstore had many travel guides, maps, postcards and books in English. Robert was soon absorbed in the computer section. Jana sought the archeology section, which contained a number of books about the Maya. She allowed herself to bring only one Maya book on the trip, trying to travel lightly, and determined not to buy any more. But her resolve felt wobbly in the presence of such enticing material.

If I buy anything on the Maya here, it's got to be unusual, not a book I can get at home, or from Amazon.com.

She pulled some books out, but already had several of them. One tiny book caught her attention, for she had never seen a similar title in her searches. It was called *Ancient Maya Traders of Ambergis Caye*, by Thomas Guderjan from the University of Texas at San Antonio.

Bet Francine Rappele knows him, Jana thought.

It was too good to pass up, and its small size was another plus. She didn't know the Maya had settlements on the cayes. And, they would be there in a few days. She bought the slender book, struck by its beautiful color illustrations of pottery.

On the way out of the bookstore, she showed her find to Robert, who chided her affectionately while she defended the book's merits. He bought some postcards, but resisted all temptation to get a book.

They walked back toward their resort, feeling hot for the first time and breaking a light sweat in the mid-afternoon sun. Jana spotted a shop featuring indigenous arts and crafts, and dragged Robert in. She purchased a small amber pendant with a tiny fossilized flying insect inside. The round, light golden amber stone had faint streaks of deeper orange tones. She was aware that amber was sacred to the Maya, who used it in ceremonies. Amber was believed to have a protective quality, perhaps to keep dangerous spirits away that could trick shamans during rituals.

That evening both Jana and Robert were reading in bed, another of their favorite pursuits. He was studying the Belize travel guide, while listening to music through earphones attached to his portable CD player. He never seemed to get enough classical music, taking advantage of any opportunity to listen, wherever he might be. Jana quickly read the 39 pages of her new book on Maya traders, then reviewed the section on Tikal in her other Maya book. Tomorrow they would go on their Tikal excursion. Although she had read this section before, she saw something as if anew, now pregnant with meaning. It was the emblem glyph of Tikal: A knot tied around stylized hair on the back of a head.

Ohmygosh! That's the image I saw during my session with Carla Hernandez—thick hair tied in a knot behind the head. She told me to watch for connections, that the meanings would be revealed to me if I stayed alert. And here it is, what I saw was the Tikal emblem glyph! That scene in my imagery must have taken place at Tikal.

In her mind she replayed the scene: the girls sat in a narrow stone room with their stately teacher. They were learning something sacred, secret wisdom they were mandated to preserve. Shivers passed over her body, bringing goose bumps to her skin.

I was identified with one of those girls. Guess I've got big-time stuff with Tikal.

        *   *   *   *   *   *

During the night Jana woke several times, unable to stay asleep. Rain was falling, making gentle splattering noises on the thatch roof and staccato drips from the corners. She hoped it would be gone by morning. But dawn was overcast with a constant misty rain. Jana and Robert dressed in layers, and she wore her new jeans, taking in the low-riding waist with safety pins. Robert got hot water from the resort kitchen; Jana carefully crimped two filters into the oil funnel, added ground coffee and managed to drip quite a flavorful brew, which they savored before going to breakfast.

The van was full for the Tikal trip, despite the unpromising weather. Six people joined Jana and Robert: an older German couple, a French couple and two college students from the United States traveling together. None of them were staying at Tikal.

The driver prepared his group for crossing the border into Guatemala. They should only change as much money into quetzales, the Guatemalan currency, as they planned to spend, because the exchange rate back into Belize dollars was unfavorable. Everyone had to disembark the van and stand in line for the border check, because the van was separately inspected. A Guatemalan guide would join them at the border; it was a government requirement that all guides to Maya sites be Guatemalan citizens, licensed for this purpose.

Raoul Chaktul, the Guatemalan guide, was a good-looking man in his mid 40's with a round face, wide cheekbones, a smallish Maya nose, and dark wavy hair. He had the casual authority of one well versed in his trade, and clearly expected his tour group to pay attention to his commentary—which was nearly unceasing during the 2 hour drive. Jana listened part of the time, but drifted into her own reverie, watching the countryside through the misty rain. She was trying very hard not to feel disappointed. Having her first day at Tikal rained out was not what she bargained for.

The road was less well maintained than the Belize highway, and the driver swerved frequently to avoid potholes. Poverty was more apparent; rickety shacks on stilts lined the road. Gently rolling hills were dotted with groves of trees and some cultivated fields. Small towns positioned buildings right on the roadside, causing the van to

147

stop as school children in navy and white uniforms, or women in formless shifts, crossed the road. An occasional military vehicle passed, carrying stern-faced militia in khaki holding rifles. The van stopped at one checkpoint, continuing after a short dialogue between Raoul and the soldier.

Following this encounter the students, a clean-cut man and his plump girlfriend who looked to be ivy-league, engaged in a lengthy discussion with Raoul about Guatemala's political situation. The gist of it was that the military had become less aggressive since the new regime brought more stability. There was still considerable guerilla activity but mostly in isolated northern parts of the country. Some headway was being made in the economic plight of the Maya people, who lived at the lowest rung of poverty, but much more was needed.

The rain lightened and became sporadic as they turned north from the town of El Remate at the junction to Tikal. The road climbed a limestone escarpment, providing a good view of Lake Yaxha to the east. Villages thinned out and the landscape became more undulating. Raoul described Tikal National Park

"The park is a protected area 370 square kilometers, surrounding the large site of the ancient city of Tikal. It has two excellent museums, a visitor center, several restaurants, and three hotels built in the area that was once the archeological camp. The airstrip used by archeologists was closed several years ago to preserve the natural quality of the site. Only a few official vehicles are allowed in the site, you will need to walk some distances. I hope you wore good hiking shoes.

"Tikal is one of the most extensively studied and excavated Maya sites. It is also one of the largest sites. Central Tikal covers 16 square kilometers, but there are ruins scattered around it at distance of at least 50 square kilometers—that's about 30 square miles for you North Americans. At the peak of population around 700 CE, the city covered more than 65 square kilometers, containing many thousands of structures. Only two other Maya sites reached this size: Coba and El Mirador.

"Although it was a large site with six very tall structures towering over the jungle canopy, the first official expedition to Tikal took place in 1848, sponsored by the district of El Peten. Over the next century, explorers visited from Switzerland, England, Austria, and the United States. Many artifacts were removed and are still in museums in these countries. Major excavation and restoration took place from the late 1940's until around 1970 through the University of Pennsylvania, which then turned the site over to the Government of Guatemala. Under the Proyecto Nacional Tikal work is continuing, but still less than 10 percent of structures known by mapping have been excavated. Though we have learned a great deal about Tikal's history, the answers to many questions lie beneath its unexcavated portions.

"The central area of Tikal is grouped around a very large triangle with a long extension from its southwestern corner, linked by causeways. The causeways are named after four early explorers: Mendez, Maler, Maudslay and Tozzer. To see the site thoroughly takes several days. You will see that the walking distances are considerable. In our half-day tour, we will visit the Great Plaza area, three well-restored temples, and the Lost World complex, ending with lunch at the Comedores."

The last few miles seemed interminable to Jana, as she watched the thick wet forest on either side of the road pass by. At last the van arrived at the parking area. The rain had stopped, but heavy clouds billowed overhead, gray contours turned to charcoal underbellies laden with moisture, threatening to disgorge at any moment. It was cool; the group wore jackets brightened by gaudy yellow rain slickers of the young students. Raoul made sure his charges had their cameras and water bottles, gave each an admission ticket, then led the way down a long path into the ruins.

Jana outpaced the others to walk beside Raoul.

"Tikal has an emblem glyph," she said. "I've seen pictures of it, a knot tied behind a head. What does it mean?"

"The tied bundle glyph," Raoul replied. "There are two schools of thought about it. One reading of the word Tikal, in Yucatec Maya, divides it into 'ti' meaning 'place of' and 'k'al' meaning spirits. But 'k'al' also means the count of 20, associated with the sacred time period called *katun*. We have evidence from monuments that the rulers of Tikal considered katun endings very significant. So rendering Tikal as 'The Place of the Count of the Katun' may be a more accurate meaning. There's also a recent interpretation involving the ancient Maya propensity for puns. Men wore their hair in a topknot. When viewed from the rear, it's formed exactly like the Tikal emblem glyph. The Maya word *mutul* is read from this glyph, meaning flower. The glyph thus refers to a flower with a visual pun for men's hairstyle."

"So the glyph itself might mean place of spirits, of the katun count, or a flower," Jana repeated, to be sure she understood correctly.

"Yes," Raoul affirmed, his eyebrows raised a little, wondering at her interest in this academic point. "In any case, the official name remains Tikal."

The small group followed Raoul along the wide dirt path leading into the ruins of Tikal. The ground was damp, brown, faintly emanating the smell of humus and molds. Tall ceiba, mahogany and copal trees rose on either side, soaring upward 50 to 70 feet and spreading their upper branches to form the forest canopy. The modest undergrowth was lush, green and wet from the rain. It was very quiet. Beside the soft crunch of footsteps, the only sounds were falling droplets and distant birdcalls. Low clouds metamorphosed into waves of thin mists that drifted among the canopy leaves. When the mists came, they moistened the tourists' faces with fine rain.

They walked for 20 minutes, mostly in silence. A sense of timelessness descended upon them. They could have walked this deserted path into the wet forest a year ago, a decade ago, centuries ago and the jungle would be the same. The jungle drew one inward, a place resonant with ancient echoes, to the stillness of that eternal core transcending mere lifetime identities.

Scurrying noises in the treetops caused them to look upward. Flashes of dark brown forms with long tails moved quickly among the branches.

"Spider monkeys," said Raoul.

Chattering monkey voices confirmed his comment.

"Don't walk underneath them, something might fall on your head," he advised the group. "Might be nut shells, or something less pleasant."

The path ended in an expansive meadow with two sets of twin pyramids arranged in east-west pairs, called Complex Q and Complex R. Only one pair was restored; five-tiers reached a modest height with steep stairs ascending all four sides. Archeologists believed this grouping had ceremonial purposes, although much information was lost due to purposeful defacing.

"These are twin pyramid complexes dating from the Late Classic period," Raoul told his group. "They were erected to commemorate the katun ending. These sacred 20-year time periods were very important to the Maya of Tikal. Few other cities built markers of katun changes. When the king had a twin pyramid complex built at the katun end, it was a public declaration of his success in seeing his people through another sacred cycle. The king always placed his stela in the north, signifying the heavens and his identification with the gods. The stela were carved with a depiction of the king dominating a conquered victim. In this enclosure are Stela 22 and Altar 10, superb examples of Late Classic sculpture. They were carved in 771 CE, or 9.17.0.0.0 in Maya dates and depict Tikal's 29th ruler, Yax Ain II, also called Curl Nose."

He pointed to an area with an open-sided, thatched roof structure enclosing the stone monuments. A short fence prevented observers from touching the deteriorating stones.

Jana stood reverently in front of the closest twin pyramid. Its stepped sides were dark gray with buff highlights. The steep stairs were well restored and slippery with a coating of moisture. She followed the group to the enclosure and looked at the eroding carving of Yax Ain II, portrayed in full regalia with enormous sweeping headdress and huge back ornament of feathers, holding a World-Tree bar. It was an impressive stela, beautifully carved in exquisite detail and deep relief. Raoul commented that defacing probably happened in Postclassic times, as people tried to weaken the lingering power of this ruler.

They walked to the adjoining Complex R, a smaller twin pyramid complex. The western pyramid abutted the Maler Causeway. Also built by Yax Ain II, it included Stela 19 to mark the 18th katun ending on 790 CE (9.18.0.0.0). Its altar was different. Instead of depicting the usual bound prisoner, the side border displayed four dignitaries, possibly a royal lineage. But the glyphs were too badly eroded to read.

Leaving Complex R, Raoul turned left onto the broad Maler Causeway, once an elevated sakbe paved with white plaster, but now just a raised dirt path. Instead of taking the usual way, following the causeway to the East Plaza, he led the group through a jungle path behind the North Acropolis. Raoul had his own purpose for this unorthodox route. He wanted to give his group the most dramatic view of the stunning Great Plaza, the heart of Tikal. He planned their entry to face Temple I, the signature pyramid of Tikal. If he had taken them the usual way, they would first see the back of Temple I and enter the plaza facing Temple II.

Ascending from the jungle path onto the East Plaza, the group came up behind the towering hulk of Temple II and climbed the broad, short stairs at its left onto the Great Plaza. They paused at the top of the stairs to take in this most famous part of Tikal.

Jana's breath caught in her throat at the sight. There was nothing that could have prepared her for it. Seeing the pyramids in person for the first time caused an electric shock to run through her body, from feet to crown. No pictures in books or film, no descriptions could possibly convey the immensity, the soaring power of the pyramids. Pulsating with over one thousand years of Maya heartbeat, the silent witnesses of untold ceremonies, of victory and tragedy, gave their mute testimony to the greatness of Tikal.

Temple I rose steeply across the plaza, its nine dark gray limestone terraces with buff highlights ascending in sloped symmetry, sharply etched against the slate gray sky. The upper terrace high above formed a platform that supported a three-room temple, each room set behind the other in tandem fashion. The ornamental roofcomb perched above the temple. Its two levels were finished with stone blocks arranged to form a monumentally proportioned person, seated and flanked by elaborate scrolls and serpents, badly eroded. The dramatic impact of the structure was increased by its single, very steep stairway leading to the solitary doorway into the temple on top. This design drew the eye irresistibly from the pyramid base to the doorway, so high above the plaza as to appear part of the sky. A ruler standing before the temple door would indeed be reaching the domain of the gods.

After giving his group a few minutes to stare in rapt amazement at Temple I, Raoul provided brief commentary:

"Temple I was built by Hasau Chan K'awil, the 26th ruler of Tikal, in the early 700's CE. He acceded as Kalomte, great overlord, in 682 CE, ending the 125-year hiatus during which Tikal fell from power and was dominated by Calakmul and Caracol. No inscribed monuments have been found in Tikal during this time. Hasau Chan K'awil"—the unusual sounds of the ruler's name fell from Raoul's lips with relish and reverence—"was the second great king in the Jaguar Claw lineage, and he built many of the structures that we see today in Tikal. His name in Maya means 'Heavenly Standard Bearer' and he was indeed a god to his people, bringing their city again to greatness. The roof comb of Temple I is 44 meters—145 feet—above the Great Plaza. It was Hasau's burial monument. When his tomb was discovered in 1962, its opulent assortment of jade, fine pottery and carvings pointed to a king. The body was laid on jaguar skin over a straw mat. A fine jade mosaic vessel was found shattered, and was carefully reconstructed. It is inscribed with 12 glyphs and names Hasau as a four-katun batab. This means that Hasau ruled for 80 years. Batab was a title used at Tikal meaning lord or ahau. The knob handle of the lid was shaped like a human head, presumed to be a portrait of the king."

Raoul led the group further onto the plaza, to the base of the wide stairs leading to the North Acropolis. They turned to look at Temple II, facing directly across the plaza from Temple I. The three-tier pyramid was broader at its base and less tall than Temple I. It had wider and less steep stairs. Carved masks flanked the stairway. A large platform on top supported a temple that also had three rooms in tandem. Crowning the pyramid was an extravagantly adorned roofcomb. A huge carved face in the center sported large circular earplugs, so badly eroded by years of weather exposure that its details were hard to discern.

"Temple II was also built by Hasau Chan K'awil," Raoul told the group. "It stands 38 meters—125 feet—above the plaza, though it might have once been as tall as Temple I. The stairs and temple doorways of the two temples directly align with each other, and are

Hasau Chan K'awil at Altar 5

connected with Altar 5, the commemorative stone of Hasau's wife. There is an interesting story about this, which sheds light on royal customs and political relations during the Late Classic period. The glyphs around the altar's side and the picture carved on top tell that Hasau retrieved the bones of his wife, probably Lady Twelve Macaw, from her home town of Topoxte eight years after her death. This town was in enemy territory at the time, under Calakmul's dominance. Hasau obtained safe passage and was escorted to the town by the Lord of Calakmul, who was a blood relative of the Lady, to save her remains from desecration. It was common practice of warring royalty to desecrate the graves of enemy rulers and their relatives. The picture carved on top of Altar 5 shows Hasau and the Calakmul lord kneeling to honor the Lady's bones.

"Hasau built a twin pyramid complex known as the N Group, and erected Altar 5 and Stela 16 on which he is shown in full regalia. A burial cache was found under Stela 16 with a collection of unusual artifacts and bones, possibly those of Lady Twelve Macaw. Altar 5 was used to determine an axial alignment for the later construction of Temples I and II. Temple II was constructed in honor of Hasau's wife. She died in 703 CE, 31 years before Hasau's death. These two great temples, built facing each other, provide an enduring monument to their love—built to last untold centuries, perhaps an eternity. Their spirits embodied in the two stone temples gaze forever at each other."

Tears came to Jana's eyes at the thought of this Maya lord, who so loved his wife that he built soaring monuments to continue expressing their love into the unfathomable future. Her heart palpitated with the strong currents of energy running between the two great pyramids. Closing her eyes, she could almost hear the distant murmur of voices, the rhythmic cadence of a deep toned drum, and the sense of sacredness filling the Great Plaza from times long ago. Present silence weighed heavily upon her ears, like high atmospheric pressure, causing a humming noise. Quickly opening her eyes, Jana looked around for the source of this humming. No creatures flew in the cool moist air of the plaza, and no person was close by except their small group, all standing transfixed by the majestic presence of the two great pyramids.

Where did I hear that sound before?

Instantly the memory flooded her mind: at the mysterious mound at Xunantunich, where she went alone. She only had time to register the recollection briefly, as Raoul led the group onto the platform skirting the North Acropolis. Standing on the platform 40 feet above the Great Plaza, they could see lines of stelae and altars in long rows along the base of the stairs. Thatch-roof shelters had been placed over some to protect them from the weather.

"The North Acropolis is the most complex grouping yet excavated in Tikal," Raoul told them. "Its base covers two and a half acres, rising in several levels with multiple layers of buildings. What you see here is the final stage of its growth. Buried underneath the 15 structures that can be seen today are a dozen or more earlier versions, one built right on top of another. Excavations found over 100 buildings buried in this mass, the earliest dating back to around 200 BCE. Pits cut deep into the underlying bedrock show traces of occupation here even four centuries earlier. By 100 BCE, the Maya were constructing successive elaborate platforms that supported large temples. They decorated these temples with beautiful polychrome stucco facades and huge masks. The architecture and vaulted tombs of this era show the sophistication of Preclassic Tikal.

"About 250 CE the North Acropolis started to take on the form that we see today. All the buildings present at that time were razed and a completely new platform was built. The new structures were step pyramids and probably functioned as ceremonial and religious sites. Each was rebuilt at least twice during Early Classic times. The older structures are in the rear of the platform. In the 3rd century CE there were four temples facing the plaza. Other structures were added over the next three centuries. This is the single greatest concentration of Early Classic architecture visible today."

"So these temples are much older than Temples I and II," Jana commented.

"That's right," Raoul affirmed. "The North Acropolis was a sacred burial area for Tikal's early kings. They believed it was the center of their world, where the three realms came together. It was designed to be a small cosmogram with all the characteristics of the great cosmos as they conceived it, a realm of the ancestors, of kings ruling as gods. But during the Hiatus, many temples and stelae were desecrated by Tikal's enemies. When Hasau Chan K'awil came into power, he changed forever the cosmic configuration honoring the ruling ancestors. He shifted focus onto the Great Plaza and triad of tall pyramid temples that he created.

"He held lengthy ceremonies to re-consecrate monuments, particularly the priceless Stela 31 that documented Tikal's early history in extensive hieroglyphics. It was carved for the 11th ruler, Siyah Chan K'awil (called Stormy Sky), when he became Kalomte in 426 CE. A new temple was constructed for the sacred burial of Stela 31. Hasau also constructed a tall pyramid, Temple 33, to cover his father's tomb. Hasau's father was Nu Bak Chak (called Shield Skull); he created an alliance with Palenque's greatest ruler, Hanab Pakal. Temple 33 became the pivot for a new cosmogram, that later culminated in the triangle it formed with Temples I and II."

Raoul paused and contemplated, while his group walked through the maze of structures. The North Acropolis with its burial vaults for a dozen or more Tikal rulers, its consecrated monuments telling the glory of ancestors, and its temples creating a sacred cosmic configuration had renewed the power of this great city. So much history was contained here that it would take weeks or months to properly experience these stone witnesses that mutely held the chronicles of royal lives. Raoul knew he had given his group of tourists as much information as they could reasonably take in.

The overcast sky enhanced the gray tones of the partially restored structures crowded together on the large platforms of the North Acropolis. Multiple stairs connected different levels. Robert took out the digital camera and shot pictures. Jana stood before Temple 33, Hasau's first major building project after he became ruler. It was much deteriorated, but vestiges could be seen of tiers and a steep narrow stairway leading to a small temple on top, with a single doorway. It was premonitory of Temple I, a new architectural style in the lowland region: tall, narrow, austere with its few decorations reserved for the roofcomb, soaring into the sky, placing the king among the gods when he ascended to perform rituals. Jana sensed the immense power, drive and will of this remarkable king who left his mark indelibly upon the city, changing forever its architecture, creating a legacy of his people's greatness that would continue to awe visitors over the ensuing centuries.

Jana wandered through the North Acropolis, climbing carefully over slippery stones, touching the walls of sacred structures, breathing in damp air poignant with history.

How much history is shaped by the drives and desires of kings, she reflected. The lives and realities of the people were molded by the ruler's choices and the resulting consequences. Deeds of greatness, shames of defeat, horrors of brutalities, suffering during famines and economic collapses—the fortunes of their cities rose and fell with the king's actions. Most of the hieroglyphs were devoted to the acts of kings. Part historical record, part political propaganda, the testimony of stelae and other inscribed monuments stood through the years; codes that unlocked doors of insight for later people.

Going past Temple 33 toward the back area, Jana tried to feel into the earlier structures now buried under superimposed versions. But the inner layers held back their secrets from her, mute stone seers in the deep earth. Something else was needed for access. She was standing in the plaza between the four facing temples when Raoul came around a corner and joined her. The German couple was in a conversation off to one side, caught up in their own concerns. Robert had disappeared from view.

"Much to see," Raoul commented with a friendly smile, already liking Jana for her keen interest in this great city, of which he was very proud.

"Its so impressive," Jana said. They both stood reverently for a moment. Then Jana asked:

"Who was the other great king of Tikal? He must have built structures here."

"Yes, he did," replied Raoul, pleased at her question. "His name was Chak Toh Ich'ak, called Great Jaguar Claw, the 9th ruler of Tikal. His reign was from 317 to 378 CE, sixty-one years. He was very old for a king. He brought Tikal to its first era of prominence in the Early Classic period. Stela 31 contains information about him as well as other Early Classic rulers. The older temples here were built then, as well as early structures in the Central Acropolis on the other side of the Great Plaza. Chak—Great Jaguar Claw—also built the Jaguar Claw family palace at the far eastern end of the Central Acropolis. This palace is one of the few royal family residences that was not partially demolished and covered with later structures. It was considered highly sacred, identified with the dynasty ruling Tikal for over 1,000 years."

"Did the Jaguar Claw family rule through that entire time span?" asked Jana.

"No, there were breaks in succession, due to the ups and downs of warfare," Raoul said. "After Great Jaguar Claw's famous victory over Uaxactun—the two cities had been enemies for decades—the next two rulers were most likely lords from Teotihuacan, México. Great Jaguar Claw was very old when this victory occurred, and he accomplished the coup with the help of Mexican warriors using spear-throwers, a new battle technique to the Maya. He died the same time as the Uaxactun victory, and the next Tikal ruler was K'ak Sih, also called Smoking Frog or Fire Born. Glyphs on Stela 31 said he was 'Not of Tikal' and other inscriptions in Teotihuacan style said he was a warrior of great strength. The ruler after him was Yax Ain I, called Curl Snout or First Crocodile. Stela 31 recorded him as Kalomte twenty-four years later. We're not sure exactly when Yax Ain acceded, since K'ak Sih was lord over both Tikal and Uaxactun for some time. Yax Ain was the son of the Teotihuacan ruler called Spearthrower Owl."

"When was this happening?" asked Jana. A sensation of sharp focus snapped through her mind, like the sights on a rifle lining with a target.

"The Uaxactun victory was recorded on Stela 31, in Long Count style, as 8.17.1.4.12; that's January, 378 CE by the Gregorian calendar." Raoul had memorized these dates carefully; he loved the rolling precision of the Long Count calendar. It proved the superiority of his ancestors in tracking time.

"Uhuh," Jana mulled the date over. "Around the height of the Roman Empire."

"Right. The long arm of the powerful Mexican empire reached into the dynastic succession of Tikal. The ruler after Yax Ain was his son Siyah Chan K'awil, called Stormy Sky. He and the subsequent rulers made a point to emphasize their descent from the founder of the Jaguar Claw lineage, the great-grandfather of Great Jaguar Claw. We speculate that Yax Ain married into this lineage to become a legitimate ruler of Tikal."

"That's fascinating. It's like the royal inter-marriages, dynastic successions and constant wars for dominance that took place in Europe."

"True. Royalty behaves much the same everywhere. During the Hiatus there were probably outside rulers, but we have no written records of that time."

Jana recalled reading about the Hiatus, when Tikal fell silent for 125 years after its devastating defeat by Calakmul. She wondered what horrors the people of Tikal suffered during this dark time, when many monuments were destroyed or defaced. She could imagine that death, torture, famine, and slavery were the lot of many. Perhaps this nasty defeat was one of the consequences of the escalated warfare Tikal had introduced through its alliance with Teotihuacan, a karmic rebound leading to a period of subjugation. When Hasau Chan K'awil brought his city out of this silent, dark phase the influence of Teotihuacan had faded and the Mexican empire was dissolved into oblivion. The new architectural expressions and art forms promoted by Hasau were uniquely Mayan, a revitalization of their culture that led to a period of even greater glory.

Robert appeared threading his way between the north and west temples. Standing uncertainly near the stairway of the north temple, he motioned for Jana to join him. She detected distress in his body movements, excused herself to Raoul and quickly crossed the small plaza to his side.

"What's up, dear?" she asked.

Robert looked pale with furrowed brow. His clear blue eyes darkened when he was troubled. He shook his head impatiently.

"Jana, this place is giving me the creeps," he said. "I can't explain it. I was behind this temple"—he pointed to the north temple—"and all of a sudden I felt queasy. Then my knees went weak and I almost fell down. I still feel shaky."

"Maybe something you ate upset your stomach," Jana suggested. She knew well how sensitive Robert's stomach was. Food that was too spicy or fatty often caused gastritis, for which they always carried antacids.

"No, I don't think so," Robert said. "My stomach doesn't hurt. I really feel ill at ease, like I just want to get away from here."

She looked at him with concern. His unusual behavior alarmed her.

"OK, lets go to the Great Plaza."

Taking his hand, she led the way. Quickly crossing the North Acropolis plaza, they climbed down stairs past the larger front temples, and found their group on the stairs bordering the Great Plaza.

Raoul led the group down from the North Acropolis onto the Great Plaza. He advised that they could climb Temple II, but the stairs of Temple I were too dangerous for ascent. Jana hesitated, concerned about Robert's strange sensations. He looked more settled now that they were standing in the center of the plaza. He nodded that it was all right for her to go up.

She eagerly began the steep climb, noticing again the peculiar shape of the stairs. Each step was considerably higher than it was deep. She could not place her feet directly toe in, but had to turn them to the side to fit on the step. Each step was nearly two times the usual stair height. In essence, one had to go up sideways, giving thigh muscles a workout. Perhaps this served to focus attention carefully on an ascent upward to sacred space.

Jana reached the top platform first, with the American couple just behind and the French couple climbing more slowly. The Germans opted to stay on the plaza. Standing some 100 feet above the plaza gave her a magnificent view. Exhilaration filled her as the moist wind blew through her hair and misted her face. Reverently she walked all around the platform, observing the ruins spreading out for miles. Only the roofcombs of Temples IV and V soared well above the forest canopy. Tikal was immense, even now with thousands of structures still unexcavated. What must it have been like when all these buildings were standing, with steady streams of Maya people going about their daily pursuits, filled with the hum of activity, enacting grand rituals at auspicious times!

Feeling the pulse of Maya life within her body, Jana completed her circuit around the platform and returned to the temple doorway.

The roof had long been missing, but the entry door still had its carved wooden lintel spanning the top. Jana stepped inside, breathed the musty odor and imagined the strong woody scent of copal incense that was used here for ceremonies. With eyes closed, she thought of Lady Twelve Macaw and acknowledged her. Turning to face the entrance, Jana opened her eyes to the stunning view of Temple I framed by the doorway.

That was Hasau's purpose!

Jana was certain of it. He used an amazing knowledge of symmetry and geometry, not to mention construction acumen, to create this view. The spirit of Lady Twelve Macaw, inhabiting this room of Temple II, could forever view the spirit of her beloved husband Hasau residing in Temple I. And no doubt his spirit had the mirror image view from the temple doorway of his monument.

Reluctantly, she sensed it was time to return to the group. Waving at Robert far below, Jana posed for pictures on the platform. At the top of the stairs for the descent, what she saw was frightening. From her position on the platform, she could not see the steps going down. Only when she got to the very edge were they visible. It looked like a sheer drop, virtually unnavigable. Her heart beat faster. Watching the American couple navigating carefully halfway down the steep stairs was encouraging. Cautiously she placed one foot sideways on the first step, then the other foot, balancing herself with her hands. In this manner Jana slowly descended.

They certainly make you concentrate on what you're doing, she thought with admiration. Nothing was casual about Maya pyramids.

Next they explored the Central Acropolis, a vast maze of buildings with innumerable rooms, passageways, courts and stairs. Over 700 feet long east to west, it covered four acres, expanding in the complicated fashion of Maya buildings, one superimposed or appended onto another. The form seen today consists of six relatively small courts surrounded by long, low-lying buildings of one, two, and three stories. According to Raoul, these were residences and administrative structures. Activities of the royal court took place here for centuries. On the far eastern end, bordering the East Plaza, was the palace complex of Great Jaguar Claw. The palace, now partially restored, still retained its nobility and grace. The two-story building had symmetrical wings flanking a wide central staircase, and an extraordinarily complex interior plan of multiple inter-relating rooms. It was occupied by royal family members of the Jaguar Claw lineage from Early Classic to the end of Classic times.

Raoul took his group next to the Lost World Plaza—in Spanish "Mundo Perdido," giving them a brief glimpse of the massive Great Pyramid, a very old structure from Late Preclassic time. Standing close to 100 feet high, it was a radial pyramid with stairways going up all four sides. It was considered one of the greatest structures of its time in all Mesoamerica. They passed a smaller stepped pyramid called the Temple of Talud Tablero, built in a distinctive style reflecting strong Teotihuacan influence. In this style, an enframed rectangular panel with an insert design (tablero) alternated with a sloping panel (talud) that also had an insert design.

Wending their way behind a U-shaped structure called the Bat Palace, they crossed through Complex N where they viewed the exquisite Altar 5, and the famous Stela 16. It was still possible to discern details of the intricately carved depiction of Hasau Chan K'awil on Stela 16, despite centuries of wearing away.

Making a short climb onto the Tozzer Causeway, they came to the base of the tallest pyramid in Tikal, Temple IV. By now the day had warmed up, offering a few glimpses of sunshine streaking through the heavy cloud cover. The group rested, taking advantage of vendors selling cold drinks. Robert was delighted to find Fanta Orange, similar to an orange soda he loved in childhood.

As the group sat on tree stumps in welcome shade, Raoul explained the climb to the dizzying heights of Temple IV, advising anyone with heart problems or vertigo to opt out of the strenuous ascent. A part wooden and part metal rung ladder had been built up the pyramid's northeast corner in a series of tight switchbacks. Except for the lower portion, the climb was nearly straight up. There was one ladder for ascent and one for descent. Raoul gave background about Temple IV:

"Temple IV stands 64.6 meters—212 feet—from the base platform that supports the pyramid to the top of the roofcomb. It's the highest standing structure in Tikal and throughout Mesoamerica. Temple IV had seven stacked terraces, with a central grand stair leading to the temple on top. These can't be seen well due to jungle overgrowth. In the signature style of Hasau Chan K'awil, the roof temple has a single door leading into three narrow rooms in tandem. The carved lintels made of heavy zapote wood and placed over the temple doorways tell the story of the pyramid. On the massive roofcomb is a sculpted figure of the seated king, facing east overlooking most of the city.

"Yik'in Chan K'awil, 27th ruler of Tikal, the son of Hasau and Lady Twelve Macaw was the creator of Temple IV. The lintels depict scenes of Yik'in in victory over two neighbor cities, and are masterpieces of Maya art. Two lintels reside in a museum in Basel, Switzerland and one is in the National Museum in Guatemala City."

Raoul could not conceal a note of disapproval in his voice that these precious carved lintels had been taken away from the site of their creation.

"From the temple platform you have an unparalleled view of the great city of Tikal. Temple IV faces east, in geometric relation to Temple I, which faces west. Temples II, III and V can all be seen. In Maya times, there were open plazas between the temples and acropolises, making visibility of the city excellent. Now trees have filled the plazas, so all you'll see are the temple roofcombs rising above the jungle. You can also see beyond the city: To the east is the Pine Ridge bordering the large Bajo de Santa Fe, the route taken by early pioneers on their way to settle this city. Beyond that in the far distance you can see the Maya Mountains in Belize.

"In building Temple IV, Yik'in created many parallels to his father Hasau's constructions. This may be Yik'in's burial place, or it might be at the Temple of Inscriptions, we don't know since excavation has not been done. Inscriptions on the lintels from Temple IV indicate the date of 9.15.10.0.0, or 741 CE."

Raoul glanced at his group, noting most were finished with their drinks.

"Ready to climb to the top?" he asked.

Jana, the two young Americans and the French couple nodded. Robert and the Germans indicated they would wait below. Raoul led the adventurers over the root-entangled terraces to the wooden staircase leading up, and they began the strenuous climb. It was difficult; Jana broke into a sweat in short order. She had to stop several times to catch her breath. Other climbers coming down encouraged her to keep going, remarking on the incredible view from the top. She was determined. Although her thighs were definitely sore and her lungs aching by the time she reached the temple platform, she managed to outstrip the plump American girl and keep up with the others in her group.

Not bad for a middle age woman, she thought with satisfaction.

Standing on the exalted platform, the body's self-preservation instinct caused goosebumps to rise on Jana's arms as she backed against the temple walls, seeking reassurance from its solid stones. It was so high. The ground was so far below. To stop the giddiness from spreading, Jana switched her view quickly toward the distant horizon. Ridge after ridge of forest rose and fell to the east, and she could just see the hazy outline of the Maya Mountains. But what caught her eye were the gray-white roof combs of the other temples, protruding starkly through the dense green forest canopy. Clouds played across the sky, gray tones darkening when pregnant with rain. The wind was strong, carrying away the voices of other climbers already hushed in awe. About 10 people were around the temple platform. Three brave ones sat on a ledge about 15 feet higher, accessed by a metal rung ladder built into the roofcomb.

Raoul glanced at Jana, nodding toward the higher ledge. She shook her head, looking with concern at the ledge, which had no rail to provide a barrier against falling down the pyramid's sheer precipice of nearly 200 feet.

Raoul reached out and took her hand.

"Come, I'll help," he said.

Jana breathed deeply a few times, closing her eyes. She allowed Raoul to draw her toward the rung ladder, feeling her resolve build. He made her climb first, staying close behind. After a quick scramble, both were seated on the ledge, which had more space than appeared from below. Jana gripped the ledge tightly, again not looking down but keeping her view on the distance. She tried to imagine the city of Tikal as it had been in Classic times, with open plazas, painted pyramids and shining white sakbes joining the main complexes in a huge triangle. Raoul seemed tuned into her imaginings, quietly supporting her.

She felt his calm, deep presence. He had no trace of fear. He loved this place, this towering stone mountain reaching into the sky, touching the gods. Their gaze met; his black eyes unfathomable Maya pools that poured mystical communion into her hazel-flecked eyes wide with unexpected joy. An instant of merging occurred, a current passed between their hearts and eyes. Who they were at this moment mattered not at all. Their essence met; two sentient beings full of awe and love for this amazing monument, this grand city, these mysterious people who created so exuberantly in the jungle depths.

*   *   *   *   *

"Dos cafés con leche. Más fuerte, por favor."

Jana ordered what she hoped would resemble lattes in the café patio of the Tikal Visitor Center.

"¿Azúcar?" inquired the waiter.

"No, gracias."

Robert faced Jana across the round table as a few rays from the late afternoon sun crept across the patio. Clouds quickly extinguished the golden streaks, and a light breeze caused him to draw his jacket tighter.

"Maybe we'll get lucky," he commented. "We are in Guatemala, hopefully we can get some good coffee."

After completing the tour with their group, Jana and Robert were dropped off at the Tikal Jungle Lodge. They thanked Raoul and tipped him generously. His parting smile to Jana acknowledged the moment they shared atop Temple IV. Both appreciated their unexpected kinship weaving through cultures, nationalities and histories, although their paths would most likely never cross again.

Leaving their luggage in their room, Jana and Robert returned to the Tikal site to explore the Visitors Center and museums. And to search for some good coffee.

"How was the day for you? Are you feeling OK?" Jana asked. She realized she'd paid little attention to his experiences, so caught up was she in her own. She was curious whether he had any other uneasy episodes.

"You know, it's been a really great day, despite the weather and the strange stuff at the North Acropolis," Robert said. "I'm frankly blown away by Tikal. I had no idea a Maya city could be so huge. Those pyramids are amazing, they just hit you with a wallop of power. How on earth did they construct them? I wonder how long it took. Years, probably."

Jana smiled, pleased at his reaction.

"Did you experience anything else that felt spooky?" she asked, wanting to be sure.

"No, I felt fine after that. It was really odd," he said reflectively. "Almost pure gut feel, very primitive and beyond thoughts. I've never quite felt anything like it before. And I never want to again!"

"Hmm. I've had some pretty powerful sensations, too, though mostly positive."

They sat in silence for a few moments, each lost in their own thoughts.

Jana broke the silence.

"For some reason, I feel deeply connected with this place. I can almost see the people who used to live here, feel their lives, hear their sounds and music."

"I feel a lot more connected than I thought I would," Robert admitted. "Like you, I have this sense about the Maya people, some connection with them. Maybe everyone who comes here feels this way. Being in this place has a real impact."

The waiter returned with two steaming mugs of coffee and a small carafe of milk. The aroma was strong and earthy. Thanking him and paying in quetzales, they added milk and tasted tentatively.

"Finally, some good coffee!" Robert exclaimed.

"This really is good," Jana agreed.

They savored the dark brew, cupping their hands around the warm mugs as the air was cooling quickly. It was a moment that felt outside of time. The patio was nearly deserted, the café shutting down. Birds were twittering in their usual fashion as they sought perches for the night. A few geese chattered at the edge of a small lake. Stillness was descending with the receding light.

Why does this feel so much like home? Jana wondered to herself.

On the walk back to Jungle Lodge light rain began to fall. Jana tried to hold back disappointment without a great deal of success. She was so ready to be warm, to feel the sun on her skin, to wear some of the numerous shorts she had brought. Lying beside Robert in bed, she listened to the rain beating steadily on the roof, some time in the middle of the night. Would this rain ever stop? After fretting for a while, an idea came to Jana. She would communicate with the Maya rain god Chak and request that the rain stop. She would send prayers to engage Maya deities, to seek their assistance in her visit to their homeland. She thought of Ix Chel, the healing goddess who sought her out in the shop, molding circumstances to catch Jana's attention and lead her to buy the round carved slate featuring the goddess.

Quietly to avoid disturbing Robert, Jana slipped out of bed and turned on the bathroom light, closing the door so just a wedge of light entered the bedroom. She found her suitcase, located the zipper pocket where she had put the Ix Chel slate, and took it out. Her fingers traced the raised, smooth carvings on its surface, the figure of the kneeling goddess. After placing it on a chair where the light glanced off its graceful curves, Jana sat on the floor and focused her attention. She took several measured breaths and made a silent invocation. With eyes closed, she envisioned a Chak mask and the Ix Chel carving.

"Chak, god of rain," Jana formed the words clearly and slowly in her mind, "Ix Chel, great mother goddess, you who shape the actions of nature, hear my request. I ask that the rain stop, I ask that tomorrow the sun will shine. I long to enjoy your magnificent city Tikal with warm sun on my face, and bright sunshine lighting up the temples. I wish to see the ground dappled as sunlight streams through leaves, to smell your dark earth when warmed by the sun. This I ask of you, as a visitor who comes to learn about and to honor the ancient Maya."

For several moments she held these images in her mind, feeling intensely the effects of sunlight. Her vision was flawlessly clear; it was already accomplished in her imagination. She felt total harmony with the natural world. Then she said mentally:

"This I ask of you, great Chak, holy Ix Chel. I thank you for receiving my request." Remembering that one must be respectful in such interactions with the spirit realm, and that in human awareness there is much we do not comprehend in the workings of deities, she added: "Be it according to your will."

Putting the Ix Chel carving away, Jana turned off the light and returned to bed. She slept soundly, dreaming in short segments, until a strange sound slowly penetrated her awareness. At first it was a distant roaring sound, like a far-away ocean. Then the eerie roars came closer, louder, lasting many minutes in rising and falling crescendos. Hovering on the edge between light sleep and waking, Jana was aware that some roars were closer and others farther away. They seemed to be calling and answering to each other. Now fully awake, Jana tuned her ears to the sounds. Otherworldly howls, long drawn out and deep voiced, filled her ears.

What is it? An animal, a jungle animal. No, many animals, she realized, listening to the overtones made by multiple voices howling together. *Were they jaguars? How could there be so many jaguars close around the lodge?*

No! They're howler monkeys.

Instantly she recognized the eerie, long-drawn-out roars echoing back and forth in the trees. Her attention was riveted to the sounds, striking such a familiar chord in her memory. But, this was the first time she had ever heard howler monkeys. She listened for what seemed a very long time. Gradually the roars became fainter as the monkeys moved to distant trees. Jana drifted into a delicious doze, images of Tikal temples, palaces and plazas wafting through her inner vision. She felt deeply reassured by the strange roars.

166

The morning was clear and sunny. A few wisps of thin mist hung in the high tree branches, and the groundcover was wet from the night's rains. By the time Jana and Robert finished breakfast and gathered their gear to return to the ruins of Tikal, the morning had become warm and steamy. Gleefully they donned shorts and tee shirts, readied cameras and backpacks, and took off along the road to the park entrance. Jana decided not to mention her midnight prayers to the Maya deities.

That sunny day wandering the ruins of Tikal was one of the peak events of Jana's life. Robert was caught up in her enthusiasm, and both were like delighted children making one after another wonderful discovery. They explored vine-shrouded pathways and crumbling stone structures, going wherever their curiosity led. They revisited the Great Plaza twice, once early in the morning, and again just before leaving in the afternoon. They avoided the North Acropolis without saying anything. Jana climbed Temple II again, spending more time inside the platform temple communing with Lady Twelve Macaw and her loving husband Hasau. They wandered inside the maze of halls, rooms and multi-level plazas of the Central Acropolis, visited twin pyramid complexes, studied intricately carved stelae and altars, explored the Bat Palace and Lost World Complex at length. Jana climbed the massive Great Pyramid there scrutinized the Seven Temples on its eastern side, remembering that these were used for astronomical observation.

Along the way they laughed at a band of coatimundis, small animals that looked like a cross between anteaters and raccoons, with lush brown coats, long noses and snake-like tails. These inquisitive animals had learned to find treats in tourists' backpacks, so they kept theirs out of reach. Several flocks of beautiful ocellated turkeys crossed their path, opalescent feathers catching the sun and shimmering in shades of blue, lavender and gold. Colorful macaws and parrots squawked in the trees. Toucans flashed their black and orange beaks like immense garden shears. Spider monkeys chattered in the branches overhead and tossed down empty nutshells, barely missing their heads.

It was a magical day.

The next morning Robert decided to stay at the Jungle Lodge while Jana returned to the ruins. His feet were sore and he wanted time to relax, read and listen to music. The van from Cayo Hills Resort was coming at 1:00 pm to pick them up. Jana was eager to spend the morning exploring two additional places, the Temple of Inscriptions and a residential palace called prosaically Group G.

Walking briskly along the road into the ruins, Jana reflected that two and a half days were not nearly enough to really see Tikal. Her destination required a 30-minute walk one way, so she could not visit the North Group, which was in the opposite direction along the Maler Causeway. And, dozens of other groupings remained unexamined.

The morning was warm and sunny with puffy white clouds overhead. Soon Jana worked up a light sweat in the humid air. Taking a path branching left from the main entrance, she cut through dense jungle to reach Group G. Sunlight dappled the path, filtering through the canopy, and she smelled the earthy damp humus. She was alone on the narrow path, the jungle stillness broken only by sounds of buzzing insects and calling birds.

Soon the narrow path joined a raised, wider road she recognized as the Mendez Causeway. Walking a short distance, she saw the dramatic front of the Group G palace situated on an elevated platform. A tall vaulted passageway rising the height of the two-story building led into a large inner court. She climbed deteriorated stairs and passed through the entry, reverently touching the dark gray stones with lighter mortar where they had been restored. The grassy inner court was surrounded on three sides by a U-shaped structure, its open side overgrown by large trees and vines. A narrow path disappearing into deep shade was tersely labeled "To Temple."

In the guidebook she read that the palace consisted of 29 vaulted chambers in a multi-room complex, with the rear entry through a passageway framed by a huge monster mask. The rooms varied in size, their configurations changed over time by different occupants. The original palace was built by Yik'in Chan K'awil as his family home.

Jana walked through rooms, halls and passageways stepping over raised doorways. The rooms were narrow and small, often at different levels, with few window openings. Some had stone ledges at thigh level attached to a wall; she assumed these were sleeping platforms. She sat on a ledge about 2 ½ feet wide and 6 feet long, feeling the hard, cool surface beneath her and trying to imagine sleeping on it.

The Maya must have put mats on the sleeping ledges. .

Instantly images of the dream flashed through her mind. The old woman was lying on a ledge just like this. But the room was not the same; it was larger with a corbel arch doorway that opened to the outside. This room had a square doorway opening into a long hall running the length of the structure.

It must be another place, Jana mused.

The musty smell of damp stone wafted from the long hall. Jana touched walls and arches, inviting them to reveal their secrets. Eyes closed, she leaned against the cool wall, palms open in full contact. She listened.

Faint humming filled her ears. An insect chirped nearby, almost obscuring the sound of clay pottery being scraped. Soft scuffling noises arose, coming from a short distance down the hall. Murmuring voices, strange tonalities with deep-throated explosive syllables hovered in the still air. A loud "clunk" as though something heavy had fallen caused Jana's eyes to fly open.

She jerked upright, heart pounding. Looking around, she saw the hall was deserted except for a large lizard scurrying over a raised doorway.

Where did those other sounds come from?

Maybe people were in the court. She walked down the hall to a passageway leading to the inner court. Her eyes squinted automatically at the bright sunshine. No other tourists were there. Closing her eyes, she imagined the court filled with Maya people, women weaving and cooking, children noisily playing, men working flint. Again she heard the strange language sounds. For an instance, she was there among the Maya, hearing their ethereal voices and sensing their ghostly presence.

Brown jays cawed in the distance. Their harsh cries grew louder, shriller.

Caw! Caw! Too loud, too close, the noise buffeted Jana's ears.

Crows? Are they crows? Jana felt confused, disoriented.

A pulling sensation made her body feel heavy, like it wanted to sink into the earth below the court. She squatted on the ground, placing palms on the short grass, worn down by many tourist feet. Her palms tingled as a rushing sensation filled her head, stilling her breath. A thick cord of spiraling energy undulated from her heart into the earth. It pulled her body to the ground, like a powerful magnet. She fell forward on knees and hands. Moments passed, she was unable to move or breathe.

Suddenly a great gasp racked her body as survival functions in the brain stem forced her to breathe. Instinctively she sat up, lifting shoulders to expand her chest, breathing rapidly, hungry for air. Shakily, she rose and looked around the court. It was empty and still.

No jays called. Now a magnetic force was pulling her across the court to the arch at the rear entrance.

She walked slowly, automatically, her mind dazed. The rear arch led to the monster mask for which this palace was famous. Vaguely she recalled wanting to see the mask. Approaching the arch, she had to navigate through a pile of rubble. Footing was unstable due to fallen stones, overgrown by vines. Jana was so focused on picking flat stones for footing that she did not notice the old man until he spoke. He was sitting in shadows, leaning against one jowl of the monster mask framing the outside of the rear entrance.

"¡Cuidado! Está en peligro. No vaya más lejos."

Jerking her head upright, Jana turned to the old man. His wizened face was dark brown, sunken lips framing a toothless mouth over which hung an enormous hooked nose. The battered straw hat seated low on his forehead nearly hid his eyes, glowing black coals in deep sockets that stared relentlessly at her. He wore a brown poncho over wrinkled baggy pants that had once been white. His feet were bare.

"¿Perdóname?" Jana ventured tentatively, hoping she remembered how to say "Pardon me" correctly in Spanish.

"¡No vaya!" he repeated fiercely, gesturing at her sharply with one arm.

Jana felt hit by a force that pushed her backward. She lost her footing, slipping down on one knee. Pain seared her knee as it scraped against a broken stone edge. She twisted to break the fall with her hands, glimpsing a ravine just beyond the mound of stones. Grasping vines to avoid tumbling into the ravine, Jana landed hard on her buttocks. Her heart pounded loudly as she let out an involuntary groan. Glancing quickly at her knee, she saw the scrape was superficial although beginning to bleed.

From her seated position, Jana had to turn 180 degrees to again face the mask and the old man. She swiveled around, wincing from the bruise developing on her butt. The old man had disappeared. Only the immense grimacing mask, its open jaws framing the doorway and its muzzle badly eroded, returned her gaze. Where the eyes would have been, the wall had crumbled away.

"¿Señor?" Jana called. "¿Donde está?"

Birds twittered, brown jays cawed, and a parrot squawked. The air felt heavy, hot, oppressive. Distant roars of howler monkeys reverberated across the canopy, eerie and ominous. No footsteps, no human voices broke the jungle sounds.

Jana felt immeasurably alone. The prickling sensation of fear crept up her spine. What had the old man said? She replayed the incident in her mind, straining to recapture his Spanish phrases.

"No va mas . . . mas . ." she repeated softly, "mas . . oh, yeah, mas lejos."

At the moment she couldn't translate the phrase into English. And what else? In a sudden flood the entire communication echoed through her mind. She repeated it several times to impress it on her memory. She would look up the translation in her Spanish-English dictionary when she got back to the lodge.

Pulling tissues from her backpack, Jana dabbed her scraped knee. It was already clotting. She got up carefully, finding that her butt and knee were not too sore and she could walk with minimal discomfort.

Thanks to the adrenalin rush—just wait until tomorrow.

Nursing knowledge came forth from hidden recesses in her mind. Its familiarity was comforting in the wake of the extraordinary events brought by the last several minutes. Her mind felt numb, insensate. She would think about all this later.

Jana returned to the Mendez Causeway. She hesitated, uncertain whether to proceed to the Temple of Inscriptions or go back to the lodge. She was shaken from her strange encounter with the old man and her fall. Jana watched the sun and clouds casting patterns of light and shadows across the wide path. The effort to go on was too much. Hints of fatigue crept through her muscles, and her knee was starting to throb.

Checking her watch, she judged that the slower pace of her return walk would take up what time was left. As she bade farewell to the jungle paths of Tikal, one resolve became clear: She would not to tell Robert about the incident with the old man until she had time to process it.

*   *   *   *   *   *

The small twin propeller aircraft revved its engines for take-off then bounced along the short runway, lifting skyward at a rakish angle. Roaring engines deafened the ears of 12 passengers during the 30-minute flight to Ambergris Caye. Jana glanced across Robert's lap, peering through the small window as the shore of mainland Belize receded.

Sitting back with closed eyes, Jana allowed the engine roar to encase her awareness like a cocoon. Holding her mind blank, she waited. After a few moments the Spanish words spoken by the old man took shape like sharply etched writing projected on an inner screen:

"Cuidado! Esta en peligro. No va mas lejos."

She had translated the words: "Watch out! You are in danger. Do not go farther." Had he been warning her that she was too close to the ravine, and might fall if she went farther onto the jumbled stones? That was the obvious meaning. She sensed that his words held a more sinister message, however.

As the airplane flew northeast from Belize City, the Caribbean Sea below took on shades of turquoise, emerald and lapis according to the water's depth. Irregular white atolls dotted the sea's surface, with a substantial island cropping up here and there. Ambergris Caye was the northernmost and largest among the 400 cayes; most were merely a stand of palms and a strip of sand.

Robert was excited about going to the cayes. There, according to the guidebook, was "Belize's spectacular barrier reef, with its dazzling variety of underwater life and string of exquisite islands." The longest barrier reef in the western hemisphere, it started south of Cancun and ran the entire length of the Belize coastline at a distance of 9 to 25 miles from the mainland. Behind the reef a limestone ridge formed the larger islands on the north end of the chain. Here flourished one of the richest marine ecosystems on earth, a haven for scuba divers and snorkellers, offering fantastic coral formations teeming with hundreds of species of brilliantly colored fish.

The guidebook explained that beaches were not as spectacular as on Hawaii, because the barrier reef protected the islands and reduced the surf action required to produce long, wide beaches. But there were some excellent stretches along the south end of Ambergris Caye, and Robert had chosen the Coconut Palms Beach Resort, promoted for its location on the best beach area.

As the small airplane descended Jana saw the irregular outline of the caye's southern tip, dotted with coves and lagoons. After a bumpy landing at San Pedro's picturesque airport, evoking images of 1930's-style adventure movies, Jana and Robert hailed a beat-up taxi for the bouncing ride through sandy pot-holed streets to their resort. Palm trees swayed in the ever-present breeze that also ruffled brightly colored orange and purple bougainvillea climbing on walls of yellow and blue houses. Their driver expertly swerved to avoid the numerous

172

bicyclers, pedestrians and electric golf carts that were the main modes of transportation.

The Coconut Palms Beach Resort was upscale and expensive, its inner patios paved with colorful tiles surrounding two good-sized swimming pools. Robert had really splurged and booked a large room with separate kitchen-living area and a balcony facing the beach. The view from their balcony was lovely; a long stretch of white sand beach with clusters of palm trees and two piers defining the hotel's beach area. Well-padded lounge chairs were arrayed in two straight lines along the beach, some with umbrellas. Sunbathers exposed oil-glistening limbs and a few swimmers splashed in the shallow water. The day was mostly sunny with a refreshing breeze. High cirrus clouds cast a thin veil across the sun from time to time, as puffy Colombo-nimbus metamorphosed at lower altitudes.

It was a great beach day. Jana and Robert put on their swimming suits and joined the sun-soaking loungers.

They settled into a pleasant rhythm during their week on Ambergris Caye. First they made breakfast in the kitchen and had aromatic Guatemalan coffee bought in San Ignacio. Now it was dripped through an actual coffee maker instead of the oil funnel. By mid-morning they were sunning and reading, interspersed with swimming in the azure Caribbean. For lunch they walked or bicycled to town, finding interesting little cafes for sandwiches, then a little sightseeing around San Pedro town, returning by mid-afternoon for another session on the beach. After a minimal sunburn the first day, they developed nice tans. Dinner out was expensive with limited vegetarian fare, so they cooked in their kitchen. Evenings were spent reading, listening to music and watching a video or two.

They went on a few water excursions, including a spectacular snorkel trip to the Hol Chan Marine Reserve south of the caye. Enthusiastic descriptions in the guidebook hardly did justice to the amazing abundance of coral reefs and fish life. Ridge upon ridge of colorful coral in fantastic shapes folded into deep canyons. Hundreds of fish swarmed around them, unafraid and seeking treats. Pocked reef ridges hid Moray eels, and in deeper crevices huge red snappers, variegated groupers and slender barracuda with long toothy jaws swam nonchalantly. They visited nearby Shark Alley, where dozens of mild-mannered nurse sharks gathered along with huge manta rays, flapping 8-foot wings gracefully along the sea bottom. Their guide caught a young nurse shark, about 3 feet long, and Robert was brave enough to hug the remarkably cooperative creature who showed no signs of wanting to bite.

Although settled into a seemingly ordinary routine, Jana's thoughts were never far from the strange events in the ruins. The scrape on her knee festered and got more painful. All she told Robert was that she slipped on some stones. For a couple of days she feared the infection might get out of control. It was worrisome, for she usually healed quickly. But, between the astringent seawater, drying warmth of the sun, and antibiotic ointment from her travel kit, the scrape slowly healed.

Jana planned one day for visiting Maya ruins on the caye. Robert was having too much fun in the sun, and decided not to go along. She booked a daylong boat trip from the San Pedro lagoon along the west coast of Ambergris Caye to the ruins of Santa Cruz, San Juan and Chak Balam, currently under excavation. The return trip went through the Bacalar Chico channel, dug by the Maya about 1500 years ago, allowing access by sea-going canoes from the Caribbean to the protected west side of the caye, and then to Maya cities in on the coast. This channel turned Ambergris Caye into an island; before that it was a peninsula attached to the Yucatan. The tour returned along the ocean side of the caye to drop off guests at their resort's pier.

Jana dressed in layers, as the morning was cool and the wind brisk when her 25-foot outboard boat departed at 8:30 am. Two guides and four other tourists made up their crew. Leaving San Pedro lagoon, a guide pointed out the underwater site of Yalamha submerged two feet under the surface. Rising sea levels worldwide, and the sinking geological plate on which Ambergris Caye and northern Belize sit accounted for the site's submergence. It was likely that other coastal Maya sites were also lost to the rising sea.

The large site of Santa Cruz was about two-thirds of the way up the west coast of Ambergris Caye. It was used for shipment of trade goods in the Postclassic period. Large amounts of exotic pottery, obsidian, basalt and ornamental greenstone including some jade were found in excavations. Formally arranged, large stone mounds were thought to support pole and thatch buildings. Small plazas between the mounds would have served as gathering places for markets selling trade goods.

Walking the flat ruins, Jana found little to catch her attention. No structures stood; many of the mounds were overgrown with grasses and small brush. A scattering of wind-blown, gnarled trees and some mangroves by the rocky shore added a little interest to the level landscape.

They proceeded to the early Maya site of San Juan, where they had lunch before visiting the ruins. Munching a cheese sandwich, chips and lemon soda, Jana tried to recall what she had read in her thin book, *The Ancient Maya Traders of Ambergris Caye*. The San Juan site, which of course had another name in Mayan times, was strategically located and jutted out into a cove making it easily visible as boats completed the westward journey through the Bacalar Chico canal. While archeologists were not sure exactly how early the Maya occupied Ambergris Caye, it was in use by the Late Preclassic if not before. Excavations of trade goods from San Juan included many luxury items from great distances, much valued by rulers and the elite. Especially exciting was plentiful green obsidian, originating in central México and brought all the way around the Yucatan Peninsula. High quality black obsidian from highland Guatemala, stone artifacts from the Maya Mountains, and ceramic pottery from the Pacific coast of Guatemala were also found there.

Chewing her sandwich made Jana think of the Maya grinding stones for maize, shaped like a large mortar and pestle. The elite favored volcanic basalt grinding stones, because these hard stones did not crumble into the maize meal to wreak havoc with their teeth. Basalt came from mountains in México and Guatemala, transported long distances to lowland Maya cities. The common people used grinding stones made of limestone that fragmented easily, leaving tiny chunks in the meal to erode teeth. The condition of tooth wear made it simple for archeologists to determine if people used limestone or basalt grinding stones, and thus their social status.

Salt was another important commodity traded by the seaside Maya settlements. In the hot tropical climate with limited meat in their diet, Maya people found salt an absolute necessity for life. Much salt was imported from large salinas in northern Yucatan, transported in ocean-going canoes along coastal trade routes through caye settlements. On northern parts of the caye, lagoons provided salt until only a few decades ago. A type of pottery called Coconut Walk, thin shallow dishes 15-20 inches wide, was used for evaporating seawater to make salt.

After lunch the group walked the site of San Juan. The flat ruins nestled between a small beach and a marshy meadow, bordered by clumps of mangrove trees. There were mounds and crumbled stone walls, with no standing structures. Although the site did not look

175

substantially different from the one at Santa Cruz, Jana felt a qualitative difference here. Something was "in the air" as she breathed deeply of salt-tinged sea breeze. Her feet on the sandy gravel paths felt light, almost like dancing. Something here delighted her, awakened her senses. The shrill calls of seagulls seemed musical to her ears. Noon sunlight glittered on the choppy water of the small cove, creating diamond sparkles that nearly blinded her eyes.

Jana stood on a small grassy mound, waiting, listening. The group moved away toward another part of the ruins. Slowly she turned in a 360-degree circle, like a radar dish seeking the strongest signal. She felt a subtle pull toward the northwest, and began walking in that direction until she found a small portion of beach sheltered by a grove of mangrove trees, their branches intertwined, roots dropping from lower branches into brackish water where a small stream flowed into the lagoon. She walked onto the beach, only about 25 feet long and 15 feet wide. The mangroves shielded her from the ruins and she could not see the other people in her group.

Listening to the gentle lap of water on the beach, Jana closed her eyes. She had a strong, irresistible impulse to take her shoes off and feel the sand on her feet. Quickly she slipped off her tennis shoes and socks, digging her toes into the damp cool sand. Her hands had to touch the sand, too. She sat on her backpack, caressing the sand with her fingers, then burying them under the sand. Waves of delight wafted through her body, every cell tingled with some unknown anticipation. She wanted to lie on the sand, but was afraid to get her clothes wet and suffer from a chilly ride back. No thoughts formed in her mind to explain these pleasurable feelings, she simply merged with the inexplicable ecstasy.

Moments passed, she didn't know how long. She opened and closed her eyes, but the delightful feeling remained either way. Her heart felt incredibly open, receptive and giving at the same time. Without summoning it, an image of Robert appeared in her inner vision. Her heart leaped and she felt love emanating from her heart toward him. The inner ecstasy exploded in a scintillating sensation, rapidly radiating outward from her body to form a golden globe around both herself and Robert. She felt their bodies merging, their hearts beating as one. Her body quivered with delight. It was a near-orgasmic sensation.

The Observer part of Jana's mind was bemused and fascinated by watching her in this experience. It made no judgments, it just watched and noted. Then it reminded her about the other people who were probably wondering where she was as they re-boarded the boat. She sat a few moments longer, savoring the slowly waning sensations. With deep reluctance, she brushed off the sand, put her shoes on, and returned to the boat.

The last Maya ruin of the tour was Chak Balam, located between San Juan and the Bacalar Chico canal with a man made harbor. Smaller than San Juan, the site had platforms with cut limestone producing a façade similar to mainland architecture. A rich burial tomb found below one platform contained finely made plates imported from the north, and bloodletting artifacts indicating a ruler or noble. Skeletal remains from burials here and at San Juan showed these were very healthy people with good nutrition and little disease.

Jana half-listened as the tour guide described Chak Balam. She was preoccupied with her unusual, intense experience on the tiny beach at San Juan. She appreciated that the Maya trading societies on Ambergris Caye led a relatively abundant life, prospering from vital trade routes and skimming some luxury goods off the top for their own use. But what really engaged her focus was her experience on the small beach—powerful physical sensations as well as emotional highs.

I've been on that beach before. It was wonderful. But what has Robert got to do with it? Jana was puzzled and intrigued.

The boat wound its way through the Bacalar Chico canal. The one-mile long waterway was narrow enough at some points to almost touch mangroves growing on the banks, although considerably wider at other places along its winding route. At the canal's mouth the reef was very close to the shore, so the boat had to cross into open sea for most of the trip back to San Pedro. The afternoon wind was brisk, a typical pattern, and the waves created swells that rolled the boat side to side as it accelerated to maximum speed. All the passengers huddled down and drew their jackets tight, warding off the cutting wind and sea spray. It was a cold and extremely bumpy ride, making a couple of hours seem like an eternity.

Jana could not talk about her experience at San Juan for a while, though she described the rest of her trip to Robert in some detail. On their last night on the caye, they went to dinner in the resort's outdoor patio grill. It was a lovely setting, bordered on one side by a half-wall with columns and trellis covered with flowering vines. Glass tables and stylish bamboo chairs added luxury. Torchlight reflecting on the pool created an aura of romance. They indulged in wine with a gourmet dinner; fresh fish prepared with imagination and style. Fine restaurants were really expensive on the caye, but tonight was special for them.

After dinner they walked on the beach, shining silver in the light of a nearly full moon. The breeze was gentle, stirring their clothes and hair. Saying little, Jana and Robert walked hand in hand, barefoot in the sand, listening to the waves making soft crescendos as they broke onto the shore.

"I've had a wonderful time," Jana said after a while.

"Me, too," Robert assented.

"Are you glad we came? I know it's more pricey than most of our vacations during semester break."

"It's well worth the cost," Robert reassured her. "I would never have imagined so many fascinating places in Belize. Tikal was truly special. And, this is an incredible beach no matter what the guidebooks say."

They walked a while longer in silence, reached wooden pilings marking the beach end, and turned around.

"Robert, there's something I wanted to tell you about my trip to the ruins on the north caye," Jana said.

"Sure," he replied, glancing sideways at her as he detected a different note in her voice. He knew this tone meant she was broaching something either difficult or very important.

"When we were at San Juan, one of the larger ruins, I felt drawn to a tiny beach. I can't explain exactly why. I went there while the rest of the group explored the ruins. I had to put my feet and hands into the sand, and when I did I had this incredible experience. It was actually physical, I had these strong physical body sensations."

Her voice caught.

"Were they bad?" Robert asked with concern.

"No, not at all," she quickly replied. "Just the opposite. They were exquisite, unbelievably pleasurable. I felt like I was in some kind of bliss. Then your face appeared, and I felt the most powerful love for you. It was like you were there, and we were embracing, merging into one. I was amazed at how much love I felt for you."

They had stopped walking and were facing each other. Tears, turned into tiny sparkles by the moonlight, moistened Jana's eyelashes. Robert cupped her face between his hands, looking deeply into her eyes. He smiled and murmured:

"That's wonderful, sweetheart. I love you too, with all my heart."

178

He bent down and kissed her, gently at first then with building passion as her body arched against his and her lips parted. Arms around each other, they exchanged long, lingering kisses on the moonlit beach. Both knew they would make love as soon as they returned to their room at the Coconut Palms Beach Resort.

The illness struck Jana first. Two days after returning from Belize, she tried to ignore a scratchy throat but it was the harbinger of worse ahead. A few days later Robert came down with symptoms. They were careful to take vitamins every day on the trip and zinc lozenges while flying, but the impervious virus slammed them with a vengeance. It marched through their bodies, from throat to nose, sinuses to lungs, muscles and joints, backtracking to create yet another set of symptoms in previously visited territory. The immune system in hot pursuit with histamines, immunoglobulins, scavengers and white blood cells wrecked havoc in virus-infested tissues, causing swelling, mucus, pressure and congestion as battleground fall-out.

Jana missed four days of work and Robert had to cancel classes for the better part of a week. This was unusual for both of them. Normally they recovered quickly from colds, but this virus was different. High fever wracked their bodies, causing teeth-clattering chills alternating with burning heat leaving them sweaty and wrung out. Jana observed wryly that hot flashes took a back seat to this fever. Draining mucus and sinus pressure made sleeping nearly impossible. An intense sore throat made swallowing painful, even coffee lost its flavor. Every cell in their bodies felt toxic. Then, as these decidedly unpleasant symptoms began to wane, the cough took over. Hacking paroxysms of cough sometimes left them breathless. It was a nasty illness.

Sleeping fitfully, Jana tossed restlessly, lost in fevered dreams. Images of a toothless old man haunted her, his gaunt face wobbling precariously on a thin neck. Huge square eyes stared ominously past a prominent hooked nose. He danced, lifting his bony legs high and waving emaciated arms, the knobby joints disproportionately large. His belly was bloated, protruding. This corpse-like wraith twirled and dipped, belt jangling with hanging shells and jaguar cape flapping. Then he became a jaguar, dancing on its hind legs, with a toothy grimace and long claws extended from waving forelegs. A gaping-jawed Chak mask enticed the dancers into its maw, stony eyes gazing with cold indifference into the distance.

Only vague memories of these dreams persisted when Jana awoke. Thankfully the need to find some relief for the illness diverted her attention.

Drawing upon her nursing background and familiarity with common alternative methods, Jana and Robert downed Echinacea and goldenseal, throat coat teas with slippery elm and ginger tea to ease throat pain, vitamin C and bioflavonoids. When sinus and nose symptoms became intense, they resorted to Sudafed and nasal sprays just to be able to breathe. Codeine cough syrup that Jana kept on hand did suppress their coughs enough to allow them to sleep a few hours less fitfully. After four days of viral misery, their symptoms began to improve.

Sipping Wellness Tea in the afternoon, they agreed their illness was definitely taking a turn for the better. Robert still had more symptoms, especially a persisting cough, having come down with the virus a day later than Jana. They could finally focus their minds enough to have a decent conversation.

"I wonder what this illness was all about," Jana said reflectively.

"Bad virus, not strong enough immune system," Robert observed pragmatically.

"Well, yes, a host-pathogen imbalance, but why?" Jana said. "We don't usually get sick after traveling, we take precautions to boost our immune function."

"Does everything have a deeper meaning?" Robert sounded a little annoyed. His reserves were depleted, lowering his normal tolerance of Jana's metaphysical theories. "Sometimes a cold is just a cold."

"This feels like an unusual illness," Jana retorted. "And, some quite unusual things happened to us on this trip. One thing happened to me that I didn't tell you about, I was waiting until I understood it better. Now I think it may be connected to getting sick."

"What was that?" Robert asked, with tentative curiosity.

"On the last day at Tikal, when I went by myself to the ruins, this old toothless native man appeared from nowhere. I was alone, drawn by a magnetic force to the back door of the palace. It opened through a carved mask. The old man spoke to me in Spanish but I couldn't understand it at the time. Then he yelled at me and I felt a force, like a strong wind, that pushed me backwards. I slipped and scraped my knee, and almost fell into a deep ravine behind the pile of stones I was standing on. When I turned around, he was gone."

"What did he say? Did you get it translated?" Robert queried.

"Yes, he said 'Watch out! You are in danger. Do not go farther.'"

Robert reached the obvious conclusion, just as Jana was sure he would.

"He was probably warning you about falling into the ravine."

"That was my immediate thought, of course," Jana replied. "But there were overtones of something else. I felt his intention was, well . . . almost evil. You should have seen how he looked at me. His eyes were so intense. And I don't know how to explain the force that must have come from him, that knocked me backward."

Robert reflected on this for a few minutes. He didn't want to discredit his wife's experience. He took a more practical approach to life and had questions about the world of unseen forces that Jana and her "New Age" friends believed. But, he had to admit there undoubtedly was a lot he didn't understand. He was aware of people who could alter the forces of nature, such as yogi masters and faith healers. He recalled his own experience at the North Acropolis in Tikal. The intensity of his momentary weakness when his knees almost buckled, and the deep-seated queasiness in his chest and abdomen were undeniable. He must have felt some kind of emanation at the pyramid that affected him physically and emotionally.

As though she were reading his thoughts, Jana brought up this experience. It was a frequent occurrence; Jana often knew what Robert was about to say, but he also anticipated her words. Maybe being together so many years, knowing each other so well, created mutual thought patterns causing their minds to work along the same lines.

Or perhaps mental telepathy actually does exist, Robert admitted.

"What about your experience on the North Acropolis?" she said. "You had strong reactions there, and we haven't really discussed it."

"I have to admit, it was very strange," Robert allowed. "It came on suddenly, out of nowhere. I was taking photos, and wanted to see what was beyond the far edge of the platform. I walked behind that farthest pyramid—the one on the north end—and as I was focusing the camera for a shot, I felt sick to my stomach and my legs started to give out. I had to grab onto the temple wall to keep from falling."

He paused, reflecting as a new memory arose, something he had overlooked before. It was very subtle, but now he could recall the feeling distinctly.

"When my hand touched the temple wall, I felt a chill go through my body. The stones were icy, way too cold for the temperature that

182

day. I pulled my hand away and then almost fell. That must be why I forgot this part of it."

Jana was watching him closely. A touch of concern played across her face.

"That sounds like the intense feelings I had, with the old man at the palace," she said. "And, I had another unusual experience when I went alone to that off-the-path ruin at Xunantunich, do you remember?"

"Uh, yeah," Robert said, "you did go off alone for a while."

"It was just an unexcavated mound, covered with grass and brush, but I was strongly connected to it. It seemed to hold some mystery that it wouldn't reveal to me. The only images I got were of plants—herbs, I think—and my work at the emergency room. Doesn't make any sense, but it had power."

She paused, weighing her next remark.

"You know, Robert, I've got business with these Maya. I'm sure its no accident that we visited those ruins. Even the one on Ambergris Caye, where I had that incredible experience on the small beach. Remember?"

"Uh-huh." He was reflective. Being slammed by the viral infection had reduced his mental guard against mysterious happenings. He was ready to admit there was some portent in their experiences in the ruins.

"The Maya did human sacrifices, didn't they?" he asked.

She nodded affirmative.

"I wonder if I tapped into some of that energy. They did use the North Acropolis for rituals, if I remember right."

"Yes, it was the major ceremonial center in the Early Classic, from before the time of Great Jaguar Claw up to the Hiatus, when Tikal went into decline for 125 years. No doubt they did human sacrifices there."

Robert nodded, a bit surprised at himself for entertaining such a metaphysical view.

"You think all this is connected with your dream about the old woman's hand," he observed.

"In some way, yes," Jana said. "I need to find out why, what it means, what it's telling me to do."

"Jana, I think you should be careful," Robert said with concern. "You don't know what you might be getting into. People have been killed with voodoo. The old man might be a Maya witch doctor. You better stay away from it."

Jana hosted the next meeting of the women's group at her home. She was over the illness, though not yet back to her normal energy level. Robert always went to a friend's house or to the Mills College library when the women met, allowing the feminine energy to stay pristine. After everyone settled down in the living room with tea, the group did their opening check-in then focused on Jana's recent trip. She gave highlights, emphasizing her intense experiences in the ruins.

"Sounds to me like you've been a Maya in prior incarnations," observed Carmen, with animated gestures.

"Or, you moved through a threshold in liminal time to tap into another dimension of reality," said Claire, recalling the group's previous discussion about portals and quantum theory.

"Those experiences you had at the three different ruins really do sound like synchronicities," added Lydia in her precise way. "For a moment your awareness passed through an opening in the fabric of space-time, as the physicists say, to have contact with another reality. You received a call through your dream to make this journey to Maya ruins, and your attunement to the ancient Maya psi-field drew the experiences to you."

"That unexcavated mound you went to alone in Zu . .Shu . ., how do you say it, the Stone Maiden place?" queried Mary, Jana's emergency room colleague.

"Xunantunich," Jana pronounced the Mayan name phonetically "Shoo-nan-<u>toon</u>-ich." She enunciated the strange syllables with relish, for she was enjoying the distinctive vibrations of the language on her tongue as she learned pronunciations.

"Whatever. That might have been a healing place in Maya times," Mary observed thoughtfully. "You had images of herbs, which would have been their main method for treating illness. And then you saw yourself in the ER, where you do your work helping sick people. Maybe you touched into the common frequency for both these fields when you were there."

"All that makes sense," said Jana. "But what I'm having trouble with is *why*, what this is all about. So I have some connections with the ancient Maya, and maybe I've had a prior incarnation there, but what am I supposed to do, if anything?"

"Did the ancient Maya believe in reincarnation?" asked Sarah, tossing her brown curls with a quick head movement and widening her tawny eyes framed by enviable thick curved eyelashes.

"I don't think so, at least not the way the Hindus do—you know, the same soul or Atma reincarnating over and over into a new body," replied Jana. "The Maya revered their ancestors and believed they could contact them when in altered states during rituals. They buried family members under the floors of their homes. Kings were buried under pyramid temples. Their successors invoked previous kings through what they called vision serpents. The ancestors would emerge from the vision serpent's mouth while the king was doing a vision quest. These ancestors gave information and advice. Images of bloodletting rituals done by kings were frequently carved on stelae, showing the vision serpent with an ancestor or god emerging from its mouth."

"Bloodletting rituals?" Mary sounded quizzical. "What were those?"

"Kings, priests and nobles would use sharp implements—mostly stingray spines—to make small piercings in their ears, tongue, fingers or penis. The blood that dripped was collected on bark papers and burned. As the smoke went up, it swirled around and became the vision serpent. The king was in an altered state, probably because of the fasting and long rituals that preceded the bloodletting, and from loss of blood. The Maya believed the king or priest actually became the ancestor or god invoked through the vision serpent. So they had access to their wisdom and power. The king was thought to be the physical presence of the god, and maybe of his ancestors too."

"These guys actually pierced their penis?" asked Mary with incredulity, her face screwing into a distasteful expression.

"Probably their foreskins, Mary," said Jana. "Though I've seen pictures of the penile shaft with a rather large elongated stone sticking through it."

"Yuk, would you two stop being so clinical?" Sarah feigned disgust, with a twinkle in her eyes.

Everyone laughed.

"The Maya pierced many body parts," Jana continued, unrelenting. "Even the noble women did bloodletting. Both sexes wore huge earplugs as decorations, must have made enormous holes in their earlobes."

"Huh, like our current youth," observed Grace, who was following the conversation with interest. "They pierce almost any area, some have multiple piercings of ears, nose, navel, tongue and nipples. You know, this does revert back to tribal customs. Lots of indigenous people used piercing for adornment and for ritual

185

purposes. Maybe the young people are looking for a connection with an older tradition, for meaningful symbols in this chaotic world."

"Yeah, maybe," observed Claire cynically, "but without the spiritual practices that accompany body piercing, all they're doing is making holes in their chakras to drain energy out."

Carmen refocused the discussion, a function she often performed for the group. Being half-Mexican, though second generation in the U.S., she was quite interested in spiritual traditions of Mesoamerica. She had traveled to the area of her family's origin in México, a small town in Tabasco not far from Villahermosa, the region's capital city. Bordering the Yucatan Peninsula, Tabasco was known for its extensive cacao plantations, lush vegetation and banana farms.

"What were the religious practices of the common people?" Carmen asked. "Did they worship ancestors and do ritual piercing?"

"I'm not sure about that," Jana told her. "It's much easier to find information about royalty than commoners in Maya books. I'm feeling confused about their spiritual beliefs and basic values. There's so much archeological information that I get lost in it. I need to know about their cosmology, their worldview, what were the principles they lived by. And," she added wistfully, "what all that has to do with me, right now."

"Have you tried to contact any contemporary Maya, the ones who are bringing their ancient heritage to light now?" asked Grace. "I've noticed in the past few years that shamans are literally coming out of the woodwork. There are several recent books from the Toltec and Native American spiritual traditions. I'll bet there are some by current Maya shamans too."

"Why didn't I think of that? It's a great idea, Grace," said Jana. "Can you suggest some books?"

"Yes, I'll give you a few titles after our meeting tonight." Grace paused thoughtfully. Her dark reflective eyes, mocha-colored skin and long wavy black hair testified to her mixed Caucasian, Native and African American genes. Slender and willowy, she moved with natural, unstudied elegance, a true embodiment of her name.

"I just got another idea," she said. "That experience you had with the old man where he gave you the warning, I think it's about more than just not falling into the ravine. My sense of him is that he's a shaman, and what he said is related to your mission with the Maya. There may be some danger. You could use help getting a better picture about this. There's a native woman from my family's tribe, a Hopi medicine woman, who is coming to Oakland soon. She gives readings and makes contact with the spirit world for people. I've met her before, her name is Tuwa Waki. I can set you up with a session, if you'd like."

Jana hesitated, remembering Robert's admonition against delving further. But, she quickly sensed this was her next step in unraveling the mystery.

"I'd really like to do that. I could use some insight, that's for sure."

"Good idea," Carmen agreed. "If the old man was a shaman, maybe he gave you what the Mexicans call 'mal ojo,' the evil eye. They believe this can cause illness and misfortune. When a shaman puts the evil eye on you, it takes another shaman to reverse the effects."

"Tuwa Waki is a powerful shaman," Grace asserted with more intensity than was usual for her.

Oakland belied its name, for there were few oaks left in the sprawling metropolis. Sandwiched between San Francisco Bay and the Berkeley hills, a low mountain range running parallel to the bay, the city was criss-crossed by freeways and densely populated. Going south, one city merged its borders into the next, making the East Bay one long strip of shopping centers interspersed with industrial and residential areas. Downtown Oakland most closely resembled a metropolitan city, with a number of tall buildings but nothing remotely resembling a skyscraper. Here and there, parks or campuses interrupted the web of streets, creating havens of cool shade and green lawns.

The older areas of Oakland had a Victorian look, with many late 19th century houses. In better residential areas, these houses had been restored. And surprisingly, a few were surrounded by large lawns still bearing venerable oak trees. It was to one of these rare homes, islands of serenity in a sea of asphalt and concrete, that Grace drove Jana for her appointment with Tuwa Waki. Grace explained that this Hopi name meant "Earth Shelter."

Jana argued that she could go alone, but Grace insisted on accompanying her. The session would only last an hour, Grace reasoned, and she would bring something to read. Deep within, Jana was grateful for this caring support from her friend.

The two women climbed a short staircase onto the wide veranda spanning two sides of the gracious two-story home, beautifully restored with white trim and gray siding. The ornate white entry door

187

was embellished with an oval, chiseled glass window. In response to the door chime, pleasing and understated, a young woman invited them inside. She appeared in her early twenties and was of moderate height. Her features were clearly Native American though her hair was short, and she wore a loose white shirt over blue jeans.

"Hi, I'm Takala," the young woman said.

Grace had told Jana about her on the drive over. She was Tuwa Waki's niece, a techno-wiz who majored in computer sciences. After a stint working in the information technology industry and quickly becoming disillusioned with self-serving ambition and consumerism, she returned to her tribal village to become the medicine woman's assistant. Takala ran Tuwa's website and managed her travels and appointments. Jana was a bit surprised that a Hopi medicine woman would have a website, but why not take advantage of modern methods of communication. Stranger things happened all the time.

Takala ushered Jana into the study while Grace settled down in the living room to read. The study was richly endowed with dark wood walls and polished bookcases filled with neatly arranged, old appearing books. There was a large executive desk in one corner, its gleaming mahogany surface reflecting the Tiffany lamp on one edge. But Tuwa Waki chose to sit in a small chair, one of a pair with burgundy upholstery trimmed in a golden fringe, flanking an oval table just large enough to hold her ritual implements and several small books. From this site the seated women looked out through two large windows, low to the floor in period style and reaching almost to the high ceiling. Across the veranda the view encompassed a well-tended lawn bordered by azaleas just starting to bud. One ancient oak tree, now devoid of leaves during winter dormancy, spread its massive branches over the lawn.

Tuwa Waki was very short and round. Her feet in soft, fringed leather shoes dangled from the chair, not reaching the floor. A cushion was placed below them for support. Her body and face matched in pleasing roundness; she wore a simple shift of peach tones embroidered with deeper pink and rose flowers around which twined green vines. A white shawl was thrown around her shoulders, and a large turquoise and silver necklace adorned her chest. Brown and weathered, her face had the typical high cheekbones and square jaw of desert southwest Indians. Crinkles formed around the corners of her black eyes as she smiled, revealing even white teeth with one gold crown. Black strands wove through her silvery-white hair that was styled in two long braids. She was old, but somehow ageless.

"We will smudge first," Tuwa said, her accent not very pronounced but detectable.

Jana stood as Tuwa got up and lighted a sage smudge stick. Using a hawk wing of brown variegated feathers, Tuwa fanned sage smoke all around Jana, first front then back, reaching up her full arms length to cover Jana's head, as the pungent smell of sage filled the room. She ended by tapping Jana's feet with the hawk wing, and indicated she should sit down.

Tuwa settled back into her chair, adjusted her feet on the cushion, and smiled at Jana warmly.

"What do you seek to know, my daughter?" she asked gently.

Jana paused for a moment, struck by the fact that two native women whom she didn't know called her daughter in the past couple of months. Maybe Tuwa called all her women clients daughter, Jana rationalized. But why would Angelina Menchu also use this term after the emergency room episode?

"Some unusual things have happened to me in the past few months," Jana began. "They all seem related, and appear to be giving me a message about something I need to do, but I can't figure it out. I need help understanding this."

"Tell me your story," said Tuwa.

Jana described the sequence of events starting with her recurring dream of the old woman's hand and the Maya connections that unfolded. She kept the retelling focused but included her physical and emotional sensations at the ruins, since they seemed so important. She ended with the old Maya man's warning and her subsequent illness.

Tuwa sat with eyes closed for several minutes after Jana finished. A few times she nodded, as though acknowledging some internal communication, making a clicking noise with her tongue at one point. Performing a subtle gesture with her right hand, her lids fluttered open and she gazed deeply into Jana's eyes for what seemed a long time before speaking.

"The old man is a Maya shaman," Tuwa said in measured tones that emphasized every word. "He is a brujo. His intentions toward you are bad. He aims to prevent you from doing what you must do. He will use strong magic if he needs to. There is danger for you."

Tuwa paused, watching Jana's response. A flicker of fear crossed Jana's face, quickly replaced by resolve.

"I thought so," Jana said. "I feel I must go forward. I am being called, I have deep connections with the Maya. Whatever I'm supposed to do, I want to do."

"Good, good," Tuwa murmured, her eyes momentarily gazing upward as if checking with an unseen force. She nodded several times.

"There is something Great Spirit wants you to do, to help the Maya people," she related. "A gathering that will not be complete without you, that fulfills a prophesy. This will heal the deep earth of the Maya and help bring harmony to the world. There are forces opposing this, forces of darkness that do not want the healing to happen. This is where the danger lies. You must call on your Spirit Guide for protection. Who is your Spirit Guide?"

Jana was taken aback. She remembered that Grace also asked her about spirit guides. But, she had not made contact with guides, at least not consciously. Quickly reviewing her relationship with deities, she realized her spiritual foundations were primarily Christian with a heavy sprinkling of Eastern philosophies, mainly Hindu.

"When you are in trouble, who do you say prayers to?" asked Tuwa.

"Jesus Christ," Jana said immediately.

"Good, The Christ is a powerful spirit being, one who upholds the light," Tuwa assured her. "He has said he will help those who call on him. Now you must tell him of your quest and the dangers. Ask him to protect you, he will know how. Do this every day, and when you sense danger, call on The Christ and feel that he is there standing next to you, walking with you."

Tuwa paused again, closed her eyes and appeared intently focused on an inner experience. Her brows furrowed, she made the clicking sound and nodded.

"There is another Spirit Guide here who will support you," Tuwa informed Jana. "She is Maya, she makes strong medicine. She wants you to know her, but she will not reveal her name to me. She says you must discover that for yourself." Nodding again, Tuwa continued: "She says she is always with you now, she is walking beside you. Call to her, even if you cannot speak her name. She is protecting you."

Jana nodded, feeling disconcerted by this new revelation. Having a female Maya Spirit Guide had simply not occurred to her. Somehow this put a more serious layer on her quest. She was indeed wandering into separate realities.

"Do you have questions?" Tuwa asked.

Sighing deeply, Jana hardly knew where to begin with her questions. A dawning awareness was creeping through her mind, however, that she would need to find answers to most of them herself.

190

"Can you say anything more about this gathering I am to attend?"

"It is in the land of the Maya," Tuwa responded. "It is happening soon. You will be given signs, you will know when the time comes. That is all I can say."

"For the next step, do you have any guidance?" Jana inquired hopefully.

Tuwa tuned inward for a moment, then laughed in delighted amusement. Her smile was contagious, causing Jana to smile also.

"Talk to my niece, Takala on the way out. She has some information for you. There is guidance from the Maya very close by here." Tuwa looked pleased.

Jana had no further questions. Her mind felt on overload, trying very hard to imprint Tuwa's specific words into her memory.

"Good, then come with me," said Tuwa, leading Jana out of the study into the adjacent room that Takala had set up as an office. A laptop computer and telephone on a card table, with a few notebooks and pads constituted the temporary office. Takala was concentrating on the computer screen, and did not notice them until Tuwa spoke.

"Ta-ka-la," she spoke each syllable distinctly. "Please show Jana the websites you found about the Maya schools."

The young woman looked up calmly, used to Tuwa's silent entrances and cryptic requests. Little explanation was needed, so closely attuned were the two Hopi women.

"Yes, please sit here." Takala indicated a folding chair next to the desk.

"My niece knows all about the new web," Tuwa said with a twinkle in her dark eyes. "The web that connects people all over the world. I know more about the web of Spider Woman, who wove the world into being. Takala will help you. May Great Spirit breathe the winds of good fortune upon you, and give you the eagle's vision for your quest."

As Jana expressed thanks, Tuwa silently ambled out of the room leaving the faint smell of sage lingering in the air.

Takala quickly brought up a website titled "Clearlake School of Maya Mysteries" on the computer screen. She wrote the *url* on a notepad and handed it to Jana. Fingers flying over the keyboard, Takala went to another site which featured a middle-age blonde woman next to a Maya pyramid, billed as a Maya priestess. Takala wrote this *url* on another notepad for Jana.

"You'll find these of interest," Takala said. "I think Clearlake is not far from San Francisco, yes? I'm not sure where the Maya priestess lives, you can find out from her website. There's a lot of information about Maya on the web, contemporary teachers and shamans. It's interesting that this ancient tradition is having such an upsurge through the modern communication medium of the internet. Check it out."

Jana thanked Takala for the websites and paid for her session with Tuwa.

On the drive home Jana told Grace the details, trying to repeat Tuwa's words precisely so she could remember them. Grace was excited about the further revelations Tuwa had given, and urged Jana to pursue the leads right away. Exchanging hugs as she dropped Jana off at home, Grace gave her a list of books.

Waving good-by, Jana walked slowly up her driveway looking at the list: Jose Arguelles, John Major Jenkins, Miguel Ruiz, Hunbatz Men, Victor Sanchez, Martin Prechtel, Douglas Gillette. Feelings of anticipation mingled with apprehension. A convergence was happening, a force unfolding that she sensed would change her life.

Another thought flashed through her mind:

Robert isn't going to like this.

Harry Delgardo's wiry form moved quickly down the tree-lined sidewalks of Mills College. Elbows lifting high and legs striding in his typical power walk, Harry covered the distance between Stern Hall and the Music Building in less than five minutes. The day was cool and overcast and the ground wet from recent rains, typical for February in the Bay Area. Bounding up entrance stairs and hurrying down the long dim corridor, he arrived at Robert's office just before the appointed time. He rapped twice on the door then entered to Robert's "come in."

The two professors often met for coffee and talks. Their friendship was a long one, and they shared many interests and viewpoints. Harry settled into the wooden chair next to the desk while Robert poured two cups of aromatic, hot coffee from a thermos. A small drip coffee maker sat in honored position on top of a file cabinet, with brewing paraphernalia and an airtight jar of ground coffee beside it. Robert would never chance being without good coffee, which was especially welcome on this cool day.

In contrast to the chaos of Harry's office, Robert maintained meticulous order in his space. Stacking inboxes held neatly arranged papers; only the documents he was currently working with sat on top the desk, which had ample clear area. Matching smoky gray desk organizers held a collection of pens, pencils, paper clips and a letter opener. Tall bookcases lining two walls were filled with books arranged by topic, standing properly in straight rows. A long, narrow window provided an angular view of trees and huge shrubs growing up the steep hillside behind the Music Building. A few pictures of Impressionistic art tastefully adorned the wall behind his desk.

Sipping black coffee, the men discussed campus affairs for a while. Election campaigns for academic senate members were underway. They reviewed qualifications of their respective department candidates and speculated about who might be elected as chairperson of the senate. In general, they held similar values about academic governance and found much accord in their views. As this conversation wound down, Robert broached the topic he really wanted to discuss with Harry.

"Harry, I'd like to get your perspective on something," Robert began.

"Sure, I've got opinions about nearly everything," Harry replied cheerfully.

"This is a little touchy, its about Jana," Robert said. "She's really going overboard on this Maya caper. In fact, she seems obsessed about it. She believes that she's got some kind of mission to carry out on behalf of the Maya—though she doesn't know quite what it is. I did tell you about our strange experiences in the ruins of Belize and Guatemala, didn't I?"

"Yes, you did," Harry replied. "I found them fascinating. Jana had several and you had one, as I recall."

"That's right. Her encounter with the old man in Tikal seemed ominous. So she found a Hopi medicine woman, with her friend's Grace's help. Grace is part Native American, and her mother has distant connections with the medicine woman's tribe. Anyway, the woman told Jana she had this mission to go to some Maya gathering in the near future, but there were dangers involved. The old man is supposedly a Maya shaman who's trying to prevent Jana from fulfilling her mission."

"Huh," Harry grunted, nodding in encouragement.

"Now Jana is setting up a trip to Lake County. She's meeting with people at this Clearlake School of Maya Mysteries. The Hopi medicine woman pointed her in this direction. Jana's supposed to be getting help from her spirit guides to keep her safe, according to what

193

she's been told." Robert paused, his brow furrowed as concern deepened his clear blue eyes. "Harry, I'm worried about this. Either Jana's getting too far out in metaphysical woo-woo land, or she's messing with supernatural forces that could be more than she can handle."

Harry sat back and stroked his chin thoughtfully, fingers hardly noticing the beard stubbles he had missed when shaving this morning. He was reviewing what he knew about tribal magic and shamanic practices.

"Indigenous people still retain strong belief in non-physical realities, a spirit world populated by both good and evil beings that often interfere with human affairs," he commented. "Central and South Americans often seek curanderas, or medicine women, for healing illness and get shamans to perform divinations about upcoming events, or to intercede with the spirit domain. They do believe there are evil shamans who can create problems or illnesses. One thing is called 'mal ojo' or evil eye—they cast a spell by using certain ways of looking at you. These people's health and lives are actually affected by their beliefs about such things."

"Like voodoo for the Haitians?" Robert asked.

"Very similar," Harry confirmed. "It's a common belief system held by the group. You know how strong beliefs are, how the mind can affect the body. There are many scientific studies that support this. For instance, medical students preparing for a difficult exam were found to have a drop in their level of white blood cells. They had less immune resistance and caught colds more easily. The whole placebo effect is created by what people believe and expect to happen. Even when taking the fake pill, their symptoms improve. When drug companies do clinical trials to get approval for new drugs, they claim success when the actual drug performs 10% better than the placebo. Pretty astonishing, eh? The power of the mind."

"Yeah," mused Robert. "But I thought you had to be part of the tribal tradition for these kind of beliefs to work. Some Haitian medicine man can stick pins in an effigy of me all day long, and I don't have any effects unless I believe in the system."

"That's what we usually think," Harry said. "But I wonder. Faith healers often say people don't have to believe in faith healing for their practices to work. There are lots of examples of that, where a person's relatives asked for healing without the patient's knowledge, and the disease disappears. And, you've got to take into account that Jana does believe in shamanic processes. She's open to it. That no doubt provides a doorway for these metaphysical things to occur."

"Harry, you're not being very reassuring," Robert complained. "I get the impression that you give credence to this interaction between the spirit and physical worlds."

"All I can say, as an anthropologist, is that I've seen too many examples of the connection to completely discount it," Harry replied.

Robert reflected for a few minutes, his reverie soon interrupted by a coughing spell. He still had lingering chest congestion from his post-trip illness.

"Still haven't completely cleared out that flu," he remarked. The cough caused him to refocus and continue pursuing the topic of healing.

"Speaking about illness, Jana would say that whenever something like energy healing takes place, it's by agreement of the person's higher self. Even if the person isn't consciously aware of what's happening, his higher self knows and interacts with the higher self of the healer. So, there's a type of consenting, of inviting these unseen energies that cause cellular changes and heal the illness. I'd venture to say Jana believes everything that happens to us is because in some way we've drawn it to ourselves. She doesn't think things happen by chance, she sees virtually everything as having some meaning in a vast interconnected cosmic web. It's frustrating, Harry, because she's sure there's an important message in her experiences and feels she is obligated to follow through, wherever that may lead."

"And you're worried about what she might run up against," Harry reiterated. "Or maybe about her mental health."

"I don't think Jana's going crazy," Robert said. "She's functioning normally and what she says fits into her belief system. I guess I'm becoming more convinced about these paranormal forces than I want to admit. People get really sick, disappear, or even get killed on strange adventures. That's what I'm concerned about."

"Have you told Jana this?"

"Not in so many words. I need to do that. But honestly I don't think my concerns will deter her. She's so independent—and incredibly strong-willed when her mind is made up," Robert said with a touch of sadness.

"Yes, so is Rita," Harry agreed with a sigh. "We're both married to some pretty assertive women. Now that I think about it, seems they're all that way. My female students are anything but retiring violets. Must be a sign of the times."

"The restoration of gender balance and the righteous end of the patriarchy, Jana would say," Robert observed wryly.

Both men sipped coffee, lost in thoughts about their immutable wives.

"What if she knew how much it meant to you, for her to stay out of danger?" Harry ventured.

"Maybe . . . I don't know," Robert admitted. "She will probably think I'm making more of it than I should. And maybe I am over-reacting. But, I will tell Jana more clearly about my concerns. Thanks for talking it over with me."

Harry nodded and the conversation turned back to campus affairs. They discussed a graduate student who was having problems with his thesis research; both professors were on his thesis committee. After about ten more minutes, Harry bid good-by and left. Robert sat musing at his desk, staring out of the window at the damp foliage made darker by the cloudy day and low angle of the winter sun. He coughed a few more times, bringing up a little mucus. The lingering cough annoyed him; usually he recovered quickly from colds. His inner sense of discomfort was greater than he had expressed to Harry. Ever since the incident at the North Acropolis in Tikal, he had felt very uneasy about the Maya quest that was compelling Jana ever more deeply into ancient mysteries—with contemporary consequences.

*   *   *   *   *   *

The day was gray and blustery. A cold north wind whistled through bare branches reaching like skinny fingers into the leaden sky, while heaving bushes scraped against the walls of the house. Spurts of rain spattered against windowpanes in synchrony with bursts of wind. Jana snuggled under a throw blanket on the couch, surrounded by a large collection of Maya books. She balanced a yellow lined writing pad on her lap, taking notes. Flickering flames from the gas fireplace gave a warm glow to the room and added welcome warmth.

The next three days, which Jana had off from work at the emergency room, were her window of opportunity to delve into Maya cosmology. Robert was away at a meeting and the weather kept her inside. Time like this to go deeply into something was precious. In addition to reading both archeological and metaphysical books, she would spend time meditating and contacting her guides.

The poetic, sonorous opening of the *Popul Vuh*, translated by Dennis Tedlock, ushered in the mystical story of Maya beginnings:

Now it still ripples, now it still murmurs, ripples, it still sighs, still hums, and it is empty under the sky. . . There is not yet one person, one animal, bird, fish, crab, tree, rock, hollow, canyon, meadow, forest. Only the sky alone is there; the face of the earth is not clear. Only the sea alone is pooled under all the sky; there is nothing whatever gathered together. It is at rest; not a single thing stirs. It is held back, kept at rest under the sky. . . Whatever might be is simply not there: only murmurs, ripples, in the dark, in the night.[7]

In this serene stillness of sea and sky, creator gods brought forth the "sowing and dawning" in the darkness before creation: The Maker and Modeler, Sovereign Plumed Serpent of blue-green quetzal feathers, the Bearers, Begetter from the water joined forces with The Heart of the Sky, Thunderbolt Hurricane, peering out from swirling clouds and lightning. Their words and thoughts started the process of creation.

The gods spoke the words that brought forth the earth, forests and mountains from the all-encompassing waters. They gave the animals homes. But when they asked their creatures to praise them, to tend shrines, make offerings and live by the sacred calendar, all that came forth were howls, screeches and squawks.

The creator gods tried again, making beings from clay, but their soft bodies crumbled and melted away in the rains. Frustrated, they consulted an old couple, grandfather Xpiyacoc and grandmother Xmucane. Where the old ones came from remains unanswered; they predated the creator gods. Mayanists thought they represented the cosmic god Itzamna and his consort, the great mother goddess Ix Chel.

The old ones were the primal diviners, the original shamans and daykeepers. They sought omens, then advised the gods to make people of wood. But the wood people were brittle and stiff, they did not pray to the gods in the required manner. The angry gods destroyed

[7] Tedlock, D. (1996) *Popul Vuh:* The Definitive Edition of the Mayan Book of the Dawn of Life and the Glories of Gods and Kings. Simon & Schuster, New York.

them with a great flood and fearsome monsters; the remnants of the wood people were left as forest monkeys.

Interesting, Jana thought. *The impious people were destroyed by a flood.*

She reflected on similarities of this creation myth to Genesis of *The Bible*. Both began with a void, a stillness that existed before the world came into being. Then the creation deities spoke a word and held a thought, this initiated the process of creation. A word was a sound, a vibration, it was movement. In Genesis, God's breath moved across the waters. In the *Popol Vuh*, the water was removed from earth like a mist when the gods said "Earth." In both stories, the creatures and plants of earth were made first, then people were added. The Maya gods wanted people to "name now our names, praise us . . pray to us, keep our days," and Jehovah created people who were "made in His image and likeness. . . to glorify the Lord." Early attempts at making proper people failed, and floods were sent to destroy them.

The story told in the *Popul Vuh* was long and convoluted. Harry Delgardo had given Jana some of the basics, but now she appreciated the rich metaphor of the tale. Though the surviving version was written in the mid-seventeenth century, she could see how Maya beliefs were reflected in its pages. The Quiche Maya preserved the story during the Spanish conquest, when nearly all the Maya codices were burned. Bishop Diego de Landa led the destruction of these books containing knowledge "from the Devil." A few Quiche were taught the alphabet, and wrote out a phonetic version in the Mayan language. This work was translated into Spanish by friar Francisco Ximenez in 1701-1703. The precious document is now housed in a Chicago museum.

The Quiche people still live in Guatemala, Jana reflected. Close to one million speak this distinct dialect. Their predecessors who preserved the story noted they were writing "amid the preaching of God, in Christendom now." They asserted that their own gods accounted for everything as enlightened beings, in enlightened words. What the Quiches wrote down was the *Ojer Tzij,* the "Ancient Word" that was prior to the Christian god's teachings.

Jana found it hard to grasp all the innuendos and twists of the *Popul Vuh's* plot. Like any oral tradition with ancient roots, much was no doubt lost over centuries of transmission. The Quiches regarded the book as a "seeing instrument" that guided them in overcoming nearsightedness imposed by the gods. Using this

"Council Book" they recovered the vision of the first humans, people who could see the four corners of earth and sky, read the signs, see what would happen perfectly. It enabled them to know whether there would be war, death, famine, quarrels.

According to the *Popul Vuh*, the world now is in its fourth creation. The fourth attempt of the creator gods was successful, but two generations of heroic deities had to struggle with malevolent forces to prepare the world. Two sets of twin brothers, the sons and grandsons of the old couple, contended with the Lords of Death, the Xibalbans. The Death Lords challenged them to play ball on the court of Xibalba in the Underworld. The first set of twins was killed, but the head of One Hunaphu was hung on the calabash tree. It spit in the hand of Blood Moon, daughter of a Xibalba lord, as she examined the odd fruit. Blood Moon became pregnant, though she denied having known any man to her furious father. Condemned to death by the Xibalbans, she was rescued by owls that substituted a lump of copal for her heart. She was taken to the old couple as their daughter-in-law. After fulfilling an omen, she gave birth to the second set, called the Hero Twins: Hunahpu and Xbalanque.

This wily pair took up the ball game again, but outsmarted the Lords of Death. They surmounted a series of trials using trickery. Their greatest trick was bringing each other back to life, after one twin severed the head and cut out the heart of the other. The Lords of Xibalba went wild at this, demanding the twins perform the feat on them. The twins happily obliged, but would not revive the Death Lords afterwards. Triumphing over death, the Hero Twins declared that henceforth the Xibalbans must be satisfied with sacrifices of copal and animals; and they could only attack humans who were guilty of evildoing.

That's interesting, Jana thought. *Here's another parallel to the Bible.*

In the Old Testament, Jehovah tested Abraham's commitment by requiring the sacrifice of the patriarch's only son, Isaac. Although he dearly loved his son, Abraham prepared to carry out what the deity ordained. Human sacrifice must have been an established practice in his culture for Abraham to follow this order without protest. At the last minute, just as Abraham's knife was about to slice Isaac's throat, Jehovah stayed his hand. Since Abraham had demonstrated his obedience, he was allowed to sacrifice a goat instead of his son. The Hebrew deity was satisfied with the lesser offering, as were the Xibalbans after the Hero Twins' victory.

The Hero Twins performed one more feat to usher in the Fourth Creation, or Fourth Sun. They had to set things right in the celestial realm. One of the stellar gods, Seven Macaw or *Wuqub Kaqix*, was aggrandizing himself, claiming to be both the sun and moon. But he was a false deity, not the true solar god. The twins battled with his sons the crocodile monster and earthquake, and then shot down Seven Macaw from high in a fruit tree where he was eating and preening himself. They used blowguns, breaking his teeth off and dislodging metal discs around his eyes. His earthly descendents became scarlet macaws, and he became the Big Dipper, whose decline across the night sky marks the hurricane season and symbolizes his fall from power.

The stage was now set for successful creation. The Hero Twins revived their fathers: One Hunahpu became the Maize God or First Father of all humans, Seven Hunahpu embodied the veneration of ancestors. Using white and yellow corn from a sacred mountain, ground into meal by old Xmucane, the cosmic midwife, the creator gods brought forth proper humans. Having finished their job, the Hero Twins rose into the sky as the Sun and Venus. There for all time, in the cycles of these stars, they re-enact their epic descent into the Underworld, to emerge again in the metaphorical triumph of life over death.[8]

Maize God and Hero Twins

The goal of all spirituality—eternal life, thought Jana.

She studied a picture she had seen in several Maya books. The striking image was painted with delicate precision on the interior of a Late Classic pottery bowl. One Hunahpu/First Father was depicted as the Maize God, with distinctive jewelry and corn foliage headdress emerging from the split shell of a turtle, representing the surface of the earth. The Maya called their land Turtle Island, Tamaunchan. On

---

[8] Ancient Maya names for the Hero Twins were Hun Ahau and Yax Balam.

either side the Hero Twins administered to the Maize God, Xbalanque pouring water from a large ceramic jar and Hunahpu offering a gift (its details had been worn off). A glyphic skull below the crack in the turtle's shell indicated that the Maize God was emerging from the Underworld.

Hunahpu. Hunab K'u.

Jana remembered that name from Hunbatz Men's book on Maya science and religion. Hunab K'u, the primary deity of contemporary Mayans, is called the "Giver of Movement and Measure." It must have derived from Hunahpu, the Solar God. This Maya Supreme Being is the architect of the universe and father of humanity, a cosmic force symbolizing form and energy, soul and spirit. The god is represented by the geometric form of a square within a circle. K'u also means pyramid. Hunbatz Men explained that humans have pyramidal energy because molecules of water, which constitute 75% of human bodies, have triangular-pyramidal structure.

Jana thought of pyramids as vortices of energy, used in Egypt, India and the Far East for initiations and sacred ceremonies. Mystical experiences inside pyramids were reported by many people over untold eons of time. She and Robert had powerful experiences at the Maya pyramids in Tikal. Did their human molecular structures strike a resonance with stone pyramids to create portals, liminal spaces?

Jana yawned, uncurled her legs and stretched. She needed some hot tea and a little exercise, for she had been sitting a couple of hours, engrossed in her studies. The rain was steady now, beating upon the roof relentlessly. After doing a few leg stretches and yoga poses, Jana sipped her favorite Bengal Spice tea. It's heady aromas of cinnamon, ginger and cardamom caused tingling sensations in her nose, and provided comforting warmth in her throat. Staring out of the breakfast nook window, she watched the rain making puddles on the patio stones. She reflected on the relationship of gods and humans.

The Maya view that the spirit world and the human world were interconnected fit better with her own beliefs than the prevailing western view. Even religious people, including most in her Unitarian church, saw God as existing in a separate domain, somewhere far above. Although one could pray and ask for help, and sometimes God responded, everyday life went on in secular fashion with little thought of the influences of spirit beings. Certainly very few people tried to have direct communications with God or spirits, and even fewer listened for an answer.

She returned to the couch and read a paragraph from Mayanist David Drew's book, which captured the essence of Maya beliefs:

> For they saw no real distinction between an everyday "natural" world in which humans lived and a "supernatural" world of gods and spirits. Indeed the universe as a whole appears to have been conceived in ancient times as one continuous existence in which all things, animate and inanimate, visible and invisible, were charged to a greater or lesser extent with what is commonly defined as a kind of sacred "essence" or energy.[9]

To the Maya, every person, animal and structure on earth was imbued with spiritual potency. Their word *k'ulel* best conveyed this idea, translated as "holiness" or "sacredness." A common title found on stelae and pottery is *k'ul ahau* or "holy lord." This sacred essence was most potent in the blood. It would not be an exaggeration, Jana concluded, to say the ancient Maya were obsessed with blood and the heart. At some point in their social evolution, despite the decree set by the Hero Twins, the Maya developed the practice of offering human blood to the gods.

To sustain their existence, the Maya people constantly praised the gods and nourished them. In return for maize and water, animals and plants that supported human life, the Maya had to fulfill a covenant with the gods that bound humans and the divine order together. People were created from and are seen to be, literally, what they eat: maize and water. Mayas made offerings of maize and other valuables, but the sacred gift of blood, which made life possible, was most precious.

That humans depend on the gods is an easily understood concept. It's central to most religions. But that the gods needed humans—that was radical.

For God to need humans was foreign to Christian thought, where God was viewed as transcending creation, complete, perfect and needing nothing. Eastern spirituality was closer to Maya views; many myths related how various gods needed human assistance and attention. To the Maya, humans actually sustained the gods. Without this human exchange, the very existence of gods and the world order

---

[9] Drew, D. (1999) *The Lost Chronicles of the Maya Kings*. University of California Press, Berkeley, CA.

would be threatened. In this process of reciprocity, recycling the substance of life, feeding the gods so they would be able to provide for humans, the whole order of the universe was maintained.

A thought bubbled up in Jana's mind: The Maya gathering that she was supposed to attend, that would not be complete without her, perhaps this was to fulfill some covenant with the Maya gods. Just possibly it was needed to help maintain the order of the universe.

Whoa, gal! Her Observer chimed in. *Don't be getting grandiose on us now.*

OK, Jana replied mentally. *So what do you want me to make of all these unusual, metaphysical experiences? Didn't Tuwa Waki give me a pretty clear message?*

She got into these internal dialogues fairly frequently. People might call it talking to yourself, but for Jana it was having a communication with other aspects of her consciousness. Sometimes she dialogued with the Higher Self, a part of her being with an expanded view that provided spiritual direction. At other times, however, the dialogue could be with archetypes such as her Inner Critic or her Saboteur, or simply doubts and fears speaking up to hold her back. The Observer was usually neutral, a part of her awareness that stood aside, watched and commented, kept her in balance.

Go inward, the Observer advised. *You will know the truth there. Keep the mind from too much speculating.*

Jana had to agree this was good advice. She planned to meditate later that day, around dusk, which was a good time to slip through the veils between the worlds. For now, she continued the inquiry into Maya spirituality.

The Maya's entire environment was imbued with spiritual energy. Certain features of the landscape possessed formidable powers. Water and caves were magical places, thresholds to other domains. Offerings were made in cenotes and caverns; archeologists found huge caches of everything from precious stones and pottery to human bones in pilgrimage sites. Mountains were potent places to contact the spirit world. Pyramids were symbolic mountains; observatories for celestial progressions and sky platforms for vision quests. Animals became uayob or naguals, giving humans extra abilities. Most powerful were the jaguar, cayman, snakes and birds of prey. Maya elite, those with very strong blood, invoked jaguar powers by wearing costumes or images of the fierce spotted cat.

The sky, sun and moon, stars and planets contained the greatest sacred essence. The Milky Way had special significance, since the dark rift was an entryway into the Otherworld. At the heart of our galaxy was the Central Sun, around which the Milky Way spun. This great "white road" across the sky was an umbilical cord between Earth, the Upperworld and the Underworld. It was depicted in Maya art as a double-headed serpent, whose markings represented celestial bodies. In ceremonies, Maya kings carried a serpent bar to symbolize their ability to travel to the Milky Way in visions. The Milky Way stood for the "World Tree," the axis of the Maya world, the giant ceiba that the gods used to raise the sky from the ocean at the moment of creation.

The god of the Central Sun, the Galactic Center, was Itzamna. This high god of ancient origin was the creator of the universe and archetypal shaman, the most important of a number of creator gods, and the source of writing and learning. His wife Ix Chel, "She of the Rainbow" was associated with healing, medicines, childbirth, and mothering energies in all aspects of earth life. Contemporary Maya saw Hunahpu/Kukulkan, the Solar God, as the son of these two.

The Holy Family again! The real Trinity: God the Father, Goddess the Mother, and the Son who "saves" life on earth.

Coming to grips with the Maya pantheon was challenging, Jana realized. They had a diffuse concept of divinity, one not easily categorized. Sacredness was a widely dispersed phenomenon: Deities often were personifications of natural forces such as lightning, rain and storms; they could represent divine qualities and powers, or might be deified spirits of important ancestors. Their sheer volume and changing expressions were daunting. As elusive and multifaceted as Hindu divinities, Maya gods and goddesses had both human and animal characteristics, possessed many and often diametrically opposed aspects, could be benign and malevolent, male and female, young and old, with different forms by day, night or season.

The idea of the one in the many, part of eastern philosophy, best enabled Jana to relate to this profusion of divinities. Some archeologists and metaphysical writers suggested that all the Maya deities represented different facets of a divine oneness at the heart of Maya religion. This yin and yang coexistence of opposites was helpful in dealing with the perplexing ambivalence in Maya spirituality—one Maya god or goddess could reconcile, within its own manifold nature, fundamental dualities. The balance of dualities seemed a key principle of Maya thought; the continuity of all life was dependent on this coexistence of opposites. Ultimately, the life of the Maya people depended on death—a cycle which, if successfully negotiated, led to eternal existence as an ancestor-god or a stellar being.

Dualities and cycles. The good hidden in the bad. Cycles of creation and destruction. Interweaving dimensions of multiple realities.

Jana felt oddly comforted by images of a vast cosmic clock, arms sweeping endlessly around, metamorphosing into a sphere that exploded into billions of scintillating sparkles, each birthing new universes.

The Maya fascination with time and its cycles intrigued Jana. She knew that calendars governed all aspects of Maya life. Her talk with Harry Delgardo provided a quick overview of the main calendars: the Tzolk'in 260 day sacred cycle that guided life day by day, the solar calendar of 360+5 days connected with the Tzolk'in in 52 year cycles, and the Long Count calendar based on multiples of 20 that could be permutated for cycles lasting thousands or millions of years.

Everything functioned in cycles, according to Maya thought. Astute astronomers, their observations of the movements of stars and planets revealed recurrent cycles, a cosmic order that was predictable according to time parameters. The stellar patterns progressed over long time periods, while solar and lunar patterns followed shorter cycles. But, everything recurred, came around again, to repeat the pattern. If the structure of the universe revealed itself in this way, as an endless process of repetition, then surely the affairs of humans and gods must follow the same course.

Keeping track of time was of utmost importance to the Maya. The Daykeeper, who tracked time cycles and offered divination according to the calendars, was highly honored in both ancient and contemporary Maya cultures. By following calendars precisely, people had information to anticipate and prepare for events. This allowed them to maintain proper relationship with the gods and the universe. In patterns of the past they found guidance for the future, from both celestial events reflecting acts of the gods and earthly occurrences that signaled sacred power. All things would recur in their appropriate time cycle.

Where did their knowledge, their ability to track incredibly long time cycles with unerring precision come from?

Several of Jana's sources pointed to the Preclassic city of Izapa as the source of Maya calendrics. Such a sophisticated reckoning as the Long Count must have taken hundreds of years to develop, so its

205

origins stretched into the distant past. Near Izapa, the earliest glyphic evidence of Long Count calendar use was found. Izapa is a large site about 50 miles from the Pacific Ocean in Chiapas, close to the Guatemalan border. Most of its monuments and carved stelae date from 300-100 BCE. Prototypes of the World Tree, the rain god Chak, and images from the Popol Vuh legend are found in Izapa. The major ritual center during its time, Izapa defined art styles and cosmological ideas for later Maya sites, drawing from Olmec antecedents. It appears to be the birthplace of the Hero Twin creation myth, for it contains the first archeological record.

Izapan astronomer-priests are credited with making the astronomical discovery of the precession of the equinoxes, and doing calculations on which the Long Count is based. According to this calendar, the present great cycle, the Fourth Sun, began on August 11, 3114 BCE (counted as 0.0.0.0.0 by the Maya) and will last for 5,125 years.

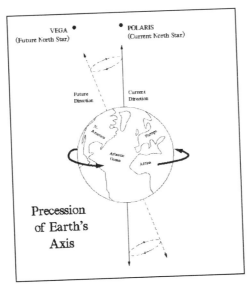

Each great cycle or Sun has 13 baktuns; each baktun is equivalent to 395 years. Astronomical information encoded in Izapan monuments points at the important alignment of the 13th baktun—the end of the 13-baktun cycle of the Long Count, known as the Maya calendar end date: 13.0.0.0.0 or December 21, 2012 CE.

The precession of the equinoxes!

It seemed incredible to Jana that the ancient Mayas had knowledge of a phenomenon that took nearly 26,000 years to complete its cycle. How could they have known this? She wondered if they had been watching the sky for untold eons, developing a sophisticated understanding of unbelievably long stellar movements, or if other advanced beings had given this knowledge to the Maya.

The Hindus also knew about the precession, she recalled. Their great cycle of four yugas or ages, each with ascending and descending phases, also lasted 26,000 years. She read an obtuse book by the Indian sage Sri Yukteswar called *The Holy Science*[10], most of which was way over her head. But she did get the basic principle that the world went through ascending ages when human consciousness was steadily increasing, leading to a golden age at the apex, then descending ages when humans gradually lost their exalted state and deteriorated into materialism, violence, brutality, fear and survival mentality. After the lowest ebb, a gradual increase in consciousness, creativity and compassion began with the next ascending cycle. The Hindus believed that great avatars or saviors took incarnation on earth during the darkest era to help humans remember their true birthright as children of the Divine.

And, we're just past the lowest point now, she thought wryly. *The world certainly seems a place of chaos and violence, though we've got strong forces for unity and peace.*

Jana was certainly no adept at astronomy, so she pulled out a book to review the basics of precession:

The precession of the equinoxes, also known as the Platonic Year and the Great Year, is caused by the slow wobbling of the Earth's axis. The Earth's wobble causes the position of the equinox sun to slowly precess westward against the background of stars, thus the term "precession of the equinoxes." . . . Modern astronomers estimate the full cycle of precession to be between 25,600 and 26,000 years. The Maya estimate of precession, if we assume that five Great Cycles (65 baktuns) were intended to represent a full precessional cycle, is 25,626 years.[11]

---

[10] Swami Sri Yukteswar (1984) *The Holy Science.* Self Realization Fellowship, Los Angeles, CA.

[11] Jenkins, J.M. (1998) *Maya Cosmogenesis 2012: The True Meaning of the Maya Calendar End-Date.* Bear & Company Publishing, Santa Fe, New Mexico.

In other words, Jana surmised, the North Pole gradually rotated as the earth changed its tilt in a long, slow circle. If you stood on the North Pole and pointed your hand directly up into the sky, the Pole Star would change during the precession cycle. Right now the earth's axis drawn through the North Pole pointed to the star Polaris, but 5,000 years ago it pointed to Alpha Draconis and by 11,000 CE it will point to Vega. Obviously from the southern hemisphere of earth, the South Pole axis would be pointing to a different set of stars.

The other truly amazing piece in Maya calendrics was the correspondence of the 13-baktun cycle with a rare astronomical alignment due to occur in 2012 CE. On the winter solstice, December 21, the sun will rise directly through the center of the Milky Way, where the dark rift is found. To the Maya, the dark rift was the birthplace of the sun, as represented in their World Tree symbolism and told in the Popol Vuh creation myth. This convergence of the solstice sun with the dark rift of the Milky Way occurs only every 5,125 years, the Maya Great Cycle. The rebirth of the sun ushers in a new age, a new Sun according to Mesoamerican people.

Milky Way-Sun Convergence

The significance of the Maya calendar end date was emphasized in the books by Arguelles, Jenkins and Men. It means the end of the present era, the close of two great time cycles. In 2012, both the Great Cycle and the Precession of the Equinoxes will be completed. Some people feared this implies the end of the world. But, the Maya worldview of recurring cycles pointed instead to the birth of a new age. This understanding was expressed by contemporary Maya shamans. They said the earth was moving into the 5th Sun, or fifth great era in Mesoamerican cosmology.

But the present world situation points to disaster. We're poised on the brink of war that could ignite global destruction. Will we make it through to the new age? Was it necessary once again to cleanse the earth of degenerate peoples?

Jana sat for a while, reflecting on these dismal thoughts and Maya predictions of huge upheavals at great cycle endings. She lost track of time, until a cramp in her leg that was folded underneath brought her attention back to present. She stretched her leg and rubbed the achy calf muscles, noticing that it was almost dark outside. The rain continued steadily, with occasional bursts of wind whistling around eaves and through branches. She stood up, extending arms above her head and arching her waist in a slow rotation.

I'd better do my meditation now, Jana thought. *It's nearly dark.*

She settled onto her meditation cushion in front of the small altar she maintained in one corner of the bedroom, lighted two votive candles and an incense stick, and took several deep steady breaths. After a short prayer of invocation, she focused on the breath moving in and out through her nostrils, stilling her mind by reciting the "Hong-sau" mantra. These Sanscrit words represented the sounds of incoming and outgoing breath, and translated as "I am that," serving as a reminder of unity with Spirit. A deep sense of calm descended, surrounding and filling Jana. It was welcome after the intense activity of her mind in study and analysis.

She set her intention. Carefully, she formed a request in her mind:

Let me understand more about my mission with the Maya.

Then she called upon her spirit guides:

Lord Jesus, the Christ Consciousness, bringer of pure unconditional love, be with me in this quest. Surround me with your light, your aura of protection, in all that comes. I want only to serve the highest good. Blessed Mary, Divine Mother, bring your grace and compassion to your daughter, enfold me in your arms of safety. Guide me in wisdom and right action. Aum, Shanti, Amen.

Jana felt another feminine presence as she invoked the goddesses. It was a subtle sensation hovering at the fringes of her awareness, not taking form, just an undefined presence. She held her attention steady, but nothing more definite emerged from this presentiment. Gradually the sensation dissipated.

Some time passed, she could not tell how long. Aside from an occasional thought straying into awareness, which she quickly dismissed, her mental field felt still, void, dark, empty. Then the

209

images began to appear. Vague and wispy at first, they moved gradually into better focus. Faint nondescript sounds slowly increased until she could hear the cries and wails of voices, dropping into piteous moans and rising to terrible shrieks. Images played across the inner screen behind her closed eyes, disturbing, confusing, chaotic. A wide river flowed between steep gorges, rocky and stark. She seemed to be flying and swooped over the river as a hawk might. A yellow-green, thick liquid languidly flowed in the river, lapping against rocky banks, creating clusters of festering bubbles—a river of pus. Soaring over the gorges, she had a bird's-eye view of the dark, dreadful place that seemed bone-chillingly cold, despite fitful fires flaring here and there in cavernous gaps. Torrents of blood cascaded down jagged cliffs, forming glowing red pools in crevices between boulders. Faint human-like figures were barely visible through fog and smoke. They waved arms in distress, some bent over under an unseen burden, others writhing on the rocky ground. Many corpses were strewn about, in various stages of decomposition or dismemberment. A terrible stench filled her nostrils along with a feeling of vast despair.

The sharp smell jerked Jana out of the imagery. Eyes flying open, Jana saw that an ember from the incense had fallen on the wool scarf she used as altar decoration. Quickly she pinched out the ember, but the acrid smell of burning wool persisted. Jana blinked several times, shaking her head to clear it. Involuntarily a deep breath shuddered through her lungs, which seemed hungry for air. She realized she had been holding her breath.

What was that imagery all about? Jana wondered. It was very disturbing, bearing close resemblance to what she had read about the Maya conception of Xibalba, their Underworld ruled by the gods of Death. But it was so real; she felt she had actually been there, although viewing it from high above as an observer, not immersed in it. She had the sense that the suffering beings trapped in that awful place were Maya, and somehow she needed to help them.

Jana felt saturated and overwhelmed. She had to back away from the intensity of her involvement for a while. Her stomach growled and she realized she was very hungry and thirsty. It was time for dinner and a break. She did an ending prayer and thanked her spirit guides for being with her.

*   *   *   *   *   *

"Hi, Mom, I'm here," called Marissa's melodic voice as she dropped two bags of groceries on the kitchen counter. "I picked up the powdered sugar and cream cheese that you wanted for Dad's cake. I got some extra raisins, too. Can't ever have too many raisins. Lousy weather, when's this rain ever going to stop?"

"I'll be right out, Butterfly," Jana replied from the bathroom. Butterfly was the nickname her parents had given Marissa when she flitted around from flower to flower in their summer garden as a toddler.

Marissa was home for the weekend to celebrate Robert's birthday on February 28. They teased him that he could have kept himself 25% younger by being born one day later, on leap year, so he would have a birthday just once every four years. They were baking a carrot cake, Robert's favorite, for the birthday dinner tonight.

Jana came into the kitchen, hugged Marissa, and the two women put groceries away and organized ingredients for making the cake.

"How's school?" Jana asked, as she added grated carrots into the wet ingredients. Marissa was combining the dry ingredients in another bowl.

"Asi, asi," Marissa used the Spanish phrase meaning "so-so." She was a Liberal Arts Major at University of California, Santa Cruz, and had taken two years of Spanish. Often she and her mother spoke Spanish to each other just to keep in practice. "My far eastern history class is pretty interesting. Chinese dynastic politics make Europe look tame. The noble warrior mentality sure crosses cultural boundaries. I wonder why acquisition of wealth and territory has been such a powerful motivator for ruling classes throughout history."

"More is good, the bigger the better," Jana quipped. "Get enough stuff, and you'll be happy."

"The American mantra," observed Marissa sardonically. She chopped walnuts as Jana combined wet and dry ingredients for the cake batter.

"It doesn't work," added Jana.

"So I've observed," Marissa said, adding walnuts and raisins to the cake batter with a little more vigor than necessary.

"Careful, you'll over-stir the batter," advised Jana, ever observant in the way of mothers and health care professionals.

Marissa sighed in mock exasperation, tossing her blonde curls and rolling her brown-flecked tawny eyes. She stood her full height, half a head taller than Jana with a slender well-proportioned frame inherited from her father. She shot a knowing look at Jana, having learned some time ago to allow her mother's advice-giving penchant to roll off her back. Over-reacting simply led to arguments, a waste of energy and a formula for frustration. She stirred the batter gently to mix in the raisins and walnuts, then poured it into the prepared rectangular baking dish Jana was holding.

"The Warrior is certainly a universal archetype," Jana said, picking up the conversation's theme as she put the cake in the oven. "But it serves people well when its energies can be harnessed and directed toward goals. I'm sure I've got a Warrior archetype, and so do you. I try to have the Peaceful Warrior on lead."

"Speaking about warriors and war, things are really heating up on campus around the Iraq situation," Marissa said. She washed up the bowls while Jana sat at the breakfast nook table. "Most of the kids are incensed about the idea of a pre-emptive war. It's invading a sovereign nation without just cause. There was a protest vigil at the student union a couple of days ago."

Jana had read about the President's proposal to send American troops into Iraq searching for weapons of mass destruction supposedly possessed by Saddam Hussein and the Iraqi military. Although given broad authority by Congress to take protective action should the U.S. be threatened, the evidence of danger was shaky.

"He should wait for more data from the U.N. weapons inspection teams," Jana said.

"Yeah," agreed Marissa, who shared her parents' liberal views. "In any case, going into Iraq should be a joint effort involving U.N. leadership. Unilateral action by the U.S. just isn't acceptable. We've never been an aggressor nation like that—though we've done a lot of meddling in other nations' affairs, I regret to say. Do you know about what the U.S. did in Guatemala in the fifties? I know you're interested in that part of the world now."

Jana looked up quizzically, her interest clearly evident.

"Tell me," she said.

"After decades of oppressive dictatorship, Guatemala finally had a reasonably fair election and put a progressive guy in office," Marissa related. "He actually created a democracy and was making all kinds of reforms, especially economic changes to help the poorest strata of society, the rural Maya people. A few Communists were elected to the legislature, however. This made the U.S. administration nervous, Eisenhower was in the White House and the Cold War was hot. It was scary to the huge American-owned United Fruit company that made a killing by paying rock-bottom wages to the poor plantation workers, mostly Mayas. United Fruit got worried that their land might be confiscated by the Guatemalan government. They put

212

pressure on our government to protect their interests, and the CIA backed a coup that assassinated the Guatemalan president."

"No!" Jana exclaimed, frowning in disbelief.

"Yes-s-s," Marissa spoke slowly to emphasize this truth. "Then a time of chaos followed, while the U.S. made sure the next president would be more sympathetic to their financial interests, and not allow any Communists in government. And you know that more decades of violence and guerilla warfare resulted, up until very recently. It's a sad story."

"That's terrible," Jana said. "We shouldn't be messing with other countries' governments like that. I understand that things are a little better in Guatemala now."

"I think they are," agreed Marissa. "Now our government's attention has shifted to the Middle East. We're serving the interests of the oil industry and the military, no matter what reasons President Bush might drum up for invading Iraq. You know, there's a lot of concern that this hot spot may launch us into World War III. Some of my friends are in a state of deep despair, alternating with outrage that our government would place the entire world on the brink of nuclear disaster."

Emotion played across Marissa's face, darkening her eyes.

"I know, Butterfly," Jana said, shaking her head sadly. "I don't understand it myself, and I share your worries. It's a hard time to be growing into adulthood. The world feels like such an unstable place."

The two women made tea and sat in the breakfast nook for some time, sharing their thoughts about the world situation and making suggestions about using prayer and heightened consciousness to shift global energies. They reinforced each other's hopes that it was indeed possible to counteract destructive forces with higher vibrations of love and compassion.

The carrot cake was a stupendous success. Rich, moist and bursting with flavor, it's dark interior framed with creamy white icing, the birthday cake was pronounced by Robert as the absolute best yet. They sipped water-processed organic decaf French roast coffee with the cake. Robert blew out the all candles, and then had a coughing spell. His chest congestion from the infection following the Belize trip still had not cleared up, though it was nearly one month. Jana made a mental note to set up a doctor's appointment if the cough lingered for another week.

The parents caught up on their daughter's school activities and interests, gently probing into any signs of romantic involvement.

213

Tossing her blonde curls, Marissa skillfully parried their inquiries and provided just enough information to satisfy them without revealing too much. It was a game they were all familiar with, knowing each other's strategies. Underlying the exchanges was a sense of respect, for Marissa had shown herself to be a level-headed young woman, capable of making intelligent choices.

The overhead light sparkled off a row on tiny multicolored ear studs lining the upper curve of Marissa's left ear. In both ear lobes she wore dangling earrings with similar tiny stones at the ends of three long gold prongs, and her right upper ear sported two ear studs. She also had a naval ring with a small pearl, often visible between hip hugger jeans and a midriff length knit shirt in the common style of her generation

"Are those new?" asked Robert, gesturing at the row of left ear studs "How many do you have there? Five? Six?"

"Five," replied Marissa, "and they are sort of new, I got them done about 2 months ago. Nifty, huh?"

"That's a lot of ear piercing," commented Robert.

Jana took a careful look, wondering why she had not noticed them earlier.

"Do they ever get infected?" Jana asked with mild concern. She had seen some badly infected body pierces in her nursing work.

"Not if you take good care of them," Marissa answered. "You know, alcohol or peroxide swabs and keeping the area clean. Its really not that hard to do."

"Hmm," said Robert, deciding not to pursue the topic. He really could not understand the attraction of body piercing.

Jana was interested because of Maya practices, piercing ears and nose for body adornment in a more flamboyant style, as well as ritual piercing for bloodletting.

"What does the body piercing mean, Butterfly?" she asked with genuine interest and no hint of judgment.

Marissa sensed her mother's sincerity and responded in like manner.

"Well, I guess it's a way of group identification," she offered. "It gives an outward sign about being part of a certain value system, a way of thinking. Such as, the body is beautiful and the jewelry enhances that. Like celebrating ourselves and not being ashamed of our physical nature. Modern society is so schizophrenic, its full of shaming messages but then uses blatant sexuality to sell everything from shaving lotion to cars. Maybe the young people's body

214

adornment is trying to express a more natural approach to sexuality, it's just a normal part of life, so get comfortable with it and make smart choices."

"That makes sense," said Jana. "Body piercing does cross sociocultural lines, and even age groups, though mainly it's done by young people."

"Body decorating also includes tattoos," Marissa added. She had a small butterfly tattooed on the outside of her left ankle. "And dress styles are statements of group identity, tastes shaped by trends in a given culture. I studied quite a bit about that in sociology classes."

"Yes, these things are tribal statements, ways to mark someone's identity with particular groups," Jana observed. "Do you think body piercing has any spiritual dimensions now? Spiritual meanings were important in these practices among ancient cultures."

Marissa thought for a moment, and then shook her head.

"No, I don't think so," she said. "At least not directly. Tattoos might do this more, some are pictures of deities or religious symbols like the cross, six-pointed star or celtic knot."

"And they're not done in a ceremonial way," Jana added. "Not in the context of a spiritual tradition, as indigenous people did."

"Like the Maya?" inquired Marissa. She and her father had discussed this new pre-occupation, and she was aware of his concerns.

"Yes, the adornments were deeply symbolic of their cosmology, worldview and religious belief system," Jana replied. "Their body piercing was for spiritual purposes."

"So, Mom, what's with this Mayan fascination?"

Jana hesitated. This was delicate ground. She glanced quickly at Robert through the corner of her eyes. He was assiduously maintaining a neutral expression, though she recognized traces of concern in the subtle deepening of the crease between his eyebrows.

"It's a little hard to explain," she began. "I'm not sure where it's actually coming from. A series of events happened that all kept pointing me toward the Maya. Then this fascination—that's the right word—just welled up inside and I've been compelled to learn everything I can about them. I feel a connection with the Maya people, their ancient civilization. Maybe it's related to a prior incarnation."

"Like karma playing out in this lifetime?" Marissa held similar views to her mother's about reincarnation and karma.

215

"It does feel karmic," Jana said. "And I sense there is a purpose, something I have to do in relation to the ancient Maya, but also connected with the current world situation. I'm still vague about what exactly."

"Do you expect your trip to Clearlake to shed light on that?" Robert chimed in.

"What are you going to do in Clearlake?" asked Marissa.

"There's a School of Maya Mysteries in Clearlake," Jana explained. "I've talked to the people there, and they invited me for a weekend. It's a special program, the Maya teacher they're affiliated with is coming. I'm hoping this will shed some light on what I'm supposed to do."

"Is this teacher a modern shaman?" Marissa queried.

"I think so. I've never heard of him before. His name is Hanab Xiu." She pronounced the name phonetically: "Hahn-ab Shoo."

"I have misgivings about this, Jana," Robert said gravely.

"Yeah, Mom," added Melissa in support of her father. "Those shamans can do strange things, like witch doctors. I don't know much about the Mayas, but didn't they do pretty awful things, like human sacrifices and cutting out people's hearts?"

Jana sighed. Her heart felt wrenched between love for her husband and daughter, recognizing that their concerns were both valid and coming from their love for her, and the deep sense of mission she had regarding her Maya quest.

"I know you're both worried," she said. "There are a lot of unknowns. But I don't think it's that risky. When you're doing what you're called to do, Spirit protects you."

"Yeah, like Joan of Arc," observed Marissa. Then she added quickly, "Just kidding, Mom. Don't take it seriously."

Both Jana and Robert appeared lost in thought. Jana was sure they were sharing the same one: fulfilling your mission was no guarantee of safety or happiness, at least not in this world.

Jana felt the need to shift the energy of their conversation.

"Hey, you two, lighten up," she said, smiling. "Good things are coming from contemporary Maya shamans. We really need the indigenous people's wisdom about living harmoniously in the world right now."

Turning to Robert, she requested:

"Sweetheart, could you pour us some more coffee?"

Robert smiled, obligingly retrieved the coffee carafe and poured three cups of the mellow aromatic brew.

Marissa watched her father, admiring his handsome appearance and vigorous body movements. When he smiled, the left corner of his mouth curved slightly more than the right, and activated a hint of a dimple. She had always thought his smile was exceptionally attractive, and the subtle dimple made it irresistible.

"More cake, anyone?" she asked teasingly.

"I'm stuffed," said Jana.

"It was delicious, but I'm too full," Robert seconded.

"Good things from the shamans, Mom?" Marissa said, picking up the conversation and cutting herself a small piece of cake.

"Yes, teachings that help people stay centered and connected with all life," Jana said. "Ways to know yourself deeply and respect spirit in nature. Like Don Miguel Ruiz' book *The Four Agreements*. Didn't you read that, Marissa?"

"I did," said Marissa, washing down cake with a gulp of coffee. "They were good principles, lets see . . . Don't take things personally, be impeccable with your word, don't make assumptions, and always do your best. Is that right, Mom?"

"Perfect!" Jana exclaimed. "Similar ideas were expressed in Hanab Xiu's website."

"Modern shamans have websites?" marveled Marissa.

"Oh, yes, most I've heard of use electronic communications," said Jana. "No reason why they shouldn't take advantage of the web that links the world. It's actually quite in keeping with their beliefs that everything is interwoven in one vast unity. But, they probably use a web of consciousness to connect with people who are receptive."

"So what are some things Hanab Xiu says?"

"Well, according to the Maya calendar the earth is in the last decade of a great cycle," Jana related. "The cosmic alignments are promoting global shifts in human consciousness as well as earth changes. People must learn the ancient wisdom that teaches alternate ways to relate to nature, so that body and spirit can live harmoniously on the sacred earth. Technological cultures are so disconnected that they actually destroy nature. We're all entwined within the web of life, so whatever we do to this web we do to ourselves. This course of destruction has to change."

"We can all agree to that," said Robert, listening with renewed interest.

"And," Jana continued, "the sacred Maya sites are being reactivated. People are gathering and doing rituals to shift political systems and personal religious beliefs that are damaging to the planet.

217

The Maya teachers who know the ancient mysteries have been called to come forth and lead this movement. They also say we need to become more aware and integrated as individuals. Certain shamanic practices are taught that tap into the forces of nature, and use these to support spiritual growth."

"Wow, that sounds pretty powerful," observed Marissa.

"Yeah, it all sounds positive," Robert added, looking a little puzzled.

"I feel that it is positive," Jana said. "The message of modern Maya teachers, as best I understand at present, doesn't seem to fit with the constant warfare and emphasis on blood sacrifices that the archeologists report about the ancient Maya. I've run across some evidence that earlier Maya culture, before the Classic period, was not involved with war and had a life-enhancing spirituality. I wonder what happened."

"The fall into darkness," Marissa ventured. "The degeneration of great civilizations that has happened over and over again throughout history."

"You may be onto something," Jana said thoughtfully.

The evening ended pleasantly as conversation drifted off to more mundane topics. The parents enjoyed spending time with their lively and intelligent daughter, laughing at her stories of professor antics and classmate foibles. Before going to bed, Jana made a mental note to check the incongruities she was finding about the Maya with Francine Rappele.

Jana and Francine had set up a private on-line chat room, so they could respond in real time to each other. At the specified time for their on-line dialogue, Jana logged on and posed her questions.

J: In the Maya sites from the Early and Middle Preclassic, there is no indication of warfare and human sacrifice. The social structure seemed egalitarian and honoring the gods was done with things like incense and gifts of jewels and pottery. What happened to cause the violent practices that were common from the Classic period on?

F: The basic cause was the institution of kingship. This was a social innovation that appeared in the 2nd or 1st centuries BCE, during the Late Preclassic. Some of the earliest evidence we have of a stratified social structure with buildings designed for high ritual are from sites such as El Mirador in the Peten and Cerros in Belize. The records in Cerros are particularly interesting because this city embraced kingship with enthusiasm for a few generations then gave it up suddenly, returning to their former lifestyles as fisherfolk and farmers. There are signs of deliberate "termination" of the temples built by kings. Power held in these sacred mountains was released systematically through smashing rituals.

J: Why did the people of Cerros decide to institute kingship?

F: The theory is that the Maya were facing cultural tensions that threatened to tear their society apart. Such forces as trade with distant cities, raised-field agriculture and extensive water-management systems created prosperity in regions with the means to organize the necessary labor pool. This led to a wealthy class, those who reaped the rewards of abundance. Trading partners who were already kingdoms, such as Teotihuacan and the Oaxaca Zapotecs from México, brought ideas of rank and privilege to the village Maya. These forces upset the Maya system of social egalitarianism, where accumulation of wealth was considered an aberration. The institution of kingship, the high ahau, was a way to make social inequality legitimate, necessary, and intrinsic to the proper order of the cosmos.

J: How did the people actually benefit from having kings?

F: The king became like the pinnacle on a pyramid of people, with his nobles or ahauob forming the next section and the common people forming the base. Everyone was an integral part of this structure, and the king's glory reflected on the lowest as well as highest in the kingdom. The person of the king was magical, a sacred conduit to the Otherworld, an embodiment of the gods. He became the means of contacting the dead, the honored ancestors, and even the means of surviving death itself. He brought spiritual guidance for conducting everyday life, from planting and harvesting to influencing illness and health. His expertise brought favorable trade agreements, he read the signs of the heavens about when to make war or maintain peace, and what allies to seek. The farmers, masons, stoneworkers, craftspeople and fishermen who paid tribute in goods and services to the king were compensated by his giving them a richer, more enjoyable, more cohesive existence.

J: So they benefited spiritually by the king's influence with the gods and materially by sharing the fruits of wealth and power.

F: Yes. This social innovation led to the brilliant culture, vast cities and soaring pyramids that were typical of Classic Maya times. But the people, nobles and commoners alike, had to be consenting for this form of government to work. Maya kingdoms never maintained standing armies or police forces to coerce people into obedience. The charisma of the king was important, but kings needed to perform

219

effectively to keep the social order going. Their performance was measured by the abundance of crops, prosperity of trade, health of the people, and victory in battle. Maya kings always faced the possibility of some kind of failure that would bring down their dynasty. Much of the public art was deliberate political propaganda, often created to deal with difficulties arising from such failures.

J: How did kings come to Cerros?

F: We read the evidence from buildings, symbols on stucco panels, and burial caches. There is very little written text, so we use carved glyphs associated with masks and frescoes. But the full meanings elude us. Given that caveat, here's the story as archeologists understand it:

Around 50 BCE the community of Cerros, located at the mouth of the New River where it empties into Chetumal Bay on the eastern coast of the Yucatan Peninsula, began a revolutionary program of building broad plastered plazas and massive temples that literally buried their village. They built new homes in a 160-acre halo around the new city center. The first temple, called Structure 5C by archeologists, was built right on the water's edge oriented to the south. The masons at Cerros probably learned how to build this low pyramid from sojourns at other cities. Each level of structure was ritually consecrated. Four elaborate panels flanked the long stairs up to the temple, two on each side. Huge masks decorated each panel, the lower two are the Jaguar Sun God, the east mask denoting the rising sun and the west mask the setting sun. The upper two are Venus as Morningstar on the east and as Eveningstar on the west.

The path of the sun and of Venus traced an arc over the temple where the king stood during rituals, easily visible from the plaza below. On the top platform, there were once four tall carved posts representing the supernatural trees at the four corners of the cosmos, holding the earth and sky apart. The symbolism of this temple evokes the Maya creation myth of the Hero Twins. The older brother, Hun Ahau was linked with Venus, and the younger brother, Yax Balam, was linked with the sun. These ancestral twins are the prototypes of kingship. When the Cerros king stood on the stairs between the four great masks, he represented both the cosmic cycle of day and night, and the lineage cycle of the Hero Twins as founding ancestors of the Maya people.

J: Are those the same as the Hero Twins in the Popol Vuh, called Hunahpu and Xbalanque?

F: Yes. Hun Ahau and Yax Balam are ancient Maya names, while Hunahpu and Xbalanque are names in the Quiche Maya language.

J: So suddenly around 50 BCE a king was put in office in Cerros?

F: We don't know exactly how that occurred, but Linda Schele and David Freidel give a fascinating account of how it might have happened in their book, *A Forest of Kings*.[12] They spin a tale about visiting traders arriving in 40-foot canoes hewn from single massive tree trunks, being welcomed by Cerros elders and townspeople who had been waiting their arrival. Leaders of both groups gathered for an all-night banquet with rituals and a lavish feast.

Late at night the patriarch of the visitors brought forth a headband of fine cotton, onto which were fastened four stones of glowing green jade carved in the images of gods. A fifth jade piece, larger than the others, was a pendant worn on the chest. These jade jewels were actually excavated from a temple at Cerros. All present recognized these as the jewels of a high ahau, a king. They were potent symbols to sanctify ahau rank, assert the inherent superiority of their wearer, and transform a noble into a divine being who can control natural and spirit forces.

The principle patriarch of Cerros stepped forth to claim the jewels, while the other nobles present silently raised their right arms across their chests and clasped their left shoulders in a reverent salute. This event, carefully planned and approved by leading families of the village, was a deliberate step to establish Cerros as a kingdom. It gave their city a more exalted presence among the other powerful city-states emerging in the wetlands of the interior.

J: Interesting. Cerros simply decided to have kings. But you said it didn't last long.

F: That's right. There were 3 or 4 generations of kings, then Cerros ritually terminated the temple complexes they had built and went back to village life, living in the outskirts of the central city area. Again, we don't really know why but can speculate. Kingship was a new system, there may have been problems in transfer of power between generations. A weak king without much charisma would not be tolerated long. The people might have become disillusioned with this novelty, finding their former way of life preferable. We know the

---

[12] Linda Schele & David Freidel. (1990) *A Forest of Kings: The Untold Story of the Ancient Maya.* William Morrow and Company, Inc., NY.

city did not collapse under some disaster, since people continued living there for a long time after. They just opted not to continue with kings.

But the mold had been set. The social vision of a high ahau as the core of his city-state, with massive architectural monuments and public ceremonies, continued to spread and endured nearly 1,000 years. It was the most geographically widespread and long-lasting form of governance in the history of Mesoamerica.

J: Before the institution of kingship, there was a highly developed, spiritual culture exemplified by the city of Izapa. I've read that the Long Count calendar and Hero Twin creation myth originated there. What do you think about Izapan cosmology?

F: That's a big subject, but I'll give you my thumbnail sketch. Izapa was one of the most prominent ritual centers during the 1st century BCE. Evidence of settlements at Izapa date back to 1500 BCE. By 400 BCE as the Olmec civilization had faded, Izapa had entered the forefront of Mesoamerican culture. Situated along ancient trade routes that connected central México with Chiapas and the Guatemala highlands, Izapa was literally in the middle of everything. It was the transitional culture of its times, drawing from the Olmecs and Zapotecs, and feeding the emerging Maya. Mayanist Michael Coe credits the Izapans with invention of the Long Count calendar, and it surely influenced cosmological beliefs throughout Maya civilization.

It was fortuitous that Izapa's monuments were found almost exactly as they were left some 1,900 years ago when explorer Robert Burkitt stumbled upon this ceremonial city of ancient sky-watchers in 1924. Izapan beliefs about the connections between astronomy and human life were expressed undisturbed in these monuments—stelae, altars, thrones, buildings such as temples and ball courts—that told the story of the Maya creation myth and its esoteric meanings. They revealed knowledge of vast astrological cycles and the precession of the equinoxes.

The monuments and buildings at Izapa were spatially related to astronomical patterns. One group of monuments aligns with a cleft in Tacana volcano to the northeast, where the December solstice sunrise occurred. The concept of mountain clefts is central to Maya ideas about the birth of Hun Hunahpu, the solar or Maize God. Tajumulco volcano, home of the ancient Fire God, looms farther east-northeast, and a group of monuments is oriented to its peak where the June solstice sun rises. Facing south, as dawn approaches, the Milky Way becomes visible. The Izapans calculated that over the next millennium, precession would bring the solstice sun ever closer to the center of the Milky Way, the dark rift. The dark rift is considered the birth canal of the Cosmic Mother. Several stelae tell of the eventual union of the Solar God, Hun Hunahpu with the Cosmic Mother as precession brings the winter solstice sunrise in alignment with the dark rift of the Milky Way.

Is this addressing your questions? Am I getting too obtuse?

J: It's all helpful. What I'm trying to grasp is how the Classic Maya civilization diverged from the original cosmology. It seems that the cult of kings led to warfare and blood sacrifice, and the eventual Maya downfall. But didn't their interpretation of spirituality also change?

F: Izapa had a more pure version of the purposes of Maya life and how the skies mirrored the principles that were central to their spirituality. The old polar deity who proved to be a false god, Seven Macaw, was represented by the Big Dipper in alignment with the north pole star. This was the configuration at the dawn of Maya civilization. The Izapan astrologers knew that the Big Dipper would precess away from the polar north, and thus Seven Macaw would "fall from his perch" revealing his falseness. The Hero Twins accomplished this by shooting him down, preparing the way for the true Solar God, First Father, One Hunahpu. When the equinox precession brought the sun and dark rift of the Milky Way into alignment at winter solstice, the creation deities—First Father and Cosmic Mother—united to bring forth a new age.

Each new age ushers in a higher level of human consciousness. After five cycles of 5,125 years, a Cosmic Cycle is completed as the equinox precesses back to its starting point; that occurs about every 26,000 years. The Izapans had calculated this timing precisely, and knew it would occur in 13.0.0.0.0 or 2012 CE by our calendar. Izapa was an initiation site, a Mecca for learning the new religion. It was a training place for priests and priestesses, and sent them out to teach all across Mesoamerica. But, as Izapa was waning in influence, the social innovation of kingship was arising. No doubt the co-opting of spiritual functions by the kings reduced the power of priests, and thus of Izapa. Somehow the view of the sacred function of shaman-priests, to keep tract of celestial events and use ritual to ensure their successful integration on earth, was distorted to serve purposes of empire building.

J: What happened to the original deities, those that preceded the creation myths, such as Itzamna and Ix Chel?

F: They lost power after kings claimed the sun god K'inich Ahau as their special patron. I believe the old religion continued in pockets throughout Classic and Postclassic times. The cult of Ix Chel always seemed present, especially as patron of healing arts. One Hunahpu as the Maize God is frequently depicted in art and carvings, remember he is a manifestation of Itzamna.

J: The practices of bloodletting and human sacrifice became associated with worship of K'inich Ahau?

F: So it appears. Blood was the most precious commodity the Maya had to offer, and the heart was absolutely central to their value system. Blood was the greatest offering they could give to cultivate the favor of K'inich Ahau, to draw Otherworld powers to the kings and nobles. Once this practice was observed to bring victory, wealth and power to one city, the others naturally took it up. So blood rituals became widespread as Maya city-states expanded and jousted for dominance. But the countdown to the Maya end times continued. The Long Count calendar relentlessly ticked forward and cycles kept repeating. Some Mayanists believe the rapid overtaking of the Mexican and Mayan peoples by the Spaniards was due to a prediction that just such a thing would occur at that time. The Maya culture, its wisdom and mysteries would then go underground for centuries and be revived just before the end of the Cosmic Cycle.

J: And that's precisely where we are now, right?

F: Exactly. This is the final decade before the end of baktun 12, the completion of the 13th cycle. The Long Count will roll over. We are in the Maya end times.

The long winter rains had finally stopped, leaving the fields soggy and tree trunks dark with moisture. A few green sprouts along the edges of the road hinted that spring was about to awaken. Puddles still covered the highway here and there, causing passing cars to throw a spray on the windshield. Jana periodically turned on the car's windshield wipers to clean away the spray, leaving streaks that caught the sunlight in the late morning. She was glad to see the sun. Its warmth against her cheek was welcome, and she rejoiced in the glistening droplets hanging onto branches and leaves. The cool air was bursting with the freshness of ozone, invigorating and full of promise for renewed life.

Twisted, gnarly grapevines wove together in neat, parallel rows, acre after acre. Their hypnotic symmetry flowed over flatlands onto gentle hillsides of the fertile Napa Valley, one of California's most famous regions for producing varietal wine grapes. A long string of wineries flanked Highway 29, which made a nearly straight line from the city of Napa at the valley's south end to Calistoga at its north end. Some were venerable wineries, their massive stone walls covered by ancient vines and surrounded by mature trees and shrubs; others were austere new structures of brick or wood siding with a few struggling plants bordering small concrete parking lots. It seemed to Jana that there were several new wineries every time she drove through Napa Valley.

She planned to stop for lunch in Calistoga, before braving the narrow winding road up to the plateau where Clearlake was situated. This weekend she was meeting with Aurora Nakin Hill, the Director of the Clearlake School of Maya Mysteries, and attending a class given by the Mayan elder Hanab Xiu. She was both excited and apprehensive. This weekend promised great insights into her Maya mission, but the specter of shamanic danger and Robert's misgivings hung uneasily around her. He had not exactly said he didn't want her to go on this trip, but that was the underlying message in his cautions about the drive.

Watching the bucolic Napa Valley landscape glide past, Jana took inventory of her values and the events that had brought her to this time, this moment, driving down Highway 29 en route to the Clearlake School of Maya Mysteries. She did believe the planet Earth was facing difficult times. Industrialized societies with their technological lifestyle were rapidly degrading the environment. There was a big hole in the ozone layer, resulting from petrochemicals, that increased the exposure of earth's surface to ionizing radiation. As huge expanses of forests were cut for farming and lumber, carbon dioxide levels were building. These along with environmental pollutants were creating a greenhouse effect, causing average temperatures to rise. The polar ice caps and glaciers were melting and raising sea levels worldwide. Warmer oceans interfered with plankton life cycles and disrupted marine ecosystems. Species were rapidly dying off as their environmental niches were destroyed by climate changes, pollution or development. These disruptions of nature were causing weather aberrations and earth changes, increasing the frequency of earthquakes, volcanoes, fires and floods.

And that was just the effects of technological civilizations on the environment. The propensity of humanity to engage in war now posed the real threat of global annihilation. Nuclear and biological weapons were more powerful and sophisticated than ever before in history. More nations possessed these arsenals. International accords for peace appeared to be shaky, and the United Nations seemed unable to move countries toward an enduring state of tolerance. Use of violence between long-embattled countries did not appear to be abating; the Middle East remained a powder-keg ready to explode. And now the U.S. was on the verge of invading Iraq on the premise that it possessed weapons of mass destruction that might be aimed against us. The Bush administration was impatient with the United Nations weapons inspections teams, and might not wait to build an international coalition to take action against Iraq. In the aftermath of " 9-11"—when the twin towers of the World Trade Center were destroyed as two airplanes crashed into them, hijacked by terrorists on a suicide mission—fear of terrorism had clouded the judgment of many Americans, and the President was being given a far too free hand.

Not to mention diseases, the new plagues, for which medicine had no effective cure: AIDS, Ebola and West Nile viruses, multi-drug resistant tuberculosis, Hepatitis C, and deadly influenza that might erupt into a world epidemic. Meanwhile the rich kept getting richer and the poor farther from a decent life, despite the capacity of developed nations to produce enough food and materials to alleviate most of the world's poverty.

It was quite a list, Jana reflected. Just tallying global problems was enough to make one feel hopeless and depressed. But, she did believe that a change in global consciousness was in process; that the

226

potential existed for enough humans to shift their values so these destructive forces could be stopped. This was often a topic her women's group discussed, and she knew each woman as an individual tried to live in ways that supported the environment and peace. The human potential movement and New Age philosophy both promoted the view of planetary unity, of bringing greater balance and harmony to the world so all people could have their basic needs met and find opportunity for growth. Internet based prayer groups such as World Puja coordinated peace vigils and prayer sessions that encircled the globe. Numerous organizations fought on their particular fronts to bring balance and justice—environmental watchdogs, human and animal rights groups, political activists, those who brought appropriate means and technology to villagers to alleviate poverty, humanitarian medical teams, food banks, and many more.

Now a new idea had dawned through her Maya experiences. There might be other ways that people could help avert global disaster and support world harmony. By tapping into a different level of consciousness, those doing sacred ceremony at power sites around the earth might be playing a critically important role. She was aware of some power sites, such as Sedona, Arizona and Mt. Shasta, California that were supposed to be portals to other dimensions of existence. Each part of the world had its unique power sites, such as the high mountains of Tibet and the much disputed center of three major world religions, Jerusalem. Though not aware of Mesoamerican power sites before, her reading had confirmed several especially potent Maya ruins, including Chichén Itzá, Tikal, Uxmal and Palenque.

According to the Hopi medicine woman Tuwa Waki, Jana was being called to a gathering in the land of the Maya in fulfillment of a prophesy. This involved doing sacred ceremony to heal the deep earth and bring harmony to the world. Hopefully her trip to Clearlake would reveal more details. She thought about the Maya spirit guide who was now with her. Although Jana tried to contact this guide during meditation, so far nothing had transpired. She was hoping that other pieces of the puzzle would fit together at Clearlake, including information about current Maya spiritual groups and deeper understanding of her mission.

We are in the Maya end times. Francine Rappele's last communication in their chat room session was emblazoned in Jana's mind. In this final decade leading to 2012, many changes were expected for the world. The Maya were not alone in these predictions. Among fundamental Christians, the end times were also supposed to occur around the millennium change. Many had dug underground shelters and stocked up on food, water and arms in anticipation of chaos at Y2K, when 2000 rolled around. But most end-timers admitted the dates could be a little off, and Armageddon might be a few years into the new century. They believed the world was now in the time of the Tribulation, and looking at world conditions, Jana had to admit they certainly had a point.

These are the times that try men's—and women's—souls, Jana thought, paraphrasing the famous quote.

The Hindu tradition in India also earmarked the present time as one of great transition, give or take a few hundred years. Depending on whose yuga cycle you followed, 2000 CE was either the ending of the lowest age, Kali Yuga, or was partway into the next ascending age, Dwapara Yuga. An important shift happened around the end of the 20th century, when the avatar of the new age mounted his golden throne pulled by seven horses. In fact, the Indian spiritual master Satya Sai Baba had done just such a ceremony a few years ago, Jana recalled. This was expected to bring about an upswing in human consciousness, leading to cessation of war and moving toward the golden age of universal enlightenment.

I'll go for that! Jana thought. *But we're not there yet. The choices people make collectively will determine whether the shift of the ages takes place with worldwide devastation, or with less drastic earth changes.*

The last part of the drive down Highway 29 to Calistoga went quickly, so involved was Jana in her musings. She turned onto Calistoga's main street, enjoying the quaint shops, art galleries, bookstores and restaurants. Calistoga was world famous for its spas and mineral springs, a Mecca for health-conscious bathers since the late 1800s. She and Robert had been there many times, relaxing in hot mineral tubs, steaming in mud baths, and luxuriating in soft blanket wraps after rejuvenating massages. Catching the smell of food, Jana realized it was noon and she was hungry. She stopped at a juice bar and ordered an avocado-Swiss cheese sandwich and a blueberry-banana smoothie.

The juice bar was busy with the lunch trade, filled almost to capacity by a colorful assortment of people. Most were wearing contemporary California casual clothing, with knit shirts hanging loosely over stone bleached jeans. Even in cool weather, the younger generation sported bare midriffs displaying their pierced navels under bulky sweaters. Older folks were dressed more conservatively, although one gentle-looking elder woman with soft gray hair cascading down her back looked like a latter-day hippie. She wore a long full multi-colored skirt and over-blouse with lacy trim accentuated by a profusion of beaded necklaces.

The murmur of voices filled the small room. Jana perched on a stool looking out the front window at the main street, watching interesting people walk along sidewalks outside. Her senses seemed heightened, enhanced by the bright sunshine and clean fresh air after the rains. Just as she finished her sandwich, she heard the pealing of a distant church bell. The clear high ring riveted her attention. Despite the buzz of activity around her, she felt immediately drawn into the stillness of her inner core. Her heart vibrated in resonance with each ring of the bell. Tilting her head slightly, she tried to locate the direction of the sound, but could not get a good sense of it.

Without thinking, Jana knew she had to find the source of the church bell. As the last peal faded away, she had a distinct sense of being summoned. Bussing her dishes automatically, she approached the young man behind the counter. After waiting a few minutes for him to finish taking a customer's order, Jana got his attention.

"Those church bells that were just ringing," she said. "Where are they coming from?"

"Oh," said the young man, thinking for a moment. "Yeah, there's a Catholic church a couple of blocks away."

"How do I get there?"

He looked slightly quizzical at the urgency of her request.

"When you go out the door, turn left and go to the end of the block. Then turn left onto the first street, its just two blocks from the intersection. You can't miss it."

"Thanks," said Jana, quickly turning toward the door.

Although the sun was bright in a nearly clear blue sky with a few puffy white clouds, the air was brisk. Jana pulled her sweater tighter and walked rapidly following the young man's directions. As she walked, a vague sense of being accompanied by a presence entered her awareness. Something seemed hovering just behind her right shoulder. Closing her eyes for a couple of steps, Jana received a flashing image of Jesus Christ.

My spirit guide is with me, Jana thought. Then she sensed another presence just beyond her left shoulder. Closing her eyes again, she focused on the feminine presence, unable to get a clear image. But she had to keep her eyes open to walk.

I wonder if that's my Maya guide. Still concealing her identity.

After the first block, she saw a small wooden church on the right side of the street. It had a white bell tower in classic chapel style with a four-cornered turret. Openings at the top displayed a modest sized brass bell. A short flight of steps led to the double doors into the church. Jana hesitated a moment at the doors, then grasped the right door handle. The large door opened silently, admitting her into a semi-dark vestibule. Another set of more elaborate double doors with stained-glass windows opened into the chapel.

Jana walked across the tiled vestibule floor, her steps echoing softly. She peeked through the stained-glass windows. The wooden pews in parallel rows beside the central aisle were empty. Cautiously she opened the door and went inside, quickly glancing around to be sure she wasn't disturbing some function. Both walls had tall, narrow stained-glass windows depicting various scenes from the life of Jesus. Filtered light cast a warm glow of mixed colors into the room. The smell of candle wax filled Jana's nostrils, igniting a deep sense of recognition, of familiarity. Images flooded her mind of earlier experiences in Catholic churches from childhood. Raised Protestant, Jana had several grade school friends who were Catholics; she went to church with them on occasion. Now memories revived with surprising intensity: Soaring cathedral walls with ornate stained-glass windows and intricate carved ceilings, clanking incense holders swinging on golden chains as priests walked down the aisle, candles flickering on altars emitting their aromatic waxy fumes, sing-song recitatives in sonorous Latin, exquisite organ chords and choir harmonies filling her with the mystical presence of a vast, regal god adorned in satin and velvet robes.

She had loved the pomp and high ritual of Catholic mass. It was ever so much more fascinating than her rather austere Protestant services. Catholic ritual spoke of mysteries, of spiritual secrets that led to deep inner communion, of esoteric wisdom accessible to elite initiates. That attraction was also a repulsion; for she had observed the soul-deadening effects of a male priest hierarchy, a huge wealthy institution driven by self-preservation, and rules that forced people to use an intermediary to access God.

Returning to the present, Jana sat down in the last pew and closed her eyes. Again she felt the profound inner silence of her deep core. She focused on her breath and meditated for a few minutes, feeling the two subtle presences just behind her shoulders. They seemed to be putting gentle pressure against her shoulders, as if to propel her forward. She opened her eyes and looked around again. A dark wooden confessional booth was against the back wall to the left of the door. On either side of the altar at the front of the chapel there were typical statues, one of the famous Pieta with Mary cradling the limp form of Jesus after removal from the cross, her face a study in compassion. The other was a saint in robes holding a large rosary, but Jana did not recognize him. In front of each statue was a rack of flickering votive candles, recent offerings made by visitors.

She looked carefully at the central altar platform for the first time. It was elevated by three wooden steps. Against the back was a carved wooden portico holding cases that contained objects for communion, the chalice and hosts. Two tall silver candelabra with unlighted candles graced the corners. A simple wooden pulpit stood at the left side. Her eyes were drawn to a small center pedestal halfway between the portico and steps. Bringing the small red object on the pedestal into focus, her eyes widened in amazement.

It was a Red Madonna. The small statue, only a foot and a half tall, was clothed entirely in red with gold trim. A tiny white face peered out from under a red veil that draped over her shoulders and fell to her feet in soft folds.

Jana had never seen a Red Madonna before. All the statues and paintings of Mary she was familiar with portrayed the Mother of Christ clothed in blue and white. Her eyes riveted on the statue, Jana felt drawn out of the pew by a strong magnetic force that pulled her irresistibly toward the Red Madonna. In a trance, she moved up the center aisle to the foot of the altar steps. Automatically she dropped to her knees, feeling an overwhelming sense of sacredness emanating from the statue. Eyes cast down, Jana muttered an inchoate prayer to all forms of feminine divinity: Divine Mother, the Great Goddess, Mary full of grace, Quan Yin, Isis, Astarte, Gaia, Cerridwin, Ix Chel.

After a few moments, Jana opened her eyes and gazed reverently upon the Red Madonna. A small gold crown was perched on her head, matching the embroidered gold trim on the edges of her rich red velvet veil and gown. Her cupped hands resting at midline just below her waist held a small golden globe covered with incised symbols. The white porcelain face appeared almost translucent, red lips formed in a sweet smile and blue eyes gazing into the distance as though contemplating something far away.

Queen of Heaven and Earth.

Jana heard this phrase as clearly as if someone had spoken it nearby. She could not exactly say she had thoughts, but these ideas swirled inside her awareness:

This is the representative of The Goddess, she is calling me to her service, she is the Queen Mother of All, she is the Divine Feminine in her regal form. She is blessing me on my mission. She is initiating me into this sacred service. I am hers.

Kneeling with closed eyes, Jana sensed an enormous presence far above her head. It seemed dome-shaped like a great umbrella, and slowly descended until it completely surrounded her form. As the umbrella came closer Jana felt increasing pressure against her body; a force that pressed steadily against her skin but also exerted pressure sensations inside her head and chest. She did not experience it as unpleasant, rather the power of this vast alive intelligence created a sense of amazement and awe.

Time passed and gradually the umbrella-dome dissipated. Jana opened her eyes and stared transfixed into the Red Madonna's eyes. Waves of love radiated from her heart to the heart of the statue, in pulsating waves that were tangible. Jana ceased feeling her physical body boundaries; her awareness stretched outward vast distances through the church walls, the earth and sky, into infinity. She noticed a deep humming sound, coming from within the centers of every body cell, and vibrating outward in all directions. It was a state of exquisite bliss.

Body awareness returned as Jana shifted positions to relieve the pain from kneeling on the hard wooden floor. She sat back on her heels and took a deep breath. She was not sure she had actually been breathing during her blissful state. The sounds of footsteps in the vestibule alerted her that this moment of intimate communion with The Goddess was about to be interrupted. Bringing her hands into prayer position in front of her heart, she silently uttered a prayer of gratitude and acknowledgement. Bowing her head once more, she rose and stepped backwards to sit in the first pew and rest her aching knees.

There was a scuffling noise in the back of the church, then silence. Jana waited a few more minutes, then rose, bowed to the Red Madonna, turned and walked down the aisle. She saw an older man sitting in the back pew with closed eyes, saying the rosary. As she passed by, he opened his eyes and glanced quickly at her, then turned away and returned to his rosary. A shiver of recognition coursed down her spine. The older man had a large nose and toothless mouth, dark wrinkled skin and sunken black eyes burning like coals. He had an uncanny resemblance to the Maya shaman who gave Jana the warning at Tikal.

232

Quickly leaving the church, Jana consciously drew her spirit guides closer. The bright sunlight assaulted her eyes, and she stumbled going down the stairs. She grasped the railing to break her fall. Disoriented, she squinted against the piercing light, glancing left and right searching for her bearings.

Where am I?

For a few moments she could not remember. Her mind felt numb, confused, unable to function. A thousand stars were exploding inside her eyes. She fumbled inside her purse and retrieved her sunglasses. Soothing blue tones filtered the sunlight and relieved the pain in her eyes.

Finally she remembered. She was in Calistoga, her car was parked a couple of blocks away on the main street. Had she stumbled from loss of vision, had a moment of menopausal brain fog? Or had the old man done something?

Shaken, she returned slowly to her car and resumed the drive to Clearlake. Concentrating on negotiating hairpin curves up the plateau, her mental state normalized. She couldn't dwell now on her intense experiences in the Catholic church. Despite the strange encounter with the old man, she felt elated. She had been initiated into the service of the Goddess by the Red Madonna.

*   *   *   *   *   *

Less than an hour later, Jana reached the town of Clearlake, its population of 15,000 wrapped around the southern tip of the 43,000-acre lake. Filling her car with gas at a service station, she reviewed a brochure about Clear Lake:

"Clear Lake is the largest natural lake in California, nearly 20 miles long with 100 miles of shoreline in the shadow of Mt. Konocti, an extinct volcano. The lake was formed 2 million years ago, making it a candidate for the oldest lake in North America, and second oldest in the world. A warm water lake, Clear Lake sits only eight miles above an active magma chamber. Several vents in the lake bottom send out thermal jets that bubble to the surface. Hot natural mineral springs riddle the area, releasing carbon dioxide and sulfur gases in their effervescent bubbling.

"The name Clear Lake is a misnomer. Its murky green-brown water is full of organic sediment, abundant plant life that sustains fish and many aquatic species. The lake is unrivaled for Bass fishing, hosting over 40 fishing tournaments at the town of Clearlake's Thompson Harbor.

"By 10,000 BCE the predecessors of the Pomo Indians were hunting, fishing and collecting food on the shores of Clear Lake. In the 1850's European families settled, and farming and ranching grew rapidly. The mineral springs became immensely popular in the late 1800's, drawing thousands of visitors 'taking the waters' to relax and improve their health. Grand resorts dotted the shoreline, the largest capable of hosting 5,000 guests at its height. This golden era lasted through the turn of the 20th century.

"By the 1920s the quality of lake water deteriorated severely. Increasing nutrient loads and overgrowth of algae caused a fetid mess on the lake surface in spring and summer. Pesticides decreased bird life, and mercury contamination from mines polluted the lake. Restoration projects gradually improved the lake ecosystem and wetlands after the 1990's. Local environmental groups and businesses combined forces with Pomo and Wappoo tribes to prevent further degradation, acting as watchdogs against pollution."

Jana recalled vacations at Clearlake with her family. She hadn't minded the murky water and her brother loved the fishing. It was a great lake for water-skiing.

After filling her car, she asked the station attendant for directions to the School of Maya Mysteries. He pointed her toward a hilly area southwest of the lake. Turning from the highway onto a narrow winding road, she flipped down the sun-visor to shield her eyes from the afternoon sun. The road led away from town, passing occasional houses. After several miles along the deserted road, Jana came to an intersection marked by a modest sign stating "Clearlake School of Maya Mysteries." Turning onto the gravel road, Jana was aware of rising anticipation, a visceral excitement in the solar plexus that felt both curious and receptive.

After winding through gentle hills spotted with bare oaks and cattails growing along a creek bed, she saw a large building in the distance. The three-story structure had covered porches bordering the first two levels and cupolas through the roof on the third story. Graceful columns supported the upper porch and roof, merging with railings that lined both porches. The structure had a distinct turn-of-the-century character, reminiscent of the gracious resorts that once abounded around Clearlake in a time when the pace of life was slower and more genteel. The white siding and green roofs blended well with the varieties of green, brown and yellow-gold of the surrounding meadows and hills.

Leaving her car in the parking lot nearly filled by 10 erratically parked cars, Jana climbed the front stairs that creaked softly as she stepped. She entered into a large parlor with wood floor and an eclectic assortment of over-stuffed chairs and couches in patterns that had no hope of being considered matching. Antique-like end tables, a 1960s style coffee table that had seen better days, and an old credenza covered with books and porcelain figurines added to the unplanned ambiance of the room. A large ceiling chandelier with dangling crystals diffused soft light onto the well-worn Persian carpet.

Jana stood uncertainly, looking around but unable to detect a registration desk. No one occupied any of the assorted chairs and couches. A stairway led up to the second story, and a couple of closed doors gave no indication of what lay behind. She sensed more than heard someone enter through the wide arch between the parlor and its adjoining room, which contained a similar assortment of unmatched furniture. Turning quickly, Jana saw the approaching woman.

"Hello, you must be Jana," said the woman. "Welcome. I'm Aurora Nakin Hill."

Aurora Nakin Hill was a tall, striking woman. The curves of her well-rounded body were enhanced by a flowing tulle skirt and over-blouse of purple-gray streaks blending softly into each other. A deep green, fringed shawl over her shoulders complimented the auburn hair tumbling haphazardly around an oval face with large, bright green-gray eyes. Her smile was not just of the lips, but was also reflected in her eyes, which seemed clear mirrors of her soul. Dangling amethyst earrings matched a pendant cluster hanging to mid-chest between ample breasts. She wore Birkenstock sandals with thick gray socks.

As the women's eyes met, Jana had the inexplicable sense of re-connecting with an old friend after a long absence. Their souls knew each other well. Without speaking, they embraced and held each other closely for long moments. Tears moistened Jana's eyes; she felt comforted in a profound way that surpassed any explanation. It felt like coming home.

"I am so glad to see you," said Aurora Nakin, still holding Jana's shoulders with hands that emanated perceptible warmth. Her penetrating eyes searched Jana's face carefully as though looking for a sign. Jana nodded, unable to find her voice, while her eyes took in every detail of the strange-yet-familiar face just inches away.

"Come, sit," Aurora Nakin made a sweeping gesture toward the larger couch with flowered upholstery and throw pillows of assorted sizes and colors. "Tell me about your journey."

Jana was uncertain whether the question made reference to the trip she had just taken to arrive here, or to her life experiences leading up to this moment. She decided it didn't matter. Almost before realizing it, Jana poured out the unusual series of events that led her to explore the ancient Maya civilization, and the synchronicities that pointed to a spiritual mission. She gave details about her encounter with the Native American medicine woman and how this directed her to Clearlake. But, she didn't mention the Red Madonna; it was too new, too precious to speak of yet.

Aurora Nakin listened attentively, her expressive face showing intense interest and hints of surprise. She nodded according to some inner knowing from time to time.

"Well, its certainly fortuitous that you have come here now," she said when Jana came to a stopping point in her story. "Tomorrow Hanab Xiu will be teaching about the true background of the Maya people, their spiritual mission on earth, and the Seven Powers of the Serpent. Many people are being called to this. You are connected with this movement; that is why you've been drawn here. Let me tell you more about the program. You are staying through the weekend, right?"

Jana nodded.

Aurora Nakin seemed deep in thought for a moment, then looked toward the closed door to their left.

"Can I get you some tea or coffee?" she asked in an abrupt change of focus.

"Coffee would be great," Jana said, a little surprised but grateful.

The tall, large-framed woman whisked away through the door, returning a few minutes later with a small tray and two cups, one of coffee and the other of tea. Jana accepted the steaming coffee and took a careful sip. It was mediocre at best, but the heat was welcome in the cool room as a few golden rays from the late afternoon sun filtered through the window behind their couch. Jana decided that, at the moment, the quality of coffee was immaterial.

"Tonight we're having chanting and drumming," Aurora Nakin picked up the train of conversation deftly. "I'll be leading it along with two other priestesses. If you have a drum or rattle, bring it, though we'll have some there. Tomorrow is Hanab Xiu's teaching, plus an orientation for the pilgrimage. Sunday morning is an initiation ceremony into the Maya Mystery School, for those who are qualified. Others may attend, you are welcome to come."

"Pilgrimage?" asked Jana, her attention caught by the word.

"Yes, oh where is that brochure . . " Aurora Nakin turned and searched the end table, found a brochure and handed it to Jana. The title read:

PILGRIMAGE TO SACRED MAYA TEMPLES & EQUINOX CEREMONY AT CHICHÉN ITZÁ.

Jana's heart made the little pinging sensation she was coming to recognize as the sign of intuitive recognition. Hanab Xiu was leading the pilgrimage that started in Mérida, México and included seven Maya temples in the Yucatan, Chiapas and Guatemala. The group would participate in a ceremony at Chichén Itzá on the spring equinox, joining other Maya elders and their groups. The Clearlake School of Maya Mysteries was sponsoring the trip, which lasted two weeks.

This is the ceremony I'm supposed to participate in. Jana tingled with excitement. There was no doubt. The link with Tuwa Waki's foretelling was unmistakable.

But, immediately her mind presented all the reasons why she could not go: It was less than a month away, she couldn't get time off work, it was a lot of money and she'd just been on an expensive vacation, Robert would never support it, it just would not work in her life.

"Are you interested in this?" asked Aurora Nakin. "It will be very powerful. We do have a few spaces left."

Jana shook her head.

"I'd love to go," she said wistfully. "But it looks impossible, I couldn't rearrange my life and obligations in that short time."

"Yes, it is coming up soon," said Aurora Nakin. "But keep the brochure, think about it. See if you are guided by Spirit, if somehow things will work out."

The women finished their drinks. Aurora Nakin showed Jana to her room. On the way upstairs, Jana asked what the Maya Mystery School was about. Aurora Nakin explained that her school, one of several in the U.S. and México, provided education about the coming time shift as recorded by the ancient Maya and their mystery teachings. Their goal was to prepare for the changes expected to occur. These teachings included sacred geometry and the role of Mayan sites, and shamanic techniques for expanding consciousness, developing telepathy and attuning to cosmic and earth cycles for balance and harmony. The upcoming equinox pilgrimage was very important in light of the current world situation, with war hovering on the horizon. She informed Jana there was more material to read in her room, and Hanab Xiu's talk would expand on the Maya mysteries. She ended by giving Jana another hug, remarking that dinner would be served at 6:30 pm in the dining room behind the stairs.

The night was dark and still, but Jana could not sleep. She rolled to one side to check the bedside clock. Its bright red digital numbers glowed 2:36 am, casting a pinkish hue across the crocheted white doilies beneath it. The four-poster bed gave a charming period feel to the room, but the mattress was soft and sagged in the center, making sleep even more elusive.

Images of that evening kept repeating, like a stack of CD's playing over and over. The buffet dinner for seventeen guests was tasty and congenial, featuring ample salads and vegetables. She met and conversed with an interesting couple, Julia and Michael, who lived near Mt. Shasta and considered themselves light workers. They were eagerly anticipating the pilgrimage to Maya sites. The spiritual focus particularly appealed to them, in contrast to their prior visit to the ruins as part of a vacation tour.

After dinner the group gathered in the adjacent large meeting room. It was sparsely furnished, having only a half dozen chairs and one long couch at the back. Many cushions were scattered on the carpet and a wicker basket in the center held an assortment of drums, rattles and other percussion tools. When the group had settled in, Aurora Nakin led them in a prayer honoring the four directions. She and two other women—all Maya priestesses, Jana understood, although they were Caucasian—took turns leading chants and songs. Most had a Native American flavor, throbbing rhythms inviting accompaniment. One woman played a thin, reedy flute at times, its tone high and shrill against the lower voiced drums and clacking rattles. The flute chants had a different character, both wilder and freer than the Native American chants. Later Jana learned these were based on actual Mayan music. There were CD's for sale featuring a professional group recording of Mayan pieces, using a close approximation of actual instruments. Jana bought a CD for Robert.

The pulsating, throbbing drums and unusual tonal melodies had a hypnotic effect on Jana. Sitting on a round cushion with legs crossed, she swayed with the rhythms, forgetting to use her rattle after a while, her mind clear of thoughts and aware only of sounds and body sensations. The chanting brought her into a timeless state that was deeply peaceful. She was surprised when the session ended; it seemed too soon.

238

Now in the middle of the night her mind would not stop, even when she tried chanting mentally, a technique that usually worked. Her thoughts kept returning to the Chichén Itzá ceremony, which brought her to a dilemma: She knew she was supposed to be there—but she could not figure out how. Every angle she considered led to some insurmountable barrier.

First, there was the issue of getting off work. Taking two weeks for the entire pilgrimage was totally out of the question, but maybe she could try getting a long weekend off. She was scheduled to work the weekend of spring equinox; that presented a significant challenge. The emergency room staff schedules were made out two months in advance. When someone needed to make a change, it caused considerable hardship for the rest. Serious illness and family death were the acceptable reasons for making changes, anything less was viewed as trivial. Without a doubt, being called to go on a spiritual pilgrimage to a Maya temple for sacred ceremony would never pass muster. Getting off for that reason would take an act of Congress, Jana concluded.

Next there was the money. She and Robert were comfortable financially, but did need to budget expenses and keep their spending in line with their cash flow. They had the house mortgage, one car payment, credit card bills, and the hefty cost of Marissa's college tuition. Their trip to Belize and Guatemala just over one month ago had been more expensive than anticipated, bumping up the balance on a couple of credit cards more than they wanted. This pilgrimage to the Yucatan, including airfare, hotel, ground transportation and meals would run at least one thousand dollars, Jana calculated.

Last and most important, there was Robert. She had no doubt that Robert would oppose her going on the pilgrimage. He was showing clear signs of discomfort with her Maya pursuits. She tried to grasp his real concerns. The most obvious was her safety, given the old man's warning and Robert's own unsettling experience at Tikal. But there was more underlying it, she was certain. He came from a very different background than she did. Although he had broken away from many of the Midwest values of his family, he still retained a pragmatic outlook and questioned the metaphysical beliefs that she held. Usually it was a good balance, she reminded herself. As a native Californian with parents involved in the early explorations of the human potential movement, she was surrounded by an open-mindedness that Robert viewed as excessive. How often had he remarked that her parents were so open-minded that their brains were in danger of falling out! Despite considering them flaky, he had a warm and kind relationship with them both. Ruefully she had to admit that his incisive reasoning had provided her many lessons in judgment, helping her discriminate the real merits of ideas and situations.

But this is different. She knew it in her heart. The string of events impelling her to this mission could not be discounted. Probably this was the very thing Robert found so disturbing. There were forces at work that surpassed his comprehension—and her own, too—and these were frightening in their power.

Jana tried to feel her inner reaction if she did decide to go on the pilgrimage over Robert's objections. At first there was just a fluttering uneasiness. She disliked facing his disapproval and feeling tension between them. She found it even harder to deal with his anger. Robert did not get angry very often, but when he did it was volcanic. He was never physical, but did unleash an explosion of verbiage that assaulted her emotions. Along with that came a blast of psychic energy that felt overwhelming. She had learned to deal with his infrequent anger eruptions over the years, but it was really hard when directed at her. If she stayed non-reactive, his anger soon dissipated and he was often apologetic.

But there was something deeper. As Jana let this come to the surface, her uneasiness soon gave way to tangible fear. It was a fear she knew well, one that had been with her throughout life. First came the sinking sensation in her stomach, then the rapidly beating heart, then tears welling up as despair and panic hit her mind. Thoughts froze and fear gripped her, as though some immense hawk clutched its talons around her heart and would not let go. After a few moments in this horribly unpleasant state, she made herself breathe deeply and slowly, remembering what she already knew about this fear from years of therapy and self-excavation.

I know you, she said mentally to the fear. *I know where you come from. You are fear of not being able to cope with loss, fear of emotional devastation. You started with the sudden death of my beloved grandfather when I was 12 years old. I was kept from his funeral because my family thought it best to spare me that painful ritual. But their intended kindness condemned me to years of emotional hell, I couldn't get resolution of this loss. So, many other losses, especially my pets, threw me into inconsolable grief until I finally grieved the real wound, the loss of my mentor, my anchor.*

She recited this litany now whenever the fear of loss showed up. It gave her a way to contain the wound, to avoid drowning in a sea of suffering. Subsequent inner work had shown her the multiple spiritual levels involved in this fear, from issues of the meaning and purpose of life, the paradox of suffering and grace, the question of immortal soul, to the ultimate loss of this existence through one's own death.

Now she acknowledged the fear of loss showing its face through worry about Robert's reaction. Would crossing him in this way destroy their relationship? She thought their love and friendship was solid, deep, reliable, lasting. They had come together well after the blush of young adulthood, after establishing their identities in careers, after enduring the traumas of divorce, after getting clarity about their values. She recalled their talks before they married, heartfelt discussions about choosing to be together through strength, not because of need. They had agreed to always support each other's individual interests and respect their differences.

But she knew intentions often melted away under the pressure of conflict. Nothing on earth could be counted on to remain unchanging.

I can't believe that would happen, Jana thought. *I know Robert loves me.*

Breathing deeply into tense parts of her body, she slowly relaxed and felt the fear dissipate. She offered the dilemma up to the Divine: *Show me the way, be it Thy will for me to go. Give me peace, be it not Thy will.*

Eventually sleep came.

The morning session was held in the same large meeting room, now supplied with additional chairs and a lecture podium. Several new people arrived, bringing the group to twenty-two. Jana sat beside Julia and Michael, with whom she shared breakfast. They chatted about their work in the manner of people getting acquainted. Julia did astrological readings while Michael practiced Reiki and other forms of bodywork. Upon finding out that Jana was a nurse, Michael inquired whether she did holistic practice. This caused Jana to pause for a moment, considering how to give an accurate answer. Although she did not do a specific holistic technique, she integrated holistic concepts, the idea of caring for the whole person, into her patient work.

Aurora Nakin appeared, accompanied by a small, slender man with very dark skin. As she was getting him set up in front, the group quieted down. She greeted the group and led an opening prayer,

241

calling to the four directions and their elements. Then she did a smudging ritual, lighting white sage in an abalone shell and using a bundle of feathers tied with a beaded cord to diffuse the aromatic smoke. The small man stood as she spread wisps of smoke all around him. After extinguishing the sage, she introduced Hanab Xiu.

"It is my great pleasure to have Hanab Xiu here with us," Aurora Nakin said. "As most of you know, he is a Maya Daykeeper and the founder of the Solar School of Maya Mysteries, of which our school in Clearlake is a branch. He is a well-known teacher of ancient knowledge and has written several books on Maya calendars and sacred geometry. His work includes bringing forth Maya wisdom to people of all cultures, so we can learn to live in harmony with the rhythms and cycles of nature. This is of great importance to the entire world, because our overall harmony with the planet and the cosmos will determine how we get through the coming shift of the ages, when the current great cycle of the Maya calendar ends in 2012. Hanab Xiu will be leading the pilgrimage to sacred Maya temples for the spring equinox, where he will join other Maya elders in a ceremony that is critically important for our future. We still have a few spaces open, please see me during break if you are interested. Now, let's welcome Hanab Xiu."

The group applauded enthusiastically as Hanab Xiu moved sinuously to stand beside the podium. His slender form was lithe and emanated contained power. Striking dark eyes appeared as wells of hidden knowledge, framed by thick black eyebrows. Equally black hair showed silver at the temples. With skin the color of rich milk chocolate, he had a typically large Maya nose with full, chiseled lips. The simple white cotton over-shirt and trousers he wore contrasted with the darkness of skin and hair.

"My grandfather was a very wise man," said Hanab Xiu. His voice was deep and resonant, as he spoke in a deliberate cadence with a moderate Spanish accent. "He taught me many things. He showed me there are lessons everywhere in nature, lessons that teach us how to live, how to think. One day we walked out into the desert. He carried a small jar with a lid. 'Where are we going, Grandfather?' I asked. 'You will see,' was all he said. We walked and walked. Suddenly he stopped, and looked around quickly, here and there."

Hanab Xiu modeled the motions, bending toward the floor, turning back and forth. He reached down quickly with one hand and made a scooping motion just above the floor. Then he stood up, his right hand closed in a fist.

"'Open the jar,' said Grandfather. So I did, and he put something inside and closed the lid. 'What do you see?' he asked me. I looked inside. At first I didn't see anything, then I saw the tiny insect. 'I see a sand flea,' I said. 'Good,' said Grandfather. 'What is the flea doing?' 'It's jumping up and bumping into the jar lid, then falling back down to the bottom.' 'That's right,' he said. We watched the flea for several minutes. It kept jumping, hitting the lid, and falling down. You know how sand fleas jump, they can jump a long distance for such a tiny insect. We waited but the flea just kept jumping. Then Grandfather said, 'Now take off the lid and watch the flea.' I did this, and the flea kept jumping but it never jumped any higher than when the lid was on the jar.

"I asked 'Why doesn't it jump out, Grandfather?' He said 'Because it has learned it can only jump so high before it hits a barrier. Now that barrier has become the top of its world. It doesn't see that the barrier has been removed, and now it can jump much higher.' Grandfather taught me how people are like the sand flea. They learn certain limitations, then they continue to believe they have them. They live their lives without thinking beyond those limits. And all they have to do is look up, and see that the lid is not there any more."

Hanab Xiu paused and looked intently around the room, his eyes quickly connecting with those of each person.

"What I am going to tell you today will be outside of the limits that most of you have. I'm going to tell you a different history of the earth. Not the history you learned in school, not the story that your religion tells. The history of the earth as known to the Maya, as told by the tradition of the Itzaes. The Itzaes were the ones who taught the Maya their wisdom, who gave them the mysteries so they could know the truth of the universe. And now you are here, by no accident, to learn of this truth."

Jana felt a shiver go up her spine. Her attention was riveted as she sat upright, her back straight, hands resting in the receptive mudra on her lap. She was unaware of any body sensations except the thrill of inner anticipation.

"This is the Maya cosmic solar memory; it will help you understand what you have forgotten, remember who you are. Being Maya is something that is in the heart and spirit, not created by the color of your skin or the place of your birth. You are all Maya. That is why you are here. As a Mayan you can remember with your cosmic mind. You are a cosmic being who has come from Hunab K'u, the

243

Creator Spirit who put the sacred measure and movement into our body and spirit according to universal law. Your body and spirit have the memory that is now ready to awaken.

"Many millions of years ago there were peoples who lived in lands that today we cannot see with the physical eyes. But we know these lands in the cellular memory of our species. The ancient Maya knew this memory, they used it to shape their pyramids and wrote of it in books and on stelae. Before the Maya arrived in the lands we are familiar with, they were in other lands, lands that are now under the waters of the sea. In very remote times, they lived in places with very high mountains and also in desert lands. The Maya remember the great sacred land of Lemuria, called Lemulia in Mayan. There were many peoples on this vast land who inherited the cosmic religion with its sacred stellar symbols, like the 5-pointed and 6-pointed stars. Many, many symbols were given that we can see now carved on Maya pyramids and stelae, and also on petroglyphs of the Hopis. The wisdom of the Maya is knowing the meanings and purposes of these symbols.

"Through millennia, Lemulia fulfilled its sacred mission to educate humanity and teach the cosmic religion. When the time came that Lemulia completed its cycle, the vast land broke apart and some parts sank under the waters. It was time for the wisdom and truth of the cosmic religion to move to a different place on earth. The ancient wise ones knew this, and they traveled to a new land with tall mountains that arose out of the waters. These wise ones were the old Itzaes, those who received the original teachings from stellar beings of the Pleiades, who visited them in very ancient times. These Itzaes were bringers of universal law, teachers of cosmic truths for the peoples of the West. They still can remember when they lived on the new continent of Atlantis, called Atlantiha in Mayan. For thousands of years they lived there among many communities of peoples that understood cosmic spiritual work. There the Itzaes developed the calendars, and deepened their understanding of the reason for their existence and the importance of the sacred symbols. They knew the cosmic timing for things on earth, and that in coming times it would be necessary to keep this wisdom secret. They saw the need for the Mayan prophesies, because this was the way they would be able to communicate the secret wisdom to initiates in the future.

"The Itzaes' knowledge of the calendar told them when the continent of Atlantiha would arrive at its end. There were forces unleashed by other stellar peoples, who had come more recently and were fierce and warlike, that created great instability on earth. The ancient wise ones in the temples tried to offset these forces, but the powerful technology of the fierce ones moved too fast. It harnassed magnetic and nuclear forces that got out of control. The electromagnetic grids that surrounded the earth, many levels of them, became disrupted. The fields spun around wildly and caused a huge rent between different dimensions of reality. The firmament of the skies collapsed. The elemental beings from deep inside the earth were unleashed. The land split into great chasms and the sea threw immense waves over Atlantiha. The continent sank into the sea.

"Before the final cataclysm, many wise ones emigrated to other lands, taking their scientific and spiritual knowledge with them. The Itzaes traveled to many places that we now call India, Asia and Egypt before they came to the new continent of America. This was because it had not yet appeared from under the waters. In India they speak of the Naga Maya who brought their land great wisdom. The Egyptians know of the Mayax who they revered as great teachers.

"What is today called America has the traditional name Tamaunchan. The first part to appear was the high lands, the Sierra Madre of Santa Marta mountains. The indigenous Kogis-Taironas arrived there in what is now western Venezuela and eastern Colombia. Later the lands of the Yucatan Peninsula and Central America rose from the waters. In these areas, the indigenous Maya people settled. The Itzaes knew these lands were destined to become the new site for the cosmic religion. They waited, and when the time was right they arrived in these lands, bringing the science, religion and symbols of the inherited wisdom of Atlantiha. They taught the indigenous Maya people, developed their spiritual knowledge. They initiated the Maya into cosmic wisdom, use of the symbols— especially the cosmic letters and animal powers of snake, eagle and jaguar—and the seven powers of the human being. They gave them the calendar and educated them in how to follow its cycles.

'That is how the Maya came to be the keepers of the ancient wisdom."

Hanab Xiu stopped to take a drink of water. He looked around the room again, not only his eyes but an energy vibration from his heart chakra making contact with everyone present.

"We are the continuation of the Itzae tradition," he spoke softly, almost in a whisper. The room was in total silence, but full of vibrant energy that caused tingling sensations on Jana's skin. She was hardly breathing.

245

Were the Itzaes the ones called the Olmec by archeologists? Jana remembered the Olmec were those mysterious people who suddenly showed up in México, the ones who were the predecessors of the Maya.

"The Mayan prophesies are being fulfilled now," Hanab Xiu said with forceful voice. Almost as one being, the people in the group shifted position and sat more upright.

"It is prophesied that initiates will return to the land of the Maya to reawaken the sacred temple sites and do the work of the Great Spirit, of Hunab K'u. These reincarnated masters will communicate with the spirits of the Itzaes, their spirits will fuse as one. The initiates will come from many places; they will be of many colors and speak many languages. Some will be old, some young, some men, some women. They will do their work in many ways. Some will sing and dance, some will remain silent, some will teach, some will entertain. They will travel around the earth like the wind and the rain; give warmth like fire and support life like Father Sun and Mother Earth. Their spirit will manifest in nature, the stars and moon, and in dreams while people are asleep.

"As the reawakened temples beckon, great multitudes of tourists will be drawn there. The masters, the Solar Priests and Priestesses, will walk quietly among the tourists who will be touched in heart and mind. Without knowing why, many people will change. Inside, they will be changed. The seven centers of power in their bodies will start growing. They will remember their connection with the earth and sun, and will care about the environment. Their hearts will start to beat in rhythm with the universe, and they will become more peaceful. Their minds will sharpen and they will see the falseness of living for material goals alone. Some will be called to become initiates.

"All this is happening now. The work is being done as prophesied. We are ending the Age of Belief and entering the Age of Knowledge, the 5th Sun, the Itza Age. As all time begins, it also finishes, and a new time begins again. The Mayan calendar Great Cycle is soon ending, as you know, on December 21, 2012. The call is put out for the light workers of earth to reunite and harmonize our planet with the cosmic rhythms, to bridge gaps between cultures, races, religions and countries.

"Don't be fooled like the sand flea," Hanab Xiu said with a twinkle in his eyes. "All your limits are only set by your own thinking. Don't believe anything that you have not tested and found to be true for yourself. And remember to look up so you can see that the lid is not there. Live out your true solar destiny."

He stopped and the group broke into enthusiastic applause.

"I would be happy to answer your questions," he said as the applause died out.

"How is the reactivation of Maya temple sites related to the Harmonic Convergence in August 1987 and other astronomical events?" asked a young man wearing black-rimmed glasses who gave the impression of being a computer geek.

"The time called the Harmonic Convergence was when the earth entered the final 25 years of the 26,000 year Great Cycle," answered Hanab Xiu. "This was also prophesied by the Maya as a time when there would be a coming together of a group of energies to create a common tone. There was an unusual planetary alignment, with all the planets in our solar system practically in a straight line. This astrological configuration opened a portal for cosmic communication. This is what happened. Those representatives of the Great Spirit, the source of our universe at the Galactic Center of the Milky Way, came to check on the earth. Humanity had been dropping in our level of consciousness, and the planet's vibrations were troubled. If this darkness were to continue, the earth would suffer a great catastrophe that would destroy much of life. So they came to check the tone, the vibrations of earth, at the Harmonic Convergence."

"Was that catastrophe the asteroid that nearly hit earth?" the young man queried.

"Yes. But enough people had chosen to follow the path of love and unity, especially in the 50 years before the Convergence, that the disaster was spared," said Hanab Xiu. "It was a signal for the keepers of the Itzae wisdom to bring it forth to the world. Many people were ready to live by the cosmic religion, to restore harmony on earth, to respect the universal laws. In 1992 a new energy came forth from the sun. It was a green spiral light that the shamans and seers could see. This light awakened people further, and awakened our Mother Earth to new life. Have you noticed how many indigenous teachers are writing and giving classes in the last 10 years? They are responding to the sun's instructions, for the sun is a channel of communication from the Galactic Center.

"Another important event was completing the repairs of the earth grids that had been disrupted by the Atlanteans. Many ascended masters worked on this. The grid for that level of human being who has what you call the Christ consciousness—Kukulcan or

Quetzalcoatl, the rainbow feathered serpent to the Maya—was completed in 1989. Now it is possible for many people to attain that level of consciousness.

"In 1995 at spring equinox, a 560 year cycle of darkness brought by the Spaniards to the land of the sun came to an end, according to the sacred Tzolk'in calendar. This prophesy was written by the Supreme Maya Council in 1475, before the conquistadors arrived. It was told to them by Kukulcan-Quetzalcoatl. Now the Maya wisdom could again flourish, according to ancient prophesy. After this time, hidden knowledge could be reawakened in the human cells, in our DNA. Many people were now capable of remembering our true history, as I have told you today.

"In November 2003 another unusual alignment happened in the skies. This planetary configuration is called the Harmonic Concordance. Six celestial bodies—Moon, Sun, Jupiter, Saturn, Mars, and Chiron—aspected each other at 60 degrees, forming a Grand Sextile pattern. This hexagon pattern creates a subtle but powerful vortex that opens a portal. It is shaped like the benzene ring, the basic building block of life on earth. Through this energy portal the structure of cells can be changed. These six bodies also form two intersecting triangles, or Grand Trines, which create a six-pointed star pattern. The six-pointed star, the Star of David, creates harmony between ascending masculine and descending feminine energies. It holds the potential for bringing a healing balance of these two energies. This is greatly needed in the world right now. The masculine forces have gotten too powerful, they have brought the earth to serious imbalance, to the brink of destruction. We must bring in the feminine forces to soften this, to remind us that the earth is our mother and our very selves. We must fuse these polarities.

"The final astrological event of this Great Cycle will be the rebirth of the Sun through the womb of the Milky Way, the dark rift, on spring equinox in 2012. This is the great transformation, the shift of ages and of human consciousness that we are preparing for. I will speak of this later. Have I answered your question?"

Everyone laughed at the obvious understatement. Jana was fascinated, her mind quickly making connections with the yuga cycles described by the Hindus and various Christian ideas of the end times. She remembered reading about a comet that passed close to Earth, and the collision of asteroids with Jupiter. A woman behind her asked the question that Jana was already posing in her mind.

"What does Maya prophesy say about earth changes around the shift of the ages?" the woman asked.

"At the end of each Sun, or era, the earth undergoes upheavals," Hanab Xiu replied. "There are cataclysms like earthquakes, fires, volcanoes, tsunamis and floods. Your Christian tradition speaks of the great flood that cleansed the earth before the age of Abraham, the father of the Hebrews. That was at the coming of the Age of Aries, at the time of the destruction of Atlantis, the beginning of the 4th Maya Sun. Each Maya Sun is about 5200 years, and after five Suns a Cosmic Cycle of 26,000 years is completed. This finishes a full precession of the equinoxes. The year of your Julian calendar 2012 marks the end of a 5200 year Sun and also the end of a five-Sun cycle, so it is a very big event. It moves us into the Maya fifth creation, the 5th Cosmic Sun Cycle. Many say it is the start of the Age of Aquarius. The dates are not exact by your astrological reckonings, but the Maya calendar is very precise."

He paused and smiled.

"But you must count like a Mayan. We always begin the count with zero, so the five Suns of the Great Cycle go from zero to four. At the 5th Sun a new cycle begins, and we count again from zero.

"Many predictions point to great upheavals on earth. Even now we see serious climate changes, shifts in the magnetic field, more geothermal activity. The earth is over-due for a pole shift. We have entered a photon belt and the sun has increased sunspot activity. The Maya elders say Mother Earth will pass inside the center of a magnetic axis around spring equinox 2012, and may be darkened with a great cloud for a few days. This darkness will degrade the environment, and she may not be strong enough to survive the effects.

"The humans of earth must help. We must change the way we live and take care of Mother Earth. This is the work of the initiates, to spread the word, to awaken others. We cannot predict exactly how severe the earth changes will be. That rests upon what humanity does in the remaining years."

He stopped and stood very still, eyes gazing into the distance. The group sat in reflective silence. No further questions were asked, and they broke for lunch.

Jana had a burning question, one that had troubled her since beginning her Maya studies. If the ancient Maya had so much wisdom and were so enlightened, why did their culture reflect incessant warfare and human sacrifice? She chose not to ask this question in front of the group out of deference for her hostess. Obviously this gathering was committed to bringing the highest of Maya teachings to light, and she did not want to disrupt the cohesive harmony of the group. She decided to ask Hanab Xiu later, if she could get a moment alone with him.

Lunch was a tasty build-your-own tortilla salad, giving Jana vegetarian options. She sat with Julia, Michael and Steve, the young man with black-rimmed glasses. All three had been involved with the School of Maya Mysteries for a year or two.

"How did you like Hanab Xiu's talk?" Julia asked Jana.

"It was pretty incredible," Jana replied. "I had no idea the Maya predecessors were at Lemuria and Atlantis. That's an interesting take on earth history."

"If you want to read earth history that will really curl your hair, check out Malwyn Melchior's books," Steve suggested.

"Who's he?" Jana asked.

"That's a complex question," said Steve. "Originally from the star Sirius, through the pre-biblical lineage of ancient priests of the Melchior order. Taught in this life by 10-foot tall angels, mentored by Thoth of Egyptian fame who taught him sacred geometry and the Left Eye of Horus mysteries, studied with nearly every spiritual teacher of note in the West. Founded the Life Flower Sacred Geometry organization to teach people how to reactivate their Mer-ka-bas."

"Mer-ka-bas?" Jana queried as Steve took a bite of his tortilla salad.

"Your light body, shaped like a sombrero galaxy, spinning around at nine-tenths the speed of light with your physical body inside," explained Steve, still chewing. He apparently had perfected the art of eating and talking simultaneously. "Adepts can use it for astral traveling. It anchors our electromagnetic field and keeps memory from being wiped out during big magnetic upheavals like pole shifts."

"That's right," added Michael, enthused by the conversation. "One definition of immortality is to preserve the memory of everything you've experienced, and who you've been in former lifetimes, regardless of what form you're in."

"Yeah," confirmed Steve. "Anyway, Melchior wrote about the real earth history in his books. It's unbelievably complex. Earth's been colonized by multiple star peoples from various places in the universe, and not always for the best reasons. A lot of the upheavals on earth came from their struggles over control and resource use. Not too unlike right now."

"We're a mix of all kinds of life forms," Julia added.

"A mongrel lot!" Michael said emphatically.

"Yeah, but now our DNA is getting upgraded," Steve said.

"Even our reptilian DNA?" asked Julia with a sly smile.

"Reptiles rule!" Michael did his best imitation of a velociraptor, hands hanging from uplifted wrists like claws as he bared his teeth, drawing a laugh from the others.

"Yeah, worse luck to us!" Steve rejoined. "Those Jurassic dinos in Washington are gonna get us into World War III."

"You guys aren't going to get started on the reptilian brotherhood conspiracy theory, are you?" asked Julia in mock horror.

"Well, there *is* this elite group of wealthy and powerful families of reptilian heritage that control the vast majority of the world's resources . . ." Michael stopped in mid-sentence as Julia made a slicing motion across his neck, laughing.

"I saw a prediction about war on the web," Julia interjected. "A group of Maya elders said if war happens after this March 21st, it will impact huge areas of the world. If it happens before that, just a small region will be involved."

"Does war have to happen at all?" queried Jana.

"They seem to think so," replied Julia.

Everyone ate silently, sobered by that thought.

Steve took up the DNA theme more seriously:

"There is support in evolutionary theory for reptilian genes in mammals. Scientists refer to the brain stem, the part supporting basic life functions, as the reptilian brain. But whatever our polyglot of genetic information and wherever it came from, things are shifting now. We can get past the lower parts of our nature and move into higher consciousness."

"At least those of us who choose to," Julia said with a sigh.

"That's hopeful," Jana observed. This connected with her own New Age ideas.

"Hanab Xiu's mission is to bring out the wisdom of indigenous peoples," Steve continued. "He teaches techniques to access deep soul-knowing in the secret chamber of the heart, an esoteric practice known to the ancient Mayas. He's going to teach it to us on the Maya pilgrimage."

"Yeah, and not a minute too soon," Michael added. "This planet really needs to wake up, I mean the people need to get it that we're one with our planet. Destroy the planet, destroy ourselves. Pretty simple."

"Greed and power are blinding," Julia remarked.

"The forces of evil have a mission to prevent things from progressing on earth," added Michael. "Their job is to keep spirits bound to earth, recycling for infinity, never finishing evolution so they can move on to the next level—which probably isn't here."

"The Hindu teachings call that process the power of delusion, of Maya," Jana offered. "It means getting lost in our senses, in our experience of living, and being ignorant of our true spirit nature. Strange that they use the word 'Maya' for this force of darkness."

That last remark stopped conversation for a while. Everyone focused on eating. Jana wondered what the others were thinking. Her mind popped up a provocative thought:

Maybe it took the Maya to overcome 'Maya.'

In the afternoon session Hanab Xiu spoke of the Serpent of Creation.

"The first form the Creator Spirit took in creating the universe was a serpent," said Hanab Xiu. "The Divine Mind, what you can think of as a transcendent force, the Infinite Oneness beyond any form, condensed the Primal Serpent out of the feminine cosmic ocean, the womb of creation. This was the first contraction of Infinite Spirit, the first form taken. The Maya believed the Pleiades were the great Celestial Serpent. The Mayan name for Pleiades—*Tzab*—means rattlesnake rattle. The Pleiades are the Divine Mind becoming the Creator Spirit for our corner of the universe. Seven aspects of Primal Serpent, first form of Creator Spirit, were worshipped in ancient times as the seven stars of the Pleiades.

"Seven is a sacred number for the Maya. It reminds us of the galactic origins of Maya culture brought to earth by the Itzae. Temple pyramids with seven tiers are most sacred. At Chichén Itzá, seven isosceles triangles are formed by sunlight on the temple steps during the equinoxes, moving serpent-like down the steps. This brings the serpent power of Kukulkán to the initiates during the equinox ceremony. You will experience this on our pilgrimage. You will become absorbed by the serpent of sacred knowledge—in Mayan, *luk'umen tun ben can.*"

Hanab Xiu explained what it meant to have the power of Kukulkán, to be Kukulkán, as knowing the seven forces that govern the human body, understanding their intimate relationship with natural and cosmic laws, and using them to live in accord with the long and short calendar cycles.

"We must know how to live, how to die, and how to be born," he said. "We must know how to transform the sacred power, the energy of Kukulcan, in our minds and bodies. Hunab K'u, the one Supreme God of our solar system, gave us the power to become Kukulcan. He gave us the seven powers. They are distributed in our bodies as the centers of movement and measure. The serpent represents the seven powers of light, which form a circuit of energy focused through the crown of the head. There the energy dances and flows into energies of the Creator Spirit. In art of the ancient Maya, this flowering of energy through the crown was depicted as brightly colored feathers in a large headdress. Kukulcan-Quetzalcoatl appears as a serpent with a rainbow colored crown of feathers."

Jana was making associations with the seven chakras of the Hindus and the thousand-petal lotus that was the symbol of the crown chakra.

Hanab Xiu's next remarks confirmed this. The seven powers of light matched the Hindu seven chakras, he said. From the crown, the energy of Spirit travels in the form of a serpent down the spine to the base, then upward through each power center to reunite at the crown. The colors of these centers are wavelengths of the rainbow, red at the base moving up through the spectrum to violet at the crown. The Maya word for the red color at the base of the spine is *chacla,* meaning "this my red." Red merging into orange of the next center is the color of the galactic force from the middle of the Milky Way galaxy.

Jana realized the Maya colors for chakras corresponded to the Hindu ones. She was further impressed as Hanab Xiu described Maya knowledge of kundalini. He said in Mayan the word was *k'ultanlilni,* a composite word made of the Mayan words for god, pyramid, coccyx, vibration and nose. Jana immediately saw the connections. Breath meditations for stimulating kundalini involved sitting cross-legged, forming a pyramid with the body. You focused on drawing Divine energy in through the nose, moving it down the spine to the coccyx and back up to the crown, and feeling the vibration of spirit inside. She smiled as Hanab Xiu mentioned that Maya sacred art depicted the nose as extremely large, emphasizing its importance for bringing in Divine breath-energy. An electric shock ran through her body when he said the Chak masks at Uxmal expressed this concept, having noses that look like elephant trunks inscribed with glyphs that held this sacred knowledge. The mandate she had received resonated loudly in her mind:

"You must go to the place of Chak."

Uxmal must be the place of Chak.

The ruins of Uxmal were not very far from Mérida, Jana recalled.

I could go there during the pilgrimage to Chichén Itzá. If I could go.

The rest of the afternoon session was devoted to learning and practicing breath techniques that moved the serpent energy through the spine and around the body. It was similar to practices Jana already used, and she was not surprised when Hanab Xiu called it "Maya yoga." He showed the group a striking picture of a Maya priest in feathered headdress sitting in meditation in the full lotus posture.

Maya Priest in Meditation

Hanab Xiu ended the session with comments that stirred Jana's heart and evoked yearning for more:

"When we practice Maya yoga, our bodies function like pyramids in processing energy. We become the integration of the seven powers of light, moving in the form of the serpent, undulating eternally with movement and measure. We are the form of Kukulkán, we are filled with the truth of sacred knowledge. We see the serpent form of our DNA, alive in every cell, vibrating in tune with the cosmic symphony. The Maya culture will endure, although many others have come and gone in our lands, because it is based on wisdom inspired by cosmic laws. To live the cosmic religion is to be Maya, to live with Maya culture is to experience cosmic laws in every day. In this way we become children of time, of solar and galactic and cosmic cycles. Then we live as the essence of universal consciousness."

Jana sat quietly as the group milled around, the room filled with a buzz of conversation. She waited until the people in front of Hanab Xiu were done with their questions. As he started to walk toward the door, she approached him, thanked him for the class, and asked if she could pose an issue that troubled her. He nodded as one heavy dark eyebrow rose slightly, creating a lop-sided quizzical expression.

Jana provided a little background about her Maya studies, then said:

"In a culture so full of wisdom and sacred knowledge, how is it that kings and lords kept their cities in constant warfare, and they used so much violence including human sacrifice?"

Hanab Xiu studied Jana's face for a moment, his black eyes probing deeply into her hazel ones. His expression was inscrutable.

"There is much archeology does not understand," he began in a thoughtful manner. "Much of Maya culture was not expressed on stelae and lintels. Those who rose to power became seduced by that power. It is the way of the world everywhere, yes? The 4th Sun had passed its apex and begun its decline. The great glory of the Maya, the culture that flowered before what is called the Classic periods, left few traces. But their knowledge of cosmic laws is reflected in the great monuments of the Classic Maya peoples. They could not have built these pyramids, their vast cities, cultivated the jungle for an immense population, without knowing these laws. Some of the priests and priestesses kept the sacred teachings pure. But the Divine Spirit must work with those vessels that are present in any given time. Not all vessels are clear, some become clouded and distorted. So we see some part of truth, but we also see the result of ambition, greed, vengeance, cruelty. A pattern begins, it brings power, it continues—until it fails and the culture collapses."

He paused, intensified his gaze into Jana's eyes and said softly but with great force:

"Do not confuse higher truth with lesser knowledge. Find the essence that you can feel within your deepest heart. That is where true wisdom lives."

Crossing his wrists over his mid-chest, Hanab Xiu nodded to Jana, turned and left the room. She stood, her body vibrating in a force-field of energy for several minutes. Her mind wanted to remember every word, but all she was clearly aware of were pulsations in the heart chakra almost like a drum beat.

Aurora Nakin, who had observed their interchange, came over to Jana. Putting an arm around Jana's shoulders, she gently guided her out of the room.

That evening Jana and Aurora Nakin talked late into the night. They shared their personal stories of how they became involved in metaphysical and spiritual pursuits, events that shaped their careers

255

and family life, and what drew them to the Maya. Although their paths had been quite different, they shared a passion to know who they really were, where this whole planetary adventure had come from, and where it was going. Both believed the wisdom of the Maya would reveal the answers.

The next morning Jana attended the initiation ceremony as an observer. At breakfast Julia, Michael and Steve told her about their year of study with Aurora Nakin. In preparation for today's initiation, they had fasted 20 hours and brought four gifts traditionally given to the spiritual teacher: a wool blanket, medicine plants (usually sage, sweetgrass and cedar), a personal item for use in ceremony (such as a rattle, drum, crystal, leather bag), and a donation of money. They explained the fire ceremony would create a vortex of energy as a portal into the Spirit world. As the Spirit enters the fire, Hanab Xiu would intercede with the conscious vibration of Creator Spirit to coordinate the dispersal of the seven powers of light to the initiates. Throughout the year of training, initiates had practiced breath techniques and meditation to prepare their energy centers, or chakras, for receiving these powers.

At mid-morning the group of 10 people gathered in the back yard for the ceremony. Six were bearing gifts, the others were observers like Jana. Aurora Nakin appeared flanked by her two priestess assistants, all wearing bright orange dresses trimmed in red, with necklaces of hollow nut shells making clinking sounds as they walked. Behind them came Hanab Xiu, also wearing orange and red, with a multi-color feather headdress. Its size was modest compared to drawings Jana had seen of Maya priests and kings.

As the procession passed Jana, Hanab Xiu stopped and called to Aurora Nakin. She came to his side quickly, and he told her while pointing at Jana:

"She is to be in the ceremony."

Aurora Nakin hesitated, wondering if Hanab Xiu was confused.

"She's not one who trained with me," Aurora Nakin said softly, hoping their dialogue would not reach the ears of others.

"She is an initiate of old. The ceremony today will remind her," he said decisively.

Aurora Nakin simply nodded and resumed her place leading the procession.

Jana was astonished, but the pinging sensation in her mid-chest told her this was intuitively right. A tiny flash of embarrassment colored her cheeks, and she silently hoped no other initiates would be offended. When the six initiates were called to stand in a circle for the fire ceremony, she joined them. No one seemed to take notice except Julia who shot her a surprised glance.

Hanab Xiu and Aurora Nakin created a mandala on a bare spot of ground, made of ensarte (tree bark dipped in resin) and copious quantities of medicine plants and herbs, all very dry. No wood was used for the fire. To this base they added copal incense and a little chocolate and honey for sweetness and to give thanks for the blessings of life. The center of the mandala was mounded up, and seven thin taper candles leaned against it. Fresh flowers were arranged around the rim of the mandala.

Aurora Nakin led them in a chant, accompanied on drums by her assistants. Hanab Xiu lit the candles and offered prayers to the four directions and center axis. Soft drum beats in the background accentuated his rhythmic incantations. He called each initiate forth by name and accepted their gifts, after which each returned to their place around the circle.

Jana was called last. All she had was the amber pendant from Belize that she was wearing and some money; he accepted these with a smile. The candles burned down and caught the dry herbs on fire. Soon a small fire burned brightly, giving off the wonderful scents of sage, cedar, copal, and sweetgrass. The complex aromas tingled in Jana's nose and she felt her state of consciousness changing, expanding, dissolving into some vast ocean of pure awareness.

The sound of Hanab Xiu's voice reciting in Mayan seemed distant. She was startled to find him standing in front of her, and realized her eyes had been closed. Placing one hand on her crown and the other on her heart, he said softly: "You are initiated into the Maya Mysteries." Their eyes locked for a moment, he placed copal granules in her palm, then he moved to the next person. After each received the initiation, they sprinkled their copal granules on the fire. Flames burst and sputtered as the resin caught fire, releasing its woody aromas into the air.

The ceremony ended with a chant of gratitude to Hunab K'u, Solar Father and Ix Chel, Earth Mother.

Those who could were invited to stay for lunch. Jana went through the motions of sharing lunch and conversation with her new friends—now fellow-initiates—but on the inside she was in a state of awe. Never would she have dreamed Hanab Xiu would virtually

257

command her to become initiated into the Maya Mysteries. It was too much for her mind to grasp.

Aurora Nakin seemed a little nonplussed, too. Saying good-by to Jana, she remarked how unusual this event was. In their long talk last night, the two women acknowledged their deep soul connections; they felt they had known each other forever. They agreed to stay in touch. In parting, Aurora Nakin handed the amber pendant to Jana and said:

"Hanab Xiu wanted you to have this back. He said you would need it."

Jana was completely surprised. It had pained her to give away the pendant, but the light amber glowing with hidden power was all she had in the moment. Her hand closed happily around its cool smooth surfaces.

"Please give him my deepest thanks."

"Sure. It looks to me like you are supposed to come on our pilgrimage."

"I know," Jana replied. "I just don't see how. The best I could hope for would be a long weekend over the equinox. Could I join the group if I work it out?"

"Hanab Xiu believes it's important to attend the entire pilgrimage," Aurora Nakin said. "For building group cohesiveness and getting everyone on the same level. I really don't know if he'd be OK with that."

She paused, adding with an ironic smile:

"But in light of what he did with you today, I'd say anything's possible."

*   *   *   *   *   *

Robert was having a hard time. He had been provoked before in his relationship with Jana, but this was the biggest challenge of all. She had ignored the not-so-subtle hints he put out against going to Clearlake. Robert was not accustomed to having his desires ignored. From childhood when his doting mother deferred to his choices, immature as they were, to his admiring students who emulated his tastes in music, Robert's point of view usually prevailed.

Meeting Jana had been a revelation. Here was an intelligent woman with a mind of her own, along with sweetness and exuberance for life, who faced him as an equal. Jana's strong sense of self and ability to stand up for her views were high among her many attractions, especially after years with a weak-willed and dependent first wife. But, her independence was also a big point of contention.

Everything about her trip to the School of Maya Mysteries at Clearlake troubled him. What did it mean anyway, Maya mysteries? This smacked of occult secrets, hidden knowledge used to manipulate and control. Although he admired the Maya's capacity for building vast cities and soaring pyramids, for taming the jungle and creating a wide network of trade and commerce, he was repelled by their practices of bloodletting and sacrifice. Their shamans might actually possess secret knowledge, but he suspected it was not used for good purposes.

After their vacation in Belize and Guatemala, Jana seemed possessed by this Maya mystique. Certain there was a Maya connection, she was compelled to keep delving deeper into the meaning of her recurrent dream of the old woman's hand. The experiences she had at the ruins affected her profoundly, tightening the connection. He could not shake off the deep uneasiness, the gut-wrenching sensations he went through at the North Acropolis in Tikal. Then, there was the strange warning from the old man and Jana's near fall into the ravine.

He did not like it at all. This seemed like something best left alone. He resolved to talk seriously with Jana upon her return from Clearlake. He would emphasize how important it was to him, that she really needed to back off this unsettling quest, so their life could return to normal.

The night she returned from Clearlake, Jana had the dream again. It was a lucid dream, the Observer knew she was dreaming and watched the dream unfold.

The girl's small brown fingers gently traced along the old woman's snaking veins, caressing the long thin fingers and big knuckles. She slipped her hand into the old palm, and the thin fingers closed around it. The night was dark and still. A few embers glowed in the center hearth. As dawn approached faint gray light crept into the stone room. The old woman lay on a woven reed mat resting on a stone slab attached to the wall. The girl withdrew her hand and the old fingers fanned outward, reaching. Moving to the door, the girl drew back a heavy curtain and the dawn light outlined the corbel arch.

The slender pre-adolescent girl wore a white shift to mid-calf. Her feet were bare and a single braid of dark hair hung down her back. Her narrow brown face was dominated by a large nose. She listened to the raspy breathing of the old woman, her face showing concern. She stepped from the stucco platform down three stone steps onto a dirt path leading through high shrubs and willowy trees. In the distance was a graceful rounded pyramid with a square stone temple on top, its exalted summit towering above a grove of tall trees.

Jana drifted in and out of the last scenes in the dream. She could feel her awareness rising toward the waking state. Summoning the Observer she requested to see more. Her consciousness lingered at the liminal threshold, a subtle tension playing between waking and dreaming. Again she asked for more of the dream.

Suddenly it was as if she were standing in a plaza facing the immense rounded pyramid. The light was dim, either dusk or dawn. It seemed that a crowd was present although she could not see them. Her vision was riveted on the pyramid. A single incredibly steep, broad stairway ascended the front face, ending in a narrow platform that supported a small temple with a single doorway. The doorway formed the mouth of a large carved mask, its rectangular eyes and elongated nose projecting above, while fangs descended on either side of the opening. Beyond that was a small turret-like structure with no visible access. Lining both edges of the steep stairway, from top to bottom, was a cascading succession of smaller masks in typical Maya style, eyes square and long trunk-like nose hanging over gaping mouths.

Torches burned on either side of the temple platform. As if from nowhere, an etheric white form appeared standing before the temple door. Lifting her arms, the dark-haired priestess with towering feathered headdress gave benedictions to those below. A quick image flashed by of a young man in royal regalia standing just behind the priestess.

Jana was abruptly awake, her heart pounding. She knew this woman, this priestess.

She is my Maya guide, the one I sensed behind me in Calistoga!

Everything was so familiar, but where was this occurring? It certainly didn't look like any pyramids in Tikal, or the Pyramid of the Sun at Chichén Itzá, a square structure with four stairways, one on each side. This unknown place was undoubtedly connected with her Maya mission. She had to find it.

Carmen Wilson sat at a round bistro table on the sidewalk outside the Uncommon Grounds coffee and deli. She spoke with animation into her cell phone while flipping through an elegant leather day planner spread on the table. Tapping its open page with a pen, she had a staccato exchange with her realty office. Legs crossed, her rapidly shaking foot revealed her irritation. As Jana approached carrying two lattes, Carmen finished her conversation and snapped the cell phone closed with a sigh.

"When will they ever get things right?" Carmen complained in exasperation. "It's a wonder I ever close any sales. You'd think they'd know to check details by now. In real estate if anything can get glitched up, it will. My office tries to make sure of that. Thanks, hun," she said as Jana put a tall steaming latte in front of her.

Jana sat and sipped the fragrant vanilla latte, appreciating the nice head of foam.

"They make a good latte here," she said.

"Um," was Carmen's retort. She was still making notes in her day planner.

The spring sun provided welcome warmth as a cool breeze ruffled the primroses growing in a nearby planter. It was too nice a day to sit inside, though the women needed sweaters to ward off the breeze.

Finally Carmen refocused and gave her attention to Jana, who had waited patiently.

"So," Carmen said, "you wanted to talk over a dilemma. To go or not to go, that is the question?"

"In a nutshell," Jana replied. She laid out the pros and cons of going to the Yucatan to join up with the School of Maya Mysteries pilgrimage.

"What do you really want to do?" Carmen asked.

"I want to go," said Jana. "I just don't know how to make it happen."

"The most important thing is being very, very clear about your intention. That is the crucial thing. When you send that clear intention into the universe, it will respond. Leave the details to the higher forces." Carmen watched Jana's reaction, sensing a slight hesitation.

"Here are the steps," she said. "I learned them some time ago from studying the Abraham Teachings. They really work. First, send your request to the universe. Make it as precise as you can. Don't include anything about how it should happen. Just say what you want. Second, the universe immediately responds, it is here to fulfill our requests, to provide us with what we want. Any gap between our asking and something happening has to do with our lack of clarity, or with blocking step number three. Third, allow the universe to give

261

you what you want. This sounds simple-minded, but most people don't know how to get into receptive mode. They keep asking and asking, and never tune into the receiving part of the equation. If your antenna isn't tuned into the right frequency, all you get is static. There you have it, the great secret of manifestation."

"That's it?" Jana sounded slightly incredulous. "Just ask for what you want, know the universe is there to provide it, and be receptive?"

"You didn't hear me," Carmen said brusquely. "The most important thing is being really clear about intention. No mixed signals. Feel it inside, feel what it is like when you have what you requested. Just like it has already happened."

"OK, I get that," Jana replied. She remembered her experience in Tikal when she wanted the rain to stop. She envisioned a sunny day, felt the sun on her skin and smelled the evaporating dew. She called on the rain god Chak and Ix Chel to stop the rain. And it happened.

"You're still not 100 percent," observed Carmen in her not unkind but penetrating way. "There's still a little doubt. When you want to manifest, you can't have doubt."

"That's hard. I really want to go, but I'm worried about how that will impact Robert, work and our finances."

"You told me this is a mission, something you feel called to do, right? Then you do what you know you have to, and leave the consequences to the Divine. And you leave the specifics of how it will work out to the Divine also. Don't try to tell the Infinite Force how to do its business. Remember what Reverend Taylor said at last Sunday service?"

Carmen paused a moment, thinking, as Jana shook her head.

"Oh, you weren't there, you were in Clearlake. Anyway, his talk was right on this point: 'My ways are not thy ways, saith the Lord.' You can't figure it out. You've got to trust the process. Geez, I wish I could apply this to my real estate office," she ended ruefully.

At home, Jana sat in meditation. She set her intention:

I want to join the pilgrimage for the equinox ceremony at Chichén Itzá.

Repeating this in her mind, she felt deeply into her heart. It confirmed the choice. When her mind started injecting doubts, worries, uncertainties, what if's, she quickly put these thoughts aside. She held an inner image of herself meeting the group in Mérida, standing beside Aurora Nakin and Hanab Xiu, doing ritual with them at the Pyramid of the Sun. During that moment, she was there, it had already happened.

She got on the internet and checked out flights and hotels. To her surprise, she found a reasonably priced Mexicana Airlines flight from Los Angeles to México City to Mérida. There were several inexpensive commuter flights from Oakland to Los Angeles. She connected with an on-line Mexican travel agency and booked into the same hotel the group was using in Mérida, as well as one overnight in Piste for the Chichén Itzá ceremony.

Piste—wasn't that the town Angelina Menchu was from? It's right next to Chichén Itzá. What an irony, or more accurately, a synchronicity.

The next day at work Jana planned to talk with her supervisor about getting off. Before she did, however, Mary approached her with an astonishing request. Mary's sister was having unexpected surgery the coming week, and Mary wanted to be there to provide support and help with the children. She asked Jana to switch four workdays with her—Thursday through Sunday, March 20-23, for Mary's four days the coming week when Jana was off.

The universe does work in wondrous ways, Jana mused. Indeed, the ways of this mysterious force were not the ways of human understanding. Of course, she agreed to the schedule change. Two parts of the dilemma had effortlessly fallen into place. The last was the hardest. She planned to have a discussion that night with Robert about the pilgrimage trip, now just over two weeks away.

After a nice dinner, Jana and Robert were ensconced in their favorite chairs. Each was rehearsing mentally what they wanted to say to the other. A barely perceptible current of tension ran between them. Jana spoke first.

"Robert, there's something I need to talk to you about."

He put down the music magazine he wasn't really reading and turned toward her.

"That's funny, I've got something to talk over with you, too."

Jana sensed what it was about, and knew it bode ill for her trip plans. She considered whether it was best to let him say his piece, or to put forth her intentions first. Deciding the former might be more strategic, she said:

"Ok, tell me."

He switched positions, re-crossing his legs and leaning slightly forward.

"Its about your Maya involvement," he said with gravity. "I don't think it's leading in a direction that's best for you, or for us. You seem obsessed by it, driven by some unseen force. I feel it's pulling you away from me, from our life together."

She felt her heart sink. This was going in the worst possible direction. She was taken aback by the emotion in his voice; she had not realized how her Maya involvement might drive a wedge between them.

"What are you suggesting I do?" It was the best she could come up with.

"Don't pursue it any more."

"But what about the dream? All the pieces that fit together linking the dream to the Maya? I had the dream again a couple of nights ago, and it went even further. After the young girl left the old woman in the stone structure, there was a scene in front of a huge pyramid, different from any I've ever seen but definitely Mayan. At the temple on top a priestess appeared and I felt I knew her, though I couldn't place where or when this was happening. I'm sure if I just go a little more into it, the dream will finish and I'll know what it's all about."

"Ok, keep exploring the dream, go back to Carla Hernandez, but don't get involved with Maya groups and other stuff," Robert acquiesced.

"Like the School of Maya Mysteries?" she asked, already knowing the answer.

"Yes."

"Robert, I can't do that," she said with a touch of irritation. "I know you don't understand it, but this is a mission for me. It's something I've been called to do, like a sacred contract with Spirit. When I was at Clearlake, I learned about the purpose of the Maya, how their ancient wisdom is going to help bring the world into balance now. The people there are committed to putting this wisdom into action. It's good, and positive, and teaches people to live according to natural laws. You know what a mess the world is now, with the U.S. acting like an imperial power about to invade a sovereign nation. We all need to do what we can to stop this power-mongering that serves the wealthy, and damages everything else."

"Jana, there's nothing you can do to change the world situation," Robert replied.

"How do you know?" she flashed back. "What if there was something I could do, some small act that would add to the momentum for change? I'd feel terrible if I didn't do it, and things continued on the road to disaster. I know, I know, you think I'm having delusions of grandeur. I'm not fooling myself about my individual power, there's a huge worldwide web of forces at play. But this I do believe: If I feel strongly called do to something for the greater good and I don't do it, I lose my honor and integrity. Whether it makes a measurable difference or not, it matters a lot inside of me."

Robert leaned back and shook his head. He was getting exasperated with her.

"So what is it you're called to do?" he asked, knowing something was up.

Jana took a deep breath, pulled into her center and prayed for courage.

"The group from the School of Maya Mysteries is going on a pilgrimage to several Maya temples. They're taking part in an important spring equinox ceremony at Chichén Itzá, along with lots of other Maya elders and initiates. I want to be there. I believe this is the ceremony that Tuwa Waki, the Hopi medicine woman, told me about. It's my mission to be there, for some reason. I guess to fulfill a Maya prophesy that will affect the planet's transition into the next age. I got some pretty powerful confirmation of this at the conference in Clearlake."

"You want to go to México when . . . the spring equinox, that's in two weeks, right?" he asked with incredulity.

Jana nodded. She watched the signs of anger play over Robert's face, signs she knew well. His eyes narrowed to slits of glinting cold blue, killer eyes of his Viking heritage, no doubt. Furrows lined his brow and his lips pulled downward into a scowl. The muscles of his neck tensed and small blood vessels on his temples stood out.

"For God's sake, Jana," he said forcefully, "the world condition is really unstable now. Bush might invade Iraq any day, setting off who knows what chain reaction—terrorist attacks, global war, breakdown of international relations. This is no time for foreign travel."

"It's just México," she retorted with rising ire. "I doubt there's going to be war in México."

"But international travel could be affected," he argued. "Terrorists can strike anywhere, and I'm worried about airport security there."

"OK, look, I do appreciate your concern for my safety," Jana acceded, " but everything in life has its risks. You could get killed driving to work."

"That's a lot less risky than flying to México on the eve of a war," he snapped back.

They sat in silence for a few moments. Jana was starting to feel desperate.

"Robert, please try to understand," she said more gently. "This is something I've got to do. I'll be all right, Spirit will protect me."

"Jana, listen," he said with deep sincerity, some of the anger fading from his face. "I love you very much, you're precious to me. It's not just the physical danger of going, it would be another thing to push us farther apart. I'm asking you now, please don't do this to our relationship. Please don't go."

Tears flooded Jana's eyes at his heart-wrenching plea.

Oh Lord, she thought, *why did it have to come to this?* She loved Robert more dearly than anyone else in her life, she treasured their marriage. The possibility of losing him was almost more than she could bear. She cried more, unable to stop the flow of tears that carried her grief and despair. Through broken sobs, without her willing it, some part of her inner being spoke out:

"I . . I love you . . so much . . . I'm so, so . . . sor-ry . . . but . . .but, I've . . . just . .got to . . to go."

Robert stood up, furious. He usually was softened by her crying, but now his anger exploded past any compassion.

"I can't believe you would choose some insane mission, this crazy Maya obsession, over me!" He paced back and forth, fists clenched, arms waving. "I can't even believe it! You're out of your mind, Jana!"

Anger began rising through her grief and tears.

"What you really mean," she said in choked voice, "is that I've got to do what you want for us to have a relationship. What gives you the right to define my life?"

"Don't our lives together mean anything to you?" he yelled.

"I don't have a life if you tell me everything to do!" she yelled back, furiously wiping tears away. "I don't tell you how to run your life."

"Don't be such a hypocrite. You're pretty full of advice," he retorted in contained fury. He was moving into his cold, sarcastic phase. "Now take some advice from me. Don't go on this trip, or you might not have a marriage to come back to."

She could feel him distancing emotionally, the threat heavy with possibility. There was nowhere to go with the argument. Tears of despair flowed again and she sobbed harder, bent over with face in hands, weaving her upper body back and forth in her chair.

"Look," he said, grabbing her shoulders and jerking her upright. His slitted blue eyes bore like lightening flashes into hers. "You think it over. You're destroying our relationship. I'm going out to have a drink and cool down. Don't do this, Jana."

He stormed out of the house, slamming the door loudly.

Jana cried, her body racked with great sobs, gasping for breath. Finally she was cried out, exhausted, depleted. Her mind felt numb. Like a robot, she washed her face, brushed her teeth, took a couple of aspirins and went to bed.

In the uinal (month) of Uo the toads came out. They waited, buried in the hard earth, its surfaces cracked from the oppressive heat of the dry season. At the end of last fall's rains, the toads wriggled their flat, wide bodies into the wet earth, digging with back feet, noses pointing up. They inflated their loose skin to fill in crevices, fitting perfectly into their underground burrows, making it hard for searching paws and fingers to pull them out. Slumbering, they waited.

Before rains came, they knew. Awakening in the burrows, their calls rose up from mud dens through the cracked earth. Thousands of toad voices wafted up from earth, singing "uooooooh" in long plaintive cries. The noise of the Uo toads was deafening. But the people welcomed their cries, for this meant the life-giving rains were coming. Languishing trees, dried grasses, drooping vines, mud-caked ponds would soon spring into new life. People rejoiced as nature's cycle of replenishment began again.

Yalucha sat on a smooth boulder, very still. Rain fell, cooling her skin and dripping from nose and ears. Little rivulets ran down her arms and droplets hung from her lashes. She blinked but otherwise made no movement. She waited for the toads to come out. Uo was her birth month, and the Uo toad was her uay, her spirit animal. Every spring she waited patiently, sitting still for hours, anticipating that magic moment when the Uo's emerged.

As the raindrops seeped down into the Uo's dens and loosened the soil, the toads began to dig, pushing their way to the surface. The dirt trembled here and there, and soon a webbed foot or a pointed snout broke through. Struggling and heaving their 2-3 inch bodies out of their burrows, the mud-caked toads emerged. At first it was just a handful, but shortly the ground was covered with the tiny creatures. "Uooooooh" cries mingled with pounding rain and the musty smell of wet humus.

Still unmoving, Yalucha sang as her mother had sung to her, from earliest childhood as far as she could remember:

"Little children of the earth,
    Rain comes to give new birth.
    Leave your dens and find the pond,
    While we listen to your song."

As the rain dissolved caked mud, she saw their colors: a maroon-brown body displaying a smattering of orange spots with a black line running down the back. Small beady eyes peered from a pointed snout and thick webbing stretched between toes. Smooth, loose skin fell like a dress from rounded sides, belly brushing the ground as the toads waddled toward the nearby pond. There, they inflated loose skins and floated out like dusky balloons. The males commenced their mating call, which could be heard for miles. The Uo toads were the pets of Chak, the rain god. They were the musicians of rebirth.

Two cycles of Uo had passed since Yalucha's mother Xoc Ikal sent her to Xunantunich to complete training as a priestess of Ix Chel.   Similar to the toads, the young woman felt she had undergone rebirth during this time. Her body had changed from a lanky slender girl into a shapely woman, with firm full breasts and rounded hips. Even more remarkable, however, was the metamorphosis of her mind. She had learned the power of plant medicine and practiced the rituals that invoked spirit forces for healing. She had journeyed to the domain of the gods and used her visions for guidance. Under the tutelage of skilled priestesses and priests, she was becoming an adept.

Ix Chel

It had not been easy. Even with the herbal lore gained from her mother, Yalucha felt overwhelmed by the vast store of knowledge needed by healers. The primary plant medicine teacher, an elderly H'men named Ubah, was exacting of her students. In the early hours following dawn, Ubah led the acolytes into the jungle to gather plants. Cotton bags slung over their shoulders, the small group of young women yawned sleepily, treading carefully on the slippery path. Within minutes they left the city border and were swallowed in dense foliage, dripping from night rains.

Ubah stopped frequently, pointing out an herb or plant needed for the day's Nine Xiv formula, or to restock their standard supplies. Xiv—medicinal leaf—was a collection of nine herbs that varied from day to day, used for baths and teas. There were hundreds of pairs of Xiv, always a male and female plant paired together. The combination was determined by the Tzolk'in calendar day, for each day held its own energies that influenced how the body responded to illness. Ubah carried all that information in her seemingly limitless memory. The acolytes were required to learn it, little by little, day by day.

No one knew how old Ubah was. Gnarled hands, still supple despite knotty arthritic fingers, hung from thin muscled arms. She was stooped from a twisted spine and hunchback, but was surprisingly agile. Tough and resilient, her energy outlasted that of her students and belied her advanced age. She walked rapidly, feet sure on the uneven paths, eyes scouting foliage like a hawk.

They called her the "miss-thrown vessel of endless wisdom" or less kindly, the "old cracked pot." But they respected her immensely.

"Each plant has its signature," Ubah told them. "If you look closely, feel and smell, it will give you a sign about how to use its medicine. Here is a pair, very important for you to learn."

She caressed a woody vine with rough dark bark, spindly but enormous as it stretched precariously several hundred feet into the dappled sunlight of the rainforest canopy. It looped itself around branches of several towering trees.

"This is Ki Bix, Cow's Hoof, used to stop bleeding of the womb and watery bowels. It counteracts poisoning, but is itself a poison when taken in excess. Here is its sign."

Deftly she cut through a stem with a sharp obsidian blade, revealing a cross pattern on the branch.

"The cross is always a warning. It tells you the plant is medicinal, but toxic. You must use it with caution. The vine is chopped and boiled as a tea, but only taken in small sips three times each kin (day). Now where is she?"

Ubah twisted around, looking intently at the surrounding trees.

"Ah, there you are," she sang sweetly, approaching another vine growing four feet from the Ki Bix. "This is his mate, Ix Ki Bix, Female Cow's Hoof. They always grow together. See how they intertwine above in loving embrace?"

The acolytes craned their necks to see the smooth-barked female vine, covered with three-inch thorns, looping around tree branches until it met and intertwined with the male vine about 50 feet above. Ubah scratched the bark then cut through a branch of the female vine. Underneath the dark bark, the vine was mahogany-red, with layers of varying hue throughout.

"See her red color? Many plants used for women's conditions have a reddish tint. Ix Ki Bix is the color of the womb membrane. She gives power to prevent making babies. But you must use her carefully. Boil a handful of chopped vine in three cups water until the color turns dark red, then drink one cup three times each kin when moon blood flows. This dries out the womb membrane, it prevents the pregnancy from sticking. Taken for one moon flow, the effects last five uinal (months). Taken for two moon flows, they last ten uinal. And, taken for nine moon flows makes a woman permanently barren."

Her dark intense eyes peered from deep sockets, appraising the young women gathered around her. She made clucking sounds deep in her throat, as was her wont when pondering some thought.

"For you, ones so young, this is not a good medicine," she warned.

Several girls giggled or drew in deep breaths of shock.

Ubah grinned lewdly, her mouth a dark cavern behind a few scraggly teeth. She made an obscene gesture, drawing more gasps from the girls.

"Do not pretend such innocence," she said nonchalantly. "When the blood runs hot and your heart is erupting, you will not be so proper. For the young ones, make a tea of cedar bark and drink three times each kin for 3 kin before the moon flow starts. The effects last only one uinal, it is not permanent."

She winked in collusion, imagining their youthful passions, then admonished: "This is knowledge best kept among women."

Yalucha exchanged glances with her friend Olal. Tints of pink blushed the high cheeks of both young women. Ubah's earthy crudeness amused and embarrassed them, while they loved her passion for healing and playful friendship with plants.

Olal fluttered around Yalucha like a moth drawn to a bright flame. Spontaneous and flighty, the shorter girl found Yalucha's steadiness had a grounding effect. Olal came from the noble family of Cahal Pech, a small city only one-half kin's walk from Xunantunich. A hint of awe colored her regard for the girl from Mutul. She had never been to a truly large city, and could barely imagine the soaring pyramid temples, huge palaces and broad plazas of the gargantuan power. Her parents had been there once to pay tribute to the ruler, bringing back endless stories of Mutul's wealth and high living.

Love for nature drew the girls to each other. Many hours were spent finding where lizards hid, coaxing blue-crowned motmots and rainbow-billed toucans from tree perches with bits of fruit, chattering with spider monkeys, and spotting iguanas in the tallest branches overhanging the river. Once they caught a glimpse of the fearful kum

271

cokoo, yellow-neck fer-de-lance, slithering into the root cavern of a fallen ceiba tree. Kum cokoo was sacred to Ix Chel, worn by the goddess on her headdress. One bite from the asper's sharp fangs injected toxin causing internal bleeding and paralysis; death ensues within minutes. Rarely did a person survive, although legend told of two miraculous cures by Ix Chel priestesses at Xunantunich.

Many villagers came to the healing temple at Xunantunich. Some traveled long distances through jungle trails, or paddled canoes up the river arcing around the high promontory on which the small city perched. A neutral sanctuary, the city ministered to any supplicant, regardless of political ties or family status. Patients and family members were received graciously, fed and housed while the sick and injured recovered. The skill of Ix Chel's healers was legendary.

It was a daunting tradition to live up to. Yalucha made some mistakes at first, nothing too serious, thank the Goddess. One of her early full-responsibility patients was a little boy with watery bowels. His mother, a broad-faced buxom villager, carried the small child in a back sling on the four-kin journey from her village. The trails were overgrown, so she used a long chert blade to slash through underbrush. Desperation had driven the village woman. The village healer had been powerless to help her child, who had been sick for three uinal.

The listless boy looked up at Yalucha, igniting her healing instincts. His hollow eyes were bright with fever, lips dry and cracked. Thin arms and legs dangled uselessly, while his belly ballooned out grotesquely. He whimpered pitifully when his bowels rumbled and ran. The mother tenderly stroked his head, saying:

"Three uinal he hardly eats or drinks, he vomits and his bowels run. Our village healer gave herb teas and poultices, but nothing helps. He is so weak! We must see the H'men, he said. Bad wind in the belly. More is needed, go to Xunantunich. He is my only boy, please help!"

Tears ran down her broad cheeks as she cradled the boy closer. Yalucha watched his heart throbbing against paper-thin skin stretched taut over protruding ribs. She held his wrists to feel pulses, which fluttered weakly against her fingers like a dying butterfly. The child was very sick and would not survive more than a few days, unless the illness was cured.

Leaving the wide platform covered with thick fiber mats on which patients sat, Yalucha entered the rectangular Xiv House where herbs were dried and prepared. She gathered a handful of fresh Epasote (wormseed) leaves, mashed them with a small mortar and pestle, then added the juice to warm water. Watery bowels were such a common problem that Epasote was picked each kin, so fresh leaves were always at hand. A pot of water simmered on the hearth all day, ready for use.

Yalucha treated the boy with Epasote juice for two kin, giving him 5 doses while he was awake. She urged sips of broth through his reluctant lips, and gave him frequent rubs with cool water to reduce fever. On the second kin she added a tea of zutz pakal (sour orange) leaves, helpful for fever, vomiting and watery bowels. The fever went down, and the boy vomited less, but his bowels kept emptying frequently. He was only a little better.

Ubah made rounds to observe the work of her charges. Yalucha explained her therapies while her mentor examined the thin boy with the big belly. Ubah listened to noises in the boy's belly then grunted knowingly.

"Siro is the problem," she pronounced. "White siro. Mucus and ulcers in the stomach. Siro jumps in the belly like a frog, makes too much wind, too much water. Everything wants to come out, both ways. Nothing wants to stay down. Right, Mama?"

The village woman nodded, intimidated by the gnarled old H'man's powerful aura.

"There are three types of siro," Ubah continued. "White siro with mucusy runs, red siro with bloody bowels, and dry siro when the stool is stuck inside. The boy also has parasites, so giving him Epasote was a good thing. Zutz pakal always helps fever and vomiting, so that is good. But what the child needs to recover from siro is pay-che (skunk root), very strong medicine. You must be careful with pay-che, lest it prove too potent in weakened patients. Come, I will show you how to prepare it for him."

As Ubah led Yalucha inside the Xiv House, she called over her shoulder:

"Have courage, Mama. Your child will be well."

In the herb pantry, Ubah grabbed a small handful of chopped pay-che root, scooped hot water into a smaller pot and mixed in the root. She stoked one side of the fire to bring the root pot to a boil.

"It must boil six hundred heartbeats," Ubah intoned. "Until you have that sense of time in your bones, you must count, Yalucha."

Yalucha felt her own pulse, counting her heartbeats.

I hope my heart does not beat too fast.

She was excited and humbled at the same time. Ubah nodded a few moments after Yalucha finished the count, removing the bowl carefully with a rag and straining the liquid into a cup.

"He must sip this throughout the kin," she instructed. "Also give him sips of water and broth very often. He will be well in seven kin. Pay-che cleanses stomach and intestines, heals ulcers and sores, and starts moon cycle bleeding. Adults must take one cup before each meal."

She paused thoughtfully, adding:

"Pay-che is the shaman's friend. It increases your powers and dispels envy and evil spirits. Study this plant, Yalucha. Come to know it. Listen to it, it will help you think, it will show you what you want to learn."

The boy was well in seven kin. He and his mother stayed the rest of the uinal, while he ate heartily, regaining weight and strength. The village woman had nothing to give but her undying gratitude. While no payment was expected, people understood that gifts to the healers allowed them to continue their work. So she swept and cleaned, cooked and sewed for the priestesses. Before returning to her village, she gave bouquets of jungle flowers to Yalucha and Ubah.

The young women sat on the cool stone floor, in welcome dimness. Summer heat wilted both plants and people. Thick stone and plaster walls held the night's dampness and allowed slivers of filtered sunlight to stream through narrow windows. Seated on woven mats, they formed a semi-circle. Lilting tones of their girlish voices echoed softly in the long, rectangular room of the House of Learning. The acolytes gathered here, bordering the main plaza, for training with the High Priestess, Zac Kuk.

Voices hushed as the High Priestess strode majestically into the room, every step worthy of a formal procession. Zac Kuk was tall and stately, features finely sculpted, thick black braids wound crown-like atop her head, white robe billowing around shapely brown limbs as she walked. She was the embodiment of her name: White Quetzal, the most pure and rare form of the Resplendent Quetzal bird, whose serpentine tail feathers were highly prized for adornment. The quetzal was the uayob of the feathered serpent god, a powerful deity associated with Venus.[13]

Zac Kuk carried a small incensor filled with glowing chunks of copal. The young women stood as she made ritual gestures to the four directions with the incensor, creating sacred space. Woody, pungent fumes wafted through the room. Placing the incensor on a low altar in the center of the room, she led the acolytes in chant-like prayers. All then sat down, Zac Kuk facing the semi-circle of eager young faces.

"We practice *panche be*, seeking the root of truth, knowing in order to understand," she spoke in clear, resonant tones. "In the codes, in the symbols, lives the essence of what these represent. When you understand the mystery of how the essence lives in the form, you become a sage, a seer. We have studied the symbol 'G' and its hidden meanings. What do you remember about these teachings?"

Yalucha and Olal exchanged quick glances, but nothing escaped Zac Kuk's piercing vision. Nodding at Olal, the High Priestess gesturing for her to speak. The smaller girl squirmed uncomfortably. She did not like having to recite, her mind was not agile and quick like Yalucha's, and her memory often proved faulty.

Priests and priestesses followed an oral tradition; it was forbidden to write out the sacred incantations and formulas. Writing was the purview of the scribes, who used syllabic and representational glyphs to glorify the deeds of rulers and powerful nobles. Hidden within complex, intricate patterns were sacred symbols, rich in esoteric knowledge for those with the vision to see.

"*Ge* is the egg, the value of zero, the creator of the worlds," Olal recited tentatively, using the Maya sound for 'G.'

Zac Kuk nodded and waited. All the acolytes seemed to be holding their breath. Yalucha sent a mental energy beam to support her friend.

"The . . the egg . . . uh, Egg-Creator is the essence . . ." Olal pursed her lips and screwed her face in an effort to remember. "The essence . . . uh, the seed from which all life springs."

"That is correct," smiled Zac Kuk, as the girls let out a simultaneous breath of relief. One plump young woman at the end of the semi-circle snickered under her breath. Yalucha shifted her gaze

---

[13] The quetzal is found carved in stone and painted on pottery throughout the Maya world. In the Late Classic period the feathered serpent god was called Kukulkán by the Maya and Quetzalcoatl by the Toltec Mexicans.

under half-lowered lids, hoping Zac Kuk would not notice, and shot forth a tiny energy missile of anger to the unsympathetic acolyte.

Ahpo Hel shifted her round buttocks quickly as if stung by an insect, swatting at her thigh. Exactly at that moment, Zac Kuk directed her penetrating gaze toward the girl, commanding:

"Tell more of the hidden meanings of 'G,' Ahpo Hel."

Yalucha wondered if the plump girl's discomfort was due to Zac Kuk's questioning, her own attack, or an actual insect. At least her action had escaped notice, she thought smugly.

"Ge is the place we have come from," replied Ahpo Hel, collecting herself with an indignant sniff. "It is far away in the skies, the great spiral of stars. It is where Holy Itzamna lives, the Blessed Creator of All."

"Very good," said Zac Kuk. "And what do we see when we look at the great spiral, the Celestial G?"[14]

Before Ahpo Hel could pull a reply from memory, another acolyte blurted out:

"We see the white dome spread across the night sky, the egg of creation, holding the Sacred World Tree!"

The High Priestess nodded calmly, while Ahpo Hel shrugged with a sour expression on her face. The plump girl was not well liked by the other acolytes. Her sarcastic manner and quick criticism made them keep their distance.

"Now, who will describe the four layers between our physical forms and the Celestial G?" asked Zac Kuk.

Silence fell upon the acolytes, as each searched memory for the answer.

"I will!" Yalucha called out enthusiastically. Zac Kuk nodded for her to continue. "The first layer is the visible form, the physical body. It is tangible and palpable, we can use our sight, smell, hearing and touch to know it. The second layer is invisible, but we can feel it emanate from living things. It radiates out from their forms, like body heat or fierceness from the jaguar. The third layer is mind and thought. We cannot see these, but we can see their effects in what people do and say. The fourth layer is pure essence, the vital energy of spirit that inhabits and surrounds our body and mind. This is the 'G' within us."

---

[14] The Maya letter 'G' represents the spiral view of the Milky Way, and zero symbolizes the horizontal view of this sombrero galaxy.

A flicker of admiration sparked in Zac Kuk's eyes, but her face remained impassive.

"You have spoken well, Yalucha," she said. "Students, hear and remember. These are the words of hidden truth, things you must never forget. Our ancestors came from the Celestial G, and we have emanated from this essence. It is our destiny to return. It is your responsibility as priestesses to visit the Central Sun in the heart of the Celestial G, the abode of Itzamna, in your visions. On this earth, the Middle World, flowers and song are the highest things that can penetrate the confines of this hidden truth. Use them to know *ge*."

When the acolytes were released for their lunch break, Zac Kuk took Yalucha aside. She waited until they were alone, then spoke softy so lingering ears would not detect her words.

"You have a calling, daughter," Zac Kuk murmured. With a knowing smile, she gently admonished: "Already the power of Spirit grows within you. Never use it for harm or in anger."

Yalucha lowered her eyes, feeling penitent for sending angry energy to Ahpo Hel.

"Ix Chel has chosen you for a great task," continued Zac Kuk. "It will not be easy for you, there will be much suffering. You do not have to accept it. If you do, your soul will reside in several bodies over many baktuns. You will remember, when others have long forgotten who they were to you in earlier times. Your heart will ache, but it will also rejoice for the good you have done to save our world."

She placed one hand over Yalucha's heart, it was beating rapidly like a startled doe. The girl gazed with awe and trust into the taller woman's eyes.

"Do not speak of this to anyone. You do not need to answer now. Your answer must be given directly from your heart to Spirit."

"Yes, Mother of My Soul," Yalucha replied in a daze. Soft warmth spread through her chest from Zac Kuk's hand, calming the palpitations.

Taking both of Yalucha's hands, Zac Kuk drew her down until both women were kneeling, facing each other. Palm to palm, their eyes locked as powerful emanations pulsated between their solar plexus, hearts, throats and foreheads. The High Priestess began a soft singing chant; soon the younger woman's voice joined in:

"Hebix u top'ol nek'e, hebix u hok'ol yalche y tipil lol,
(As the seed buds, as the flower emerges and blossoms,)
Beyo hebix u zihil le wuinice.
(In this way is born the human being.)

277

Ix Chel, ti tech in dzama in wuinclil yetel in vol."
(Ix Chel, to you I surrender my body and my spirit.)

Golden beams of sunlight filtered through the forest canopy high above, forming lacy patterns on the moist humus covering the ground, dancing as wind ruffled through leaves. A crimson streak flashing through the sea of green announced a scarlet macaw, screeching in irritation at the young woman sitting below his favorite perch. Squawks and chattering replied to his outburst, then the jungle fell silent again. Tall tree sentinels stood in quiet repose, supporting voluptuous vines twining along branches, drooping long trumpet-shaped white flowers. Tiny, delicate ferns peeped shyly behind thick surface roots, coated with lime-colored mossy lichens. An insect buzzed softly in the distance.

Yalucha sat cross-legged on the soft humus, facing a copal tree. Its trunk was as large as two stout warriors, covered with smooth, pinkish gray bark. Two rivulets of sticky sap dripped from where the trunk had been tapped for its sweet resin. Hardened copal resin formed granules that were burned as incense for sacred ceremonies. Dark green, leathery leaves with distinct veins lifted skyward, reaching up through the canopy for the sun's kisses. A rainbow-billed toucan deftly plucked the small, smooth fruits with his extravagant beak, sharing the upper limbs with the disgruntled macaw.

Her assignment was to communicate with a tree. In this process, she would learn the hidden knowledge, the root truth, the *panche be* of the letter "T." The stately Ceiba was the sacred tree of the Maya, they called it *yaxche*, "first the tree." It was made first during the creation of the world, used by the creator gods to raise the sky from the waters, making space for things to live. The sacred Ceiba rose through the center of the four directions, it was the axis of the world, called *Wacah Chan*, "raised up sky." The roots plunged deep into the watery Underworld, the trunk went through the Middleworld, and the branches stretched to the highest level of the Upperworld far away in the sky.

The Sacred World Tree, Wacah Chan, was not located in any one earthly place; it was of the Spirit domain. Through ritual, shamans could materialize it into existence during ecstatic visions, opening the awesome doorway into the Otherworld, both lower and higher. There they could communicate with gods and ancestors.

Te, "T" stood for this Sacred World Tree. Humans emerged from a split in the branches of this tree during the final stage of creation, as they entered the world. The tree and the human were of similar substance; trees have reactions similar to humans. Trees sustained life with the Breath of Spirit, forming the air and wind that feed human breath. *Uinic,* to be human, was literally being the tuber, *ui,* of the immense cosmic root, *nic.* Trees gave people shelter, fruits and nuts, and medicines. Like humans, they produced sounds, emitting screams, cries and moans when buffeted by strong forces. Trees also had psychic abilities, they could produce visions and evoke apparitions. The Trickster, *x'tabay,* always appeared near a tree when tempting solitary travelers off the road into the dense jungle.

Two intertwined serpents around the World Tree were the positive and negative energies of the life force. They maintained the tension of dualities, the sustaining cosmic essence and the activating, outward forces of physical life. The Maya were the children of the tree; the split from which they emerged symbolized the garden of Tamuanchan, the place of birth, the mystical West where gods and humans originated.

Eyes closed, Yalucha concentrated intently on the copal tree. Behind her were two young Ceibas, their sacred essence quietly supporting her effort. She had selected the copal tree for communication, because she wanted to understand why its resin had such power to invoke expanded states of consciousness. As she meditated, her breath became shallow and so slow that her rib cage barely moved. Not a muscle twitched. An imperceptible heartbeat moved just enough blood to keep tissues from anoxia.

Whispering leaves tantalized her with a language she did not grasp. Deep humming emanated from the trunk, distinct from buzzing insects. Without words, she asked the tree to speak to her. She sent it love and respect. She waited.

We are the guardians.

It was simply an awareness in her mind, not actual words. But it came from the copal tree in an arc of telepathy.

The guardians of spirit. Our sap is cosmic essence. The blood of gods. The mystery of creation. The itz through which gods become manifest.

Yalucha's body vibrated with the frequency of the humming sound. Boundaries of body and mind melted away, she merged with the tree, entered into its core. She felt thin veins of sap flowing through her body like tiny undulating snakes. Tingling, exciting, filling her cells with life force. Beneath she sensed a web of roots probing deeply into the soil, felt droplets of water entering and

279

flowing upward. Deep, grounded, solid. Rising rapidly from the base of her spine to her crown, the tingling energy burst upward into a profusion of billowing leaves, dancing with the sunlight, breathing out the breath of life, breathing in the wastes of creatures, keeping the wind in perfect balance. She felt the force of Spirit—the *itz*, gift of life—forming into resin, imbuing the sticky sap with mystical powers. The strong sweet woody smell of burning copal incense filled her nostrils.

Slowly the intense sensations dissipated. Body awareness returned as the young woman and the tree became separate beings. Musty humus odors replaced the sweet copal incense. The scarlet macaw screeched with irritated impatience; his domain too long intruded upon. Tickling sensations on her bare arm caused Yalucha to open her eyes. A small iridescent bug wandered aimlessly along her forearm. Gently she brushed it off.

Sliding onto her knees, the acolyte bowed before the copal tree, wrists crossed over her heart. Saying a prayer of gratitude, she buried a round blue stone streaked with white between the roots, her offering of sky and wind to the sentinel spanning the worlds.

*   *   *   *   *   *

Olal burst into the room, calling in an excited flurry:

"Yalucha, Yalucha, foreigners have arrived! They're all men! Merchants and warriors from Uaxactun, and one of them injured his leg. Come quickly, Zac Kuk is treating him now."

Yalucha looked up from the side of the girl she was treating, applying medicinal packs to the patient's wrinkled abdomen draped like thin cloth over a gourd-sized womb. Barely old enough for moon cycles, the girl had conceived too soon. She labored hard and long, the womb struggling to push out the baby that was almost too large for passage through her small pelvic bones. The labor lasted three kin, too long for the child to survive. It was only through the grace of Ix Chel that the young mother was alive, although seriously depleted from blood loss and exhaustion.

"Be calm, Olal," Yalucha admonished her excitable friend. "You disturb the little mama, she has suffered enough. I will come in a moment."

Carefully securing the herbal packs of rue leaves, grated ginger and basil, she felt the patient's pulse and was reassured by the full, even stroke. The herbal packs were effectively relieving cramps and keeping the womb contracted to control blood flow. The girl had

280

drifted into sleep, breathing steadily. It was safe to leave her for a while.

Olal led the way, scurrying hastily up the path to the main plaza. Yalucha needed big strides to keep up, amused at the shorter woman's excitement. Bring a few men near, and Olal went into a flutter.

Bordering the main plaza was the residence house for guests. On the low stairs leading up to the platform, a group had gathered, a mixture of familiar acolytes and strangers, all young men. Nodding politely, the two young women passed the group and squeezed into the acolytes clustered around the door, peering into the room where Zac Kuk attended the injured foreigner.

The lump and slight indentation on his left shin were sure signs of a displaced fracture. The well-muscled young man lay still, already sedated with relaxing herbs. Zac Kuk had one hand over his heart and one on his forehead, as she chanted softly. Two priests prepared his leg for setting the bone. The High Priestess spoke in the man's ear, his eyelids twitched in acknowledgement. She placed a smooth leather strap between his teeth, putting her hands on his temples and nodding at the two priests. One grasped the knee, the other grasped the ankle, and almost before the man had time to bite the strap, they straightened the broken bone with a deft twist. It slipped into place with a subtle grinding noise. The man moaned once, then drifted into drugged sleep. Under Zac Kuk's expert guidance, the priests applied a wooden splint bound with cotton wraps and strong leather cords.

Yalucha and Olal exchanged admiring glances. Zac Kuk always handled the most difficult cases, combining extensive healing skills with mystical incantations that drew in the power of spiritual forces. All that was needed now was time for the bone to mend.

Olal tugged on the short sleeve of Yalucha's huipil, drawing her toward the young men lingering on the platform and stairs. Several acolytes were flirting with them already, a mutually pleasurable activity. Olal quickly engaged one stranger in conversation, but Yalucha held back, walking slowly to the far edge of the platform. She sensed a presence behind her, turned suddenly and nearly bumped into the young man.

He stood a half-head taller than the young priestess. Warm brown eyes, lively and intelligent, scanned her with appreciation. His nose was straighter than most, though prominent, blending into the elongated flat forehead considered attractive by Mayas. Full, curved lips hinted of passion. As he smiled, the stones embedded in his teeth sparkled and a subtle dimple winked in his left cheek.

As their eyes met, Yalucha felt a whirring sensation in her mid-chest, like the wings of a tiny hummingbird lightly brushing her heart.

"Greetings, Lady," he said in a rich baritone voice. "May I ask, are you a priestess here?"

"A priestess of Ix Chel in training," she demurred, dropping her eyes.

"Ah, the priestess-healers of Ix Chel are most respected in my city, and all around," he enthused. "I am certain my comrade will recover fully. How long do you think it will take for his leg to mend?"

"At least 40 kin, perhaps a little more," she replied. "It was a bad break, displaced. Zac Kuk and the priests set it very nicely."

"That long! We may need to shorten our trip, to return while the river still runs high," he reflected.

"Where are you going?" Yalucha was quite curious about travel.

"To the Great Water in the East, across a large bay to an island. There we meet with traders from long distances up the coast. The place is called Nohnab Hol (Great Water Portal)."

He flashed his dazzling smile again, setting off the pleasant whirring around Yalucha's heart. She noticed that his even teeth were square, not filed into points as were her warrior uncle's. Perhaps that custom had not yet arrived at his city.

"Have you been to the Great Water in the East?" he asked.

"No, I have not traveled much. My heart would be pleased at seeing it."

"Then you must come with us," he offered impulsively.

Yalucha laughed at his forthright manner.

"Oh, I do not think Zac Kuk would permit me," she said. "We follow a rigorous schedule of training and caring for the sick. And, she would never allow her acolytes to travel with a group of men. It is not fitting for maidens."

"Yes, yes, of course," he murmured, but his lively eyes danced with schemes.

"Are you of Uaxactun?" she inquired.

"I am," he replied with pride. "It is a great city of many people. Where is your umbilicus buried?" This phrase was commonly used to refer to the city of birth. It was the Maya custom to bury the afterbirth under the central hearth in one's home.

"I am of Mutul," she spoke slowly, carefully watching his reaction.

Two visitors standing not far away turned their heads sharply upon hearing the huge city's name spoken. The young man's eyebrows lifted, though the rest of his face remained neutral.

"May I ask, what is your name, Lady of Mutul?"

"Yalucha, daughter of K'an Nab Ku and Xoc Ikal. What is your name, Lord of Uaxactun?" Their status as nobles was evident to both young people.

"Chan Hun, of the Ac Tok family, kinsman to the ruler of Uaxactun."

"All are welcome here, Chan Hun. The temples of Ix Chel are places of peace, sanctuaries from all enmities and conflicts."

Her tacit recognition of their cities' enmity and proffering of sanctuary defused the tension that had been building between them.

"Indeed, it is so," he acknowledged. "I and my men are most grateful. Your temple's healing powers are a great boon for our injured comrade."

Several of his men had gathered and were staring impatiently, stomping to get his attention. He waved to them, and bowed slightly to Yalucha.

"I must go, Lady Yalucha. We will meet again soon."

Three kin of heavy rain kept the dwellers of the hilltop city inside. Bounding rivulets coursed down steep slopes, adding their impetus to the swiftly flowing river below. When the sun came out, the jungle steamed clouds of mist. Birds and monkeys chattered, lizards and iguanas came out to bask, people sang and moved about as life resumed its daily pace.

Yalucha descended carefully down a slippery path to the river, at times balancing by grasping trailing lianas. On level ground, she followed a well-worn path to a small clearing bordered by zapote, chakaj and aromatic allspice trees. Several times she stepped carefully over narrow paths of leaf-cutting ants, tiny sakbeobs criss-crossing the jungle floor along which the industrious insects carried their burdens of clipped leaves, waving like sails over their backs. Long-tailed monkeys skittered in the treetops. The distinctive double tap of a pale-billed woodpecker caught the young woman's attention. She paused, searching tree trunks for a glimpse of the large bird's brilliant red head and black body with a white V on the back. All her effort returned was the elusive woodpecker's voice clucking "kuk kuk kuk-uh-uh" punctuated with repeated "chuk" cries.

283

She placed her woven reed mat in a small clearing near the river's edge. Sitting cross-legged, she watched the swift current making swirls and eddies where it encountered roots protruding from the bank. The water was dark and mysterious, meandering past low mountains through the long plains to the east. Eventually it reached the Great Water of the East, she knew. How she would love to go there! It was hard to imagine this vast body of water that stretched beyond the distant horizon; the very edge of the world. The largest body of water she had seen was the bajo next to Tikal.

Chan Hun asked me to accompany him to the Great Water, she remembered. As unlikely as this was, simply the idea caused her heart to leap. Was it the thought of seeing the vast water, or being with the young warrior? She was bemused by her interest in him.

I must study, she reminded herself.

Pulling a small figurine out of her pouch, she focused her attention on carefully examining every detail. Only as long as one finger, the ivory-hued bone carving depicted a stubby-legged, short-armed female figure bare to the hips, where flounced pantaloons hung to the feet. Two shoulder-length braids framed her face, and a smooth round turban perched atop her head. From her forehead to her vulva was a line of seven circles. She wore round ear-flares but otherwise had no jewelry.

The figurine was to teach Yalucha deeper understanding of the letter "O," the symbol of spirit. The line of seven circles represented areas of the body where the force of spirit entered and enlivened tissues. These were the Seven Centers of Power, and each had a particular vibration with which the acolyte must attune to understand and draw in spiritual energies. The sound used was *ol.* The letter "L" represented vibration; when combined with "O" into *ol,* a resonant frequency was created that awakened consciousness, attuning acolyte to the infinite cosmic consciousness.

Yalucha closed her eyes and focused on the forehead circle of the figurine, also imagining a circle on her own forehead. She intoned "ol" with a high, soprano note. Sitting silently after toning, she allowed the vibration to sink deeply into her head. Then she focused on the circle at the figurine's throat, imagining a circle at her own throat. Again she intoned "ol" at a slightly lower note, then silently drew the vibration into her neck. This process repeated until she had intoned progressively lower notes through chest, mid-abdomen, pelvic region, and at the base of her body. After completing these six centers, she reversed the process back up to her forehead. She ended the exercise by focusing on the very top of the figurine's turban, where another "O" was hidden in twists of fabric. In tandem, she focused on her crown, toning "ol" in falsetto at an impossibly high frequency. It had taken many uinals of voice training before she could hit this note precisely. Then she meditated on the infusion of cosmic consciousness into her power centers, feeling intimate connections with far-off stars.

The sound of rustling in the underbrush brought Yalucha out of meditation. She glanced around as a tapir broke through the dense foliage and skirted the edge of her small clearing to disappear again into a dim sea of green. She smiled at the large brown animal with creamy underbelly, weighing as much as two grown men. Standing at chest height, the tapir was the biggest animal of her homeland, using its long tapered snout to scavenge under fallen leaves and forest humus for young roots and tender leaves. Grunts and soft whistling noises trailed off as the tapir continued deeper into the jungle.

The young woman placed the bone figurine back into her pouch, taking out an oval chunk of amber. She held the smooth, crystallized-resin stone in her palm, allowing its soothing emanations to travel up her arm, into the chest and then spread throughout her body. Amber was the protective amulet of priestesses; it served as a portal for focusing spiritual allies when facing difficult work or shamanic threats. She liked to use her amber stone daily, building up vibrational strength in the energy egg surrounding her body, so she would be prepared in times of challenges.

Suddenly, as if from the still air, a form materialized at the edge of the clearing. Yalucha startled, rising quickly to her knees.

It was Chan Hun.

She let out her breath in an audible sigh, and sank down onto her heels. Their eyes met across the clearing, setting off the whirring around her heart.

"Greetings of the morning, priestess," he said. "I hope I do not disturb you."

"All is well," she replied, "although my heart shakes—*xnik kolonton*—at your sudden appearance."

"I am sorry to have surprised you," he said as he walked toward her. "May your heart be seated, be calm—*nakal kolonton*."

"Were you tracking the tapir?" she inquired, gesturing toward where the large animal had re-entered the jungle. "He went that way."

"No," replied the young man, crouching beside her. "I was tracking you."

Chan Hun flashed his irresistible gem-bedazzled smile at Yalucha. In a rush of strong sensations, she caught his male scent as her eyes took in the powerful thigh muscles bulging between loin and breechcloths. An exquisite tingling sensation filled her pelvic region, a pleasing excitement creating instant moisture in her vulva.

Why does he affect me so? She blushed and lowered her eyes.

"May I sit beside you?"

She nodded, still avoiding his eyes. He settled himself on the mat, so close that she felt heat radiating from his brown skin. Her heartbeat quickened and she sucked in a tiny breath, then made herself breathe slowly and regularly.

"What are you doing?" he asked softly. His rich baritone voice played musically in her ears, setting off resonances as intoxicating as balche.

"I am studying," she managed to say, sounding more calm than she felt.

"What do you study?"

"The hidden truths of the letters, the sacred symbols of wisdom," she replied. "We are required to know these things deeply, from our inner experience, not just with our minds. So, I come here alone to study, to concentrate and open to deeper ways of knowing."

"And I have disturbed your study." He sounded sincerely sorry.

"Oh, no, no!" she quickly responded, looking at him again. "Truthfully, I had completed my studies. It was the tapir that disturbed my meditation. But I was done."

"Then I am welcome to stay," he concluded, looking pleased. As she nodded, he added: "Tell me what it is to become a priestess of Ix Chel. I am little schooled in such religious matters. My pursuits are of a more worldly nature, hunting, training for warfare, learning to oversee workers in my family's fields. My heart reaches to know of your life."

Yalucha felt relieved to enter more familiar territory. Ever facile with words, she enthusiastically discussed her two tuns of training at Xunantunich. She was careful not to reveal secret knowledge, according to vows taken by acolytes. Still, there was much she could share, from healing studies to public rituals. Chan Hun listened attentively, smiling and nodding when particularly taken by her descriptions. From time to time, he asked intelligent questions, showing he clearly understood her points.

Their talk evolved into exploration of their lives growing up in cities only a hard day's walk apart, but separated by a huge chasm of

286

long-standing enmity. Both young people were surprised to learn that every-day family life and public ceremonies were very similar. Neither actually knew the source of their cities' enmity, only that it had persisted several generations. It was indeed strange, they concluded, with so many shared values.

The sun was hot and bright overhead, the morning dew long-dried on the grasses in the small clearing when Yalucha remembered her healing duties.

"Chan Hun, I must return to the Ziv House," she said. "There are patients I must attend, already I am being negligent for staying away so long."

"Of course," he replied. "My heart rejoices at the time we have spent together. You are not only a woman of beauty, but of great intelligence and skill."

She blushed at the compliment. Before she could move, he reached toward her exposed ankle, tracing its graceful curve with a fingertip. She caught her breath, transfixed at his touch. The hummingbird around her heart fluttered its tiny wings wildly.

Chan Hun smiled as he observed her response; it was too strong for her to conceal. The energy between them was as charged as a bolt of lightening. Like magnets, their bodies leaned toward each other. Her hand, acting on its own accord, reached to stroke his cheek, smooth and brown with strong jaw muscles.

"Oh!" The sound burst out of her lips, as she quickly withdrew her hand, confused and embarrassed.

He laughed and backed away, rising to his feet. His eyes lingered on her, devouring every detail as his full lips curled in a sensuous smile.

"We will meet again, Lady Yalucha," he promised, disappearing almost as suddenly as he had appeared.

*　　*　　*　　*　　*　　*

The last ten kins were unusually torrid for the rainy season. An unrelenting sun blazed on wet jungle foliage and saturated soil, causing a steam bath effect. In the sweltering humidity, it was impossible to keep anything dry. In the kitchen of the Ziv House, the acolytes kept a constant fire burning, placing dried herbs on racks nearby in an effort to prevent mildew from ruining them. The large room was hot as an oven, despite several windows and two doors opening outside.

287

Yalucha wiped a stream of sweat from her brow as she stirred boiling ziv, the herbal tea made especially for that kin. Making ziv for the kin was a daily routine, rotated among the acolytes. Wet strands of black hair hung down her neck and temples, escaping from the long single braid. Her white huipil clung to her body, thoroughly damp. She could not remember when she had been hotter.

"Ya-LU-cha! Ya-LU-cha!" sang Olal's voice from outside. "You are WANT-ed, Chan Hun re-QUESTS you!"

The shorter girl stuck her head into the oven-hot room.

"Oooh, so hot!" she said, quickly withdrawing her head. "Come out, Yalucha."

"One moment," the young woman called to her friend. "I must finish making ziv."

Although she thought it impossible for her blood vessels to dilate any more, she did feel a flush in her cheeks.

Chan Hun is here to see me! Why?

It was unusual for a man who was not a priest to come to the Ziv House. Quickly she set the tea aside to steep, grabbed a less wet cloth and wiped her face, neck and hands. Stepping outside, the temperature was a few degrees cooler and felt almost refreshing.

Chan Hun was sitting on the low stairs leading to the side platform of the rectangular structure. Only priestesses and workers used this entrance. He rose and smiled as she approached. Tiny beads of sweat glistened on his bare, muscular chest. The wide-eyed look of admiration he gave her reminded Yalucha that her huipil was clinging to every curve of her well-developed body. She tried in vain to pull it away from her breasts, but gave up as her curiosity overcame embarrassment. Olal was lingering not far away.

"Greetings, Chan Hun," she said. "For what purpose have you come?"

"I have some news you may find of great interest," he replied. "Your High Priestess, Zac Kuk, is planning to accompany our expedition to the Great Water. She has need for ritual implements and special herbs found only along the coast. And, she needs some assistants to come with her. I hear she is going to bring you."

"Bring me? To the Great Water?" Yalucha's excitement was palpable.

"You are among her most accomplished acolytes," he noted with surety. "Indeed, it appears she wants to provide you additional training in these unusual healing methods."

"How do you know these things?" she asked with genuine surprise.

He smiled enigmatically, and shook his head causing his topknot of hair tied with a white band to sway to and fro.

"A warrior must always be alert, must learn the terrain well. I have my own secrets that I cannot reveal." He grinned playfully. "You are pleased?"

"Oh, yes! My heart jumps to see the Great Water, to travel on the river, to see the coast and the creatures of the sands."

"Tell her, tell her about me!" interjected Olal, who had been listening and watching their interaction. She could tell there was a strong attraction between them.

"Olal will be coming, too," he added obediently.

The two young women exchanged glances, smiling happily. It would be wonderful to share this adventure together.

"I am sure you will receive official word soon," Chan Hun said. "We have only 15 more kins to prepare. Already Nunbak is walking, his leg has healed so well he barely needs a crutch. I am most grateful for the excellent care he received here."

Yalucha was acutely aware of the short time remaining before the expedition from Uaxactun would be leaving. Deep sadness had tugged at her heart when she thought of not being able to see Chan Hun again. But now she was going to the coast! She thanked him for the news, and before he left, reminded him about the ceremony for the full moon. She would be invoking the vision serpent that night along with Zac Kuk and several other priestesses. It was a great honor, and she wanted him to be there. All residents and visitors at the city were invited to attend.

"I will be there," he vowed. "Nothing could keep me away."

The night of the full moon was cooler, the heat wave had abated to every person, plant and animal's relief. Only a few wispy clouds floated overhead, there would be a perfect view of the shining orb rising shortly after dusk. Gradually the main plaza filled with people as darkness fell. Attendants lighted torches at the four corners of the plaza, and along the tall, wide stairway rising up the front of the square pyramid in the center. Though short by Mutul standards, this sacred mountain had a wide flat top permitting many priests and priestesses to participate in rituals. A single thatch-roof temple, open on all sides, perched in the middle of the flat top platform.

Yalucha fasted and meditated in preparation for her vision quest. She purified her consciousness, taking a ritual bath in an infusion of payche (zorillo) and kaba yax nik (vervain) to enhance her psychic receptivity and ward off evil spirits. After that, Olal doused her with copal incense to heighten her vibratory frequencies and connect her with the *itz* of the spirit domain. Olal helped her don the long, flowing white robe used for ceremonies, and braided her hair tightly around her crown to support the colorful feather headdress. As the final step, Yalucha tucked her amber stone into the waistband above her navel. All was in readiness.

Drumbeats from the plaza summoned the priestesses. Thirteen in all, a sacred number in the 13:20 kin-tun cycle of the tzolk'in calendar, gathered at the plaza's edge. Yalucha was placed halfway in the double line behind Zac Kuk, a position of honor for an acolyte not yet finished her studies. Several of her classmates followed behind her. In front were the prominent priestesses of the Ix Chel temple. A choir of female voices sang ethereal chants as the procession moved across the plaza and ascended the pyramid stairway. Thin reedy flutes joined the steady drum rhythms, carrying minor melodies an octave above the voices.

Chills ran up Yalucha's spine, her heart beat in eager anticipation. She had taken the vision brew before, but in less significant rituals than tonight's full moon ceremony. Ix Chel was a moon goddess; the celestial orb was one of her forms. Tonight the priestesses would journey to the moon in their visions, to unite with the goddess. It was her heart's deepest desire to become one with her beloved deity.

On the top platform, the priestesses fanned around the periphery, facing the crowd below. The plaza was almost full of people surrounding the square pyramid. Zac Kuk recited incantations to the four directions and the Moon Goddess form of Ix Chel. The priestesses echoed her phrases, their voices carrying the blessings of sacred sounds to the people in their portion of the plaza. As the recitative progressed, the moon began to rise, yellow-gold as she broke past the horizon, paling to silvery-gold as she cleared the treetops. Ephemeral moonbeams lit the plaza and square pyramid with an otherworldly gleam, casting shadows as distinct as during the day. Zac Kuk's lifted arms embraced, surrounded, cradled the moon. She sang lilting melodies, open-throated and wild, in counterpoint to the measured chanting. As the chants finished, the mother drum took up her deep throated, insistent beat. The time for the vision quest had arrived.

Thirteen temple assistants ascended to the top platform, standing beside their assigned priestess. They were the anchors for the journeyer's soul; their focus would provide the thread of consciousness by which return to the physical body was accomplished. Each priestess came in turn to the center structure, where Zac Kuk had blessed the brew of spotted mushroom, a hallucinogen long used in the Izapa tradition. She poured just the right amount into a cup for each, then took her own cup. At her slight nod, all priestesses drank the brew simultaneously.

The bitter, astringent taste filled Yalucha's mouth. Slowly she released small swallows into her throat using the technique she had been taught. Over several moments the bitter liquid trickled down until it was all swallowed. If taken all at once, it caused severe vomiting and disorientation, making it impossible to follow the vision. After this, she sat on a reed mat next to her anchor.

Just as the hallucinogen began changing her body awareness, Yalucha wondered if Chan Hun was positioned where he could see her. Then all thought ceased, and she entered the disembodied world of spirit. Her essence, pure consciousness, floated above her body, looking down as a bird would upon the pyramid platform and plaza below, full of people. It hovered for a moment, enjoying the expansive view of the structures and plazas of Xunantunich. Turning toward the moon, halfway to its apex in the night sky, she zoomed like a shooting star toward the round beacon of silver light.

Liquid silver, she swam in a whirlpool, its vortex pulling her inward. Falling, falling weightless through twinkling star-clusters, vast spaces of empty darkness. Brilliant light flashes, celestial bells pealing, high ringing echoes, harmonies of the heavens. Blood-red rivers of molten gasses, swirling pulses of insipient life. Wraith-like visages, changing as clouds in the wind, whispers of spirits and ancestors half-recognized.

Ix Chel, where is Ix Chel?

Some sentient part of her vast awareness sought focus.

Moon Goddess, come to me. I am your daughter, your priestess.

With sudden force a huge presence burst into her awareness. She was consumed by it, buried within it, but knew this was home, the goddess's celestial body. It was pure, vital, primal life force, the serpent of creation writhing and twining into a double helix. It danced in every vibration of her consciousness and she saw it enlivening every cell of her body. Conceiving, incubating, birthing, suckling, nurturing, comforting, crying, dying. The Moon Goddess was the creation of life itself.

Waves of overwhelming love radiated from her disembodied awareness. Love of the goddess, the celestial bodies, the three worlds, all beings, all life. There was nothing else, no other thing. This was the highest truth of being—all is one, all is love.

Ix Chel, Mother of All, Moon Goddess, I give myself to you. I am you. Ask what you will of me, I wish only to serve you in truth and love.

The face of the goddess became clear to her altered vision. Round, glowing silvery as the moon, eyes like shining stars, lips of honey, fullness of radiant beauty. As the goddess kissed her daughter's ephemeral form, and the essences of both merged into one, a message imprinted within this beingness:

The contract is sealed, the mission is set. The goddess lives in the daughter of earth. We are one. We are eternally together.

* * * * * *

The expedition of 20 men and 6 women floated in two large canoes down the swiftly flowing river, weaving eastward through palmetto-dotted plains. Carved out of a single massive mahogany trunk, each canoe was the length of three men and as wide as half a man. The dark hardwood trunk withstood weathering from water and wind, and was resistant to insects. Six paddlers were required for each canoe, plus one helmsman at the rudder behind. Warriors and merchants doubled as paddlers, spelling the others who served as bearers for overland portions of the trip. At home the distinctions between nobles and the serving class were sharper, but during travel an easy comradeship blurred these boundaries.

Each massive canoe easily held its burden of people, trading goods and supplies. The women from Xunantunich were divided, three in each canoe, given the most comfortable center seats. In a natural grouping of age and interests, Zac Kuk rode in the first canoe with her two serving women, and three young acolytes rode in the second. Chan Hun, whose natural placement was in the first canoe, thought long and hard about how he could justify riding in the second, but could not come up with a plausible argument. He consoled himself by spending much time gazing back, checking on navigation of the follower.

To Olal's chagrin, the third acolyte chosen for the journey was Ahpo Hel, the dour plump girl whose sharp tongue made her unpopular. Yalucha suggested this provided an opportunity to rise above petty judgments, but Olal was unconvinced. Still awed by her vision quest experience, Yalucha carried the impetus of universal love in her heart. She resolved to be kind and accepting toward Ahpo Hel.

The many rivers and swamps that crisscrossed the landscape were the major arteries of transportation for the Maya. When on land, they used multiple paths coursing through deep forests, across cultivated fields and wide coastal plains. The rivers were hazardous at the height of the rainy season, turning into raging torrents. During the driest time, many became too shallow to navigate. The Uaxactun group had planned their trip accordingly, but their 40 kin delay for Nunbak's healing set them back. Now the river flowed calmly, its swollen infusion from heavy rains already deposited in the sea. There was little danger that this river would run too low at the east end, but the stretch from Xunantunich west might be tricky on their return.

The trip to the coast took three kin. In the evenings around the campfire, after setting up camp and eating a frugal meal of maize cakes and dried fruit, the travelers clustered in small groupings to talk. Chan Hun and Yalucha made occasion to sit together away from the others, at the edge of the campfire's light. They were still in sight of the High Priestess' watchful eyes, but distant enough that their conversation could not be overheard. Olal felt rising jealousy at her friend's preoccupation with the young man.

It was the last evening before the canoes would reach the coast. The two young people sat near a clump of tall marsh grasses, flickering shadows from the campfire playing across their faces. They kept a proper amount of space between them, although the powerful magnetic attraction of their bodies wanted to draw them closer. Electric energy like tiny flashes of lightening passed back and forth, heady and exciting. Tonight's conversation ventured into the dangerous territory of the gods and sacrifice. Yalucha explained the rituals performed for Ix Chel, wanting to share what she could about the full moon ceremony.

"Did you see me there?" she asked.

"Yes, I followed you around the pyramid so I could stand close-by. You were a precious white flower, more lovely than the rarest orchid hidden in the deep jungle. You were more radiant than the moon herself," he replied with heart-felt sincerity.

Yalucha blushed at the extravagant praise.

"Did you feel her, Ix Chel, the Moon Goddess? She came to me, united with me. It was a wonder beyond what words can tell," she said pensively.

"I felt you. For me, you were the Moon Goddess." His intense emotions threw the tiny hummingbird of her heart into a bout of riotous wing-beating. Their eyes met, holding, plunging into each other's depths.

"You exaggerate, sweet Lord," she said demurely, looking away to quiet her heart. "Do you not honor the goddess in your city?"

"K'inich Ahau is our main deity," he said, reining in his passion lest it cause him to act indiscreetly. "The women h'men call upon her for their healings. Men do not much think of her."

"That is your loss," retorted Yalucha, bristling at the slight to her beloved goddess. "Men would do well to cultivate more kindness and less warfare."

Chan Hun laughed heartily. The firelight flashed on the gems and gold set in his teeth, the mark of warriors. Dancing shadows emphasized the rippling muscles of chest and forearms as he gestured.

"You know not the ways of men, little doe," he observed. "Are there not warriors in your family?"

"My uncle is one. My father and brother are stone-carvers. I like not the ways of war and the blood sacrifice of K'inich Ahau."

"These are the tools of power, of satisfying the sun god," he replied, sounding perplexed. "Your great city of Mutul uses them with expertise, we have suffered their fierce attacks for many tuns."

"I regret this, Chan Hun," she said sincerely, looking again into his eyes. "Why must our cities be enemies? The old religion of Izapa is peaceful, the gods keep the world in harmony. Itzamna and Ix Chel did not birth the world for its people to destroy each other."

"But K'inich Ahau demands these things," argued Chan Hun. "He cannot be fed otherwise, he must be sustained by blood or he will destroy us. Blood gives life to the gods, the gods give life to people. It is the way of things."

"But the victory of the Hero Twins over the Lords of Xibalba changed the tribute, and they could only demand offerings of copal and animals," Yalucha reminded him.

"That was long ago," Chan Hun reasoned. "The needs of the new gods are different. Now the offering of blood is necessary to satisfy them. Royal blood especially, and the heart of noble captives are what ensures victory and power."

"My heart is swarming—*xch'ach'on kolonton!*" Yalucha declared furiously. "This is the lust of K'inich Ahau, fired by the ambition of kings in an unholy bargain."

"K'inich Ahau is the most powerful god now," argued Chan Hun.

"Who is this K'inich Ahau? Nothing but an upstart, a lesser god who aggrandizes himself, like the false bird *Wuqub' Kaqix*. His time of ascendance will also come to an end. It is the great Itzamna, source of all, and mother Ix Chel who will endure. They teach us to love life, to cherish all creation, not to destroy it."

Chan Hun thought he had never seen a woman so beautiful, so passionate as Yalucha when speaking her deep convictions with flashing eyes and strong gestures of her long slender fingers. But he was concerned that she overstepped human bounds, even for a priestess.

"Take care, Yalucha," he cautioned her. "Do not offend the sun god, for he may bring revenge against you. Consider, count in your heart, be realistic about the present times. You are among the few who still follow the old religion of Izapa. Of course, I am grateful," he added sincerely, "for your healing skills and dedication to helping those who are sick or in need."

She sighed, accepting his overtures for peace. Glancing secretively at Chan Hun, she wondered why her heart was so drawn to the young warrior from an enemy city, whose religious views were so different from her own.

"Can you see it? Can you see it?" cried Olal, balancing carefully behind Yalucha.

Both young women were standing in the center of their canoe, craning their necks to catch the first glimpse of the Great Water of the East.

"No, not yet. The mangroves are too thick," Yalucha replied.

Although the river was wide, thick stands of mangrove trees narrowed the passage with their arching branches that dropped thick roots into the water. The canoes threaded carefully through, avoiding entanglement with mangrove roots and reeds along the bank.

"Lady Priestesses, please sit down," called their canoe scout Nanbak, standing effortlessly on his healed leg at the prow. "The waters have Cayman with long teeth, you must not fall in."

Obediently the women sat. After several more moments that seemed endless, the canoes swept clear of the mangroves and glided into an immense bay. Covered with small waves, the bay stretched to the eastern horizon. Never had the women seen such a vast body of water, nor one covered with waves.

"Its so huge," marveled Olal.

"Oh, yes," agreed Yalucha. "And the waves, how they move. See, some break and spray white foam!"

"I am afraid," moaned Ahpo Hel, gripping the canoe frame tightly as surging waves caused a rolling motion. "We will be thrown out, it is too far to swim!"

"Ladies, calm your hearts," Nanbak said. "These waves are small and cannot tip over the canoe. The island to the east protects the bay. Wait until you see true waves in the immense waters beyond the island. Some are taller than a man."

"Oooh, oooh," cried Ahpo Hel. "How can this be? Taller than a man? I cannot go there, surely I will fall out!"

"You will not have to go there," reassured Nanbak. "The city of our destination, Nohnab Hol, sits on the bay side of the island. We will stay there for trading, then return again this way. And, this canoe is too small to travel in the rough outer waters."

"Too small? There are even larger canoes?" queried Yalucha in amazement.

"Oh, yes. The true Great Water canoes are as long as 8 men, and wider than one man. They carry over 30 people and vast quantities of goods. The coastal traders from Mexica regions use them." He paused, pondering his next point, as the women would have no frame of reference. "To move faster, they tie large sheets to a pole inside the canoe, it catches the wind and pushes the canoe. They call it a sail."

Yalucha immediately understood.

"Like leaves flapping over the back of leaf-cutting ants," she offered. "Only much, much bigger."

Nanbak laughed at her example, but saw the similarity.

"Yes, Lady Yalucha, that is so," he replied. "But the men use ropes to change directions of the sheet, to better catch the wind."

"That is clever," Yalucha observed.

The paddlers strained against wind and waves, gradually advancing their canoes across the huge bay. Ahpo Hel watched the coastline recede with trepidation, but could not speak as she fought nausea from the rolling action of the waves. For some time, the two canoes floated in a world of water, no land visible in any direction.

Yalucha found it exhilarating. Her skin tingled from the whipping wind, and she loved the taste of salt spray on her lips. The canoe's rolling motion set her body into a hypnotic rhythm, stilling her mind. She dwelled in pure awareness, senses acute to every nuance: the shrill call of seagulls, the lapping sound of waves against the hull, the metered splashes of oars. The vast blue-green, undulating expanse from horizon to horizon mesmerized her. Suspended between worlds, devoid of thoughts, beyond sense of self, she simply was.

Men's voices brought her out of this pleasant floating state. Focusing her eyes, she saw the faint outline of land in the distance. As they drew near, white stone structures of modest height could be discerned. Soon the two canoes entered a half-moon protected harbor in which an assortment of canoes were moored. They arrived on shore as the sun dropped into the west horizon, casting a golden glow on the white stucco of the city.

Nohnab Hol, Great Water Portal, was a small city at the northwestern edge of a long finger, reaching from the great peninsula into the warm tropical sea to the south. A huge barrier reef lined the western coast of the finger, posing hazard to sea-going canoes. Coastal Maya dug a long canal across the narrow section of the finger, to avoid danger from the reef and facilitate passage into the bay, giving faster access to the main rivers used for transportation. Nohnab Hol was situated just south of the canal, on land jutting into the bay where canoes completing the trip could see it readily. The city and its canal had been there for several katuns, a well-established trade center that maintained its independence, refusing to ally with any mainland power. Astute traders, the coastal Maya kept options open. Their affluent lifestyle was testimony to the success of this approach.

The city teemed with traders and merchants from far away, including central Mexica regions, the inland areas far south, the mountain dwellers of the west coastal range, and the western coast, the land of the Great Water of the West. Many rare and highly valued commodities passed through the city, almost anything could be found here. It was a major supplier of salt, essential to survival in the hot jungle inlands where meat was a small part of the diet. Creatures of the sea were a specialty of the coastal city, including precious red spondylus and a vast number of other shells, stingray spines for bloodletting, sponges and coral. It was one of the few places where fish and crustaceans were eaten regularly.

The three young acolytes from Xunantunich were astounded at the rich collage of peoples and diverse products offered. They stared and gaped at heavily laden stalls, asking repeatedly what some object

297

might be. Watching Zac Kuk make selections was in itself an education. She kept them at the herbal stall for nearly a kin, explaining various unusual plants and their uses, purchasing large quantities while supervising her students as they filled cotton sacs. Back at the guest house where the women stayed, she kept the acolytes busy sorting and decanting herbs into smaller bags, labeling them with identifying marks for future reference.

The High Priestess laughed at their reactions as the young women tasted shellfish for the first time. Yalucha preferred spiny lobster, saying it had a nutty flavor. Olal could not get enough of the dense-textured, tan-colored flesh of large clams. Ahpo Hel found the chewy saltiness of oysters much to her liking. None cared for octopus, revolted by the suction caps and tough flesh. They argued the merits of shrimp and crabs. It was astonishing to have such a variety of sea creatures to eat.

Whenever their duties permitted, the young women asked to go to the shore. Under the wings of Zac Kuk's serving women, they walked beside the marshy bay and gawked at the great water canoes in the harbor, immensely long and wide, twice the size of the river canoes. Following much pleading, they forayed across the island to the eastern shore, exclaiming in amazement at the high waves crashing upon the coral reef. After several trips supervised by the serving women, the High Priestess allowed her charges to go by themselves. Sometimes men from the Uaxactun group joined them; they had become friendly during the voyage. The women's status as priestess acolytes drew respect from the men, it was a social code all understood well.

Chan Hun saw an opportunity in these coastal excursions. Since arriving in Nohnab Hol, he had been separated from Yalucha. Zac Kuk kept her students so busy during the first several kin that he could find no way of making contact. Now that the women were allowed time for sightseeing, he would seek out the young priestess who fired his passion and touched his heart deeply. He had known women before, but none captured his free-flying spirit but the gentle healer from an enemy city.

Several times Chan Hun joined Yalucha, her two companion acolytes and several men from his group for walks along the coast. The grassy flat land dropped suddenly into rocky shores, or spread into salty marshes crossed by raised footpaths. There were no nice beaches near the city. Though the young warrior managed to walk beside and converse with Yalucha, he burned to be alone with her.

The beaches provided a ruse. Without letting the others hear, he described a small sandy beach where they might find little treasures, pretty shells and smooth stones. That it was well-hidden and little known he kept to himself. He pleaded with her to meet him alone, so they could share this special beach. Her ready acceptance did not surprise him; he could feel her magnetic attraction matching his, merging into the electrically charged field between them.

Yalucha was not naïve. She understood the consequences of being alone with Chan Hun. The intense power of their mutual attraction was not lost on her. A sensible young woman, she had taken tea of cedar bark for 3 kin before her last moon cycle. Its effects would protect against conception for one uinal.

If it comes to that. She mused while sipping the tea. Given the passionate responses he invoked in her body, she could not trust herself to resist him. It was indeed better to be well protected and not need it, than to risk bringing difficulty to herself and her family.

The afternoon was balmy and warm, the sea breeze unusually light. A festival had drawn most visitors to the city center for feasting and dancing. Chan Hun stood impatiently at the north edge of town, near a rocky outcropping. He had been very clear in describing it to Yalucha, giving her precise directions.

What is keeping her? Did she change her mind?

These thoughts tormented Chan Hun. He wavered on the edge of anger, shifting quickly to a dropping sensation in the pit of his stomach. He had anticipated this so much, schemed so avidly, it must work out! Had he been mistaken about her attraction to him? Uncharacteristic doubts flooded his mind, disturbing and confusing. No woman had ever affected him this way, pushed him off balance.

I would be better off without her, he thought petulantly. Instantly a powerful surge of feelings for Yalucha erased that thought. He stepped up on rocks to see farther down the path to the city. Aching moments passed as he strained his eyes.

There she was! He had no difficulty recognizing Yalucha's graceful walk and her slender willowy form although at some distance. Hopping down from the rocks, he waited with pounding heart.

Smiling happily in greeting, he did not admonish her lateness. All that mattered was that she was here, and that they were going to the secluded beach. They walked in silence for a while. Yalucha remarked on an egret and a cluster of pink flowers by the path. They

299

talked then, about the wonders of the island and the sea, the new discoveries in the markets. A glow of anticipation surrounded them, magical and sweet, making every sensation heightened.

The tiny beach was hidden behind a large stand of palms and a cluster of mangroves, hovering over a shallow creek that flowed into the bay. Chan Hun offered his hand to help Yalucha cross the slippery creek stones. The heat between their palms surprised them both; they exchanged glances, laughed and dipped their hands into the cool creek water. The beach was lovely. Warm golden sand formed a narrow crescent, bay waves lapping gently in the protected cove. An abrupt ledge bordered the land side, half a man's height and covered with twisted roots and vines. The beach could not be seen until you were right upon it.

"Its so beautiful!" Yalucha exuded. "How did you find it?"

"From spending many kin walking about this area, waiting for trading to be done," he replied. "I was here two tun ago, and found it then. I have never showed it to anyone before."

"Oh, thank you for showing me," she said. "It is very special, very precious. Are there many shells? Come, let's look."

She crouched and ran her fingers through the sand, picking up a few shell fragments. Chan Hun searched and found one nice spiral shell, which he handed to her. After admiring it and thanking him, she slipped it into her pouch. They searched a little more, but soon gave up and sat with feet in the bay waters, taking off their sandals. Neither could make conversation easily.

"The water is warm," Yalucha said after a period of silence.

"Um," replied Chan Hun. "It is shallow here. Do you want to go in?"

She laughed, as if the idea was utterly surprising.

"Yes, I suppose . . ." her voice trailed off.

He looked at her full face, flashing his gem-toothed smile that caused a faint dimple in his left cheek. Her heart melted. Taking her hand, he helped her stand and they waded into the shallow water. Gentle waves surged around their calves. He tucked his loin-breech cloths into his waistband and went into thigh level water. She lifted her huipil carefully to the upper thigh, but would not go farther. He beckoned her, she shook her head. He called her name, but laughing she backed away toward the beach. Suddenly he scooped a handful of water and threw it on her. She squeaked in surprise then returned the water attack. Soon they were hopelessly wet, laughing, breathless.

They splashed back to the beach and stood dripping, facing each other on the warm sand. Yalucha's wet huipil clung to her firm breasts and shapely hips, Chan Hun's mid-thigh pants and hanging loin-breech cloths concealed little of his well-muscled form. Their eyes scanned each other, then met, merged, became lost in deep pools of desire. He reached to touch her upper arm, caressing her shoulder and neck. She placed one hand on his chest, feeling the pounding heart beneath bare, hard pectorals. Slowly he drew her toward him, folding her into his arms, quivering as her body pressed against his.

Her supple form did not resist, she arched into his hardness and slipped her arms around his waist. Caressing with fingers eager to know each other's every curve, they swayed in the soft breeze and cool wetness. His breath was hot in her ear as he whispered:

"Oh, Yalucha, I am aching for you, my heart aches—*xk'uxub kolonton.*"

"You perfume my heart—*chamuibtasbon kolonton,*" she murmured back.

Keeping one arm around her, he ushered her toward the pack he had dropped near the palm grove. Spreading out a cape, he gently drew her down. Fingers entwined they knelt knee-to-knee, gazing deeply at each other as surges of energy passed between heart, navel and pelvic regions. His building passion was ready to burst, pushing at his capacity for control. He lifted her loose, wet huipil carefully over her head. Eyes closed, she remained kneeling as he sucked in an admiring breath.

"You are so beautiful, the flower of perfection," he breathed out.

She trembled as his hands cupped her breasts, moaning softly as he nuzzled the hollow of her neck, eyes still closed.

"Look upon me, Yalucha," he gently commanded. "Am I fitting for you?"

Almost reluctantly, she opened her eyes and saw he was naked and fully aroused. She had never seen a man so, having only tended to very aged male patients.

"Oh!" she gasped in surprise.

"Do I not please you?" he asked with concern.

"Oh, yes, yes, Chan Hun, you are magnificent," she replied in honest admiration for the perfection of his male form. "I have never seen a young man."

"Good," he murmured, stretching out on the cape and drawing her to his side.

301

His knowing hands stroked the curves and hollows of her body, causing shivers of unfamiliar pleasure to course through her pelvis and breasts. Feeling the wetness between her thighs, he tasted her moisture on his fingers.

"Your taste is good, sweeter than honey," he whispered. The insistent throbbing in his groin could not be restrained, he carefully lowered his body onto hers.

Their lovemaking was full of passion and tenderness. After a moment of sharp pain, she released herself to the rhythms of his movements, lost in waves of indescribable pleasure. Sinuously, their undulating bodies slowly increased rhythms until a fierceness possessed his thrusting. Every nerve and muscle taut, his body released in ecstatic shudders as she felt wondrous, exquisite surges deep inside.

They lay beside each other, holding hands. A sense of profound peace, complete fulfillment enveloped them. It was meant to be, emblazoned in the stars.

"You are the ruler of my heart," Chan Hun stated softly. "I want no other woman."

"My heart is yours," Yalucha replied. "You have found a home in my being."

The lovers were able to slip away to their crescent beach sanctuary three more times before the expedition from Uaxactun was scheduled to depart. They were intoxicated with each other, wrapped in the effervescence of new love. Magic moments passed as they searched for hidden treasures on the beach, swam in naked abandon, cracked green coconuts and savored their milky nectar, explored the marshes for birds and reptiles, laughed and told stories. Both marveled at the simultaneous intuition that their souls had long known each other. Being together was coming home, in a way almost too profound to grasp.

One afternoon, in the quiet after lovemaking, Chan Hun asked:

"Are you not concerned that we are making a baby?"

Yalucha was stroking his brows and tracing the profile of his nose. He was more handsome than any man she had ever seen.

"There is no need for this worry," she said casually.

"Ah, you have ways . . ."

She quickly laid a finger across his lips.

"Shush, dearest heart, I cannot speak of these things," she stated.

"Ummm," he purred, putting her hand back on his forehead. "That feels so good, do not stop." He was relieved and impressed by her sensible precautions, and content not to know women's secrets.

Ahpo Hel bustled into the room where Olal was wrapping ceremonial implements for the return trip.

"Where is Yalucha?" she demanded in bristling tones.

"Gone on an errand," replied Olal, annoyed at the plump girl's bossy manner.

"You cannot deceive me, Olal," said Ahpo Hel disdainfully. "She is with Chan Hun."

"Do you say?" retorted Olal, averting her eyes.

"I do say!" Ahpo Hel sounded full of herself. "And so do his men. They all know Chan Hun and Yalucha slip away together. They are up to no good. I will tell Zac Kuk."

"No!" Olal turned toward the younger girl, her eyes flashing. Her loyalty spurred her to cover for her friend, although she was hurt by Yalucha's indifference.

"Ah, you reveal yourself."

"It is not true."

"It is so true. Zac Kuk must be informed, and I will do it," said Ahpo Hel smugly as she departed.

Olal tearfully warned Yalucha. Hugging her friend, the taller women apologized for her neglect and shared some things about her love for Chan Hun. Olal was wide-eyed at the prospect of lovemaking, but was too embarrassed to pursue details.

That evening Zac Kuk summoned Yalucha. They were alone in the High Priestess' quarters. The acolyte bowed, wrists crossed over her chest, in the Maya gesture of respect. Both stood in the narrow, small room.

"You have been seeing Chan Hun." It was a statement, not a question.

"Yes," admitted Yalucha.

"Alone."

"Yes."

"This is not in accord, you have broken trust," Zac Kuk said firmly. "Do you know what you are doing?"

Unflinching, Yalucha met her mentor's eyes.

"Yes, I do know what I am doing," she said in a deliberate manner. Her confidence was unwavering as Zac Kuk's gaze bore into her eyes.

The barest hint of a smile played at the edges of the older woman's lips.

"Yes, you do know," she acquiesced. "Yalucha, you are brave and headstrong. The goddess has chosen you as her vessel, that pact is sealed. So, what of this young man?"

"He has captured my heart, Mother of My Soul," Yalucha admitted. "It is a deep connection of our spirits, I sense this strongly. Our love burns brightly, I cannot resist. But, I will make no mistakes to cause my parents anguish."

Zac Kuk understood at once.

"That is good. Few young women in the blush of first love would be so sensible. Let us be practical, my daughter. Do not be cause for gossip on the return trip. Contain your emotions and keep your young man's passion from flaring. I will assure his group is detained one extra kin at Xunantunich, for your time together before parting."

A distant look swept over the High Priestess' face, her eyes turned up slightly. She sighed deeply, shook her head and looked again at Yalucha.

"It is true, your souls and spirits are deeply entwined. But it will be a difficult path. Find joy when you can. Call on Ix Chel, keep her presence ever with you."

Yalucha was the picture of discretion on the river voyage back to Xunantunich. Without her having to say anything, Chan Hun kept his distance. She suspected that Zac Kuk had primed him and obtained his cooperation. His warm smile and dancing eyes, when they met in passing, hinted that he knew the arrangements.

Ahpo Hel stared sourly at Yalucha from time to time, but she made no rude comments. Yalucha used the time during the return to infuse Olal with energy and attention. Sharing adventures and discoveries while on the island, the two friends laughed often and sang to the splashing rhythms of the paddlers. They taught the men chants and entreated them to sing along. Olal basked in the radiance of her beautiful companion—who was even more glowing than usual.

True to her word, Zac Kuk found reason to detain the Uaxactun expedition for one kin, but her needs did not involve Chan Hun. The lovers spent the free kin together, disappearing into jungle trails where Yalucha showed the young warrior how she found herbs and medicinal roots. They worked their way through crossing trails until they arrived at the small clearing by the river, Yalucha's place of study and meditation.

Dusk was falling as they settled into the clearing, glad to be sitting after so much walking. Chan Hun drew Yalucha into his arms, nuzzling her cheeks and throat as she stroked his shoulders and back. Their bodies thrilled again to the little lightening flashes that caused such tingling pleasures deep inside. While the last sunlight glinted across the river, Chan Hun brought out his pouch.

"I have a gift for you," he said, almost shyly.

Yalucha blinked with surprise at the new tone in his voice.

Opening the pouch, he removed a jade pendant and gave it to her. Trembling, her fingers felt the shallow carvings on its smooth surface. Half the size of her palm, it was pale green, the color of spring's first leaves, almost translucent. A finely woven thin white cord was attached to one end. Holding it close in the dim light, she saw a stylized flower with a distinct "O" in the center.

"Oh! Chan Hun, it is so beautiful, so special! My heart is pleased completely."

"You are the flower of my heart," he replied smiling. "I knew this pendant was for you. But it is more. Here, I will put it on you."

Tenderly he slipped the white cord around her neck, and the pendant settled between her breasts, over her pulsating heart.

"This is my pledge to you." His voice sounded more serious than she had heard before. "My pledge for our marriage. Will you have me?"

"Yes, yes!" she cried joyfully. "You are master of my heart, there can be no other."

There on the soft carpet of grasses, they made love with abandon. Their passion was fueled by their pledge to each other, as well as acute awareness of tomorrow's separation. Several times they melded together in the ecstasy of heart communion merged with exquisite physical union. After Chan Hun had spent himself—and it took quite a while for the virile young warrior—they lay in each other's arms gazing at the half-moon shining overhead.

Nuzzling her lips into the hollow beneath his strong jaw, she tasted his salty skin and drank in his male scent.

"How can I live without you?" she murmured.

"Goddess of my heart, you will live *with* me," he replied sleepily.

"How can that be? Our cities are enemies. Our families would never agree," she said mournfully.

305

"I will come to you."

Chan Hun sounded confident. Rising on one elbow, he covered her face with nibbles from his sensuous full lips. She giggled. He smiled, looking deeply into her eyes in the moonlight that gave her face a wondrous silvery sheen.

"Yalucha, anything is possible. You must believe. We will be together."

The Boeing 747 swung in a lazy circle, like a great bird surveying its terrain. Far below, nestled between mountaintops, the terrain could not be seen. A brown pall hung over México City, an inverted bowl of noxious chemical soup smothering the high plateau. The airplane appeared suspended, like a silver quetzal hovering above its desecrated nest, the once shining City of the Sun, Tenochtitlan, Aztec jewel of the mountains. Now her broad avenues were choked with fumes, the wastes of technological civilization that had lost its connections to the self-restoring balance of nature. As if suddenly finding courage to plunge into the murky complexities of modern life, the airplane lowered its nose and began to descend.

The sharp voice of the stewardess crackled through the intercom: "Vamos a llegar al aeropuerto en diez minutos. Favor de prepararse para el aterrizaje."

Jana startled out of heavy-lidded dozing, grasping the initial advisory about arriving in the airport in 10 minutes and preparing for landing, but the long rapid-fire stream of Spanish that followed completely escaped her. She shifted uncomfortably after the six-hour flight from Los Angeles, welcoming the chance to walk when she changed planes for the journey's next leg to Mérida. Gazing out the window, she watched buildings, streets and trees gradually materialize out of the smog. Everything below had a brown hue, despite the brightly shining sun in a cloudless sky. It appeared that México City had not accomplished much in solving its air pollution problem.

The contrast of bright sun and murky smog fit Jana's mood perfectly. Like these opposites, her life felt polarized by two conflicting forces. She was en route to join Hanab Xiu and Aurora Nakin Hill on the Maya Mystery School pilgrimage. When she focused on this, every fiber of her being vibrated with excitement and eager anticipation. In curious juxtaposition, in the stillness of her inner core a deep contentment spread calmly. She was following the call of Spirit, the mandate of the Goddess, to attend the Spring Equinox ceremony at Chichén Itzá. A series of amazing synchronicities had put this trip into place, overcoming what looked like impossible hurdles.

All except one. The other side of the polarity, the dark part that ached inside her heart. Robert was strongly against the trip. It had provoked the worst argument of their marriage, pushed them into irresolvable conflict. She was wrenched between two important values, torn between her greatest love and sacred duty. His threat that she could be destroying their relationship by choosing to follow her conscience left her shaken to the core. It was one of those dichotomies that could not be bridged; an impossible choice, a no win situation, a ticket to misery either way.

Tears moistened her lids, though she wondered how any were left. It had been years since she cried so much. Robert remained steely cold and distant as she prepared for the trip. They hardly spoke. It was the most painful two weeks she could recall, except the time she went through grieving her grandfather's loss. So much pain. That the human spirit could endure it was a testimony to our capacity for blind perseverance.

The flight from México City to Mérida was a three-hour episode of the sun-smog polarity. Jana waited for the brown pall below to thin and dissolve away, as they flew farther into the Yucatan Peninsula. But it persisted, albeit less thick than over the Mexican capital. She was puzzled that the pollution extended so far.

The airplane landed in Mérida in the late afternoon. Waiting for a taxi, Jana sniffed the smoky air and wondered at the hazy orange-brown glow produced by low-angle sunbeams. On the way to the hotel, she asked the taxi driver, who spoke reasonable English.

"The farmers burn maize," he replied. "This time of year, for two-three months, much smoke from fires."

Still burning maize stalks to return nitrogen into the soil, Jana thought. *Like the ancient Maya did centuries ago.*

Mérida was a bustling, expanding city with colonial roots. Capital and commercial hub of the Yucatan state, its population surpassed 800,000 people of mixed heritages. It was a curious combination of the modern and the timeless, conveying an air of sophistication. Called the "White City" for good reason, virtually all its buildings presented glistening white stucco or warm pastel walls, with muted pinks, blues, yellows and tans dominating. The soothing pastel colors created a feeling of serenity and cleanliness, a needed balance for the narrow busy streets.

Located in the western corner of Yucatan state, Mérida was founded in 1542 on the site of T'ho, an ancient Maya city. Crumbling temples and deteriorated palaces were leveled to provide the base for Spanish cathedrals, ornate mansions, shops and parks. An extremely wealthy class developed as large haciendas farmed the versatile Henequen, an agave plant from which twine, burlap, furniture stuffing and hammocks were made. They had a monopoly on these products, as the tough, thorny plant thrived in the rocky soil and seasonally dry climate of the northern Yucatan peninsula. The product, called Sisal after the port town from which it was shipped, gave Mérida more millionaires per capita than any other city in the world by the early 20th century.

This international market brought European and oriental influences to the city, giving it an exotic cosmopolitan flavor. Imposing mansions built in Moorish and rococo style with arched doorways and marble tile interiors lined wide boulevards. Ornate cathedrals graced expansive town squares, flanked by museums, shops and elegant public buildings. City life focused around these squares and the many parks dotting the city, busy with activity day and night. In the evenings, families gathered to stroll, shop, visit and listen to music of mariachi bands and folklorico groups. This agreeable lifestyle continues to present times.

Jana braced herself as the taxi swerved around slow-going trucks, narrowly missing pedestrians. The route to the hotel was circuitous due to many one-way streets. Still, she enjoyed seeing the lovely pastel buildings and tree-filled parks in the fading light. The taxi dropped her at Hotel Los Aluxes, in the downtown area a few blocks from the main Plaza de la Independencia. The five-story structure of pale pink was tucked discretely between tall buildings on a narrow side street. One could easily miss its modest sign on the recessed drive-through entry. Aurora Nakin Hill had told Jana their group was staying at the Los Aluxes part of the equinox weekend, and had given her an itinerary.

When checking in, Jana left messages for both Aurora Nakin and Hanab Xiu. The concierge informed her their group was still out on tour, but he had no knowledge of where they would be that evening. It was March 20, two days before Spring Equinox. She had to find the group this evening, to gain acceptance into their events over the next two days. Tomorrow was the sunrise event at Dzibilchaltún; after that the group was leaving for the Mayaland Hotel near Chichén Itzá. On that evening was an important class with Hanab Xiu in preparation for the equinox ceremony. If she missed them tonight, Jana did not know how she would make contact.

Scouting the hotel's layout, Jana selected a central place where she could watch the hotel entrance and most interior traffic. The tall wings wrapped around a center plaza with patio and swimming pool, open to the sky. On one side was a meeting room with large windows facing the pool, on the other the glass-walled dining area. Jana sat in a lounge chair by the pool, pleasantly bordered by planters with palmettos and birds of paradise. She engaged in people watching. Teenage girls splashed in the pool, the temperature remained very warm as darkness settled. Nattily dressed young adults chatted in rapid-fire Spanish over drinks on the patio. Men in business suits conversed as they walked toward the elevators, matriarchs loaded with packages herded bouncy children. Several distinct languages blended in the general hubbub of voices.

A group of about 20 European-looking people gathered in the meeting room. A middle-aged man whom Jana did not recognize was talking to them. It appeared to be a class. Discretely, Jana slipped close to the window to listen, but the language sounded German. Looking among the seated people, Jana saw no familiar faces. This could not be Hanab Xiu's group. She returned to her vantage point near the pool.

It was quite dark now, nearly 8:30 pm by her watch. Where were they? She worried that she would miss them, and felt clueless about what to do if that happened. Suppose she had come this entire way, causing a dreadful crisis with Robert, and failed to connect for the ceremony. It was a disheartening thought. Quickly she countered:

No! I will connect with them. It's got to happen, I'm called to do this.

In the continuous flow of people passing the pool to and from the elevators, a woman caught Jana's eye. She was probably in her forties, though her age was hard to determine due to heavy make-up. Orange-gold hair, obviously dyed with frizzy ends, hung in waves to her shoulders. Her sensuous lips blazed with intensely red lipstick in a face that was well proportioned, quite attractive. Creamy mocha skin, dark brows and eyes suggested a Latin heritage. Walking beside a tall, portly older man, her swaying high-heeled gait exuded sexuality. Tight Capri pants clung to her shapely legs like a second skin, accentuating the full hips and small waist. A thin sleeveless top molded to her impressive upright breasts, showing off her hourglass figure to perfection.

Wow! Observed Jana in appreciation. *A luscious ripe woman in the fullness of her overblown sexuality.*

But, there was something else besides sexual energy. The woman's presence held a sinister quality, something that felt wild, out of control. Jana's skin prickled. Deep inside she felt ill at ease; this was an energy that she wanted to avoid.

310

Her eyes followed the couple until they disappeared into the elevator. A tiny wave of relief flowed through her as the elevator door closed. She shifted her focus toward the hotel entrance. Activity was slowing down. Worried, she checked the time again: it was 9:05 pm. She got up and paced around the pool to dispel her tension, wondering if the group had changed plans and left for Chichén Itzá already. Swinging past the glass walls of the dining room, she noticed a sizable group milling around a long row of tables placed end-to-end. Suddenly, her gaze rested on Hanab Xiu. He was standing near the end of the long table, in conversation with two people. Quickly she scanned the group, soon finding the tall, auburn-haired form of Aurora Nakin.

Murmuring a prayer of thanks to the Divine Mother under her breath, Jana entered the dining room and approached Hanab Xiu.

"Hi, I'm Jana Sinclair, I left you a note," she said when he finished his conversation. "I don't know if you remember me."

"I remember you well," Hanab Xiu replied. Smiling into her eyes, he hugged her warmly.

"I – I wondered if I could join your pilgrimage for the equinox ceremony, for the next couple of days," she said, a little surprised by the hug.

"Of course. It is in keeping, it is proper. I was expecting you." A slight twinkle lit his dark eyes. "These next two ceremonies, at Dzibilchaltún and Chichén Itzá, are more public. Many other people are joining us, many elders. You are most welcome. After the equinox will be the inward part of our pilgrimage."

"Thank you so much," Jana replied with great relief. "I would have come for the whole time, but I couldn't get off work. I have to be back on Monday"

"Ah, yes" he said. "Will you sit with us during dinner? I cannot invite you to partake, as you are not in the tour."

Jana hesitated, not wanting to impose. But Aurora Nakin swept in, hugged her and said she must sit with them. Sitting down beside her, Jana soon saw Julia, Michael and Steve across the table. Her acquaintances from the Clearlake School of Maya Mysteries gave enthusiastic greetings, exclaiming upon her being there. As the meal progressed, Aurora introduced Jana to other nearby participants. Leaning forward to better see down the table, Jana almost gasped as she was introduced to Evita, the sexy ripe woman she had just observed, and her husband Jorje. She learned in conversation, though

311

their English was as limited as her Spanish, that they were from Columbia.

Aurora Nakin was absolutely beaming over Jana's arrival. She kept repeating how she "just knew" Jana would make it there, and how happy she was about it. Jana felt a little awed at the effusive welcome and being accepted into the group; the whole thing had the flavor of a minor miracle. But, there were some details she needed to clear with Aurora Nakin.

First was transportation. Jana hoped she could catch a ride on the group's tour bus; it would simplify things greatly. Aurora Nakin replied that would not be possible, only those registered for the pilgrimage were covered by the tour company's insurance. Jana would have to take a taxi or bus. In addition, Jana must pay $50 fee for tomorrow's dinner and teaching in preparation for the equinox ceremony. Part was a donation to support Hanab Xiu's Mystery School in México. Payment was needed tomorrow morning in pesos, before the group left for the Mayaland Hotel. The dinner was at the Ik Kil resort restaurant just below Piste. Jana already had a hotel room in Piste for that night, but getting from place to place was going to be a real challenge.

Weariness began to settle over Jana. It had been an incredibly long day, starting with the 5:00 am flight from Oakland to Los Angeles. Waiting and worrying had further drained energy. Her last meal was on the Mérida flight, over seven hours ago. Hunger was gnawing at her stomach, provoked by smelling food and watching others eat. She told Aurora Nakin she needed to get some food and rest.

The priestess from Clearlake slipped a dinner roll into Jana's hand.

"We're leaving at 4:30 am for Dzibilchaltún," Aurora Nakin advised. "You'd better line up a taxi tonight. It takes about 45 minutes to get there, and sunrise is around 6:00 am. Its spectacular, you don't want to miss it. Hanab Xiu will give brief instructions before, he wants us to make it an inner experience, to receive infusions from the rising sun as an initiation for this equinox process. Then I believe there's going to be a ceremony at the cenote with a crystal skull later. Things are pretty fluid with these shaman-priests, you know."

Giving her thanks and a hug, Jana waved good-by to the others and went to make arrangements. She scheduled the taxi with the front desk, feeling pretty sure it was actually set up. In her room, she munched trail mix and dry fruit along with the roll Aurora Nakin had given her. The room was comfortable but not plush, offering all important air conditioning and bottled water. Showering and requesting a wake-up call at 4:00 am, she settled gratefully into the cool sheets.

Although exhausted, Jana had trouble staying asleep. She was worried about the taxi and wake-up call actually happening. Just drifting into sleep, painful memories of her conflict with Robert surfaced, disturbing her emotionally. Her fatigued body was unable to completely relax, the over-stimulated adrenal glands pulsing out untimely bursts of cortisol that activated her. Periodically checking the clock was no help. Twice she drifted into deeper sleep, only to be jolted into awareness by the ringing phone. A man's voice in rapid Spanish made no sense, she tried to communicate "wrong number" but couldn't find the words.

The wake-up call did ring at 4:00 am; Jana had been sleeping fitfully. Getting up was actually a relief. In the lobby by 4:15 am, she checked on the taxi and was assured it was coming. The group gathered, voices muted and sleepy, sorting through backpacks then boarding their large tour bus, which pulled out with engine roaring.

Shortly afterwards Jana was in the taxi, using a Spanish-English dictionary to attempt more accurate communication with the driver, who appeared to understand almost no English. He nodded and repeated "Vamos a Dzibilchaltún," taking off with a jerk. Jana struggled to determine the price; she read you should establish price with taxi drivers before leaving.

"¿Cuanto cuesta?" she said several times. "Por ir a los dos direcciónes." She was trying to get price for both directions.

The driver rattled several lengthy phrases. She shook her head, not understanding, and repeated her questions. Suddenly he pulled over to the curb, hopped out and went to a telephone booth. Alarmed, Jana hoped this did not bode some huge difficulty. When he returned, he smiled and confirmed he could take her both directions for 300 pesos in half-Spanish and broken English. She grasped that he had spoken to his father and received approval. This surprised her, as her driver appeared to be in his fifties with graying hair. Perhaps the patriarch just would not give up running the family business.

"OK, está bien," she agreed. "Three hundred pesos, trescientos pesos." At the current exchange rate of 10 pesos to one dollar, it was not a bad price for a long taxi ride.

Having settled the price, Jana relaxed and observed her surroundings. The taxi was wending through nearly deserted streets. The sky was dark, no stars visible, and the lights of the city cast an eerie yellow glow into the smoky air. Traffic picked up as they entered a highway leaving the city. Jana's taxi was among the slowest moving vehicles, causing some honking and swerving as commuters rushed to work. After about 30 minutes, the taxi turned onto a small blacktop road, nearly straight on the flat landscape. No other vehicles traversed the black ribbon going into quiet darkness as they left the highway.

Jana glanced at her watch; it was 5:22 am. She hoped they would make it on time. Already the faintest graying on the eastern horizon prefaced the dawn. On both sides of the road, thin scraggly bushes about 10 feet high reached snaky tendrils into the dim sky. The only sound was the chugging taxi engine. It was a surrealistic scene, a lone voyager en route to ruins of a once-great civilization, wending through a deserted countryside in the graying of dawn, snake-like branches hovering overhead.

They reached the parking lot at Dzibilchaltún, where several cars and a couple of tour busses parked randomly. The taxi driver agreed to meet Jana at the drop-off spot at nine o'clock, *aqui a los nueve.* She spotted the group near the park entrance, sidling in line beside Michael and Julia, who gave her a welcoming hug. Everyone was casually dressed with sweaters or long sleeve shirts for the morning cool. Soon after sunrise the temperature would climb drastically. Jana wore her Belize jeans, which she thought most fitting for the event.

A few moments later the group moved through the entrance into the park, heading east toward the Temple of the Sun. Dzibilchaltún was one of the oldest Maya cities in the Yucatan, settled around 500 BCE. It was occupied for 1500 years, becoming large and prosperous in Late Classic times because of salt trade. Archeologists identified the city as a political center in its region, probably allied with Chichén Itzá. It collapsed in the Terminal Classic period, about 900-1000 CE.

Hanab Xiu stood on a large rock near a long, raised path that was once sakbe. A corridor had been partially cleared on either side, leading to the small temple at the far end. Stubby brush struggled to re-establish itself in the dry, rock-strewn terrain. At the corridor edges were the same thin scraggly bushes that lined the road, now dark against the gray dawn sky. The group surrounded the Maya elder.

"Dzibilchaltún is an old, old spiritual center," he said. "It was built by the Maya for a special purpose, for solar initiations. Here we

314

see, very clearly, how they used their buildings to converge with astronomical events, to draw their power. See, the Temple of the Sun." He gestured toward the simple, square structure on a low raised platform at the end of the sakbe. "The sun rises exactly through the central door on each equinox. Year after year, century after century, this holy thing happens. The temple doorway focuses the sun's first rays, it is a portal that alters these rays, gives a code that initiates can understand. It relays the message of the sun, Hunab K'u, our First Father, to his earth children. The sun, this great flaming star that brings earth to life, is a cosmic transducer. Our ancestors, the people of the distant stars, send us messages through the sun. They taught the Maya this way."

He paused, eyes scanning the group, lingering momentarily as they met Jana's eyes, now wide and alert.

"This is the main initiation center for the Mystery Schools of the New World. It is for initiation into the solar mysteries. Today, you are here for this solar initiation. Find a place in line with the temple doorway. Meditate, go inward, prepare breath and mind for stillness and receptivity. Open your heart to receive, connect with your Mother Earth and Father Sun. Ask to be initiated. It is an inward thing."

He waited for a moment, letting his words sink in. Then he concluded:

"After the sun is above the temple, come back here and we will go to the cenote for ceremony. May the blessings of Hunab K'u be with you."

The group slowly dispersed, mingling with other people who had come for the equinox sunrise phenomenon. All together, about 80 people were there. Jana walked pensively along the raised path, reflecting on centuries of Maya feet treading this same sakbe for their solar initiations. She found a place just off the path and settled into a cross-leg position, using her backpack for cushioning the rocky ground. Entering into meditation, she focused breath and concentration, feeling her heartbeat and breathing becoming slow and regular. She placed both hands on the parched, hard soil to connect with earth, consciously sending energy down into its depths. After sensing earth's vibrational field, she focused upward through her crown, sending a stream of conscious energy into the sky and cosmos beyond. It was an expansive, soaring sensation. Her awareness flew past the planets of the solar system, into the vast Milky Way galaxy, and out into the infinite universe. The darkness of immense empty

315

space and the twinkling stars felt like old friends. After a while, she focused on her heart chakra, felt it opening, tuning to the sun.

Increasing light signaled her to open her eyes. She saw a rosy glow on the horizon behind the temple. The atmosphere was hazy, smoky and thick. It hung heavily, muting the sun's brilliance. She kept her eyes on the temple doorway. As the rounded glowing curve appeared at the bottom of the doorway, people in front of Jana rose to their feet, blocking her view. Quickly she stood, transfixed as the rising sun was perfectly framed by the temple doorway. A powerful rush of energy bombarded her heart, activating intense pulsations. She sensed cords of liquid golden light arcing between her heart and the sun.

Intense feelings of love exploded in her heart; love for the sun, the earth, the austere terrain and its crumbling stone ruins, all the people present, and Robert. Tears moistened her eyelids as she thought of her estranged husband. The sun was pulsing such powerful, universal love into her heart that her sadness dissolved quickly. She was swept up in a wave of unconditional love for everyone and everything. Human mistakes and enmity of countries seemed insignificant, only this unshakable unity was really true. Through sacred structures interacting with the cosmos, the ancient Maya were communicating their real values.

This intense sun connection continued for several minutes, then the pulsations diminished gradually. With mind still, but with acute awareness, Jana watched the sun climb upward through the temple doorway. Everyone present stood in hushed concentration, nothing moved in the morning silence. For a few moments, the sun disappeared behind the square doorway frame at the top, reappearing just above the central roofcomb. The pink glow of dawn faded into hazy blueness. People began moving around. Jana waited respectfully a few moments, and then followed the raised sakbe for a closer look at the temple.

The Temple of the Sun was a simple square structure perched on broad, short stairs. Two tiny windows peered out of the forward facing walls on either side of the center doorway. Long-nosed masks at the corners, and a larger mask over the doorway embellished its flat roof. The modest roofcomb had two bands of eroded glyphs. Viewed as a whole, the temple itself had a mask-like appearance, the visage through which the sun god appeared to speak with his people.

Jana retraced the path along the sakbe, following her group across a large open plaza covered with short dry grass. Several structures lined the plaza on all sides, long buildings with wide stairs and multiple doorways, none very tall. Near the central plaza was a rectangular round-top structure with remnants of a façade supporting three short towers, open at one end. Quickly reading the sign, she learned this was a Catholic church built by the Spaniards in the 16th century, over an older Maya temple. Striding across the plaza, she joined the group gathered around a modest sized ruin with small courts at three levels. Crumbling stonewalls allowed easy access. Beside it was a large, tree-lined cenote, slightly recessed from ground level. Deep blue in color, the clear cenote water was gracefully adorned with water lily pads.

Finding Aurora Nakin, Jana stood by her side, receiving a quick hand squeeze. Everyone was focused on Hanab Xiu and another man standing beside a round stone altar at the base of the structure. The other man was a full head taller than the Maya elder, and appeared Caucasian. His receding slate-gray hair was tied in a ponytail, giving his pale forehead striking height. Prominent, straight dark eyebrows made two slashes over clear, light golden eyes, giving him a hawkish look. A thin beak-like nose added to his raptor appearance. He was slender but muscular, wearing a Native American woven serape in patterns of purple, red and pink over a simple white tunic and pants. A large turquoise pendant hung down to mid-chest.

"Who's that?" Jana whispered to Aurora Nakin.

"Fire Eagle," she replied, equally softly. "He's an American shaman from Sedona, knows a lot about Pueblo Indian traditions and Maya temples. Hanab Xiu asked him to co-lead the pilgrimage."

"What are they doing?"

"Starting the crystal skull ceremony," said Aurora Nakin. "Listen, you'll see."

As they were whispering, Hanab Xiu laid a white cloth on the altar, and carefully placed a quartz crystal skull on it. The finely carved skull was human size, of milky white smooth crystal with a translucent quality when the sun struck it. It magnetized everyone's attention.

"This is an ancient Maya crystal skull," Hanab Xiu said. "It is older than anyone knows. It came to Fire Eagle when he was in Chiapas several years ago, in a very unusual way. He was staying in a village near the ruins of Yaxchilan. An old Maya woman came to him, told him she had something for him. It was the crystal skull, and the Maya spirits wanted him to be its caretaker for now. She had been caretaker for most of her life, but a new circumstance was needed for it to do its work. She could not tell him much more, just that her mother and grandmother had taken care of it before. How old it was, where it came from, she did not know. But, it did have Maya spirits in it, and they told her to give it to this stranger from North America."

He nodded at Fire Eagle, who spoke in a strong, surprisingly high voice.

"There are two Maya spirits within the crystal skull, a man and a woman. They love each other very much. When they were young, they agreed in solemn ceremony to consciously die, and at the moment of death to enter the crystal skull. There they would live, in eternal union with each other, to hold the knowledge and experience of the ancient Maya people. This was from the time period when Maya culture first blossomed, a time when love, compassion and cosmic wisdom guided their every moment. The young lovers offered their lives to communicate these extraordinary truths to people at the End of Time, the end of the Great Cycle, the time that is now."

He paused, moved by emotion. After a moment, he continued:

"Their purpose is now being fulfilled. We are those modern people, both modern-day Mayans and people from all corners of the world, people who want to live in love and harmony with earth. People who want to live in keeping with the truths of the ancient Maya."

Fire Eagle looked around the circle, his golden eyes glistening, radiating passion for these ancient Maya truths. Then he lowered his gaze onto the crystal skull again.

"There is one more thing I want to tell you about the skull," he said softly. "After I had sat meditating with it for some months, I became aware that there was another person inside. It is an old grandmother, sitting quietly in the background, supporting the young lovers. She had arranged this eternal marriage between them, she had prepared and instructed them, she had planned what this crystal skull was to do. The grandmothers of ancient Maya times devised this method of holding and transmitting information across the ages. They have been the guardians of the skulls.

"This is an ancient mystical practice, used for millennia, the infusing of human spirit into stone or rock to hold a vibration, a consciousness for those in the future. There are only a few truly ancient crystal skulls, some say only thirteen exist. Scientists can't figure out how they were carved, against the natural axis of the crystal. It should have made the crystal shatter. Crystal is so hard, diamonds are needed to cut it. But there are no microscopic scratches to indicate carving. Some believe these skulls came from Atlantis. Most of the authentic crystal skulls were found in Central America, and are now in museums. But now, the skulls are being drawn together, to re-ignite our hearts with love, compassion and wisdom."

The group of pilgrims stood silently, transfixed by his story and the glowing power of the crystal skull. Many had tears in their eyes, including Jana.

"The love of this young Maya couple is showing us what we must do now," said Hanab Xiu, his face softer than usual. "They are keeping the masculine and feminine energies in perfect balance, they are together in sexual union and eternal love. The world now needs this balance of the masculine and feminine. For over 5,000 years the world has been out of balance, the masculine has dominated. This is not good for the planet. Male power must be softened by female compassion. Male technology must be tempered by female natural cycles. We must touch the earth again with love, not just with desire to control her and exploit her gifts. We must love each other, all people, all creatures, the world, and beyond. That is the teaching of the crystal skull."

More tears were flowing. Jana noticed a young man next to her wiping his eyes. Aurora Nakin put an arm around Jana's shoulders, many people joined hands.

"Let us now send silent prayers and blessings to the entire world," said Hanab Xiu. "Pray for harmony among people, the end of war, respect for the earth, honoring indigenous wisdom. Then come forward, two or three at a time, and place your hands on the crystal skull, touch it and feel its power."

After a few minutes, those closest to the altar on which the skull sat moved forward to touch it. Most of the others stood in silent prayer, many with closed eyes. Slowly they switched positions and those located on the higher courts climbed down. Jana was among the last to approach the skull. She stepped up to the altar beside Fire Eagle, who was standing in silent vigil. Hanab Xiu had moved to the edge of the group, in quiet discussion with Aurora Nakin.

Jana placed her right hand on the smooth cranium of the translucent milky white skull, closing her eyes. It felt cool to touch, but soon tingly sensations prickled her palm and coursed up her arm. Sweetness settled over her heart, as it opened even more to receive the love from the eternal couple. Another woman also had one hand on the skull.

Suddenly a scuffling noise to Jana's right pulled her out of this sweet reverie. Her eyes flew open as a woman's voice screamed in Spanish:

"*Ese mi! Ese mi! No tiene ese!*"

("It's mine, it's mine, you can't have it!")

Before she could take in the situation, Jana was shoved to the ground by the screaming woman. Hitting hard on the rocky ground, Jana broke her fall with elbow and hands. The force of the fall whipped Jana's head around, narrowly missing a large rock and instead landing on a nearby foot wearing a tennis shoe. More screaming and scuffling ensued above her. Two group members helped Jana to sit, asking if she was all right. Looking up, she saw the portly older Columbian man, Jorje, and another two women restraining his sexy wife Evita. Fire Eagle was cradling the crystal skull and backing away. Two other men quickly ran to Evita, who was fighting, scratching and writhing while spitting out vituperative phrases in Spanish. Her body seemed to convulse, she stiffened, then started sinking to the ground. The men supported her, pulling her upright while Jorje held her in his arms. Her screams faded to moans and whimpers.

The little group around Evita herded her to the structure's steps where she sat, sobbing and moaning. Fire Eagle put the crystal skull back into its protective leather bag and checked on Jana. Her elbow was scraped and bloody, and both palms had open scratches. She responded that her head was OK, although she felt dazed and shaken. Aurora Nakin hurried to her side with tissues for the blood and a drink of water. She encouraged Jana to just sit for a few minutes, but advised her they needed to leave the park very soon.

"What happened?" asked Jana. "What was that all about?"

"I can't talk about it now," Aurora Nakin answered. "I'll explain when we get back to the hotel."

The sound of motorcycles pierced the air. Aurora Nakin spotted Michael and Julia, asked them to walk Jana out, and left to join Hanab Xiu who was having an intense discussion in Spanish with park police. As Jana stood a little shakily, supported by her friends, she saw three motorcycles crossing the large plaza. The park police wore tan uniforms with combat boots, and looked imposing. They had guns strapped to thick belts. It was clear that they wanted the group to leave at once.

Walking as rapidly as possible toward the park entrance, Jana asked why they were being escorted out in such a militaristic fashion.

Julia told her they had stayed too long, the sunrise event had been free and people were expected to leave before official park hours began. If the group stayed any longer, everyone would have to pay an entrance fee. Mostly the park police were suspicious about the strange behavior of the group.

At the parking lot, Jana waved good-by as the tour bus left. She looked around for her taxi, but it was nowhere in sight, although her watch said 9:00 am. Sitting on a bench near the entrance, she waited. Reflecting, she wondered what had provoked Evita's outburst. From Aurora Nakin's demeanor, it was evident that the group leaders were concerned. She sensed a deep issue around the Columbian woman.

The taxi pulled up a few minutes later, her driver smiling and waving her inside. As they left the parking lot, she caught an unsettling sight out of the corner of her eyes. An old man was squatting, hunched against a telephone pole, wearing a battered straw hat and a brown poncho. He seemed to be napping, but lifted his head just as the taxi passed, giving a toothless grimace. The taxi turned into a curve and she lost sight of the man before any other details were visible.

Was that the brujo, the evil shaman from Tikal?

Doubly shaken from Evita's attack and the sight of the old man, Jana grabbed her forearms and held herself tightly for a while. The taxi's motion and chugging engine plus her own fatigue eventually put her into a semi-hypnotic state. She dozed most of the trip back to Mérida.

The taxi's radio blaring brought her back to foggy-brained awareness. They were traveling along a busy city street divided by an island. Glancing out the window as they waited at a stoplight, Jana saw the headlines of newspapers young boys were proffering to passing drivers. It caused her to sit bolt upright with a gasp.

BAGDAD: ¡ATENTADO CON BOMBA!

The United States had bombed Baghdad. Front page pictures showed black smoke billowing above buildings full of flames. Several times she caught the words "Los Estados Unidos" and "Iraq" and "guerra" in the rapid Spanish newscast on the taxi radio. The United States was at war with Iraq. The invasion of a sovereign nation based on questionable evidence, the first pre-emptive U.S. attack on another country, had happened. Sometime during the night of March 20th, American airplanes dropped bombs on a city full of civilians. Less than a day before the cut-off date given by Maya elders for a war of global destruction.

War. The ultimate folly of humankind—or more precisely, mankind.

Jana reflected somberly that war might be the immediate result of men's actions, but too many women supported them in aggression, or at least did not stand up in opposition. She was always amazed that women, whose bodies formed and carried their babies for nine months, who went through the suffering and risk of giving birth, who gave years of their lives nurturing and protecting children, would willingly send their sons to war. What happened in a woman's mind that could justify support for devastation of homes, destruction of cities, maiming and death of people? Her heart cracked at the thought of Arab children in Baghdad, horribly wounded, killed, orphaned in the carnage of bombing. Images flooded her inner vision of crumbling buildings, flames bursting through windows, smoke swirling into the sky, roaring jets, ear-splitting explosions, people running, screaming through chaotic streets. She could see black-clad Muslim women frantically gathering children, animals, maybe a few possessions and rushing out of toppling houses, but to where? No place was safe in a city under siege.

She thought of the young men and women, the American troops, who would suffer or die in the conflict. Lives full of potential, crushed before full bloom, altered by indescribably hideous experiences that would leave indelible imprints on the psyche. Missing limbs, damaged functions, post-traumatic stress syndromes, broken bodies and minds; the horrible fruits of war. Yet this ultimate use of force, this maximum thrill of risking everything continued to fascinate human beings. Certainly they used emotion-racking imagery and called up the most primitive tribal values to fuel the impetus to war. But the basic, underlying dynamic was fear. If people could be made fearful enough, they would consent to unbelievably horrible things.

The U.S. administration had certainly played on the American public's fears. Capitalizing on the terrorist bombings of the twin towers, the fear of further terrorist attacks in the U.S. was the emotional pivot used to manipulate public opinion. Through a series of devious twists, the source of that threat was shifted from Al Qaida and Bin Ladin, and somehow related to Sadam Hussein's amassing weapons of mass destruction that might be directed toward our country. Weapons that had not been found, that were still being investigated by the United Nations team, but the process was pre-empted by this invasion of Iraq.

Fear for our safety. Fear for our opulent way of life, that exploits and depletes other nations, that creates pollution with global effects, that sustains a growing gap between the obscenely wealthy and the profoundly poor. Fear driven by flag-waving patriotism that sets us against the rest of the world. When will we learn that we are citizens of the world, that we cannot set ourselves apart, thinking only of what's good for us? As if destroying the planet that gives us life is good for us! Better we should try to understand why terrorist actions are directed against our country, and make reparations that give people in poor countries a decent standard of living.

Jana sighed as the radio continued to blare in Spanish. She knew the underlying reasons for war were power, wealth and control of resources. The Iraq war was about oil, not terrorism. The safety fears engendered in the American people were the intoxication that kept them from seeing the leader's real motives. Fear, hatred and distraction were the techniques of leaders through untold centuries to numb the minds and manipulate the hearts of their people.

No doubt similar tactics were used by Maya rulers during the Classic and Postclassic periods, when warfare characterized their civilization. She recalled her email discussion with Francine Rappele. War became a key factor in the fortunes of Maya cities, with shifting alliances and enmities, different cities rising to power then falling, and the eventual decline of Maya civilization. Tikal was a prime example of this process, using a new technology for warfare they obtained through alliance with Teotihuacan to conquer Uaxactun and become the dominant power in the Peten. After several decades of wealth and expansion, Tikal was defeated by the Kalakmul-Caracol-Naranjo alliance and sent into 125 years of silent subjugation. Rising back to power, Tikal defeated its old enemies and had another period of fluorescence, but went into decline two hundred years later.

And so it went for city-states and nations. Rising and falling, wealth and power, destruction and subjugation. When would the utter futility of this way, the way of warfare and dominance, of polarization and enmity, dawn within the psyche of enough people on the planet that it would end?

This is what the pilgrimage is all about. This is why we are gathering at Chichén Itzá to do sacred ceremony.

Jana felt immense sadness and a sense of shame about her country's attack. As the taxi approached her hotel, she tried to express it to the driver in halting Spanish:

"Está . . . está terrible, estoy muy . . triste," she said. "Mi pais está muy mal."

He nodded without looking back, repeating "terrible" several times. His warm smile and handshake as he let her off at the Hotel Los Aluxes confirmed that he did not hold it against her.

Jana found Michael, Julia and Steve at breakfast. She hungrily downed scrambled eggs and tropical fruit, along with decent black coffee. The conversation focused on the Iraq invasion.

"Well, it happened despite all our prayers for peace," said Julia, her voice laden with dejection.

"Yeah, but before March 21st," Michael reminded her.

"At the eleventh hour," observed Steve.

"So the fallout is supposed to be limited, right?" said Michael. "It won't be World War III, according to the Maya elders. Boy, I hope they're right."

"It's still going to have awful consequences for people in Baghdad, and the soldiers on both sides," Jana added. She sipped the strong coffee, already feeling the caffeine zinging between brain synapses. It was a much-needed pickup for her fatigued mind.

"Yeah, war is ugly. But is it sometimes necessary? How do you deal with aggression, with use of force, without fighting back?" pondered Steve, ever philosophical. "Look at dictators determined to take over neighboring countries, and eventually the world, like Hitler. We might all be slaves if the allies hadn't attacked in World War II."

"What led to Hitler?" Michael asked rhetorically, answering at once: "A series of mistakes, an attitude of vengeance against Germany after World War I, a climate of oppression and economic hardship that paved the way for an Arian supremacy movement. Hitler was masterful in taking advantage of the people's fears and suffering."

"There are similarities to what's happening now in our country," Jana ventured. "Playing on people's fears and insecurities, I mean. Its hard to know how real the threat is from Iraq."

"Terrorism is pretty real," Michael commented. "We don't want another 9-11."

"But is more violence the answer?" countered Jana. "You get into a never-ending spiral of fighting until one side is totally destroyed."

"Remember, Jesus said to turn the other cheek," Julia added. "And to love your enemies as yourself."

"Yes, and nonviolent tactics can be used to oppose what you believe is wrong," said Jana. "Like Gandhi and Martin Luther King."

"I don't know about that," said Steve doubtfully. "If Gandhi and King were here now, and had their people do sit-ins against the terrorists, I think they'd all be wiped out. It's a different ball game now. Suicide airplanes and bombs go way beyond any sensitivities about killing or being killed. The propensity for violence has escalated."

"It's a total dehumanization of the enemy, the target," Michael added. "An extremist way of thinking that's foreign to us. Fueled by hatred of what we stand for and fundamental religious views."

"But it's a distortion of what Muhammad taught!" exclaimed Jana. "Jihad, holy war, meant defending your city against attackers, not sending out terrorists on suicide missions to other countries. Muhammad taught love and tolerance, devotion to God and family."

"Yeah, I know," said Michael. "Another example of leaders manipulating their countries with religious interpretations that serve their lust for power. Unfortunately, all the great world religions have been used this way."

"So, is there such a thing as a just war? Or noble warriors?" asked Julia.

Everyone fell silent, pondering those ideas. After a few more sips of coffee, Jana spoke thoughtfully.

"The Bhagavad Gita is all about war between two branches of the same Hindu family, pitting uncles and cousins against each other. But it's considered the Hindu 'bible' and contains some of their greatest spiritual teachings. Arjuna was the epitome of a noble warrior, with Lord Krishna as his charioteer. Arjuna didn't want to fight his kinsmen, but Krishna told him he had to, it was his duty and karma. So he led his forces and won, restoring the kingdom to its righteous leader."

Jana looked around at her friends.

"But," she added, "it's supposedly a metaphor for every person's inner struggle against desires and worldly attachments that keep them from union with God. They have to slay the 'enemies' who would take over and lead them astray, even though these habits feel like old friends and relatives."

"Maybe that's how we need to look at this situation, the war in Iraq," mused Steve. "As a metaphor, a symbol for something deeper. When we meditate and do ceremonies, I feel in touch with a greater reality, it transcends the happenings on the material plane."

"Yes, I know what you mean," replied Jana. "Hindu teachings call this world a dream, an apparent reality that isn't what we really are. When we wake up, see things clearly, become en-lightened, then we know nothing that happens in this world has lasting effects, or truly harms our essential being."

"So war and killing don't really do harm?" queried Michael, wrinkling his eyebrows dubiously. "Pollution and raping the earth doesn't hurt us? Blowing up the planet is OK?"

Jana shook her head.

"I don't believe that, Michael," she said. "But there's so much I don't understand. Everything matters immensely and doesn't matter at all, depending on the reality from which you're viewing it. If earth is the planet of choice, of maximum experience, anything goes, whatever you want you can get, do I have the right to deny others the experiences they choose?"

"But what if their experiences are harming others?" said Julia.

"Exactly. Can we help them make better choices, seek higher experiences, that are supporting life and keeping the planet healthy?" Jana suggested.

"I think that's why we're on this pilgrimage," Michael observed. "We're trying to affect the collective consciousness of people around the world, so they can make more loving, more life-supporting choices."

"Yeah," added Steve. "Maybe we actually can move the global mind to dream a new reality, a world of peace and harmony. It's sure worth a try."

They sat in silence for a few minutes, sobered yet heartened by their discussion. It was time to move on. The three group members talked about the next stop on their journey that afternoon, the caves at Balancanche on the way to Chichén Itzá. No one mentioned the Colombian woman's outburst at the cenote. The tour bus was leaving in an hour; they had to get ready. Jana remembered she had to give 500 pesos to Aurora Nakin before the group left, and she needed to find transportation to Chichén Itzá.

The morning was already steamy when Jana left the hotel, stepping out onto Calle 60 for the four-block walk to a nearby bank. She obtained directions from the hotel desk, where she also inquired about buses to Chichén Itzá. There were several, the deluxe bus that took an hour or local busses that meandered through villages and stopped frequently. She needed a taxi to get to the bus station, and for moving between her posada in Piste, the Ik Kil resort, the Mayaland Hotel at Chichén Itzá, and back. She was not sure when the ceremony ended, and catching a bus back to Mérida in the evening looked dicey. Considering how critical timing was to arrive at events promptly, it looked like a rental car was the best solution. Jana felt a little uneasy about driving in México. The tour book warnings and friend's stories about police hassles made her cautious.

Just as these thoughts were in her mind, Jana turned at the intersection a block from the hotel, and spotted a rental car sign another half-block down Calle 60. The name made her laugh: *Turista Car Rentals.*

That's bound to be a tourist trap, she thought. *But it's really close.*

She skirted the pleasant plaza, bordered by large shade trees with rectangular steps leading to a recessed center with a fountain. Benches located under trees invited pedestrians to rest their heels. Pigeons and small brown birds scouted the ground for crumbs. It was mid-morning and businesses were open. Although the sidewalks were mostly empty, auto traffic was brisk. She glanced in shop windows, admiring ceramics, jewelry and clothes displayed in the bright pastel buildings.

The bank was an imposing edifice set well back from the street, up several tiers of wide stairs bordered by plants. A uniformed guard stood in the antechamber where the ATM was located, between two sets of heavy glass doors. He nodded to Jana as she entered, she smiled back saying "Bueno dias."

It only took a few minutes to figure the process out. The ATM had instructions in several languages on its plaque with international codes for accepted cards. She inserted her debit card, keyed in her code and requested 1,000 pesos, to have some extra money. The machine calculated the day's rate of exchange and soon spit out a huge wad of bills.

That was frighteningly easy, Jana thought as she put the money in her purse. *No problem getting money to spend in Mérida!*

On the way back, she stopped at an internet shop to send Robert an e-mail. Soon the young man had her set up at a computer. She sat for a moment, focusing her thoughts. He would be worried, given the Iraq war. But what other emotions was he having for her? Was he still as angry and distant as when she left? She typed:

Dear Robert,

I'm in Mérida and doing fine. I've connected with the Maya Mystery School group, they let me join them for the next two days. This afternoon I'm going to Chichén Itzá. Got the news of the war this morning. People here do not seem very upset and life goes on as usual. I think of you often, you are so dear to me. I love you with all my heart. Jana.

She decided to keep the message short and avoid bringing up their conflict. It would not do any good at this point, but tears glistened as she felt the anguish again. She could only hope that something would shift inside Robert to dissolve away these issues.

Back at the Hotel Los Aluxes, Jana found the group gathered in the lobby, flooding it with luggage and bodies. She looked around for Aurora Nakin; it was not hard to find the tall, stately woman with an authoritative air. Jana gave her 500 pesos, asking if she could take a minute to talk about the outburst at the cenote. Aurora Nakin drew Jana outside the lobby to the central pool patio. They stood partially shielded by a palmetto to talk in privacy.

"The problem with Evita started to show up yesterday, our first full day together as a group," Aurora Nakin said softly. "She is, well . . . hard to miss and pretty 'out there' both physically and emotionally. At one point when we were in circle doing silent focusing in the ruins, she started making noises, like moans and sighs that turned into near shrieks. Her body twisted around, it took a couple of us to quiet her. Hanab Xiu sensed that a dark entity was inside her body. He and I and Fire Eagle talked about it, he's sure the entity intends to do whatever it can to disrupt our pilgrimage and derail our ceremonies. This morning was another example of that."

"Wow!" Jana said, eyes wide. "Why did she attack me?"

"You're important to the mission of our pilgrimage," Aurora Nakin said. "I'm not clear about how or why, but it's karmic for you to be here. That was obvious when Hanab Xiu initiated you at Clearlake though you hadn't taken the training. I suspect you have deep, ancient connections with the Maya. When you touched the crystal skull, that was going to reawaken those connections for you. I think the entity using Evita was trying to prevent that from happening."

"Yeah," Jana said reflectively. "I was just beginning to feel a deep heart connection with the lovers in the crystal skull when she shoved me down."

"How is your elbow? Are you OK?" inquired Aurora Nakin with concern.

Jana had forgotten about her injuries. Now she noticed a dull throbbing in her elbow, and glanced at the scratches on her palms.

"I'm OK. It's just superficial."

"Let me know if you need anything for them," Aurora Nakin said. "To finish about Evita, we're aware that something has to be done before the equinox ceremony at Chichén Itzá. I think Hanab Xiu is planning to deal with it tonight after our meeting. Jana, stay away from her. I don't know what she is capable of doing—rather, what the entity could do through her. You have a way to Ik Kil?"

"I think I'll rent a car, that will be simpler than trying to figure out bus schedules," Jana replied.

"OK, well be careful," Aurora Nakin advised. "We're facing pretty strong forces. I've got to get the group on the bus, see you there."

The women hugged and Aurora Nakin strode back into the chaotic lobby, a beacon of order and calmness in the hubbub of disorganization.

Jana stretched out her weary body on the bed in her dark, cool air-conditioned room. She planned to rest a couple of hours before checking out and driving to Piste. Smiling inwardly, she replayed her experience at Turista Car Rentals. Still uncertain about renting there, she checked with the hotel concierge for other options, but the agencies were quite far away. With some trepidation, she walked the block-and-a-half to Turista, just catching the proprietor as he left for early lunch. He was an agreeable young man who spoke English well—and he should, with a business name like that! In record time, she was signed up for the economy car, an older red Volkswagen with stick shift and no air conditioning. The 24-hour rental cost 600 pesos, without extra insurance. Jana wanted to be frugal on this trip, and hoped she was not also being unwise.

It took a few tries to get accustomed to the wobbly four-speed shift on the floor. The glaring red VW lurched forward like an epileptic beetle, its engine roaring, the muffler backfiring several times. After going around the block, she managed to coordinate the clutch and shift reasonably well. The proprietor gave her a map, pointed out the numerous one-way streets and marked her route out of town toward Piste. There were two ways to go for the hour and 45-minute drive, one a toll road with few exits, the other a free road through several villages. He noted all dents and scrapes on the VW, and the gas level that needed to be replaced upon return. By the time

329

she deposited the venerable red bug in the hotel parking lot, Jana felt fairly confident.

Breathing deeply a few times, she relaxed into the soft covers and felt herself drifting toward the delicious, drugged sleep of midday. Her awareness floated just under the surface of semi-waking, dropping into luscious nothingness then bubbling up again. Every little movement pushed her awareness up just enough to enjoy falling back into pleasant oblivion. Dreams and images swirled in layers of unconsciousness, until she became dimly aware of a presence.

Eyes closed, not wanting to emerge from semi-sleep, she sensed the ephemeral presence standing at the foot of the bed. Her foggy mind struggled to grasp it.

Lord Jesus?

Peace be unto you.

Faintly the shimmering image materialized to her inner vision, like wisps of fog as sunlight evanesces the droplets. Someone else was there.

Who is it?

Before the ephemeral Christ spoke into her mind, the thought crystallized:

The Maya priestess!

It is so. From the Christ image came the affirmation, wordless.

Chills of fear rippled up Jana's spine and her neck hairs stood on end.

They do human sacrifice!

The thought burst forth, exploded into awareness before she could filter it. She felt only calm acceptance emanating from Christ. The dread quickly dissipated. Eyes still closed, her awareness was now acute and focused on the images.

Is it OK to know more about her?

Ask, and you will receive.

What is her name?

Yalucha.

Please spell it. She wanted to be sure.

Y-A-L-U-C-H-A.

Yalucha. She repeated the name to familiarize her mind with the unusual sound. Without forming thoughts, she opened her awareness to receive visual images of the priestess. Slender, dark hair, warm brown skin, intense black eyes in a Mayan-looking face with softer features than usual. She wore a white sleeveless robe with a deep v-neck, clasped at the waist by a woven shell-encrusted belt. Large earrings and multiple strands of beaded necklaces adorned her. On her head a tall plumed headdress waved, sporting a collection of inky blue feathers reflecting rainbow shimmers as two long, slender red feathers curved and danced above.

Do you wish to tell me something? Jana felt the priestess had a message.

Go to the cathedral near the main plaza.

It was a communication directly into Jana's mind from the Maya priestess, as Christ had done. An image of a large, pink stone cathedral appeared with a small plaza to the left, facing a very large square plaza across the street that had three-story buildings all around. Jana was certain she had seen it in the guidebook; it was the main plaza of Mérida. And, it was four blocks away from her hotel.

OK.

Jana did not have to ask when, she knew it was now. The two images faded away. She roused herself over the protests of her tired body. She had to go to the cathedral before she left Mérida.

It was a few minutes after 1:00 pm, checkout time for the hotel. Jana quickly re-packed her suitcase and assembled her daypack. Seeing the small, embroidered jewelry pouch reminded her of the amber pendant. She hooked it around her neck, feeling comforted by its smooth cool touch against her chest. She checked out, booked a tour of Uxmal for Saturday, the day after her return from Chichén Itzá, and put her luggage in the red VW bug.

Stepping outside onto the sidewalk was like entering an oven. A wave of heat enveloped her body, immediately bringing a fine sweat to her skin. At the intersection she glanced at a street map to orient herself, then walked slowly along Calle 60. The sidewalks were deserted and only a few vehicles traveled the baking streets. Shops were closed for afternoon siesta time. Jana appreciated the need for this custom, as the heat was enervating. Just breathing seemed an effort, and walking was an exercise of willpower. No wonder people stayed inside in the midday heat.

Jana's clothing was wet when she arrived at the imposing facade of the cathedral. Built in the 16th century exactly atop the site of a Maya temple, the pink-hued stones used for much of the exterior walls came from ruined structures. On either edge triple towers soared skyward in diminishing tiers, accented by arched doorways and carved stone railings, each successively smaller. Three doors opened to the flat plaza, the towering central entrance decorated with columns

331

and crosses. The simple, medieval lines of the exterior lent an aura of Benedictine antiquity.

The large central door admitted Jana with a protesting creak, and she entered the coolness of the dimly lit antechamber. Grateful for relief from the outside heat, she stood a moment letting her eyes adjust. The cathedral's interior was stark, a surprising contrast to the usually ornate colonnades and ceilings of Catholic churches from colonial times. There were few windows, blanketing the huge nave in velvety darkness. Dim streaks of light from the small chapel left of the main altar drew Jana's attention. Her footsteps echoed in the cavernous silence; the stillness was palpable. She entered the small chapel and sat in a forward pew.

The chapel featured a replica of a famous native wood carving of Christ, called Cristo de las Ampollas (Christ of the Blisters). Legend told that the Maya Indians, converted to Christianity by the Spanish conquerors, witnessed the carved figure burning repeatedly without being consumed by flames. The fame of this figure drew pilgrimages to the village church in Ichmul, until a fire destroyed the church without burning the image, although it caused blisters on the wood. The blistered carving was brought to the cathedral in Mérida in 1645 CE.

Jana sat in meditation, eyes closed. The scents of candle wax and incense filled her nostrils, sending her into a spontaneous imaginal journey.

Images of colonial Mérida played across her inner vision: stately mansions with gracious patios, horse-drawn carriages wending through narrow streets, families promenading along the plazas in the evenings, mustachioed cavalry in ornate uniforms riding in close formation, priests saying mass in sonorous Latin, brown-skinned servants scurrying on endless errands, dancers twirling and clapping to rhythmic guitar melodies.

Next came images of natives toiling on plantations of agave and tropical fruits, dusty villages where women labored all day drawing water and grinding maize, barefoot children running in ragged clothes followed by scrawny dogs, Spanish overseers riding sleek horses with crop tucked under arm, and the inescapable priests and monks drilling a fearful god into the minds of a conquered people. Image fragments of violence and unbearable cruelty flashed and flickered, but her consciousness rebelled and sought to keep them out of full awareness.

Suddenly the inner screen shifted, swirled like nebula in space, full of exploding stars and rotating galaxies. Two images began to coalesce amid the cloudy star-studded swirls, moving gradually closer. These were female figures, emerging from the cosmos, shimmering into form. It was Mary and Ix Chel. The faces of the two goddesses bore expressions of profound sadness, weeping with tears streaming. Their hearts were each pierced by long swords with gem-encrusted handles formed like a cross. The two forms merged together, the hearts and swords becoming one, enlarging until they filled her entire image field. The huge pierced heart opened, forming a tunnel-like window through which battle scenes raged, conquistadors and natives pitting swords, cannons, spear-throwers, lances, daggers, maces, arrows against each other. Sweating, cursing, groaning, screaming they locked in combat, writhing with wounds, falling from rocks and neighing horses, bodies trod underfoot, burning buildings, running in defeat, roaring in victory. Streams of blood ran through wide stone-paved streets between soaring pyramids, brightly colored feathers tossed fitfully in winds blowing through empty plazas. The sharp clack of horseshoes on stone and the clanging of metal armor broke the silence of deserted, once-great cities.

The jungle grew over the cities of stone. Vines twined through corbel arches, palms grew on wide stairways, lichen and weeds found footing on stonewalls now bare of colorful plaster. Bats found homes in quiet, dark palace rooms. Once soaring pyramids crumbled and eroded, stelae tumbled and cracked, plazas became grassy fields. Soon only the tops of slowly deteriorating roofcombs appeared above the jungle canopy.

The people of the cities dispersed, melted into the jungles, or merged with the culture of the conquerors to become its servants. But many souls entered the deep earth, descended into the underworld, were trapped in Xibalba. Especially the souls of the warriors, the leaders, those fighting in fury and desperation against forces they knew brought inevitable defeat. Trapped in cold darkness with fitfully burning fires that gave no warmth, subject to repeated suffering and foul odors from rivers of pus, tormented by the Lords of Death.

Jana remembered her dream in which she envisioned just such a scene. It was the Maya depiction of Xibalba, the underworld. Numerous rituals were enacted during life, but especially at death, to provide means for outwitting the Lords of Death and empowering the soul to avoid being trapped in the underworld. But many Maya had been unsuccessful or unable to accomplish this; they remained trapped in the deep earth.

The frightful images gradually faded from Jana's inner vision. Indistinct stellar swirling played for a while, then the image of a rounded pyramid began to emerge. As it became clear, she saw the Maya priestess in white robes standing on the high platform.

It was Yalucha. The priestess she had encountered in her semi-dream state in the hotel room, accompanied by The Christ. This was her Maya spirit guide. The majestic figure emanated profound calmness, complete acceptance and radiant love. Gazing with deep black eyes, pools of infinite wisdom and compassion, the priestess communicated directly into Jana's mind:

Love the men.
Love them for who they are, not what they do.
See the pure essence of their souls, not the ugliness of violence.
Call forth their inner beauty, for all souls are innately perfect.
Heal their wounds. Pain underlies all fear and violence.
Only forgiveness leads to deep healing.
You must be strong to truly forgive, you must be whole, healed within yourself.
You can only forgive from strength, which comes from being whole.
This strength does not cower before threat. It knows when to stay and when to leave.
Use your strength for healing our people. Release them from the deep earth. In doing this, the middle world will also be healed.

The sweetness of acceptance and forgiveness poured through Jana's being. Her heart felt immense, huge enough to hold all the suffering and pain of the world. Everything merged into a blissful unity. She felt one with Source. That Infinite Consciousness, for a moment, was hers.

She wanted to sit in the quiet chapel, in front of the Christ of the Blisters, forever. Although the image of the priestess had dissipated, she still felt every cell resonating with Yalucha's presence. She had met her Maya spirit guide, and she was powerful.

A sense of time surfaced, an awareness of her schedule. She had to get to Piste, check into her hotel, and arrive at Ik Kil resort by 6:00 pm. Her observer watched dispassionately, but Jana's emotions regretted the inevitable shrinking of her consciousness as the necessity of time entered. She said a silent prayer of gratitude to Christ and Yalucha, and to the cathedral for being the portal to this extraordinary experience.

Leaving the cathedral, brilliant sunlight assaulted her eyes and she quickly put on sunglasses. The heat pummeled her skin and nose, almost taking her breath away. Glancing at her watch, she saw it was 1:48 pm. It was amazing how much could happen inside one's mind and consciousness in a short time. But, she reflected, you were in a timeless state during those experiences.

Returning along Calle 60, she passed several closed stalls of vendors in the small plaza beside the cathedral. One stall was open, to her surprise. She did not recall noticing it when going to the cathedral. Drawn by curiosity, she went to the open stall. At first she could not see into its well-shaded interior, but in a moment the form of a tiny, bent old woman appeared. She was sewing a costume on a doll; the stall contained numerous dolls of varied sizes wearing traditional Mexican and native clothing. Jana was about to turn away when the old woman spoke:

"Señora, this doll is for you." Her English was impeccable.

"¿Perdón?" said Jana, completely surprised.

"Si, mire está muñeca," the woman said, reverting to Spanish as she told Jana to take a look at this doll. She stood creakily, taking a doll from a shelf in back of the stall and holding it out to Jana.

Jana gasped. The six-inch tall doll had ceramic brown skin with a Maya-looking face and black hair braided and twisted around her head like a crown. She was dressed in a simple white gown with a deep v-neck, trimmed in gold with a sequin-decorated waistband. Her features bore uncanny resemblance to the Maya priestess of her images, Yalucha.

"W-where did . . . how did you do this?" Jana stumbled over her words.

The old woman, strands of wispy gray hair straggling from her headscarf, hobbled to the stall counter. Deep wrinkles cut grooves in her bronze face, and two whiskers stuck impishly from a large mole on her hooked nose. Her heavy-lidded eyes were almost buried under folds of skin. Gnarled fingers proffered the graceful doll to Jana.

"The priestess is with you, yes?" she said in lightly accented English. "This is her spirit doll. The doll must go to Chichén Itzá. She must be present at the ceremony, she brings the priestess back. It is very important, muy importante!"

Jana took the doll in her hands, eyes devouring every detail. Tiny beaded necklaces adorned the doll's neck and her feet bore painted sandals. The robe was made of gauzy, opaque material that was smooth and silky to touch. She looked up again at the old woman, who smiled with still full lips invaded by dozens of tiny wrinkles.

She's a shaman! Jana thought immediately. *Like the old man. But she's on my side.*

"Yes, I will take the spirit doll to the ceremony at Chichén Itzá," Jana said slowly.

"Bien, very good. The ceremony fulfills an ancient prophesy. It is of utmost importance to the world now. It was predicted from ancient times, through this priestess. You have inherited this mission. You must do this for the world to pass successfully through the ending years of the Great Cycle."

Jana was so astonished by the old woman's message that she forgot to marvel at her impeccable use of English. This was indeed a strange encounter!

Holding the doll uncertainly, Jana did not know what to do next. The old woman nodded a couple of times, saying:

"Ciento cincuenta pesos, one hundred and fifty pesos."

Jana tilted her head quizzically, and then remembered this was a vendor's stall. Pulling the money from her wallet, she felt amused at the interplay of material and spiritual forces. There could hardly be a more fitting metaphor.

"Gracias, señora," the old woman said, taking the money.

"Estoy agradecida, I'm grateful," Jana replied. "Muchas gracias."

"Oh, momento," the old woman muttered, bending over. "Tome. Put this headdress on her for the ceremony."

She handed Jana a tiny feathered headdress, dyed rainbow colors, with a tie string to fasten it on the doll's ceramic hair. Jana marveled at the exquisite workmanship and vibrant tones of the wispy feathers.

"It's beautiful, muy bonita," Jana murmured.

The old woman nodded in contentment. She gave Jana a bag for the doll.

"Si, bonita. Keep her close, Señora. You will face danger in this mission. Remember to wear amber, it protects the priestess."

In a reflex motion, Jana's hand touched the amber pendant hanging inside her shirt. She nodded, speechless. It was too much for her logical mind to accept. Placing the doll and headdress carefully in the bag, she turned and continued back to the hotel.

*   *   *   *   *   *

Robert sat morosely in front of the television, trying half-heartedly to focus on the tennis match. Since Jana departed for the Yucatan yesterday, he had been unable to focus on anything for very long. He took a long draught from the bottle of beer, his third that evening. He was drinking too much, but he didn't care. He grunted in appreciation as the match point was skillfully taken, but quickly returned to his mental preoccupation. She had left on her quest, despite his strong opposition, despite his point-blank asking her not to, despite his warning that she would destroy their relationship.

He still found it hard to believe. Up until the last minute, when her car pulled out of the driveway, he held the inner belief that she would relent. He was sure that her love for him would win over her sense of mission about this trip. What mission could be that important? It seemed crazy to him, this idea she had about being called to be part of a ceremony in a Maya ruin. Maybe she had lost her mind. He found a little comfort in that.

But he really did not think Jana had gone crazy. Some mysterious inner force was driving her, pulling her away from him, causing her to put this "calling" above him. To be sure, there were a lot of unusual circumstances that pointed to some paranormal process. But he saw that as even more reason to avoid further involvement. The vague sense of danger he felt around the Maya hinted at uncanny forces that were best left alone. Jana, however, did not seem intimidated by these forces, and he had not been able to convince her that getting in their path was unwise.

The couple of weeks between their blowup and her trip had been agony. They had each gone about their daily activities, although the tension was draining. He wanted several times to cry out, to beg her not to go, but his pride stopped him. He would not grovel, and even worse, what if he did and she went anyway? He simply could not fathom it. Nothing in his life experience had prepared him for this kind of conflict: he knew Jana loved him, and he loved her. It was her damned idea of a sacred mission that blocked her from understanding how much it meant to him. He could not stand being relegated to second place.

Waves of anger flooded through his body. Unable to sit, he jumped up and strode aimlessly around. After several minutes of pacing, he stopped to consider his options. He could get drunk—well, he was already halfway there. Then he would have a hangover tomorrow and he had a class to teach. He could prepare more for the class, but he had tried that earlier and found it impossible to concentrate. The material was familiar, he could just "wing it."

Thinking about the class invoked the image of Veronica. The sexy blonde student was taking a second semester with him this spring. She seemed really fascinated by music theory and had a talent for it, or . . . maybe she was fascinated by him. Letting his mind savor Veronica's sensuous curves and luscious lips, he fantasized having sex with her. It did capture his attention and gave some satisfaction to his injured ego. And he sensed she would welcome his advances . . .

Hold on! What the hell are you thinking?

Robert's rational mind fairly screamed at him. Sexual intimacy with students was anathema to him, a code he valued so highly that never before had he actually contemplated breaking it. This showed him the desperate straits to which he had come.

OK, he said to himself. *If you're looking to get laid, it's not going to be a student.*

Just thinking it out clearly brought relief. This little problem-solving session had defused his anger, but made him somberly aware of his coping options:

Alcohol or sex. That's a pretty sorry pair of coping mechanisms. I've got to do better than that.

With sudden focus, he picked up the phone and called Harry. They talked for an hour. Robert reviewed all his reactions and the issues as best he understood them. Harry listened and offered other interpretations from time to time. The bottom line of Harry's advice about dealing with headstrong women—such as Jana and his wife, Rita—was to endure and wait it out. They would come around in time. Things would settle back in and go on, pretty much as before. Robert was not sure he believed that. At least the long talk allowed him to decompress his intense emotions. He thanked Harry and went to bed.

The next morning the phone rang as Robert was about to leave for class. It was his daughter, Marissa.

"Hi, Dad," came the cheerful melodic voice. "I'm coming home tonight for the weekend. Lets have dinner. I'll pick up a pizza. Got beer?"

Just hearing Marissa's voice gave him a boost.

"Sure," he said, making a mental note to replenish his beer supply. "That's great, Butterfly. I'll look forward to seeing you, about what time?"

"Six-ish OK?"

"Done deal."

The day went better than Robert had anticipated. His class was rich with memory-stored detail, almost brilliant if he had to say so himself. It was funny how some of your best classes happened during times of duress. Perhaps some mental barrier dropped that allowed unexpected synapses to fire, bringing forth heightened creativity. Veronica hung on his every word, her limpid violet eyes lingering on his body just a little too long. He did not miss the implicit invitation; he just chose not to respond. And he felt good about it. After a faculty meeting he and Harry had a latte, talking some more about handling challenging wives, but nothing new emerged to help Robert grapple with the situation. Their conversation moved to discussing the Iraq bombing, which had just happened that morning. Both men were deeply concerned about global implications.

A traffic snarl slowed down his drive back home, dampening his mood and increasing his irritation. He did remember to pick up a six-pack of Corona, Marissa's favorite beer.

By 6:30 pm they were enjoying pizza and Corona beer together. Marissa's blonde curls tossed as she spoke with animated gestures about her studies and friends at college. Robert half listened, glad for the entertaining distraction, a little bemused at how good his appetite was despite his emotionally distraught state. Jana was just the opposite. When she was upset, she could hardly eat at all. As if sensing his train of thought, Marissa suddenly changed the conversation.

"So, Mom's in México," she said abruptly.

"Uh, yeah," Robert answered, caught off guard.

"And you didn't want her to go."

Robert was not sure how much Marissa knew about their blowup.

"Yeah, I'm worried about her safety. Especially now that Bush has invaded Iraq. Timing couldn't be worse." It had been all over the news that day.

"I know," Marissa agreed. "Dad, its so terrible. What on earth are they doing?"

For a while they discussed the Iraq situation, reviewing the arguments for a pre-emptive strike and the questionable evidence for

339

weapons of mass destruction. Both agreed it was an ill-advised action, opposed by most of the rest of the world. The consequences could be catastrophic.

"Bet this makes you more worried about Mom," Marissa commented.

"It does. I tried to talk her out of going, but nothing could stop her." Frustration leaked into his voice despite his attempt to conceal it.

"Are you really upset about it?" queried Marissa.

"Well . . . I am upset, Marissa. Guess I can't hide it." He ran his hand through his hair, shaking his head. "I just don't understand why she had to go. She said she had this mission, this sacred contract about being present at a ceremony . . related to the ancient Maya. It's all too nebulous for me."

"You told her not to go, right?"

"Yeah . . ."

"Did you have a big fight?"

At times Marissa's intuition was too accurate for Robert's comfort. He sighed and shrugged despondently.

"Yeah, we had a big fight. The biggest we've ever had. I said some pretty harsh things," he admitted.

"You didn't give her an ultimatum, did you?" asked the incisive Marissa.

"What do you mean?" parried Robert.

"You know, something like your marriage or your mission. Did you say that?"

"Not exactly. But I did say I felt she was damaging our relationship by doing this, when I felt so strongly against it." He felt defensive.

"And that's the way it stood when she left?"

"Uh-huh."

"So she went away on this trip, which might be risky, to fulfill her sense of mission, and for all she knows your relationship could be on the rocks?" There was a touch of incredulity in Marissa's voice.

Robert frowned and nodded. He thought Marissa was too much like Jana.

Marissa jumped to her feet, almost knocking over her beer bottle. Gesturing dramatically, she waved her hands overhead and nearly yelled:

"Dad, you blew it! How could you give Mom that kind of ultimatum? That's about the most impossible choice any human being could have!"

Robert pushed his chair back from the table, recoiling at his daughter's outburst.

"She didn't have to go on this crazy mission! Why did she put it above us? Above our marriage? I really don't get that, Marissa."

"She's not putting the mission ABOVE the marriage! Ye gods, can't you see? Why does it have to be one or the other? Look, Dad, I know Mom loves you. She would never do something to hurt you, unless it was very, very important and there wasn't any other way. I'm sorry, but why do men think in boxes so much? Life isn't either-or, it's both-and. She loves you, she treasures your marriage, AND she has to carry out her mission. One thing doesn't negate the other. Why did you set it up that way?"

"Me set it up that way?" Robert said, full of incredulity. "What do you mean, I set it up? She made the choices."

"Think about it." Marissa calmed herself and sat down. "She felt called to do something, it came from within or from spirit or whatever, anyway it was really important. It didn't mean she cared less about you. It wasn't directed against taking anything away from you. You're the one who made it either-or, if you do this then you can't love me. I'll bet she never said anything like that."

Robert was taken aback. He had never seen their conflict in this light. He leaned on the table and took a few more swallows of beer. Placing his forehead in his hand, he murmured:

"No, she didn't. She never said that. She kept saying she loved me, I just couldn't understand how since she was ignoring my feelings."

Marissa came around the table and put her arms around his shoulders. He hugged her back, feeling tears stinging his eyes.

"I'm really sorry this happened with you and Mom," she said softly. "And I'm sorry that I yelled at you."

"Guess I deserved it," he said, his voice strained.

After a while, Marissa released her hug and got them each another beer. Robert collected himself, becoming pensive. He had a lot to think about. She sat opposite him at the table again, saying:

"Let's go through it again. Maybe that will help you get a different perspective."

They talked late into the evening. Sometimes it was heated, sometimes poignant, sometimes humorous. Robert had never

341

unburdened his heart in this way before to his daughter. Her maturity and deep insight into human behavior astonished him. At times he felt another presence was there, a wise counselor much experienced in the difficulties of navigating this emotionally charged, experience-loaded life school. And he did have a different perspective when their talk ended.

Robert read Jana's email from Mérida the next morning. Profound relief swept through his body and his eyes moistened just knowing she was safe. Her simple statement of love touched his heart deeply. No apology, no excuses, no arguments. It was better that way, clean and uncluttered. He sensed that his mind was a huge obstacle, getting in the way of truly understanding Jana's commitment to the Maya mission. Yearning to connect with the inner passions that drove her, he searched the house for some inspiration. When he found it, the path was so obvious he could kick himself for being so dense.

Music.

Music was Robert's passion. It had shaped his whole life, opened his inner world of experience, modeled his career, brought solace and inspiration, stimulated and comforted, connected him to other times and people in magical ways. There beside the stereo lay the CD that Jana had brought him from the Clearlake School of Maya Mysteries: *Codex: Music of Ancient México.*[15] It featured instruments as close to Maya originals as possible, using melodies and rhythms taken from ancient musical codices. The group of indigenous musicians was led by Xavier Quijas Yxayotl, a native man with an unpronounceable name combining Spanish and Maya words.

Robert poured another cup of coffee, slipped the CD into his high-end audio system, and settled into his favorite chair.

Shimmering sounds of thin waterfalls blended with echoing roars of distant surf. Sounds of the jungle played over; bird chirps and squawks, long twitters trailing into snaky rattles, the hint of a jaguar's roar. The drums came in, slow and insistent. The gradually building rhythms spoke directly to Robert's cells, his foot tapped automatically to the beat. Music always had the power to bypass his mind, to put him in touch with feelings in the blink of an eye. He was immersed in

---

[15] Xavier Quijas Yxayotl. *Codex: Music of Ancient México.* Canyon Records & Indian Arts, 1997.

the interior world of sensations, impressions, images, feelings beyond ideation.

Cellular. Primeval. Roots sinking deep into the earth. Pulsations of the living planet, the global organism. A time before and beyond mechanization.

The music evoked the very fiber of his soul, he felt at one with nature, blending with its natural cycles, ebbing and flowing cycles of seasons, crops, people, continents, creatures. There was no inclination to dominate nature, to control her. It was enough to be one with her.

She was wild and free, as the music. High sweet flute notes hovered above the pulsating drums in simple, pure melodies. Mellow wood flutes, clear ringing ceramic flutes, tight harmonics of ocarinas. Unstructured, unfettered sounds. Abandoning all need for rigid tonal patterns and prescribed scales. It spoke to his own wild, untamed nature, free of civilized hierarchy.

The pieces flowed one into the next, connected by jungle calls and wails, along with spattering raindrop sounds from some curious types of percussion instruments. He was amazed by the quantity and diversity of percussion: deep voiced drums from hollow trunks, multi-voiced drums from logs that gradually narrowed, resonant turtle shells, high pitched water gourd drums. Joining these were rose wood sticks that clacked sharply, rasps, rain sticks, and an assortment of rattles from seeds and shells. At times a low base sound uttered guttural moans and sighs, similar to Australian didgeridoos. Some very long wooden trumpet-like instrument must be producing those sounds.

Robert was connected through music with the indigenous heart. It was natural, subtle, open, free, generous, joyful, creative, intuitive. It rejoiced in the abundance of life sustained by the earth mother, fed by the sun father. This must be what Jana felt in her devotion to the Maya.

But there was something else in the music. The patterns changed, shifting to an ominous, fierce cadence. At first the base drum sounded deep and low in a relentless rhythm. Its driving beat accelerated gradually, as accompanying percussion instruments intensified in quickening, complex patterns. Eerie voices echoed wailing tones and explosive grunts. Crinkling rattles sounded warnings as fearful as a rattlesnake before striking. Sharp, piercing and sustained notes from ceramic flutes vibrated eardrums to the point of pain. The frenzied rhythms moved faster and faster, heart-pounding, mouth-drying, raising hairs as muscles tensed in apprehension.

Robert felt distinctly uncomfortable. It was not just the ear-splitting flute notes and chaotic percussion noise. Faint echoes of ancient memories danced at the fringes of his mind. Eyes closed, he almost saw images inside his eyelids. Ghostly apparitions swirled and instantly dissolved before he could grasp a pattern. The pounding resonances held him in their power, trapped him like a prisoner. There was no escape.

Suddenly the music stopped. Robert's eyes flew open, like birds released from the bondage of cages. He sat up straight and quickly looked around, almost expecting an ancient mystical presence. But the living room appeared the same as always, except not quite as neat as when Jana was around. His tense muscles relaxed and he settled back into the chair.

The jungle sounds began once more, joined by gentle syncopated drums and percussions. The sounds were playful and light, joyful and spirited. Faint background voices hinted of harmonious villages at peace with their natural environment. Mellow wood flutes spoke of maize dances, native trails, moonlight on open plazas, pyramids reaching to the sky. It was timeless as the ancestral soul.

Robert knew he was connected to this ancestral Maya soul. Mayan music had communicated to him in a language that his heart understood. He realized he was in his mind when reacting, when formulating his opposition to Jana's mission. She was drawn to the Maya by feelings and intuitions, in a way foreign to his experience. But the music drew him in, entered his cells, opened his intuition.

He wanted to know more, to have the actual experience of his Maya connections. As quickly as this idea coalesced, guidance came for implementing it. He would schedule a session with Carla Hernandez.

The night sky arced overhead in a liquid velvet dome. The moon, now at first quarter, had disappeared behind the horizon. Millions of tiny strobes flickered from distant reaches of space, the vast Upperworld where the gods and goddesses, the ancestors and spirits resided. The stars arranged themselves in patterns to communicate with observers below. Their trajectories across the night sky informed those who understood, gave counsel about the right time for actions, for beginnings and endings. Success or failure, victory or defeat depended upon correctly reading the stars.

Chitam drew his cape closer around his shoulders, shivering as a light breeze blew across the high platform of the Observatory Complex pyramid. In the late night darkness, cool and mysterious, he was tracking signs for the appearance of Venus. This assignment was important for the son of Mutul's (Tikal's) Chief Daykeeper Priest. It was an honor, a testimony to how much his skills had advanced over the past two tuns. Venus was the star of Hun and Vucub Hunahpu, twin fathers of the Hero Twins Hun Ahau and Yax Balam. The Hero Twins were the progenitors of Chitam's people. They had battled the Lords of Xibalba, the Underworld, and triumphed over Death. They had resurrected Hun-Vucub Hunahpu as the Maize God, First Father, so the Maya people could find life in the Middleworld. And now they guided their descendants in every phase of life. The boys ascended straight into the sky, Hun Ahau as the sun and Yax Balam as the full moon, the sun's counterpart in the night. Their fathers reappeared in the sky as Venus, reborn every 584 kins as Morningstar, traversing the night sky and then sinking into the Underworld, dying as Eveningstar.

The guidance sought tonight from Venus—Hunahpu—was about war. The ruler of Mutul, Chak Toh Ich'ak was planning an attack on the long-time rival city of Uaxactun. This upstart city was making forays against the outlying settlements of Mutul's large domain. It was insulting and humiliating for the dominant power, the great city-state of Mutul, to have its territory nipped around the edges. Of course, the ruler of Uaxactun would never attack them directly, would not pit his forces against Mutul's greater power. But soon Uaxactun would taste that power, and this would leave bitterness in its mouth.

Venus as the guide for waging war was an innovation brought by the warriors from Teotihuacan. They had learned to align with Venus' appearance at Morningstar, the moment when its power rose to the greatest height. Power drawn from Tlaloc, the goggle-eyed rain god of the Mexica people, but also the power of Hunahpu. Attacking an enemy when Venus re-emerged over the eastern horizon as Morningstar guaranteed victory. Warriors drew the force of the invincible Hero Twins into their arms and legs, their minds and hearts, becoming fierce and undefeatable. The Teotihuacan god Tlaloc knew of these things and informed his people. Tlaloc taught them how to use the atlatl, their fearsome spear-throwers that sent deadly missiles flying far distances with impressive accuracy. The foreigners trained Mutul's warriors in this technique, and two years' practice had made them experts.

Craning his head around, Chitam fixed his sight on the distant twinkles of Jupiter and Saturn. These two stellar bodies held stationary points in the night sky during the important heliacal risings of Venus as Morningstar and Eveningstar. He located the stellar bodies against the background constellations depicting The Crab (Cancer) and The Twins (Jemini), hanging near the eastern horizon just before dawn. A few more days must pass for Venus to ascend over the horizon, shining as the brightest dawn star in the east. How many days? This was critically important. Chitam must mark what he observed on the bark paper scroll beside him, so he and his father could make calculations during the day. Chitam moved to the far side of the platform where a small torch burned. Using a carved wood pen dipped in plant pigment, he drew symbols that represented the positions of Jupiter and Saturn and the constellations just before dawn.

The calculations for Venus' appearance as Morningstar had to be accurate. This would decide the day on which Mutul launched its first Venus-Tlaloc war, the first Star War among the Maya people.

Several hours passed as Chitam made adjustments in his drawings. When the eastern horizon became lighter, heralding dawn, his work was finished. He could no longer see the stars clearly due to the sun's early glow, first creating soft gray tones that gradually became brighter. With a sense of relief, he gathered his materials and put out the torch. Standing on the tall platform, he waited expectantly for Mutul's spectacular dawn. No matter how many times he had seen it, the breath-taking beauty always thrilled his heart.

Along the flanks of the swamps, the eastern bajo, ground mists gathered. Hovering low and still, the mists were born of night coolness embracing the retained warmth of water and ground. Just before sunrise, the air became filled with expanding moisture forming a thick ground fog. For lingering pre-sunrise moments, the view was obstructed by a fog blanket across the horizon. Then the magic occurred. As the sun broke the horizon, its rays struck the low fog and the world turned into liquid gold. Misty golden haze floated upward, glowing vibrantly, giving trees and structures an ethereal quality. Snaking rivulets of fog seeped through low passages as if trying to escape the sun's brilliance that would dissolve them away.

Amidst this golden amniotic fluid, K'inich Ahau was reborn. The Sun God appeared for the start of a new day, new kin. Kin not only meant day, but also was the root of the Sun God's name. K'inich Ahau's blazing face was deep red when it first ascended behind the morning mists, the same color it took when sinking at day's end in the west, the direction of death. The color of the east was red, the color of birth, dawn, and a new start.

Chitam murmured the morning prayer to K'inich Ahau. He watched until most of the mists dissipated, and then descended the pyramid stairs. His heart was singing, full and happy. His step was light and springy as he quickly walked along the deserted sakbe back toward his home. He had many reasons to be happy. As the Chief Daykeeper's son, he was positioned for a successful career with close ties to Mutul's rulers. Already his skills were recognized and he was given increased responsibilities. Mutul, this great city of his birth, had received excellent predictions for the new katun; more abundance and wealth, greater power and influence. And, to his immense delight, the young priestess Yalucha had recently returned from training at Xunantunich.

In his heart Chitam held the secret, soon to be revealed, of his betrothal to Yalucha. It was agreed between their fathers, it was a good alliance for both families, and even Yalucha's independent-thinking mother saw the wisdom of the match. Xoc Ikal's approval was essential. After many discussions with her husband K'an Nab Ku, she had been convinced to support Chitam's suit. Her one caveat was that Yalucha must agree to the union of her own accord. Chitam could not think of any reason why the young woman would not consent. There could be no better match for her in all Mutul.

A frown of annoyance clouded Chitam's countenance, drawing heavy black eyebrows almost together on the high bridge of his huge hooked nose. This frequent expression made his thin bony face even more severe, but he was not aware of it. Chitam never looked in mirrors. He prided himself on his lack of vanity, never preening before mirrors, as did many nobles and rulers. They sometimes used

347

mirrors for vision seeking, but he had no need of such deceptive paraphernalia. Mirrors simply directed visions back to one's self-concepts, in his learned opinion. It was not true communing with Spirit.

This frown, however, was caused by his thoughts about marriage to Yalucha. He was irritated that women had so much say in the process, which was primarily for profitable alliances and properly pedigreed progeny. Inheritance of rank and title passed from father to son, making the male line of descent most important. Women had too many rights, too much freedom, he reflected. They could make unilateral decisions about wedding and divorcing, and could inherit wealth and property. Chak Toh Ich'ak, the ruler of Mutul, seemed much in support of these liberal practices.

And for good reason, Chitam thought. *He has no living sons, only one daughter now. He wants his direct descendants to rule Mutul, his daughter's future children. So he plots to defy our customs of direct male line descent, to make his daughter's future husband Mutul ahau, ruler of our great city.*

Though not spoken about openly, this topic was the focus of much gossip in Mutul. The ruler was very old, his nephews and cousins jockeying for favor and scheming alliances to support their ambitions. But he had not named a successor. There was much speculation about whom he would select to marry his daughter, and how he might seat that man as ahau of Mutul. The situation did not bode well. Infighting among contenders would weaken Mutul and make the city vulnerable to attack from hostile neighbor cities. The pending attack on Uaxactun fed into the ruler's scheme, but Chitam did not know exactly how.

The young priest's thoughts turned again to his personal match, certainly much less controversial. But what if Yalucha did not want to marry him? Again the frown exaggerated his severe features. She was always kind and polite when they met, but nothing really intimate had passed between them. Chitam had to admit he really did not know how Yalucha felt about him, or about their marriage. The lovely young woman was much of an enigma to him. She and her mother were both priestesses of Ix Chel, the remnants of the old religion, followers of a dying goddess cult. The important deity now was the sun god, K'inich Ahau, who brought power and victory. The other male gods, the many forms of Chak, the Jaguar God, and Hunahpu had more influence in people's lives in the present era. Of course, he revered the Great Goddess Ix Chel, Earth Mother, weaver of life for

348

the Maya world, Tamuanchan. But, her domain was primarily the world of women, moon cycles, healing and birthing. The male gods enlivened the world of men, especially those who were leaders. Chitam knew he was in line to inherit the Chief Daykeeper Priest position from his father. He would become a leader himself in due time.

This thought reassured him. His thin lips parted in a smile as he strode forth with increased confidence. He was as good a match as Yalucha would find in Mutul. Her father was in strong support, and her mother consenting. And, they did share priestly dedication to serving the gods and goddesses. Yes, it was a good match that any sensible young woman would be pleased to accept.

As the sun reached mid-morning position, Mutul's morning mists evaporated, leaving a clear blue sky. The day promised to be hot. Already the two women working in their home garden wiped sweat from their faces. Systematically they harvested herbs, deftly placing small piles of each variety on separate cotton squares. Cultivating with stone digging implements, sharp and pointed on one end with a smooth, rounded handle, they loosened soil and pulled weeds. Nearby two boys played, rolling a rubber ball back and forth, scuffling to direct it with legs and feet. After a particularly hard kick, the ball bounded into the herb garden close to the women.

"Be careful, boys!" admonished Xoc Ikal. "Your ball will scatter the herbs. Take it farther away, back by the avocado trees."

She tossed the ball to her sons, who resembled each other enough to be twins, born just one year apart. Smiling as they retreated to the back of the garden, she reflected how much they had grown in the two tuns that Yalucha spent in Xunantunich. As if reading her mind, her daughter remarked:

"They are so big, Mother. They have grown an entire head since I left. Soon they will be taller than I am."

Xoc Ikal nodded. Raising three sons was an interesting experience for the priestess of Ix Chel. Boys, and men, she had learned, definitely had different perspectives than women. Her older son, Hunbatz, was modeling himself closely after his father, a respected carver and stonemason. Hunbatz shadowed K'an Nab Ku whenever possible, even developing similar mannerisms. Only recently had the young man forayed out on his own, obtaining independent commissions for carving family monuments. The two younger boys, pre-adolescents, were much taken by their warrior uncle K'in Pakal. They pestered him to take them hunting and teach them to use battle implements such as spears, knives and axes. None of her sons were drawn to the old religion from Izapa, despite her instilling its spiritual teachings over the years.

She used a cotton cloth to wipe rivulets of sweat from her forehead, as the salty moisture stung her eyes.

"The morning is too hot for this work," declared Xoc Ikal. "Come, let us sit on the steps and have water. We can finish picking herbs before evening, when it becomes cooler."

Tying the herb bundles carefully, the women gathered up their gardening tools and retired to welcome shade under the thatch roof awning projecting over the low house platform. Yalucha went inside the adjoining kitchen, scooped water with a hollow gourd from a tall, wide-mouth pottery jug, and brought two cups back to the platform. She sat beside her mother on the upper steps, both sipping cool water with relish.

It was good to be home. She had missed her mother and family more than she let herself realize during her stay in Xunantunich. The young priestess acknowledged silently what an anchor Xoc Ikal was in her life. Simply sitting beside her mother, doing mundane household tasks was immensely comforting. Sharing about her many experiences during priestess training brought the two women even closer together. Their passion for healing, for doing the work of the Mother Goddess, created a strong bond.

Yalucha brought small gifts for everyone in her close family, but chose her mother's with special care. Seeking unusual but meaningful things, she found a perfectly shaped sea clamshell, its smooth interior shining with opalescent mother of pearl. The large shell was an ideal container for holding dried ceremonial herbs. Her mother had never been to the Great Water in the East, or seen medicinal plants from the seashore. With the help of Zac Kuk, the High Priestess of Xunantunich who was her mentor, Yalucha obtained both dried herbs and living plants that might survive inland. These would expand the healing repertory her mother offered in Mutul.

Xoc Ikal was delighted with these gifts. Yalucha enjoyed playing the role of teacher, informing her mother of the herbs' properties and uses in healing arts. Now both priestesses provided care to the steady stream of clients who came daily to the small temple on the west edge of their home complex. In one side room the dried herbs, healing tools, and ritual objects were stored. Clients sat on the wide temple stairs to wait, while the priestesses tended others on the raised platform. The daily ziv, herbal tea mixture, was made each morning in the kitchen.

The women lingered in the shade, enjoying its coolness before facing the heat of making ziv over the central hearth fire in the kitchen. The two boys, tiring of their ball game, had run off around the corner to find other amusement in the complex's plaza.

Yalucha drank the last of her water, sighed and looked off in the distance. Xoc Ikal glanced at her daughter's profile, heart swelling at the young woman's exquisite beauty. She had matured into a striking woman with delicate features and long, graceful limbs. Often she seemed preoccupied, deeply immersed in some distant vision. Xoc Ikal sensed her daughter had not shared everything that happened in Xunantunich with her. That would come in time.

Now, Xoc Ikal had an agenda. She must discuss the proposed marriage to Chitam. Her husband was strongly in favor, and had extracted the promise of her support. Although Yalucha had never shown particular interest in the young priest, neither had she seemed taken by any other men in Mutul.

Yalucha turned to her mother before she could broach the subject.

"Tell me more of Chuen's marriage and pregnancy," said Yalucha. "It seemed she had no interest in family life before. Her music was everything when I left."

Chuen, K'an Nab Ku's independent-minded sister, had raised many eyebrows by divorcing several years ago, although it was within her rights as a Mutul citizen. Indeed, teaching and performing music did seem to be her life. Gossip had it that she might never marry again, so devoted was she to her career. Everyone was surprised at the sudden marriage just over one tun ago.

"The ways of the heart are mysterious," observed Xoc Ikal. "The son of the artisan from Tayasal, who married into a Mutul family and made our city home, perfumed Chuen's heart, *chamuibtasbon kolonton*. He is also a musician; they came to know each other during performances. She does not speak of the details, but they were constantly together for months, then they married."

"They simply fell in love," Yalucha commented. "It happens, often quickly. *Xk'uxub kolonton*, my heart aches, they say when they fall in love."

"True," Xoc Ikal replied, surprised at the surety with which Yalucha spoke of love. "Soon after, Chuen became pregnant. She wants the child very much, but the pregnancy is difficult. It is not going well. She still has the sickness of morning every day. I am concerned that her labor will come early. She has contractions of the womb, although the pregnancy is only eight moons along."

"You have given her mango syrup to stop contractions," said Yalucha.

"Yes. The herbs help but do not take the contractions completely away. I have pressed upon her to rest and stay off her feet, but she gets too restless. It is hard for Chuen to be still. Perhaps you will spend time with her, distract her with stories of your adventures in Xunantunich," Xoc Ikal suggested.

"Oh, yes, I am happy to do so," replied Yalucha. "I will go this afternoon to visit."

The women sat in silence for a few moments, each lost in their own thoughts. Xoc Ikal spoke again first.

"Yalucha, I must speak to you of an important thing."

The young woman looked at her mother quizzically, catching the gravity in her voice.

"Your father wishes you to marry, he waited on this until you completed priestess training at Xunantunich," said Xoc Ikal. "Chitam, the son of Yo'nal Ac, Chief Daykeeper Priest has made suit for marriage. Your father and Yo'nal Ac are much pleased by this match."

"Chitam?" Yalucha said in genuine surprise. "My heart is unmoved by him. I hardly know him, and had no idea of his interest in me."

"He has been interested for several years. He is shy, and does not express his feelings openly. Your father and I have spoken several times with him. I feel his caring for you is sincere, and I have agreed to support his suit."

Yalucha sat in stunned silence, her heart pounding and her mind racing. Images of Chan Hun filled her inner vision, his handsome face and strong muscled body, the captivating smile flashing gems in white teeth, setting off a slight dimple in his left cheek. Reflexively her hand leapt to touch the pale jade pendant, token of their betrothal, which never left her neck.

Xoc Ikal noticed her daughter's reaction and the gesture. The jade pendant must hold special significance, as Yalucha always wore it. The thought already had occurred to her: it was a gift from a man.

"Are you not inclined toward Chitam's suit?" she asked.

"Oh, Mother!" cried Yalucha, bursting into tears. After collecting herself and wiping the tears away, she continued with

352

hesitation. "I do not dislike Chitam . . . I do not want to disappoint you and Father, but . . . I . . I want to wait . . . I'm not ready yet, for . . for marriage."

Placing an arm around her daughter's shoulders, Xoc Ikal said gently:

"You have only just returned, only a few kins. It is too early for considering such a big decision. It is reasonable to wait, I will tell your father."

"No! I mean, yes . . . . oh, waiting will not do any good," moaned Yalucha. "I do not want to marry Chitam, or any man in Mutul. I . . . I . . ." Her voice trailed off as she broke into tears again.

Xoc Ikal pulled her distraught daughter into her arms, holding her as the sobbing girl buried her face in the contour of her mother's shoulder. Now she was certain. The jade pendant was from a man, with whom Yalucha was in love. Patting her and stroking her hair, the mother waited until the girl's sobs died away.

"Tell me," Xoc Ikal murmured. "Tell me what wrenches your heart."

Yalucha swallowed, wiping her eyes and face, wet with tears and sweat, using a spare cotton cloth. Avoiding eye contact, she took a deep breath, letting it out with a long sigh. Her fingers caressed the jade pendant.

"I met a man in Xunantunich," she said in measured tones. She knew this would have to be said, and was almost grateful that the time had come. "We fell in love. My heart aches, *xk'uxub kolonton,* more than I can say, more than I dreamed possible. He is more precious to me than life. I cannot live without him. He is wonderful, brave, strong, a leader, handsome, tender, loving. Oh, I cannot bear it! I cannot be with another!"

She began crying again, and then caught herself. It was unbecoming for a fully trained priestess of Ix Chel to dissolve so completely into emotions. Sniffing, she dabbed her eyes and looked at her mother.

Xoc Ikal's expression was full of compassion. There was no judgment, just calm acceptance and tenderness. She nodded her head slowly.

"I thought as much," she said. "You wear the token of his love, the jade pendant. Is it his pledge?"

Yalucha nodded, looking down.

"Tell me about him," continued her mother. "I know he must be wonderful, to capture your heart."

A smile brought light into Yalucha's eyes, brightening her face.

"He is wonderful," she said with enthusiasm. "He led an expedition of traders to the coast, the Great Water of the East. They stopped at Xunantunich because one of his men had a broken leg. While the leg mended, Chan Hun—that is his name—and I met many times, talked about so many things. He has intelligence, and wit, and humor and was so much fun to be with. He asked about my priestess studies and attended ceremonies. The High Priestess took me and other acolytes with his expedition to the Great Water. And we . . we were drawn to each other. It was so powerful, a force in my body and heart I never knew existed. Our hearts opened to each other, and we . . . loved each other. Before he left to return to his city, we pledged our hearts and he gave me the pendant."

"It is a truly lovely pendant," observed Xoc Ikal, "of the finest jade. He has good taste, both in jewelry and women. Is he a trader?"

"No, he is a warrior. He and his men were protecting the traders on their journey," Yalucha replied.

"A warrior. From which city?" asked her mother.

It was the moment Yalucha was dreading. She hesitated, closed her eyes and blurted:

"Uaxactun. He is a noble warrior from Uaxactun, related to the ruler."

Xoc Ikal caught her breath. This was worse than she had imagined. Mutul was at this very time preparing for war against Uaxactun. She took Yalucha's hand in hers, squeezing gently. The girl looked up, her eyes dark pools of agony.

"You know war is pending," Xoc Ikal said softly. "It will happen in a few kins. Your beloved is back in Uaxactun?" Yalucha nodded, mute.

Xoc Ikal sat in thought, stroking her daughter's hand. The intensity of the young woman's love for Chan Hun was obvious. For him to make a definite betrothal pledge and seal it with a costly jade pendant testified to his sincerity and commitment. This was no passing infatuation, forgotten as soon as a new romance appeared. The priestess intuited a deep soul connection between the young lovers. To reach across their cities' long-standing enmity required no less.

"Let us not speak of this to your father yet," Xoc Ikal said after consideration. "It is a time of uncertainty, with war soon coming and our aged ruler having no clear successor. We need to wait, to see what happens. I will tell your father that you are thinking about Chitam's suit, but need more time."

"Yes, thank you," murmured Yalucha. "That is best. But my heart is clamoring, *xk'opk'on kolonton.* I am afraid for Chan Hun, he will certainly be in the battle."

"Come, we will go to the temple and say prayers," urged Xoc Ikal. "Find comfort for your heart in communing with The Goddess."

Torches flickered around the small plaza of K'an Nab Ku's family compound. The U-shaped home structures surrounded the plaza on three sides, square stone buildings set on low raised platforms with five wide steps leading up. Three men sat on cushions placed in close proximity on the stairs of the central home, just outside the entrance. Their strong features were highlighted by the play of light and shadow from torches. Simply dressed in beech-cloths with bare chests, they relaxed in the early evening cool while discussing events of great portent for their city.

K'an Nab K'u and his eldest son Hunbatz listened intently as K'in Pakal related his observations while attending at court that day. Hunbatz' eyes glistened with admiration for his warrior uncle, muscular and broad chested. The heady excitement of pending battle hung around the warrior, whose body conveyed the poised tension of a stalking jaguar. In contrast, Hunbatz was small and slender, with long agile fingers, perfect for his career in stone cutting.

As they talked, the men drank pepper-laced cacao from tall clay cups. Local artisans had painted the outsides with picturesque scenes from domestic life. Ochre-red figures wearing garments of white, blue and yellow stood by verdant gardens or stooped to play with brown and white spotted dogs. A jug with pouring lip sat on the stairs between the men with more of the stimulating muddy liquid.

"When did the king's runner appear?" asked K'an Nab K'u.

"Before the sun was at half-apex," replied K'in Pakal. "He must have run most of the night. He reported that the Teotihuacanos are one kin's walk away. They will arrive in Mutul tomorrow."

"Umm." K'an Nab K'u took a sip of cacao and reflected. "This is what Chak Toh Ich'ak is waiting for, yes? Before our warriors set out for Uaxactun?"

"Yes, but also he awaits the appearance of Morningstar," said K'in Pakal. "Venus-Hunahpu gives invincible power to our forces, when properly invoked. His priests do ceremonies daily at dawn. They track the dawning sky closely for signs of Morningstar."

"When do the priests say it will be reborn over the horizon?" asked Hunbatz.

"Two days hence. We are ready. Many warriors have perfected use of the atlatls that give spears a greater range. We will take many captives in this battle, but also defeat Uaxactun's forces soundly, kill as many as we can. The Teotihuacano warriors under K'ak Sih join forces with us to accomplish this."

"It is different, this war," mused K'an Nab Ku. "This we have not done before."

"True," agreed K'in Pakal. "The king plans to bring Uaxactun under Mutul rule, to stop their frequent forays against us. Their city will pay much tribute for its arrogance."

"He must have gotten this idea from Teotihuacan," offered Hunbatz. "They are a great empire, many cities are under their dominance. Their king sets his own lords as ahauob of conquered cities. Do you think this will happen at Uaxactun?"

"Yes, we must be careful of the ambitions of Spearthrower Owl," K'an Nab K'u agreed. "The long arm of Teotihuacan's king may be reaching toward Mutul."

"Never will they rule us!" exclaimed K'in Pakal. "Our forces are too strong, our power too great. They are our allies, both kingdoms benefit through conquest and trade. You are imagining too much, brother."

"Let us hope you are right," K'an Nab K'u retorted.

"What other news, uncle?" asked Hunbatz, breaking the tension between the two older men.

"In the company of K'ak Sih is the son of Spearthrower Owl, Yax Ain, called First Crocodile," replied the warrior. "He is a young man, not yet of age, but word has it that he is brave and wise. He will fight in the battle, he is trained as a warrior."

"That is interesting," observed K'an Nab K'u. "We have an elderly king and a youthful prince who need protecting in battle. Your warriors will have much on their hands, K'in Pakal."

"We are capable, and our forces are augmented by Teotihuacan," replied the warrior, expanding his chest and sitting more erectly.

"Well, the omens for Mutul in this new katun are all favorable," said the older stonecutter. "Victory in war, expanded power, greater abundance. All will go well, K'inich Ahau provides for Mutul as we honor him in the required ways."

Thin cloud cover created a glowing halo around the morning sun, dampening the heat slightly. Crowds filled the East Plaza of Mutul, their murmuring voices blending with clinks of wood and shell adornments as they moved about, seeking a better view. An aura of excited anticipation hovered over the crowd. They awaited the arrival of K'ak Sih and the expedition from Teotihuacan.

From the distance came a cadenced drumbeat. The crowd's murmuring peaked as Mutul warriors formed a wedge making an opening from the east end of the plaza. Falling silent, the people backed away opening a long corridor curving through the broad East Plaza to its juncture with the smaller court fronting Chak Toh Ich'ak's palace, the home of the Jaguar Claw dynasty. There in the inner throne room behind the eastern chamber, the King of Mutul sat on his Lord's Bench, flanked by leading nobles and priests, prepared to perform the royal function of receiving the visitors.

The thuds of marching feet in cadence with the drumbeat soon filled the air, which felt heavy with humidity and tension. The Mutul warriors stood tall and straight, their festooned spears held points up at their sides, ribbons and feathers drooping listlessly in the still air. Almost as one being, the people sucked in a breath as the Teotihuacanos ascended the short stairs onto the East Plaza.

Row upon row of warriors, four abreast, marched in unison behind a core of eight drummers. The warriors were dressed in Tlaloc imagery, the apparel of their fierce storm-war god. Helmet headdresses with protruding chin guards were decorated with mosaic monsters, flower-like sun discs, and long tassels cascading behind raised wedges. Small masks of the goggle-eyed, big-nosed, fang-toothed Tlaloc adorned forehead or jaw pieces. Metallic and shell collars of gold, white, red and blue hung over bare chests, brown and heavily muscled. Breech and loin cloths sported multicolored strips of fabric with round hip ornaments and long feathered tails. Metallic wristbands glittered with embedded stones, as one hand grasped an atlatl and the other a fabric shield decorated with a Tlaloc image wearing a tasseled headdress. Boots and leggings of beaded leather protected their feet.

The discipline and ferocity that made Teotihuacan the greatest empire in the land of Tamaunchan was clearly apparent in these warriors. Just looking at their fearsome visages was enough to chill one's blood. Instinctively, the crowd drew back as the warriors passed. It was a large contingent, over 200 warriors, very similar in appearance.

A cheer rose from the crowd as the leader, K'ak Sih, appeared walking at the end of the rows of warriors. Beside him was a youth, not quite at full stature, of noble demeanor. Both were attired in full royal regalia. They wore the Teotihuacan balloon headdress, made of deer pelt and rising well above the intricate metal and fabric crown set into a headband with stylized cloven hoof protruding over their foreheads. A trapezoidal design, the Mexican year sign, held the balloon headdress in place. Chin guards protruded small goggle-eyed Tlaloc masks in front of their mouths. Over an elaborate metal-beaded collar hung a pectoral bar decorated with a human skull, the sign of Venus-Tlaloc war. Strapped around the solar plexus was a jaguar mask with a small owl covering the forehead. Wide embroidered and beaded loin, beech and hip cloths sported more Tlaloc images, while jaguar pelt boots covered their feet. Heavily adorned wristbands matched their collars. The royal nobles carried tall spears and flexible shields with goggle-eyed Tlaloc faces.

Behind the leaders came several emissaries bearing large vases and packages with gifts for the ruler of Mutul. Simply dressed with neck collars and colorful waistcloths, the emissaries wore disproportionately large headdresses flaring over their faces like huge hats. Flouncing fabric strips danced like large bubbles atop several layers of flat round bands, the bottom layer bordered by swaying fringes that hung almost to their eyes. Balancing their burdens carefully, the emissaries did not attempt to keep in cadence with the drumbeat.

The procession moved through the open corridor onto the court of the Jaguar Claw palace. There the Teotihuacan warriors stood to one side, while their leaders handed spears and shields to attendants and then approached the palace stairs. With pomp, Maya trumpeters standing atop the palace stairs blew deep, echoing notes through four-foot long wooden trumpets. The crowd answered with a roar, although a line of Maya warriors kept them from surging onto the palace court. The two royal men ascended the stairs with dignity, passing through lines of Maya nobles into the eastern chamber. The gift-bearing emissaries followed, navigating the steep steps carefully and straining with the weight of their burdens.

At the far end of the eastern chamber was the corbelled vault entrance into the throne room. K'ak Sih glanced around as he and the youth moved through the cluster of Maya nobles, nodding to one or another whom he recognized, his manner self-assured to the point of haughtiness. K'ak Sih was brother of Spearthrower Owl, King of

Teotihuacan. The power of the mighty empire sat upon his shoulders, he was equal to any Maya ruler. Beside him was the king's second son, Yax Ain. This visit to Mutul would fulfill an agreement made in secret with Chak Toh Ich'ak, to be sealed with the anticipated victory over Uaxactun tomorrow. The jaguar of Mutul and the owl of Teotihuacan would unite.

The two Teotihuacanos entered the throne room, where Chak Toh Ich'ak held court. The Maya ruler was seated on the Lord's Bench, a raised stone platform with backrest. A finely woven mat covered the bench and a large, lavishly decorated pillow supported his thin back. Several attendants hovered behind and at the sides of the bench, holding paper strip fans and jars of *utz,* good tasting drinks made from honey, cacao, and sweet atole. A richly dressed dwarf held a mirror ready, into which the ruler could glance as desired. Lords and nobles of highest rank—ahaus, cahals, bacabs—sat on cushions and stood beside the walls of the throne room. From the door into an adjoining room, musicians peered with drums, trumpets and flutes ready.

Chak Toh Ich'ak was simply clothed in a fine white waistcloth with gold threads and glass beads sewn into the loin and beech cloths. He wore a large jade pectoral over a beaded collar. Jewelry adorned wrists and ankles, sparkling with inset gemstones. His headdress signified status as ruler: A jester god headband on the forehead, supporting a tall cylinder carved with intricate scrolls and embedded with jade and shell plaques, from which spouted a train of long quetzal feathers. Round white beads attached near the end of the brilliantly colored, gracefully waving feathers. The large headdress seemed almost too much for the aged king's thin neck to support.

The hum of conversation died out as the Teotihuacanos strode across the distance to the foot of the Lord's Bench. Their booted feet made clacking sounds on the smooth plaster floor as metal adornments clinked rhythmically. The hush of the throne room was pregnant with anticipation, the atmosphere crackling with tension.

The foreign Lords clasped right hand to left shoulder in the prescribed gesture of homage, bowing only the minimally acceptable amount. The Mutul ruler's expression remained inscrutable. He waited in the tense silence, keeping the visitors in homage position almost to the point of insult, before speaking.

"We of Mutul greet you, Lords of Teotihuacan. Welcome again to our city, Lord K'ak Sih." Turning to the younger man, he added:

"It is our pleasure to receive you, Lord Yax Ain. I trust you will find your stay here agreeable."

"Thank you," replied Yax Ain. "My father Spearthrower Owl, King of Teotihuacan, sends his greetings and most high regards."

Chak Toh Ich'ak nodded graciously to the prince. Body postures of the Maya nobles relaxed and the tense atmosphere diminished. The ruler waved one hand, signaling attendants to bring forth large cushions for the guests. These were placed in front of the Lord's Chair, leaving an opening for receiving the emissaries with gifts. Servants offered the seated Lords tall cups of *utz,* assisting them to remove the headdresses that covered their mouths.

"Your journey was uneventful?" the ruler continued.

"All went well," replied K'ak Sih. "With our contingent of warriors, none dared attack us. Our men are well armed and highly trained for warfare. We have come to join forces with the renowned warriors of Mutul, as agreed, for the Venus-Tlaloc war. I trust we are in correct timing with the stars?"

"Yes, Venus rises as Morningstar tomorrow," said Chak Toh Ich'ak, glancing toward Yo'nal Ac. The Chief Daykeeper Priest nodded solemnly.

"Good, we will be ready," the warrior replied.

"May it please you, Great Ahau of Mutul, to receive our gifts," said Yax Ain, his manner poised and assured. The young prince was of slighter build than his warrior companion, but his muscles were hard and developed. He had the broad face and square jaw of the Mexica people, with prominent cheeks and a flat nose, by Maya standards. Long dark hair was wound into a topknot to fit inside the headdress. His mouth was broad with well-defined full lips.

Chak Toh Ich'ak nodded, signaling the musicians to begin playing. The procession of emissaries was ordered by Yax Ain, who announced the content of vases and packages. There was dark blue maize, favored by Ek-Xib-Chak, god of the west, the place of the dying sun, portal to the black waters of the Underworld. This offering brought the god's power to dispatch many souls of enemies to Xibalba, the realm of the Lords of Death. Precious honey filled vases, from rare highland flowers near Teotihuacan which sat upon a high mesa. Bundles contained prized black obsidian and hard chert mined in distant mountain veins that could be worked into extremely sharp knives and spear points. These war implements invoked the red-hued god of the east, Chak-Xib-Chak, patron of warriors and sacrifices. There were ceramic vessels of many types, with flared bases and abstract leafy patterns, thrown by the master potters of the Mexica Empire. Reams of fine woven fabric in bright colors, predominately red and yellow, would be turned into royal clothing. Other gifts included jewelry heavy in gold and precious stones, and carved wooden implements for household and ceremonial use.

It was a worthy offering, fitting for the ruler of the great Maya city of Mutul. Murmurs of approval rose from the Maya nobles as each gift was announced. The king nodded graciously and smiled slightly, enhancing wrinkles in his deeply etched cheeks. When all the gifts had been received, he called forward his war chief and entered a dialogue about tomorrow's battle. K'ak Sih joined in the planning as nobles craned to hear details. Excitement was rising in anticipation of the new strategy for warfare, the first Maya battle using atlatls from the storm god Tlaloc, aligned with Venus as Morningstar to draw the power of Hunahpu into the warriors.

The Venus-Tlaloc battle against Uaxactun, the first Maya Star War, would happen tomorrow.

＊　　＊　　＊　　＊　　＊　　＊

The leaders of Uaxactun knew that Mutul was preparing for battle. Scouts forayed through dim jungle paths, finding hidden observation spots in dense thickets or high tree limbs concealed by heavy foliage. Spies visited Mutul's international marketplace, asking discrete questions and overhearing conversations as they browsed and shopped. Over four tuns had passed since the last encounter between the enemy cities, and tension was building on both sides.

These intelligence gatherers detected something unusual about the pending battle, but could not discern exactly what this was. They watched Mutul warriors training, and observed their practice with the spear throwers, atlatls, brought by the Teotihuacanos. But they had no frame of reference for using these slings except for hunting in the open savanna. The implements were useless in dense forests, which deflected their flight. And, there was no association with warfare, so the scouts assumed Mutul planned a large hunting expedition for savanna game.

The arrival of the Teotihuacanos was the signal that war was imminent. A runner was dispatched to the ruler of Uaxactun that morning, so the city's warriors could prepare for battle. Uaxactun was eager to regain prestige by taking many noble captives to use in victory ceremonies. In the last clash, Mutul had predominated and Uaxactun's honor was in need of restoration.

The city buzzed with excitement as the ruler, his royal relatives and noble warriors underwent rituals of purification and sacrifice to draw the gods' favor in battle. Through the night, in the flickering torchlight of the multi-chambered men's hall, the warriors adorned each other with black and red paint, making patterns on face, chest and arms to frighten adversaries and invoke spiritual charms. The king himself painted the men of his royal clan, each paint stroke increasing their solidarity and dedication.

Chan Hun stood among a group of lesser relatives at the end of the king's chamber. The men had battle jackets of thick woven cloth, tied loosely across their muscled chests. Thick padded waist and hip cloths extended protection to mid-thigh. Fringed and decorated knee-bands added color, heavy cloth and leather boots covered lower legs and feet. As the king moved methodically, painting repeating patterns and exchanging terse comments, the young warrior felt a heady mixture of excitement and dread. The pre-dawn hours of preparation for battle were always the hardest.

At last it was his turn. For a moment, Chan Hun's dark eyes locked with those of his ruler. The king was an experienced leader and brave warrior. He exuded confidence that bolstered the young man's courage. Each paint stroke on Chan Hun's face and body infused him with purpose and commitment. He would fight fiercely for the glory of his king and Uaxactun.

As the darkness faded into pale gray dawn, the final rituals for war took place. The wives of the king and his highest-ranking captains brought forth long stone knives and flexible shields of dense, many-layered cloth, handing these ceremoniously to their men. Next the wives presented long heavy spears with great flint blades, ridged sharply to slice effortlessly into enemy flesh. Each spear had unique decorations, beaded ribbons and feathers that dangled and danced with every movement.

The king's principal wife, pregnant with their second child, brought forth his battle gear after the other royal warriors were prepared. Nearby, his second wife held their newborn baby and tended his firstborn son by the principal wife. The toddler clung to his stepmother's legs, dark eyes wide with fear and fascination. Already his child's mind grasped that his father's place in this great pageantry was a model for his own future. All present stood at attention and silently focused upon the pregnant wife's ritual arming of her husband, a symbol of infusing her uayob or animal spirit powers into him.

362

The final step was placing war helmets upon the men's heads. These closely fit headdresses, adorned with emblems of animal and god protectors, were strapped in place. The seasoned warriors donned chest and belt straps with wizened, shrunken heads of dead captives and fearsome masks of Chak-Xib-Chak and other denizens of the Underworld. Entering the main plaza just before dawn, the king and his relatives were greeted with a low-throated roar from the assembled warriors. The royal palanquin awaited him, six hefty bearers ready. The wooden structure was emblazoned with symbols of his royal lineage and Uaxactun's emblem glyph. Mounting the palanquin, he signaled for the procession to the battlefield. Amid cheers of the gathering crowd, the warriors of Uaxactun marched out of the city at sunrise, filled with anticipation of glory, toward the open fields where they would face their archenemy.

The ground mist quickly dissipated with the rising sun's warming light. Uaxactun's forces gathered at the northern edge of the field, standing in tense silence, straining eyes southward for the first sight of the enemy. Chan Hun shifted weight from foot to foot, his body quivering with adrenalin, tightly wound muscles aching for action. No clear thoughts formed in his mind, only brief bursts of images from prior battles and strong desire to overcome the enemy and take a noble captive. A faint, ephemeral image of the young woman he loved, the priestess of Mutul, flashed before his inner vision. There was no place for such thought in battle, and he quickly dismissed it. A sudden roar from his companions drew his attention sharply to the forest edge across the field. The forces of Mutul had just emerged from the dense greenery.

At once the long wooden trumpets blasted low vibrating notes that carried long distances and penetrated every fiber of the men's bodies with ominous warning. The bass thunder of the great war drums, the *tunkul,* set a fearsome cadence that raised hairs along the neck and set hearts pounding. Hundreds of Mutul warriors filled the far end of the field, undulating like some great multi-colored serpent. Sunlight glinted off metallic adornments on armor and sharp spear tips. The sound of war drums from both sides melded in pulsing cacophony.

Facing each other across a knee-high sea of grass, the warriors shouted insults about each other's ancestry and lack of prowess in battle. Individuals leapt and twirled, making fighting gestures by brandishing long knives and spears. Small groups charged onto the battlefield, screaming insults and making battle gestures, then drew back to their ranks. This bravado pumped up their courage, the insults built their anger and rage until the men on both sides were transformed into hot-blooded killers, hysterical with blood-lust, faces contorted and bodies trembling.

It was the way of Maya battle. It followed more than twenty katuns of honorable precedent, an unspoken agreement about the goals of war. Each warrior would seek an opponent of similar status, engage in close combat, and attempt to take the other captive. Some would be killed, of course, and others wounded in the process. These were the risks of war. But taking captives was the main objective, a necessary demonstration of ability that permitted a ruler to take succession and provided required sacrifices for important ceremonies in the sacred calendar.

As the warriors' raging emotions peaked, they exploded into action almost as one being in a frenzied release. The two forces charged across the grassy field, screaming and waving weapons. Heavy feet trampled the grass into a flat mat as the two lines struck and merged into a writhing, surging mass of swinging arms and thrusting spears, grunts and screams. Slashing and thrusting in crazed chaos, men tried to inflict injury and protect themselves while looking for a worthy captive. Sharp blades ripped through fabric armor and sliced into chests, arms and thighs. Warriors deflected blows with woven shields, twisting and turning, shoving against sweating opponents. Bright red blood soaked the trampled grasses. A few men fell to the ground, wounded. Warriors not immediately engaged in struggles pulled them back toward safety at the field's edges.

After some time, the entangled mass of fighting men separated, each group drawing back to their side of the field. In the glaring blaze of mid-morning sunlight, the exhausted warriors drank water from jugs to refresh their dry throats and replace moisture lost through sweating. They bound oozing wounds with cloth strips. More serious wounds were attended by healer-shamans who had litters ready for transportation back to their cities. A few captives had been taken by each side. These unfortunates were stripped of battle finery, left naked or with only loincloths, and tied down to prevent escape.

The lull in battle was temporary. Soon warriors converged and re-entered the fray, taunting their opponents to meet for one-on-one struggle. A determined group from Uaxactun formed a wedge and drove through Mutul's line toward the old king, Chak Toh Ich'ak, sitting on his palanquin. They almost reached him, but a nimble cadre of Mutul warriors joined forces with the king's guards and deflected the attack. Chak Toh Ich'ak descended from the palanquin during the struggle, armed and ready to fight in a display of great bravery. Several Teotihuacano warriors appeared and surrounded him, joining the struggle and giving added protection, including the young prince Yax Ain.

Clusters of sweating, bleeding, panting and cursing warriors engaged in hand-to-hand struggle, some taking captives when overpowering their adversary. The fierce Teotihuacan warrior K'ak Sih was among the most daring, slashing and thrusting, taking on several men at a time and felling them with his enormous strength. He sighted Uaxactun's king not far off, and signaled his cadre of warriors in that direction. Quickly they moved through writhing bodies and engaged the warriors around the king. The action was bloody and violent, the Teotihuacanos intent on killing any warrior standing

Ruler and Noble Taking Captives
Bird Jaguar on Lintel 8, Yaxchilan

between them and their goal. Swords pierced through fabric armor into heaving chests and bellies, spears sliced faces and throats. The king's guard fell, screaming and gurgling life out through open chest and throat wounds.

Chan Hun saw what was happening, and signaled his group to the king's defense. Their courageous fighting delayed K'ak Sih for long moments, but too soon he reached the king's side. The two royal men faced off then leapt at each other, wrestling with bulging muscles and aching lungs. They did not want to kill each other, for each was a highly valued prize. Around the thrashing arms and legs, warriors from both sides fought without constraints, using their sharp weapons mercilessly on each other. Chan Hun mustered forth every last ounce of his strength to ward off the ferocious attack of a thickly muscled

Teotihuacano. Searing pain across his right thigh brought him to his knees; another adversary had lanced him with a spear.

As the young warrior fell, he caught sight of K'ak Sih overpowering the king, tearing off his helmet and grasping his topknot while forcing him into a position of kneeling subjugation. Then Chan Hun was himself sprawled on the bloody grass mat, his own helmet and weapons torn away. Several enemy warriors grasped the king and Chan Hun by wrists and legs, quickly dragging them toward the sidelines where they were stripped and bound.

The battle still raged between the opposing cities' forces. It would last most of the day with such large numbers of warriors who could spell each other. But with the sound of Mutul's long wooden trumpets, everything changed. Sitting bound at the southern end of the battlefield, the ruler of Uaxactun and his kinsman Chan Hun had clear view of the unspeakable treachery.

At the sound of the trumpets, hundreds of hidden warriors materialized out of the forest, primarily Teotihuacanos but many from Mutul. They stood in eerie silence, never uttering a sound. Shouts and challenges were expected from new forces joining battle. At the trumpet sound, the men in battle stopped and looked, then Mutul's forces quickly withdrew to their sidelines as the new warriors lifted their weapons, the atlatls. Almost as a man, they simultaneously hurled a cloud of short spears into the ranks of Uaxactun. For a moment the Uaxactun warriors stared in stunned silence, frozen. The enemy was using spear throwers—hunting weapons—in battle.

The sky overhead was dark with rapidly descending spears, lethal black rain that would cut the warriors down like animals at slaughter. Sudden panic gripped them, they broke into milling chaos as the spears pierced hundreds of throats and torsos, felling most of the forces at the center of the battlefield. Screaming in fear and disbelief, those still standing began running at top speed toward their side line, but another wave of sailing spears decimated their remaining numbers. Bodies sprawled everywhere, many writhing in agony, screaming and pleading for help, but more lying still in the distorted postures of violent death. The next volley from the spear throwers reached the warriors resting at the field's edge. In total rout, what was left of the Uaxactun forces retreated rapidly into the bordering forests, running back to their city with horrifying news of unbelievable defeat: their king captured and their forces destroyed by foreign weapons not meant for noble warfare.

366

But Uaxactun's defeat was even more final than any Maya could possible imagine. Mutul's long wooden trumpets, conch shells and war drums began sounding across the battlefield strewn with corpses and dying men. The high voiced chant of victory rose from the throats of all Mutul's forces, carrying well into the distance, chasing the fleeing warriors of Uaxactun even to the borders of their city. With the sun glaring relentlessly in the mid-afternoon sky, Mutul's forces pursued the retreating enemy. Bursting through the forest, they surprised the shattered remnants of Uaxactun warriors gathered in the main plaza that was filled to capacity with city residents awaiting news. The atlatl throwers unleashed another barrage of short spears into the crowd, killing about half and sending the rest running in terror through the city's streets. Pursuit by the victors was merciless, their intent to kill all warriors and most nobility.

It was an unheard of takeover, an unthinkable disaster. Smoke billowed from fires of destruction, consuming pyramid temples, palaces, public halls and spacious homes. A contingent of Teotihuacanos led by K'ak Sih stormed the ruler's palace, set it afire and captured the royal family: the pregnant primary wife, the second wife, and both children. Later they would be sacrificed ceremoniously and buried in a special vault under the monument created to commemorate the Teotihuacan lord's victory. The king of Uaxactun would meet a similar fate in Mutul. They would all be killed, his line of descent ended, his sacred mountain portal to the gods and ancestors taken over by ruthless foreigners.[16]

K'ak Sih would rule over Uaxactun. A new line of descent would be established. The old, honorable way of Maya warfare was ended. Venus-Tlaloc star wars had begun.

The forces of Mutul camped overnight at the edge of the battlefield, too spent to attempt the hard day's walk back home. Food was distributed by attendants as the warriors sat around campfires.

---

[16] Archeological evidence for this scenario was found in a burial vault under Temple VIII in Uaxactun. The tomb contained an unusual grouping of five skeletons, an adult female who was pregnant when she died, a second adult female, a child and an infant. The vault was located under the temple celebrating Tikal's victory, built by K'ak Sih. The dead women and children were surely the wives and progeny of the defeated king, ending forever his line of succession as rulers of Uaxactun.

Jugs of balche were brought around and the men drank copious amounts of the intoxicating liquor. They nursed wounds and traded stories of their valor during battle. Shaman-healers ministered to the more seriously wounded men, who would be transported by litter tomorrow.

Many of the Teotihuacano forces occupied the conquered city, burning and plundering. A few Mutul warriors accompanied them and would later tell stories of unimaginable horror as the once beautiful city of Uaxactun was thoroughly routed. K'ak Sih and Yax Ain returned by evening to the Mutul camp for important business.

The Mutul warriors' triumph was marred by one serious happening: their venerable ruler Chak Toh Ich'ak had been wounded. No one knew how it happened. After descending from his palanquin, the king insisted on getting closer to battle. On at least two occasions Uaxactun warriors engaged in conflict with his guards, who tried to keep a second circle around the king with the help of Teotihuacanos. Maybe the circle was penetrated, it seemed the king did exchange blows a few times with an adversary, but in the melee it was impossible to be sure how the wound occurred. It was a deep penetrating wound in his lateral lower chest, and had punctured the lung. Shortly after that the lung collapsed, and the king had difficulty breathing. Occasionally he coughed frothy mucus tinged with blood.

Chak Toh Ich'ak became weaker as the day waned, despite incantations and herbal remedies applied to the wound by shaman-healers. Perhaps a younger, more vigorous man could have withstood the punctured lung, which would gradually repair itself. But the aged king had little reserve to recover from a serious wound. Word passed around camp that the king would likely die during the night.

As soon as K'ak Sih and Yax Ain returned to the Mutul camp, the king summoned them to his side. He was surrounded by his chief captains and highest nobles, as well as his royal relatives. Seated silently, their faces were grave in the twilight. Torches were lit as the two lords from Teotihuacan knelt beside the frail, thin body of the dying king stretched out on a litter. As the king spoke in a gasping whisper, all present leaned forward straining to hear. They were all witnesses to the king's statement of his succession. The royal relatives and Mutul lords tried to conceal their shock and anger at what they heard.

Chak Toh Ich'ak stated that Yax Ain was betrothed to his only daughter. They would marry as soon as possible. The Jaguar Claw dynasty of Mutul would be passed down through the king's daughter,

368

a shocking breach of tradition. Until Yax Ain came of age in two tuns, K'ak Sih would be regent and rule in his stead. The king declared K'ak Sih kalomte, high king, over both Uaxactun and Mutul. In a weak breathy voice the ruler called upon his nobles, relatives and warriors present to vow allegiance to this decree.

At that moment K'ak Sih rose to his feet and stared defiantly into the eyes of each man present. Materializing in the deepening twilight as if from thin air, a cadre of twenty Teotihuacan warriors still in full battle regalia appeared. They stood a respectful distance away from the group gathered around the king, but the message was clear. The foreign lord was ready to carry out the succession decree of Chak Toh Ich'ak with force, if necessary.

The Mutul lords each in turn gave assent. What they felt in their hearts, each kept to himself. They had observed well the prowess of the Teotihuacanos in battle that day, and were cognizant of the foreigners' capacity for ruthlessness. It had been a day of world-shattering changes: conquest war and altered royal succession.

Chak Toh Ich'ak, Great Jaguar Claw, the first truly famous king of Mutul, ruler for 61 tuns, died that night. When the victorious forces of Mutul returned to their city the next day, they had a new ruler: the fierce foreign warrior lord from the Mexica empire of Teotihuacan.[17]

*   *   *   *   *   *

Nearly all the adult members of K'an Nab Ku's extended household gathered near the wide stairs of the compound temple. K'in Pakal had returned that afternoon with the forces of Mutul, fresh from their decisive triumph over Uaxactun. The family warrior had incurred minor wounds on arms and legs, and was being treated by Xoc Ikal and Yalucha on the temple platform. As the two priestesses applied a paste of chaka bark and payche root to his wounds to reduce swelling and prevent infection, K'in Pakal related his experiences in battle to the rapt audience.

No details were spared, and K'in Pakal relished this story-telling opportunity, emphasizing the bravery of Mutul warriors and his own personal struggles with worthy Uaxactun opponents. He had captured

---

[17] Stela 31 of Tikal records the victory over Uaxactun on January 16, 378 CE (8.17.1.4.12) and the death of Chak Toh Ich'ak the same day. The glyphs cryptically say "he let blood" and was succeeded by K'ak Sih "not of Tikal" and Yax Ain "the noble of" K'ak Sih. The date of Yax Ain's accession to the throne as 10th ruler of Tikal was Sept. 13, 379 CE.

369

a brave enemy warrior who was now among the twenty-five captives confined in chambers adjacent to the Palace of the Ahauob. The listeners gasped in horror as he described the slaughter wrought by Teotihuacan atlatls, and the subsequent sacking and burning of Uaxactun. Eyes wide in amazement, the listener's minds grappled with the dying king's succession decree and the instillation of foreign lords as Mutul rulers. Intense, mixed emotions flooded through them: pride in victory, sorrow for their king's death, confusion over the upheaval of their world, excitement about coming ceremonies and unpredictable dramas at the highest echelon of society.

Upon hearing the vivid, bloody description of enemy slaughter, Yalucha blanched and sat quickly on a mat in the temple doorway. A wave of nausea swept through her solar plexus as her skin broke into a cold sweat. Xoc Ikal shot her daughter a warning look, then moved strategically to stand between the seated young woman and the closest family members. All were so engrossed in the battle re-telling, however, that no attention was paid to Yalucha's faintness. As K'in Pakal continued to spin hair-raising stories, Xoc Ikal brought a cup of cool water to her daughter, again admonishing her with cautionary eyes to contain these emotions.

As dusk fell, the group began to disperse to their respective homes. It was dinnertime, and the tempting aromas of bean and vegetable stews and roasting maize cakes beckoned. K'in Pakal thanked the priestesses for tending his wounds, declaring they felt already healed. K'an Nab Ku and Hunbatz lingered for a few more words with their kinsman. Yalucha had recovered enough to assist her mother putting their healing materials away in the temple side room.

"The king's wound," said K'an Nab Ku softly to his warrior brother. "How came that about?"

K'in Pakal shook his head.

"I do not know," he replied. "Nor could I find any of his guard who had a clear understanding of it. No one saw the wounding thrust delivered to his side."

"You said the Teotihuacanos joined the king's guard, to reinforce them as enemy warriors attacked him," K'an Nab Ku repeated.

"Yes, that is so."

"The king's death advanced the plan of succession, bringing K'ak Sih at once to power as regent for young Yax Ain," observed the astute stone carver.

"Yes." K'in Pakal looked sharply at his brother, moving closer to see his face better in the twilight. "What are you saying? This disturbs my heart."

K'an Nab Ku glanced around to be certain no other family members were still in the plaza. His face close to his brother's, he whispered:

"K'ak Sih is ruthless. This foreign lord does not respect our ways. He will do anything to advance his goals. Think, K'in Pakal. Who benefits the most by the death of Chak Toh Ich'ak?"

The warrior drew back, his brow furrowed. His mind did not easily follow the machinations of royal politics.

"I like this not," he said thoughtfully. "In truth, brother, my heart shakes, *xnik kolonton*, I am greatly disturbed by the seating of foreigners on the throne of Mutul. But you are right, the Teotihuacanos are capable of such deeds. There was much opportunity in the confusion of battle to slip a thin dagger into the king's side. Even he would not know from whose hand the death thrust came."

"Exactly so," agreed K'an Nab Ku.

Xoc Ikal and Yalucha joined the men, having overheard this whispered conversation. An image from her vision quest at the katun end ceremony two tuns ago burst into the older priestess' mind: the jaguar of Mutul with the owl of Teotihuacan on its back, the merging of the two animal's traits, the people of Mutul bowing to the owl-jaguar. She now understood the vision, and what it foretold had happened. The foreign owl bloodline was entering the jaguar claw lineage.

"These are dangerous times," said Xoc Ikal softly. "We do not know whether the king's nephews and cousins, those in traditional order of succession, will accept this situation. They may rise to overthrow the foreigners."

"Yes," agreed her husband. "Mutul could see internal warfare."

"K'ak Sih may have more Teotihuacano warriors already en route," mused K'in Pakal. "I have no doubt he will use force to maintain this succession, if necessary. Perhaps his ambitions are to subsume Mutul under the Mexica empire."

"Mutul will never submit to that!" exclaimed Hunbatz, worried and worked up by the older men's discussion.

"Quiet yourself, son," admonished his father. "No, our great city will not become a vassal to this foreign empire. We must wait to see how events play out. It was the ruler's decree that Yax Ain marry his daughter and become Mutul ahau. There may be enough support among our people for this; Chak Toh Ich'ak is the only ruler most have known, he is respected as a god."

"K'ak Sih also commands great respect," admitted K'in Pakal. "He captured the ruler of Uaxactun himself. His men took many of the captives brought back today. Our warriors hold these foreigners in high regard for their battle prowess."

"Were other of the Uaxactun rulers' relatives captured?" asked Yalucha in a shaky voice.

"Yes, three others," said K'in Pakal. "Two by Mutul warriors, cousins to the king of the Ka'nab family, great prizes. K'ak Sih's foremost captain took the other, a young warrior defending the king. His name, I believe, is Chan Hun; a distant relative who fought bravely." Proud to show his knowledge, K'in Pakal went on to describe the lineage and names of the king's cousins.

Yalucha ceased to hear any more of her uncle's answer once Chan Hun's name was mentioned. She struggled to keep her face expressionless, as her heart leapt with joy.

Chan Hun is alive! He is here in Mutul!

At least he was not killed by the deluge of spears that decimated his comrades. Although she knew fully what being a war captive meant, she blocked those thoughts that were too painful to allow into awareness. For now, she rejoiced in the knowledge that her beloved lived. Somehow she would find a way to see him.

Xoc Ikal considered her strategy carefully. In the kins following the conquest of Uaxactun, the city of Mutul simmered in a volatile state of uncertainty. K'ak Sih and his captains were ensconced in desirous quarters in the Palace of the Ahauob, while his troops camped at the city outskirts. The foreign leader was holding court, of sorts, in a chamber there. So far, the nobles of Mutul were attending this new nexus of power and the warriors seemed content to accept the new ruler. Murmurings of disapproval could be heard among the dead king's relatives, but none were openly opposing the unorthodox succession mandated by Chak Toh Ich'ak. Plans were being made for the victory ceremony with K'ak Sih presiding, and events had been set in motion for the marriage of the Mutul king's daughter to Yax Ain.

A current of unrest seeped through the broad plazas and wide sakbeob of the great city, however. The prevailing attitude toward the Teotihuacanos was a mixture of fear and admiration, with subtle uneasiness over what their ascendance to power meant for Mutul. The possibility of internal warfare hovered at the fringes of most people's minds. They were careful about what was said and who might overhear words of dissidence. Each kin the presence of Teotihuacan warriors striding purposefully on unknown missions throughout the city kept the people on notice. These were uncertain times.

The priestess of Ix Chel knew that shaman-healers often cared for the wounds of captives, to keep them alive and healthy. Some royal captives were kept alive for years, displayed at important ceremonies as a reminder of the king's prowess. Those intended for sacrifice were not infrequently subjected to torture, but paradoxically these unfortunates were kept healthy and strong as possible. Thus they were more fitting offerings to the gods, and could withstand their ordeals better.

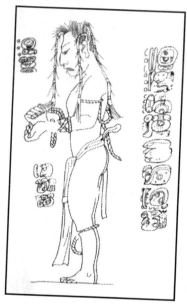

Noble Captive
Bone Carving, Cakalmul

Gathering information carefully, Xok Ikal learned that the king of Uaxactun was imprisoned in a small chamber alone, his closest relatives in another room, and the remaining warriors divided between two rooms. She approached the head shaman-healer and offered to attend wounded captives with new poultices she had created from plants growing by the Great Waters of the East, brought by her daughter after completing priestess training. This request was granted.

Although she had misgivings, Xok Ikal was moved by her daughter's heart-wrenching plea for assistance in finding a way to see Chan Hun. She prepared Yalucha thoroughly. The priestesses spent a kin doing purification and meditation, calling upon their patron goddess Ix Chel and their uayob assistants, and preparing herbal poultices. Before departing the morning of their mission, Xoc Ikal again gave strong warning:

"You must call upon every drop of your power to remain implacable. Do not reveal emotions, keep your speech measured, remember your time is short with him. I will prepare him, he is in the second chamber which I will enter first. You will attend the warriors then come later to his chamber." She looked at her daughter with immense compassion and firmness. "Do not place our family in danger by revealing your heart, Yalucha. These are dangerous and uncertain times. We do not know what measures the foreign rulers may take to maintain control."

Xoc Ikal paused, searching her daughter's face. Only wide, unusually bright eyes gave hints of the young woman's strong emotions. Her face rested in an expression of composure.

"Good," murmured the mother. "Maintain that expression. This may be the most difficult thing you have ever done, my child. Have courage, call upon The Goddess."

The women arrived at the captives' chambers by mid-morning. Guards stood outside the narrow corbelled doorways, barred by thick beams held horizontally by grooved stones. Xoc Ikal explained their mission, noting that the guards were a mixture of Mutul and Teotihuacan warriors. The foreigners were maintaining a presence in all the key processes of governance. The priestesses were not allowed to attend the king, but could attend wounds of the other captives. Two men were needed to lift each beam from its rest. Yalucha went into the warrior's chamber while Xoc Ikal entered that of the royal relatives.

It took a moment for Xoc Ikal's eyes to adjust to the dim light inside. The three royal captives had risen to their feet, bodies tense and guarded. She explained her purpose, inquiring about their wounds. Gratefully the men accepted her ministrations. The most serious wound was in the thigh of the youngest man. As the priestess cleansed the wound of the now seated warrior, she asked his name.

"Chan Hun," he replied.

Xoc Ikal looked into the young man's face. He was as comely as her daughter described, and she immediately liked his energy. The thigh wound was deep and beginning to fester.

"I am sorry, Chan Hun," she said softly. "I must cleanse this wound, and it will give you pain."

"Yes, I understand," he replied. "Pain is now my lot in life. But you give pain from kindness, and my heart is pleased to accept it."

She smiled at his nobility of spirit. There was no sign of torture as yet, but she knew this practice could be started at any time. The confrontation with suffering and facing fear of death were the two greatest challenges of warriors—or any of her people, she reflected. Life certainly provided enough of these experiences to test the mettle of any living person. In this way the soul was refined and developed, brought into its power so it could outwit the Lords of Death.

The young man held still through the wound cleansing, although his jaw muscles tightened and he winced from pain. Finishing this work, Xoc Ikal applied a soothing poultice with antibacterial properties, and wrapped a white cotton cloth around his thigh.

"This will bring relief and stop infection," she told him. Glancing around, she saw the two other men were preoccupied, gazing out through the door. Lowering her voice, she whispered close to his ear:

"Chan Hun, brace yourself. I am the mother of your beloved. By her pleas, I have arranged this visit to tend wounds. She is coming to you in moments. The fire in her heart compelled her, but she must contain it. You also must contain your feelings, or our family will be in great danger. The foreigners have usurped the throne of Mutul, all is unstable, we do not know where danger lurks. There must be no exposure of your relationship. Do you understand?"

The young warrior's expression of surprise quickly changed as he allowed the significance of her words to sink in. He nodded gravely, setting his face into a neutral expression.

"Thank you," he said. "I understand."

The two men at the door stepped aside to allow the young priestess entrance. Xoc Ikal quickly went to them, taking the men to the near corner of the chamber to check their wounds. Yalucha slowly walked to Chan Hun, seated far inside the chamber. Her eyes gradually adjusted to the dim light as she knelt beside him. Not yet looking into his eyes, she took an herbal packet from her basket and held it toward him.

"These herbs will keep your blood pure," she said. "Chew them three times daily."

Lifting her eyes, Yalucha felt a wave of faintness sweep over her body. Her heart was pounding, beating fiercely against her chest like an imprisoned dove. A fine tremor in the hand extending the herbal packet was the only sign of these intense emotions. As their fingers touched and their eyes met, a burst of indescribable sweetness flooded through her, so powerful she could taste nectar deep in her throat. Almost tangible energy arced between their hearts, a bolt of lightening sending tingling sensations throughout their bodies as both felt the familiar magnetic attraction.

For a long moment they gazed deeply into each other's souls through the windows of the eyes. Eyes speaking of unending love, of total commitment, of bone-aching anguish. The young woman looked away first, furiously blinking back tears.

"How is your wound?" she inquired, noting his bandaged thigh. Her voice was husky with emotion.

"Much better since your mother's ministrations," he replied, voice steady and calm.

The sounds of Xoc Ikal in conversation with the other two men provided background noises that muted the young lover's voices.

"My heart is clamoring, *xk'opk'on kolonton,* to see you such," Yalucha said softly.

"I said I would come to you," Chan Hun replied with a sardonic smile. "But I did not think it would be this way."

Her heart leapt at the flash of gem-embedded white teeth and subtle dimple in his left cheek set off by his smile. Despite her sorrow, a slight smile played across the corners of her full lips at his irrepressible humor.

"Nor I," she replied. "The ways of the gods are unfathomable."

"Heart of my heart," Chan Hun said with intensity, his voice just above a whisper, "know I love you always. Whatever may come, you are goddess of my heart, companion to my soul. You perfume my heart, *chamuibtasbon kolonton.* There will never be another."

"*Xk'uxub kolonton,* my heart aches with love for you," she whispered back. "I am yours forever. You are in my heart every moment, I yearn for you . . . oh . . ."

Her voice trailed off as she stifled a sob. Chan Hun furrowed his brows and shook his head slightly in warning, glancing at his comrades still occupied by Xoc Ikal's chatting as she cared for their wounds.

"Time is short, beloved," he said. "Soon I face my final battle in the Middleworld. After that I face the Lords of Xibalba on their home territory."

"Speak not of that to me, I cannot bear it," she murmured.

"That I might embrace you one more time," he continued, eyes devouring her face, muscles quivering as he held them back from gathering her in his arms. "To hold you again, press your breasts to me, join with you, feel life pulsing between our bodies . . . ah, Lords of Darkness, you tear from me this treasure! Too soon, I have only just tasted the *utz,* the flower of love. This I regret more than death itself."

Burning fires of intense passion bounded through Yalucha's body, along with cold currents of fearsome dread, running alongside

376

each other like her veins and arteries, twining into every cell in the eternal struggle of life and death.

"I will find you, wherever you go," she whispered breathlessly. "The Lords of Death cannot keep us apart. We will be together, in all the worlds."

"You must live, heart of my heart," he replied with concern. "I must be able to think of you alive."

"Life is nothing without you," she said in a forced whisper.

"Life is everything, in each moment," he rebuked. "I am learning how precious every moment of life is, this gift of the gods, this walk in the land of terrible beauty. Live your life in my honor."

Now she could not stop the tears, so she turned away and rummaged in her basket. Putting her face close over it, she surreptitiously dapped away tears with a cloth, then pretended to hand him something else. By some deep well of willpower, she knew not from where, she quelled the tears and set steely resolve for calmness.

Their fingers touched again, tips brushing gently, lingering, savoring the tiny jolts of lightening dancing in-between. Inhaling simultaneously, they relished the scents of each other mixed with pungent dried herbs and dank odors of damp stones. Eyes locked and pouring out unexpressed longing, for a few moments the lovers enjoined in consciousness, their souls united and merging. Hovering in another reality, time and place suspended, an eternity of soul-communion swept them away into realms of bliss.

"Yalucha, we must go."

Xoc Ikal's stern voice summoned the reluctant young woman back into the present. Without speaking, but keeping her eyes on her beloved, Yalucha took the herb basket and rose to her feet. Xoc Ikal pressed her arm firmly, turning her toward the door.

One last glance. Chan Hun's dark eyes, wide with anguish, watched the woman he loved slowly move toward the doorway. She turned her head away, bowing it low. He could read in her body language the Herculean effort it was taking to keep from crying out, from running back to embrace him. Tears stung the young warrior's eyes, and he turned away, hugging his knees tightly, impervious to the pain from his thigh wound.

Outside the bright noon sunlight stunned Yalucha. She covered her eyes with one hand, a good excuse to conceal her tears. Mind numb with pain, she walked slowly toward the passageway to the Great Plaza as her mother thanked the guards and bid farewell.

Mutul was in a festive mood, a good antidote to the constant tension prevailing since the death of Chak Toh Ich'ak and accession of the foreign lords to rulership. The city was preparing for the victory ceremony to acknowledge Mutul's triumph over Uaxactun. The ceremony was timed halfway through the Venus synodic period, 4 moon cycles after the star of Hunahpu rose as Morningstar and led the forces of Mutul and Teotihuacan to resounding victory. The city had mourned their king with great ceremonial pomp several kins after his death, and buried him with opulent grave paraphernalia in the chamber already prepared for this purpose under the north pyramid temple of the Sacred World Tree Complex. Now the time of mourning was over, and Mutul could celebrate.

But one household in Mutul could not join fully in the celebration. The immediate family of K'an Nab Ku was caught up in the strange illness that gripped his only daughter, Yalucha, since she and her mother had ministered to the captives from Uaxactun. Xoc Ikal speculated that her daughter had contracted an "evil wind" from one of the men, a form of spiritual illness that the young healer was not experienced enough to ward off. These things sometimes happened to inexperienced priestesses. The older priestess prepared the prescribed potions, but she knew the true cause of Yalucha's suffering.

Yalucha had sickness of the heart. Her love for Chan Hun and the inevitability of his fate raged in ceaseless battle within her inner being. She was tossed on turbulent storms of conflicting emotions, plunging into the vast abyss of despair, raging against the cruel injunctions of the gods, grieving a sorrow so profound that it catapulted her beyond tears into the shattered remnants of her very soul. Then a ray of light would glimmer faintly, beckoning her heart to hope, daring her to dream of a possible future. Sometimes captives were kept for years. Although not common, some men from enemy cities were eventually released and integrated into their captor's society. Most often these were scribes, artisans and carvers, put into service of the victorious ruler. But even warriors had escaped sacrificial death and lived to serve a new master. She grasped desperately at this straw, allowing herself to imagine a life with Chan Hun, making a home together, having children, just the daily joy of living with her beloved.

But it was not to be. As word of the planned victory ceremony spread, the ruler's intentions for captive sacrifice became clear.

Yalucha's father and uncle brought home news from their attendance at royal court. K'ak Sih would himself let blood to honor the Maya royal tradition, and he would offer the ultimate sacrifice of human life as the climax of the rituals. The three royal kinsmen of the ruler of Uaxactun, and half the captured warriors, would be sacrificed to K'inich Ahau and Tlaloc. The ruler of Uaxactun himself and the other warriors were reserved for a later ceremony, the accession to Mutul's throne by Yax Ain when he came of age. The marriage of the Teotihuacan prince and the daughter of Chak Toh Ich'ak would take place shortly before this.

Her faint hopes crushed, Yalucha felt paralyzed, helpless, hopeless. There was nowhere to turn for relief, no source of comfort. She could not pray. Ix Chel had deserted her devotee, abandoned her to oceans of sorrow, she was drowning. On some days, the young priestess' mind became nearly blank, her feelings numb. Then she could go about daily tasks, usually assisting her mother with healing work at the compound temple or tending the herb garden. Soon, however, the black pall of despair again descended and she withdrew to her room, curled into a ball and slept fitfully.

Xok Ikal wisely did not try to alleviate her daughter's grief. There was nothing one could say, no counsel that might shift perspective, for a process so immediate and raw. When Yalucha would permit, Xok Ikal simply held her daughter in her arms, crooning softly as she might to a distraught child. She made *xiv* to support overall health, and relaxing brews to promote sleep, urging these upon the reticent young woman. As the date of the victory ceremony approached, Xoc Ikal made sedating teas, hoping to blur the edges of awareness that kept re-piercing the heart wound of her daughter.

Hearing of Yalucha's illness, Chitam came to visit several times. It was obviously not the right time to press his suit, and he made no mention of this. He brought tasty maize cakes and dried fruits, honey *utz* to drink, and offered to do divinations to combat malevolent spirits that might be involved. Xok Ikal was gracious to the young Daykeeper Priest and asked for his prayers. Yalucha said very little, often declining to leave her room, and never eating his gifts. At times Chitam became the unknowing target of her inner fury: when alone she railed against the gods; why did Chitam live and prosper while her beloved suffered torment and faced certain death?

The Lords of Xibalba played with stakes that were too high for her. She lad lost her ability for spiritual focus, her entire world in all

379

its multiple dimensions was crashing and dissolving, she wanted no more of life but did not want death either. She wanted simply not to be. Void. Oblivion. No thought, no feeling, no thing.

On the day of the victory ceremony, Xoc Ikal stayed home with Yalucha. All extended family members left for the Great Plaza, except Chuen who was near term pregnancy and having mild contractions. Xoc Ikal would tend to both of the women. The older priestess prepared a very strong brew with sedating herbs and a small amount of ground hallucinogenic mushrooms. She wanted her daughter thoroughly drugged, perhaps for several days, as Chan Hun went to his sacrificial death on the stairs of the pyramid temple. After that, she did not know. Waiting for the execution had been devastating for Yalucha. Only time would tell about her ability to recover.

Faint crowd roars and drumbeats signaled the ceremony was in process. Xoc Ikal checked on Yalucha, who was asleep on the padded ledge in her room. The young woman's breathing was regular and slow. She was deep under the influence of the mind-altering substances, in some other realm. Gently brushing a stray tendril of hair from across her daughter's face, the mother sighed deeply. Leaving the room, she placed the thick woven drape across the door, checked on the herbal brew she was preparing for childbirth, and went to see how Chuen was faring.

As the afternoon wore on, Chuen's labor became active and Xoc Ikal needed to be in closer attendance. It was good that the young woman had carried nearly to term, thanks to her sister-in-law's herbal remedies. The labor was a hard one, however, as Chuen's pelvis was narrow and her muscles tight from years of dancing. Dashing repeatedly between the two homes across the compound plaza checking on her charges made Xoc Ikal wish she had requested another woman to stay home. Yalucha was starting to toss fretfully, but Xoc Ikal could not get the sedated girl to drink more brew. Finally her daughter dropped back into drugged sleep, allowing the mother to return to Chuen, whose cries could be heard across the plaza.

The drums became frenzied, driving, wild. Roars rose from hundreds of throats like distant crashing surf.

The surf. The Great Waters of the East. Yalucha's drugged mind grasped at surging images of water, beach, waves. Blissful sensations filled her as memories wafted upward, lying with Chan Hun on the warm sand. Screams broke into this sweet reverie, screams of pain.

Pain. Death. Drums beating, pounding, driving daggers of fear into her brain.

Where was he? Where? The drums, the drums of sacrifice. Chan Hun was being sacrificed!

No! Oh, stop them! Who is screaming? Chan Hun, Chan Hun . . . oh gods . . .

Yalucha lurched up, swaying dizzily. She grasped at the wall to steady herself. She had to leave this place. She had to get away from the drums, the killing drums, stabbing her brain, pounding deeper and deeper into every cell until her entire body was bursting with the drumbeats. The screams came again, confusing her more. Staggering, she made her way through the door, tangled with the heavy drape and fell with a thud. Dazed but driven, she pulled herself to her feet, weaving through the kitchen to the garden behind, running, slipping and falling, grasping trees for support.

The drugged young woman reached the jungle edge. The incessant drumming drove her mad, she had to get away. Clasping hands over ears, she plunged into the verdant density of jungle growth. Propelled by rushing adrenalin giving unfathomed strength to slender muscles, she shoved low branches and hanging, twisted vines away. These denizens of the forest depths fought back, slamming against her body and slapping her face, throwing her back and forth. Falling repeatedly, she crawled over a thick mat of humus and plant litter, moist and earthy with decay as millions of molds and fungi competed for existence. Interlocking networks of roots created a sea of brown ripples, trapping her hands and feet like thousands of terrestrial octopus tendrils. Disentangling herself, the dazed young woman clung to hanging vines, pulling herself upright, thrashing and lunging once again through leafy walls.

Everything was green in her blurry vision, dancing and leaping, twirling and spinning. Even the sky above was green, painted with waving leaves of jade, now deep and dark, now pale and translucent. Huge tree trunks appeared out of nowhere, coated with mosses and aerophytes, obstructing her progress. She climbed unsteadily over huge flaring roots taller than she was where they fanned out from trunks. The sharp serrated leaves of palmettos sliced her bare arms and face, leaving little streams of bloody droplets. Thorny vines tore at her loose night shift, shredding in into multiple streamers and embedding their stinging points where she pressed against them, trapped momentarily until she yanked herself away. Bumping against needle palms, she was barraged with a shower of hair-like poisonous spikes, like miniature sea urchins. The tiny spikes released toxins into her skin, which began swelling immediately, and soon produced a feverish achy reaction through her entire body.

The drums kept pounding in Yalucha's ears. She batted these offending auricles, trying to drive away the agony of this death messenger. Insects swarmed around her face and stung her eyes, adding their incessant buzzing to the unbearable drumbeats. Gasping for breath, swiping gnats and mosquitoes from already blurry eyes, she pushed on, deeper and deeper into the jungle. She was lost in caves of chlorophyll, a dense exuberance of life forms, sprouting and spreading, spawning and flowering, killing and rotting, eating and breeding, singing and screaming, hiding and sleeping, flying and creeping, slithering and digging. Hundreds of eyes watched the struggling creature that disturbed the foliage and made unusual noises, unlike the silence passages of the jungle's natives.

Darkness fell abruptly. The exhausted young woman collapsed on the humus mat, clothing almost completely torn away, welts and cuts oozing on all exposed skin surfaces. The rapid pounding of her heart replaced the drumbeat in her ears, accompanied by the sounds of night insects: high-pitched whistling cicadas, rhythmic cricket chirps, syncopated bleeps of frogs, hissing noises of beetles. In the distance roars of howler monkeys set an ominous tone, enhanced by the rumbling and coughing of prowling jaguars. Before sinking into feverish sleep, Yalucha realized the drums had stopped. She knew Chan Hun was dead. Semi-conscious, she was dimly aware of jaguar noises and felt strangely comforted, releasing herself to their jaws.

Fangs surrounded her neck. Smooth sharp teeth punctured skin, as warm blood dripped down her back and chest. Strong musty odor of the big cat, snuffling noises. Limp aching body dragged across bumpy roots. Pain, sharp mingled with burning and stinging, all over but especially the neck. Warm jaguar saliva mixing with blood. Release into death, death the comforter, the end of suffering. She welcomed death.

Sudden shouts and crashing noises disturbed the insect chorus. Brandishing torches and long knives, a small group of men slashed furiously through thick underbrush toward the retreating jaguar. Opening his mouth to roar angrily at these intruders, the great spotted cat dropped his prey abruptly. Staring defiantly with torchlight glinting across his amber eyes, the jaguar gauged the situation. The men continued their headlong rush toward him, shouting and waving torches. Deciding to abandon his meal, the jaguar turned and leapt with ease through the tangled jungle, disappearing into the heavy blackness.

*   *   *   *   *

Half a moon cycle passed as Yalucha hovered on the brink of death. The toxins injected by poisonous plants and infections from the jungle organisms that entered her multiple wounds caused a long period of high fevers. The jaguar's teeth had penetrated deeply, just missing the jugular vein. For several kins the young woman did not move a muscle, causing worry that her neck might be broken. As the state of fevered torpor drained her body of precious fluids, muscles twitched involuntarily and limbs jerked. Lost in an inner realm between worlds, she moaned piteously.

The taste of death was sweet, cloyingly sweet. She floated in a sea of nectar. Thick, sticky, holding her limbs captive, making each breath an effort. She breathed nectar, fully immersed in delicious waters like a fish. Everything was dissolved in this vast sea, melting and merging into oneness. All that was, was here. All could be known, every meaning of every event was revealed, each detail in each moment of life showed how it fit into the whole picture. Like an immense circular river, the current of death nectar flowed from what seemed before to what seemed yet to come, emptying into the vast sea yet to circle again. All life dissolved into this sea of soundless merging. Boundaries melted away; times, places, beings lost their separate existence in this viscous oneness. Oneness that was noneness, all knowing yet incapable of using knowledge. No desire, no caring, no feeling, no purpose. Just the stunning sweetness of mindless death.

She was sinking deeper, deeper into the honeyed goo. It was delicious, effortless. But a tiny point of awareness formed like a bubble, slowly rising from an unfathomable depth. It wanted something, it sought something. Far, far away came an infant's cry. The bubble listened. It desired to meet the cry. Struggling upward through thick nectar currents, the bubble aimed itself toward the baby's cries. A baby meant life. Life anew, life refreshed and coming forth to blossom in nature's diversity. A ripple of caring moved deep inside her dissolving being, concern for the babies unborn and born, the bright little souls who sought the life experience. Her being was a vessel for those babies, for the very force of life itself. In that moment she made a choice. She wanted to live.

383

It was hot, unbearably hot. Every joint and muscle was wracked with pain. Revolting stomach and bowels spasms forced sparse fluids out as she retched and strained. Neck stiff, burning deep inside, unable to turn. Soothing cool packs upon her face and body, drops of astringent liquid forced between cracked lips slowly took the nauseatingly sweet taste of death from her mouth. The sticky currents released their hold and she followed the expanding bubble to the surface of consciousness, back to life.

With Xoc Ikal's skillful care, the fever finally broke and a lengthy period of recovery ensued. Slowly the festering cuts and wounds healed, leaving many small scars as reminders of the jungle's fearsome armamentarium. Daily herbal baths and frequent doses of blood cleansing teas drew toxins out. Nutritious soups gradually restored strength. The young woman's hollow-eyed look and gaunt cheeks filled out, and she began putting more flesh on her thin frame. Another full moon cycle was needed before she was able to be up and walk around. Still she was weak, and rested often.

The men in Yalucha's family hovered around, hoping to find ways to be helpful. Sometimes her father simply sat by his semi-conscious daughter's side, holding her hand. He spoke words of love and encouragement, words that penetrated into the dim reaches of her mind, calling her back. Hunbatz too spent time with his sister, and K'in Pakal visited often. It was her warrior uncle who led the group of men into the nighttime jungle, braving serious danger to themselves, to save her from the jaguar's jaws. He relished re-telling this story, as dramatic a rescue as he could recall. When Yalucha was alert enough to grasp the sequence of events, she too marveled at the exact timing of the rescue party. Apparently the gods did not want her to enter the Underworld yet.

During Yalucha's protracted recovery, Chitam visited regularly. He brought simple gifts and plied her with stories about the stars, relating how Daykeeper Priests tracked cycles and used hidden information to gain knowledge and advise people. At first she dozed through much of his chattering, but as she recovered she became intrigued, listening with attention and asking questions. This spark of interest encouraged both the young priest and Xoc Ikal, who worried about the deeper causes of her daughter's illness.

Chuen brought her infant girl over frequently. Despite the difficult labor, both mother and baby were doing well. Yalucha enjoyed holding the tiny tan-skinned being, admiring her curving lips and tiny nose, and laughing at how she grasped a finger so tightly with her miniature hands. More than anything, playing with the baby brought life back into Yalucha. Chuen retold the story of her pregnancy and labor again and again to the rapt young priestess, who seemed never to get enough of hearing every detail. They shared dressing and bathing the baby, and Yalucha often entreated Chuen to breastfeed her there before leaving for home.

Even when they were alone, Yalucha did not speak to Xoc Ikal about Chan Hun. Something had shifted in her jungle ordeal. There was a quality of calmness and determination in the young woman's manner that had not been there before. Perhaps facing death, meeting the Lords of Xibalba head-on in two very different ways in rapid succession had matured her soul. And, the lovely jade pendant given as his pledge by the young warrior was lost, taken by the jungle, ripped away in her drugged struggle with viney tentacles and grasping branches.

But Chan Hun was nearly every moment in Yalucha's awareness. He lived in her heart as surely now as ever. A plan began to form in her mind, slowly taking form. She would contact him in the Otherworld. Using her secret knowledge as a priestess and shaman, she would journey to wherever he was to meet with him. It was this resolve that underlay her calm determination. She needed to return to her spiritual practices, to revive her techniques, to re-ignite her connections with Ix Chel, her patron goddess.

Within four moon cycles, Yalucha was again providing healing care to supplicants at their compound temple. She started accompanying her mother in temple rituals, and then led smaller ceremonies herself. She spent long times alone communing with Ix Chel, making offerings and burning copal, calling upon the Great Mother Goddess, the Moon in all Cycles, Weaver of the Worlds. After appropriate preparations and purifications, she undertook vision quests with the temple assistant as anchor in the usual way. She used the hallucinogenic mushroom drink that was traditional in the old religion of Izapa. But the journeys of her soul followed already established routes: she soared among the stars in the sky, merged with the Moon Goddess, frolicked with the forces of creation as the cosmic serpent danced life into manifestation. Looking, seeking in the swirling star showers of the Otherworld, she could not find a hint, any faint clue, about her beloved.

Yalucha reflected upon these vision quests and prayed for guidance. One afternoon while in deep contemplation under the avocado trees in her family garden, the soft calls of a frog wafted into her awareness.

"Ruuuop, ruuuop," the tiny tree frog chirped.

She allowed her consciousness to follow the frog calls. A calm pond covered with water lilies filled her inner vision. Upon a lily pad sat a small uo toad, her *uay* or animal familiar. It called her with the mournful "uoooooh" sound she loved, the signal that rains would soon relieve the parched heat of the dry season. Moving closer, she looked into the toad's beady eyes and it communicated to her soul:

Holy sister, you enter the wrong portal. Here is the surface of the shadowy region below, the deeper realm of Underworld gods and demons. In these hidden depths you will find what you seek. You must take the southern portal of the Sacred World Tree, the place of White-Bone Snake, the Black Transformer. You must enter the Black Dreaming Place.

The young priestess had suspected as much. Cold fingers of fear crept around her heart. Techniques for entering the Underworld were reserved for High Priestesses and Priests of the Ix Chel tradition, and her training had not included these. This was an extremely dangerous journey, one she had not felt prepared to undertake. Could she do it now? Was this fearsome vision quest necessary to contact Chan Hun?

She knew it was. She also knew from within her intuitive core that the technique must involve bloodletting. This was the requirement of the Lords of Xibalba. It was not the way of Ix Chel, of the old religion, but it was necessary. Chan Hun was a follower of K'inich Ahau, the new Sun God, who also required blood sacrifice. It was the only way.

Yalucha prepared in secret, not sharing her intentions with her mother. From the lessons she learned while listening to Chitam, she selected a time when Venus was hidden. The bright star dropped beneath the western horizon, the direction of endings and portal to the Underworld. While Venus sojourned in the watery depths, she also would make her visit. She assembled a small packet of the gifts favored by K'inich Ahau: kernels of the finest maize contained in an exquisitely decorated small urn, a thin obsidian blade, several glittering gems, and wrapped them in a beautifully worked cloth with red and black designs. In another wide-brimmed cup, she placed bark paper for catching blood and copal for burning.

In the middle of the night, the young priestess stole silently to the compound temple, her way lit by the moon just entering its waning phase. She performed invocation prayers before the round altar, first to Ix Chel and then to K'inich Ahau.

"K'inich Ahau," she whispered, hands lifted in a gesture of supplication, "I do not understand your ways. But this is clearly your time, your Sun age of our people. I will give you the blood tribute you require, but in a way that keeps honor with myself. Accept my offerings, may they please you. Be my guide, open the portals to the quest that I seek. You know my heart, lead me to my beloved."

She went into the small chamber of vision quests. Sitting upon a woven mat, she positioned herself so the wall supported her back. Opening the cloth holding her offerings, she carefully arranged and blessed each object. Immediately in front of her crossed legs she placed the wide-brimmed cup with its contents, and the sharp obsidian blade. She retrieved a few glowing embers in a small cup from the temple's ongoing supply. Using a series of incantations, she began shifting her consciousness into the spirit domain. With strong intention, she anchored her soul through the base of her spine deep into the earth. She called upon Ix Chel, the Great Mother, the very body of earth, to protect her and keep her anchored so she could return to the Middleworld.

The sound of her heartbeat became the drum that propelled her consciousness farther and farther from body awareness. She focused on images of K'inich Ahau, blazing as the sun, fully armored for battle, wielding tasseled spear and wearing a riotous immense headdress with lightening flashes replacing feathers. The god's fire spouting eyes beckoned her, millions of exploding light crystals radiating from teeth as he smiled. It was time for blood.

In a trance state, she watched her arms in slow motion moving her hands toward the obsidian blade. The right hand grasped the smooth rounded handle, lifting it. The left hand uncurled palm upward over the wide-brimmed cup. Slowly, deliberately these hands acted of their own accord. The sharp blade cut a straight line across her palm. Dimly she was aware of pain, but it was so distant that it mattered not. No wincing or reflexive withdrawal of the hand happened. In fascination, her observer watched the droplets of blood form along the cut like ruby gems on a necklace. The precious itz droplets became fatter and coalesced into a flow, trickling to the edges of her palm and dripping down on the waiting bark paper. She turned the palm downward to allow the small current to flow. Soon the bark paper was saturated, bright red with the blood of life.

Laying the blade back on the cloth, she took a thin stick and plunged it into the cup of glowing embers. It burst quickly into flames, and she applied the hungry little tongues to the copal granules scattered around the bark paper. The resin immediately embraced the flames, giving them added life. The copal's sweet earthy smell filled the room, and a curl of smoke began to rise from the burning bark paper.

Lady Six Tun Invoking Vision Serpent,
Lintel 15, Yaxchilan

Eyes closed, Yalucha inhaled copal and paper smoke. The pungent smells loosened her soul even more from its bodily habitat. The White Flower Thing of her soul hovered on the swirls of smoke, waiting. Waiting. She felt it more than saw it, the Vision Serpent forming from the undulating smoke. Languidly the thick scaly body swayed and curled, rising and extending its length, lifting its flower-bedecked fanged head, mesmerizing her with its slanted amber eyes. Opening its toothy jaws wide, it protruded a forked tongue that flickered a secret code, beckoning her, summoning her.

Suddenly a whirling funnel formed that sucked her downward with breath-taking force. She was falling into the vortex, spinning along its sides as the centrifugal force pulled her deeper and deeper. It spat her out the far end into a place of indigo-blue, watery darkness.

The beady eyes and long calls of uo toads, millions of the small creatures, surrounded her. Their soulful "uoooooh" calls sounded like wails, poignant with the suffering of all creatures. Their calls reached crescendo and suddenly stopped. The uo toads disappeared and were replaced with a barrage of weird and fearsome uayob, intermediary beings between the world of ordinary consciousness and the domain of Underworld gods.

Dancing grotesquely around her were fantastical animal combinations: deer-headed monkeys, monster-dogs, hawk-headed and winged jaguars, enormous mosquitoes with human-like arms and legs, snakes with huge dragon jaws, crocodile-headed birds. Human bodies sported an assortment of animal heads including lizards, jaguars, and birds. Fish with square-eyed human features swam by. In the distance a rabbit scribe was busily writing in a codex, while dogs and deer played musical instruments.

These gatekeepers of the Underworld seemed to threaten or challenge her. Some dove toward her, hovering eye-to-eye or brushing wings against her. The young priestess held steady, not allowing fear to unleash its power of soul-undoing. She knew of these uayob and how shamans could transform themselves into these shadowy monsters to use their supernatural abilities for navigating the dimension halfway between the daylight world and the abysmal domain of the gods. Grasping the antlers of a deer-headed macaw, she urged the Underworld denizen to fly her past the gatekeeper monsters.

With dizzying speed, her unnatural transport plummeted even deeper into the murky dark blue waters. Banking abruptly, he deposited his passenger on a cold slimy rock beside a Lord of Death. Leering with jagged teeth and hollow round eyes, the skeleton-limbed form with grotesquely bloated belly let out a foul-smelling fart in greeting. He nodded in recognition, twirling a wand of clacking jawbones in his own bony fingers.

What do you want here? You returned to life. Your time is not yet.

I come on a vision quest, she replied. No words were spoken, their consciousnesses communicated. The decay-smelling, disgusting Lord nodded for her to continue.

I am here to see Chan Hun.

He is not finished here. He is still cooking.

I demand to see him.

By what right do you speak such to a Lord of Death?

By the right of my love. Bring him forth.

Ha! The Lord of Death laughed heartily. *You will not like what you see.*

Bring him forth in the form that I last saw. She had no idea where this bravado came from, but she was extremely clear about what she wanted.

You have courage. Your goddess stands behind you. The required blood rituals have been done. I will comply.

Suddenly she was on a beach, where tall crashing waves made ripples of foam on the sand and a vast sea stretched to the far horizon where it blended into a slate gray sky. The atmosphere was still colored hazy gray-blue and seemed to be watery. Wind blew against her face, refreshing salt-tinged gusts that washed away the Underworld stench. It was the eastern shore of the island she visited with Chan Hun's expedition, the edge of the Great Waters of the East. She felt his presence. He was nearby.

Looking right and left, at first she saw nothing. Then gradually a form materialized out of the haze, standing ankle-deep in the water as waves made eddies around his feet.

Chan Hun!

The young warrior stood straight, his muscled chest and thighs bare; only a small waist and loincloth covered his middle. The wind whipped long strands of black hair hanging from his topknot across his face. As she moved closer, for he seemed unable to move, he smiled and her heart melted as his full sensuous lips parted to reveal shining gems in white teeth, and brought out his faint dimple. His eyes danced with joy to see her. He spoke wordlessly, directly into her consciousness.

Beloved, goddess of my heart, you have come to me!

I promised I would find you, wherever you went.

What love you have to brave this fearsome place, for me.

The depths of my love for you will never be plumbed, Chan Hun.

This I believe. Nor mine for you. Are you well?

Now I am. I almost died. I thought my heart was dead when you were killed.

But you live. I am consoled, you shape my heart, xapatbon kolonton.

She hesitated, but had to ask.

Was your dying terrible? Did they torture you? I could not bear to think of it, and became sick of heart and body.

Dying is easy, Yalucha. His face was grave and calm with the peace that passes all understanding. *It is living that is difficult. Yes, I was tortured. What is torture? People torture themselves every day with diseases of body and mind. They are tortured by emotions, by lacking, by jealousy, by impossible yearnings. Women endure torture in childbirth, and shed sacred blood to bring a new life into the world. Suffering is part of the human condition. When we take life we seek suffering, so we can mentor our souls. Here in the Underworld the soul cooks more, remnants are stewed away, until we become the refined essence of divine ch'ulel.*

What then? Will you come back? She had always wanted to understand this mystery.

The perfected soul-essence is never lost. The tests of the Lords of Death can be won with cunning and determination, but you must understand and play their game, as did the Hero Twins. In the deepest reaches of Xibalba the worlds turn back upon themselves. From the womb-tomb of First Mother at the very heart of Xibalba, the Underworld becomes the Overworld. The dying sun in the west is resurrected into the rising sun in the east. The soul likewise is resurrected, we become ch'ul ahauob—Lords of Life-Force. Then we choose. Life on earth again or return to cosmic source.

He looked at her with profound, soul-permeated love flowing from endless depths in his black eyes. She felt their soul-essences merging, uniting, enveloped in raptures that surpassed all ecstasies she had ever experienced. They were one, forever, indelibly.

I will come again to live and love you.

The wind whipped more strongly, tossing strands of his unruly hair like snake tendrils dancing wildly around his head. He turned his head slightly as if listening to a faraway call. The sea waves were rising up his legs as if the tide was coming in.

Beloved, I am called back. I must finish my work here. He looked again intensely at her. *You must live your life fully, Yalucha, in all its terrible beauty. Do not hold back. Marry Chitam, have children. Do your healing. Honor your goddess.*

No!

She cried desperately, sensing his form becoming less distinct.

I love you! I cannot marry another. My body was meant to bear your children, not Chitam's.

What is the difference? We are all of the same star-seed. The blood of the same First Mother and First Father flows in our veins. Is your love so narrow that it cannot include Chitam? He is a good man and he loves you. Have his children, Yalucha. I will be there; I will always be with you.

Now he was backing into the crashing waves, his form fading and dissolving. Throwing her one last captivating smile, he turned and dove into the high surf, disappearing from her vision.

Chan Hun! Chan Hun!

"Chan Hun! Chan Hun!" The sound of her voice startled Yalucha into dazed awareness. Blinking, she looked at the crumbling embers in the wide-mouthed cup that gave a faint glow in the small vision quest room. She was back in her family's temple, sitting in the moonlit night. Owls hooted softly in the distance. A nearby cricket chirped rhythmically. She had returned home, after venturing into the horrifying domain of the Underworld. She had found Chan Hun as she promised.

He loved her from beyond the portals of death, through all the worlds, until the ends of time itself. And he had given her a mandate: live and love.

*   *   *   *   *

Yalucha settled herself carefully on a cushion placed upon the woven reed mat covering the outer platform. Her perineum was still tender from childbirth, so she sat off center onto one hip. Leaning back against the wall, she loosened ties of her over blouse and put the baby to her breast with a contented sigh. Glancing down at the tiny face with eyes tightly squeezed shut, the new mother smiled as the baby's little mouth hungrily latched onto her nipple. She released herself to the mildly erotic sensations of the baby's strong suckling. Her daughter, only a few kins old, was perfect, beautiful, and vigorous. It was good that her second child was a girl.

Looking up from where she sat, Yalucha's eyes scanned the small garden behind the house for her son. The toddler was stooping between tall squash bushes, already bearing bright golden gourds. Something crawling on the ground claimed his undivided attention. The boy was now nearly two tuns old, and was growing rapidly. He glanced up momentarily at his mother, assuring himself that she was close by, and babbled unintelligible syllables in some melodic language of his own. Then he re-focused on the insects drawing his small mind into fascination with nature's wondrous creatures.

As her eyes met her son's across the garden, Yalucha felt the faint whirring of hummingbird wings around her heart. From the moment of his birth, she had seen Chan Hun in his eyes. It was just a hint, a whisper of that indomitable spirit whose unfailing love surrounded her whenever she opened her awareness to its presence.

392

The boy's slender angular face with thin beaked nose and lips clearly carried the heritage of Chitam. He would never be handsome as Chan Hun. But her love for her son was full and complete, nothing was held back.

She enjoyed her house, an addition to the family compound of Yo'nal Ac, the Chief Daykeeper Priest and her father-in-law. Chitam was quite proud of the home that he had constructed. There was a separate small chamber set aside for prayers and meditation. He wanted his wife to have space for practicing her religion and keeping talismans of Ix Chel, her patron goddess. This and many other smaller concessions to her differing views never ceased to warm Yalucha's heart. Chitam was a good man, sensitive and caring. He was also ambitious and opinionated, but she did not fault him for that. So were most men, to some degree. At times his constricted views of women's place bumped uneasily against her free-spirited ways, but his deep regard for her and desire to make her happy loosened him considerably.

Chitam was grateful that Yalucha had agreed to marriage. He had come close to losing her, first to serious illness and then to her independent-mindedness that he feared would override her parents' wishes. For uinals after her illness she seemed off in some distant world, disinterested in him and everyday life. But to his unending delight, once he began courting her more intently, she accepted his suit and the marriage was arranged.

Yalucha did come to love Chitam. Not with the soul stirring, cellular magic of her love for Chan Hun, but with a gentle love of kindness and regard. Her love deepened as the children arrived and Chitam became a playful, caring father. Their life together was good. She often joined her mother at their family compound temple to minister to the sick and perform ceremonies sacred to Ix Chel. In this, Chitam was most supportive.

The young mother reflected on the indomitable human spirit that could overcome so many griefs and wounds. The embodied soul seemed to adjust to life, however tenuous or difficult it might be. Miraculously, it found some sources of happiness welling up through pools of suffering and muck of despair. Or, was happiness simply the soul's normal state when it released itself from the bonds of suffering? Suffering, she concluded, was not the price of living, but part of the gift of being alive. As Chan Hun had told her, suffering and death developed the soul, honed its mettle and prepared it to transcend all lesser qualities until it became the perfected White

393

Flower Thing, sak-nik-nal. In this state it was one with the Overworld gods. Then was produced the wondrous blossom, the being who embodied dignified grace in the face of both triumph and disaster, in all the three worlds.

Mutul prospered and its people lived in abundance. Under the astute leadership of the lords from Teotihuacan, the city-state became the dominant power in the lowlands. The city enjoyed relative peace due to the widely reputed strength and ferocity of its warriors, who remained loyal to the succession decreed by their deceased king. Yax Ain married the daughter of Chak Toh Ich'ak and mingled the royal bloodline from the Mexica Empire with that of the Jaguar Claw lineage of Mutul. He gained accession as Mutul ahau in the long-fabled opulent ceremonies of 8.17.2.16.17 (September 13, 379 CE). His descendants went to great lengths to reaffirm on many stelae and monuments their direct descent from the founder of the Jaguar Claw lineage. In the long run, the jaguar subsumed the owl.

Eighteen tuns after the conquest of Uaxactun, Mutul prepared for katun end ceremonies once again, the katun of 8.18.0.0.0 (July 8, 396 CE). K'ak Sih conducted the high rituals at Uaxactun and Yax Ain led those of Mutul.[18] In the family compound of K'an Nab Ku the priestesses of Ix Chel performed their traditional katun end rituals in their small temple. Yalucha now took primary responsibility, as her mother was older and less vigorous. In this ritual, the priestesses sought to look farther ahead than the coming katun. An unrest within Yalucha from a subterranean current, running silent and deep, ushered forth this quest.

As the tuns went by, the longing in her heart for her soul-companion increased. This surprised her; she had imagined it would be the opposite. Memories of Chan Hun and subtle awareness of his spirit presence became more frequent and strong. Despite her full life, raising children, overseeing a household, doing healing work and sacred ceremonies, she felt incomplete. She sensed there was something more, yet other layers in the endless creative process of developing the soul. And her soul was inextricably connected with Chan Hun's soul. When her children matured and left home, she delved with growing urgency into the domain of the Otherworld.

---

[18] Stela 4 at Uaxactun and Stela 18 at Tikal depicted the katun end ceremonies, naming K'ak Sih (Smoking Frog) as Uaxactun ahau and Yax Ain as Mutul ahau, calling him "the noble of" K'ak Sih.

Many times the lightening bolt of K'awil cracked through her forehead sending her into ecstatic trance. She did shamanic work more often now with this third-born son of First Mother and First Father, brother of the Hero Twins, the divine life force they used to triumph over death. The serpent-legged lightening-struck god transmitted the creative force of the great mystery in its most powerful form, the powers of manifestation, energy transformation and enlightenment. She drew itz, life-giving substance into her being, and increased her abilities as a seer. Though often left dazed and reeling from the immensity and violence of the self-resurrecting universe that she experienced in these trances, she knew the secrets she sought would be revealed there.

In these numerous visioning journeys she undertook, none had taken her again to direct contact with Chan Hun. Where he might be, and how to navigate the multi-layered domains of the Otherworld to find him, perplexed and eluded her. She sensed that a vast unfolding of time was destined to take place before their souls would be reunited. But they would find each other, they would be reunited, of this she had no doubt. This was the sacred promise, the vow of unending love, they had made.

The priestess took advantage of the special energetics of the katun end, a moment in the cycle of sacred time when stellar bodies and time currents aligned magically. She plunged more deeply into the misty world of unmanifest potential than ever before. Swept forth on the currents of time, she peered into Mutul's future. The rising and falling fortunes of her great city played out like sand castles forming and dissolving in the capricious surf. Periods of immense power, nadirs of brutal subjugation, and a culminating phase of deterioration and decline were shown to her. Sky-spearing pyramid temples of unimaginable majesty, legacies of remarkable Jaguar Claw kings yet to come, rose above the verdant jungles to be slowly overtaken by climbing vines and squatter trees, turned into forested mountains. Deserted capitals once teeming with life, vast plazas reclaimed by jungle brush, long sakbeob leading nowhere into a sea of greenness. Pride and conquest of kings, katuns of warfare, failing crops, denuded landscapes, droughts, abandonment by the gods, deprived peoples rising against nobles, all played into the decline and disappearance of the great Maya civilization.

But the Maya wisdom must not be lost. They must preserve their profound understanding of the workings within celestial cycles and earthly rhythms, and how the Three Worlds of humans and their gods interplayed. This knowledge and the techniques through which it was accessed were the legacy of her people. She was given the charge to do her part in keeping this legacy alive, in saving it from obliteration through the churning upheavals of the devouring earth, swallowing and digesting her creatures in endless cycles of comings and goings, death and rebirth. She saw the Maya wisdom going underground for long time periods, kept secret and hidden from naïve and destructive foreigners. In some way that was not yet made clear, she would perform service to this necessity in the future.

In a heroic outpouring of willpower, she wrestled with the Otherworld denizens for information about Chan Hun. Was her beloved still struggling with tests in the dark chasms of Xibalba? Had he been outsmarted by the wily Lords of Death, become another human soul-prize stashed away in the deep earth of the Underworld, food for their blood lust? Or, had he perfected his soul, this White Flower Thing of exquisite beauty and radiance, and joined the Overworld gods as an ancestor? Perhaps, but then she could invoke him through the vision serpent. Might he have chosen to return to source, past the Central Sun, to the Star Sisters who seeded her people? No, for he promised that he would come to her. He might be once again in the Middleworld, growing up in a distant city, his soul calling forth another human body.

The pure power of her love drew a small hint from the secretive tricksters of otherworldly domains. Brief images of a handsome young king, in a city of lovely symmetry, in a land of dry and open terrain, appeared before her. And there were other glimpses, different faces, lands she could not fathom. Chan Hun would return. And she knew, from this place of shadowy potential holding the seeds of every manifestation, that she would be there also.

Mérida, the White City, was laid out in a grid. Streets radiated like spokes from the downtown core, El Centro Historico. Many streets were narrow and one-way; taking unexpected twists that easily disoriented unfamiliar drivers. A loop road, Anillo Periferico, encircled the city borders, providing a bypass of the crowded interior and access to regional destinations without struggling through downtown congestion.

In the blazing heat of mid-afternoon, Jana maneuvered the old red VW bug through narrow downtown streets congested with heavy traffic. She kept the marked map from Turista Car Rentals on the seat beside her, glancing at it frequently to assure her directions but loath to take her eyes off the road. Driving was made challenging by trucks parked in traffic lanes to unload, a practice that was rampant judging from how often she had to stop, wait for an opening, then scoot around the obstacle. Vespa motor scooters and beat-up bikes with grocery-laden baskets wove between cars at risk of life and limb. Autos, taxis, busses, trucks roared and rambled erratically as everyone jockeyed for passing positions. At least horn use was modest, a small boon to her rattled nerves.

Calle 59 seemed interminable. It was the spoke taking Jana from El Centro to the loop road, where she would connect with the highway to Chichén Itzá. Buildings gradually changed from lovely pastel structures to shabby brick and wood of dull brown or gray. People were everywhere, crossing streets, walking on curbs, browsing at shops. The siesta time was over, but the heat had not diminished one degree. Jana worried that she had taken a wrong turn, as street signs were unreliable, often missing or bent at rakish angles. Finally arriving at Anillo Periferico, she drove along the wide multi-lane road to the highway intersection. There she pulled into a gas station to fill up; the VW bug had less than a half-tank and she felt uncertain about finding gas in the smaller towns.

Standing outside the car, a slight breeze under the shaded overhang evaporated some sweat, providing a touch of coolness. Her clothes were wet and stuck to her skin. As she loosened them and cooled down, she realized she was hungry. There had been no time for lunch. She had brought along a bag of trail mix from home, and taken the bottled water provided in the hotel room. She munched the nuts and dried fruit thankfully, taking long sips of luke-warm water.

Because she was sweating so much, very little was collecting in her bladder but she went to the bathroom anyway, preventively.

Leaving Mérida, Jana took the free road to Chichén Itzá, not feeling confident enough to handle a Mexican toll road. She had the hang of driving the VW bug, but was unprepared for heat blowing up from the floorboard. Waves of oven-temperature heat coursed up her feet and legs, baking her body and face. Hot wind blowing in through the open windows was only a degree or two less intense than what was coming from the floorboard. Ironically, it felt to her like one continuous maximum level hot flash. Inside her core temperature must be elevated, giving the same uneasy, irritating feeling. Maybe she was having hot flashes, too. Who could tell—heat outside, inside, all around.

The drive to Piste was the hottest, wettest experience Jana could remember. Every inch of her body was covered with sweat. Her clothes did not have a dry ounce. Although the moisture covering her body evaporated, she immediately sweated more in the searing humidity. Salty sweat dripping over her elbows caused the raw scrape from her fall that morning to burn. It brought her to the point of sincere regret that she had not paid additional for an air-conditioned car.

Small villages dotted the two-lane road at regular intervals. Stucco and wood buildings abutted the road in dense clusters, relieved by occasional open, grassy plazas. Large cement speed bumps, called *topes,* marked the passage through villages. Jana could readily appreciate the need for reducing traffic speeding along the highway, as the villages had considerable pedestrians and loose animals. The VW bug bumped and groaned as she eased it over the mountainous obstacles.

Although she looked around for village names, most did not have signs. Even storefronts were sparsely marked, giving few clues to their merchandize. In the fifth or sixth village along the route, she stopped at a plaza with several open stalls. Spotting a stall with textiles, she bought a colorful striped tote bag just the right size to hold her newly acquired spirit doll of the Maya priestess, Yalucha. Another booth offered cold sodas. Drinking a Fanta orange in honor of Robert, who loved these overly sweet citrus relics of his boyhood, she wistfully wondered what her husband was doing at that moment. It was Friday mid-afternoon; he would be finished with his class. Maybe he was having a latte with Harry at the Rothwell Center patio, a practice he was fond of doing. A distinctly clear image of this scene materialized momentarily in her vision. Her heart yearning rushed out to Robert as his handsome features appeared to her.

With a sinking sensation in her stomach, she recalled their conflict before she left for the Yucatan. She had never seen Robert so angry. Alienation and tensions had never before persisted between them for such an extended time. His emotional coldness frightened her. Had she done irreparable harm to their relationship? Was following this calling worth losing Robert? Maybe she had made the wrong choice. Despite her dehydration, a few tears slipped from her eyes, adding to the wetness of her face.

She continued the grueling, roasting drive. There were long stretches of open countryside between villages. The mostly flat terrain baked tan and gray-green in the relentless afternoon sun. Scrubby brush struggled to survive, short trees lifted scraggly limbs as leaves hung listlessly in the still air. Dry grasses and rocks gave no indication of life. It was a harsh, unsightly environment.

The heat and monotonous countryside put Jana into a semi-hypnotic state. She drove the noisy heat-spewing VW bug on automatic pilot, her mind blank and hazy. There were longer stretches between villages, with little around to attract her attention. Subliminally, her vision caught and barely registered an intersection sign on the right. Instantaneously the thought of Yalucha, the Maya priestess erupted into her mind along with an intense sense of danger. An explosion of adrenalin jerked her into total awareness.

It was just in time to turn her head slightly to the right, and see through the corner of her eyes that a car was pulling out from the intersection, directly in her path. With split-second coordination, her reflexes leapt into survival mode. Her foot slammed on the brakes while her hands jerked the steering wheel right, acting upon lower brain commands beyond thought. The VW lurched and screeched, sliding sideways onto the shoulder and barely missing the rear of the other car as it turned onto the road. Hard bumps from the rocky shoulder jarred her teeth, while she clenched the steering wheel to brace her body. Swerving left, she maneuvered the VW back onto the highway, still moving forward at a moderate speed.

She glanced in the rear-view mirror, able to see the battered dark blue car weaving erratically in the opposite direction. There did not seem to be a driver. She could not see a head above the seat, but the car's windows were cracked and dusty, reducing visibility. A trail of black smoke belched from its tailpipe.

Jana gunned the VW bug and roared off. She wanted to get away from that car, to put distance between them. Soon she rounded a curve and lost sight of it. Then she slowed down, realizing she was driving much too fast for road conditions. Another village with large speed bumps caused her to focus on driving carefully. She cautiously scanned each intersection before proceeding. Her heart was still pounding, and she was sweating even more profusely, as impossible as that seemed. A wave of faintness and shakiness caused her to pull to the roadside and sit for a few minutes, though she left the engine running.

Where did that car come from? Who was driving it—was anyone driving it? Maybe someone so small and stooped they could barely see through the steering wheel . . . like the old shaman—brujo— from Tikal!

The omens of destruction, death and war were all around her. The parched lifeless landscape, the suffocating heat, the war in Iraq, the close call with a driverless car materializing from nowhere—eerie forces were at work. Would she have to forfeit her life to fulfill this mission?

Her mind tried to wrap itself around the near-collision. She replayed events leading up to the encounter, seeking every possible detail. She was sleepy, driving on automatic, not paying close attention. Then she barely noticed an intersection sign. What happened next? It was all so fast, she didn't have time for thoughts. Right before the car pulled out in front of her, something alerted her to danger. What was it?

Oh, yes! It was an image of Yalucha. She must have warned me.

Jana recalled it clearly now, how the image of the priestess flooded her mind and brought her to instant alertness. She felt immense gratitude flowing through her heart, and said a prayer of thanks. And the amber pendant. She touched it under her wet shirt, feeling comforted and protected. She recalled the old woman's words, at the booth by the cathedral where she bought the spirit doll:

"Amber protects the priestess."

Despite the frightening experience, she felt oddly calm. Her guides were with her. She had allies against the dark shamanic forces trying to dissuade her from continuing. Breathing deeply and slowly, she spread this calmness into her nerves and cells. The shakiness and weakness resolved; she shifted the VW's wobbly gears and proceeded along the highway to Piste.

The pleasant hacienda-style posada (small hotel) in Piste wrapped long rectangular wings around verdant grasses lining the geometric swimming pool. Stunning aqua waters contrasted with white flagstones, arching palm trees hung serrated fronds over umbrella shaded patio tables. It was an oasis of cool green and blue calmness in the busy, steaming town. Inside a refreshingly darkened room with window air-conditioner, Jana threw off her wet clothes and went straight into the shower. Rejoicing, refreshing cool water streamed on her over-heated body. It was physical bliss beyond words. She then lay naked on the bed, allowing cool air to blow across her tingling skin.

She drifted into delicious semi-sleep, exhausted yet strangely invigorated. It would be a power nap, focused and short, taking only one hour since she had to meet Hanab Xiu's group at Ik Kil by 6:00 pm. Although part of her brain stayed alert to time, and she did not fall into deep sleep, when the hour was up she felt refreshed.

Ik Kil was a fifteen-minute drive from the posada, taking Jana past the entrance to Chichén Itzá and the Mayaland hotel. She noted the guard house and lift gate that protected the entrance to the upscale hotel, wondering how she would get in tomorrow to meet the group in the hotel lobby. It was too far to walk from the posada.

The grounds at Ik Kil resort were lovely and well tended. Dark wood structures with palm thatch roofs gave a mysterious jungle feeling. Profusions of flowering plants added exotic color: bright pink bougainvillea, yellow and red birds of paradise, creamy white tree blossoms, purple salvia. A huge banyan tree sent limb-roots into the ground below, making its massive girth larger than the VW bug that Jana parked next to it. The tour bus had not yet arrived. Slinging the colorful tote bag containing the priestess spirit doll over one shoulder, Jana followed signs to the cenote next to the restaurant.

A solid stone wall, waist-high, protected visitors from stepping over the edge into the 50 foot limestone sinkhole. Jana peered over the wall, admiring the deep blue water far below. White limestone cliffs offered narrow perches for small clusters of plants. Long gray roots hung down from ground level like thick strands of hair, their distant ends dipping into the water. Swallows chirped and cut graceful acrobatics around hanging roots to find their nesting places. At the back of the cenote a stairway led down to water level. Paved with small flagstones, the well-maintained stairway descended to the cooler depths, a welcome respite from the still hot afternoon.

Jana stood at the water's edge, enjoying the dampness and trickling liquid sounds. Looking up gave a better view of the hanging roots that lined the entire round sinkhole. Formed by the collapse of underground caves that were carved over centuries by deep rivers under the limestone terrain, cenotes were the life-sustaining essence for Maya cities in the Yucatan. Called *tz'onot* in Mayan, cenotes were always filled with water percolating through the limestone, although some could be as far from the surface as 100 feet. Often cenotes were accessed by rope ladders suspended from ground level. Jana imagined the strenuous daily task of descending into cenotes with clay jugs, hauling them up while heavy with precious water, and carrying them to the village.

The sound of a bus engine alerted her that the group had arrived. She quickly ascended the stairway and found the tour bus unloading in the nearly empty parking lot. Greeting Aurora Nakin and her friends, she fell in line as the group went into the restaurant for dinner. A couple of carloads of new people pulled up and joined their group. Julia informed Jana these were members of the European group who would be participating in the ceremony tomorrow. It was certainly going to be an international affair; there were German, Italian, French and British members, all connected in some way with Hanab Xiu. Jana was impressed by the unassuming Maya elder's following.

Dinner was a real treat for Jana, who by now had developed a voracious appetite. The buffet offered an abundance of vegetarian dishes, and she thoroughly enjoyed the mixed steamed squashes, pureed black beans, rice, fresh fruit and salad. There were at least two meat dishes prepared in ways that bore no resemblance to what Americans thought was Mexican cuisine. A hubbub of voices in several languages filled the dining area, where about 80 people sat at long tables. Jana was happy just to be there.

It was twilight when dinner ended and the group moved outside to gather on the green lawn beside the restaurant. A makeshift sound system had been rigged with two speakers and a hand-held microphone for Hanab Xiu. Two Germans set up a video camera and lights behind the group, as people settled into a large semi-circle on the ground. The hum of conversation died down as Hanab Xiu began the teaching in preparation for tomorrow's equinox ceremony at Chichén Itzá.

"We are in the Baktun of the Transformation of Matter," began Hanab Xiu. "Baktun 12, the thirteenth cycle, the closing of the Maya

Great Cycle, the ending of the Maya Long Count Calendar, the shifting of the ages. What comes next? The end of the world and of life as we know it? Many of you will be surprised when I say 'yes.' But this ending is also a beginning. The world that ends is the world of materialism, of technical progress, of believing humans are separate from nature. The life that we know of, where machines and artificial foods dominate industrial societies, where most people live in poverty and lack while the privileged few drown in a wealth of excesses, where the environment is destroyed as its gifts are exploited, this is the life that is ending.

"And it needs to end. Its time is over. It is told in the star patterns, in the cosmic cycles, in the process of planetary evolution. Earth is soon entering Baktun Zero, the first Baktun of the next Great Cycle, the Fifth Sun, the start of another round in the Precession of the Equinoxes. That will happen in your Gregorian year of 2012, at the Winter Solstice. For the Maya, it is said in this way: 13.0.0.0.0. The solstice sun, First Father, will rise through the dark rift of the Milky Way, the birth canal of Great Mother. Together they will conceive the New Age, the Fifth Sun, their child of consciousness upon the planet. This great event will be nothing less than the collective re-patterning of human consciousness. Our cells, our DNA, they are changing as the sun bombards us with rays that alter our very essence.

"We are being changed through the electromagnetic field. This field that surrounds the planet has decreased rapidly in the past several years. When it was stronger in the past, it affected human consciousness by creating the illusion of separation, it protected the underdeveloped human mind from energies outside ourselves. Most of us were not prepared to deal with outside energies. We could not handle expanded consciousness and feeling oneness with all. The planet's very vibrations were slow and heavy. But since the Harmonic Convergence in 1987, there's been a measurable increase of energy. Earth resonated, vibrated at a base frequency of 8 Hz per second for thousands of years. During this time Earth was essentially asleep, we were asleep to our true being. Now Earth's resonance has risen above 13 Hz per second. She is vibrating faster, higher, with greater energy. Humans are waking up. Many of us are thinking in different ways, we are feeling our connections with each other and the planet. We experience energies coming into ourselves. Our barriers are dropping, we are getting more sensitive. This is hard for some people. Their bodies and minds suffer from being too sensitive.

403

"You are all here because you are sensitive." He waved his arms to include the entire group. "You are sensitive to the pain of others, to the suffering of creatures, to the Earth's cries for harmony. You are here because you want to help. You know, deep in your bones, that what was known to the first people, those who lived in accord with nature, is still known by the indigenous people of the world. You want to use your sensitivity to become united with this indigenous wisdom, so you become a vessel for it. And you are a vessel. Tonight you will learn to become a more perfect, a more powerful vessel.

"I will tell you some things. Things you need to understand, things you need to practice. So you can be sensitive, so you can be open to energies, be in unity while still keeping your physical vessel healthy. You cannot help by becoming sick or weakened yourself. To do this work you must be strong and healthy."

Hanab Xiu paused. It was almost dark, a few stars beginning to flicker in an indigo sky. The video crew turned on spotlights, making his white-clad form glow against the velvet darkness.

Jana was sitting between Julia and Steve, her mind making rapid associations as Hanab Xiu spoke.

Being strong, caring through strength—that was in the message from Ix Chel in the cathedral. This sensitivity . . . must be the things I'm experiencing inside, the communications from the spirit domain . . . and the impossible outside events, the old woman by the cathedral, the apparently driverless car in my near-accident— sensitivity that makes me receptive, able to link with liminal energies moving through portals, openings to other dimensions.

The everyday world of people with these kinds of sensitivities would be totally different than what most experienced, Jana thought. She glanced around at the 80 people from multiple countries sitting in rapt attention, listening to the words of ancient wisdom from a contemporary Maya shaman, preparing to enact a ceremony in a ruined city with mystical ties to cosmic forces. It was as unlikely a scene as she could imagine.

At the far edge of the group she could barely recognize Evita, sitting by her husband Jorje where the shadow merged into darkness. Very nearby sat Fire Eagle, his erect posture revealing unwavering vigilance. A shiver went up Jana's spine; she was grateful for Fire Eagle's monitoring presence.

"This is something you must understand, must know inside from your heart," continued Hanab Xiu. "It is a most difficult teaching. I will say it then I will explain it.

"Choose love in every circumstance.

"That sounds simple, yes? But it is not simple. If you have any anger, any fear, any criticism, envy, blame, doubt, frustration, hopelessness—then you are choosing the energies of fear. You are letting fear vibrations attune your consciousness. When fear is there, it crowds out love. Here is the challenge:

"Mother Earth has two sons. The older son is the indigenous peoples, the younger son is the technological peoples. Both sons want to experience a different relationship with her, their Mother. The older son wants to live in harmony, to nurture and caretake her. The younger son wants to explore and experiment, to create things himself from the mother's materials. He wants to push the limits of nature and to experience everything possible. The Mother doesn't see one son as good and the other as bad. She loves all her children the same. She offers all her children everything they want. Any experience they want, they can have it. But she knows there are consequences for what the children do, and they will meet those consequences.

"You are all worried about this war. I tell you this: it was inevitable. The energy patterns that produced it were formed long ago. This was known to the elders, to the indigenous sons. There were two potentials in those energy patterns. One potential was a war that set off global disaster, that killed millions and decimated the land, that changed life forms on the earth. The other potential was a limited war that brought great havoc and suffering to people of the involved countries, but did not spread across the world. The timing of the war was critical—if it happened before the equinox it would be limited, if it happened afterwards it would be global.

"And you see, it happened before. Just before, at the last moment. But before the shift of cosmic patterns that would lead to disaster. Was this just a coincidence? Did we all simply get lucky?

"No. You see, the choices that are made by Mother Earth's sons, all her peoples, influence what shape her material reality takes. They affect what kind of relationship she has to all her children, creatures as well as humans. It was close, but the collective choices of enough people, the conscious energies of their thoughts, the vibrations of their hearts affected which potential came to be.

"Enough people were choosing love and harmony over anger and fear and hatred. Maybe it wasn't a perfect choice, maybe a little cloudy, but enough. Now I will teach you to make more perfect choices, use more pure intentions, so the reality we collectively create on Mother Earth is what we truly desire. You all, and millions of people, pray for peace. You all desire harmony with nature, balance and compassion in relations with others. Why is there so much conflict? Why do wars continue to happen? Why do so many people suffer and why is the environment getting more disrupted?

"Because you are praying from your minds. When you create anything from your mind, you set in process the energy of opposites. That is because the mind operates in dualities, it cannot help but perceive this way. It is the nature of the mind. The mind separates things into parts, it breaks them down into little sections, it compares them with other things in order to understand them. All duality must have its opposite: love-hate, hot-cold, up-down, light-dark, peace-war. Desiring the one inevitably produces the other. You cannot create from the mind without also bringing forth the opposite of what you seek. This secret of creating was long known to indigenous peoples.

"To create without duality, you must use the heart. You must pray from the heart, express your intentions through the heart. Then what you truly desire can come into being. I will now teach you a very ancient way of praying and creating from the heart. This was also known to indigenous peoples from long-ago times. But it has been forgotten by many."

Hanab Xiu paused and looked around. He signaled for a chair, and settled onto the small folding chair an attendant brought forth.

"Sit upright, feel your body relaxed but alert," he said. "Close your eyes. Can we get the lights dimmed?"

The video crew quickly lowered their floodlights. Velvety darkness of tropical night settled on the group. Myriads of stars twinkled overhead, but the moon had not yet risen. Chirping night insects sent forth their calls on the gentle breeze, just enough to provide refreshing coolness. Intense anticipation emanated from the group.

"Now we will journey to the sacred space of the heart.

"With eyes closed, focus attention on your breathing. Make the inbreath and outbreath equal, rhythmic, smooth. Let go of thoughts, of worries for now. Keep breathing for a few minutes until you feel relaxed, releasing all tensions."

Silence ensued for several minutes. Jana felt calmness enveloping her as she followed her breath, a technique she used quite often. Her mind was empty, open, receptive.

"You must prepare yourself for entering the heart, which we do for any important ceremony, by making connection with Mother

Earth and Father Sky," Hanab Xiu continued. "The indigenous people always do this, it creates the proper state of mind and heart, it connects you in love and honor with your sources of being. If you do not make this connection, the sacred space of the heart becomes elusive. You will not find it.

"To connect with Mother Earth, bring into your awareness a place on earth that is most beautiful to you. A place where you feel peaceful, safe, joyful, full of delight. It can be anywhere, real or imagined. Maybe a magnificent snow-covered mountain, a lovely meadow full of flowers, a serene lake or babbling brook, deep forests, seashores, vast desert expanses, islands in an azure sea—whatever you perceive as beautiful. See as much detail as you can. Not everyone sees with inner vision. Some sense or feel the beauty of this place, some hear the sounds it makes. Everyone has their own way. Just be with your beautiful place in nature, feel the love you have for it and for Mother Earth who gives you this place. Let this love fill your heart and flow into your entire body. When you are so filled with love that it is bursting out, use your intention to send it down deep into Earth, to the very center of Earth. Send your love to Mother Earth, your Divine Mother, who gave you form to walk on this planet. Let her know how much you love her. Then wait, and receive, the love Mother Earth sends back to you."

He paused for a moment. Jana was vibrating with profound connections to Earth, feeling energy tendrils pulsing deep into its core. Her heart ached with the exquisite beauty of this blue and green planet, wrapped in white clouds. Soon she felt indescribably sweet emanations, full of love beyond measure, vibrating upward from Earth into her body. This loving connection flowed back and forth between Jana and Mother Earth. She had never felt so deeply united with Earth before, or so appreciative of the precious gift of life on this planet.

"Now, without breaking your connection with Mother Earth, gradually shift your awareness to the night sky," Hanab Xiu said softly. "Become aware of the stars, moon and planets, the Milky Way, swirling galaxies, the entire vast universe. Feel the immense power of the Sun, our star, which awakens life in our world with its light and heat. Feel the love you have for the rest of existence beyond our world, for Father Sky, the Divine Father. This is the cosmic intelligence that organizes the universe. This intelligence dances in our DNA, informs every cell of its unity with the source of all creation. Let this love fill your heart, and when your heart is full, send your love up to Father Sky. With your intention, send it directly to the Divine Father, to the Sun above or to the Central Sun in the middle of our galaxy. Let him know how much you love him. Then wait and receive the love Father Sky sends back."

Jana's consciousness was soaring in outer space, flying among stars and nebulae. The indigo darkness dotted with shining stellar bodies and glowing gasses was unbelievably beautiful. She felt powerful cords of energy spouting from her crown into the vast distances of the universe. Upon Hanab Xiu's instruction, she directed these cords toward the Sun in awed respect. Like a spinning vortex, the Sun projected her energy into the center of the Milky Way. Immediately she felt energy returning, bringing an immensely expanded awareness that was pristine and impersonal. It seemed to include all potential, all time, all manifestations of being in the entire universe. She could only sense this immensity of awareness, for it over-arched the mind's capacity. It felt infinite, unending, without beginning, without condition. It simply was.

And, it was an infinitely, unconditionally loving consciousness. Although very different, it was no less loving that the palpable, cellular sweetness of the Mother's love. These two love sources joined together inside Jana's heart, as Hanab Xiu spoke again.

"When the Divine Father and Divine Mother's love unites inside, you become the Divine Child. The Holy Trinity becomes alive on earth, within you, at this moment. It is most sacred. You are a tiny drop of the sky and the earth, spirit and matter, joined together. In this state, you can directly know God, the Divine Being. Just feel this union of cosmic forces, know you are one with Spirit.

"Now you are ready to enter the sacred space of the heart.

"Place your awareness inside your head, position yourself behind your eyes. You may want to open your eyes briefly to orient yourself to this ordinary way of seeing."

Jana opened her eyes, but everything looked blurry. She blinked then rubbed moisture from her lids. The lighting was dim, making Hanab Xiu appear as an ephemeral white shadow while those at the edges of the group were lost in darkness. Quickly she closed her eyes again, but kept herself oriented behind her outward looking eyes.

"Inside your head, feel how hard your skull is. See or sense the brightness inside your brain from incoming light signals and firing nerve cells. The skull space has a vibration, it is the sound of 'Om.' Make this sound with your voice, feel how it resonates inside the skull."

408

The group sounded "Om" softly, in varying keys blending into a multi-toned swell.

"Then, begin to allow your awareness to slip down from your head to your throat. Sense yourself in your throat, slipping farther down into your upper chest. You are a tiny point of awareness inside a vast body. If you look up you can see your neck, chin and head above, like a huge statue towering overhead. Now look down and slightly left inside your chest, where your heart is located. It is beating, pulsating. It's very big, much, much bigger than you. Set your intention to enter the heart. Move toward it, then slip right through its membrane into its interior.

"You are there. You are inside the sacred space of your heart. It is dark, warm, moving, pulsating. It is very soft, not at all like the hardness of the skull. If there is not enough light to see, just say 'Let there be light.' Look or sense around, notice what is there inside your heart. Listen to the vibration, the sound of the heart. It is the sound of 'Aah' and you may want to make this sound."

Soft breathy "Aah" sounds in lower registers wafted from the group.

"Some of you will know you have been here before, maybe many times. For others this may seem like the first time. In truth, this sacred space is our essence. It is older than anything that exists, before galaxies, before creation. Within this space is memory of everywhere you have been in all creation, everything you have been, your deepest desires and your true purpose for being on Earth. Any question you have can be answered here. Any intention you have can be brought forth from here. I will give you some time to explore the sacred space of your heart."

Jana easily slid inside her throbbing heart, feeling the warm, soft darkness. The rhythmic beats created vibrations that filled the darkness, pulsed against her. Following Hanab Xiu's words, she asked for light inside the heart space. Gradually, like a dimmer switch being turned up, light appeared. It had no specific source, but seemed to emanate from the walls themselves. Jana was surprised at how large the heart space appeared. It was a circular space with glowing walls, almost transparent. What appeared to be two doorways were shrouded in darkness at opposite sides. As she turned to look all around, her amazed awareness noticed a bank of TV or computer screens covering a large section of wall, from top to bottom. Approaching them, she saw each was running a different scenario, like a TV control studio where operators could select from multiple views. Intuitively she knew these screens provided views of her present life, as well as other existences. There were perhaps one hundred screens, and she found it difficult to focus on any one. She remembered to ask a question.

What is my relationship to Yalucha?

Her vision was drawn to one screen. In rapid sequence a series of images played across the screen: a young brown-skinned girl walking across broad white stucco plazas as pyramids towered in the background, dense forests where the girl gathered plants, a young Maya woman in white robes surrounded by smoking incense on a pyramid temple platform. Scenes merged one into another; the young woman was laughing and embracing a young Maya man, running wildly through punishing jungle brush, cooking meals and comforting children, caring for sick people, sitting in silent meditation. Next an older Maya woman appeared, sitting in council with leaders, performing ceremonies on high temple platforms, teaching acolytes, walking alone toward the setting sun.

There was no doubt. This Maya woman was Yalucha. And in some mysterious way, she was also Jana.

The screen darkened, as if it had no more to reveal. Jana continued turning to view her sacred heart space. Opposite the wall of TV screens was a huge picture window. Beyond the window was a white mist, so thick she could not see through it. She went closer and peered through. Faint outlines of terrain were visible, but she could not identify its characteristics. A powerful cord of energy leapt from her heart through the window, toward the filmy landscape. She intensely wanted to go there, to pass through the window but it would not allow her passage. She intuited that she belonged to this landscape, it was her very essence, and she yearned to be there.

This place is my true home, my place of origin.

This came to her as deep knowing, without doubt. And she immediately intuited that if she was allowed to go there now, she would not return. The time was not yet. She was a little surprised at how quickly her heart accepted this knowledge.

Turning more, she continued to examine her heart space. A passage led toward one darkened door, around which she felt swirling, tumultuous energies. Something was in there that was difficult.

It must contain my own darker parts, she thought. Later she would return and explore this passage. It did not feel right to enter now.

Hanab Xiu's voice worked its way slowly into her awareness.
"Now that you have entered the sacred space of the heart," he said, "know that you can return again. There is a great deal you can learn about your life, your purpose on Earth, your past and future existences in this space. For now, I want to bring you to yet a deeper place in your heart, the place where you create without duality. Some call this the heart's secret chamber. It is a small space within the sacred space of the heart. Use your intention, and your intuition, to allow yourself to be guided there. This space is different for each person, but it has very similar qualities. The vibration goes up in pitch. What you feel in this small space is different from other places in the heart. This is the space where creation begins, where the infinite Creator of all life resides within you. It is your point of divinity. All potential, all possibility exists within this space.

"Intend now to be in the secret chamber of your heart."

Jana set her intention and waited. She had been dimly aware that something was in the very center of the round heart space, but had not focused there before. Now her attention was drawn to the center. At first it appeared to be a fountain. A round low wall contained a watery substance, and a tall projection stood in the center. But it was not a fountain and no water cascaded down into the pool below. The tall structure did not have a distinct form, its sides were gossamer strands that undulated slowly, changing shape like filmy cords swinging against each other. Glowing light emanated from the strands. Inside was a flame-like image, but it had crystalline qualities that changed rapidly, moving and shimmering. Focusing more intensely, Jana saw a rapidly spinning clear diamond-faceted object shaped like two pyramids joined at the bases, one pointing up and the other pointing down. As soon as she saw it, her consciousness was sucked inside. She was looking out from the diamond pyramids at the surrounding heart space.

An amazing profusion of spirals, circles and geometric patterns filled her awareness. In an instant she understood the sacred geometries of creation. But it was not something her mind could ever explain. Within this secret chamber, the dynamics of creation already existed, fully perfected and needing only activation.

She brought forth in awareness an image of the world at peace. People of all races and nations sharing, communicating, cooperating. People in harmony with nature, animals, all creatures. Loving awareness that we are all one, one with Earth and the cosmos.

411

Recognizing and acknowledging the divine essence in everyone and everything.

As she sent out this prayer of pure awareness, from the secret chamber within the sacred space of the heart, she understood in some deeply intuitive way that it followed a certain trajectory. Originating from she knew not where—that infinite source of creation—it passed through the seven star cluster of the Pleiades, to the Central Sun in the center of the Milky Way, and from there passed through the Sun of Earth. From the Sun it rained like liquid light onto the Earth, spreading like shining dewdrops along a network of grids that completely surrounded Earth. These grid structures emanated energies that affected vibratory frequencies upon and inside Earth. Atoms, molecules and cells of Earth beings resonated with these vibrations, and were changed.

As if from a vast distance, Jana heard Hanab Xiu's voice and realized he was calling them back. It was hard to leave this sacred space. Slowly she felt her consciousness moving away from the heart's space, going out through the membrane around the heart, retracing its path through the chest, to the neck, throat, and back into her skull. Brightness through closed eyelids alerted her that the floodlights had been turned up. She waited a few moments, adjusting to the light, before opening her eyes.

"So, this is how you consciously co-create with God," Hanab Xiu said. "This is how you create without duality. Only from the deepest place in the heart, the secret chamber in the heart's sacred space, can you bring forth what you truly desire. The heart creates through dreams and images. It does not use logic. There is no reason, no rationality, in this heart space creation. Here you dream into existence what you want. It finds expression through your images, your feelings, your emotions. In a state of purity, in sacred space, you dream and feel into being a new life, a new world.

"This is your divine inheritance, your birthright as sons and daughters of God, the Great Cosmic Spirit. You are always creating; it is your nature to create. Now you can create consciously, aware of the process by which you draw Divine Creation through your body vessel. You become a pure vessel for creating with love, in unity, free of duality. Let us close with a prayer."

He led the group in a simple prayer of gratitude and honored the directions. Aurora Nakin came forth at his signal, took the mike and reviewed instructions for the ceremony tomorrow. Slowly, with little conversation, the group of international pilgrims gathered their belongings and walked to the parking lot.

Leaning against the red VW bug in the Ik Kil parking lot, Jana felt a wave of exhaustion sweep through her body. She glanced at her watch in the lights of the tour bus; it was 9:40 pm. Her mind was on complete overwhelm, though her spirit felt exultant. Beyond a doubt she needed some sleep, some down time. Waving to her friends boarding the tour bus, she started to get in the VW when Aurora Nakin walked over.

"Jana, something important has come up," said Aurora Nakin. Her voice sounded more throaty than usual.

Closing the VW door, Jana nodded for her to continue.

"Hanab Xiu wants you to come tonight for . . ." Aurora Nakin hesitated. "For a special process that we have to do before tomorrow's ceremony. He says you are needed, that your connections are important for what has to be done. It will be at the Mayaland Hotel, probably will take about an hour."

Mind numb and body fatigued, Jana resisted for a moment. But her inner being knew she could not decline this request.

"OK," she heard her tired voice saying. "But, I don't have a pass to get inside the Mayaland gate."

"I'll ride there with you, and use my pass," Aurora Nakin replied. "Wait for me, I'll let Hanab Xiu know."

Wearily Jana slumped into the driver's seat of the VW, resting her head. She started to drift off into light sleep, jarred awake as Aurora Nakin got in the car beside her. Fumbling with the key in the darkness, she got the VW started after a couple of tries and drove out of the parking lot.

The two women were silent for a while. There were things Jana wanted to discuss with Aurora Nakin, experiences she wanted to share but the topic seemed too big to begin. Maybe there would be time tomorrow.

Aurora Nakin broke the silence.

"This involves the Columbian woman, Evita. I'm sorry about how she pushed you down this morning at the cenote. That's part of the problem, how the dark entity uses her body. Tonight Hanab Xiu is going to remove the entity. He doesn't want it to disrupt tomorrow's ceremony. He says he needs you for this."

"Me?" asked Jana, astonished. "I don't know anything about removing entities."

"He'll guide you in what to do. You may be surprised that you know more than you think. Several people will be involved, and I'll be there too."

The Maya priestess Yalucha flashed into Jana's mind. This was something she would know about. And, it was clear through the TV screen images in her sacred heart space that she and Yalucha were merged in some way. She needed to know more about the Maya understanding of reincarnation, or whatever their process of soul movement between lifetimes might be.

They soon arrived at the Mayaland gate and were given entrance by Aurora Nakin's pass. As Jana handed it back, Aurora Nakin waved her hand, saying:

"You keep it. Use it tomorrow to get in when you join us in the Mayaland Hotel lobby."

The long driveway curved through stands of trees, floodlights accenting the sinuous outline of twisted branches. Rising to a low hill, it passed several parking lots. Aurora Nakin pointed to one.

"Here, turn right into the parking lot, go to that big RV parked over there."

They joined three others standing beside the RV. It was relatively isolated at the far end of the parking lot with only a few nearby cars. Aurora Nakin whispered to Jana that these three men were standing watch, in case hotel guards appeared. The RV belonged to a member of the European group. It was selected because it would muffle the screams that Evita was sure to make. If such screaming occurred inside the hotel, undoubtedly police would be called. After a few minutes, Fire Eagle stuck his head out the RV door and summoned them inside.

The living room area inside the RV had been cleared, the folding table put up against the wall. Couch-seats were attached to the two side walls. Evita was lying on one couch-seat, as Hanab Xiu, Fire Eagle and another man stood in the small center space. Her husband Jorje was seated at the far end of the opposite couch-seat, looking decidedly uncomfortable. Hanab Xiu nodded to Aurora Nakin and Jana, saying:

"Let us begin."

Fire Eagle lighted copal incense in a bowl, using a single feather to smudge everyone with its woody smoke. Hanab Xiu intoned chants in the Mayan language, turning to face each direction as the others followed suit. He made several hand gestures at the end. From a small pouch, he removed a jar containing a thick herbal paste. Turning toward Jana and Aurora Nakin who stood in the adjoining kitchen area, he remarked:

"This is a blend of dried Skunk Root, *Zorillo,* Rue and Esquipulas powder. It is plant medicine the Maya use for spiritual healing, for clearing out evil forces. The entity who is inside knows the powers of these. I use them to increase the force of my intention as I work with this entity."

He turned his head slightly to the right.

"See, it is upset already. It knows our intention. This is a very strong entity, it was once extremely powerful among the Maya. It carries the consciousness of the Death Lords, the Lords of Xibalba; it was connected with the ancient practices of sacrifice. This is the dark spirit force behind the Maya use of human sacrifice. For centuries, since ancient times, this dark spiritual force has been woven into this land and peoples. It exists in other people now in the land of the Maya. It caused the Maya people to do things that they knew in their hearts were wrong.

"Its purpose is destruction and chaos. It wants to keep the souls of many Mayas trapped in the Underworld, the deep inner earth. It knows why we are here. That we have come to free these Maya souls, to let them return to the Middleworld and complete their purpose. In any way it can, it intends to prevent us from releasing these souls, from creating balance for this land. Its attachment is strong, so we will need great spiritual power to get it to leave her body."

Turning to Evita, who was beginning to whimper and toss her head, he applied the herb paste to her forehead, throat, wrists, umbilicus and ankles while murmuring incantations. Watching this process evoked oddly familiar sensations in Jana, not thoughts but cellular knowing. Her body knew this procedure, this incantation. As Hanab Xiu moved his hand over Evita's abdomen, she started writhing and jerking her limbs. Fire Eagle and the other man gently restrained her so she did not fall. Soon her moans turned into shrieks that were earsplitting in the small confine.

Aurora Nakin stood with eyes closed, hands lifted and palms facing toward Hanab Xiu and Evita. Jana followed suit, focusing intensely, hoping she would get some inner direction about what to do.

Immediately she sensed the presence of several spirit beings. Some appeared angelic with large arched wings, glowing golden amber and pearly white light, emanating love and grace. Others had warrior energies, darker with black and silvery hues, radiating

415

protective forces. She sensed they represented the spirit energy of the herbs. They were assisting and supporting the healing work being done.

Jana's inner sight picked up a golden octahedron pyramid that Hanab Xiu had created around Evita's body, along with other powerful angelic beings she did not recognize. One had sun-like brilliance, sparking golden light and fiery tendrils but emanating immense benevolence. It had Maya qualities; she intuited it must be Hanab Ku, the Sun God who was the manifestation of infinite creator spirit in our galaxy. The golden pyramid appeared as a portal, a dimensional window through which beings could move to other worlds. Jana immediately understood that Hanab Xiu, with the assistance of these angelic spirit beings, was intending to move the entity dwelling in Evita out through this portal into another dimension.

Then she got a sense of the entity. It was terrifying in its fury and violent energies. With no distinct shape or form, this presence exuded bone-chilling evil. Destruction, chaos, terror, suffering and death were its clear intentions. The Xibalban force was ruthless, savage, merciless. Thick tendrils of energy connected brutally into Evita's body, causing it to distort and bulge as she thrashed desperately. The entity clearly did not want to leave, to let go its attachments to her. Hanab Xiu and his spirit assistants summoned in more power, and sent a series of energy waves through Evita and into the entity to force it into the dimensional window.

Jana summoned up reserves of inner strength she was not aware existed, from depths of spiritual rivers running from source. Her guides were there, adding their strength to hers—Lord Jesus, the Maya priestess Yalucha, and the goddess Ix Chel whom she served. The amber pendant radiated heat against her chest; the pouch with the spirit doll hanging at her side vibrated against her hip. Every fiber of her being strained with the effort of projecting energy toward the entity, shoving it into the portal against fierce resistance. Beads of sweat broke out along her upper lip and brow.

Blood-curdling screams filled the RV, more like the roars of some wounded animal than human sounds. Thumps and scuffles sounded as Evita kicked the RV walls and writhed on the couch. Hanab Xiu kept his hands near her umbilicus, pulling upward as though against a deeply anchored rope. The woman's body arched, then fell against the couch repeatedly. After one final deep-throated yell, she collapsed into silence.

It was done. Jana felt lightness inside the RV, a clean peaceful energy. Opening her eyes, she saw Aurora Nakin kneeling beside Evita, making stroking motions over her body. The Columbian woman appeared asleep, her breathing deep and regular, her body relaxed. Hanab Xiu sat beside Jorje, patting his arm comfortingly. Fire Eagle was quietly putting things back into a pouch. The other man went to the door as a soft knock sounded. It was one of the outside watchers.

"Are you done? No, the guards haven't shown up," the man said, anticipating the question. "Something weird just happened, right when the screams stopped. The trees on both sides of the parking lot started shaking, like they were suddenly hit by a big wind. A branch broke off one tree. It lasted a few seconds and stopped. We didn't feel any wind."

From inside Hanab Xiu responded:

"That was caused by the force of the entity leaving. It would have done more destruction if it could have, but we contained it. It's over now, the evil entity has been taken to a realm where it belongs. It is actually better off in its home world, but it did not truly understand this."

He rose and walked closer to the door, where the second watcher had approached. Slowly the Maya shaman looked into the eyes of everyone present, turning in a circle to see everyone.

"You are free to share this with others in the group," he said. "But do not tell people who might not understand. Remember this well: Every being serves a purpose in this Divine play, this dream of life that we are living. This dark energy was among us for a reason. It was necessary and inevitable, just as the war was. This consciousness is part of the problem we are seeking to heal. We must treat it with love, compassion and even feel gratitude for what it provides. And, we need to honor this woman for the courage to play such a difficult role among us. At a higher level, her soul agreed to be the vehicle for this experience. It teaches us something we need to learn, and allows her to advance her own healing and provide a service to the world.

"Thank you all for being here. This healing would not have been possible without each one of you. Go now, and rest."

Aurora Nakin walked Jana to the red VW. The women hugged each other warmly, holding their bodies close, feeling comforted. Jana was both exhilarated and fatigued. One question burned in her mind, and she had to ask it.

"How can we be united as one—which I felt so clearly during the heart space meditation—and still have these forces of evil? Does it mean we are also one with evil?" Jana asked, perplexed.

"It's something the mind will never understand," said Aurora Nakin, shaking her head. "In some way we are one with evil, with all destructive forces in the world. If God, the Divine is everything, then it encompasses these things too. I believe it's all about perception, the lens through which we view the world. Where is our consciousness vibrationally tuned? The state of consciousness we are resonating with shapes what we experience. "

"So there are multiple states of consciousness we can enter," Jana mused. "Different levels of reality, different dimensions of being. In some of these we can have the experience of evil."

"Right. You choose, either knowingly or through conditioning and habits. What you experience in life is the result of this question: How conscious do you want to be?"

     *   *   *   *   *   *

Carla Hernandez greeted Robert in the waiting room of her office. She observed that Jana's tall husband looked distinctly uncomfortable, although he smiled amicably in return greeting. There was urgency in his request for this session with her. Seeing clients on Saturday was not usual, but an inner sense of its importance led to her acquiescence. Carla was long accustomed to following inner guidance. Honoring the voice of intuition was what kept it alive.

Seated comfortably facing each other in Carla's consulting room, the two began a dialogue about Robert's experiences in the Maya ruins and listening to Maya music. He brought the therapist up to date on Jana's excursion and his concerns for her safety. With hesitation, he described their conflict about this and the new perspectives he gained after talking with Marissa. Robert was as honest as he could be without totally losing face. He was still hurt by Jana's choice, and confused because it seemed such disregard for his deep feelings. He did believe his views had validity.

With the skill of a seasoned therapist who bridged both traditional and metaphysical fields, Carla honed in on what Robert was seeking. Soon it became clear that his goal was not processing feelings about the conflict, but gaining insight into the unusual sensations brought up by the music and how that might relate to the Maya.

As Robert described these, he broke into a coughing spell. Shaking his head after the coughing stopped, he remarked how unusual it was for an illness to linger so long. He told Carla that Jana suspected both their illnesses after the Belize trip might be caused by shamanic forces. Although he found that notion hard to accept, he was perplexed about the persistent cough.

"I'm hardly ever sick, and get over it right away," Robert said in exasperation. "This cough, along with an array of unsettling feelings and strange coincidences are making me really concerned about what's going on. My mind can't make sense of it. That's why I've come, Carla. I need to get to the bottom of all this."

"I don't think just talking about this is going to get you deep enough," Carla advised. "What you're feeling comes from experiences deep in the psyche, or held within cellular memory. You must go beyond the mind to access these. Are you open to doing guided imagery?"

"I've never done it before, though Jana's talked to me about it," Robert replied. "Sure, I'm open to it. I don't know if I'll be much good at it, but I'm willing to try."

"Do images of things easily come to mind if you close your eyes and think about them?" Carla asked.

"No," answered Robert. "Not easily, but sometimes that happens. Especially if it's a very vivid memory, it can replay like I'm there again."

"Good," said Carla. "I think it's important for you to be really relaxed. We'll do a relaxation exercise first then go into imagery."

She clicked on a CD that played dreamy, melodic music and dimmed the lights. Reading Robert's body language, she sensed discomfort and asked:

"Is anything wrong?"

"Uh, I hope you're not offended, but . . . it's the music," Robert explained. "Music is my profession. I can't help analyzing it, that's what I do. But I'm somewhat of a classical snob, and this wallpaper music drives me nuts. I'm afraid it will draw my focus away from what else we're doing."

"Oh, sure. How about nature sounds, or would you prefer silence?"

"I think silence would be best."

Carla turned the CD player off. She sensed Robert would find sitting up through the imagery preferable to lying on the massage table, so she coached him to find a comfortable sitting position and close his eyes. Then she led him through progressive muscle relaxation, tensing and relaxing muscle groups from feet upward through the body to his scalp. Even the tiny muscles around eyes and mouth were included. After this, she had him breath deeply and slowly, feeling his breath moving deeper and deeper into his body until it reached his toes. She asked him to scan his body for any tense place, and tense-relax that area.

From her many guided imagery techniques, Carla selected one that she believed would be most comfortable for Robert. She discerned that beginning from a secure, familiar place would provide a safety net for riskier areas.

"Bring to mind a place in nature where you have been before, a place that is familiar, that you find beautiful or relaxing, where you feel at home," she directed in soothing tones. "See as much of your place as possible, look around, note details. Feel how much at home you are here, how safe and comfortable it is. This is a wonderful place for you, and it is always there when you want to return."

She watched his face. The muscles appeared relaxed and his expression was peaceful. His breathing was slow and steady.

"You are in your familiar place, yes?"

He nodded. It was the big meadow at his grandparents' farm in Ohio, where he spent many summers as a boy. Tall golden grasses waved gently, a few cows and horses grazed contentedly in the distance. The meadow was a place of wonder, full of creatures and offering many adventures. Crossing to the farthest fence was his ambition when small. And then, more fields opened to the horizons in all directions, an endless land to explore.

"Good. Stay there a little longer, feeling calm, relaxed, secure," Carla continued. "This place is the base from which you are going to explore a deeper level of yourself. Now go to the edge of your place, and look around for an opening. It might be a cave, a hole, some opening going down into the earth. Do you see some kind of opening?"

After a moment, Robert nodded.

"Can you describe it? Remember to keep your eyes closed," she advised.

"It's like a trapdoor, opening at the end of a narrow path. There's a hole under it, going down, like a rabbit hole but bigger. It disappears into darkness," he said.

"OK, you now need to go down into the hole, but leave the door open. It will not trap you below. You will easily be able to come back up to your special place."

Carla was alert to the symbolism of the trapdoor, and did not want fear of being trapped in the dark reaches below to prevent Robert from accessing them. Slowly she guided him down the hole, telling him to bring along a flashlight so he could see. She had him go down as far as possible, and tell her when he was at the end.

"You are a child now," she said when he reported he was as far down as possible. "Try to get a sense of how old you are."

"Ummm . . . I'm pretty little, maybe around five or six," Robert answered dreamily.

"Good," said Carla softly. "Now look around and see something about your environment, where you are."

"It's, uh . . . dirt, I'm sitting on the dirt and playing with some . . . uh, bugs or something, they're scurrying around and I'm trying to direct them into little grooves I made in the dirt."

"Uh-huh. What else?"

"Lots of trees, thick growth, must be jungle. Hot. It's really hot and humid. I'm sweating a lot. I try to wipe sweat from my forehead but there's some kind of board, I've got a board strapped to my head. Huh! That's weird," he remarked.

"Is that some punishment?" Carla asked.

"No, its just what my family does," he said with a touch of surprise in his voice.

"Can you see your home?"

"White . . . made of white stone, smooth walls, big with lots of rooms . . . a few windows but no glass, the windows are open. The roof has some kind of palm leaves, it's a thatched roof, and . . . Oh wow, there's the door and its got a corbel arch!" he exclaimed.

"What does that mean?" Carla asked.

"It's a Maya home," Robert responded. "That's how they built with palm thatched roofs and corbel arches. It's definitely Maya."

"OK, good," Carla said. "Now lets go forward a little, to when you're older, maybe a teenager."

There was a pause, the silence charged with an almost electric quality.

"I'm with a group of other boys and men," Robert said slowly. "We're not wearing much clothes, some wrapping around waist and thighs. We're practicing a technique, learning to use these spears, throw them at targets. Training for fighting. We use these spears for fighting . . . and hunting too."

"What are you feeling?"

"I . . . I'm, uh, I like it. I like throwing spears, it's exciting. Soon I'll be among the men, the warriors. It's something I've been waiting to do, or at least this boy has been waiting to do." He hesitated, moved a little in the chair. "I don't know who this Maya kid is, he sure doesn't think like me now, but somehow I'm connected with what he's doing. What's going on?"

"Just try to stay with the imagery," Carla said with a soothing tone. "We don't know exactly where these images come from, but they are delving into your deep psyche. We'll talk about this afterward. Are you OK to move forward again? See yourself a little older."

"Yeah, I guess. What age now?" Before Carla could respond, Robert sucked his breath in sharply. She waited.

"Oh boy, this one is great!" Robert said enthusiastically. "Think I—the Maya guy—is in love. Beautiful, mysterious young woman, long black hair, she's exotic even to him. They've really got a thing for each other. Not just physically, it's very intense emotionally, a deep caring, it's so . . . they're really committed to each other. They love each other so much, but something's keeping them apart, some conflict."

Robert became lost in his imagery, unable to voice it. A chord was struck in his heart that went to his very core. There were no words for it. Inside, part of his being knew this same love was what he felt for Jana. The young Maya man and woman's relationship was woven into a web that stretched into his and Jana's lives now. Tears moistened his eyelids and deep remorse swept through him over his harsh words to Jana.

"Can you tell me what you're experiencing?" asked Carla gently.

"Their love—the Maya couple—it's like me and Jana, I don't know exactly how, but we're all connected," Robert said, his voice husky with emotion. "It's like we've always been connected, at least for a long, long time."

"Can you see where it goes with the Maya couple?"

Robert took a deep breath. His psyche resisted, a huge wave of over-powering emotions felt poised to crash over him.

"Oh, God this is awful!" he choked out.

"If you can go with it, it will unlock things for you," Carla gently urged. "Take a step back, become the observer of a scene playing out in a movie. It's OK, I'm here with you."

Scenes erupted onto Robert's inner visual screen, confusing, chaotic, full of turmoil.

Men in battle, close, face-to-face, slashing with spears and knives, grunting and yelling, blood splattering each other and the ground, limbs hanging partly severed, bodies crumpling in heaps of glittering armor. Then his army was pelted by a downpour of short spears falling from the sky, from nowhere, wave after wave. Sharp points piercing throats, penetrating into eyes, belly, limbs; sudden screams descending into the throaty gurgles of death, men running with shields raised against the sky-borne missiles of doom, but no escape. The ground was covered with writhing bodies soon to collapse into frozen distorted poses, limbs askew in puddles of blood.

Dark coolness, sitting on bare stone, leg throbbing. Prison, he was a prisoner. A captive. Haughty guards, derisive, cruelly taking pleasure in suffering. Impending death, certain and inescapable. It was the way of things. Die with courage, die with nobility, that was all he had left. She came, she soothed his wounds and ministered in unspoken ways to his soul. Anguished heart, yearning beyond imagining, love's first blossom crushed as a tender bud. Ever to meet again? The gods were capricious, who could know. The drums, beating insistently, calling and calling him to his death. Dazed but head held high, he walked up the steep steps. Numb, no thought, no feeling. It was the way of things. Sudden rip of searing pain across the chest and darkness, nothingness.

High on a platform, wind whipping his face and hair. Young, vigorous, full of life and power. Many subjects below, chanting voices and pulsating drums, waves of adulation floating up the tall pyramid, the ruler communing with his people. And the older woman, the holy woman, was there. She stood beside him, as always, supporting, guiding, mentoring. She was his anchor and she loved him beyond all accounting. This he knew. Not the way his comely wife loved him, but in a way he did not understand. He accepted this love for it fed his soul, and his soul fed his people. But his heart ached, felt incomplete, sadness hovered around the edges.

The images faded. Robert's body quivered as it began restoring the cells' chemical balance after their infusion of arousal peptides and hormones caused by his intense waves of emotion.

"Do you need to return to your special place now?" Carla observed his body signals. He nodded. She talked him back up the hole, through the open door and into his place of safety and comfort. He stayed there a few moments, as she advised. With a deep, sighing breath he opened his eyes and suddenly broke into a coughing paroxysm that racked his body. Carla rose and got a glass of water for him. The sips calmed his cough, he thanked her and looked at the therapist.

"Can you talk about what you were experiencing?" she asked.

"I've never felt anything like it," he said, bemused and in awe. "What's going on deep inside? Pretty amazing, like I was really there. It's hard to tell you about it. Everything happened so fast, one scene merging into another. But the emotions, the feelings that went with what was happening, they were so intense. Lots of war and battles, war was brutal then. The Maya guy—me, who knows? He and the woman were in several scenes, but they kept changing, I'm not sure they were the same people . . . but some thread linked them through the whole thing. That thread links them to me and Jana. I just know this, I can't explain how."

Carla probed for a few more details, which Robert described as best he could. Then she observed:

"When you—the Maya warrior—was a prisoner and was going to die, that sounds like he was a human sacrifice. Did you get that sense?"

"Yes, definitely," Robert answered. "And . . . wait a minute, I just remembered something. He had to walk up a tall stairway, must have been up a pyramid. Like the pyramids I visited in Tikal, when I had that uncanny physical faintness and almost fell."

He paused, frowned and looked searchingly into Carla's eyes.

"Do you think I had that reaction because I was this Maya warrior who got sacrificed, there at that spot?"

"That's possible," Carla answered. "Do you believe in reincarnation?"

"I'm not sure," said Robert. "Jana does, and we've discussed it often. I believe the soul, our essence, does keep on existing after the body dies. But I really don't know in what form, what process that existence takes."

"Nor do any of us with certainty," said Carla. "We don't know, at least most of us don't, whether that essence, the soul or spirit, of a certain person keeps re-inhabiting a new body in a series of lifetimes in linear progression, or whether some other dynamic occurs. Valerie Hunt, a leading edge psychologist doing research at UCLA thinks there is an information field that connects us to other lifehoods. These lifehoods carry information about the soul's experience in a material body, and that information is always part of each new life. Because lifehoods operate like fields, their information is always now, in present time. The past, the present, and maybe the future are all accessible now through these fields, like soul sparks flashing around a person."

"So, what we went through in other lifetimes is still present inside?" Robert queried.

"In the information field, which carries the memories, patterns and beliefs set up through the soul's experiences. These become our emotional residue, the source within the deep psyche that directs our lives," Carla responded. "The lifehood field intersects with other fields that have similar resonances. I believe this draws certain people and experiences into our present life. When lifehood fields become activated, we can remember things from other incarnations."

"Do you think that's what I've just gone through?"

"Yes, I do."

Robert fell silent, reflecting. Maybe he had been a Maya in the past, as he knew Jana believed she was. Maybe their lives had been interwoven over and over again, as he glimpsed in this imagery. And perhaps this lifehood field had drawn the experiences they both went through in Tikal, in other Maya ruins, and since returning from the trip.

And, maybe not, his doubting rational mind piped up.

"Couldn't some other process be operating?" he suggested. "Some psychological phenomenon, like reading another person's mind or creating imaginary scenarios in our minds?"

"Well, yes," admitted Carla. "But where does imagination come from? How does the mind create these images, what does it draw from? Another theory holds that we inherit memories through DNA passed down through generations. This is tribal or group memory, it contains residues of information that were formed by collective experiences. We also call this cellular memory. It holds information from both an individual and a group's consciousness, so that includes beliefs and ways of seeing the world as well as important events in their histories."

"Hmm, that's an interesting theory," said Robert. It appealed to his logical mind. "I remember Stephen Hawking once saying that the laws of science do not distinguish between past, present and future. And Einstein's theories of space-time certainly make it a fluid condition, not at all linear."

"Yes. But whatever the mechanism, our human consciousness has the ability to tap into a vast realm of memories and experiences. The ones that come to us have particular significance for our lives, whether this is symbolic or from actual past events. The information is important; it gives insight into our present issues and problems. Which brings us back to why you're here," concluded Carla, smiling.

"Right," replied Robert.

"What have you gotten out of this?" she asked.

Robert gazed off in the distance, contemplating. Then he nodded and smiled slightly.

"OK, there is a past connection with the Maya, both for me and for Jana. Whether this was an actual past life, or some consciousness field or carried in DNA cellular memories, there were experiences that are affecting us now. She's gone off to fulfill a mission that is going to help the Maya people, and perhaps the world in some way. I'm dealing with intense reactions—not my best moments, I'll admit—that seem related to my own Maya experiences. There's been lots of conflict and sadness in those experiences."

"Good, perfect," said Carla. "And here's one additional piece of information that might help you working through all this. Your cough, you said it's been present since you returned from the trip to the Maya ruins. On a symbolic level, coughing and mucus in the lungs represents weeping of the heart. There is a heart wound that was reawakened on this trip, from traumas your being had. If you can bring this wound into your awareness, and find a way to forgive those involved, your physical body can heal."

Robert sat up straight, his attention sharply caught by Carla's comments. Intuitively he knew she had hit upon a truth, it clicked into place in his mind.

"Yeah," he said slowly. "I know what you mean. The Maya music, one track had this incredible drumming that was ominous and fierce, really made me scared. Then today's imagery, the battles and being sacrificed, I think it's all related. My real reason for being so

426

upset about Jana's going on this trip is being afraid I'll lose her—like I did before."

Tears flooded his eyes and he felt intense pain around his heart as he said this. Carla placed a hand on his arm and sat, quietly supportive. Robert cried, beyond caring what anyone thought. Waves of sorrow flowed from his heart, eons of loss and grief. Great sobs racked his body. He was lost in the flood of emotions for a while, and when it started ebbing away he realized Carla had wrapped her arms around him, holding him, comforting him. He was deeply grateful. His heart felt cleansed.

He took the tissues she offered and wiped his tears, coughing a little. When he felt reasonably self-collected, he thanked her.

"I . . . I really appreciate your seeing me today, Carla," he said. "This is very important to me. I needed to get a handle on my reactions, you've helped a lot."

"I'm glad to have been helpful," Carla responded. "If possible, stay quiet the rest of today. Let this process keep working through you. A door, actually a portal has opened for you and more information may come forth. As well as more feelings. Do you pray?"

"Yes, not every day, but I do pray," Robert replied.

"Good, spend some time in prayer. Ask for the grace to accept and forgive all injuries done to you, and all injuries you've done to others. Pray for the greater good of all those involved. If feelings arise, just try to endure and be with them. They will pass. If it gets too difficult, call me. The number's on my card, I'll get back to you." She gave him the card with a warm smile.

"Thanks so much," he replied. "I'll also pray for Jana's safety, that she comes back safely to me."

11   Uxmal

The boy stood impatiently at the beginning of the footpath leading away from the city into nearby woodlands. He pushed a few pebbles around with his sandaled foot, a temporary distraction from his annoyance at having to study with the High Priestess this morning. A group of warriors was taking the other noble boys of Uxmal on a hunting trip today, and he wanted to accompany them. Perhaps he could talk his way out of this obligation, if he was clever.

Chan Chak K'ak'nal was dressed simply but in finely made clothing that bespoke his high rank. Geometric embroidery bordered his waistcloth and the edges of loin and beech cloths. On his bare chest was an expertly carved pectoral ornament bearing the face of Chak, his namesake god. Just entering puberty, the boy's limbs were straight and strong, his chest developing muscles that promised to rival those of any Uxmal warrior. Gold and precious gems embellished his wrist cuffs. Bright dark eyes gazed from under straight hawk-like brows, emphasized by a prominent curved nose and high forehead. Black hair was secured to his crown by a colorful woven band around the topknot.

The first son of the Uxmal king was a handsome boy, by all accounts. He was adventuresome and strong-willed, not a readily compliant student. Now, with the igniting fires of approaching manhood warming his blood, the boy had even less tolerance for these esoteric matters. He passionately wanted to practice warfare and hone his hunting skills. He wondered if that old woman, the High Priestess, would ever show up. She was nearly twice his age, and although her shamanic powers commanded his respect, he was much more interested in the nubile young women of the city.

The sound of sandaled feet crunching on pebbles caused him to turn. She was approaching, walking with an energetic gait that conveyed vigor and health. In the prime of life, the High Priestess radiated subtle power that naturally drew deference. Her black hair showed one or two strands of gray; her honey-gold skin was taut and nearly free of wrinkles. Of medium height, her body well developed with full breasts and hips, the High Priestess embodied the qualities of feminine divine, creative forces. The moon glowed in her dark eyes and her smile sang of the sun's warmth. The men of Uxmal much admired her beauty, but to the young prince she was old.

"Greetings of the morning, Lord Chan Chak," said the High Priestess. "How does this kin find you?"

"Quite well, Lady Yalucha," the boy replied.

The High Priestess of Uxmal bore a family name of considerable antiquity. It had been passed down through her family since the times long ago when they lived in the great cities of the southern jungles. The Maya people who built Uxmal, the Tutul Xiu, had migrated from the south many generations ago. Leaving the dense jungles of their former homeland, they settled in the drier regions of the north peninsula. Uxmal, the "three-times-built" city, sat at the base of the Puuc hills rising dramatically to the north, towering above the rolling savannah. A vast limestone shelf underlay the entire region, and surface water was scarce. There were underground rivers flowing deep and cool under the white limestone, but in the Puuc region these precious sources of life were too deep to access. Using their ingenuity, the Tutul Xiu created the *chultun,* a cistern carved into the limestone with wide lips to gather rainwater into a funnel neck that minimized evaporation. The chultun was lined with plaster to prevent water from seeping through porous limestone. Each household had its own small chultun, where water collected during the rains to sustain them through the dry season. Chak, the rain god, was ever-present in Puuc cities, his long-nose mask decorating most buildings.

Chan Chak was named in honor of the god of rain and storms, as were many men in his lineage, rulers of Uxmal for several generations. Ah Koy Tok' founded the city in the katun ending 9.16.0.0.0 (751 CE). The founder's name meant "he of the owl-flint." The combination of an owl, a shield and an atlatl spear made from flint honored his ancestors whose fame was still legendary among Maya people. This symbolism represented the many victories of combined forces from the great jungle city Mutul and the vast Mexica Empire Teotihuacan, and their Venus-Tlatloc methods that changed the face of warfare.

The High Priestess began to walk along the path that curved over low hills toward a woodland cluster in the distance. Chan Chak stood his ground, calling to her:

"Lady Priestess, if you will."

She stopped and turned, looking back with a quizzical expression.

"I mean no offense, I know these lessons are valuable," the boy continued. "But today my heart is called elsewhere. I request your release, that I may pursue this call."

"Ah," she said with a knowing smile. "You wish to accompany the warriors on the hunting expedition."

"Yes." He stood tall, his eyes already level with hers. Unflinching, he returned her steady stare. The priestess' dark eyes dove deeply into his; he was certain she could read his soul. Since he was very young, as far back as he could remember, she had been his spiritual mentor. There was nothing about his life that she did not know intimately. The knowledge necessary for shaman-kings, and the discipline required to commune with the realm of gods and ancestors, were the focus of her relentless instructions. Despite how demanding she inevitably was of him, the boy knew she loved him from unfathomable depths, far beyond his ability to understand.

"Chan Chak," she said gravely, "your life is different from the lives of your companions. You have a greater responsibility. In time you will be ruler of our city, supreme guide and leader for your people. There is no place in your life for avoiding duties. Today your duty is to further your studies of the spirit realm. For you, this is far more important than hunting. No, you cannot go."

Disappointment clouded his eyes. His willfulness rose in a hot surge, coloring his cheeks, as he struggled with how to respond. But, he did not argue. He was well aware that his destiny required forgoing many personal desires and pleasures. The regal boy set his shoulders, nodded and followed the High Priestess along the path. They walked in silence as the path wound through low hills. Topping a rise, he glanced back toward the city he would some day rule.

Uxmal spread like a white jewel in the green tree-spotted hills, red soil breaking through in places where erosion washed away sedges and grasses. The rainy season had just ended, and the grasses made a variegated carpet over the landscape in shades of golden-yellow to gray-green. Groves of tall oak trees spread thick dark leaves to provide welcome shade for squirrels, peccaries, white-tailed deer and agoutis that fed on its acorns. Nance trees growing gnarled and low to the ground were bearing tiny orange and yellow flowers in twin rows along stems. These would form into thumbnail sized sweet yellow fruits shortly, enjoyed by people, animals, birds and the food of Seven Macaw, the *Wuqub Kaqix* of creation mythology. Stubby palms and rough-leaved chaparros spaced themselves in small clusters across the rolling hills.

At the eastern side of the city rose the majestic *Itzam Ka'an*, the sky pyramid of conjuring magic.[19] Its steep western stairway was bordered on both sides, along the entire length, by Chak masks. Atop the stairway was the most sacred temple of the city, with an entrance formed by the gaping mouth of a huge monster. Yalucha as High Priestess, along with the High Priest and the Uxmal ruler performed rituals in this magic sky place. The pyramid's sides were gracefully rounded, creating a feminine flow to balance the angular, erect and fierce masculine constructs of the stairway and masks. Itzam Ka'an was one of the city's oldest structures. Katuns of ceremony, visitations by gods and ancestors during vision quests, and repeated lightning strikes by the god K'awil to crack open the foreheads of seekers creating a portal to the Otherworld, had imbued it with immense *itz,* the sacred substance that carried *ch'ulel,* the divine soul essence.

Chan Chak admired the well-constructed structures of his city, but already vague ideas swam in his imagination about making it even more beautiful. His soul yearned for symmetry, for balance in these stone creations of humans that would speak to the great mysteries of being and emanate eternal truths. A faint inner vision of the city expressing perfect harmony between masculine and feminine forces played at the fringes of his awareness. He knew his future held constructions of stone to manifest this vision.

They reached the first groves of woodland oaks as the sun climbed midway in the clear blue sky. The oaks were tall but well spaced, with grassy areas in between. Limestone rock outcroppings appeared here and there, bordered by low nance bushes. Yalucha chose a grassy opening that was nearly round, with flat rocks for sitting. The High Priestess and her royal student settled down to begin the lesson.

First she murmured a short prayer to invoke the presence of Scribe Gods, the divine rabbit and monkey scribes who chronicled esoteric wisdom. Focusing intently on Chan Chak, she asked:

"What are the five enemies of the soul, Chan Chak?"

"The soul has five enemies," he replied confidently. "These are disease, death, stupidity, arrogance, and fear."

---

[19] Called "Pyramid of the Magician" by archeologists. Legends tell that it was built overnight by a magical dwarf, or perhaps the great primeval god Itzamna.

"Very good," said his mentor. "Which of these are under our control?"

"Clearly we have the ability to control the vices of stupidity, arrogance, and fear. This is learned through education to become a real human. Disease may be prevented to some degree by how we live. But disease may be visited upon people by evil shamans, or by curses of the gods. Disease may result from necessary actions, such as battle and bloodletting rituals. That is where the healing arts of the priestesses of Ix Chel come to our assistance, Lady Priestess," he added with a smile.

She nodded but made no response to the compliment.

"So death is beyond our control," she observed.

"I would say so," he confirmed. "All that is alive must die. That is unavoidable."

"From the human point of view, this is correct," Yalucha said. "The soul, the White Flower Thing, separates from the body at death, and the maize and blood of the body return to the soil. The goal of the shaman, however, is to gain control over death. The shaman masters the magic of turning death into resurrection. He learns how to overcome the Lords of Death, to outwit Xibalba, and turn nonbeing into Eternal Being. By practicing oneness with the Cosmic God, the Source of All Being, you have nothing to fear from either life or death."

"How does one accomplish this, Mother of My Soul?" asked the boy, his attention now fully engaged. Any lingering thoughts about hunting had disappeared from his mind.

"By growing your soul through the experiences of life," she replied. "By perfecting the White Flower Thing, the *sak-nik-nal*. The qualities of the ideal soul are the qualities of the life force, *ch'ulel*, Being Itself. These qualities are shown to us by the Hero Twins, Hun Ahau and Yax Balam. They are our models for descending into the jaws of the Underworld, and overcoming all tests given by the Lords of Death. What qualities did they use to outwit their opponents in Xibalba?"

He thought for a few moments, recalling details of this story told by his family repeatedly since his early childhood.

"They used fast thinking and cleverness," he said. "They were very resourceful, and used creatures of nature to assist them in meeting the tests. The Twins used the quality of intelligence to outwit Death."

"Yes. Intelligence is essential. It is the antidote to stupidity or ignorance. One must pursue spiritual education, the study of Divine Truth, to overcome a dull mind and naïve incompetence. One must understand the true nature of existence, and not be deceived by what appears to be on the surface. Remember, Chan Chak, always to delve more deeply into any thing you wish to know. Seek layer after layer of meaning. Appreciate the inescapable dualities of life in the Middleworld, while embracing the underlying unity of the Overworld." The High Priestess continued her inquiry, saying:

"What other qualities, perhaps not so obvious, are qualities of the ideal soul?"

"Courage," he replied quickly. "In life and in the Otherworld, courage is needed to overcome fear."

"Ah, excellent!" Yalucha replied. "Fear is perhaps the greatest enemy of one who seeks to become *ch'ul ahau*, a Lord of Life, an authentic human being. What ways have you found to overcome fear, Chan Chak?"

The boy searched his limited experiences for an example. He had been well protected during childhood, carefully watched over by constant attendants. There was no lack or hardship except his struggles to control desires that went against the training for leadership that began very early. One occasion when he eluded his attendants and embarked on an excursion into the savannah, he did encounter a frightening experience. To retell it accurately, he allowed his feelings to slip into that place of excitement and fearfulness.

"When I was six tuns," he related, "I ran away from home to explore the surrounding hills. They would never let me be alone, and seldom took me outside the city. I wanted to see what was there. The grass was dry and brown, as high as my shoulders. I searched for lizards, toads or birds and scared a few. It was so much fun, I kept wandering around until suddenly I heard a strange sound. I had never heard such a sound before, the sound of small dry rattles, almost like dry grasses tapping against each other in the wind. Curious, I walked toward the sound, parting the grasses and leaning down toward the sound that seemed to be coming from the ground. There, next to a group of rocks, I saw a rattlesnake. Its snout and round amber eyes were only an arm's length from my face. The diamond patterns on its coiled body were very clear, and it held the tip of its tail straight up, rapidly shaking the rattles. Every so often it stuck out its tongue at me.

"I felt sudden intense fear. My body went stiff and cold. I knew the bite of this snake was deadly, and I was far from the city. The muscles of the snake's body rippled and I knew it was about to strike. The only thing I could think to do was to become fierce. If I quelled my fear and instead showed the snake my strong willpower, I could command it to back away. I stared with all my strength into the snake's eyes, willing it to stop its attack. For what seemed a very long time, the snake and I were frozen, staring into each other's eyes. Then it turned away, stopped rattling and slipped off into the grasses."

Yalucha looked thoughtfully at the boy, almost a young man. The innate power of this soul was clear to behold. He was destined for great leadership.

"You have learned well, Chan Chak," she said sincerely. "Look fear in the face, stare into its eyes, know it for what it is, and it loses power over you. Strength of will, determination, and courage turned danger away. Even as a child you showed wisdom."

He smiled, pleased at this acknowledgement from his mentor.

"Courage will serve you well in many situations," she continued, "but look more deeply. Peel off the layers, see courage for what it really is. Courage is educated fear. Reflect on this, Chan Chak. Yes, courage is a quality of the wise soul and absolutely necessary for a great leader in this world. You must continue to develop courage. And, you must learn to go beyond courage to become a shaman. The shaman has a different relationship with nature."

"What is that relationship, Lady Priestess?" inquired Chan Chak. Going beyond courage was a new idea to him.

"It is to *become* nature, to become everything in this world," she replied. "This brings a different level of power. You can use willpower, determination and courage to overcome creatures or natural forces, as you did with the snake. At times this is what is necessary and right. But to attain the powers of the creatures and forces of nature, you must become them. To command the winds and rains, the animals and plants, you must become what you seek. In doing this, you discover your own true being, you open the soul-space to realizing beyond knowledge. Nature does not need knowledge, because nature is knowledge. It is knowledge manifest in the Middleworld. Our human knowledge comes from the investigation of this manifestation.

"Through this investigation, you will come to understand that nature and forces are the imagination of the gods. The gods have dreamed this world into being. Your human nature is hunting your own soul inside this vast realm of imagination. Your soul is the imagination of the ancestors living within the imagination of the gods. And all are living within the vast mind of our Cosmic Source of Being. When you discover this, you know the soul's secret of eternal life. Through the imagination you merge with nature, forces and the gods. You become one with the Source of All."

Yalucha paused, allowing these ideas to sink into the boy's eager mind. His eyes were wide, deep pools of potential, receptive. She continued.

"It is time for you to learn calling. You have practiced focus and learned to observe life, becoming aware of everything around you as one organism with you inside it. Calling can be done once you are merged with nature around you. Calling brings animals and birds to you, changes weather and growth of plants. A shaman must possess this power. To do calling, you find that place within you that calls different creatures, the place where they become trusting and unafraid, where the mind is still and you are in the remembrance of deeper layers of being. In this practice you come to understand that your heart contains the whole world. Shamans do not simply observe nature, they become nature. To become nature, shamans become a charmer of all that exists in this world."

She rose to her feet, and Chan Chak followed suit.

"Come, we go deeper into the woods," the priestess said. "You will find a place to do calling. Tell me when you are aware of the right place."

They walked off the path, feet crunching on twigs and pebbles. The sounds of birds twittering and chirping, of humming or clacking insects, of soft breezes stirring leaves and grasses filled their awareness. Chan Chak slipped into the consciousness of full perception, every sense alert, attuning his being to nature. He felt the sun's warmth on his skin and the light caress of the breeze. Smells of the woodlands wafted into his nose, warm bark, grassy perfumes, pungent humus, and sharp acrid berries. He tasted wind and woodlands, cooled in shade, felt moist near thickets. A triad of oaks seized his attention. This was the right place.

Without speaking, he nodded toward the triangle formed by the oaks. The small area was filled with damp green grass and shaded by a canopy of intermingled branches. Yalucha assented with her eyes, and found a place not far away to sit as he settled down in the center of the triangle. She spoke the instructions softly, a melody of rippling sound carried on the breeze, blending with rustling leaves.

"Fill yourself with every sensation of this place. Listen to nature's voices, that you may be in this place well. When you are full and one with nature, call a creature with your heart. Your heart will tell you which one to call. Get behind the eyes of the creature you are calling. Become its vision; see the world as it does. Know its likes and dislikes, what it is drawn toward. Become what it desires, what is attractive to it, and the creature will find you irresistible.

"The important thing, Chan Chak, is that you are not chasing the creature. You cannot actively go after it or order it to come, even in your mind. To do calling, you must be humble. Arrogance makes a sound that is offensive to nature. The thinking of the human mind causes a low grinding sound that scares away most creatures and natural forces. So fill your mind, your awareness, your total being with nature herself, until your resonance is attuned to hers. Then you can envision what you are calling, become its own vision that is looking for what is desired. As you become the thing it desires, it will appear to you. Do you understand?"

He nodded, already immersing himself in the beauty and diversity of nature around and within the triangle in which he sat.

"I will remain close by, but make myself invisible," Yalucha added. This was an extremely valuable shamanic skill for use with both nature and humans. Pulling her consciousness into a tiny point, and stilling her metabolism to just enough activity to keep the body alive, the priestess seemed to disappear into the dance of shadow and light in the dappled sunlight under the oaks.

Chan Chak closed his eyes and allowed nature's expressions to permeate his senses. A cacophony of sounds filled his ears with twitters, pops, chirps, clacks, creaks, groans, liquid notes of birdsong, whispering breeze in the leaves. His skin felt each subtle change of checkered shade and sun, coolness and warmth, hairs stirring in wind currents. The moisture of the grass and hardness of earth below spoke to his muscles and bones. Smells wafted in delicious contrasts, sweet, acrid, pungent, woody. There were no images in his mind, just sensations. His soul began to merge with nature around him, melting the boundaries of his being.

Suddenly his mind jumped alert, rebounding into self-awareness. He was this boy sitting on the ground in this woodland doing this exercise. The mind did not want him to slip too far away. He calmed his mind, as he had learned, reassuring it that he would come back. Then he slipped into nature awareness again, going farther into oneness, pulsing with her vibrations, being her vibrations.

Something tickled his left knee. It was only a hint of touch, the softest brush of presence. Opening his eyes, he looked down and saw a vivid blue *pepen*—morpho butterfly—perched nonchalantly on his knee. Its open, slowly flapping wings were the most pure, intense blue, like the cloudless sky after rain. They were edged with cocoa brown, and as they closed together he saw the big, brown circles underneath that looked exactly like eyes. The butterfly uncurled its long, thin feeding tube and probed against his skin as if expecting to find nectar.

Instantly the boy's consciousness was inside the butterfly, he was looking through prisms of multi-chambered eyes at his own knee, the pores distinct and small hairs standing erect here and there. From this view he watched the feeding tube move, probing skin pores. No openings into the nectar inside. He felt the wings beating faster with stronger flaps, as the butterfly lifted into the air and proceeded through the triangle in typical bouncy flight that made it difficult to catch.

He was back behind his own eyes, but not entirely. Rapidly changing perspectives gave him views of himself from inside a tree and looking upward at his towering statue form from pebbles on the ground. He closed his eyes and merged again with nature. A fox. He was calling a gray fox. The butterfly had come of its own, but now he deliberately formed intention to call a fox. A clear image of the small canine formed, standing about knee height, its reddish-gray coat sporting a black stripe down the back and a creamy underside. Its bushy tail was full and half as long as its body. A lighter tan mask highlighted its almond eyes and black nose. Trotting rapidly, it panted with small pink tongue protruding, paws fanning for balance on the rock-strewn grasslands.

The gray fox preferred to hunt at night, but might be seen during the day skirting along the edges of clearings next to wooded forests. This agile creature could climb trees by grasping the trunk between front paws and scooting up the shaft. Often it perched on branches, using its long tail for balance, while scouting its territory.

Chan Chak was inside the gray fox, looking out through its eyes, low to the ground. The brush and trees seemed much taller, the grass served as cover. Eyes scanning back and forth, it watched for movement of prey such as mice, rabbits, insects and birds. It liked birds, but these were hard to catch. Chan Chak assumed qualities of a bird, feathered, flittering, chirping, hopping, making sweet song and

437

sweet meat. He felt himself as a bird, sitting very still, a succulent morsel for a gray fox.

An animal odor, pungent in a different way than the woods, struck his nose. Faint panting sounds and footsteps cracking tiny twigs reached his ears. The fox was there.

He opened his eyes, staring into the masked face of a gray fox sitting a short distance from him in the triangular clearing. Boy eyes and fox eyes met and merged. Moments of utter stillness passed, neither creature moving a muscle. The fox did not pant and Chan Chak held his breath. Fox *itz* flowed into the boy's heart. He had called the gray fox and its qualities were now his: cunning, speed, wiliness, endurance.

*   *   *   *   *

The education of Chan Chak K'ak'nal, future ahau of Uxmal, was entrusted to three prominent leaders in their separate domains. Yalucha, High Priestess of Ix Chel, esteemed healer and shaman, keeper of the Old Religion of Izapa and she who remembered the ancient ways, was responsible for mentoring the young prince in the timeless wisdom of harnessing the powers of the natural world. The High Priest of Uxmal, Mac Ceel, guided the young man who would inherit rulership through rites of manhood, the techniques necessary for invoking the vision serpent, and the divinatory responsibilities of the king. Huntan Pasah, the Captain of Uxmal's forces and Chief Warrior, was charged with training him for leadership in battle, honing skills with knife and spear to rival those of any warrior of the city, and developing the requisite skills to inspire and direct groups of strong-willed men toward common goals.

His father, the King of Uxmal, modeled the finesse of diplomacy and the intelligence of negotiation when relating to the city's nobles as well as leaders of allied cities. Uxmal had become the most powerful city in the Puuc region well before Chan Chak was born, dominating its neighbor cities of Kabah and Nujpat. Streaking from the hub at Uxmal like raised white spokes, long sacbeob linked these cities. During the tuns of Chan Chak's growing into manhood, Uxmal formed a key alliance with the upcoming power in the northern peninsula, Chichén Itzá.

Settled by a shadowy people from the eastern coast, the Putun Maya, this large city was an amalgamation of various Maya and Mexica groups. The hybrid creation blended their different architectural styles and religious practices. It was a synthesis of Maya

438

and Mexica iconography, dress and customs. Chichén Itzá made a striking departure from the traditional Maya system of governance, in which a king from a ruling lineage inherited leadership, and coalesced around him noble families who provided warriors for battle and tribute for sustenance. The rulership of the new city was shared among a group of *yitah*, "companions" or "brothers." Actual brothers and cousins of the Kokom family were co-rulers, joined by others allied through common purposes and beliefs. These men formed a *multepal*, a joined reign. This governance by a collective was an innovation, never seen before. It appeared to inspire followers to high levels of dedication, and espoused a cult of warriors that had significant influence on the governing council.

Uxmal, based on the traditional royal lineage form of governance, initially struck an uneasy alliance with the innovative Chichén Itzá. But the arrangement served both well, and the cities became more comfortable with their different styles in time. A large confederacy formed with alliances to Dzibilchaltún and Izamal. Shortly it grew into the most formidable power in the Maya world, and Chichén Itzá became the largest and most renowned city in Mesoamerica, controlling most of the northern peninsula.

Chan Chak underwent rites of manhood at the end of his first katun, twenty tuns after his birth. The High Priest, Mac Ceel, initiated him in his first bloodletting ritual. After a preparatory period of fasting and seclusion, and induction with a hallucinatory mushroom brew, the young man used the traditional stingray spine to pierce his penis. In the trance induced, as smoke rose from the burning blood-soaked bark paper, he sought the vision serpent for communing with ancestors and gods. Just seeing the vision serpent was enough in the early stages of this art; later as ruler he would be expected to receive messages of importance for his people.

The next stage of manhood rites was directed by Huntan Pasah, the Chief Warrior. Chan Chak was required to stalk and kill a jaguar, to obtain the skin as his cloak of rulership and to assume the animal's powers. A small band of warriors accompanied the young prince, but they could not protect him from the risks of hunting the jaguar alone. This was a fearsome time, as he might be killed or fail in his quest. Either way, the omens would be bad for his city. The King of Uxmal, the young man's mother, the High Priest, Yalucha and the rest of the city spent a few tense kins awaiting the results of this test. To everyone's relief, the young man succeeded in stalking and single-handedly killing a mature male jaguar with a magnificent pelt. Great feasting and much balche consumption marked the celebration of this confirmation of his manhood.

After these rites of manhood, Chan Chak was changed. Yalucha became acutely aware of these subtle differences that also changed their relationship. The young man's new presence conveyed an inevitable ruthlessness that would be used when necessary. The High Priestess was well aware of this quality in powerful men, and realized it was required for the decisions they must make. But she missed the heart-opening innocence of his boyhood. An emotional gap was created between them, one that could not be bridged completely. While she could support him in kingly undertakings, the decision points were places where he would travel alone.

This was not surprising. It was a stage in his maturation that she anticipated. She was surprised, however, by the impact of his full male sexuality upon her. When he was a boy and adolescent, she loved him deeply as a mother would and beyond that: her dedication was to expanding his mind, growing his soul, bringing out the finest in his character. This love was simultaneously personal and impersonal, a strange marriage of sensitivities. Her heart touched his through multiple levels of being, including the sensuality of nature's beauty and wonders. But this raw sexual energy was something else.

Yalucha had chosen not to marry, although most priests and priestesses did have families of their own. She had been a striking beauty as a young woman, pursued by several eager men, but something inside kept her from accepting their intimacy. Containment of sexual energies provided the inner fire to propel her spiritual quest, and she advanced rapidly through the priestly hierarchy to become the youngest High Priestess the city had seen. This sexual, creative life force inspired her teaching and fueled the power of ceremonies and rituals that she conducted. She did not regret this decision for celibacy—except now.

The torrents of sexual desire thundering through her body as Chan Chak came into manhood left her shaken. Her mind was perplexed; she knew this was inappropriate for her relationship with the young prince. It was also ridiculous; she was twice his age and he obviously saw nothing sexual about her. Gossip spread around the city about which noble maiden would be chosen as his wife. He was clearly looking around, appraising the young beauties of the city. Catching a glimpse of Chan Chak flirting almost brought Yalucha's heart to a sudden stop: His dark intelligent eyes glowing with the embers of passion, the hard muscled body of admirable proportions, the charming smile parting full sensuous lips over straight white teeth, forming just the hint of a dimple in the left cheek.

He was heart-wrenchingly handsome. She was hopelessly in love with him, desire burning in every cell. This unsettling and unseemly attraction had stolen her serenity of mind and thrown her unruly body into clamoring turmoil. She had to do something about it, to get a grip on this process and to overcome it.

The High Priestess prepared for a vision quest in which she would seek answers about the source of this ill-advised passion for the young prince. She was experienced enough to need little preparation time, and to undertake journeys without having someone serve as an anchor back to the Middleworld. But because her emotions were running so high, she took the time for careful preparation. Ruefully, she recognized the need to follow her own advice to acolytes: purify body and mind, practice austerities, empty out in order to create sacred space inside. Without that sacred inner space there was no room for spirit information to enter.

She waited for the dark of the moon to undertake the quest. She sought what was hidden, out of sight, deep and dark recesses where secrets abided in timeless silence. In the cool darkness of midnight she retraced familiar steps to the Ix Chel temple not far from her house in the Complex of Priestesses. Only a small oil-wicked shell provided flickering light, but she could walk this path in total darkness, so often had she come here. Inside the temple set on a low platform, she prepared the altar with her gifts and the hallucinatory mushroom brew of vision quests. After invocations and taking a few sips of the brew, she pinched out the wick to sit in near-total darkness.

Come, Serpent of Visions, she called silently. *Rise within, rise without, all is one. Bring me the answers I seek, known to you. What is my soul's connection with the soul of Chan Chak, through all eons of time and timeless being? Whisper to me, Serpent. Hiss these truths into my waiting ears. I am ready. I await you.*

Gradually her sense of self melted away, her boundaries dissipated until only pure awareness floated on a vast sea of consciousness. A waterspout began rising from this sea, twisting and swaying, turning into a sea serpent of immense proportions. Rivulets flowed down its smooth silvery-blue skin, and it fixed her with glistening slitted eyes, opened its huge fanged mouth and spewed out fine mists that formed a rapid sequence of ephemeral impressions.

Dark vast reaches of space. Twinkling stars and glowing nebula dust. A dream in the Cosmic Mind, coalescing into tiny comets,

*raining into sombrero galaxies. Globes twirling around a brilliant
sun. The void empty under the sky, rippling, sighing, murmuring,
humming. Endless sea pooled under the sky, at rest, nothing stirring.
The world in potential, waiting. Words of the gods whispered across
the waters, clouds swirled above, lightning flashed. Land gathered in
the space between raised sky and water below. One huge land,
immense, unfathomable.*

*Beings walked the huge land, very tall and transparent.
Complete beings, needing nothing else. Totally aware and one with
each other and The Source, dreaming its dream of the world.
Lemulia, land of first beings. The dream became denser. The beings
drew apart, aware now of separateness. They were unified souls, not
male or female. They were still happy and close to The Source. The
huge land broke apart, forming smaller lands. Volcanic mountains
erupted, deep chasms formed and the sea filled them, forming
channels. Beautiful white cities draped over cliffs dropping
precipitously into the sea. The tall beings came and mingled with the
new star migrants of Atlantiha.*

*The dream became denser still. Magnificent structures, powerful
crystals, flying palanquins, beings structuring reality. Her tall unified
being entered the round water chamber, agreeing as it must be.
Dividing in two, mirror forms, one female and one male. The soul
split and gave up its wholeness. The unified being became two. They
knew intimately, but were strange to each other.*

*Through many lives, in many lands, through cataclysms and re-
forming, sinking and rising, dropping farther into denseness, the split
soul wandered apart and sought itself. Again and again, until it
forgot. Only deep in the infinitesimally small, intertwined cell
serpents did remembrance continue. And sometimes in the intuition.*

*Lifehoods in which these split souls sought each other,
sometimes finding and sometimes not. Masters from the sunken land,
bringing high knowledge to Turtle Island. Early times of the Maya
predecessors. Izapa lifetimes, nurturing the seeds that came into
brilliant bloom as the wisdom and ways of the Maya people. The split
soul was there, close at times, intimate, joyful. At other times one soul
walked the Middleworld alone, or could not find the other. Her
priestess ancestor of the same name in Mutul, the young enemy
warrior of a similar name, the deep love and explosive passion, the
tragic loss and acceptance, the never-ending yearning. It was all
clear now. The pledge, the promise to find each other, dancing*

442

*through the Three Worlds, unconsciously looking for clues, lives
linked inexorably. Souls seeking union.*

Yalucha's self-awareness gathered together just enough to pose
another question. The sea serpent continued to undulate before her
inner vision.

What now, Serpent of Visions? What else lies ahead?

*Distressing images of deteriorating conditions, worsening
warfare and abandonment of the lovely city of Uxmal appeared. The
time was not that far away. The king and the priestess went separate
ways. Something of great import must be done before this. A ritual at
Chichén Itzá, at the Pyramid of Kukulkán, to preserve and hide Maya
wisdom, the esoteric teachings, the shamanic practices. She would be
there, and the High Priest of Uxmal with six others. This was her true
mission. Times of great travail and suppression would descend upon
her people, brought by those who could not respect the ancient
wisdom. So it would go underground, into dimensions inaccessible to
those who were not adepts, and safely kept until conditions were right
for its re-emergence.*

*And, if conditions did coalesce for this re-emergence, her soul
would be there again, in this far distant future time. As would the
others participating in the ritual. There was uncertainty, however.
Many beings would be involved in setting the right conditions in the
world. Several potential futures existed.*

And her split soul? Would it be united?

*That was in the domain of potential. The opportunity would be
present, but the capacity for recognizing it was the unknown factor.*

*Unknown . . . hanging in the domain of potential . . . choices,
awareness . . .*

The High Priestess reflected for a long time on the messages of
the Vision Serpent. These were things that went beyond what she had
been taught, but that rang true with her intuitive nature. Remembering
the lifehood of Yalucha of Mutul, her ancestor, brought deep
understanding about her soul connection with Chan Chak. He had
forgotten, however. Despite his considerable psychic abilities, this
elusive strata of memory remained outside his awareness. Perhaps
this was for the best, she conceded. He had his work of this lifetime,
creating a magnificent city and leading his people. In this
understanding, and in accepting the bittersweet reality of being so
close to her eternal beloved yet kept apart by their roles in life, she
found comfort.

Slowly she transmuted the intense, consuming sexual passions into the serpent fire of soul awakening. The secrets of existence revealed themselves. She knew the paths to all the worlds and traveled them with acumen. Other qualities of the ideal soul came forth, those not fully developed before. She knew and embraced the quality of necessary ruthlessness. Ruthlessness meant killing what was in the way. Things dear to the self that impeded the soul's growth, habits, sentiments, points of view, comforts, were slashed away with the sharp discrimination of ruthlessness. In telling the truth to those seeking her guidance, she often had to say things that appeared hurtful or cruel, things that disturbed their way of life. But without themselves using ruthlessness to cast out what no longer served, people could not make changes to attain their goals for healing or insight.

She became an unparalleled seer, whose counsel was sought far and wide. She walked daily with the gods and goddesses. The Otherworld presence hovered around her, not just during vision quests. The people of Uxmal sensed this and accorded her the respect and also the distance given to great shamans. Her soul found peace, and balance, and centeredness. She lived a life of dignified grace.

In the works of Chan Chak after he became ruler of Uxmal, she could see his remembrance of the once-unified soul. Not in a personal way, but in the symbolic language of glyphs and carved images, in the perfect symmetry of the Spirit Quadrangle and the stellar elegance of the Royal Palace constructed under his inspiration. Within his artistic being this vision was born, and through his skillful leadership it was materialized into large-scale form to evoke awe in all who visited these structures of Uxmal—for ages not yet dreamed of.

When Yalucha stood in the center of the wide plaza enclosed by the Spirit Quadrangle, she felt most intimately connected with Chan Chak's soul. The beauty of the frescoes and the profound symbolism in every detail of the structures were breathtaking. The Spirit Quadrangle adjoined the towering Sky Pyramid, Itzam Ka'an, to the east, with a small plaza in between. Four long, narrow buildings framed the Quadrangle, each standing on a different level and varying in form and design according to its purpose. They blended into a harmonious whole, united by long horizontal vistas of wide stairways, platforms, and the medial and upper moldings that defined the plain lower section of each building from the richly ornamental, carved mosaics of the upper section. Symmetrically placed doorways caught the viewer's eye; each building had uniquely meaningful numbers and sizes of doors.[20]

The formal entrance into the Spirit Quadrangle was through the South Building,[21] where a towering corbelled arch above a wide stairway gave passage straight through the center of the building. This

Spirit (Nunnery) Quadrangle, Uxmal

ceremonial entrance funneled processions of elaborately costumed lords, musicians and dancers into the plaza. Its huge frame focused upon the center of the North Building, the imposing royal structure standing highest of the four. Each side of the South Building had eight evenly placed doors, each leading into a single room, four on each side of the corbelled arch. The number eight represented universal harmony in duality, the unified perfection of Spirit reflected in the opposites of the natural world. Adding the central corbelled arch, there were nine doors, which stood for the nine layers of Xibalba, the Underworld. The South Building also had the lowest placement in the Quadrangle complex; this together with the number nine signified its association with the cycles of life and death.

The medial and upper moldings enclosed an entablature full of symbolic meanings. Small *itz* flowers were placed at regular intervals on the upper molding. *Itz* was sacred nectar, spirit energy, to make magic. This symbol marked the South Building as an *Itzam Nah,* a "Conjuring House" where magic was made, where *itz* was

---

[20] This complex was named "The Nunnery Quadrangle" by Spanish explorers, as it reminded them of nunneries in Spain.
[21] Capstones on three of these structures provide a building sequence: The South Building was dedicated on 10.3.17.3.19 (April 23, 906), the East Building on 10.3.17.12.1 (October 2, 906), and a small structure near the North Building on 10.3.18.9.12 (August 9, 907). The last inscription notes that "the writing of Chan Chak K'ak'nal Ahau was raised."

445

experienced. Small mosaic sculptures of thatched-roof houses stood over each door amidst a lattice pattern, with the Maize God's face carved above. In this building, representing the house where the first people were made from maize and water, rituals were done to remember First Father in his guise as the maize plant, the Maize God, and his resurrection from Xibalba by his sons the Hero Twins. It carried special energies that enhanced seekers' abilities to conjure the history and mythos of their people.

The North Building, facing across the plaza, rested on the highest platform that was approached by a grand stairway flanked by two colonnaded smaller buildings. This platform stood at the level of the medial moldings of the East and West Buildings, creating a flowing visual continuity. Eleven doorways punctuated the front wall, with additional doors at each end of the building giving thirteen doors in total, each leading to a double-chambered room. Thirteen was the number of sacred cycles, the base of the tzolk'in calendar, the way the universe revealed itself. It was the number of the thirteen layers of heaven, the celestial realm. The imagery and symbolism of this building contained the most important aspects of Maya life.

The most immediate impact upon viewing the North Building came from nine towering stacks of masks, one over every other door. The uppermost masks soared well above the roof like sky sentinels. The face was that of Tlaloc, with goggles around eyes, a nose bar and curving upper lip containing a mouth full of teeth. Tlaloc evoked a long history of conquest wars, honored the powers inherited from Teotihuacan, and declared Uxmal a "Place of Reeds," a source or origin place intimately connected with creator gods. Under the Tlaloc masks were four phantasmagoric images with long beak-like noses, intricate and varied, most wearing flower ornaments on their foreheads that identified them as *Itzam-Ye*, the bird avatar of Itzamna. The central mask towers were flanked by stacked snake heads and twisted cords of the sky umbilicus that connected Maya leaders to their sacred source of power in the Overworld. S-shaped cloud scrolls around the masks emphasized their place in the cosmos above, and foliated maize plant scrolls depicted their creative link with the earth below.

The entablature contained a flowered lattice, marking the building as a *popol-nah* or "mat house" where ruler and nobles gathered to sit on mats and conduct affairs of state. This was an assembly house, used for council meetings and for dancing important stories in public festivals. The elevated platform provided a site where the king, nobles and priests would conduct community events, visible to all gathered in the plaza below. Alternating with the flower lattice were square S-shaped cloud scrolls, with glyphs that read *muyul,* cloud. The activities that occurred here were of the highest domain, connected to the sky gods of the Overworld. Small, carved thatch-roof houses sitting over doors 3, 5, 7 and 9 were adorned with rearing double-headed serpents, marking them as places where vision rituals took place: *kan-nah,* a "sky house" or "serpent house." Under the door of each little house was a small jaguar throne, unusual in its configuration of two crouched jaguars sitting back-to-back with tails entwined. This testified that the king was a central figure in rituals and conjuring taking place in the North Building.

The North Building was wrought with high purpose and powerful symbolism. Many times over the tuns since its construction, Yalucha participated along with the High Priest Mac Ceel as Chan Chak K'ak'nal, ruler of Uxmal, led community ceremonies from the high platform of the North Building.

The East Building sat on a platform that was level with the medial molding of the South Building, giving a sense of integration between the structures. A wide stairway ran along the entire front of the East Building, lifting the plaza up toward its five doorways and front facade. The largest central door opened into a complex of six rooms; the other four doors led to double-chambered compartments with no back access. *Itz* flowers decorated the upper molding, marking this as an *Itzam Nah,* conjuring house. Three stacked *Itzam-Ye* masks rose above the central door, and similar stacks perched at the corners of the roof. Lattice patterns covered the entire front entablature, interrupted by six V-shaped double-headed serpent designs. Called *kan che'* or "snake wood," these represented inverted cribs for holding dried maize. Small mosaic masks sat near the top of each kan che' with scaly faces, feather and jewel headdress, a protruding tongue and spear-thrower darts crossed behind. This lizard-warrior mask and the eastern location signified the struggle of life as the sun is reborn each morning. This building served as a conjuring place for nature spirits who influenced birth, weather, rain and growing crops.

The West Building rested on a platform level with that of the East Building, and its medial molding aligned with the high platform of the North Building. A wide stairway ran across the entire width, mirroring the east stairway across the plaza. Seven doors led into double-chambered rooms with no back entrances. A spectacular entablature spanned the entire upper section, running between stacked corner masks. The upper molding was decorated with *itz* flowers, and the masks had flower headbands from which two snakes emerged, one having diamondback patterns and the other with a feathered body. Cloud scrolls and flower-lattice panels as background marked the building as a community house and a sky house. Small, carved houses sat above doors 1 and 7 with masks wearing flower and feathered serpent headbands, indicating the building was also a conjuring house, an *Itzam Nah*. Large masks of *Itzam-Ye* birds over doors 2 and 6 confirmed this.

The community-cloud-conjuring house purposes of the West Building were concerned with the soul's growth in the Middleworld. The number seven represented the mystic surfaces of the earth, and the power centers within the human body, *chaklas*. In this building, acolytes in priestly training received instructions and underwent mystical experiences. People of the city seeking assistance with their personal soul development, needing to deal with spiritual issues, and undertaking vision quests came to the West Building. Other symbols conveyed this process: Carved human figures on cloud scrolls with bloodletting sticks penetrating skin of thighs and penises, or wearing feathered capes and *Itzam-Ye* masks; kneeling figures inside sky palanquins; god images emerging from flowers, being born in visions through flower *itz*.

Four feathered serpents undulated and intertwined across the entire span of the entablature, wrapping around masks, houses and cloud scrolls. Ancestor figures emerged from the gaping jaws of raised snake heads, and the four tails had rattles. A "drummajor" headdress wrapped in the serpent's coils near the tail conveyed the image of war, and evoked connections with the Temple of the Feathered Serpent at Teotihuacan, now lost since the collapse of the great Mexica Empire many katuns ago. On a personal level, this symbolized the "war" for one's soul against the dark Underworld forces.

Yalucha did most of her teaching and personal guidance in the West Building. As High Priestess, she oversaw the training of both female and male acolytes, and worked with advanced students herself. Standing in the center of the cool double-chambered room, surrounded by young women seated on mats on the floor, Yalucha explained the use of several ritual objects. Light from the entry door penetrated the first chamber well, but the second remained dim. It was used for storage of objects and materials. Glancing at the alert faces of her students, the High Priestess found herself hovering between two worlds, living in two simultaneous realities for long moments.

One part of her consciousness was present in another city, at another time. It was a jungle city, surrounded by dense tropical foliage and very humid. The calls of parrots and myriad birds wafted through the heavy air. She could see the place through the eyes of a young girl, not yet at puberty. The room was a long rectangle with one door and a few small windows. A group of girls sat on mats around their teacher, a stately woman with commanding but gentle presence, wearing a white huipil with embroidered hem and sleeves. The young girl's eyes—her eyes—were fixed upon the priestess, full of love and admiration. Her mother? Someone very close.

This priestess was imparting the hidden wisdom of the old religion, the great teachings from the Izapa tradition. These were acolytes of Ix Chel, even as Yalucha's students were now. She perceived the long chain of women, of Ix Chel priestesses, reaching across baktuns, transmitting sacred knowledge, keeping the truth alive. Her heart swelled and overflowed with appreciation and profound gratitude. She was honored to be carrying forth this tradition, and was comforted to see its continuity. But she knew forces were gathering to threaten this continuity, to destroy this ancient wisdom. She prayed silently:

It must be preserved. Show me the way, what I am to do in the coming darkness.

*   *   *   *   *

Uxmal was busily preparing for katun end ceremonies, the end of Katun 12 Ahau and beginning of the next katun on 10.4.0.0.0. (January 20, 909 CE) The city had much to celebrate, having completed a katun that saw expansive construction under the inspired guidance of their young king, Chan Chak K'ak'nal. Their confederacy with Chichén Itzá dominated the landscape of the northern peninsula, having defeated all rivals except the eastern city of Coba, which they held at bay. Residents led prosperous and healthy lives, their greatest concern being the favor of Chak in bringing adequate rains to fill their chultunob. The king's wife had recently given birth to their third child, the second son, a vigorous boy. With succession guaranteed, strong military alliances, and sacred structures that were widely acknowledged as the most beautiful ever raised in the Puuc, the city was in at an apex of success. During the katun end ceremonies, the ruler Chan Chak would undertake a vision quest for predictions about the coming katun. The people felt certain all omens would be good.

In the early evening, with torches flickering around plazas and cooking fires glowing inside dwellings, the High Priestess wound her way past the graceful structures of the city to the Royal Palace. Chan Chak had summoned her to his residence, several kins before the katun end ceremony. In the morning he would begin purification rituals, fasting in seclusion, to prepare for invoking the vision serpent.

Passing the ball court facing the ceremonial entrance through the corbelled arch of the Spirit Quadrangle's South Building, Yalucha climbed the wide stairway onto the high platform of the Royal Palace. The magnificent residence and administrative complex built by Chan Chak never failed to take her breath away. The long, straight building was of epic proportions, longer than the Spirit Quadrangle. It stood on three distinct raised platforms, divided with exquisite balance into three sections linked by grand corbelled arches. Twenty rooms with separate entrances faced the plaza in front, approached by a stairway covering the middle third of its length. In keeping with Chan Chak's building style, the lower façade was plain, and the upper contained elaborate mosaics with powerful symbolism. Several seated human figures appeared among lattice patterns, cloud scrolls, and Itzam-Ye masks. The most impressive figure sat over the central doorway, depicting the ruler seated on a throne and wearing a huge feathered headdress. Nine double-headed serpent bars radiated outward horizontally from this figure, signifying his royal authority.

The Royal Palace was oriented at a different axis than all other structures at Uxmal. It faced east-southeast toward a solitary mound 3.5 miles (5.6 km) away. Over this mound, Venus rose as Morningstar at its southerly extreme. Hieroglyphic inscriptions on the double-headed serpent bars depicted the constellations visible in the night sky at the time of this Venus alignment, toward which the building was oriented. Chan Chak was the living expression of the cosmic Venus cycles that played out the fortunes of the Hero Twins, their earthly representative in the person of the king, and the Maya people.

Yalucha ascended the stairway and stood politely at the doorway into the ruler's quarters, waiting to be acknowledged. In the main chamber, the central hearth fire danced against the three traditional hearthstones, a pot of cacao drink bubbling with an enticing aroma. Chan Chak was sitting on a plush woven mat, holding his little daughter. The toddler was a sunny-natured girl, already much loved by the community for her bright disposition. Her laughter sounded like tinkling seashells as she played with his ear flares. The young king chuckled, tossing his head about to entrance her with the dancing baubles. Across the hearth fire sat his wife, nursing their youngest infant boy. She looked up and smiled greetings to Yalucha. The voice of their older son carried from a rear chamber where he conversed with his attendant.

Yalucha's heart warmed at this scene of family conviviality. She was thoroughly pleased at Chan Chak's happiness in this moment, her heart full without bitterness. In another lifehood, another circumstance in the vast play of life's dreams, she would be mothering his children and sharing his bed. But that was not her lot now, and she had long ago come to peace with it.

"Greetings, Lady Priestess," said Chan Chak, his smile as charming as ever. "I will join you in a moment." Turning his head, he called softly to his daughter's attendant standing in the shadows, nearly invisible as were skillful servants.

"Would you have cacao?" asked Chan Chak's wife.

"Yes, thank you," replied Yalucha. She enjoyed the hot, peppery beverage.

"And I also," said Chan Chak.

The attendant deftly poured two cups, handing them off before gathering the protesting girl from her father's arms.

Chan Chak rose, nodded to his wife and led Yalucha outside onto the expansive platform of the King's Palace. They sat on the stairs, watching stars appear like tiny lights in the indigo sky, sipping hot cacao. Chan Chak mused for a while, and Yalucha waited silently.

"Yalucha, Mother of My Soul," he said gravely, "I am troubled. All is going well, yet inside I am ill at ease. The cycle of Katun 7 Ahau portends difficulties, it has been the pattern in times past. The vision quest I am to take soon gives me concern. What think you of these things?"

"Katun 7 Ahau is a difficult cycle," she confirmed. "There are trials coming for Uxmal. You do well to be aware of this."

She paused, thoughtfully looking at his profile etched by torchlight. He wore the mantle of rulership well, his high forehead and prominent nose classically handsome, his strong jaw conveying determination and resolve. The ideal soul qualities of fierce courage, passion for his mission, noble grace, and humility that maintained centeredness emanated from his being.

451

The High Priestess considered carefully how much to say. His vision quest must be his own, not colored by her perceptions. She would be there to support him, but not to interfere. The closeness of their souls, however, gave her clairvoyance into his inner processes. She knew what he was thinking, what he was feeling. His intuition had already foreseen hints of what was to come.

"There is great darkness ahead, Lord Chan Chak," Yalucha said. "You are correct that Katun 7 Ahau leads into difficult times. And, Katun 8 Ahau to follow brings widespread disruptions for Uxmal, Chichén Itzá and our allies. More I cannot say. You will know in your vision quest."

Her words settled into patterns already forming within his awareness. He nodded, glancing off into the distance. Even in the moonless night, he knew exactly where the mound of Venus rising sat, picturing in his mind the brilliant Morningstar hanging like a sparkling gem just above the eastern horizon. Venus, his symbol, his stellar mentor.

They sipped hot peppery cacao in silence. Draining his cup, Chan Chak shifted restlessly, and then expressed what lay deeply below his discomfiture.

"Although I am in the fullness of my life, and my people of Uxmal prosper, yet my thoughts turn to death, Holy Mother," said Chan Chak said, his voice deep with emotion.

"The fleeting nature of life is never far from the thoughts of the wise person," Yalucha replied. "But the nature of death, too, is temporary. Your soul knows this, Chan Chak. You are well versed at overcoming the Lords of Death. I have watched the soul in its journeys through the Underworld and back into the land of light. I have talked with the ancestors in the Upperworld, as have you. You know the path."

"Yes," he replied. "And I will take that path again soon. I know these things you speak are truth, Yalucha. Yet, in this moment, life is too sweet. I yearn to stay here in this precious time. It is my failing, Mother of My Soul."

Dropping his head, Chan Chak covered his eyes with one hand.

Aching, throbbing love welled up in her heart for the young king, her split soul. His pain was her pain, his yearning tore at the core of her being. Tears glistened on her eyelids, bespeaking strong emotions she had not felt for some time. The irony of his desire to remain in this life that kept them separate brought a little smile despite the waves of sadness. Indeed, the duality of life in the

Middleworld played trickster to them all. Yet, she could understand. She, too, remembered that powerful attraction to the terrible beauty of earthly life.

"It is not a failing, Son of My Heart," she responded after a few moments. "It is the price of being human. The real measure of how you have grown your soul is this: you will feel the anguish over the beauty of life, and you will live your life to the fullest, and still do what the gods require of you. This I know without doubt."

"I thank you for this kindness, Yalucha. You are always beside me to gentle my heart and champion my soul. My life would not be complete without you. It is truly your wisdom that has brought forth the best of this White Flower Thing, my soul."

Chan Chak sat in silence, watching the stars, musing upon the gods' requirements. He continued:

"I must find guidance from the vision serpent about how to lead my people through these coming times of darkness. I will invoke the ancestors who have seen the fall of the great jungle cities. They will know what must be done. My heart does ache for the beauty that is Uxmal, and my life here, and my people," he said sadly.

"Reflect upon the harmony, balance and sacred mystery you have captured in these great structures," advised Yalucha. "Uxmal is the jewel of the woodland savannahs, a more lovely city has never graced our lands. All the symbols that whisper secret knowledge to those with eyes to see are here. This beauty and wisdom will stand, Chan Chak, long after we are gone. People of a distant future, from unknown lands, will come and be moved into their authentic hearts. You have created a thing of blessing, of eternal *itz*. Let your heart be seated, be content, *nakal kolonton*."

The west plaza of the Sky Pyramid filled with people as the sun descended toward the western horizon, flooding the underbellies of low-hanging clouds with a deep red-orange color. Heavy dark thunderclouds hovered above the topmost pyramid temple, sitting atop three-tiered rounded cones rising in diminishing proportions from an oval base. There were no square corners in the structure except those on the west and east stairs and the two temples, one atop the other, facing west. The Sky Pyramid, *Itzam Ka'an,* was built in five installations following 52 tun cycles that made a complete tzolk'in calendar round. The smaller top temple had only recently been completed.[22]

In the larger second temple, the ruler Chan Chak would conduct ceremonies for the katun end. These were to begin at sunset. From the late afternoon until dusk, processions wound through the Spirit Quadrangle plaza. Lords and their retinues strode in feathered splendor, bringing offerings to place before the jaguar throne of the North Building, where the young king sat in full regalia, already in an altered state of consciousness. Musicians and drummers played rhythmic, plaintive and rousing melodies with flutes, ocarinas, conches, trumpets and many types of percussion instruments. Shaman-priests performed energetic, spellbinding dances in costumes of the jaguar, feathered serpent, Itzam-Ye bird and turtle. The entranced dancers became the uayob they impersonated, leaping, slithering, flapping and ambling in perfect mimicry, and by this

Sky Pyramid (Pyramid of the Magician), Uxmal

process invoked the powers of these creatures into the ceremonies.

After the pageantry concluded, the king and his chief attendants retired into chambers of the North Building for the final preparations. The crowd gradually moved to the smaller plaza facing the Sky Pyramid, where they pressed closely together. Shortly before sunset, the royal procession skirted the plaza, staying largely out of view, to

---

[22] Called the Pyramid of the Magician, or Temple of the Dwarf, this immense structure stands 117 feet high on a base 240 feet long by 120 feet wide. The lowest portion has been carbon dated to 569 CE, and the structure was completed around 900 CE.

ascend the Sky Pyramid by the east stairs and proceed through the inner passages to the recessed rooms of the lower temple.

Chan Chak, the High Priest Mac Ceel, and the High Priestess Yalucha joined in the ancient incantation that began the quest of the vision serpent. They were alone in this most sacred moment, their attendants waiting in the adjoining room. The secret words passed from one set of lips to another, repeating magical syllables known only to the highest adepts. They wore the costumes of their offices, the priestly white robes long and flowing, trimmed in wound silver and gold threads, the king in gem-encrusted waistcloths and collar with spectacular pectoral, arm and leg ornaments. All sported magnificent headpieces with soaring multi-colored feathers, but the king's several-layered drum major crown was by far the most intricate and symbolic.

Thunder rumbled in the distance and a rain-perfumed breeze blew across the elevated temple platform. The mother drum began a deep-throated cadence as the sun slipped behind the distant tree-covered horizon. Mid-voiced drums took up a counterpoint rhythm in building anticipation. Attendants lit torches on either end of the temple platform high above the waiting crowd. An open-ended "Ahhh" resounded from hundreds of throats as a figure appeared on the platform. The upper structures of the pyramid seemed to merge with the black roiling clouds in the darkening sky above. Necks craning back, the people looked up the steep west stairs, bordered on each side the entire length by Chak masks, long hooked noses hanging over gaping mouths, rounded eyes staring fiercely ahead.

The figure in white robes contrasted starkly against the gathering darkness. Spiraling torch flames tossed by wind gusts cast glittering sheens off silver and gold trimming. The High Priestess lifted her arms as the wind whipped her robe into undulating swells. In a high, clear voice that carried easily across the plaza below, she sang the eerie tones of moon invocation long part of the old religion. She called to the great goddess Ix Chel, mother of the world and all beings, consort of Itzamna who was the first and most powerful sorcerer in this Creation. As the last few notes floated into the night, the High Priest stepped out next to her and intoned in his rich bass voice, invoking Hunab Ku-First Father, Itzamna, Chak in his four forms, K'awil the god of divination, and a litany of lesser gods. In the final stanzas, the priest and priestesses' voices joined together in exquisite harmonies, haunting minor melodies that resolved into a transcendent major chord. It bespoke perfect balance of masculine

455

and feminine forces, even as Uxmal's beautiful structures conveyed that same balance and harmony.

Barely visible to the crowd below, the ruler stood behind the priest and priestess. As their intertwined voices came to the final crescendo, Chan Chak K'ak'nal stepped forward to the platform edge. Torchlight on his resplendent costume created rainbow sparkles; light seemed to radiate out from his form in a halo of brilliant quetzal feathers. The crowd gave a sustained loud roar, punctuated with rapid-fire drumbeats and echoing conch shell blasts. Cradling his serpent bar in one arm, he made gestures of benevolence with the other raised arm. The great pulsating devotion of king to subjects, subjects to king arced with the drum cadence into a tangible force of transcendent love. Making the cross-armed gesture over his chest, the king signified his acceptance of this charge to lead and provide for his people. They in turn chanted his name with reverence.

Chan Chak backed slowly into the temple door, a huge mouth framed by the jaws of the Cosmic Serpent in the visage of Itzamna, half-closed eyes focused on a distant vision in the far reaches of space. Yalucha and Mac Ceel bowed with crossed arms to the people below, and then turned and followed the king inside the temple. As they disappeared from view, a many-forked streak of lightning blazed across the sky above the temple, quickly followed by an ear-splitting crack of thunder. Within seconds fat raindrops began to fall, splattering on pyramid and plaza stones and bouncing off heads and shoulders of the people below.

It was an auspicious omen. K'awil, god of lightning and opener of visions, spoke loudly from the black night sky and transferred his divination powers to the three seekers.

Quiet fell upon the crowd; the drums were still. In flickering torchlight, spurred on by the heavy rain, people quickly dispersed back to their homes. The king and his priestly attendants would undertake their vision quests during the night. In the morning, the king would convey messages brought by the vision serpent to his people in the Spirit Quadrangle.

Inside the first chamber of the temple, the three seekers removed their robes of office and donned the simple garb of the vision quest. Chan Chak sat in the center on a low four-legged square bench, the "birthing throne" used by kings since time immemorial to bring forth their visions. Two attendants brought bloodletting paraphernalia, one standing by with bark paper in the collection bowl, the other behind to support his back. With calm, unflinching resolve, the king used a stingray spine to pierce his penis. As the royal blood, most sacred to gods of lineage and earthly power, saturated the bark paper, the attendant used glowing coals to ignite it and produce twisting threads of smoke. The king moved quickly into trance state on the swaying coils of the smoke-vision-serpent.

Yalucha and Mac Ceel followed the ancient Izapa tradition of taking hallucinogenic mushroom brew to invoke their visions. They sat cross-legged on low benches on either side of the king. Accepting the cup from her assistant, Yalucha barely touched the brew to her lips. She had taken this journey so many times she hardly needed the botanical aid. The priestess set her intention for this vision quest with invocation prayers and incantations: to receive guidance about the coming times of darkness, and how to preserve the ancient wisdom of the Maya.

Softly, gently her awareness escaped her body. Drifting upward, rising above the Sky Pyramid, she saw its steep stairs descending into the empty plaza below, rivulets of water cascading down in miniature waterfalls. Lightning flashed among the dark clouds, highlighting their contours for an instant. K'awil had split her forehead with his cosmic lightning, opening her consciousness to the Otherworld. As she drifted higher, the entire lovely city of Uxmal appeared below in momentary flashes of illumination—the Spirit Quadrangle, plazas, ballcourt, buildings on broad raised platforms, the Royal Palace, other pyramids, streets, houses, chultunob, sakbeob leading like white spokes into the woodlands.

Higher and higher she went, pulled at increasing speed away from the land below into the night sky. Billions of brilliantly sparkling stars and glowing planets surrounded her. The blissful sound of the celestial spheres enfolded her, a high-pitched hum that came from everywhere simultaneously. This she knew was the sound of creation, of nascent potential waiting to be vibrated into existence. A force pulled her consciousness toward the dark rift in the Milky Way, the Cosmic Mother's birth canal and sacred conduit between earth and the innermost planes of the galaxy. This passage led to the Central Sun, the Galactic Center, home of Itzamna, Father of the Gods, original creator of the Maya people, first priest and greatest shaman, inventor of writing and books for sacred knowledge.

Yalucha had not directly encountered Itzamna before, although she and all shaman-priest-healers used his essence or sacred *itz* in their conjuring and healing processes. As Yalucha's consciousness entered the center of the Milky Way, incredible golden-white brilliance of the Central Sun consumed her. All traces of awareness dissolved, melted into blazing light. Beyond any form, beyond any thought, her essence merged into oneness with the Cosmic Intelligence and she *was* the stars, planets, consciousness and beingness of all that was.

And she was merged into the Cosmic Heart of Itzamna.

Sea of bliss, light of infinity, without beginning or end,

Breath of Eternity, exhaling and inhaling universes in the boundless cycles of creation, all intelligence, all knowing, all being.

All life, the body of the universe,

Infinitesimally small and greater than the sphere in which the cosmos breathes.

Molten light coaxing the stars, planets, water, earth, trees, matter, true people into existence,

To dance through worlds in the play of love-hate, health-disease, life-death

Shadows on the screen of duality until awakened into memory divine.

True humans—halach uinic—of the Fourth Sun, sparks of the Cosmic Creator bringing forth shining white cities in the green forests,

Sacred calendars of vast eons, cycles within cycles that know the timing of stellar wisdom and the earth's fecundity,

Secrets of how to honor the divine in perfect harmony, to commune with unimagined realms where past, present and future are one,

Seed the world for the next era.

Empty white cities crumbling into dust, swallowed by jungles, inscriptions of proud lineages toppling into rubble,

Legacy of greatness hidden in tombs, secret knowledge concealed in indecipherable codes, waiting for curious intelligence to probe the jungle's treasures.

The World Tree cross in bare wood towering above floating cities of white-faced, bearded strangers,

Metal swords and studded boots crushing the Feathered Serpent,

Black books in unutterable tongues with stern proclamations, words of a distant god capturing and vanquishing the true humans,

The white god of tribute and strife, of trampling on the people with violence and oppression and subjugation, assault on the old gods and sacred knowledge,

Killing diseases devastating the true humans, who fled to forested mountains.

Until a future time, the closing of the World of the Fourth Sun.

When the birth canal of the Cosmic Mother, the dark rift of the Milky Way, aligns above the dawn horizon with the rising Father Sun in the plane of the ecliptic, the Winter Solstice,

The Maya long count of 13.0.0.0.0—completion of the equinoctial cycle, alignment with the Heart of the Galaxy.

Then will open a channel for cosmic energy to flow through the earth, cleansing and healing it and all that dwells upon it, raising all to a higher level of vibration.

Rebirth into a new age, the World of the Fifth Sun.

Prepare for the coming baktuns of darkness.

Hide the cosmic wisdom, the secret knowledge of creation cycles, in the inter-dimensional chamber beneath the Pyramid of Kukulkán at Chichén Itzá. There it will be safe. It must be kept alive in the hearts and souls of the shamans who live through the times of darkness, so they can remember and reawaken the sacred temples.

Within the heart of every human is a secret chamber. Hidden inside this chamber is, literally, all creation, the entire universe. This Heart of the Cosmos is inside. Know this place. Learn to enter it during earth life. From here, all is manifested without duality.

When the wisdom and knowledge of the Maya are placed underground, beneath the Pyramid of Kukulkán, the individual secret heart chambers of eight true humans, four men and four women, must merge into one, become the collective heart of the Maya people. Only by perfect balance of male and female energies, and creation of the collective heart chamber, can this be done.

The time of reawakening, of re-emergence of the Maya wisdom, is the final two katuns before the end of the long count calendar.

Many shamans will heed the call, listening to the whispers from the Cosmic Intelligence, and emerge to become teachers for diverse peoples across the earth. The souls of the eight who placed the wisdom underground will be summoned, through their beings of that future lifetime. These beings will gather at the Pyramid of Kukulkán to revive and bring forth the hidden wisdom and knowledge of the ancient Maya.

The Maya people are the keepers of the sacred cycles, knowers of galactic movements that bring enthronement of First Father-Sun in the Cosmic Mother's heart. And so they give birth to the new age, the World of the Fifth Sun.

459

This is an age of unity. The greatest Maya wisdom conveys how to live a life of unity and harmony with other beings and the earth, to grow the soul, to become a true human.

Take this and place it below the Temple of Kukulkán at Chichén Itzá.

The morning was clear and bright, with puffy white clouds sailing serenely across the deep blue sky. Freshness was everywhere, in the sparkling white plaster on plaza and stairs newly washed by the night's rain, on the shadow-enhanced carved frescoes decorating upper portions of buildings. Oak and fiddlewood leaves, serrated palms and tiny bushes glistened many shades of green with life-giving moisture. Birds called happily and lizards scuttled over stones to warm in the sun. The woodland gem that was Uxmal luxuriated in the blessings of the gods and awaited their message given last night to the ruler in his vision quest.

Chan Chak K'ak'nal sat inside the central room of the North Building, surrounded by the High Priest Mac Ceel, the High Priestess Yalucha, the Chief Warrior Huntan Pasah, and a cadre of leading nobles and priests. The king's mood was thoughtful; he pondered how much of his vision message to reveal and what to keep secret. His revelation today to the people of Uxmal would contain the positive aspects. Later he would discuss the troublesome aspects with his chief advisors. The coming katun was favorable, but the next katun after would bring increasing difficulties—warfare, drought, and food shortages that put increasing pressure upon the city, and the entire northern peninsula. He had foreseen his grandson leading remnants of the city's population back to the southern jungles, to the mountainous regions where lakes provided reliable water and food. To the land of their ancestors, for renewal and survival. Of this, he would not speak to the people.

Catching the eye of Mac Ceel, the ruler intuited that his High Priest also had received an important message, not favorable. Glancing at Yalucha, he read the same quality in her energies. So it was, even as he had sensed before this ritual. Uxmal, and the Maya world, was heading toward dark times.

Nodding readiness to the chief steward of ceremonies, Chan Chak lifted his head and squared his shoulders that supported magnificent but heavy regalia. The drums began and the procession of priests, priestesses and nobles poured out onto the raised platform. The crowd gathered in the Spirit Quadrangle court murmured greetings and admiration as the splendidly attired leaders spread across the platform, and the king appeared at the center. As he raised his arms, the drums stopped.

"People of Uxmal," resonated the rich baritone voice of Chan Chak, "the spirits of ancestors have appeared to me. The greatest leaders of the Jaguar Claw lineage of Mutul, my progenitors of many katuns ago, the founder Yax Ch'aktel Xoc, and the restorer of power and master builder Hasaw Chan K'awil, spoke through the mouth of the vision serpent. They commend the structures of Uxmal, the work of carvers and builders, that express the essence and truth of our beliefs. They wish us to erect the World Tree, *Wakah-Kan,* in the center of this plaza with a jaguar altar to commemorate our ruling lineage. All honor to the ancestors; into your hands we surrender ourselves."

"*Ta k'ab c'k'ubicba,* into your hands we surrender ourselves," repeated the crowd.

"This katun brings more good fortune to Uxmal," Chan Chak continued. "Food and rain will be plentiful, our strength in war is upheld with many victories, and our alliance with Chichén Itzá continues in good measure. Rejoice, people of Uxmal, and enjoy the fruits of our righteous actions.

"As this katun draws to a close, clouds of adversity gather around our beloved city. We will be tested by the gods and the forces of nature. Our children, and our children's children, must be prepared and strengthened for these times. In our abundance and stability, let us not be lulled into complacency and forget the needs of the future.

"It is of utmost importance that each person, each one of you, devote yourselves to growing your soul. In the first part of this katun, you have been given an opportunity. Do not allow it to slip away. This is the message brought forth by the gods. First Father-Sun, Maize God, Hunab K'u also appeared through the vision serpent. He wants all his children of Uxmal to become true humans, *halach uinic.* This is the most important thing; become an authentic human. No greater legacy can any person give to our people and the world. In this way, we are prepared for coming challenges. Our soul is strong and pure for any tests.

"Let us honor the bounty of the gods this kin with feasting, dance and celebration."

Long wooden trumpets sounded and multiple drums broke into frenzied cadences, as the crowd roared its pleasure with the favorable katun messages. For now, they would not dwell on the coming

461

challenges. The king and nobles danced on the raised platform, twirling, bowing, legs extending in intricate movements, arms waving and gesturing to represent their *uayob* and patron gods. Steaming pots of stew, trays of maize cakes, fresh fruits, jugs of balche and honeyed cacao were set up around the courtyard periphery by the king's cooks. Thousands of cups and bowls appeared from pouches, carried for the feasting, as the people pushed and surged to partake the king's bounty. Between eating and drinking, many people broke into dance and song as the kin-long celebration proceeded. At sunset, the stela commemorating the ruler's deeds during the past katun would be erected in front of the North Building.[23]

In the late afternoon, Yalucha sat alone on the western stairs of the Complex of Priestesses. She often sat here to watch the sunset. The raised platform provided an unobstructed view across gently rolling woodlands and savannahs stretching to the horizon. In the background she heard music and voices raised in revelry, as the people of Uxmal continued their celebration. Deep in reflection about her vision quest, she did not hear the quiet approach of the High Priest until he stood beside her. Even so, she was not startled. She knew he would come.

"May I join you, Lady Yalucha?" inquired Mac Ceel.

"Yes, please do sit with me," she replied.

The elder priest settled his portly frame with a sigh. That he much enjoyed feasting was all too evident, and he could imbibe balche with the stoutest of warriors. But this kin he had indulged very little, he had no heart for it.

"The sunset is lovely," she commented wistfully. "It brings me peace."

Mac Ceel nodded, gazing at the glowing red orb that dipped halfway below the horizon, casting streamers of golden-pink light amidst the distant treetops. Bedding swallows cooed along roof eaves, crickets chirped in the lengthening shadows.

"We must go to Chichén Itzá," Mac Ceel stated unequivocally.

"This came also to you in the visions," Yalucha stated, already knowing it was so.

---

[23] Stela 17 on the north stairway, though badly eroded, refers to a birth, probably that of Chan Chak K'ak'nal in the tradition of the southern lowlands. It records events taking place during the preceding katun of 12 Ahau, which ended on 10.4.0.0.0 (January 20, 909 CE).

"Yes, and to you. Itzamna has shown what the keepers of wisdom must do in the coming times of darkness. Know you of this method for entering the secret chamber of the heart?"

"I recall a teaching from very long ago, before the time of Izapa, that was written in a small red-and-black codex," she answered. "This method was rarely used after the old religion declined. The codex was passed in my mother's lineage; so far back no one could remember its origins. Yet it seems so important now, why did we forget?"

"Much is forgotten in the dramas of our lives," Mac Ceel observed. "Multiply that by hundreds of people's lives, over many generations, and it is easy to see how wisdom gets lost. Do you still have it?"

"I think so. There is an old, oddly decorated box in which many inherited things stay," Yalucha said. "Perhaps it is inside. I will search for it."

"Did you also receive instruction for male-female balance in the ceremony for interring our people's wisdom and knowledge?" asked Mac Ceel. When Yalucha nodded assent, he continued: "Good. I will select one priest, and you one priestess who are best able to do empowered ritual. But the others must be from Chichén Itzá, their High Priest and Priestess and another pair they select. Since the Pyramid of Kukulkán is the place above the magical chamber, the energies of the Itza must be engaged in the process. Do you agree?"

"Yes, I sense this is essential for the balance of forces that we must engage. I will find the codex, Mac Ceel, and we will learn this secret heart chamber method together. Will you make arrangements with the Kokom of Chichén Itzá?"

"I will do this, Holy Sister. We will gather on Winter Solstice at Chichén Itzá."

*   *   *   *   *

Chichén Itzá, the "Mouth of the Well of the Itza," spread across the flat plain of the north central peninsula. Capital of the hegemonic empire that forged alliances with Uxmal and Mayapan, the city's amalgamation of building styles and decorative symbols reflected the blending of Maya and Mexica religious and cultural traditions. Like a huge quetzal bird hovering low over the ground, the city spread two wings out from the central plaza. One wing led north to the sacred cenote, the well of the Itza, the other wing fanned south to the stellar observatory and noble residences. Serpents were everywhere, decorating stairs, roof corners, doorways, and murals. Together, the

463

quetzal and serpent united into the symbol of Kukulkán, the Feathered Serpent—Quetzalcoatl of the Mexica and the Vision Serpent of the Maya.

No stelae depicting kingly deeds and lineages stood as stone trees in the city of the Itza. Thrones, when pictured in murals or carvings, were empty. Instead, groups of leaders appeared as a brotherhood that shared joint or confederate type of government, *multepal*. Tradition held that Kukulkán established the city, and passed leadership down through the Kokom family in men with *yitah*, or sibling relationship such as Kakupacal and Kin Cimi. These leaders did not care to celebrate their births, accessions, and triumphs as Maya rulers had done for untold generations before them. Rather, they created structures that honored the group, the leaders being "first among equals." Nowhere was this better illustrated than at the Temple of the Warriors, an assembly house with a long rectangular gallery containing over 200 square columns, their intricate carvings showing warriors with Tlaloc-warfare spears, clubs and studded ax blades; each portrait an individual with unique characteristics, differing in detail from the others. In another grouping, captives dressed in rich regalia with bound hands indicated the choices often made by the Itza to respect and absorb their enemies, rather than destroy them. Another grouping of columns displayed priests and shamans, with one intimidating old matriarch marching among the men, the Moon Goddess Ix Chel, called Lady Rainbow, in her old form.

The majestic Pyramid of Kukulkán, The Feathered Serpent, whose Temple of the Sun crowned its heights, rose like a solitary sentinel in the vast central plaza of Chichén Itzá. Every detail of the astounding structure had significance for Maya religion and science. The pyramid represented Snake Mountain, the mystic place of origin where creation first occurred at the legendary "Place of Cattail Reeds," called *Tula* by the Mexica and *Puh* by the Maya peoples. The four-sided square pyramid was formed by nine large tiers with a central staircase on each side leading to the square temple on top. Each stairway had ninety-one steps and all shared a single top step, the temple platform—denoting 365 kins of the solar tun (year). Each side of the pyramid had fifty-two rectangular panels, the number of tuns in the sacred tzolk'in calendar round. The stairways divided the tiers into 18 groupings on each side, corresponding to the 18 uinals (months) of the calendar.

On the north facing side, the stairs were distinguished by two large serpent heads at the base on either side. These were the expression of the serpent form of Kukulkán. Every spring and fall equinox, when the length of daylight and evening hours is equal, a light phenomenon occurred along the western side of these stairs as the sun set. Seven triangles formed, cast on the stairs by shadows of the tiers, becoming the undulating body of the serpent with its head at the base. Sixteen kins before fall and after spring equinoxes, nine complete triangles of shadow and light appeared on the stairs, and 17 kins after fall and before spring equinoxes there were six triangles visible; also times of important ceremonies. At the Winter Solstice, the shortest day, the southern and western faces of the pyramid were bathed in sunlight; while at Summer Solstice, the longest day, the northern and eastern faces caught the sun. To produce these solar phenomena, the northeastern point of the pyramid's square base was oriented exactly 18 degrees from true north.

The sun on Winter Solstice shone dimly through layers of streaky clouds. The air was cool and moist from recent rains that were thankfully absorbed by clusters of oak trees dotting the austere landscape. In the late afternoon, as the sun cast a pale glow on the southern and western faces of the Pyramid of Kukulkán, a small group gathered before its massive bulk. Diminutive forms at the foot of the stone mountain, four priests and four priestesses, half from Uxmal and half from Chichén Itzá, began the ceremony to inter sacred Maya knowledge beneath the pyramid.

The High Priest and Priestess of Chichén Itzá had at once recognized the importance of this ceremony. The coming times of darkness were foretold in their prophesies, and they received omens in their visions portending the need to preserve their traditions from the culture-rending assault of a lengthy reign of oppression. Although this time was still far in the future according to the sacred calendars, the Itza people and their descendents were ordained to confront the bearded white strangers from the east. The holy ones knew they must use their shamanic abilities to save the esoteric teachings, the cosmic knowledge, before their civilization was swept into its declining phases of disruption and dispersal.

Several kins before the Winter Solstice, Yalucha and Mac Ceel traveled to Chichén Itzá and sequestered with the other priests and priestesses. During this period of preparation, they delved deeply into the prophesies and omens. They decided upon rituals, underwent rites of purification, and learned the resurrected method for entering the secret heart chamber, brought by Yalucha from their ancient ancestors, kept in a faint but constant thread of inheritance through the women of her family.

Now they would enact the ceremony at the Pyramid of Kukulkán. It was not a public event, only a few residents of the city walking through the great plaza in the late afternoon cast curious glances at the small cadre of priestly adepts. The High Priest had informed his city's leaders about the joint undertaking with Uxmal, and received their blessings. But there was no fanfare; most citizens of Chichén Itzá never knew the ceremony was taking place.

In keeping with the reclusive energies of the ceremony, the priests and priestesses were simply dressed in unadorned white robes. They wore no headdresses, and left their hair loose and flowing as unobstructed conduits for the most refined and subtle vibrations. Their feet were bare, to connect into the earth without barriers. They chose not to wear jewelry or to use talismans in the ceremony. The only vessels for transmuting spiritual power would be their own bodies and minds. Indeed, it was the very cellular knowledge, the encoded wisdom of these vessels that were to be preserved below the pyramid. Nothing material could enter that inter-dimensional space, and no icon could make it accessible—only the secret chamber of their collective heart.

The priests and priestesses divided into male-female pairs, one couple facing each side of the square pyramid. Yalucha and Mac Ceel stood at the base of the north stairway, with the large serpent heads stretching open-jawed onto the plaza floor. Setting their intention and focusing awareness, each couple slowly ascended the steep stairways up the four sides of the pyramid. Four was the base number for creating forms in the Middleworld, the intelligent vibration of the Creator God in its four manifestations as earth, water, fire and air. The serpent was the form in which that vibrational energy traveled, from the etheric undulations of the Vision Serpent to the miniscule intertwined snakelike double helix of cellular information.

Magical numbers of the Maya calendars—nine, eighteen, and fifty-two—were likewise activated during the ascent up the stairways. The sacred geometry embedded within the pyramid's structure reverberated into the bare feet of the climbing adepts. As each couple stepped onto the temple platform atop the pyramid, the 365th step, their feet engaged the annual solar cycle. The kin after the Winter Solstice, that solar cycle renewed itself and began again. The enduring power of these sacred cycles, the ebb and flow of nature and of earth's relation to the universe, seeped into their bodies.

The adepts entered the simple flat-roofed temple through the four doors facing the four directions. In the center of the low-ceiling temple was a raised round altar with deep relief carvings of feathered serpents and *itz* flowers. The altar stood for "O" and for oneness. It signified *lol*, the white flower, and *lil*, vibration. "O" meant consciousness combined with spirit; the White Flower Thing that was the soul, *sak-nik-nal*. They sat in a circle facing the altar, alternating men and women. Their number was eight, the symbol of harmony and balance, of union of the seven bodily forces with the One Universal Spirit. Sitting cross-legged with hands resting in laps, the eight adepts intoned the prayer of invocation for the setting sun:

"*Dzu bulul H'yum K'in, dzu tip'il X'yum Ak'ab,*
Pepenobe cu lembaloob ichil u lol caan,
C'tucule tian ti teche c'Hunab K'u,
Tumen teche c'azaholal, ta k'ab c'k'ubicba."

"Already the Master Sun has set, and the Mistress Night has risen,

The butterflies shine amid the heavenly flowers,

Our thoughts are in you, Dear God,

Because you are our hope; into your hands we surrender ourselves."

They sat in meditation as the sun dropped behind the horizon and dusk fell upon the earth. The wall torches inside the temple were left unlit; they would do this ceremony in darkness, guided by the inner light of awakened consciousness. Each activated their seven internal power centers—chaklas—vibrational vortices along the spine. Using breath and awareness they filled each center with divine energy, starting at the base of the spine and moving upward through the pelvis, solar plexus, heart, throat, forehead and crown. In this process they activated the cosmic serpent of the human energy body, the *k'ultanlilni*. Each syllable of this mystical word carried meaning and actually was the process of raising the cosmic serpent:

K'u—God, pyramid; *K'ul*—coccyx; *Tan*—place; *Lil*—vibration; *Ni*—nose.

The breath of the Sun God entered through the nose, connected to the coccyx, the earth base, through the seated pyramid form of the body, vibrating the divine essence of Spirit. The soul and spirit were thus united within the form of the human body-mind, making it a perfected vessel for Divine transmissions.

It was totally dark when Yalucha sensed this process was complete in each person. She murmured the agreed upon signal for the group to begin entering their secret heart chambers:

"*Tz'ib kolonton*, be wise in your heart."

As they had learned, each adept moved their awareness from inside the skull toward the heart. The sense of aware focus slipped down through their throats into their upper chest regions, next to the pulsating heart. With intention, each slipped awareness into the heart, into that warm, dark, throbbing organ where the greatest human *itz* concentrated. They were to merge this human *itz* with the Divine Source of all *itz*, Itzamna. When all felt this had occurred, they were to seek the most secret, sacred place of the heart—the secret chamber—and follow its guidance to form the collective heart chamber of the Maya people.

Yalucha was there quickly. She could sense in this tiny spot, this infinitesimally small place, the entirety of all creation, the universe, the cosmos and beyond. All the gods and goddesses, all the knowledge and wisdom, all the love ever possible for timeless ages, all the Infinite Intelligence that was the All, were contained there.

And all the pain, suffering, cruelty, inconceivably horrible atrocities, every possible thing and Nothing, no-thing-ness, were there too. She heard distant cries, moans of distress, screams of agony, calling for help, calling her, calling . . .

Yalucha! Come back! You cannot help them now, that task falls to compassionate people of a later time, people who re-discover our sacred temples and learn the heart chamber meditation, who release souls trapped in the deep earth out of universal love. Your work is here, now. We cannot accomplish it without your complete focus here.

The ethereal voice of Mac Ceel commanded Yalucha back into her present mission. She immediately knew the truth of this, and turned her focus onto the held potential of her secret heart chamber. She sensed all were ready to form the collective heart chamber.

As one organism, the eight adepts extended hands sideways toward the person on either side. Palms touching, they intertwined fingers until all were locked into a continuous circle, energies flowing from one to the other through the palm centers. Male to female, female to male, a double spiral was formed with feminine energies moving to the left and masculine energies to the right. These vortices flowed up arms into chests, through hearts, and out the other arms. Faster and faster it moved, pulsating in a giant heartbeat, filling the

468

inside temple with red-gold light. Their hearts merged and became the heart of the Maya people.

Throbbing to the drumbeat that was the pulse of the Cosmos, the collective Heart of the Maya People contained everything that allowed them, shaped them into what they were: Intimate lovers of nature, familiars of animals, suitors of plants, seers of the stars, readers of cycles small and immense, artists of stones and structures, tamers of jungle wildness, gatherers of peoples, conceivers of great cities, mythologists of humanity's hidden forces, dancers of life-into-death-into-life, embracers of unity, knowers of shamanic secrets, growers of souls, lovers of the Three Worlds. Vibrational strings of the collective Heart that never lost connections to the Infinite Source. The Heart that knows its place upon Earth, in the galaxy and the universe.

The double spiral of the Collective Maya Heart formed a vortex that elongated into a funnel, its bottom point passing through the center altar and suddenly streaking down through the entire length of the pyramid into the ground below. A crystalline chamber opened, its clear walls glistening and emanating otherworldly light. This crystal womb opened itself to the phallic vortex, the sacred tantric creation of enlightened sexual energy in the service of highest truth. Into the crystal womb chamber were deposited, from the minds and bodies of the adepts into the Collective Maya Heart, and then through the phallic vortex, the most revered and sacred wisdom and the most esoteric knowledge of the Maya people:

Remembrance of stellar origins, star-seeds planted into earth's Three Worlds, dancing through soul-evolving destinies;

Sacred calendars that spoke the cycles of time, of Worlds and Universes, with unparalleled precision attuned to the Cosmic Clock of Creation;

Intimacy with Nature, knowing how to become the natural world, to call creatures and command elements;

Knowledge of how to live in a sacred cosmos, infused at every moment by spiritual intelligence, full of rich meaning, immense force and unimaginable beauty;

Shamanic secrets for traveling between Worlds, embodying animal spirits—uayob, taking vision quests and soul journeys, empowering objects with spirit force;

Growing the soul into a god-being by fully embracing life's duality, shadow and light, pain and pleasure, master of the power and terrible beauty of existence;

Qualities of the ideal soul, the gentled heart—often forgotten in the kingly quest for domination—that produce an authentic human, a real person;

Ability to see how all life is related, and how each being's conscious-vibration-emotions-actions join in a unity field around the earth, affecting everything else;

The dance of resurrection that overcomes death, as destruction betrays itself into creation, darkness transforms into light—and also the reverse—in the service of a deeper, richer, more whole light that ultimately ascends into dimensions of Eternal Light, returns to Source, and eventually takes all the Worlds and Cosmos along.

There would be a time of emergence, when the Maya wisdom and hidden teachings could be summoned out of the crystal chamber. The adepts at Chichén Itzá sealed the chamber with conscious vibrations that must be matched exactly to re-open it. At a time near the end of the present Great Cycle, the closing of the Fourth Sun, the potential would exist for future adepts to access the inter-dimensional space of the crystal chamber. These future adepts would, of necessity, be connected with the soul-being of the performers of the ceremony.

When earth's people again chose to call nature spirits, to harmonize with the natural world, to remember how all life is related, to honor traditions of indigenous peoples, then would be the time of emergence. When shamans came forth to reawaken the sacred pyramid temples, when many people from places around the earth made pilgrimage to ancient power sites, when enough souls cried for unity and dreamed of peace—then could the crystal chamber be opened. Then could they dream the Maya Fifth Sun.

The young mestizo security guard slumped against the hard back of a metal chair, the solitary furnishing inside the Mayaland Hotel entrance booth. With deliberate eagerness he lit a cigarette, inhaled deeply then released twin curls of thin smoke from his nostrils. Fascinated with the serpent-like coiling, he observed the smoke streams for several puffs. Soon the nicotine, clasped by hungry receptors in his brain neurons, brought the expected rush of alertness and lifted his mood. The heaviness of brain fog began to clear with the dissipating smoke.

Last night had been bad, the worst in a while. He stayed too long in the cantina, drank too much cerveza, smiled at too many saucy-eyed girls. His wife yelled too loudly when he finally staggered home, balancing their crying infant on one hip while gesturing wildly with her free arm. Even in bed with the pillow over his ears, and buffered by alcohol-dimmed awareness, he reeled under her verbal assault. Hitching one shoulder, he winced from bruises inflicted when she pummeled his back. Yes, it was a bad night.

The cigarette was helping; he was starting to feel better. As soon as his shift ended, he would get some food and a cerveza, then he would really feel good again. It was going to be a long day, however, with lots of activity around Chichén Itzá. It was the spring equinox, a national holiday, and thousands of people were flocking to the ruins. Already tour busses, vans and autos were filling the adjacent field used as parking lot for these events. His job was to prevent intruders from sneaking into the Mayaland Hotel parking lot, trying to get closer access to the ruins.

He looked up as an old red VW bug turned into the Mayaland driveway. Resort guests usually drove better cars, so he was suspicious. As the lone woman driver stopped at the gate, he stepped outside. The woman was attractive with wavy light brown hair, but his interest dropped as he saw her middle age face, eyes slightly puffy as if she had not gotten enough sleep. She presented a Mayaland pass and said in imperfect Spanish that she was joining her group there. Obviously a foreigner with a rental car. He studied the pass for a while, but could find no fault with it. The dates were correct, it was signed, and it appeared to be authentic. The young guard shrugged, returned the pass, lifted the gate and waved the woman in.

Jana let out a breath of relief as she proceeded up the winding driveway. Finding a parking place at the far end of the lot, away from the check-in structure, she quickly locked up and took the first path toward the large main hotel. The grounds of the venerable Mayaland Hotel were works of arboreal art, a harmonious marriage of lush tropical vegetation and white stucco-walled, thatched roof bungalows resembling up-scale Maya dwellings. Paved pathways wound gracefully around grassy knolls, passing through flower-draped arbors and between tall palms. Colorful bougainvillea climbed porch columns, broad-leafed pathos and orange-beaked birds of paradise arched from neat border gardens. Birds chirped and twittered in a variety of well-spaced native trees. Around the well-manicured edges of the resort, dense thickets of trees and shrubs contended for space in the riotous tropical jungle.

Small electric carts were used to transport guests and baggage from parking lots to the main hotel and the numerous bungalows nestled within the 100-acre gardens. Jana stepped aside to allow a cart to pass, waving and smiling to the porter who gestured that she hop aboard. She managed to convey in simple Spanish that she wanted to go to the reception area. After winding through what seemed a maze of intersecting paths, the porter arrived at the large two-story main hotel and let Jana off.

The Mayaland Hotel was an anachronism turned into an elegant, genteel resort. Situated amidst the temples of the ruins, it was the first hotel built at Chichén Itzá during a time when only the most ardent archeology buffs were visiting ancient sites. In 1921 the scion of an old Yucatan Spanish family, Ferdando Barbachano Peon, himself enchanted by the majestic presence of the long-abandoned city that still drew pilgrims for sacred ceremony, brought the first tourists to Chichén Itzá. He persuaded the group to leave their cruise ship at the Gulf Coast port of Progreso, on the northwest edge of the Yucatan peninsula, and follow him for a several days long excursion into the jungle. For this accomplishment, Peon is considered the pioneer of organized tourism and father of México's travel industry. In 1923 he built the Mayaland Hotel to host an ever-increasing stream of tourists venturing to the remote site.

Still owned and operated by descendents of this family, the resort expresses the style of hacienda nobility of 19th century. The two story main house of white stucco with red tile roof is beautifully proportioned, with an air of genteel hospitality and old-fashioned charm. Dispersed through acres of gardens are 50 bungalows built in traditional Mayan style with wood, stone, native marble and thatch, and decorated with works of local artisans. Most are graced with wide verandas and some have small pools. There are Mayan sites on the grounds; four buildings are being excavated and restored. The hotel has its own entrance to the main archeological park.

The arcade leading to the hotel lobby was buzzing with people as Jana ascended the wide, low stairs. Graceful arches opened to an interior patio and dining area, potted palmettos brought a touch of the jungle inside. In the lobby, a dark wood staircase swept upward to an open mezzanine. Heavy Spanish-style antique furniture tastefully positioned around the polished tile lobby continued the colonial period feeling. A huge portrait of an older couple with Spanish features dominated one wall, their high foreheads accentuating long straight noses, intense black eyes, and an air of multi-generational nobility. Jana was sure this unsmiling but kindly appearing couple was the founder of the Mayaland Hotel.

Over the heads of the milling crowd Jana caught a glimpse outward through the open-arched doorway facing the ruins. There, framed perfectly by the arch, was the rounded carapace of the Caracol, known to be an observatory. It was certainly no accident that the main house central lobby was situated in this precise position. Only a few hundred feet of tree-entangled jungle separated the Mayaland Hotel from the ruins of Chichén Itzá.

Although it was just nine o'clock the lobby was full of white-clothed pilgrims, conversing in at least five different languages. Jana recognized several from last night's session, and soon connected with Julia, Steve and Michael. Although she had not been instructed to wear white, Jana knew this garb would be the protocol and donned a t-shirt and walking shorts in the color of purity—and, for the Maya, the color of the soul. Moving closer to the arched door facing the ruins, she saw Aurora Nakin sitting beside Evita at the edge of the outside stairs leading down to the cobbled auto entrance. The women were engaged in an intense conversation, so Jana kept her distance. A few phrases reached her ears, however.

"I don't know . . . what could have come over me . . . so sorry for the disturbance . . . still feeling shaken . . . you're so kind . . . " as Evita apologized and processed her experiences, reassured by Aurora Nakin that all was well. Jana could hardly imagine what it must feel like, to be relieved of a monstrous dark force wreaking havoc both within and through uncontrollable actions. Evita did look brighter, her energy field felt lighter, although her face showed fatigue.

The appearance of Hanab Xiu descending the curved stairway from the mezzanine brought the group to a single focus. He instructed them to stay together, keep alert for further instructions, and follow him into the ruins. Reminding them that their purpose was sacred ceremony, and that they were not visiting the ruins as tourists, he requested they keep a quiet inner attunement and refrain from taking pictures during ceremonies. The group formed a long line and filed slowly through the Zona Arqueológica entrance into the park. The wide gravel path led through dense forest, terminating at the broad expanse of the Main Plaza, facing the south base of the breath-taking Pyramid of Kukulkán.

Everyone stood transfixed for a few moments at the grandeur of this sight. The square-based pyramid rose nearly 100 feet, topped by a square stone temple on the summit platform. Steep symmetrical stairs ascended each of the nine-tiered sides, giving the pyramid balanced, harmonious proportions. At the foot of the north stairs were the famous serpent heads, huge open-mouthed and fanged carvings that were flooded with light at the culmination of the light serpent's descent during equinox. This biannual phenomenon drew thousands of visitors to Chichén Itzá, now as in ancient times.

Hanab Xiu led the group to a shaded area halfway between the Pyramid of Kukulkán and the Temple of the Warriors. A cluster of oak trees fanned their limbs to make circles of shade, welcomed by all, as the morning was already hot and humid. Here they waited for the appearance of other Maya elders and their groups. People sat or stood in small clusters, talking softly and looking around at the immense gleaming buff structures in the bright sunlight, standing in sharp contrast with yellow-green of grassy plazas and dark green trees.

The Temple of the Warriors was approached from the south by a 45-foot long colonnade—over 1000 carved pillars standing in erect formations on a raised platform base. This Group of 1000 Columns once supported a thatched roof, and was thought to be a meeting place for the joint rulers of Chichén Itzá. Most of the round columns were carved with warrior images, but several depicted priests in full regalia and a few showed high-rank women. Nothing like this structure was found elsewhere in Mesoamerica. The sheer orderliness of the straight, evenly sized columns standing row after row conveyed a strong sense of power and intention.

These Itzae knew what they were about, reflected Jana. A strong sense of determination and purpose permeated the colonnade. The energy was very masculine.

Three thick tiers supported the Temple of the Warriors, sitting upon a thinner platform base. A single, wide stairway on the front side, facing the Main Plaza, led to a broad top platform on which sat the rectangular temple. In front of the opening was the well-known statue of the Chak-Mool, a reclining god holding a bowl over his abdomen in both hands, ready to receive offerings. Common parlance held that the still-beating hearts of human victims were placed in the bowl, but archeologists noted there was no substantial evidence for this sacrificial ritual at Chichén Itzá. They believed the bowl held other types of offerings, or perhaps an oil torch. Flanking the Chak-Mool were two serpent-headed columns, mouths open against the floor and bodies aimed skyward to support lintels that once spanned the entrance. The inverted snakes of Chichén Itzá, found in several structures, were the *kuxan sum* or "living cord" that connected the Itza lords to the heavens. Behind the Temple was another set of 200 columns depicting warriors, some still bearing faint traces of paint from years past.

A flat, smooth boulder near a tumbled rock pile beckoned Jana to sit. Listless breezes rustled tree leaves faintly, as the morning temperature climbed. Looking across the immense Main Plaza, Jana watched a colorful procession of people wandering erratically through the open expanse. Some kept to the paths and passed close to the group of pilgrims. A lot of human feminine energy was infusing into the site, perhaps nature's attempt to balance the intensely masculine structures. Jana admired the nubile beauty of slender cocoa-skinned girls, long dark hair flowing around shoulders as bare bellies winked above tight hip-riders. Black eyes sparkled with animation, earrings danced and jewelry clinked as they strode and talked, sly glances catching the appreciative eyes of young men nearby.

One remarkable young woman ambled slowly across the plaza in front of Jana's view. She was obviously pregnant, six or seven months, Jana estimated. Her swollen belly protruded through a thin wispy blouse that made no effort to conceal her enlarged breasts and prominent nipples, bouncing exuberantly as she walked. A multicolored flowing skirt hung below the taut belly. Disheveled light brown hair flounced down her back, and her skin was several tones lighter than most of the locals.

Perhaps European or American, Jana thought. *Exuding ripe mothering fertile generative feminine energy. And proud of it. Good for her.*

Babies and children were everywhere. Sable-eyed, black-haired, mocha to dark chocolate skinned, they laughed and gamboled across the plaza. Young mothers balanced startled looking babies on hips as toddlers clung to their shirts. Fathers chased older children in games of tag and herded strays back to the family fold. The Mexicans loved children, keeping alive a child-like playfulness that allowed them to have fun with life. Though they might not be affluent, they displayed a spirit of inner abundance.

Nearly all families included elders. Jana observed many older women, interacting intently with children and parents, demonstrating strong energies of balance and containment. The grandmother was important, a source of wisdom and guidance, a link with the ancestors. One short, square elder woman who looked distinctly Mayan walked to the base of the Pyramid of Kukulkán. Park guards had assembled and roped off the stairs on all sides, but they deferred to the woman who stood with her back against the lower pyramid tier, away from the stairs. She spread her fingers wide and placed palms solidly against the stones, tipping her head up with closed eyes. In silent inner communion with the ancient Maya whose blood ran strong in her veins, her meditative stillness reached across the plaza to Jana.

What reverence for her roots, thought Jana, deeply moved. *It's wonderful that modern Maya feel so connected with these power sites, the incredible heritage of their ancestors.*

She watched the elder woman, la viejita, for what seemed a long time. Two adolescents joined her, imitating her stance. Both the boy and the girl appeared sincerely absorbed in communing with the pyramid stones. They finished before the grandmother, who finally completed her ritual and joined the family nearby.

Jana shifted her position and glanced at her group of pilgrims. Hanab Xiu was conversing within a small circle, but there was no sign of the other Maya elders. A fine sweat covered Jana's skin, t-shirt damp against her back. She took a drink from her water bottle, reflexively touching the amber pendant hanging inside her shirt. Carefully she placed the water bottle beside the small spirit doll inside her pouch. Turning to gaze left toward the Pyramid of Kukulkán once again, Jana saw a large iguana crouched on the rock pile, only a few feet away. His round beady eyes were fixed on her, unblinking. Gray-

476

brown skin blended into black stripes along body and tail, with a serrated fin from neck to mid-back.

The iguana had a hypnotic effect on Jana. As she stared into his eyes, her vision softened and she slipped into a semi-conscious reverie. Part of her remained in present time and aware of her physical body, while a mysterious aspect of her consciousness entered another time and scene at Chichén Itzá.

It was dusk. A small group of priests and priestesses approached the towering Pyramid of Kukulkán. Its walls were covered with smooth plaster, gleaming yellow-gold in the sun's setting rays. Stripes of green and red accented the edges of the steep stairs on all four sides. The serpent heads facing north were brightly painted; red tongues, blue eyes, green skin with red stripes, white fangs. Her awareness was drawn to one priestess, she knew this woman, had seen her—where? In the church in Mérida, on the TV-like screen inside the secret chamber of her heart . . . it was Yalucha!

They were ascending the stairs in pairs, climbing slowly up to the temple on top. Their purpose was grave, their intention strongly set. This was a ritual of extreme importance, a mandate they had received. Their people's survival depended upon doing it successfully. It was nearly dark as they entered the temple on top, but no one lit a torch. They were inside, doing what? She could not see it. But this was a ritual that she knew, she sensed this knowing to her very core. Gathering intention, she projected her consciousness into Yalucha inside the dark pyramid temple high in the evening sky. She felt union with the Maya priestesses' heart, a rush of profound love. Her heart pulsed with each beat, two hearts as one, one mind and consciousness.

The priests and priestesses were bonding in a vortex of love, merging their hearts, creating a mutual chamber. A secret heart chamber of the Maya people. Through this, they were hiding and preserving their ancient teachings, putting these in a safe place to endure through coming times of darkness and oppression. In the pyramid . . . under the pyramid . . . She could not see the process clearly, but she knew it was successful.

The iguana jerked his head up suddenly, breaking eye contact with Jana and throwing her abruptly out of the reverie. He turned quickly and slithered between crevices in the rocks, disappearing into shadows. Three people from the group had walked over to sit on the rocks, impervious to the iguana and Jana's presence. Their conversation jarred her ears, and she blinked rapidly to clear her vision.

Jana tried to piece together information from this vision. It was in Chichén Itzá long ago, when the city was vibrantly alive. Maya holy men and women were doing a critical ceremony, and Yalucha was taking part—the enigmatic priestess with whom Jana herself was linked. The rituals were done atop the Pyramid of Kukulkán, at dusk. They involved using the secret chamber of the heart. Was the ceremony she had been called to take part in related to this ancient one? A troubling sense that the two were significantly connected stirred within Jana. She had no idea where today's ceremony with the Maya elders was to take place. But, seeing how the park guards had roped off the stairs to the pyramid, she seriously doubted anyone would be allowed to climb up.

Pyramid of Kukulkan, Chichén Itzá

A disturbing discomfort formed around Jana's solar plexus, a sense of anxious foreboding. A yearning in her heart pulled her toward the Pyramid of Kukulkán, and she looked again at the magnificent structure, noticing with surprise how deteriorated its west and south stairs were. Even if the guards allowed it, climbing these stairs would be very dangerous. Perhaps the stairs on the north and east were in better condition.

Her attention was diverted by the excited stirring of the pilgrim group. Hanab Xiu was striding quickly toward two remarkable figures that had appeared from around the bend of the entry path. A Maya man and woman were approaching wearing colorful garb. The middle-aged man was tall for a Maya, with shoulder-length straight black hair held in place by a beaded headband from which rose a cluster of arched feathers. His costume was solid yellow ochre, bright and earthy, over shirt clasped around the waist with a wide beaded and woven belt. Blue, red and green fabric expressed geometrical patterns, with long strands continuing into a sash that hung in front. Around the lower legs were leather straps covered by clanking wooden pods from ankle to mid-calf. A pleasant clacking sound was created with each step.

Walking beside him was a Maya woman, also middle-aged, emanating a powerful aura of vitality and strength. She was wearing a similar costume, the exact shade of yellow ochre with an over shirt and full calf-length skirt. Her belt matched his in color and design, except it had hanging adornments around the entire circumference. Small shells and shiny metallic discs clinked melodically from the belt and a large necklace hung nearly to her waist. Wavy dark hair with a few gray strands cascaded around her shoulders. She wore a similar headband with feathers. It was obvious to Jana that these warm, radiant beings were of the Maya priesthood. An vibration of wonderful grace surrounded them.

As they met Hanab Xiu on the path, each bowed slightly in acknowledgement, and the three engaged in animated Spanish conversation. After several minutes, they proceeded to the cluster of trees, where the groups of both Hanab Xiu and the German pilgrims gathered. Another group of Mexicans appeared who seemed to have been waiting for this event, swelling the collective number to over one hundred. The Maya priest stood on a rock cluster and delivered a long, energetic talk in Spanish, interrupted by periodic cheers from the groups. Jana moved closer to listen, but hardly understood anything due to the rapid-fire speech.

The sun was nearly overhead when the Maya priest concluded his talk. He and the priestess led the combined pilgrims through the Group of 1000 Columns into a grassy plaza, nestled between the L-shaped arms of colonnades abutting the Temple of the Warriors. Scattered thin-leafed trees filtered the blazing sunlight, creating dappled patterns of shade and light. The pilgrims formed a large circle, filling the plaza area. Inside the circle, the Maya elders began creating an altar. First a multi-colored altar cloth was spread on the ground, and then sacred objects were positioned according to some protocol that completely escaped Jana. Conch shells, wooden rattles, carved figurines, beads and feathers, bundles of *itz* substances, flowers, crystals and rocks were set at various corners. Members of the pilgrim group stepped forward to put out their objects. The elders moved some objects around, announcing that certain things belonged at one or the other corners or must be placed on certain colors of the altar cloth.

The Maya priest motioned for Fire Eagle to join the elders inside the circle. The American shaman came forward, and reverently placed the milky quartz crystal skull that had been given into his care, near the center of the altar. He remained with the elders. From among the pilgrims, several more crystal skulls appeared of varying colors and sizes. Some were half-human size of clear transparent crystal, others as large as human skulls of lovely pink and green opaque quartz. These were gently arranged in an outward-facing circle in the center of the cloth. The placing and re-placing of objects took considerable time; apparently everything had to be just so, and this took some reflection.

The circle of international pilgrims stood patiently in the sweltering heat. It was clear that the ceremony was waiting for something.

"What's going on?" Jana asked Steve, who was standing next to her.

"I'm not sure," he replied. "All this moving around of things on the altar cloth is a mystery to me."

"I think they're waiting for some more elders," said Julia, on Jana's other side. "Hanab Xiu said several indigenous groups were sending representatives to the ceremony. So far, it looks like only the Maya and Native American ones are here."

"Native Americans?" queried Jana, looking at the people in the center and not seeing one.

"Fire Eagle," Steve offered. "He's the representative for Native Americans. He's a recognized shaman, you know."

"Oh, yeah. I should have remembered that," said Jana.

Jana was already beginning to feel weak and woozy, it was a long time since breakfast and she had lost a lot of body fluid from sweating. That was why her brain was not functioning so well. Looking around the circle, she saw that some people sat, drank from water bottles and munched on snacks. Jana decided to eat her final, partly melted energy bar for a little sustenance. Washing it down with the last of her water, she noted to herself that after the ceremony she would need to find more to drink.

The mystery of the wait was solved with the appearance of several indigenous people in different costumes. There was a young Inca shaman in exotic feather headdress and beaded clothing, an Aztec elder wearing a gold-embossed tunic and sundial pectoral decorations, and two very short, nearly black-skinned Toltec men from distant mountains, wearing simple white suits with no adornment. One more Maya priestess joined the group, in typical yellow ochre garb.

When nine people were in the center, the ceremony began. The first Maya priestess was in charge. She placed granules of copal over burning embers in a deep metal cup suspended by three small chains joined at the top. Moving it in concentric circles, she chanted an opening prayer in a dialect of the Maya language. The rhythm was punctuated with deep glottal sounds and sharp clicks, not melodic but compelling. Copal smoke wafted across the plaza, sweet and woody. When the slightly acrid scent caught Jana's nostrils, she felt a wave of near-ecstasy and drifted into an expansive, timeless state.

The first Maya priestess honored the directions, starting in the south and moving north, west, and then east. Her invocations were lengthy and involved, repeated by translators in Spanish, English and German. At each direction, she raised the copal censor and swung it back and forth in precise patterns. The honoring of the three Maya worlds was completed by invocations for the Thirteen Heavens above and the Underworld below. For the last two, other elders added prayers or chants. The surrounding circle of pilgrims stood in quiet concentration, holding sacred space and supportive energy for the elders performing the rituals.

In the teaching last night, Hanab Xiu had suggested doing the Mother Earth-Father Sun meditation and entering the sacred heart chamber as the rituals were performed. This would anchor the vibrations into the earth and link with the cosmos, merging these realms through the human heart, the Divine Child. From the position of the heart chamber, prayers or intentions for peace and global harmony would create these qualities non-dualistically, so as not to also invoke their opposites. Jana went through the techniques twice, dropping into the heart chamber easily and staying there most of the time. On occasion, she felt simultaneously in both her head and heart, an interesting phenomenon that itself seemed non-dualistic. Using the mind, the head, was necessary for navigating through life's challenges, she reflected. Perhaps the ideal way to harness the mind's abilities in service of higher good was to blend it with the heart's capacities for unconditional love.

After the ritual of the directions, the elders gave a series of speeches. Each elder said a few sentences in his or her native language, which was then translated into the three other languages. The theme of these speeches focused on a call for world brotherhood and sisterhood, the unity of all people, the desire for peace and harmony, and the blessing of all creation including humans, animals, water, trees, air and earth. Honor was given to the important role of indigenous people in preserving knowledge of how to live in harmony with earth's cycles and the natural world.

Hanab Xiu emphasized that people *could* all live from the heart in total acceptance. This present time, he noted, was a critical period in the transition of the planet, the final decade of the Long Count Calendar before the shift of the ages. He reminded the pilgrims that each was here doing an important work, that for the sake of the world they were not allowed to succumb to doubt and fear. They had to be holders of the vision, creators of the dream that would birth the Fifth Sun as an age of universal harmony.

Staying focused and attentive was hard for Jana, standing there in the torpid heat, sweating, feeling weak at times despite the energy bar. Her experience ranged from being totally unaware of her body, intensely concentrated in a state full of stillness, to moments when her intense bodily discomfort demanded nearly all her attention. Concentration slipped at these moments and she was immersed in the physical sensations of suffocating heat, dripping sweat, faintness, weakness, hurting feet, aching legs. Wryly she noted that doing the sacred work of a priestess was hard. One had to endure difficult physical conditions, and find ways to push beyond them. This was simply what one had to learn. When her focus slipped, she caught it as quickly as possible, refocused and held the energy as much as possible, and just stayed with it.

The ceremony went on for about two hours, by Jana's best estimate. For closure, the first Maya priestess led the group in a prayer in Spanish, which everyone repeated as best they could. The Maya priest blew a conch, its long honking sound reverberating in the plaza and vibrating eardrums. Surprised tourists looked around at the unusual sound. People removed their objects from the altar, and the elders folded the cloth. The pilgrims broke into a buzz of conversation, clustering in small groups around various elders for

482

thanks and hugs. Jana went to the first Maya priestess, bowed and expressed sincere thanks in Spanish, receiving a warm hug. She really felt connected with this magnificent woman, so noble and impressive, yet centered, warm and grounded. The priestess murmured to Jana *"Mi hermana,"* my sister.

People began dispersing slowly, lingering with much conversation, loath to leave the sacred unifying energy of the ceremony. Aurora Nakin called for her group to gather around Hanab Xiu. He was going to visit the older part of Chichén Itzá, if anyone wanted to accompany him there. He advised the best time to see the serpent of light descending the stairs of the Pyramid of Kukulkán was between 4:30 and 5:00 pm, at the northeastern corner. Jana wanted to see more of the ruins, so she joined the cadre following Hanab Xiu to the Observatory complex.

Trailing along behind the 12 or 15 people following Hanab Xiu, Jana again felt uneasiness and confusion arising. The ceremony with the indigenous elders had been wonderful—inspiring and uniting, with colorful offerings and deeply symbolic ritual. Her heart was warmed by the international gathering, people from many countries around the world coming together to respect, honor and support the wisdom of indigenous peoples. The pilgrims had endured a hard physical process, yet kept hearts open and minds focused—for the most part—to join with spiritual forces in behalf of the planet.

But something feels incomplete, she thought. *Was this the ceremony I was called to participate in? Have I fulfilled that mission?*

Following the small group past the west side of the Pyramid of Kukulkán, Jana experienced a burst of energy emanating from the towering structure, pushing against and into her. She stopped for a moment, looking longingly at the temple on top.

They went up there, Yalucha and the other holy ones, she reflected. *To do an important ceremony. Why was this shown to me, just a few hours ago? Yalucha, the Maya priestess, and me . . . we're connected, our lives somehow intertwined . . . with this great pyramid.*

The group was already some distance away, so Jana broke her train of thought about the pyramid and hurried to catch up. Yet she felt, irrefutably, that what she had come to this place for was not yet finished.

Hanab Xiu set a brisk pace through wide pathways toward the southwest area called the "old Puuc Maya" part of the city, in contrast to the northern Main Plaza with its complement of the Pyramid of

Kukulkán, great ball court, temples and colonnades which was deemed the "new Toltec" region. The building and carving styles of these two areas appeared distinctly different, leading archeologists to think that the Toltec region was added later, as the Mexican conquerors imposed their preferred architecture. More recent archeological evidence showed that Chichén Itzá was always a single city, occupied by a cosmopolitan nobility of mixed heritage, both Maya and Mexican. The "old" section buildings were dated by pottery excavation as contemporaneous with the "new" section. Networks of stone roads linked principal groups into a whole, and blending of styles could be seen in the use of Maya hieroglyphic texts along with murals and sculpture in the northern "new" complex.

The group passed a refreshment stand featuring soft drinks, which caught Jana's eye. She made a mental note to stop for some liquid on the way back. Passing between a moderate sized pyramid with intertwined serpents carved into its balustrades, and a low square platform, both with stairs on all four sides, she hardly had time to read their plaques. The temple was called the High Priest's Grave, *el Osario,* as the interior led to an underground cave in which human remains were found. Two impressive serpent heads at the front stairway base stared fiercely at by-passers. Swinging past a smaller structure called *La Casa Roja,* the Red House still sporting remnants of original ret paint in a strip below the ceiling, they entered the grassy meadow that was once the lower platform supporting *El Observatorio O Caracol,* the Caracol.

The Caracol, which means "snail" in Spanish, was an unusual structure. It was once perfectly round, set atop three tiers of platforms. Small windows perforated its sides at irregular intervals. Archeologists identified it as an astronomical observatory. The small windows were precisely aligned with various stars and constellations as these moved across the night sky nearly one thousand years ago. Hanab Xiu addressed this very point:

"Inside the Caracol there are several levels, with narrow stairs winding along the walls. The last time I was here, about five years ago, you could enter inside and climb the stairs to the dome. Now, it is not permitted any more. From the inside, each window you see starts as a tiny hole in the wall, just about the size of your eye. This guides your sight exactly to the group of stars. This is amazing, that the ancient Maya knew the times and paths of constellations so perfectly that they could build such an observatory. Movements of the stars set the stage for almost every important event in their lives.

Keeping pace with the cosmological cycles was of vital significance. Everything depended on right timing."

Right timing.

The phrase echoed inside Jana's mind. Rituals had to be timed precisely, to engage the cosmogenic forces. A gnawing sense or urgency troubled her; she had to figure out why she felt incomplete, why she was so drawn to the sun pyramid, why she had envisioned the ancient Maya ritual there.

"Take a moment now to tune yourself to the Maya sacred cycles, the 13:20 rhythm that is the primal time frequency of our universe," continued Hanab Xiu. "This is the natural timing of earth rhythms, set to the rest of the universe. This pattern exists in our genetic blueprint, it connects us to earth and the universe, it is Divine Timing. It connects us to Source, Great Spirit, the Infinite Oneness. Thirteen intermeshing with 20, the pattern of the tzolk'in calendar. Feel those rhythms."

Everyone stood still, eyes closed. Jana imagined pictures she had seen of the tzolk'in calendar, where the cogs of a small wheel of thirteen numbers fit into those of a larger wheel of 20 day glyphs, turning in opposite directions. It took 260 unique combinations before the original number and day glyph met again. Dividing 260 days by 20 produced 13 "months." The tzolk'in was the most sacred time device used by all Mesoamerican peoples. Each unique combination had a spirit and symbol, giving it characteristics that influenced events in repeating cycles. Thirteen was a venerated number, holding the mystery of re-creation, the cycle-setting pulse. Twenty was the rhythm of regularity, of symmetry, of infinity, and it drove the Long Count calendar system. *Uinal, katun, baktun*—these major time divisions of the Long Count were based on multiples of 20. And the Great Cycle that marked points of major transition for human cultures was made up of 13 baktuns, just over 5120 years.

Jana felt the pulsing of 13:20 within her blood, setting the rhythm of her heartbeat, invoking subtle vibratory ripples in cells. The soles of her feet tingled against her sandals, sending and receiving energy waves into the ground. Around her head swirled the inverted dome of the night sky, its starry inhabitants arcing in slow, graceful lines on their ordained trajectories. The great, mysterious, beautiful clock of the cosmos echoed around and within her.

The sun! The Pyramid of Kukulkán—the pyramid of the sun!

Uncalled for, this awareness burst into her mind as her eyes flew open, blinking against the bright sunlight.

"We must also attune to the sun," said Hanab Xiu, as if reading her mind. "The Maya recognized the solar year and especially here in Chichén Itzá, paid great homage to the sun. They developed the Haab calendar based on the earth's rotation around the sun. The solar cycle was also broken into "months" of 20 days, there are 18 of these. The rhythms of the Haab guided them about happenings in the natural world. It told them when to plant corn, when to expect rain, when fruits would ripen, when animals would appear. This observatory, the Caracol, also had methods for tracking the sun's movements. It helped them know when to expect equinoxes and solstices, times full of power for contacting the gods. Today's equinox celebration is a remnant of those long-ago rituals."

He paused, looking around the group. When his eyes met Jana's they lingered, pools of dark portent. She felt he wanted to communicate something to her. But there was some barrier. Instinctively she whipped off her sunglasses, still staring into his eyes. A shock of recognition hit her—she had known this being, been close to him, before. Her mind groped for more information, but all she could be certain of was that their association had been as Mayans.

Gazing away, Hanab Xiu finished his visual sweep around the group and turned back to face the Caracol. He stood in silence, as if wrapped in his own thoughts.

Jana tilted her face upward to feel the sun's rays. Their angle had changed, and she turned slightly west, squinting and replacing her sunglasses as brilliant orange orbs assaulted her closed eyes.

The sun is dropping, it must be late afternoon. Jana remembered that the time for seeing the light serpent descend the stairs of the Pyramid of Kukulkán was around 4:30 pm. She glanced at her wristwatch, noting that it was nearly 4:00. Surely it must be time to return to the Main Plaza.

Suddenly Hanab Xiu turned, saying:

"Let's go to the Sacred Cenote, you should see it."

He led the group away from the Caracol, returning along the path they had entered.

Jana was confused. She thought they should be going to the Main Plaza.

Why is he going to the cenote? What's going on?

Feeling dazed, tired and incredibly thirsty, she trailed after the group. Hanab Xiu had set a grueling pace and she could not keep up. When she got back to the refreshment stand, her need for liquid took precedence over staying with the group. As she stopped to buy a soda,

486

she watched them disappear down the path. No one looked back or seemed to notice that she was no longer with them.

Gratefully, she relished the wet coolness of a lime soda sliding down her parched throat. In long gulps, she drank it quickly and returned the glass bottle to the vendor. Although only a few minutes had elapsed, Hanab Xiu and the small group were nowhere in sight. Jana slowly retraced her steps back to the Main Plaza. As she approached, the crowd and noise both swelled to surprising proportions.

Passing through tree clusters on either side of the path that obstructed the view, Jana stopped short at the sight that greeted her. The northwest portion of the Main Plaza was awash in a sea of people. Swaying, bobbing, weaving to and fro, thousands upon thousands of bodies pressed upon each other, crowding closely to obtain a side view of the north stairs. Faces mostly in shades of brown, clothing of every imaginable color, occasional umbrellas like oddly colored mushrooms, their voices mingled many languages into an incomprehensible babble. Over this steady roar was an ear-splitting PA system, blaring forth popular Mexican tunes from a grandstand set up in front of the Temple of the Jaguar by the ball court. Between songs, an equally loud announcer chattered rapidly in Spanish. The over-amplified sound system distorted the usually melodic cadences of the language. The scene created a fair-like climate, absent rides and games. The main attraction was the anticipated light serpent.

Taking the scene in with assaulted senses, Jana tried to get her bearings. The pyramid was closely guarded by uniformed men with pistols holstered to their belts, probably police there to augment the park guards. Swarming masses of people were engaged in various pursuits: some families with babies sat on blankets, eating and drinking from ice chests; clusters of young men laughed and shoved each other; couples leaned together with mooning eyes and lingering kisses; children chased and cavorted between legs and around bodies. A steady stream of wanderers passed around the edges of the dense crowd, craning to find friends or looking dazed and lost. Behind the grandstand smaller groups gathered at the entrance to the Great Ballcourt, where there was less press of people.

Jana scanned the crowd for a few minutes, looking for members of the pilgrim group. Quickly she realized this was fruitless; it was impossible to recognize anyone in the throng of blending faces. She needed to sit down, to reconnoiter. Wending along the edge of the crowd, she worked her way to the less populated Great Ballcourt. The wall of the western temple cast a thin line of shade. Finding an open spot, she sat beside a portly American couple that appeared totally enervated. The stones of the wall were warm against her back but she cared not. Sweat coated her skin and every inch of her clothing felt damp. A little more heat hardly mattered. For a moment, she surrendered to the profound fatigue flowing through her body, slumping listlessly.

Conversation in English from nearby tourists perked her flagging mind. Lifting her head, she realized that from this vantage point, she was looking directly into the ballcourt toward the small eastern temple. A man with an American Midwest accent was reading from the bronze plaque raised on a stone platform. She caught most of its description of the Great Ballcourt.

El Juego de Pelota, The Ballcourt, was immense, the largest in all Mesoamerica. Its dimensions were gargantuan: 545 feet from end to end, and 231 feet wide, it was larger than a modern day American football fields. The angled benches were low and shallow, in contrast to the usual gently slope and deep benches. High vertical walls rose sharply above the benches. No other Maya ballcourts had similar vertical walls. Three sets of relief panels decorated the benches, depicting scenes from ball games. Huge single stone hoops were set 20 feet above the ground, halfway between the two ends. Most ballcourts had more hoops that were smaller and set lower.

The ballcourt and its game, played with a large, hard rubber ball represented the act of creation. The angled benches represented the crack in the top of Creation Mountain. The Mayan word for crevice—*hom*—is also the word for ballcourt. Representing a crevice in the surface of the earth, the ballcourt gave humans access to the Otherworld, where the gods and ancestors lived. The ballgame re-enacted the events of the Fourth Creation, in which the Hero Twins set the stage for the gods to bring forth successful humans who would worship them properly and keep their ways.

The Fourth Creation is the one in which we now live, mused Jana. *I wonder if the Maya gods still find humans keeping their ways, following the natural order, worshipping the right principles.*

She doubted it. Most people in the modern world had become disconnected from natural cycles, alienated from the living body of earth. Instead of respecting earth, they were destroying it. Instead of realizing the underlying unity of existence, they were creating enmities and conflicts in selfish attempts to control resources and garner whatever they could for themselves. War seemed as prevalent as ever, and divisions between countries vitriolic and hostile. Much of supposedly progressive civilization had lost touch with the natural order—something the indigenous people were now trying to reawaken in their "younger brethren."

Closing her eyes and fighting despair, Jana prayed silently:

Divine Mother, Ix Chel, give this body the strength to endure the ordeals it is going through. The body is so tired, the mind feels numb. I don't know what to do now. This uncertainty is wearing me down. Help me to find guidance, to act rightly in the moment, to be trusting of the outcomes of things. You have brought me here, and I have tried to do what has been asked of me. If there is more, I humbly request that you make the way clear. And, give me the physical and mental capacities to do what I must.

She sat quietly for a while, reflecting on the sensations of fatigue and wondering how her body was going to manage. At that instant she could not imagine even standing up. But, she held onto faith that her body and mind would respond as needed.

Music blared loudly, distorting the sweet tenor voice of a popular singer crooning a Mexican love song. Jana caught phrases, "mi corazon," my heart, "muerta," death; something about dying if my heart cannot be one with hers. Underlying these musical strands was the rolling murmur of the immense crowd, a low roar rumbling across the plaza. Inexplicably, Jana was drawn into the crowd. Activated by some hidden current of energy, she hoisted her exhausted body up and walked slowly into the crowd of over 50,000 celebrants enjoying the national holiday.

The pyramid was calling her. Like a monstrous magnet, it pulled her toward its hulking mass. The living electromagnetic fields of her body responded, biological oscillators honing in on a compelling command source. Without thinking why, she wove into the crowd, twisting between moving bodies, stepping over extended legs, bending to avoid swinging arms. Going was very slow, as the people packed densely together. Large family groups seated on blankets presented barriers that had to be circumnavigated. Waves of rapid Spanish conversation and choruses of shouts rebounded all around; she was totally surrounded by a sea of Mexicans.

There was no use going any farther. Progress was impossible through the increasingly thick press of bodies. Jana found a tiny vacant spot and sat down, hugging knees to chest in order to fit. She was immersed, inundated, overwhelmed by the press of human presence and incessant noise. Closing her eyes, she sought that place of calmness within, where she could exist in a peaceful state despite storms raging around her. Slowly a gentle wave rose through her body, quieting and soothing her jangled nerves. There was nothing to do but surrender to the situation.

People around her were playful, in good humor. There was a sweetness about these holiday celebrants, once she allowed herself to settle in and see it. Teenage boys behind her were having a good time, assuming silly poses and taking pictures with some friendly shoving. From time to time, an outbreak of water splashing occurred. The boys poured streams from water bottles on each other, unavoidably splattering nearby people. Everyone just laughed and enjoyed the coolness of evaporating water. Empty bottles were tossed into the air like plastic fireworks, forming random arcs then falling who knew where in the crowd. Annoyed shouts of *"!Basta! Basta!"* came from adults hit on the head by falling bottles. Jana deflected a falling bottle and smiled. All was perfect.

The crowd's excitement was building. When groups stood to look around and check the sun, they were pelted with hollers and gestures to sit down. Crescendos of blaring sound from the grandstand became more frenetic. Jana squirmed in her constricted space to change position, pushing knees against neighbors who seemed oblivious, or perhaps simply accepting of body contact in such a tangled mess of humanity. She checked the time on her wristwatch; it was 4:25 pm. The light serpent should show up in minutes.

As the greatly anticipated moment arrived, a bank of clouds appeared near the western horizon and obscured the sun. A groan of protest rose from the crowd. They waited for about ten minutes, noisy as ever, but the clouds did not clear. Suddenly, almost as one person, all the Mexicans around Jana stood up and started moving around. Confused, she stood also, happy to stretch her numbed legs. Maybe they were giving up because too many clouds blocked the setting sunrays, and the light serpent would not descend that day.

From her location, Jana could see the west and north facing stairs of the pyramid. She fixed her eyes intently on the right side of the north stairs, craning her head to see through the crowd, seeking even a trace of sunlight against the stones tiers. As her eyes followed the stairs up toward the top, she gasped with surprise.

Hanab Xiu was standing at the top of the stairs, on the edge of the temple platform.

What's he doing there? How did he get there?

Riotous feelings burst forth; her heart was pounding. She could see the park guards still barring entrance to the stairs, surrounding the pyramid base. Looking toward the west stairs, another adrenalin surge hit as she saw two forms slowly climbing up the steep ascent. A man and a woman—the woman seemed familiar. With a jolt she recognized Aurora Nakin.

What . . . how did she get there . . . what's she doing? Jana's mind was in turmoil trying to grasp the meaning of this totally unexpected happening. Then it hit her.

It's the ceremony! This is the ceremony I've been called to do! In the ancient temple on top, like the one I envisioned Yalucha doing. I must be there!

Just as this realization occurred, the clouds parted and shafts of brilliant gold sunlight streamed onto the north stairs. An immense roar rose from the crowd, cheers and yells adding high overtones. An excited voice babbled in warp-speed Spanish over trumpeting musical fanfares. The multitudes turned back to the pyramid and began pressing in closely, jostling and pushing for a better view. Slowly, deliberately, a sinuous line of light took shape on the highest stair edges, dropping minute by minute to the next step.

Frantically, Jana tried to shove through the crowd. She had to get to the north stairs, to climb up and join Hanab Xiu. This she knew beyond doubt, but exactly why escaped her. From atop the pyramid, a signal of amazing intensity emanated from the Maya shaman directly to Jana. It reverberated in every body cell, it took over her mind, it pulled heartstrings of arcing ephemeral energy. Without thought or need to consider her actions, she wriggled between bodies, murmuring *"perdón"* and *"permitanme pasar"* as she bumped against them.

A group of teenage boys blocked her way. They were clustered with linked arms, swaying back and forth, laughing and singing. She could see no possible opening around them; people stood shoulder to shoulder, absorbed in watching the light serpent descend. Pushing, pleading, she could not make headway. She was shoved from behind, accompanied by a cackling laugh. Glancing over her shoulder, she caught a glimpse of a short old man fading back into the crowd behind. Dark smoldering eyes briefly joined hers as he shot her a toothless grin, thin lips curling into a sneer under large hooked nose. Then he disappeared magically, as though melting into surging bodies of the crowd.

491

The brujo! The old man from Tikal.

She immediately knew the old shaman was preventing her from joining the ceremony, doing his evil work for the forces of darkness, serving the Lords of Xibalba. They had tried repeatedly, in various ways, to keep her from fulfilling her mission.

The sunrays were lower and the light serpent had nearly reached the bottom of the stairs. Jana realized from that place of intuition, of ancient knowing, that the ceremony must begin as the sunset. And sunset was just minutes away. Desperately she flailed against the pack of boys, yelling at them to let her through. They just tossed water bottles and laughed more, as if delighting in blocking her progress. Tears of frustration stung her eyes, joining the salty coating on her sweaty face.

Standing completely still and closing her eyes, Jana prayed with all the strength and passion she could muster:

Ix Chel, Great Goddess, help me! You have brought me here to do your work, open the way!

Startled by sudden silence, Jana's eyes flew open. The crowd and the bandstand were still, quiet, unmoving. The sunlight had just begun to illuminate the neck of the huge serpent head carved at the base of the stairs. Everyone was transfixed.

A woman's low-pitched voice cried out loudly:

"¡Niños! Apártense! ¡Permitan pasar la señora! ¡Ahora mismo! ¡Anda! ¡Anda!" ("Boys! Move apart! Permit the lady to pass! Right now! Move! Move!")

The stout diminutive matriarch waved her arms commandingly. She glared fiercely at the boys. Without making a sound, the teenage pack split into two sections, opening a corridor straight through their midst to the foot of the pyramid stairs.

Jana's amazed eyes met those of the Mexican woman momentarily. Her features were familiar, Jana had seen them before, somewhere, recently . . . the memory clicked into place. It was the old woman from the emergency room, the Maya curendera from Piste whose hand was exactly like the one in Jana's recurrent dream. In that moment of recognition, she bowed slightly in "namaste" gesture with palms together in prayer, sending a wave of profound gratitude. The old woman's dark eyes twinkled.

Jumping into motion, Jana bounded at top speed through the corridor provided by the boys. In seconds she was at the pyramid base, confronting the armed police standing beside the thigh-level rope closing off the stairs. Those nearest her extended their arms to bar her passage. Just behind them, the huge serpent head was halfway illuminated by sunlight.

Jana stopped, looking upward. Hanab Xiu had been watching her struggles. He motioned her to ascend the stairs. The urgency of his gestures was unmistakable. From deep within Jana's core, a voice boomed forth with jolting force, loud and deep, not at all her own:

"¡Soy sacerdote de Ix Chel! La diosa me llama por ceremonia sagrada en este templo. ¡Permitanme pasar!" ("I am a priestess of Ix Chel! The goddess calls me for sacred ceremony in this temple. Permit me to pass!")

Shocked by the compelling voice, the stunned police dropped their arms and moved aside. Jana did not hesitate one instant, but leapt over the rope onto the stairs before they could recover their senses. Everything went into slow motion for Jana as her feet floated over the tall steps, barely touching them as she jaunted upward. Ordinarily, climbing Maya stairs was an effort, requiring a high step-up and demanding more muscle power. But now the ascent was effortless. Infinite energy coursed through her body, as if she could fly wingless to the top. Her peripheral vision caught glimpses of the vast sea of people below, waves of rich colors rippling in the last golden rays of the setting sun. Eternal moments later, she stood beside Hanab Xiu on the high temple platform of the Pyramid of Kukulkán.

Without speaking, he took her hand and led the way into the square stone temple just as the sun dropped below the horizon.

Six people were gathered in the western chamber of the temple, three men and three women. As Jana and Hanab Xiu joined them, all appeared visibly relieved, releasing tension held in tight muscles. Quickly each pair moved into a square configuration at the four cardinal points, facing the center. Jana's eyes met those of Aurora Nakin, who stood opposite. Wordless knowing flowed between the two women; eons of soul bonding and shared lives, of interchanging roles weaving through each other's history whispered of barely discerned memory traces. The magnificent, yellow ochre clad Maya priest and priestess were present, as well as Fire Eagle and other Mayas from the earlier ceremony. A hidden ache in Jana's heart was soothed. Her soul was again at home with family. She had arrived to complete the adept group mandated to do sacred ceremony.

Hanab Xiu chanted resonant Maya phrases, echoed by the seven other voices enacting the ancient invocation to the directions. Then all sat on mats that had been spread in a circle on the stone floor. The

493

musty odor left by bat guano wafted through the gathering darkness. The Maya priestess lit her copal censor, performing ritual movements then placing it in the circle center on a small round cloth. The woody scents of copal smoke diffused through the room, replacing its mustiness with sweet acridity.

Jana tangibly felt the energy loops forming around and within the group. Her self-awareness began dissolving, as something very ancient filtered upward, a pure intelligent essence that was formless, ageless, unbounded. This ancient intelligence knew what to do. As the breathing of the eight bodies became coordinated, their heartbeats synchronized and formed one large oscillator creating a powerful electromagnetic field. When Hanab Xiu began the first phrases of the invocation for the setting sun, the seven other voices joined immediately drawing from deep cellular memory:

"Dzu bulul H'yum K'in, dzu tip'il X'yum Ak'ab,
Pepenobe cu lembaloob ichil u lol caan,
C'tucule tian ti teche c'Hunab K'u,
Tumen teche c'azaholal, ta k'ab c'k'ubicba."

"Already the Master Sun has set, and the Mistress Night has risen,
The butterflies shine amid the heavenly flowers,
Our thoughts are in you, Dear God,
Because you are our hope; into your hands we surrender ourselves."

Faint traces of light crept through the western doorway, gradually diminishing until only the glowing embers of the copal censor could be seen. The group's synchronized heartbeat became a drum, sounding timeless compelling rhythms; the throbbing core of ancient Maya peoples, the pulsating resonant field of earth herself, the cyclic cosmic patterns emanating from the galactic center and informing earth life.

Re-mem-ber . . . re-mem-ber . . . re-mem-ber . . RE-MEMBER!

A tiny part of Jana's mind remained in present body consciousness. Like slit-screen physics experiments, the photons of expanded awareness left traces on the photographic plate of this mind-part. She existed simultaneously in multiple dimensions, notes of experiences dancing along octaves of being, creating liquid

494

patterns of rapidly changing melodies but blending into a symphonic wholeness.

So vast . . . so incredibly vast . . . beyond the wildest imaginings . . . this beingness . . . encompassing everything . . . eternal, unbroken . . . never apart from Source.

Through closed lids, Jana's eyes detected a luminescent glow. Barely parting her eyelids, she perceived that the stone walls of the small chamber were emanating ethereal light. It seemed to originate from within the stones themselves, softly lighting the space around with soft glowing brightness. She could just make out the figures of the adept group, seated in pairs according to the four directions. The copal censor in the center began producing more smoke and light. It became a brilliant nexus, causing her to squint reflexively. Eyes adjusting, she opened her lids a little more, watching the curls of smoke. White-gray plumes danced and swirled, swaying and twisting into exotic forms.

Forms! Human-like forms!

In the circle's center, fused with incense smoke, two Maya forms began taking shape. They wore long white robes and feather headdresses, ghostlike wraiths made of transparent fumes, billowing and morphing. As these wispy forms ascended and moved aside, two more rose, then another two, until eight Maya apparitions hovered in the small chamber. Four were men and four women. The ghostly couples took places behind each seated pair of humans, male behind male and female behind female. Expanding ripples of ethereal energy encompassed the paired groupings in a bubble of light. Ghostly forms and human forms merged.

Yalucha! Standing behind Jana was the familiar presence of the Maya priestess, her soul-companion of lifehoods.

Yalucha has returned to be with me . . . to become me!

The astral form of the Maya priest accompanying Yalucha stood behind and merged with Hanab Xiu. Jana realized he was Yalucha's male counterpart from that long-ago lifetime when the ceremony at Chichén Itzá was originally performed. Now his soul-companion was the contemporary Maya shaman leading the pilgrimage to reawaken sacred sites. Yalucha's inward smile reached Jana's awareness and drew forth the already-present knowing of the ancient priest's name: *Mac Ceel.*

Waves of unspeakable joy flooded Jana's semi-conscious form, melting her beingness in a sea of bliss. The bubble frolicking on the waves became one with the sea. Ancient memories and present being were united.

While the tiny body-based portion of Jana's mind watched all this in awe-struck wonderment, her deep ancient self performed the prescribed rituals impeccably, with full and complete remembrance.

In accord with all the others present, her chakras activated in the union of body, mind, soul and spirit: the Maya White Flower Thing, the soul, *sak-nik-nal*, in full awareness of both its earthly vessel and its divine source. Without willed intention, her voice spoke the instructions for the group to enter their secret heart chambers:

"*Tz'ib kolonton*, be wise in your heart."

Together, the merged astral and human forms performed the heart chamber procedure and became filled with Divine *itz*. In one accord, they extended hands sideways toward the person on either side, palms touching and fingers intertwined. Male to female, female to male, the feminine and masculine energies intertwined and blended into a spiraling vortex. As its spinning accelerated, their hearts merged into a huge pulsating heartbeat, the heart of the Maya people. From this giant vortex a funnel descended through the pyramid into the earth below.

Deeper it went into the darkness, cold and heavy, through flowing underground rivers and dense layers of limestone and metamorphic rock. Distinct forms began dissolving into a state of swirling substances, amorphous yet charged with force. A faint glimmer of brightness beckoned the collective vortex. Hovering within the other-worldly currents was a large crystalline chamber, shaped like a cigar. Slipping rapidly toward it, the vortex appreciated the chamber's central bulge; it appeared as a sombrero galaxy of shimmering crystal floating in the underworld currents. Approaching its surface, no opening or seams were apparent. Like a space monitor, the vortex of collective awareness scanned all around the crystalline chamber, but it was completely smooth.

Something beyond the chamber was calling. Deeper in the underworld, caught in suffering and torment, something called for help. A tendril of awareness snaked out from the vortex toward this call.

Maya souls trapped in Xibalba are begging for release. They have been waiting for centuries, waiting for this time. Waiting, pleading for shamans of the future, adepts who could move between worlds as in ancient times, to come and open the portals of the

496

Underworld. They are waiting for us, the time is now. This is the work we have come to do, out of compassion.

An immense gaping jaw materialized out of the swirling darkness. Huge bony serpent jaws opened wide, fangs as stylized white columns on either side of the center teeth, decorated with Maya scrolls and symbols. The Maw of the Underworld, *Sak Bak Nakan,* the White Bone Snake invited the collective vortex to enter. Cries and pleas for rescue, for release from suffering, became louder. The vortex tendril moved closer, glimpsed inside the maw where faint humanlike forms writhed and jumped, contorted into grotesque shapes as they tried to avoid cold fires of torment and fetid pools of punishing pus. So long they had waited, so many eons. Compassion flowed through the collective heart of the vortex.

We are coming . . .

No! It's a trap! Return, return to the crystal chamber!

The larger awareness of the vortex summoned its tendril, pulled it away from the Maw of the Underworld. Yalucha and Mac Ceel, Jana and Hanab Xiu, remembered. The first ceremony had almost been aborted by this compelling cry for help.

The time for releasing Maya souls is soon, but not now. Our work is to open the chamber, and our time is immediately or the portal will be lost. Return!

The tendril snapped back into the vortex like a bungee cord. Howls of fury mixed with screams of anguish from the Underworld. Skeletal Death Gods hovering just inside the maw flailed their emaciated limbs, jiggling bloated bellies as they hopped furiously, their skull countenances grimacing fearfully. As the image of Xibalba faded, the face of an old Maya man with deeply sunken black eyes and huge hooked nose flashed through the swirling substances. Opening his toothless mouth wide, he gave a long screech of defeat, projecting his intense fury at Jana. Buffeted by the collective heart of the vortex, her awareness deflected his destructive missile and it bounced off into the amorphous darkness.

The vortex created by the group's collective heart refocused upon the crystalline chamber. It sent waves of unconditional love, accepting the mysterious ways in which the universe expressed compassion. All was well, all was perfect. They would do what they had been called together to do.

The crystalline inter-dimensional chamber opened. The crystal womb chamber received the phallic vortex, as it had so long ago, because of the love held in the collective Maya heart. And it released its sacred wisdom, the most esoteric knowledge of the Maya people, to be born once again as the Divine Child of earth.

To be birthed in the consciousness of all who would receive it.
To reveal the lost knowledge of living in harmony with earth and galactic cycles.
To understand the secrets of Time.
To keep proper relationship with all creatures.
To know and speak rightly the name of God/Goddess.
To remember stellar origins.
To grow the soul through life's experiences.
To dance between worlds, knowing the resurrection that overcomes death.

An eruption of astral energy burst forth from deep earth, up through the Pyramid of Kukulkán, and out the temple roof. The Sacred Mountain became an exploding volcano, sending huge streams of golden-red light high into the night sky. Like incandescent fireworks, the ethereal energy cascaded down upon the Yucatan, reaching a spread of hundreds of miles. All those within its scope were affected. Sleeping or awake, oblivious or aware, conscious or mind-numb, seeker or agnostic, the DNA of their cells responded to this irresistible mandate for the psychic awakening of the contemporary Maya people.

An even vaster eruption of celestial light zoomed at warp-speed into the stratosphere, connecting about 90 miles above earth's surface with the Christos Grid. This grid was shaped into stellated dodecahedrons around the entire planet. Beneath it hovered the light-vibratory grids of all living beings on earth. Every insect, every bird, animal, reptile, plant, mineral, person—all that existed on earth, had energetic strands connected with their specific grid. Each species and group shared a common grid, which brought all members into instantaneous communication. This was the energetic dynamic of the "Hundredth Monkey Effect" and allowed for psychic transmissions. From the Christos Grid the effects of the Pyramid of Kukulkán activation coursed down to the individual and collective grids of all earth beings. The consciousness of all would be affected, in small or large ways, according to receptivity of each.

Grids of sparkling dewdrops, gossamer strands of light- *diamonds twinkling in the indigo skies, droplets trickling along*

498

arcing strings, strings crossing and twining in millions upon millions of meeting points, points of connection and interaction. Strings—string theory—everything coiling and uncoiling in miniscule strings so densely interwoven that where one began and the other ended became impossible to discern.

The web of Spider Mother, the weaver of creation, web strands the portals by which earthly things come into existence. The weaver, the web and the woven all one; the one in the many, unimaginable diversity out of unity.

Pyramid portals into the deep earth, many of them to come. Grids of the vortex, the liberating tornado into the Underworld, offering the path of ascension to souls trapped below. Like Ariadne's golden thread leading Theseus out of the labyrinth in Crete, guiding him to escape the dark clutches of the Minotaur, the light-vibration grids beckoned to long-interred Maya suffering under the tyranny of the Death Gods of Xibalba. Come out! Ascend! Return to life in other worlds. Your banishment is reprieved, your transgressions absolved.

The Hero Twins, in the new guise as male-female pairs doubling themselves in mystical numbers, won again the game with the Lords of Death. Two as one, four as two, eight as four back into one—eight the number of perfect harmony and balance, the endless symbol of infinity.

The Twins as the two faces of each human being, the unitary soul divided into male and female halves. The split self realizing integration of masculine and feminine—creating a pathway that leads to the wedding of all polarities, the union of opposites, the balancing of receptive and outgoing energies, and a new way of being for human women and men living upon planet Earth.

It was done. The ceremony was complete; the sacred mystical ritual was successful. The mission was accomplished. The ancient prophesy had been fulfilled.

Stillness descended upon the Pyramid of Kukulkán at Chichén Itzá.

The shrill double ring of the hotel telephone jarred the sleeping woman into reluctant awakening. Light brown curls spread over the pillow as she turned toward the irksome sound, arm reaching out robotically. Fumbling and clutching, she managed to pull the headpiece to her ear. Eyes still squeezed shut, she mumbled with thickened tongue:

"Hello, hola."

"Jana? This is Aurora. Did I wake you?" The warm alto voice of her friend penetrated the fog of Jana's mind, sparking neuron synapses into action.

"Aurora . . . hi, yes you woke me but thanks, I need to get up," she acknowledged. Opening her eyes, Jana glanced around feeling momentarily disoriented. A shaft of brilliant sunlight crept through a slit between heavy drapes, with dancing specs floating along its golden ray. After hovering in that delicious state of suspension during which one's location might be anywhere, anytime, she recalled where she was. This was the hotel room at Los Aluxes in Mérida.

"I wanted to check in with you before our group leaves the Mayaland," Aurora Nakin continued. "How was your drive back to Mérida last night? I know you were exhausted."

"Yeah, I was." Jana paused to take a deep yawn. "Sorry, I'm hardly awake, but getting there. Actually, the drive back was really great. The best thing was that I finally got cool. Can't remember when I've been so hot. It was dark and the air blowing into the car was actually cool."

"Did you take the toll road?" Aurora Nakin asked.

"I did," Jana replied. "I just couldn't face driving through the villages again, going over all those topes. After I got a bite for dinner at my hotel in Piste, I asked directions and got enough pesos for the toll road. It was a breeze—ha! Double entendre meant." Her mind was working better.

"You didn't have any trouble finding your way back to the hotel?"

"No, I had a little map from the car rental people, and it led me straight here, no problem. I can't tell you how wonderful taking a shower and lying down in bed felt. I was out like a light."

"I can imagine, I was awfully tired too. Quite a day."

There was a pause as both women dipped into recollections of the momentous events of the equinox ceremonies at Chichén Itzá.

Neither seemed to know where to begin talking about their profound experiences.

"It was all so amazing," said Jana, her voice full of wonderment.

"Uh-huh. Beyond my wildest imaginings," confirmed Aurora Nakin.

"We've known each other so many times before," mused Jana. "I feel so close to you. Like you're my mother or something."

"I have been, undoubtedly," said Aurora Nakin with a little laugh. "And you've probably been mine. And who knows what else!"

"Seems like we—not just you and I, but other important people in our lives—keep shifting roles through our earthly sojourns, but keep remaining in each other's lives," Jana observed, a bit surprised at her mind's ability to be philosophical so shortly after a hazy awakening. "Like Hanab Xiu. I realized during the pyramid ceremony that he and I were *sacerdotes*, in the priesthood, together in some Maya city."

"I've known for some time that you two had deep soul connections," observed Aurora Nakin. "Ever since he gave you such special treatment at Clearlake. He and I have some pretty deep roots, too. It's not all perfectly clear, but I know it's there."

"Amazing," reiterated Jana.

"Did you get the sense of opening a hidden chamber under the pyramid, that had been holding ancient Maya wisdom?" asked Aurora Nakin.

"Exactly!" exclaimed Jana. "I'm so happy you said that. I felt we were re-enacting a ritual done centuries ago to place Maya wisdom in safekeeping. Now the time was right to excavate it and bring it up into the world. Then there was this explosion of light and energy, like a volcano erupting, spewing the hidden knowledge into the ether for miles around. . . somehow affecting the consciousness of lots of Maya people, and other people here, too."

"And all around the world," added Aurora Nakin, "through the grids around the earth. You know about those? Wow, that energy eruption was really something."

Jana sighed, feeling affirmed and relieved.

"So I wasn't just imagining all this," she said thoughtfully. "Yeah, I've heard of the energy grids, surrounding earth like meridians of light. Malwyn Melchior writes about them, and others too. I guess this is what we were here for."

"Uh-huh, and more."

"What else, Aurora?" queried Jana.

"Well, our group is going to several more Maya sites, as you know," said Aurora Nakin. "Though he's not actually saying it, I know Hanab Xiu is going to activate these ancient sites and allow their energies to be accessible once again to the world. He'll do it through ceremonies using the group's emotional and psychic fields. And also, we'll be releasing trapped Maya souls from the Underworld. Did you sense that we almost got sidetracked into that during the Pyramid of Kukulkán ritual?"

Jana thought for a minute, re-playing as best she could the incredibly intense and complicated imagery of the ritual.

"Oh, yeah, we were getting pulled away from the crystal chamber . . it was the last rally of the old brujo," she said. "Those Xibalbans don't give up easily."

"Right. They're still fighting to hold onto their victims," retorted her friend. "But already the grids are reaching into the deep earth, setting up the process to release the trapped Mayas. We'll be supporting that during our ceremonies."

"I wonder where they'll go?" mused Jana.

"Some may return to Source, and others will be free to reincarnate and keep serving the world, I guess," ventured Aurora Nakin. "Hey, no doubt you and I are reincarnated Maya souls. Probably everyone on this pilgrimage is."

"The dance of life and death," observed Jana. "I wish I could go on the rest of the pilgrimage with you, to do more ceremonies at Maya sites."

"So do I, but mainly just to have more time together," replied Aurora Nakin. "You accomplished your assignment. You've completed what you were called to do; of this I'm sure. Everything is perfect as it is."

"I guess," sighed Jana.

"When do you return?"

"My flight back is tomorrow morning. I figured I'd need a day to recover before jumping back into my life at home."

"Good idea. What are you doing today?"

"I booked a tour to Uxmal and Kabah," Jana answered. "Thought it would be better to have someone else doing the navigating, and I need to return the VW this morning."

"That's great. Uxmal is very special, you'll see. Our group went there the day before you joined us. Listen, sweetie, I've got to go. We're about to hit the road for our next ruin. Ha," Aurora Nakin

502

laughed. "At this pace we'll all be ruins before this trip is over. I'll call you when I get home."

"OK, please do. Have a great rest of the pilgrimage." Jana paused, taking a deep breath. She could hardly bring herself to end the conversation with her soul sister-mother-daughter-who knew what?

"I love you, Aurora," she continued, voice husky with emotion.

"I love you too, Jana." The sweetness of Aurora Nakin's melodic alto tones was balm to Jana's heart. "We'll be together often. Bye for now."

"Adiós. Vaya con los dioses y diosas." (Go with the gods and goddesses.)

Jana lay in bed for a while after hanging up the phone. With pensive curiosity, her mind reviewed the events of yesterday at Chichén Itzá. Memories commingled in no particular order, following their own secret neural linkings. Rich, intense, mysterious, these inter-dimensional happenings. She was grateful to have been part of the two ceremonies, to learn about and experience her own Maya self. Prayers of gratitude arose spontaneously:

Thank you, Ix Chel, and Itzamna and Hunab Ku, all dioses Maya. Thank you Divine Mother-Father God for helping me do my mission. Thank you for bringing me safely here. I know you are with me.

Stretching to relieve stiffness in still-recovering muscles, she appreciated how good it felt simply to be lying flat and resting. Her night's sleep had been deep and restorative. Lifting on one elbow, she checked the time: almost 9 o'clock. The tour van would pick her up in the hotel lobby at ten. She better get up and get going. In that hour she needed to get dressed, return the rental car and have breakfast. Yes, especially coffee. Then tomorrow was the early morning flight back home.

Home. . . Robert! Oh, my beloved Robert. . . what are you thinking? Will we still have a marriage when I get home?

Wrenching pain tore at her heart as the pit of her stomach knotted. Tears welled up, dampening her cheeks and causing stinging in the right eye. That eye had felt prickly last night on the drive back to Mérida. Now it was distinctly uncomfortable. Sniffling, she brushed the tears away carefully and breathed deeply into the heartache about Robert. Whatever the situation was at home, she

503

would just have to handle it. But her solar plexus took little comfort in that thought, refusing to unknot yet.

In the bathroom, she checked her right eye. The medial aspect, that part between the iris and the inner corner near the nose, was completely covered with bright red blood. From her nursing experience she recognized the bleeding as a sub-conjunctival hemorrhage. This was a common and harmless condition, she knew. It occurred when a tiny blood vessel on the surface of the eyeball ruptured, releasing blood under the conjunctiva, the eye's transparent outer membrane. The membrane trapped a thin layer of blood and held it in place for several days, while the red blood cells were slowly absorbed. Although it looked awful, there was usually very little discomfort.

Almost immediately upon seeing the sub-conjunctival hemorrhage a thought popped into Jana's mind:

You must have your letting of blood. The expected tribute for powerful Maya gods. The requirement for sealing the covenant, for accomplishing the ritual. So be it.

She blinked at herself in surprise, watching the bloodied eye with new respect.

I'm just glad you didn't require letting blood in a more dramatic way!

She sent this thought into the ether with another wave of gratitude, shuddering to think of what might have happened on the nighttime drive from Chichén Itzá. Yes, she got off easy.

Breakfast and coffee restored her stomach to more normal sensations, though she hurried to get everything done in time for the tour. Thoughts of Robert were never far from her awareness, however. Sadness pulled at her heart, and the strange admixture of regret around Robert and gratitude for the Maya ceremonies strummed her emotions.

* * * * *

Verdant, rolling hills gradually replaced the flat, scraggly terrain around Mérida. In the distance the Puuc Hills rose gently, their soft curved mounds like arboreal breasts of the Green Mother. The land felt richer, more fertile and inviting. The Puuc Maya had made a good choice for locating their cities. Lush vegetation still bright green well into the dry season bespoke productive soils and more abundant rains than in the flatlands. The air was less smoky although a thin haze still reduced the sun's brightness. Puffy white clouds drifted slowly across a pale blue sky.

The road to Uxmal unfolded like a narrow charcoal ribbon before the tour van. Dipping into hollows and curving over low hills, the two-lane highway was well maintained and had little traffic that day. Jana sat in the front seat next to the driver, whose name was Bernal. Reasonably well-functioning air conditioning kept the van comfortable as the morning heat built up. Four other people were along on the tour, a young French couple and a middle age Mexican couple from Champoton, a gulf town on the southeast edge of the Yucatan. From time to time on the forty-five minute drive, Bernal broke into commentary in both English and Spanish, often mixed indiscriminately.

"These Puuc hills are called the little mountains of Ticul by the locals," he informed them, pronouncing syllables distinctly in the Mexican style. *"Pequeñas montañas de Ticul.* The Puuc region covers over 7500 kilometers—4700 miles—and is defined by two chains of hills in a V shape. The soil is very fertile from erosion, soil coming down from the hillsides during rains. But water is a big problem—*problema grande.* No rivers, no cenotes. The Maya were *ingenioso,* how you say ingenious. They built cisterns, artificial holes to catch run-off from the rains. Many can still be seen today."

Bernal nodded to himself with satisfaction over his ancestor's accomplishments.

"This area has many Maya sites," he continued. "Kabah, Sayil, Labna, Oxkintok, Xlapak, Chacmultun. Uxmal was the largest and most important city. Together they formed a political and spiritual unit that had great influence from the seventh to the ninth centuries of the present era. Very much influence, comparable to Chichén Itzá and Mayapan in the following four centuries. Uxmal and Chichén Itzá were overlapping for some time, and probably formed an alliance."

"When did Uxmal begin?" asked Jana.

"They think a small village was built on the site as early as 800 BCE," Bernal replied. "The city really developed after the Xiu Maya migrated there from the south, maybe from the great lowland cities of the Peten region in Guatemala. By 200 CE they had large buildings and a system of government. The city was at its height from 600 to 900 CE, with a population over 20,000. The kings and lords had many luxuries and lived in fine stone palaces. Uxmal has some of the most beautiful buildings in all of the Maya lands. Its name, Uxmal, means 'three times built or three times fruitful'. We know this is actually its Mayan name, from written documents and glyphs."

"Was Uxmal deserted like so many other great Maya cities?" Jana queried.

"Yes, and we still do not know exactly why," said Bernal, shaking his head sadly as if he personally felt responsible. "It was declining by 1000 CE and abandoned a little while later. There was warfare, but it seems that Uxmal was not invaded by an enemy. No, their society must have collapsed from the inside. Maybe because the elite did not share their artistic and technical knowledge with the common man. When the elite were killed in battles and those with knowledge disappeared, there was no one to continue the ancient arts and sciences. No one knew how to keep the cities alive. So they had to leave. *Quién sabe? Que magnifico, que tragico.*"

This guy's quite the philosopher, thought Jana.

Bernal did indeed appear lost in the matrix of his thoughts, falling silent for several miles. The two couples behind engaged in murmuring conversation, each in its own language. Jana watched the green forests slip past, dense trees interrupted by cornfields and citrus groves accompanied by an occasional stucco and thatch roof house. Her thoughts turned again to Robert, evoking feelings of intense yearning along with trepidation. Tomorrow she would know something, for better or worse. Tomorrow would be here soon, almost too soon. She both desired and feared seeing her husband.

"The Puuc style of architecture is very distinct, very lovely," Bernal said suddenly, with no overtures. He appeared to have come out of some kind of trance.

Startled out of her own reverie, Jana shot the driver a quick look, hoping he was not having petit mal seizures that temporarily rendered him semi-conscious. No, he had kept the van on a straight trajectory, driving smoothly and evenly. No sign of seizure activity.

"It this style of building, the lower portion of walls are left plain, and the upper portion decorated with intricate designs," he continued, oblivious to his passengers' attentiveness or lack thereof. "The roof combs are frontal, light and airy. Vertical columns and friezes are decorated with mosaics of masks, lattices, drums, snakes, animals, flowers and geometric designs that had religious meanings. Another unique characteristic is what they call 'fastening moldings,' carved ropes running the length of buildings. These were stone replicas of actual rope fasteners used to hold up the walls of Maya huts. The elite builders like using village themes. One frieze in the Nunnery

506

Quadrangle has inverted lattice bins for holding maize kernels, just the same as the villagers used."

"That's very interesting," said Jana with sincerity. His descriptions of architecture had captured her attention.

Bernal smiled and glanced at her, happy to have someone paying attention.

"Words cannot describe the architectural beauty of Uxmal," he stated simply.

Jana nodded. She had read exactly those words in guidebooks.

"How much longer until we get there?" she asked.

"Another ten minutes, *diez minutos,*" he called to the passengers in back.

Jana's mind raced ahead to the site of Uxmal, envisioning pictures she had seen. Instantly she felt that subtle fluttering in the heart chakra region, a tiny signal she had learned foretold something of great import. An eager anticipation was forming inside, ushering her into unreasonable happiness. Happiness for no apparent reason. Why should the thought of visiting Uxmal make her suddenly happy?

Ten minutes later the van turned into a lovely corridor, bordered by gracious resort hotels and manicured landscaping. The park entrance bespoke of harmonies with nature. Passing through a nicely arranged square patio with shops, museum, restaurant and information areas, the small group entered the turn-style gate into the *Zona Arqueológica de Uxmal.* The stone-paved walkway ascended tiers of stairs, past flowering greenery, to the top of a small hill.

Jana gasped at the sight from the hilltop. An immense oval structure arose abruptly in front of her; tall as any pyramid she had seen but with soft, rounded sides. From pictures she recognized it as the Pyramid of the Magician, but was unprepared for its impact. She could hardly catch her breath, and it wasn't from the easy climb or the 98- degree heat.

She knew this pyramid, she knew it intimately. She had been here before, inside the chamber whose eastern door she could see, three-quarters of the way up. She had stood in the main temple near the summit, which she knew was on the other side, although not visible from her present vantage point. There were Chak masks lining each side of the steep stairs leading to that main temple, also hidden from her view. This structure was emblazoned in her primal memory. Dimly, she heard Bernal describing the pyramid.

"It is the only Maya pyramid of this shape. No other one has rounded sides. And it is the most massive in total size. The platform

507

that it sits on is 279 feet long and 164 feet wide. It stands nearly 115 feet high, higher than El Castillo at Chichén Itzá. Only one pyramid in the Yucatan is higher, that is Nohoch Mul in Coba, which reaches 138 feet. On the western side is a central platform over 11 feet wide, and a square shaped temple sits there. Come, let us walk there."

The group followed Bernal around the southern side of the pyramid into the plaza on its western side. Jana lagged behind, caught by the pyramid's magnetic pull that made walking seem like hauling her body through thick syrup. Once inside the plaza, the large Chak masks of the stairway all seemed to train their glaring eyes on her. But she felt they were smiling, welcoming her, in spite of the fierce-looking open-mouth grimaces under overhanging nose. Her heart thundered as she looked up at the central platform. Its single door was formed by the mouth of a huge mask—the portal of Itzamna. Beyond any doubt, she had done ceremony there, in some distant time.

"These masks are of the rain god Chak," intoned Bernal to the group. "He was very important because if there was not enough rain, crops would fail and people would starve. Sacrifices were made to Chak in that smaller structure up there, called the Chenes Temple." He pointed to the central temple. "The outer walls of the pyramid were once carved with sacred symbols, other gods, snakes, maize, lattices, figures of rulers and priests. You can see such carvings around the temple. Its doorway is framed by a big mask, see, the door is its mouth."

Bernal paused while the two couples took pictures of each other. Jana stood motionless, taking in every detail of the pyramid. It was like superimposing a skeleton over the mirage of a fully fleshed form. There were hints, suggestions of what once was, tantalizing but elusive. It was so familiar, but at the same time so different. Faint memories were clicking into place like a computer accessing remote files, mostly subliminal. The overwhelming impression that she had been here before flooded through her mind, throwing her into a reverie.

Sky pyramid of conjuring magic, of vision journeys. . . Itzam Ka'an!

The Maya-name echoed through Jana's awareness. Through half-closed eyes, her vision blurred and the pyramid morphed into a shining spectacle: Rounded sides were covered with smooth white plaster, so brilliant that it nearly hurt your eyes. Chak masks, effigies of gods and rulers, gargantuan faces with doorway mouths were painted in vibrant colors of blue, green, red, and yellow. The temple above had red-painted columns with intricate carvings symbolizing maize, Itzam-Ye birds, snakes and cloud-scrolls in a riotous mix of colors.

The pyramid was alive; Jana could feel intense life-force energy emanating from its depths. Her vision darkened as if the sun was setting, causing the white pyramid to glow and shimmer. She sensed a large crowd of ghostly figures around her, filling the plaza and fanning around the pyramid base. Torchlight flickered on the temple platform and a white-clothed figure wearing a tall, feathered headdress appeared from inside the mask-mouth.

Yalucha! As she appeared in the dream of the old woman's hand! This is the rounded pyramid in my dream.

Instantly her perspective shifted and she saw the crowded plaza from a vantage point high above. In the fading light her eyes—the eyes of this being standing on the temple platform—viewed the descending stairway, heads of people, and multiple other large structures spreading in all directions arranged around many wide plaster-paved plazas. The ancient city of Uxmal, in all its loveliness with intact roof combs and classic Maya colors over smooth white plaster, unfolded before her. It left her awestruck, even as the heart of the Maya priestess burst with love and pride. Yalucha's heart, her heart?

Standing beside the priestess was the commanding form of a Maya priest. This stately man wore matching white robes and feather headdress. His intense visage was familiar, a face Jana had seen often, and recently. The priest joined the priestess in graceful ritual gestures accompanied by exotic chanting—echoes of melodies long known and revered.

From inside the temple chambers a young man emerged and stood behind her. His regal bearing and gorgeous attire announced a king, the ruler of Uxmal. Torchlight glinted off semiprecious stones and shells, feathered headdress danced and ornaments clacked with his movements. She knew him well, loved him boundlessly. He was her spiritual apprentice now grown, he was her twin soul. He was known as Chan Chak K'ak'nal. And many other names in their intertwined lifehoods.

A loud burst of laughter jolted Jana back into present time. Bernal had amused his group with some humorous comment. Laughing at his own wit, the cheerful guide threw back his head and waved both hands.

"Yes, that is what they say," he continued. "The legend of this pyramid says it was built in one night by a dwarf magician, hatched from an egg by an old grandmother witch. The dwarf was being tested by the king of Uxmal, but he outsmarted the king and himself became ruler for a long time. That is how the pyramid got its name. This structure actually was built in five layers, over older structures during a time period of about 400 years. The last addition is on the very top, Temple V. It is carved like a hut made of poles, the typical Maya house, which you still see today in rural areas of Yucatan. The western face is decorated with intertwined serpents and lattices."

"Can you climb up?" asked the young French tourist.

"No, that is not permitted now," said Bernal in a sincerely regretful tone. He waited a few minutes as his charges craned necks to see the topmost temple. Then with a gesture, he said:

"Come, we go now to the quadrangle."

Wending his way through narrow passages and up uneven stairs, Bernal led the group into the wide plaza of the rectangular complex dubbed by early explorers the "Nunnery Quadrangle." It reminded these Spanish men of monastic quarters for nuns in their home country. Or, perhaps they unwittingly tuned into the sacred purposes of this splendid place.

Upon entering the quadrangle, Jana instantly knew this was hallowed ground.

The four long buildings that comprised the quadrangle borders were unique but formed an exquisite symmetry. Shapes, lines, stairways, doors and entablature designs joined in point and counterpoint rhythms, amazingly oppositional and yet harmonic at the same time. While Jana could not analyze why this complex was so visually pleasing, she at once appreciated its fusion of dualities. Masculine and feminine symbols blended in perfect balance; all polarities were reconciled. It communicated fusion within separateness, unity out of diversity. Every part of each building was full of sacred symbolism, infused with spiritual energy.

The Spirit Quadrangle. All the important aspects of Maya cosmology and religion are expressed here. In Maya times each building had a special focus for conjuring spirit guides and seeking visions. But all were Itzam Nah, conjuring houses, where magic was made. Yalucha, the priest and the young king all worked here.

Jana just knew these things, without thought or question. She loved this place. Un-summoned happiness delighted her as she turned in a complete circle, looking at each structure in turn, feeling into the vibrations. Bernal was expounding to the group about Puuc architecture, but she hardly heard a word.

"Here you see all the Maya carved art of the Puuc style," Bernal intoned. "Many people think this is the most outstanding example in the entire region. On each building we have Chak masks, Maya huts, entwined serpents, frets, and many geometric designs. The skill of the stone carvers is outstanding. These structures were used for civic and religious purposes. So many sacramental spaces—see all those doorways, they lead into little rooms, not joined together like in residences—these must have been places where priests were trained."

Still in a dreamy state, Jana added automatically:

"And priestesses, too."

Bernal looked oddly at Jana.

"There were no priestesses," he said with absolute assurance. "Only Maya priests were trained here."

Jana returned Bernal a look of incredulity, but he had turned away and was pointing out other attributes of the buildings.

Little does he know! thought Jana. *Too bad that his machismo blinds him, and his compatriots, to these truths about their indigenous ancestors. No priestesses, my eye! What a nerve. Oh, well. Guess I've got to endure his bias, no point arguing.*

The group wandered around the expanse of the Nunnery Quadrangle for a short time, not nearly long enough for Jana. Bernal summoned them to follow him to the Governor's Palace, leading through the corbelled arch passage that pierced the center of the South Building, down the wide stairs and past the modest-sized ballcourt. He made a few comments about the Mesoamerican penchant for the ball game as a re-enactment of the saga of creation, but did not let them tarry. Soon they ascended the deteriorating wide stairs leading up to the immense platform, now a grassy meadow, on which rested the Governor's Palace.

Vast, expansive, and serene, the great structure covered the west end of the meadow. A few widely spaced trees lifted tall limbs at distant edges, and two peculiar stone monuments rested directly in front. Bernal explained that the small square platform with steps on all four sides served as a throne. The ruler would sit on the two-headed jaguar bench, formed by the joining of the animals' chests as each faced in opposite directions. The jaguar was the major symbol of royal power, and the two heads referred to the dual nature of the king: both human and divine, with both civic and spiritual obligations.

He glossed over the second structure, between the throne platform and the stairs of the central wing of the Governor's Palace. Resting almost on its side was a large stone column, completely unadorned. A square of small stones had been formed around it. The plaque nearby described it as a stone phalanx of unknown ceremonial significance. But, the symbology was inescapable.

It was a phallus, a large stone phallic symbol now lisping to one side. When erect, it would be taller than a man, and larger in girth. Jana intuited this was a dramatic expression of sexual creative energy, representing the World Tree/Cosmic Phallus thrusting up from the ground in front of the king's palace. She looked at the palace in a direct line from the erect stone, and saw the middle doorway of the central wing, larger than the other six doors and carrying a magnificent sculpture above. Focusing carefully on the intricate sculpture, she could make out a lordly figure festooned with luxurious plumage headdress fanning outward around a partly eroded body. Seven stylized double-headed serpents projected straight out in a trapezoid pattern behind the carving. Three Itzam-Ye masks sat above the top serpent bar. Jana knew who it was:

Chan Chak K'ak'nal, ruler of Uxmal, builder of this palace and the quadrangle. Uxmal's greatest shaman-king, the living form of First Father-Maize God, would emerge from this central doorway of his home, and stand on the platform shimmering with snake-energy as his enthralled subjects gathered around the giant erection that proclaimed the sexual powers of creation as part of his divine essence. When First Father raised the World Tree, Wakah K'an, it was the orgasmic rapture of this cosmic phallus penetrating up through Earth Mother that separated earth and sky, and brought forth life in the world. From union, separateness; all separateness seeking union.

Bernal was busy with more mundane descriptions of the remarkable palace.

"The Governor's Palace is considered the most beautiful building in Uxmal because of its exuberant decorations," he informed the group. "It is also most impressive in size and proportions. The building is 328 feet long, 40 feet wide and 30 feet tall. Great triangular arches divide it into three sections. At one time they were corridors to pass through the building, but now they have been filled in to prevent them from collapsing. The rooms inside are multi-chambered; they have inside passages between outer and inner rooms.

512

The complexity of rooms makes experts think this was a residence, as well as administrative center.

"The friezes on top are the finest in all Puuc sites. You can look for hours and still not see every detail. It has 103 Chak masks along the length, mixed with geometric patterns, lattices, and many serpents. These decorations emphasize how important the rain god, Chak, was for people in this arid climate. They also relate to movements of the sun and Venus, a very important planet for the Maya. Now I will allow you to see more on your own. There is much more to see, you have your maps, yes?"

Bernal looked around receiving affirmative nods.

"*Bueno*. Please return to the park entrance in one hour. *Hasta luego.*"

One hour! Jana felt it was not nearly enough time. *I could stay here all day, all year, a lifetime—and I probably have.*

Checking her wristwatch, she pleaded with the second hand to move slowly, to extend each tiny jerk in its 60-second sweep. 12:60, the artificial time beat of the Julian calendar. She longed to slip into the symbiotic rhythms of 13:20, to move in harmony with stellar patterns and know time as did the Maya.

The mosaic of Uxmal's great ahau beckoned her, drawing her up the wide stairway toward the middle door. Thighs reaching high, she ascended the tall steps to the long expanse of the palace platform. The enigmatic figure's facial features were obscured, but the grandeur of his being was easily felt. She walked inside the door and was immediately struck with the rank odor of bat guano, stronger here than any chambers she had visited. Holding her nose, she wandered around in the semi-dark interior, noting inside doors on both ends of the large main chamber. There appeared a string of rooms going in each direction, quite large by Maya standards. This did appear the dwelling of royalty, no doubt lavish in its heyday.

Finally the offensive smell drove her back outside. Sitting on the top steps, she looked back at the main chamber then turned her gaze pensively across the meadow.

Once the home of the greatest rulers, now the residence of bats, she thought dolefully. As her mind attempted to picture what home life might be like for the Uxmal king, the image of Robert popped into her inner sight. Robert was smiling, relaxed, looking well fed and well rested and quite self-pleased. His charming off-center smile activated the subtle dimple that she so loved.

He's looking awfully well, she thought. *What's making him so happy?*

Eyebrows screwing in concentration, Jana's sight dimmed as she focused intently on Robert. His presence was strongly here; she sensed his energies almost tangibly. Surprising herself with the sudden movement, her body twisted quickly to look again at the middle door, as if she expected to see him standing there. But, only a young tourist peered inside the musty chambers, recoiling at the smell and moving on. Closing her eyes, Jana leaned forward and rested her chin in both hands, savoring the image of her husband that remained so vivid in her inner vision.

Suddenly Robert's face morphed, changing its architecture but retaining basic characteristics that let her identify him. His skin now was deep cocoa and hair jet black, eyes dark as ink but shaped much like at present. The cheeks were higher and broader, and the nose amazingly large. But the same sensuous lips smiled over even white teeth and brought out a tiny dimple.

Who on earth? That's got to be a Maya man—but also Robert! Somehow this guy's connected with the Governor's Palace. . . wow, could it be the ruler Chan Chak?

The implications of this thought boggled Jana's mind. If she could really believe this imagery sequence, then Robert had once been the Uxmal king so beloved by Yalucha, her own soul-companion. He'd been here before, his soul essence somehow embodied in this Maya person. Swirling half-thoughts mixed with amorphous images in a confusing collage inside Jana's awareness. Rapid flashes of different Maya faces, costumes, building styles and vegetation cascaded through her inner vision. She sensed the intertwining of lives, over and over again, of these women and men. But always the same basic beings, the same split souls, the same memory banks carrying experiences and beliefs of lifehoods.

In that moment she felt the bittersweet quality of Yalucha's life in Uxmal. She entered the poignant awareness of the priestess who nurtured the young prince to become an adept, a true shaman-king for his people, but who could never realize her own love for him. The priestess' memories filled her, telling of those prior lives when these two souls united as lovers but were torn apart, the precious moments of rapture and the anguish of loss. Again and again, who knew how long or how many times?

Was there ever a happy ending? Jana's mind rebelled and demanded to know.

The opportunity is now, replied an unseen voice.

Now? Well things aren't looking too good just at the present, Jana replied to whatever part of her consciousness gave the cryptic message. Robert had been quite estranged emotionally when she left on this trip. She had never before experienced him being that angry and rejecting. All she could do was hope for the best, and pray, and continue to love him with all her heart.

In this disconsolate mood she wandered around the structures behind the Governor's Palace. Her interest was perked by the House of the Turtles, an austere rectangular building with a simple upper entablature distinguished by turtles on the cornice molding. Evenly spaced, the turtles were carefully sculpted with fine detail and minimal variation in size. The building imparted a tranquil feeling and a deep connection with nature.

Continuing along the multi-level platforms behind the Governor's Palace, she passed an older structure sporting a large Chak mask, done in whimsical but elaborate Chenes style. Past this area soared the huge Great Pyramid, composed of nine platforms with a flat stone temple on top. The front side and steps had been recently restored and gleamed light beige in the blazing midday sun. Earth, vegetation and tumbled stones still made up the other three sides. Jana climbed the high, wide stairway to the top platform, dripping with sweat as she finished the ascent. From this lofty perspective she was treated to a stunning view of the entire Uxmal site.

It was breathtaking in its symmetrical beauty. The harmonious design of the Nunnery Quadrangle blended with the Quadrangle of the Birds resting at the western base of the towering Pyramid of the Magician. From the South Building's corbelled arch entryway, wide stairs led to the parallel lines of the ballcourt, and beyond this plaza stairs rose to the impressive high platform of the Governor's Palace. Flowing lines stepped down from the back of the Governor's Palace in a cascade of partially restored stairs, embracing the Turtle House level then dropping into the lowest plaza that fused with the base of the Great Pyramid. Beyond the Governor's Palace stretched its vast high plaza reaching to the eastern border of the forest. Gleaming beige roofcombs soared above forest greenery to the west and north, airy fretwork of open niches and offset edges resembling dovecotes. Tucked into the forest, hints of other structures farther west could be seen.

Jana feasted her eyes on the sight of this lovely city, imagining what it might have looked like when Yalucha and Chan Chak lived here.

When Robert and I lived here—at least some portion of our consciousness, of who we now are, in the beings of these Mayans. Our souls embodied, or some part of that essence that continues to exist and know itself life after life.

From the uppermost platform of the Great Pyramid, she climbed the few stairs to look inside the temple door. Ensconced there was a huge Chak mask, taller than a person, its long nose forming a chair. She imagined a priest or priestess sitting there, invoking the all-important Rain God whose benevolent sky-waters brought renewed life to the arid region. Faint traces of red paint on the stone mask reminded her that once the sculpture was adorned with brilliant colors, itself vibrant and alive with *itz*.

The entire façade of this temple was covered with decorations, but these lacked the perfection seen in the entablatures of the Governor's Palace and Nunnery Quadrangle. Nonetheless, the carvings were interesting and contained lattices, floral rosettes, dados, and anthropomorphic faces. Three masks were set into the corners; those on the northwest corner had a man's face emerging from their mouths in the Maya symbolism of the supreme god Itzamna as creator of life.

Not the slightest breeze stirred in the simmering midday heat. Jana stepped back into a small line of shade offered by the corner of the temple, her skin covered with a fine film of sweat and her clothes thoroughly damp. She could feel the flushing of her cheeks and wished she had a hat. Her right eye smarted as salty droplets irritated the sub-conjunctival hemorrhage, concealed by her dark sunglasses. Then she remembered time, 12:60 western-world time. She had been immersed in the flowing rhythms of 13:20 indigenous-peoples time, simply following her urges moment-to-moment. Checking her wristwatch, she noted only about ten minutes remained until time to rejoin the group at the entrance, a walk that would take almost that much time.

Descending the pyramid stairs, she felt drawn to the left, away from the return route. A small structure half-hidden by trees, about 150 feet from the pyramid base, seemed to beckon her. Although her mind told her there was not enough time to go there, her feet disobeyed and led her onto the dirt path descending left past the lower plaza. It wound through clustered trees and past rubble piles, and then forked not far from the small structure. A narrow, uneven path branched off the main fork to the deteriorated structure 15 feet away. Carefully picking her way closer, Jana arrived at the summoning site.

The structure was about 20 feet high and 10 feet wide, with what appeared to be a round roof now completely covered with vegetation. It merged into the hill behind, probably formed by erosion and settling of the abutting plaza. A corbelled arch led into the small one-room chamber inside. Hesitating, Jana peered into the dimness of the windowless room. Heaps of crumbled mortar and stone pebbles that had broken off the walls filled the interior. There was a cleared section in the center, so she stepped through the doorway and stood, quietly feeling into its energies. This little place was so familiar, so homey, that she knew she had once lived here. Or rather, Yalucha had lived here.

This must have been Yalucha's home during her time in Uxmal, thought Jana. The amber pendant that she constantly wore seemed to vibrate against her chest. Heart chakra emanations joined the pendant, radiating outward through the interior space and into the stone walls. The spirit doll seemed to thump in its pouch against her hip. *Yes, we know this place.*

Jana fell into reverie, images of the priestess' later life playing across her inner vision. Yalucha was very old, the most revered High Priestess of Uxmal, now serving as a wisdom oracle for the priestly leadership and the ruler. She no longer performed rituals, as her creaky knees could not ascend steep pyramid stairs and her voice had lost its high crystal ring. Lovingly tended by young acolytes, she spent much time alone communing with the spirit world. Her greatest earthly joy was an occasional visit by Chan Chak, the inspired king-shaman-architect of Uxmal's beauty. He was now almost an elder himself, grooming his older son for dynastic inheritance, imbuing him with strength and vision to handle the approaching difficult times. Already weather patterns were changing with shorter rainy seasons and decreased crop yields. Unrest percolated through the grand alliance with Chichén Itzá, and hostile cities were growing in power.

Cycles, inevitable cycles, the rise and fall of fortunes, the comings and goings of souls, the dance between the three worlds . . .

Suddenly present awareness hit Jana, catapulting her out of reverie.

Yipes! I better get back to the entrance!

She breathed deeply, committing the smell of dry stone dust to deep cellular memory. Crossing arms over her chest, she bowed to the spirit of her ancestor who lived in this derelict of times long past. Turning and carefully treading over the loose rocks of the narrow entry, she picked up the pace once on the wider path, going as fast as her body would permit in the searing heat. She knew she was late, and that Bernal would be annoyed. But in typical Mexican style, he would cover his peeve with light humor. His was a culture that disliked unpleasant confrontation. Instead, they used the flowery phrases of creative wordsmiths, dissipating their annoyance with their own self-admiration.

Como si nada hubiese pasado—as if nothing had happened.

*   *   *   *   *

A multitude of tiny sparkling lights far below spread across dark landscape as the Boeing 737 slowly descended for landing at the Oakland Airport. Sharp edges bordering solid blackness outlined the shores of the San Francisco Bay and the Pacific Ocean coast. Smoothly the silver and blue airliner dropped along its landing pattern as the ground seemed to rise rapidly, as if yearning to receive the metal bird on its bosom.

"Flight attendants, prepare for landing," intoned the gravely voiced captain.

When the metal bird flies, the indigenous prophesies will be fulfilled. Who said that? Chief Seattle? Or maybe it was the time of accounting, when white men must face the consequences of their actions. I read somewhere that the techno-masters of Atlantis would reincarnate when the world's technology started matching theirs, so they could work out karma created by misuse of that power. Hmmm, maybe that's why we're in such trouble now; the Atlantean boys haven't figured it out yet and are misusing technology once again. We've got to take indigenous ways to heart, and learn to relate in a different way to our world, our precious Earth.

Jana's thoughts followed an un-reined stream of consciousness in the final minutes of her flight home. Nearly ten hours of travel, including two airplane changes, had turned her brain to mush. There was actually something nice about an exhausted mind—it couldn't worry or problem-solve or conjure up worst-case scenarios about her personal life. She'd already spent enough hours doing that. Now she simply allowed her thoughts to wander.

The mere fact that a 69-ton chunk of metal could take to the air and soar miles above the earth always intrigued her. She decided that Atlantis had a different method for flying, probably some type of antigravity force that effortlessly lifted and propelled their air-borne vessels. Not this massive combustion produced by burning fossil fuels, sucking air through enormous turbines and pushing the hulking metal faster and faster until the aerodynamics of wind flowing over curved wings created an uplift. At any rate, landing was fascinating, a process requiring more finesse than force as the pilot skillfully allowed gravity to pull the airplane down. She was always grateful for the first bump of tires on runway, signaling once again a happy earth embrace.

Blinking against the bright lights inside the Oakland terminal, Jana felt that strange disorientation of arriving in a different city, another country, and a certain way of seeing the world. It was definitely apart from the rhythms and sounds of México. Her short stay in the Yucatan seemed a world away, another lifetime, or a different dimension of existence. Had she been there only five days? It seemed an eternity.

As Jana neared the security checkpoint, her heart began beating faster. Although she tried not to think of it, her secret hope was that Robert would be there, waiting for her. They had made no agreement for him to meet her at the airport; in fact, she had driven herself and parked in the long-term lot. He did know her flight arrival information, she made certain of that before leaving. But, he avoided any implicit agreement to meet her, remaining aloof and disengaged.

Passing through the exit corridor at the checkpoint, she quickly scanned the few people waiting beyond the guards. Pausing, she caused other departing passengers to step around her in their hurry to get wherever they were going. But, it was clear after only a few moments that Robert was not among the small group waiting for their people. Acknowledging a twinge of disappointment, Jana followed the queue down escalators to the baggage claim area. She had checked her small suitcase to avoid having to handle it during two airplane transfers en route.

Her flight number flashed above a nearby baggage carousel as a rude buzzer sounded and the conveyor clacked into action. Disconsolately, she watched baggage burping out of the subterranean conveyer onto the round carousel. So many looked alike, too many little and big black bags, with only an occasional interesting design or shape. Her eyes flickered from one bag to another, searching for the multicolored woven cord she had tied to hers for easier identification. Deep sadness ached in her heart and her legs seemed too heavy to move. It was too pitiable being alone at the baggage claim, no loving

519

friend happily greeting her. No husband, no companion there to welcome her back home.

Someone moving through the edges of the crowd clued Jana's peripheral vision. Her gaze jerked up as her body snapped to alert. She knew that form! Though only seen through the corner of her eye, she immediately recognized the body movements.

It was Robert!

He was smiling, the unique smile that always melted her heart. His eyes smiled too, shining clear blue fountains of caring. Moving quickly as he could through the crowd, every movement of his body conveyed eagerness to reach her.

Jana turned toward her approaching husband, hesitating. Was she misreading his signals? Did her intense yearning for reconciliation cause her to project her own desires upon him? Was this a mirage, created by her overwrought mind?

Before she could pursue these doubts, he was there. Both stood utterly still, drinking each other in through wide eyes. Electricity snapped between their poised bodies, tingling fingers and toes and causing skin to prickle. Jana's heart was pounding wildly, throbbing with such force in her ears that she almost couldn't hear his words.

"Welcome home, Jana."

Robert smiled more broadly, making his dimple quite evident, and opened his arms. A rush of magnetism pulled her insistently toward him. Still almost unbelieving, she held back another instant, then literally leapt into his arms. Avalanches of joy shuddered through her body as he enclosed her, holding her tightly against his chest. She buried her head into one broad shoulder and started sobbing uncontrollably. Joy and relief, bliss and surrender flooded Jana's being as her pent-up emotions burst out in tears. She was crying for happiness and at the same time, crying for sorrow.

A few people around glanced curiously at the embracing couple, but most paid no attention in their single-minded quest for luggage. Robert gently ushered Jana apart, guiding her behind an adjacent vacant carousel. She kept her face pressed tightly to his chest, hugging his waist with both arms. He stroked her hair, keeping the other arm securely around her shoulders, waiting and comforting.

"Sweetheart, are you all right? Is anything wrong?" he asked when her sobs quieted.

Jana finally lifted her head, wiped her eyes and looked up at him with tear-streaked cheeks. All she could think of was how wonderful it was to see him, feel him, be held by him once again. He was here!

He had come to meet her. Still unable to find her voice, she shook her head.

"What happened to your eye? Are you hurt?" he sounded worried.

"N-no, no . . . " she finally managed to whisper. "I-I mean yes, I'm OK . . . it's just a little ruptured blood vessel, you know . . I get those sometimes. It doesn't hurt."

Robert cradled her face between his hands, leaning down to meet her eyes closely with his. Jana felt his gaze penetrating into her soul. She opened her eyes wider, blinked away tears, and received his soul into hers.

"I love you, Jana," Robert murmured. "I'm sorry for what happened."

"Oh . . . oh, Robert, its OK, I love you so much . . . " her voice trailed off as she melted again into his arms.

He tipped her chin up and smiled, eyes twinkling with delight. Bending closer, he kissed her long, slowly and passionately.

Jana felt delirious with delight. Salty tears tasted delicious against Robert's wet lips. Immense surges of pleasure coursed through her body as she arched against his warmth. Somehow all was reconciled. It was a miracle. And, it was a healing of losses more profound than she could have imagined.

Lying in bed, they talked long into the night. Neither felt the least bit tired; a vital energy of infinite source animated them. They made love with rapturous abandon, finding new ecstasies of emotions and sensations, rejoicing and celebrating each other's beingness. They were immensely grateful that they were together again. Each shared the processes they had gone through and the experiences they had encountered. It was like discovering each other all over, uncovering layer after layer of wonder and richness in the multifaceted, magical self of the beloved.

Neither would ever forget that night. It was the moment of completion, the perfection of cycles fulfilled. Their circumstances and choices had brought them to this time of indescribable joy and unimaginable beauty. So many fibers in their relationship were re-woven into the promised pattern, long sought but never before realized. It was the closest joining of their split soul in all sojourns upon Planet Earth. Intertwining lifetimes and memories of lifehoods, layers upon layers of existences at cross purposes, eons of anguished yearning—these were healed that night.

It was so much more than Jana could have hoped for, in her wildest imaginings.

"This coffee's really good, sweetheart, what kind is it?" exuded Jana, peering over the rim of her steaming cup at Robert, seated across the table in the breakfast nook.

"Its Mexican shade-grown coffee, in honor of your adventures south of the border," he replied, smiling warmly. He was surprised at how good it felt to have her home. Almost as if a missing part of himself had rejoined the corpus, he reflected.

"Nice bright tones, subtle spice aroma, with a clean finish." She mimed coffee tasters, swirling her cup deftly and sniffing aromas.

"You'll like this," he added enthusiastically. "Its called Tres Hermanas, made by a women's growing co-op in Chiapas. They hardly touch the jungle, the coffee bushes are half-hidden by trees so you can't tell it's a cultivated area. The bushes are a special type that grows well in shade. Sustainable, local production. Neat, huh?"

"Three Sisters," Jana translated. "I do like it. Thanks for getting it. The coffee in México was OK, but nothing like this."

She smiled and reached across the table, touching his hand. He quickly enfolded her hand in his, twining fingers together. Little electric charges tingled between their palms. They were newly in love again, caught in the magic of fascination with each other. And, to their delight, novel aspects of the other kept unfolding, unplumbed depths full of precious experiences and rich insights. They had not shared so deeply in years.

"Tell me again about your session with Carla," entreated Jana. The synchronicity of this event satisfied her mystic bent. Her own sessions with Carla, exploring the meanings of the recurrent dream about the old woman's hand, had launched this amazing Maya drama.

"Well, like I said last night, she guided me into past lives—or some information field that contained memories of this Maya man's experiences—and I had these incredible images." Robert shook his head, still surprised by the intensity of what he felt. "In only seconds, huge parts of his life re-enacted along with what he was feeling. It was so powerful, Jana, like I was there. Some pretty awful stuff, too. Fighting, people dying in battle, being a prisoner, torture and sacrifice—but all that wasn't as bad as losing the woman he loved. I got the sense they came together and were ripped apart lots of times over who knows how long."

He paused, drifting into the images still fresh in his awareness, and still evoking gut-churning reactions. Pulling back into the present, he looked deeply into Jana's eyes.

"There were some wonderful things, too," he said softly. "The way they loved each other, through thick and thin. The way I love you, Jana. My bad reaction to your going was because it tapped into those past losses, brought up deep-seated fears in my psyche; at least that's what Carla said. She's right, though. I know that now."

Tears misted Jana's eyes as she squeezed his hand tightly. What he was describing matched perfectly her own inner experiences of Maya lifetimes. It confirmed everything. She had told him about these in great detail last night. Heartaches and ecstasies merged into one immense resolution of peace beyond all reason and love without bounds.

"It's so good to be home," she murmured. "Home on every level. If home is where the heart is, I guess we've had lots of homes. And still have lots of them"

"Funny you should say that," he rejoined. "I've had the same sensation, like something within me has finally come home. There's been some kind of completion, and it brings me a deep sense of peace."

"The karmic cycle has finished," she added dreamily.

Robert raised one eyebrow and cocked his head quizzically.

"You really think so?"

"Yes, this time we can be together for life. Until we're tottering old folks, creaking slowly around and barely able to make our own coffee," she added with a laugh.

"Oh Lord, I hope it doesn't come to that!" he said, joining her laughter.

Robert came around the table and knelt before Jana. He kissed both her palms then hugged her closely to him.

"Whatever happens, wherever we go, I'll always love you with all my heart," he whispered into her ear.

She snuggled into his embrace, kissing his neck and whispered back:

"Cycles closing, cycles opening, we're linked for eternity, my love. We're the two parts of one soul on this incredible voyage to who knows where."

Slowly lifting out of a heavy sleep, Jana reluctantly rolled out of bed and shuffled semi-consciously to the bathroom. By the nightlight's faint glow she could just make out the time. It was 1:20 am—again. For most of the week since returning from México, she had awakened each night at this time. Curiosity tickled her fuzzy brain, but she was too sleepy to ponder the significance now. Slipping back under warm covers, she softly stroked Robert's back, reassured and profoundly comforted by his sleeping presence.

As she drifted back toward sleep, the number repeated in her mind: 1:20 am, clock hands moving past 12:00 into the first hours of the new day. Or was it the down-cycle of the night moving toward morning? She was confused, muddled. Who decided the new day started at 12:00 midnight? Why not at sunrise, that was probably when the Maya started the new day.

All of a sudden it hit her: the time wasn't 1:20, it was 13:20! The sacred Maya rhythms that attuned earth to celestial cycles.

Now her mind was alert, for something was trying to happen. Lying very still, eyes staring into darkness, she was attentive for the slightest hint. Soon she sensed a faint presence at the foot of the bed. Hovering, its faint outline appeared, wraithlike. The presence seemed to have a female essence, illuminated by the mere suggestion of a translucent light. It was bringing her something, a gift . . . something needful . . .

Yalucha!

The instant of recognition immediately catapulted Jana into the dream. Waking or dreaming, she could not tell the difference. The liminal threshold was wide open and her consciousness moved between dimensions easily. She was in the dream, and watching herself in the dream, simultaneously.

The adolescent girl's small brown fingers traced the snake-like veins of the old woman's hand. The aged hand, skin thin as crepe paper, closed its long, slender and big-knuckled fingers around the smaller hand. Embers glowed from the center hearth, faintly lighting the inside of the small rectangular room, its walls simple white plaster over stones. The dim glow cast a reddish shadow on the old woman's face as she lay on a woven reed mat, resting on a stone slab attached to the wall. The face was hollow and wrinkled, the closed eyes nearly disappearing in deep sockets, but its features were unmistakable—it was Yalucha.

The Maya priestess was very old, at the end of her life. Her breathing was rasping and irregular. Long minutes elapsed between erratic clusters of labored breath. The young girl looked concerned, uncertain what to do. It was clear that the old woman was dying.

Withdrawing her hand, the girl moved toward the door and drew back a heavy curtain. Soft dawn light outlined the corbelled arch of the doorway.

The old woman's fingers fanned outward, reaching, seeking something. But the girl did not see, as she quickly stepped down three stone steps onto a dirt path leading through high shrubs and willowy trees. In the distance, unnoticed by the girl intent on getting assistance, the graceful rounded Sky Pyramid lifted its exalted summit well above the tallest trees. Golden beams of sunlight glanced off the simple roofcomb of the small temple on top, highlighting its rectangular shape with radiant streaks against the pale gray sky.

The old woman—Yalucha, High Priestess of Uxmal—summoned her waning awareness for one final action. Drawing upon years of spiritual discipline, and invoking shamanic powers as an adept, she called forth the spirit of her successor. Not the next High Priestess of Uxmal, that succession had already been installed. She summoned the one who inherited her mission in the far distant future, the woman who was ordained to re-enact the sacred ceremony at Chichén Itzá and fulfill the prophesy. The one who would enjoin the mandate to bring forth once again the wisdom of the ancient Maya. The one who would merge with her soul.

Fanning her fingers again, the priestess performed the mystical ritual gestures of summoning. Her powers were diminishing rapidly, she feared there was not enough force flowing through her feeble being to accomplish this task. Mustering all her remaining energy, the priestess sent forth the thought-form call and invoked the ritual gesture again. Suddenly a shadowy image appeared under the corbelled arch.

A woman stood there, not very tall but bigger than most Maya woman. Her light brown hair fell in soft waves to her shoulders, and her hazel eyes were shining with love and remembrance. Jana hovered in the shimmering fourth dimension, where all forms were transparent and nothing was solid. She saw herself simultaneously from both dimensions; Jana in trance state in her bed in Piedmont, Jana in astral form in the hut in Uxmal. And she also existed, inexplicably and miraculously, in the old Maya priestess lying on the mat breathing her final few breaths.

Jana floated across the floor and took Yalucha's hand. Fingers intertwined, the two women exchanged arcs of loving vibrations, acknowledging each other's beingness and their simultaneous oneness. One and separate, the myriad in the unitary. They knew these dynamics of existence and nonexistence well.

Sucking in one more rattling breath, the old woman released her soul with a final expiration. Her hand loosened and dropped from Jana's grasp.

In a powerful surge, Jana's essence joined Yalucha in her exit from the body. Jana felt life energy withdrawing, flowing rapidly upward from the first chakra, ascending along the central vessels of subtle energy, withdrawing sequentially from pelvic, navel, heart, throat and medulla centers to leave through the forehead center, the spiritual eye between the body's eyebrows. This was the route of corporeal exit taken by adepts, by masters who died consciously. This route gave them choices about their next incarnations, and if their state of realization was great enough, they had the choice of whether or not to return to earthly life.

As she flowed out with Yalucha, moving through portals between the worlds, she flew quickly past a dark and ominous place. From a giant wormhole, grotesque Lords of Xibalba roared and shook their fists in exasperation. It pained them to see a soul soar past, free of need to descend and battle the Lords of Death. The disembodied essence of Yalucha seemed to wink knowingly at, or perhaps with, Jana's consciousness. Whatever perception is set up, it informed her, that is what one obtains. Heaven or hell, these are ours for the defining.

The ephemeral essence of the departing priestess became fainter and fainter, dissipating away into nothing. In the instant before it completely disappeared, it sent another message to Jana:

Dying is easy, beloved. It is living that is difficult. The secret is to live fully, to embrace every instant of existence, beautiful and ugly, blissful and painful. And remember to dance between the worlds, for that is your heritage as a child of the infinite Oneness.

   *   *   *   *   *

Tilden Park was nearly empty on the late afternoon of Summer Solstice. The day was unusually hot for the Bay Area, the dry air strongly perfumed with pungent eucalyptus oils. Even the numerous birds were lissome and kept their counsel in shady tree branches, save a few chickadees that chirped dolefully against the heat. At higher elevations, oaks, sycamores and coast redwoods stood utterly still, not a hint of breeze touching their branches. The stillness was intense, almost tangible, and full of portent as if waiting to burst forth into riotous action. It was the kind of day that Californians dubbed as "full of positive ions," meaning that the electric charge of air molecules had shifted to the unsettling positive polarity that created this crackling dryness. Most people felt edgy and irritable in this climatic condition.

The small group of people gathering in a clearing among mixed trees seemed unaffected by the climate. Setting up folding chairs and opening ice chests, they chatted jovially and shared picnic snacks, washed down by lots of cold sodas and icy beer. The group appeared in a celebratory mood, their laughter full of unfettered delight. It was apparent that the few men and mostly women knew each other well, and enjoyed each other's company.

Jana organized this solstice gathering of her women's group, along with a few select men who could appreciate the ceremony she had planned. It was very important to have this masculine presence, provided by Robert, his Mills College colleague Harry Delgardo, and the open-minded husbands of Mary and Sarah. This brought the group's number to eleven, not a number of particular significance that Jana could think of, but it was what worked out. In this launching of her new work, she was accepting of whatever configuration the universe provided and grateful for her friends' participation.

Most had been to solstice ceremonies before, at least among the women. But this one was different: it linked to the traditions of the ancient Maya. During the picnic, Jana discussed this connection with her friends.

"The solstices and equinoxes were important times for the Maya," she said. "Like the earth based religions of European pagan traditions, the Maya tuned into the special energies created during the sun's transits. They planned rituals for these times. We don't know exactly what meanings they gave or how the rituals were conducted. So what we're doing for solstice today is partly based on what I've learned from contemporary Maya shamans, and partly what Spirit has inspired me to do."

"Jana took part in some rituals while she was in the Yucatan during Spring Equinox, at Chichén Itzá," Robert added, showing admiration for his wife's adventures.

"Right," Jana said. "I've already told my women's group about these, but for the guys present, here's a brief version. The first ceremony was led by what are called elders from different indigenous groups: Maya, Inca, Toltec and Native American. They had planned it to bring together energies from these groups, in order to honor native

527

traditions and wisdom. They wanted to send these out into the world, so they needed the help of a larger, international group. I was part of that support group, probably a hundred people from many different countries. We formed a large circle around the elders who made an altar on the ground with lots of sacred objects. They did incantations and prayers in four languages while the larger circle held sacred space."

"It wasn't easy for her," Robert interjected. "Several hours standing in roasting midday heat, having to stay concentrated."

"Yeah," Jana admitted with a small laugh. "Today is nothing compared to that heat."

"The other ceremony was really fascinating," said Grace, who had been deeply touched by Jana's sharing with the women's group. Everything Jana described resonated powerfully with Grace's Native American roots. And, Grace knew that she had been instrumental in helping Jana unravel the threads that eventually brought her to the ceremonies at Chichén Itzá.

"It was done at sunset," Jana continued. "In the temple on top of the famous Pyramid of Kukulkán in Chichén Itzá. I was one of four women who paired with four men from among the indigenous elders who did the previous ceremony. This group had the mission to re-open a portal that ran down through the center of the pyramid, to reach an inter-dimensional chamber beneath it. Several centuries before, an identically matched Maya group had created this space to hide and preserve ancient wisdom and esoteric knowledge, because they knew about the coming of the Spaniards. They knew these sacred Maya teachings had to be hidden, because the conquistadors would destroy much of their culture. In fact, the Catholic priests who followed did burn most of the Maya books—codices—that contained this knowledge."

"That was terrible, and what they did to the Maya people was tantamount to genocide," Sarah observed with intensity. Her own Jewish people had suffered the oppression and destruction of hostile conquerors. "They slaughtered thousands of them, but wiped out lots more with diseases like smallpox."

"I hate to think of the treasures lost when that Spanish bishop gathered up and burned all those codices, De Landa was his name, right?" said Claire. Her academic sensitivities were especially offended by book burning. "The codices were so beautiful, full of Maya glyphs, written on bark paper, and who knows what technical knowledge they contained! The Maya were master astronomers and understood the workings of the universe in a more organic way than we do now. To me, its as great a loss as the burning of the famous library at Alexandria in Egypt."

"It was an immense loss, and a serious setback to our understanding ancient Maya culture," said Harry, taking his usual anthropologist's perspective. "Even so, since the Maya hieroglyphic code was finally broken in 1955 by the Russian epigrapher Yuri Knorosov, we've learned quite a lot about their civilization, at least during Classic times when this form of writing was widely used. One interesting aside about Spanish and Maya relations: after the conquest they became the most blended people of all the southern Americas. Over ninety percent of contemporary Mexicans are mestizos, a mixture of these two. It's shaped their national character and accounts for cultural contradictions, such as sensitivity and machismo, or grandiosity combined with insecurity."

"You're right on, Harry," commented Carmen. "Perfect description of my family back in Tabasco. They're a little schizophrenic."

"Back to the ceremony," interjected Mary's husband Sam, a quiet and introspective man. "You said there was an inter-dimensional chamber beneath the pyramid. What do you mean?"

"It's not a physical place, Sam," Jana answered. "If archeologists excavated under the pyramid, they wouldn't find it. It's in another dimension of reality; some call it the fourth dimension in comparison to our physical world that's the third dimension. Some kind of veil, maybe the membranes that physicists speak of, separates the dimensions. You can think of it like parallel universes; two different layers right beside each other, maybe even superimposed, but which usually don't interact. Certain people discover ways to cross over between these dimensions. Mystics and clairvoyants do this; so did the ancient Maya shamans and kings."

"And you actually, uh . . . went there?," said Sam.

"I wouldn't say my physical body went there," replied Jana thoughtfully. "My consciousness, that essence of ourselves beyond the body, went to the chamber. But it was incredibly real, as real as what you see around us here. It's hard to explain. You're in this vast sea of awareness that seems connected to everything. You interact with multiple worlds and disincarnate beings."

"You either believe it or not, honey," Mary advised her husband. "Lots of people have been in these other worlds and say they exist. Saints, mystics, psychics and so forth."

"Or maybe psychos," quipped Sarah, adding quickly: "Sorry Jana, don't mean to imply you're crazy. Just a joke, OK?"

Everyone laughed. They were used to Sarah's humor.

"I hear what you're saying," Sam continued to Jana. "But those things are outside my realm of experience. I guess I'll just have to take it on faith."

"Maybe you'll get a taste of these other realities in our ceremony at sunset, at least that's my intention. I hope that can happen," Jana said earnestly.

"So, Jana, finish telling about the pyramid ceremony," urged Lydia.

"OK. The eight of us joined hands, men and women alternating, and formed a group heart, going into the sacred heart chamber—I'll be teaching you this process in a little while. It felt like the collective heart of the Maya people, holding all their love of nature and ability to use universal laws. We created an energy vortex that shot down the pyramid's center into the hidden chamber below, deep inside the earth. It opened the chamber, or rather the chamber opened itself, in some mysterious way. That released the ancient wisdom and esoteric knowledge of the Maya to come back to the surface, so people could learn it and use it now."

Jana paused, glancing around the group. She felt hesitant but knew it was necessary to tread this mysterious ground.

"This was the most mystical experience I've ever had," she shared pensively. "I was linked to an ancient Maya priestess who was my counterpart in the original ceremony. So was everyone; each person had a counterpart from Maya times. This group of eight spirit beings surrounded us and then seemed to merge with us. Without any instructions we all knew what to do for the ritual."

The group sat in silence, respecting her timing about continuing. For a few moments she was lost in the compelling recollection. Finally Robert's enthusiasm about Jana's work got the best of him.

"Jana's a priestess, she was initiated into a Maya Mystery School, and now has a mission to carry out in the world," he said with a mixture of admiration and solemnity. "Now guys, I know this sounds really weird, but Jana and I have been Mayans in the past. We had several lives together. We were really close but kept getting separated by circumstances. I actually have some memories of these."

Sam and Sarah's husband Morey cast appraising gazes at Robert. It was new territory for the men, and they watched him as a model. Harry nodded with understanding; he and Robert had been through lengthy discussions on the subject. Claire tried to help by anchoring these unusual experiences in science.

"Think about quantum physics," she said. "The behavior of subatomic substances violates all the laws that rule the Newtonian universe. From three-dimensional perspectives, we hardly understand anything. The world of our five senses is only a tiny fraction of what's actually out there; physicists now say over ninety percent of existence is either dark matter or dark energy, and we know very little about this stuff. To quote Hamlet after seeing the ghost of his father, 'There are more things in heaven and earth, Horatio, than are dreamt of in your philosophy.'[24] The ability of our essence—soul, consciousness, whatever you call it—to persist and change form, and to relate to different realities, is beyond our imaginings. And the mystery of time melts into timelessness, everything existing simultaneously. It boggles the mind."

"So Robert and Jana have been Mayans, or in some way intimately connected with previous Mayan people," Morey said. "OK, lets go ahead and accept that. You two certainly don't look like you've fallen off the deep edge. And now Jana has a mission to carry out in bringing their ancient wisdom to the current world. What's that consist of, Jana? What are we to learn from the Maya that'll help us now?"

Jana took a deep breath.

This was it. This was the beginning of her work, the unfolding of the sacred contract for which she incarnated this lifetime. It was a small first step, dipping a toe into the sea of potential. Faint images of further classes, journeys, writing and mentoring tumbled in rapid succession. She was going to co-teach a program with Aurora Nakin at the Maya Mystery School in Clearlake in the fall. But here it began.

While her mind raced to find a suitable trajectory into the rich complexity of Maya wisdom, a flush of self-consciousness colored her cheeks. She still couldn't get completely comfortable with her new identity as a priestess. The mantle seemed too great to wear; it was not a role she had ever envisioned for herself. A spontaneous inner prayer arose to Ix Chel, to Yalucha, for their help.

Jana felt the precipitous descent of the goddess-priestess archetypal field around her. This intelligent force seemed huge and amorphous, and her skin prickled as it pressed against the surface,

---

[24] Shakespeare: *Hamlet, Prince of Denmark.* Act I, Scene V.

permeating through layers of energetic and physical structures. The archetype took over her awareness and directed her mind. She lost most of her sense of ego-identity as the archetype activated its willing vessel.

"I'll begin with the core concepts, which may seem esoteric," she said in tones more resonant than usual. "As you'll see, I hope, the Maya teachings show us how to live—moment to moment—in perfect balance with our world, which exists on several levels.

"The Maya understanding of the cosmos portrays an intelligent universe with multiple levels. All that exists is sacred, alive, imbued with *itz*—divine life force. These multiple dimensions are interconnected and interact with each other. Nothing exists in isolation; the action of each affects the whole. When we rightly understand this, and learn the methods for interacting with various levels, we become powerful influences on our world. We can act with intention to benefit or damage the whole.

"The basics of the Maya message are:

"Be in right relationship with other beings upon the earth, with the planet herself, and with the divine cosmos from which we came.

"Learn to live with integrity and inner congruence; there can be no peace without until there is peace within.

"Bring together and integrate your soul fragments, wherever they may be scattered along the course of your lifehoods, to attain a unified soul-Self.

"Harmonize with the cycles of the soul-Self and the cosmic-celestial patterns that program the workings of our universe. Live by cosmic time and natural rhythms.

"Here is the guiding principle: *perception is everything.* All truths are relative to how we see and understand the world. How we believe and how we imagine shapes reality. Not just for ourselves, but for others, too. This is the world-shaping power of collective consciousness. The 3-D, physical planet that we live on is a reflection of the most pervasive group images held in our collective consciousness. And, the images we hold are ours to choose.

"I've come to believe, along with the great spiritual traditions of the world, that there's only one Absolute, Infinite and Incontrovertible Truth, with a big 'T'—that all is One and all is Love. However, the One expresses in a myriad of ways. These many expressions of the One in the universe and on our planet are the products of perception, of imagining, of intention. In the normal way that our perceptions become manifest, at least on Planet Earth, we end up with dualities. The polarities of electromagnetic fields are the very forces that keep the atoms of existence clumped together. In this way, whatever we envision will of necessity bring about its opposite, that's the law of duality. Seek peace and war also results; ask for happiness and you must also get its opposite, sorrow. Pour out love and it calls forth hate, its opposite vibration.

"So, are we trapped in duality with no way out? Not when we find our path into the Infinite Heart, the sacred inner heart chamber that exists beyond duality. When we create from this space, we don't invoke polarized energies. I'll teach you how to do this Heart Chamber Meditation as part of our ceremony. This method of invoking, of praying, was known to the ancient Mayas and other indigenous peoples.

"But, paradoxically, we must forgo dualities. Ultimately everything is sacred, since all that exists is an expression of the Infinite One. When we judge something as good or bad, holy or evil, we are manifesting duality. Not that duality in itself is negative, just that it means being separated from Oneness. All experiences in the world are basically neutral, they're just something we're going through. No matter how horrible things appear, they're imbued with significance for those involved, who have invoked the experiences as part of their life journeys. Who are we to deny others the experiences they ask for? And if we're affected strongly, we also drew these experiences into our life journey.

"The Maya knew all this very well. It's much the same as Hindu understandings of the dream nature of reality. Some say the Maya were obsessed with death, with heart and blood sacrifices. It's true, at least during Classic times that human sacrifice was practiced on important occasions. But Maya imagery around the life-death-resurrection cycles goes way beyond this sensationalism. The dramas of how the world was created, how people came into being, and how individuals navigate their personal journeys were recreated in art, dance, ceremonies and the famous ball game that re-enacts the creation myth told in the Popul Vuh. For the Maya, life was about preparing for death and creating a state of consciousness that transcended the ending of cycles in all three worlds. The ancient Egyptians also had a revered death technology and spent inordinate amounts of time and resources applying it during their lives.

"A key concept for the Maya was 'growing the soul.' All life's difficulties, triumphs, challenges, joys, mysteries were lessons that produced the compost for growing this White Flower Thing, *sak-nik-*

nal as they called it. There is a lot of symbolic imagery in this, so let me give you a little background."

Looking around, Jana saw that her group was sitting in rapt attention. All appeared intent upon absorbing the messages being conveyed through her priestess vessel. Giving a quick thanks to her spirit guides, she continued:

"The giant ceiba tree produces white blossoms high in its uppermost branches. The ceiba was sacred to the Maya. It was the symbol of the World Tree, raised by First Father at the moment of creation to bring the world into existence. The branches of the World Tree lifted up the sky from the sea, so the Middleworld could have room. The white flowers of the ceiba-World Tree are in the 'Raised-up Sky" of the Upperworld, indicating that the soul comes from the place where all creation began. Just as blossoms are given life and nurturing by their parent plant, the White Flower Thing in the Upperworld existed effortlessly, fed by the World Tree, in the blissful dimension where it originated. Perhaps worldwide myths of paradise, Gardens of Eden, reflect faint echoes of soul-remembrance of this wonderful state.

"The White Flower Thing, the soul, eventually had to leave this place of unaware innocence. It was called to meet its destiny as a human in the Middleworld, where it became incarnated through the womb of a Maya woman. There it took on a body of maize, water and blood and formed into a proper human. The maize also came from the World Tree in its aspect as the Cosmic Corn Plant. The human child was born through the mother's birth canal that was the earthly embodiment of the snake-energy portal, the jaws of the great vision serpent through which souls passed from their Upperworld existence into earthly life.

"Faces were often depicted emerging from jaws of vision serpents in Maya art and sculpture. These jaws were portals for beings from the Otherworld such as gods and ancestors to communicate with shamans during trances. The Maya also depicted the White Flower Thing as a stylized bell-shaped ceiba blossom, often with a square-nosed snake emerging from its center. This shows that they saw the soul itself as a portal for creative snake-energy, an indomitable force continually manifesting through the earthly life of the soul. Shaman-kings wore flower-shaped earflares when they assumed the mantle of First Father/World Tree, to mark their agency as worldly incarnations with power over the life process.

"Going through life, the White Flower Thing entered the world of pain and pleasure, sorrow and happiness, cruelty and kindness. It faced all the experiences a human could encounter on earth. Subjected to devious trials set up by Underworld demons, it became caught up in the battle between the forces of creation and destruction. In its human vessel, it had to contend with outer evils of disease and death, and inner evils of stupidity, arrogance and fear—the five enemies of the soul.

"The purpose of the soul incarnate was to overcome these enemies, thereby expanding and growing itself. When it was successful, this added to the overall life force or *ch'ulul* of the world, making the world a better place for all. The soul could grow itself through education, learning to discern truths on finer and finer levels, and by ecstatic bonding with Spirit in which it remembered its divine nature. If you persevered and mastered this process, the result was a wondrous blossom, what we might call a self-realized being. This matured White Flower Thing was a blessing to all those around, a spiritual adept whose life demonstrated dignified grace in the face of both triumph and tragedy. Like a yogi master, such a one lived in a state of unruffled inner peace and boundless compassion, no matter what outer circumstances prevailed."

Cooling shadows assisted by a slight sunset breeze refreshed the small group sitting among pine and eucalyptus groves. The last rays of the sun painted the uppermost branches in rich shades of gold and orange. Long double hoots of quail cocks were answered with descending chirps as the flock gathered for nesting. Crows cawed faintly in the distance. The creatures of the park were settling into evening.

A sense of magic, of hovering on the brink of unmanifest dimensions, shimmered around the group.

"A most remarkable discovery at the ruins of Tonina gave archeologists immense insight into the Maya's conception of the soul," Jana continued. "Tonina was a small city that reached its height in the Late Classic. It's known for violent and fearsome public art, showing war, torture and decapitation more frequently than other sites. The great ballcourt there was named for the Cosmic Turtle Shell, from whose cleft First Father was reborn after his twin sons outwitted the Death Lords and paved the way for successful creation of real people. The shaman-king Baknal Chak who built this ballcourt regarded it as the earthly replica of the Otherworld where death turned into life.

"To understand this, we need to accept the Mayan shamanic belief that all forms of darkness and death, as well as all forms of light and life, arise from and return to the same mysterious unitary source. The ceiba-World Tree imagery also shows this, since its roots went deep into the Underworld, while its trunk rose through the Middleworld and its branches soared in the Upperworld. The ceiba blooms only at night, and when the day heats up the flowers fold. The night stood for the Underworld. Thus the White Flower Thing actually came into being in the darkness, the Underworld. Xibalba, the place of death, was also where the ceiba roots wrapped around into the tree's highest branches that arched through the Upperworld. There the soul cycled from Underworld-death to Upperworld-resurrection.

"When excavating the ballcourt at Tonina, archeologists dug through layers of tangled vegetation and soil and uncovered the center marker. Made of carved limestone, the center marker was a disc set in the dirt floor of the ballcourt. The disc formed a lid that covered an opening into a hollow stone cylinder several feet deep. Symbolically, the disc with its lid marked a portal to the hidden dimension under the earth, representing the Underworld-Otherworld. The archeologists knew these center markers were considered transparent; they offered a view of what could be seen in the Otherworld.

"On this center marker was a beautiful and astounding carving. It depicted a young man sitting upon a cosmic partition in a cross-legged position, identified by glyphs around the disc rim as Six Sky Smoke. The glyphs further said he had died on September 5, 775 CE and had been entombed on May 22, 776. He appeared to be in an ecstatic trance, with a bird deity headdress, probably Itzam Ye, the animal spirit of the chief god Itzamna. He was clasping the traditional symbol of the ecliptic, a double-headed serpent bar to his chest. But instead of having a serpent head on each end, the hieroglyph for white flower emerged from either end of the magic bar.

"It was obvious that the white flower bar was incredibly precious to Six Sky Smoke. He cradled it to his heart in an attitude of awe and wonder. After more decoding and learning the meaning of *sak-nik-nal*, the White Flower Thing, archeologists were truly amazed at the powerful spiritual symbology.

"Six Sky Smoke had successfully transited into the Otherworld, where he found his own soul and rapturously joined with it. By replacing the serpents with white flowers, the artists conveyed that the human soul *is* the Vision Serpent and the celestial bodies of the ecliptic. The ultimate result of ecstatic visions, of mastering death, was conjuring one's Divine Self, one's own essence. And there, within that Self, one would find the entire universe. This was the process of destruction and renewal through self-sacrifice, letting go of the smaller identity of the ego-persona to realize the expanded Self.

"Imagine how moved the discoverers of this deep Maya mystery were. The image is so full of power and poignancy. This long-dead Maya man, visible through the center disc in the Otherworld, was holding his soul in his arms—his White Flower Thing, the Divine Self, one with the Infinite Source."

White Flower Thing, Sak-nik-nal
Central Ballcourt Marker, Tonina

Jana paused, deeply immersed in the symbolic image. The group's stillness bespoke its enrapture with this profound realization by an ancient peoples. The spiritual quest was much the same in all ages, after all. The same great Truth echoed throughout centuries.

After a moment, Jana checked the western horizon. It was time for the sunset ceremony. Looking around the group, her eyes invited questions.

"So the core of Maya teachings, all this incredible framework of multiple worlds, tuning into cycles, and navigating life and death, boils down to perfecting our own souls," mused Claire.

"And realizing how we're all linked with the natural world, and how the earth is linked with celestial bodies," added Lydia. From her biologists' view, this was a beautiful cosmology.

"Yeah, and that we're all in the same ship, spaceship Earth, so we better treat her right," commented Sam wryly.

"Which brings up the last days of this Great Cycle, the ending of the Maya Calendar in 2012," Robert interjected. "Say a few words about that, Jana."

"OK, but just a few, because we need to do the ceremony at sunset," Jana responded. "The Long Count, the Maya galactic calendar, pinpoints a rare alignment in the Milky Way due to occur on

537

Winter Solstice 2012. On that date, the solstice sun ecliptic conjuncts with the Dark Rift of the Milky Way. The Maya called this rift the *Xibalba Be*, road to the cosmic underworld. Remember that where the Underworld and Upperworld meet, resurrection or rebirth occurs. The solstice sun rises exactly into the Dark Rift, which hovers just above the eastern horizon that day. Father Sun enters the Cosmic Mother's birth canal, bringing forth the birth of the new age. In essence, rebirthing the world. The precession of the equinoxes is then complete, Earth's north axis has finished another 26,000 year cycle, and a new age begins.

"The sun entering the Dark Rift activates an enormous magnetic field, considered a great galactic power station by the Maya. The earth's electromagnetic field shifts, which changes cellular programming among humans. We're supposed to undergo a shift of consciousness then, and become more enlightened as a species. Some say most of the planet ascends into another dimension, where we can manifest things instantly with our thoughts. According to Maya cosmology, the world moves into the Fifth Creation, or the Fifth Sun. We are now living in the Fourth Creation or Sun. In their thinking, a new type of human will emerge in the Fifth Sun—along the lines of New Age beliefs about activating more strands of DNA and becoming 'galactic humans' with vastly expanded consciousness. If all goes well, we move into a golden age.

"So, by this account, we've got less than a decade to get ready for the big shift. This new Maya work of mine—calling, actually—is to assist in the process of bringing forth the Fifth Sun. Does that make sense?"

Robert smiled at her warmly as the others nodded.

"OK, lets do the sunset ceremony."

As the sun dropped below the western horizon, the group moved the chairs aside and stood in a close circle for the ceremony. Jana explained they would first create sacred space by calling in the cardinal directions, a widely used ritual among indigenous peoples with origins lost in misty antiquity. She asked them to face each direction with her and mentally draw upon its energies. Grace beat her Hopi drum in a slow, steady rhythm, to which Robert added the high plaintive notes of a reed flute. He had quickly learned to play the simple instrument, not much of a challenge for a professional woodwind musician. Now that his cough had resolved, his breath control was back to normal.

As the minor melody of reedy notes faded, Grace dropped the drumbeat to a soft and very slow pace. She continued this under Jana's invocation:

"North, place of white corn, you are air, breath and consciousness. Each breath is a new beginning, a new opportunity to do the right thing. Let us create peace and harmony in our bodies and emotions with each inbreath, and release tensions and conflicts with each outbreath. Guide us to breathe properly, to take the breath that blesses all life."

As Jana turned to face east, Grace accentuated drumbeats and Robert repeated melody variations on the reed flute. As these faded, Jana continued.

"East, place of red corn, you are fire, blood of life, heart and emotions. In you we purify the life force of our blood and keep our emotions healthy. We honor the sun, our father, bringer of life, and the gifts of creation. Let us give thanks and keep good relations with the web of life, all our relatives that share this world."

The music repeated for each direction turn.

"South, place of yellow corn, you are abundance and growing things that sustain our lives. Guide us to love all things on earth, take care of all things, and act to keep the earth healthy. We honor the Earth, our mother, sustainer of life and giver of nourishment. Let us give thanks and share earth's abundance with all our relatives, peoples and creatures.

"West, place of black corn, you are the sacred waters that flow upon the earth and through our bodies. These waters are healers, purifiers and destroyers; they are life-sustaining and life-destroying. Guide us to be like water, diverse, adaptable and fluid that we may flow with the cycles of life and death. Let us maintain good relationship with the powerful forces of water, ever prepared to surrender to the depths through which comes rejuvenation and rebirth."

She lifted arms upward accompanied by music.

"Sky above, blue mystery of the cosmic realm, star clusters of origins, uplift our vision and open our perceptions to the whispers of eternity. Let us always remember that we are little drops of frozen sky, whose destiny is to merge again into infinite vastness."

Lowering arms toward the earth, Jana concluded as the music faded:

"Earth, our planetary home, and realms deep below, guide us to celebrate our sojourn in earthly life, and to release it gracefully when times of transition are upon us. In your lessons we find our wholeness and bring our being into perfect balance."

The group reformed a circle, Jana standing at the north. A soft pink glow warmed the western horizon as light slowly waned in the lingering midsummer twilight. There was still another hour of illumination, during which the veils between worlds thinned in the mystical transition into evening.

"In this ceremony, we'll focus on integrating and harmonizing male and female energies within each person," Jana said. "As each of us becomes more balanced, we help the world come into greater unity. The major expression of polarity consciousness in the human experience has been the duality of male and female. When we merge these aspects in ourselves, we reduce planetary polarization. This is one part of what the ancient Maya wisdom has returned to teach. First, I'll ask all the men to sit inside the circle, women around them."

The four men sat on the grass, backs close together facing out toward the women, who remained standing.

"Men, now release the negative side of masculine energy. Women, join hands and create support for the men in this process. In all human history, in times before history, for all ages and peoples, let go and release into the earth all cruelty, violence, aggression, and horrible deeds men have performed. Men, allow this to pass through your body and energy field, and descend deeply into the ground below. For yourself, for all males."

Closing her eyes, Jana mentally created geometric pyramidal forms with points in all directions, and a larger point thrusting deep into earth's center. She added her psychic support to the women's circle, soon sensing the movement of emotional energy through the four men's energy fields into the ground. At one point, there was a distinct shift, a sense of relief accompanied by a collective sigh from the group.

"Good, it is accomplished," Jana said. "Together let us honor the highest expression of the masculine principle: Right action, commitment, honor, enduring strength, protection, generosity, kindness."

She waited until she sensed that both sexes had enjoined these qualities. A healthy and whole man was indeed a being of wonder and admiration. She continued:

"Now men, call forth the best of feminine qualities, your own inner female. Feel this long-buried part of yourself. Accept the gifts

540

of the feminine principle: Receptivity, compassion, commitment to life, flexibility, forgiveness, attunement to Spirit."

After a few minutes, she signaled the men to rise, and spontaneously the woman began hugging them. Tears moistened many eyes as they embraced, men accepting forgiveness and nurturing, allowing their vulnerability to create a bridge across the gap that existed between the sexes for so many millennia.

"Now, women please sit in the center," Jana instructed. "Men, stand at the four directions and extend arms to each side, palms toward the women. You will hold energetic space for us. Robert will guide our process."

Jana joined the women as Robert provided the women's charge that had been previously worked out.

"Women, now release all negativity that has become attached to the feminine consciousness," Robert intoned in rich baritone voice. "Allow yourself to contact all the unspeakable things that have been done to women throughout civilization, all the physical and emotional pain and grief that has burdened the feminine spirit. Allow this to pass through your being into the earth. Discharge the anger of centuries. Release, and forgive, all desecrations of women's bodies and minds, all dishonoring of the feminine principle. Cleanse the female temple of the suffering of the ages."

Jana mentally maintained the geometric pyramidal forms, joining the other women as hideously dark memories rushed in, things none could bear alone. Collectively, they allowed a flash of soul-searing pain to move through. Several women choked back sobs or gasps as their bodies shuddered with the powerful release. A few experienced waves of nausea. Jana psychically directed them to let this go, to be as sieves so nothing stuck, to pass it into the ever-renewing, ever-cleansing core of Mother Earth.

It was quickly over, and they took a simultaneous in-breath of relief. Still trembling slightly, Jana signaled Robert. He continued:

"Now release the negativity inherent in the distorted feminine: victimization, blame, manipulation, seduction, lies, destruction of those in your charge."

He waited until he sensed the women were complete with this process.

"Together, we honor the highest of the feminine. Think of those qualities you each want most to find expression through you." Robert paused, giving time for all, men and women, to reflect. When this was done, he brought forth the final integration.

"Women, now call forth the best of masculine qualities. Embrace your own inner male, this long-denied part of yourself. Claim the gifts brought by the highest expression of the masculine, gifts that empower you to bring forth your own greatest abilities, to live life fully."

Robert led the men, who each enfolded a couple of women in his arms. Wordlessly the men consoled and comforted the women, holding them tenderly. Tears were flowing as their energies merged closely, blending male and female together, feeling deeply their pristine unity, the uniting of the two sides of the self.

It had been accomplished. Each felt polarities being drawn together, merging the male-female duality, bringing wholeness. Wholeness for themselves, balance for the world.

With sweetness that none present would ever forget, Jana led the group in the Heart Chamber Meditation. They learned the simple technique easily, dropping into hearts already open wide, and creating their own unique blessings for the world. Perhaps duality could be transcended. Perhaps the coming of the Maya Fifth Sun, the turning of the vast cosmic clock into another 26,000 year cycle at 2012, would be an age of love, peace and unity.

*   *   *   *   *

Cascading liquid notes of a classical guitar permeated the room with romantic melodies, hinting at simmering passions waiting to be unleashed. Two tall candles burned at the center of the dinner table, one red and one white taper. Gleaming gold-rimmed china and finely scrolled silverware contrasted nicely against the royal blue linen tablecloth. An aura of mystery and romance hovered in the atmosphere.

Robert poured a garnet stream of Merlot into two long-stemmed goblets. With a flourish, he lifted his glass to meet Jana's as she matched his gesture. The two goblets clinked with the clear resonant ring of fine crystal.

"Happy anniversary, sweetheart," Robert saluted Jana.

Smiling appreciatively over the rim of her goblet, she replied:

"Happy anniversary to you, my love."

Swirling the wine around deftly, both savored its intense aroma then sipped the earthy flavors mingled with hints of berries and a long ripe finish.

"Twenty-four years, has it been?" he queried.

"Yes, and I hope it hasn't seemed like an eternity," she laughed.

"It's been an instant and an eternity. Both in the best possible sense. Our relationship seems as fresh as if just beginning, yet it's like we've been together forever. Probably we have, too."

Their eyes met knowingly, hazel into blue, mirrors of the split soul finding itself. Jana was impressed anew at how handsome her tall husband was, especially when smiling. He obliged this thought, the left corner of his mouth curving slightly more and activating his subtle dimple. Around Jana's heart, the whirring sensation that he so often evoked took wing.

"I don't know how a love that's lasted so long can get deeper, but it seems I love you more and more," she told him.

"I feel the same way. There's always more depth to you, like an undiscovered facet of a diamond," he observed with a mixture of wry appreciation. "You've taken me on a few adventures, and I've certainly grown through them. The ceremony you did last week in Tilden Park was very beautiful. Everyone was touched and changed by it."

"Thanks, you and Grace added so much with the music. And your leading the women through our process made it really powerful."

He nodded, accepting the acknowledgement. Thoughtfully sipping wine, he watched the soft candlelight play across her face. The lovely contours of her cheeks glowed as loose curls of light brown hair reflected shining highlights. He had never seen her look more beautiful, more mysterious. His wife, the Maya priestess yet again. In a lifetime when their relationship could reach fulfillment. Maybe.

"Will we ever have a world of peace and harmony?" He voiced the concern of eons, that circumstances would pull them apart.

"I just don't know the answer to that," she replied pensively. "Maybe we *can* dream into existence the Maya Fifth Sun that will launch a higher age, and bring about 'new humans' who can live in perfect balance with nature and the cosmos."

"If enough of us can 'grow the soul' to its greatest perfection," he observed, "and expand our ability to live peaceably within ourselves and in our circle."

"Exactly, my dearest. You are a fast study. I've always admired your mind, not to mention your body."

She flashed him a big smile, lifting her goblet. They clinked the ringing crystal again and savored the complex, fine wine.

"And, not to mention our souls, together again," he said, his voice soft and rich.   Robert reached down and brought up a small present wrapped in silver foil with a red bow. He presented it to Jana, his eyes alone revealing his excitement.

"Here's a little something for you, a token of my love," he murmured.

She smiled with pleasure, and eagerly unwrapped it. Gasping with surprise, she slowly lifted the small pendant out of its cotton nest.

"Oh . . . oh my gosh, where did you find this? Oh, it's so exquisite . . ."

The pendant was made of smooth, light green jade that seemed almost translucent. One surface was subtly carved with a flower pattern arranged around an "O" in the center. It dangled gracefully from a silver chain, shimmering in the candlelight, turning in slow hypnotic arcs.

The jungle closed around them. Tall vine-covered trees provided a leafy canopy overhead; lush green foliage densely closed around the small grassy clearing. Night insects hummed soft harmonies and hidden frogs chirped expectantly. The air was heavy with moisture, rich with the odor of humus and tropical flowers. The young Maya man bent close over his lovely black-haired companion, drawing her into his arms. Electrical tingles coursed over warm brown skin as pleasure surged in their bodies.

"Xk'uxub kolonton, my heart aches for you," he whispered in her ear.

"Chamuibtasbon kolonton, you perfume my heart," she murmured back.

"Was I dreaming?" asked Jana, startling out of reverie.

"About being in a jungle?" Robert responded in a perplexed voice.

"Two lovers in a jungle? Did you go there too?"

"Uh-huh. It must have been us, Jana. The jade pendant must have tapped into some deep hidden memories. That was awesome. It sure felt good, didn't it?"

She savored the delicious sensations. The electrical energy pulsed between their hearts.

"Wow, I'll say. It reminds me of how incredibly much I love you, Robert. And how incredibly long I've loved you," she intoned softly with heart-felt intensity.

"Priestess of my heart," he said huskily, eyes darkening with passion, "across all the ages, through all lifetimes, I'll always come to you."

Dancing Jaguar Lord
Late Classic Painted Vase